D0204948

SOLOMON'S SONG

Bryce Courtenay is the bestselling author of *The Power of One*, *Tandia*, *April Fool's Day*, *The Potato Factory*, *Tommo & Hawk*, *Jessica*, *Solomon's Song*, *A Recipe for Dreaming*, *The Family Frying Pan* and *The Night Country*. He was born in South Africa, is an Australian and has lived in Sydney for the major part of his life.

BRYCE COURTENAY

SOLOMON'S SONG

McArthur & Company
Toronto

First published in Canada by McArthur & Company, 2000
This paperback edition published in 2001 by
McArthur & Company, 322 King St. West, Suite 402,
Toronto, Ontario, M5V 1J2

Copyright © Bryce Courtenay, 1999

The moral right of the author has been asserted.

All rights reserved. Without limiting the rights under copyright
reserved above, no part of this publication may be reproduced,
stored in or introduced into a retrieval system, or transmitted, in
any form or by any means (electronic, mechanical, photocopying,
recording or otherwise), without the prior written permission of
both the copyright owner and the above publisher of this book.

National Library of Canada Cataloguing in Publication Data

Courtenay, Bryce, 1933-
  Solomon's song

ISBN: 1-55278-206-9

Title.

PR9619.3.C598S64 2001   823   C2001-901672-7

Design & digital imaging by *Ellie Exarchos, Penguin Design Studio*
Cover photography by *Maikka Trupp and IPL Image Group*
Typeset in 9. 6/11. 7pt Sabon by Post Pre-Press Group, Brisbane
Queensland.
Printed in Canada by *Transcontinental Printing Inc.*

The publisher would like to acknowledge the financial support of
the Government of Canada through the Book Publishing Industry
Development Program (BPIDP) and the Canada Council for our
publishing activities.

10 9 8 7 6 5 4 3 2 1

For my grandsons
Ben and Jake Courtenay

ACKNOWLEDGEMENTS

One of the advantages of being older is that one has had the good fortune to meet a lot of people who are experts on a great many topics. I never cease to be amazed and gratified by friends and acquaintances who so willingly part with their hard-earned knowledge.

Quite often a younger person, having read one or another of my books, says to me, 'How do you know all those things, Bryce?' Well, of course, I don't. My friends do. Authors steal stuff, most of us have 'news-stand' minds, we accommodate knowledge for very short periods.

Here now are some of the generous people from whom I 'borrowed' information and who allowed me to appropriate the wisdom I don't have. I have also included at the end of the book a bibliography of those writers without whose books it would have been impossible to write this one (see A Note on Sources).

To Margaret Gee, my line editor, proofreader, confidante and often fearless critic, my heartfelt thanks for being at my shoulder when I needed help and quiet as a mouse when I didn't.

To Benita Courtenay, who reads each chapter while it is still warm from my desktop printer and is never afraid to comment usefully, I am, as always, grateful to you.

My admiration and gratitude go to two great professionals, Bruce Gee, who is best described as a polymath, and John Arnold, Deputy Director, National Key Centre for Australian Studies, Monash University, who, assisted by David Green and Robin Lucas, became the mainstay of my research.

It has always been my contention that the historical facts in a work of fiction must be accurate and that readers should be able to rely on them to obtain a knowledge of the times in which the narrative takes place. In this regard Bruce and John and my editor Kay Ronai have done me proud.

I have a special debt of gratitude to Bill Fogarty, Senior Curator – Photographs, Sound and Film at the Australian War Memorial. Bill was with me at Gallipoli and together we covered the battlegrounds where, in a true sense, Australia forged many of those unique elements which make us who we are as a nation today. For the many bottles of cheap and utterly atrocious local red wine shared as we pondered over maps and explanations, for reading and correcting the military detail in this book and for the willingness to help at high speed, I shall be forever grateful to you, Bill, and also to those of your colleagues who worked with you.

There may be some who will disagree with my perspective of Gallipoli and France, but I would be very surprised if Bill Fogarty, Ashley Ekins, Historian, Official History Unit, and Graeme Beveridge, Education Unit, all of the Australian War Memorial, who supplied material and painstakingly detailed my narrative, have got any of the hard facts wrong.

And now for those who helped in a hundred different ways: John Waller, Managing Director of Boronia Travel Centre in Melbourne, who generously allowed me at the last minute to accompany his official tour to Gallipoli. Essie Moses, of Woollahra Library, who never fails me in matters Jewish and others. Owen Denmeade, Dr Irwin Light, Christine Lenton, Sylvia Manning, Sardine, Ethna Gallagher, Alex and Brenda Hamill, Tony Crosby, Danny Persky, Cheryl Bockman, John Robson, Robbee Spadafora for help with jacket designs, Alan Jacobs of Consensus Research, Harry Griffiths for further material and for the good companionship on the Gallipoli tour. To Peter Darnell, who generously allowed me the use of personal family papers and letters concerning his granduncle, Major Aubrey Darnell, who was killed in France in 1918. ETT Imprint, for their kind permission to reproduce Mary Gilmore's poem 'Gallipoli' from *Selected Poems* (Sydney, 1999). Wilfred Owen's poem 'Arms and the Boy' from *War Poems and Others* (Random House) was first published by Chatto & Windus. The epigraph to Chapter Seventeen is Rudyard Kipling's 'Common Form', from 'Epitaphs of the War, 1914–18'. The poem 'Gallipoli' on page 573 is by W. S. Pakenham-Walsh, 1916.

Then there are the Mitchell Library, State Library of New South Wales, and the State Library of Victoria, two of the most splendid, resourceful and co-operative institutions in the land, without which this book could not possibly have been contemplated. I thank you for your scholarship, dedication and the many examples of the best possible library practice.

My thanks to my old friends Sir William and Lady Dulcie Keys, who will launch *Solomon's Song* and, I know, will do so with great aplomb.

At Penguin Books I thank the staff who support me so generously and those backroom people who quietly make things happen, in particular my gratitude to Ali Watts, Senior Editor, Beverley Waldron, Production Manager, Leonie Stott, Design Manager, and her people in the Design Studio, Ellie Exarchos, designer, you were all inspired.

To Peter Field, Peter Blake and Gabrielle Coyne who are responsible for the marketing and publicity, I know of no publishing house that does it better.

Then there are the Penguins who boss me around, my publishers, Bob Sessions, Julie Gibbs and Clare Forster, with Clare in the hot seat responsible for this book, you have all been patient, supporting and, as always, a delight with whom to work. Clare, I simply couldn't hope for a better working publisher.

As always, the best is left for last, my editor Kay Ronai. Kay, will you please edit my next book with me? You are simply the best. Absaloodle!

BRYCE COURTENAY

ARMS AND THE BOY

Let the boy try along this bayonet-blade
How cold steel is, and keen with hunger of blood;
Blue with all malice, like a madman's flash;
And thinly drawn with famishing for flesh.

Lend him to stroke these blind, blunt bullet-leads
Which long to nuzzle in the hearts of lads,
Or give him cartridges of fine zinc teeth,
Sharp with the sharpness of grief and death.

For his teeth seem for laughing round an apple.
There lurk no claws behind his fingers supple;
And God will grow no talons at his heels,
Nor antlers through the thickness of his curls.

– Wilfred Owen, 1918

BOOK ONE

Chapter One

WHAT HAPPENED TO
TOMMO

Sydney 1861

On a dull early morning with the cumulus clouds over the
Heads threatening rain, roiling and climbing, changing
patterns and darkening at the centres, the incoming tide
washes a body onto Camp Cove, a small inner-harbour
beach within Port Jackson which is becoming increasingly
known as Sydney Harbour.

Paddy Doyle, the shipping telegraph operator stationed
at South Head, out with his dog hears its persistent and,
what seems to his ear, urgent barking coming from the
beach below him. He makes his way down the pathway
onto the small jetty to see his black mongrel yapping
beside what, even at a distance, is plainly a human body
lying high up on the wet sand.

Doyle, a stout man not given to exertion, hesitates a
moment, then jumps the eighteen inches from the jetty onto
the sand and breaks into a clumsy trot, the sand squeaking
and giving way under his boots. Commonsense tells him no
amount of hurrying will make a difference, but death has a
haste that ignores the good sense of walking slowly on a
sultry morning. He is puffing heavily by the time he arrives
at the wet bundle of wool and limbs from which trail several
long ribbons of translucent iodine-coloured seaweed.

3

Immediately he sees that those parts of the body not protected by clothing are badly decomposed and much pecked about by gulls, crabs, sea lice and other scavengers of the deep. But not until he comes right up to it does he realise the body is missing a head.

The neck of the dead man protrudes from a dark woollen coat, a grotesque stump, ragged at the edges, torn about by the popping mouths of countless small fish. It is an aperture made less grisly by the cleansing effect of the salt water but more macabre by its bloodless appearance. It looks like the gape of some prehensile sea plant designed to trap and feed on small fish and tiny molluscs rather than something made of human flesh and blood.

Paddy, an ex-convict, brought to New South Wales on the barque, *Eden*, the last transport of convicts to Sydney in November 1840, thinks of himself as a hard man. But twenty years of half-decent living have increased the size of his girth and heightened his sensibilities and he vomits into the sand.

After a fair endurance of spitting and gagging he rinses his mouth in the salt wash and stands erect again, kicking the sand with the toe of his right boot to cover the mess he's made at his feet.

The sun has broken through a break in the clouds and almost immediately blowflies buzz around the corpse. A sickly stench starts to rise from the body, but with his belly emptied of his breakfast gruel, Doyle is now better able to withstand the smell and he squats down to make a more thorough examination.

A narrow leather thong around the base of the headless neck cuts deep into the swollen flesh and disappears inside the neck of a woollen vest. Doyle, reverting to his darker instincts, tugs tentatively at the cord. At first there is some resistance, then a small malachite amulet, a Maori Tiki, is revealed.

Doyle, like all past convicts, is deeply superstitious and is alarmed by the presence of an amulet known to ward off evil spirits and put a curse on those who harm its wearer. He hurriedly tucks it back under the wet vest, afraid now even to have touched it. Without thinking, he rubs the palm of the offending hand in the wet sand to cleanse it, then crossing himself he mutters, 'Hail Mary, Mother of God, protect me.'

The body is that of a white male of unusually small stature. The fingers of both his hands are clenched to form puffy, clublike fists. Whether from the sudden heat of the sun or the drying out of the corpse, the right hand begins to open and Doyle observes that the nails have continued to grow after death and are deeply embedded into the fleshy upper part of the dead man's palm. As the fingers unlock and open there is no sign of blood oozing from the fissures the nails have made. Each finger now wears a hooked talon with the finger pads puckered and raised from the immersion in sea water, so that the skin surface seems to be covered by nests of tiny white worms.

The nails are smooth and clean with no cuts or scars nor is there any permanently ingrained dirt etched into the lines on the palms to indicate a man accustomed to physical work. The skin on his arms is bluish-white from the sea water, but shows no signs of having ever been exposed to the sun. 'Some sort of toff,' Doyle thinks, 'no doubt up to no good and come to a sticky and untimely end, good riddance. Still an' all, choppin' off his 'ead's goin' a bit bloody far!'

Later, when he has pulled off his boots and placed them on the stone steps of his hut to dry and dusted the sand from his feet, he telegraphs Sydney to report the headless corpse. Then, in what Paddy thinks is an amusing appendage to his message, he taps out, *Best get a move on it don't take long for them blowflies to lay their maggot eggs.*

Two hours later, with the threatening clouds now well

out to sea and the sun hot as hades in a clear blue sky, a steam pinnace from the police mooring at Circular Quay with two police constables aboard puffs up to the Camp Cove jetty to claim the body for the Pyrmont morgue.

While searching the corpse, the morgue attendant, observed closely by Senior Detective Darcy O'Reilly of the Darlinghurst Police Station, discovers a small leather wallet inside the jacket. It contains four pounds and several personal calling cards which identify the headless man as Tommo X Solomon.

Detective O'Reilly immediately sends a constable to Tucker & Co. to inform Hawk Solomon that he is required at the city morgue to identify what may be the remains of his brother.

Hawk, at Mary's instigation, had reported Tommo missing in case any of Mr Sparrow's lads might have seen him entering his lodgings on the night of Maggie's death and declared his presence to the police.

A further search of the victim's clothing reveals a deck of DeLarue cards, the kind generally used by professional gamblers of a superior status. Finally, a gold hunter watch, with the ace of spades enamelled on its outer lid and a sovereign hanging from its fob chain, is discovered in a buttoned-down pocket of his weskit. It has stopped at twenty minutes past ten o'clock. Senior Detective O'Reilly writes this down as the presumed time of death and then pockets the watch. The corpse is left clothed for the pathologist to examine and is lifted onto the zinc dissecting table in preparation for the autopsy by the Chief Government Medical Officer, William McCrea M.D., who will closely examine the clothes before removal, noting any tears or stains that may help to define the method of death.

Conscious of the corpse's advanced state of decomposition Dr McCrea loses no time presenting his findings to the coroner, Mr Manning Turnbull Noyes, known in the magistrates courts as M. T. Noyes and by the hoi polloi as 'Empty Noise'.

The hearing and its immediate aftermath is best summed up by the following day's *Sydney Morning Herald* report on the murder by its popular senior crime reporter, Samuel Cook. Although Mr Cook's name is not used in the paper his style is easily recognised by his many readers who know him for his fearless reportage. He enjoys their respect for his ability to ask awkward questions which have a habit of greatly embarrassing nobs and government officials of every rank. Cook has even been known to take on the governor when a wealthy merchant of dubious reputation was included in the Queen's Honours List. There are some who believe he wouldn't back down to the young Queen Victoria herself.

Samuel Cook is the scourge of the police force, in particular of Senior Detective Darcy O'Reilly. And while every magistrate in New South Wales, given half a chance to nobble him, would cheerfully sentence the *Sydney Morning Herald* reporter to a ten-year stretch in Darlinghurst, it is Noyes who would call in the hangman. Like O'Reilly, M. T. Noyes is a special target for his remorseless and acerbic pen.

HEADLESS BODY WASHED UP ON CAMP COVE BEACH

A special report.

The headless body of a white man thought to be that of Mr Tommo X Solomon was discovered yesterday washed up on the beach by Mr Paddy Doyle stationed at the Camp Cove telegraph office.

Mr Doyle reported that he had initially been alerted by the unusual barking of his dog and had walked down to the beach to investigate, thinking perhaps a seal had come ashore on the rocks at

7

the far side of the beach as they occasionally do at this time of the year.

Upon discovering the murder victim Mr Doyle lost no time alerting the authorities and the body, sans head, was recovered by the police some hours later and taken to the city morgue at Pyrmont.

The investigation into the murder is under the direction of Senior Detective Darcy O'Reilly of Darlinghurst Police Station.

Dr William McCrea M.D., Chief Government Medical Officer, successfully applied to the magistrates court at Darlinghurst to submit his findings immediately to the coroner, Mr M. T. Noyes, citing the humid and inclement weather and the decomposed nature of the corpse. Permission was granted by the stipendiary magistrate and the inquest was held late yesterday afternoon.

In his coroner's report Mr Noyes stated that the head of the deceased had been removed by an instrument thought to be an axe with the blade prepared to a razor-sharp edge.

Senior Detective O'Reilly stated in evidence that, as the victim had not been robbed of his wallet, or his gold watch and chain, he appeared to be the victim of an execution-style murder.

The coroner, well known for his acerbic wit, remarked that in his experience on the bench he had not yet heard of a suicide where the deceased had entirely removed his own head with an axe. He hoped the senior detective might in future restrict himself to any information which might be useful to the constabulary in their efforts to solve the case.

The senior detective then stated that the murder may have taken place on board a ship at sea. However, the more likely conclusion was that the head had been removed from the body and the body taken outside the Sydney Heads and dumped at sea.

'I would be most surprised if the head isn't

buried deep somewhere ashore, Detective O'Reilly,' Mr Noyes opined.

The detective sighed audibly. 'Yes, your honour, we are most grateful for your opinion,' though what he really thought of the coroner's gratuitous insight this correspondent dares not even suppose.

The coroner made a finding of murder by person or persons unknown and the court was adjourned.

Asked outside the court who he thought might have done such a grisly execution Senior Detective O'Reilly stated, 'Decapitation is not a common method of murder, but is known to be used among the celestials. Though I have not heard of it used against a white man before.'

When it was pointed out that the victim, Mr Tommo Solomon, was a user of the opium poppy and well known in Chinatown, he refused to speculate further on the matter.

'Our enquiry will determine soon enough what we need to know,' he stated.

'Did you know that the murder victim was a partner in a gaming syndicate run by the well-known "sports-man" Mr F. Artie Sparrow?' he was then asked.

'No,' came the prompt and surprising reply.

'Did you know he was a member of a regular illegal card game that was known to take place in Chinatown on the premises of Tang Wing Hung, the Chinaman importer?'

Not entirely surprising, his answer was 'No' again.

Your correspondent then asked if the murder of Mr Solomon might be linked with the deaths on the premises of Mr Sparrow's lodging of the boxing pro-moter known as Fat Fred and the prostitute Maggie Pye, the latter suffocating under the weight of the dead body of the former.

Senior Detective O'Reilly replied that the coroner's report on the state of decom-position of the victim's body supported the theory that Mr Tommo Solomon might have been murdered at

9

around the same time, but that it would be foolish to link the two incidents.

He stressed that the coroner's findings of the two previous deaths had been that Fat Fred, while involved in sexual intercourse, had died of a sudden and massive heart seizure and Miss Pye of asphyxia while trapped beneath his body.

'We have no reason to suspect foul play.' Senior Detective O'Reilly added, 'We are hoping that Mr Sparrow will help the police with our enquiries but, as of this time, we have been unable to locate him. I ask anyone who knows of his present whereabouts to come forward.'

The good detective was then asked if he thought it a mere coincidence that the murdered man was the twin brother of the professional pugilist Hawk Solomon who, in turn, was betrothed to the murdered prostitute, Maggie Pye?

'All coincidences will be carefully examined,' O'Reilly replied loftily.

Your correspondent then asked if Senior Detective O'Reilly was aware that Mr Sparrow was also known to owe Mr Tang Wing Hung and Miss Mary Abacus, the mother of the adopted twins Tommo and Hawk Solomon, a considerable sum of money, this being their winnings from bets made on the prize fight between Mr Hawk Solomon and the Irish pugilist who goes under the sobriquet, The Lightning Bolt?

Senior Detective O'Reilly declined to comment, but pointed out gratuitously that both barefist boxing and wagering on such contests are illegal in the colony of New South Wales and that no such claim, if true, would stand up in court.

'Did this not then suggest a reason why Mr Sparrow might have "gone missing" and wasn't it worthwhile following up the evidence of the lad known as Johnny Terrible, who stated that Mr Sparrow had sent a note to Maggie Pye suggesting she be the emissary between himself, Tang Wing Hung and Miss Mary Abacus?'

'Sir, you are fully aware that the particular note found on the premises belonging to Maggie Pye was tabled and read out in court. It simply contained the words, *Come and see me, my dear*, and was signed by Mr Sparrow.'

'And the evidence of the boy, Johnny Terrible?'

'The magistrate chose not to take into consideration the boy's evidence as he has been in trouble before and is known to lie under oath.'

Senior Detective O'Reilly then looked at your correspondent with an expression suggesting some bemusement. 'I find myself surprised at your questions, sir. Given the known occupation of the deceased woman, the magistrate, I believe, has correctly concluded that she was acquired by Mr Sparrow for the purposes usually associated with women of her profession. The note received by Maggie Pye can possess no other explanation,' he concluded.

Your correspondent then countered with the suggestion that it was common knowledge that Mr Sparrow was not known to favour the fairer sex and that his preferences lay, to put it in the kindest terms, 'elsewhere'. Furthermore, it was a well-known joke among the Sydney lads employed by Mr Sparrow that Fat Fred was usually incapable of dalliance of any sort and that drink rendered him impotent.

Senior Detective O'Reilly then said, 'You are raking over old coals, sir,' and declined to answer any more questions from your correspondent.

Miss Mary Abacus and Mr Hawk Solomon, who had earlier visited the morgue to identify the body and later also attended the coroner's hearing, declined to be interviewed by this correspondent, pleading that they be allowed the right to mourn the loss of a beloved son and brother.

Hawk stops off first at the Hero of Waterloo where Mary has her temporary lodgings, and together they go to the Pyrmont morgue to identify Tommo's corpse. Here they are made to place a tincture of camphor oil to their nostrils to kill the unmistakeable odour of decaying flesh before they are taken into the morgue's coldroom to examine the corpse which has been stripped of its clothing but, at the suggestion of Senior Detective O'Reilly, the Tiki remains with its leather thong about the tattered and truncated neck.

A square of canvas has been neatly arranged over the top of the neck to conceal the absence of a head, though the Maori amulet can be clearly seen resting on the exposed chest three inches below the base of the neck. A second square of canvas in the form of a loincloth covers the private parts. Mary scarcely pauses to examine the body before confirming to Senior Detective O'Reilly that it is her adopted son, Tommo.

She notices O'Reilly's bemused and doubtful countenance at so quick an identification of a corpse, which, after all, lacks a head, the most common method of recognition. She points to a large mole high up on the left shoulder. 'Born with it, big as sixpence, can't mistake it, looks like a map of Tasmania,' she states. Remembering her grief, her voice quavers slightly and she touches the corner of the small lace handkerchief to her right eye and then her left and returns it, perhaps a little too hastily, to cover her nose, for the stench rising from the body has even defeated the efficacy of the camphor oil.

Hawk is hard put to contain his surprise for, almost at once, they have both seen that the naked body isn't that of Tommo. Hawk's twin has a small but distinctive birthmark on the calf of his left leg and no such mark can now be seen. Hawk bends down to examine the amulet and immediately sees what he is looking for, a small 'M'

12

has been scratched into the surface of the green malachite. 'The Tiki,' he points to the amulet. 'That's his, my brother's.' It was given to his twin by his Maori wife, who died in childbirth, and the 'M' scratched onto the surface is for her name 'Makareta'.

It is a certain sign to Hawk of Tommo's efforts at deception and his determination to make the murder victim seem to be himself. Tommo would have thought long and hard before parting with the Tiki which he greatly cherished as his talisman, the equivalent in his own mind of Mary's Waterloo medal. Then Hawk realises that it is a message to him, Tommo's way of telling him that he is still in the world of the living.

In fact, having received Johnny Terrible's message that Tommo was going after Mr Sparrow, they have each silently concluded the corpse must belong to Ikey Solomon's most accomplished graduate from the Methodist Academy of Light Fingers, the infamous Sparrow Fart, alias F. Artie Sparrow, the odious Mr Sparrow.

Tommo has completed what he had vowed to do and avenged the death of Maggie Pye. The sudden tears Senior Detective O'Reilly now sees streaming unabashedly down the tattooed cheeks of the giant black man are not, as he supposes, for the grotesque corpse on the zinc tray, but for Maggie Pye and the love of his twin. They are also tears of relief that Tommo is still alive.

Using the only currency he knows, this headless corpse lying on a slab of ice is Tommo's payback for all the mongrels who have blighted his life. The ghastly manner of Mr Sparrow's death is paradoxically also Tommo's last gift of love to his brother. Hawk cannot help but think that the pressure on Tommo's brain from the wound to his head has finally driven him insane. For this notion as well, he now weeps.

O'Reilly brings his fist to his lips and clears his throat.

'Hurrmph, er missus, if you'd be so kind as to turn yer back, a matter o' some delicacy,' he says, looking directly at Mary.

Mary turns away from the corpse and the detective lifts the canvas loincloth and nods to Hawk. 'It's another common way o' identification,' he says abruptly, then supposing Mary can't hear him, he whispers *sotto voce* to Hawk, 'Pricks are like faces, every one's different.'

Hawk sees immediately that, unlike Tommo's, the penis is not circumcised.

'Well, what does you think?' O'Reilly asks.

Hawk sniffs and nods his head, but does not reply, not wishing to openly commit perjury. O'Reilly sighs and pulls the small canvas square back into place. 'It's all right to look now, missus,' he says to Mary. As if he is anxious to conclude the identification, he casually produces a gold watch from his pocket. Clicking it open so that the ace of spades on its lid can be clearly seen by both Mary and Hawk, he pretends to consult it.

'Goodness, that's our Tommo's watch,' Mary says quick as a flash, for indeed it *is* Tommo's. Senior Detective O'Reilly grins, the identification of the headless victim is complete, it's been a satisfying afternoon's work all round. He nods. 'Good.' He turns and calls over to the morgue assistant who brings him a clipboard to which is attached a form. The assistant also holds a small glass pen and ink stand. Holding the clipboard in one hand and with the pen poised in the other, O'Reilly asks officially, 'Are you, Hawk Solomon, and you, Mary Abacus, quite certain this is the body of Tommo Solomon?'

'With me hand on me heart,' Mary lies, bringing her hand up to cover her left breast. The question is perfunctory, O'Reilly has witnessed a mother's quick and positive identification and the copious tears of grief still issuing from the giant nigger.

14

'You'll sign here then,' he says all businesslike, dipping the pen into the open ink bottle and handing it to Hawk. Mary and Hawk sign the paper confirming their identification and the morgue assistant takes the clipboard and departs.

'When can we take possession of the body of our loved one?' Mary asks plaintively, her eyes taking on a suitably sad expression. 'Give it a burial decent folk might attend?'

Hawk is amazed at her assertiveness, her complete presence of mind, she wants the body buried and out of the clutches of the law as soon as possible. 'It ain't in a nice state and we wish to preserve the best of our memories, sir,' she adds, putting the finishing touches to what she hopes O'Reilly will see as a mother's anxiety and grief.

The corners of the detective's mouth twitch slightly and Mary reads this as a sign of his sympathy. 'See what I can do, missus. It's in the hands o' the coroner. He don't like being told his business, though.'

Mary takes a sovereign out of her purse and offers it to him. 'A small contribution to the Orphans Fund,' she says in a half-whisper.

O'Reilly now gives her a genuine smile, knowing himself to be the orphan of particular benefit. 'Might be able to give him a bit of a hurry up, eh?' he says, taking the gold coin Mary holds out to him.

'Most grateful, I'm sure,' Mary says, batting her eyes.

'Mother, that were a bribe,' Hawk says to Mary on their return to the Hero of Waterloo.

'Blimey! And him a detective, fancy that,' Mary laughs.

The coroner, magistrate M. T. Noyes, is happy enough to oblige and he orders the body's release from the authorities and also the immediate return of Tommo's personal effects from the police. Though, unable to resist the temptation to display his infamous wit, and first

15

determining that Mr Cook of the *Sydney Morning Herald* is not present, the magistrate quips, 'In making this decision we have lost our head and must quickly bury the evidence or the case will stink to high heaven!'

By sundown every pub in Sydney will be repeating his *bon mot*. 'Have you heard the latest from his nibs, Empty Noise?' they will say gleefully to every newcomer.

Mary, never one to take chances, orders an expensive black basalt tombstone engraved in gold with the words:

Tommo X Solomon
1840–1861
R.I.P.

In a simple ceremony conducted by the Reverend Hannibal Peegsnit, the eccentric Congregationalist, with only Mary and Hawk in attendance, the remains of Mr Sparrow are duly buried.

Ikey's best pupil, Sparrer Fart, the lightest fingers in London Town, the small boy who never knew his real name, ended the way he'd started his life, unknown, unwanted and unloved, his final epitaph a beak's joke in bad taste. He will lie headless beneath a tombstone, which, when Satan asks him for a reckoning of his life, he won't even be able to call his own.

Hawk wishes Mary 'Long life', which is what Ikey would have done in the same circumstances.

Mary returns to Hobart after the funeral. Hawk gives Maggie's two-room home and all her possessions to Flo, Maggie's little friend, now married to the grocer's son, Tom. He visits Caleb Soul, who accompanied Tommo and himself to the gold diggings at Lambing Flat and has since become one of Hawk's dearest friends, to say his farewell. Then, after telling all at Tucker & Co. that he is going home to Hobart, and attending a gathering in the dock area of the entire company where he receives a handsome crystal goblet in gratitude for his services from Captain Tucker, Hawk sets sail for New Zealand.

On his arrival Hawk makes his way to the stretch of Auckland Harbour where the Maori boats moor and catches a coastal ketch that will take him to the Ngati Haua tribe under Chief Tamihana, in whose household Tommo's daughter, Hinetitama, is being raised.

Hawk discovers that Tommo is dying from the wound to his head and is in constant pain. Often he sinks into a delirium but even when he is conscious, the pressure on his brain renders him incoherent, so that the words in his mouth twist into gibberish. But sometimes he has brief periods in the early mornings when he is quite lucid.

During one such period he asks Hawk to leave his daughter with the Maori until she comes of age and can decide for herself whether she wants the life of a pakeha or wishes to stay with her people.

'The Maori be her family now, even if her name be Solomon. Let her choose later, though Gawd knows why she'd want to be one of us.' In these coherent periods it is the same old sardonic Tommo, ever on the alert for the mongrels.

'I shall see she never lacks for anything,' Hawk promises. 'I will respect your wish, though Mary pleads she would very much like her, as her granddaughter, to be brought up well at home with every privilege and the very best of education.'

'Tell her then to leave something in her will for my daughter, my share,' Tommo replies. 'Although from what I've seen of privilege and education it breeds only greed and superiority.'

Hawk protests and Tommo laughs. 'The Maori have all but lost their land and it has been took from them by educated men, men of the Church, committing a crime in the name of God and the governor himself doing the same in the name of the Queen. These are all educated men, all greedy and superior, all mongrels.'

Hawk, ever the rational one, replies, 'That is an oversimplification, Tommo, goodness is not replaced by greed when a man becomes educated nor is greed absent in the poor. Man is by his very nature rapacious and wealth has forever been the precursor of power, the need to be seen as superior. Hinetitama must have some learning, you would not want your daughter to be shackled by ignorance and superstition.'

Tommo looks wearily up at Hawk. 'You are the only good man I know what's keen on book learnin'. Let my daughter grow up the natural way of her people, she will be taught to read and count and that will be enough.' Tommo grins, it is near to being the old Tommo grin and Hawk's heart is filled with love for his dying twin. 'Unless you can teach her how to handle a pack of cards, eh? You must give her my Tiki.' He touches the Tiki Hawk has returned to him and his expression grows suddenly serious. 'Hawk, there is bad blood in me and it will be in my daughter also. If she stays among the Maori it will not come out so soon. Please tell her to wear it always, that the Tiki will protect her.'

'Your axe? Is this the bad blood you talk of?' Hawk does not wait for Tommo to reply. 'Tommo, there is no bad blood there, what you did was for me and in memory of Maggie Pye. It was justice. You are good, Tommo, as good a man as ever had a conscience.' For the first time the death of Mr Sparrow has been mentioned.

'Conscience?' Tommo smiles ruefully. 'That is the difference between you and me, you would carry the murder on your conscience forever and I have but scarcely thought about it. Mr Sparrow was a mongrel and when I

chopped him there was that much less evil in the world.'
Tommo looks up at Hawk. 'But it takes bad blood to
murder a man, any man, even a mongrel. If they should
string me up for it, it would be a fair bargain.'

Hawk sighs and then looks at Tommo somewhat
apprehensively. 'Tommo, will you tell about that night?'

It is Tommo's turn to sigh, 'Aye, if you wish, but it
weren't a pretty thing to tell of.'

'Tommo, I grieve for Maggie every day, every hour of
my life, it would make it more, yer know ah . . . complete
. . .' Hawk shrugs, not knowing how to continue.

Tommo sees his confusion and starts right in. 'It takes
me five or six minutes to run to Kellet's Wharf from the
World Turned Upside Down, the pub where Mr Sparrow
stayed. It's fourteen minutes to nine o'clock with the tide
turning at some time shortly after nine when the Kanaka
ship, *Morning Star*, will sail. I have little time left to swim
the two hundred yards out to where she's moored.

'I'm sweating and panting from the run and I remove
me clothes and shoes and using me belt I wraps them
around the axe holster and returns it to my back. Then I
wades in and starts to swim. I'm still breathing 'ard from
the run and me 'ead's hurting terrible. It's a calm night
and dark with cloud cover, so the moon is lost. The
harbour water's cool and welcoming and I strokes me
way to the dark shape o' the *Morning Star*, a trading
schooner about eighty feet stem to stern. I can see she has
her head to the wind, facing the land breeze coming down
the harbour and is preparing to sail.

'As I reach the port side I can hear the Kanakas starting
to sing as they lean into the capstan bars to take up the
slack and begin to raise the anchor. I can hear the click of
the pawls and if I'm any judge it's a task that will take
anything up to fifteen minutes. It means I can't climb up
the anchor rope as I had supposed. But, ah, there is a God

in heaven, as me eyes clear I see they've already raised the dinghy but the ship's ladder has not yet been pulled up. Glory be, it's a doddle to climb on board up the rope ladder and soon enough I sticks me 'ead up to take a look over the deck. I'm panting hard but there appears to be no one about. They've already set the mainsail which is luffing in the light breeze and will cover any sound I might make coming aboard. From where I am at the waist of the schooner the Kanaka standing at the ship's wheel and the captain on the quarterdeck can't see me and I can hear the first mate on the quarterdeck urging the men on with the raising of the anchor.

'I look around, there are a dozen or so barrels lashed to the starboard side and the dark shape of the deckhouse with the dinghy atop is to me left. Then I hear a snuffling sound and I go rigid, somebody's coming. But it don't take long to realise, like all Kanaka ships, they've taken pigs on board. Island folk, as you well know, don't like to go to sea without a pig or two. Then I see it, the pig pen, close to the fo'c'sle, Kanakas, the only folk happy to put the pig pen near where they kips down. There's another shape next to it and o' course it's the chicken coop, chickens the second thing them silly buggers like to have on board. All the bleedin' 'ome comforts. The rest o' the deck is the usual mess what come about before sailing. It will be to my advantage, nobody moving quickly, plenty of time to see 'em coming and if I has to, use me axe.'

Hawk looks aghast. 'Tommo, you'd not kill an innocent?'

Tommo grins. 'Nah, just tap him light with the blunt, put him down for a bit. Anyway, it don't happen. It ain't necessary. There's nobody on the main deck and I slips aboard and find good concealment behind the barrels on the starboard side. I'm tucked away so when they tidy the deck there is little chance I'll be discovered.

'I can see the deckhouse leading down to the saloon

where I figure I'll find Mr Sparrow. It looks to be a typical trading schooner with the one cabin below decks for a passenger or two and the captain and the first mate in their own quarters aft where it be the most comfortable to sail. From what Johnny Terrible's told me, Mr Sparrow is on his own and does not wish to be recognised, not even by the captain or the crew, let alone a fellow passenger, so it will be him and me alone, if I can get down to him.

'I undoes me swag and removes me axe from the shoulder holster so it's at me side. I'm still bollocky and I starts to shiver again, now me panting's stopped. As best I can, I wring out me wet clobber and get back into it, me clothes clinging to me skin, feeling 'orrible and me feet squelching in soaked boots. Now it's waiting time and me 'ead's hurting real bad.

'The anchor's up at last and the ship turns with the outgoing tide with Sydney now, same as me, on the starboard side. I can see a few lights and I thinks of you and Mama and of Johnny Terrible breaking the news o' Maggie's death to you and giving you the magpie feathers and I silently hopes that me going after the mongrel what done it will some day be of true comfort to you.'

Hawk's eyes fill with sudden tears. 'I thought that I'd lost you too, that of the three people I loved with all my heart, that I had lost two of them on the one night. If it were not for the strength of Mary, our mama, I don't reckon I'd have wanted to go on living another hour.' Hawk grins through his tears. 'She saw how I was and she come right out and says, "Hawk Solomon," like she'd say when we were little 'uns, stern o' face, the scar on her cheek pulled down to the corner of her mouth, "I didn't rescue you from the wild man in the wilderness just so you could snuff it by yer own miserable 'ands! I've lost me beloved Tommo and you, your lovely Maggie, but you ain't gunna do the dirty on me now, so get that inta yer thick nigger 'ead!" She points a crooked finger at me. "Dying is easy, son. It's living what takes the character. Orright? Now, let's get on with it."'

'Yeah, that be our *I shall never surrender*, Mary, that's our mama,' Tommo laughs. 'She's right, yer know, livin's what's the bastard.'

Hawk, hoping to change the sudden feeling of melancholy, changes tack. 'You're on deck, but, with the ship moving down the harbour soon to be out of the Heads, how ever did you think you'd get back to shore?'

Tommo gives a rueful smile. 'Mate, with me 'ead gone an' all, I reckoned there weren't much point to hangin' around any longer. Just so long as I can get a crack at the miserable mongrel. Tell yer the truth, I didn't think much about the next part o' it.'

'Tommo, you were willing to give your life for me and you tell me you've got bad blood. It just isn't true!' Hawk protests fiercely.

'Wait on, it ain't pretty what comes next.'

Hawk can see Tommo is tiring. 'You sure you want to go on?' he asks, concerned.

Tommo nods his head and takes up where he left off. 'It's getting bloody cold with spring not yet come and me sittin' shivering in me wet clobber. A couple of Kanakas pass by and I reckon if I coughs I'm a goner, me teeth are chatterin' that loud I think they must surely hear me loud as a chisel chippin' stone.

'But they goes about their work getting the sails up and trimmed and several others come to join them. We've passed the Sow and Pigs, them cluster o' rocks that stand inside the harbour, and we're just about through the Heads, they've got the flying jib going as well as the topsail with the main and staysail up and under way. I reckon the breeze from the land is now moving us about four or five knots, a perfect night for sail, they'll all be in the fo'c'sle abed not long after we've cleared the Heads. You know how it is, yiz pretty knackered after getting under way.

'Well, it were just like I just said. Bloody ship would sail itself on a night like this. We clears the Heads and turns to port and hugs to the coast to take advantage o' the shore breeze and the crew turn in prompt as I had supposed.

'Now it's only the creaking o' the ship, the bow waves and the sails luffing that breaks the silence. I reckon the only man left on deck is the helmsman and he's got the light from the ship's compass in his eyes, so there's no way he can see the main deck from the quarter. It's dark as hell anyway, best you can see clearly is about ten feet. Besides, the deckhouse is cutting off his line o' sight, so I reckon I am clear to make me move.

'Then I see him, Mr Sparrow, he's coming up from below. I watch as he turns, walking towards me. Gawd in heaven, he's walking straight into a trap I didn't even know I'd set. But o' course he sees the barrels and turns to the right, coming up to the starboard rails not six feet from where I'm hiding. Me heart starts to pump. Jesus H. Christ, I can take him right here and now with the axe, throw it and put the blade into the side o' his skull and he'd be dead 'fore he hit the deck or could even grunt.

'He's wearing a long coat just like the one Ikey used to wear, his 'at is pulled down to his eyes and he's got a woollen scarf wrapped around his phiz so only his eyes are to be seen between his 'at and the scarf. He's looking out to sea and all you can hear is the wash as the bow cuts through the waves. I've got F. Artie Sparrow standing still as a scarecrow, the perfect target, and him no doubt lamenting the good life he's left behind in Sydney and not knowing the next port o' call will be the flames o' hell itself.'

23

'So that was it then?' Hawk says, sighing, glad the telling is over.

'Nah, too easy, I want the bastard t'know it was me come after him and that he's gunna die. No point him being alive one moment and dead the next without him knowing why. I want to see the fear in his miserable mongrel eyes. I want to see it for Maggie, for you, for meself. It's like he's all the mongrels that ever were and I want to see how their kind take to dying.'

Hawk can scarcely believe Tommo's courage. 'But he could have shouted and alerted the crew as he saw you coming, anything!'

'Not before I'd a nailed him he couldn't have.' Tommo pauses. 'After that I couldn't give a shit.'

'So, what did you do?'

'I creep up and lift his 'at and give him a light tap on the skull with the blunt and catch him as he sinks to his knees. He's about the same size as me, but I know I'm the younger and stronger, so I slips me axe into the holster across me back and lifts him over me shoulder and crosses to the companionway. It's a bit of a struggle getting him down below and into the saloon. I'm already knackered but I dumps Mr Sparrow on the floor and locks the cabin door and sits down to recover and to await his return to this shitty world. But first I take the precaution of wrapping the woollen scarf tight about his mouth so that he won't wake with a scream and can still breathe through his nostrils.

'Then I takes a look about me. It don't take too long to find his stash what's in a leather saddlebag. There's more in it than even I supposed, gold coin o' course, but mostly it's stuff what's light but can be quickly converted into cash. Diamonds, several gold rings with large ruby and emerald stones and a box o' the finest South Sea pearls you can imagine, maybe two hundred o' the little beauties. There's a stack o' them new five pound banknotes which I can't get both me 'ands around. A fortune carefully put together to be transportable and, I'm telling yer straight, it ain't been gathered in a few days. I am forced to conclude that F. Artie Sparrow has long contemplated there might some day come the need to scarper and was ever ready to escape at a moment's notice. But then I find true paradise, a ball o' opium big as yer fist wrapped in cheesecloth. Mr Sparrow has brought along with him six months supply from Tang Wing Hung.'

Tommo laughs. 'Here I be with a fortune of ill-gained and half a year's supply o' the poppy and I can't do nothing about it. I'm sitting there thinking how bloody typical, Tommo's usual luck, eh? I think I'll find Sparrow's pipe and kill the pain in me 'ead for a while. Then I realise that if he come to while the Angel's Kiss be upon me, I'm history. The craving for opium and the pain in me noggin be so bad I almost think to chop him right there and prepare a pipe and smoke it at me leisure. Then the idea come to me all of a sudden, out o' the blue like. With me craving the poppy I can't think how there be room for such a plan to come into me terrible aching 'ead, but it comes quite sudden and complete and is worthy o' the cunning o' Ikey Solomon himself.

'I begin to remove Mr Sparrow's clothes, first his Ikey coat, which I can see will fit a treat, then his jacket, weskit and blouse, then the fine leather boots and next his trousers and then his long johns and hose. He's bollocky and there's even less of him than me and I wonder how so much evil can be contained in such a little bag o' skin, bones and misery.

'His clobber fits me like a glove and I'm warm and snug and feeling much better for the change from me own wet garments. Mr Sparrow is beginning to stir and so I pulls him up until he's sitting with his back against the cabin wall and his head lolling, chin on chest.

'His eyes open, bleary at first then with sudden light, he can't talk o' course but the surprise they show is speech enough. He looks down and sees he's naked and jerks backwards against the cabin wall and quickly brings his 'ands to cover his little blue worm.

' "Good evening, Mr Sparrow," I says. I can hear him whimper behind the scarf. So I lifts my axe and puts me finger to me lips so he'll know to stay stum and removes the scarf, though he could have done as well himself his hands not being bound.

' "Tommo!" he says, all surprised. "Where am I?" he asks, still lookin' dazed like.

' "Shush! Where you was before, but now you've got company," says I.

'He looks about the cabin and I can see he's thinking what to say next. Then he turns to me, "How much?"

'I laugh and point to the saddlebag, "Too late for that, mate. I've got the lot and what's stashed in this coat, but you might oblige me by takin' them rings from your fingers."

' "Don't know that they'll come free," he says, still a bit cheeky like. I got to 'and it to him, little bugger's got spunk orright.

'I shrugs and wave the axe. "Easy, always cut 'em loose, makes no bloody difference to me, do it?"

'He gets the rings off without too much trouble and I takes them and drops them in me coat pocket.

' "Righto then, up you gets." I point to me wet clothes, "Put 'em on."

' "But they're wet?" he protests.

' "Never mind, where you're goin' they'll soon enough be dry." I grins, but I don't think he gets the joke. It takes him a while to get the wet clobber on but what fits me fits him fine. I point to a wicker chair what's in the cabin. "Sit."

'He sits in the chair with his hands folded in his lap

shiverin' like a captured mouse. I know how he feels in the wet clobber, so I takes a blanket from the bunk and throws it at him and he wraps it around himself, his 'ead an' all. He looks like a scrawny old crone begging for alms.

'I don't reckon he'll make a sudden jump for me, I don't see it in his eyes. I can tell he still thinks he'll use his noggin, talk hisself out of trouble. But he's forgot I were brought up by Ikey Solomon, what could talk hisself out o' the condemned cell with the hangman's noose already 'round his neck. F. Artie Sparrow ain't in the same class o' spruiker. Besides, with the blanket wrapped around him it will be harder if he tries to 'ave a go at me.

' "What you going to do to me, Tommo?" he asks at last.

' "Well now, let's see. I reckon about the same as you done to Miss Maggie Pye. What say you, Mr Sparrow?"

' "She were a whore, Fat Fred fucked her to death, that ain't got nothing ter do with me."

' "Fat Fred couldn't get it up at a whore's Christmas party, yer bastard. What you did was murder Maggie and you thought it were funny, a bit o' fun for the Sydney lads and you, at the same time, gettin' your revenge on me brother Hawk!"

' "No, no," he pleads, "It were no such thing. I swear on me life!"

' "Your life? Right now it ain't worth a pinch o' shit. I've 'ad a chat to Johnny Terrible, he's told me everything, you bastard!"

' "Please," he says, "spare me and you'll not regret it, Tommo!"

' "Spare you? Jesus! Whaffor?"

' "We could go into business, son. I'll cut you in for 'arf o' everything, we'd make a bleedin' fortune you and me." He cocks his 'ead to the side, "You with the flats and me managing the game. There'd be none better in all the colonies." He tries to smile, to crawl right up me arse. "Mr Ace o' Spades, you're the best, the very best there is with the cards, never seen better, a bloody miracle them 'ands. Miracle o' motion and deception. You've got talent nigh to genius, no, correction, you *is* genius."

' "And both of us needin' the poppy regular, eh? A fine threesome, you, me and the opium pipe. Bullshit!" His nose is running and he's commenced to snivellin' and shiverin' and I can see that the courage 'as suddenly leaked out o' him, there's wet tears runnin' down his cheeks.'

' "What say you, then?" he whimpers, his teeth achatter. I don't know whether the shaking is from the cold or his fear, both perhaps. Mr Sparrow spreads his hands and shrugs and appeals to me with the wet eyes, "Please, Tommo, spare me," he cries.

' "Mr Sparrow, I didn't come to bargain, as I see it right now, I ain't got too much time meself. I come to do what I've promised I'd do since I were seven year old and four of you mongrels, you dog fuckers, stretched me over a Huon log in the Wilderness. Pulled down me torn britches and threw me over that fallen log. I remember its lemon-yellow bark were stripped, just like me, me and the pine, both bollock naked, me with me face kissin' the damp forest earth and it fallen to the same by the cruel axes o' the wood fetchers. Then them buggering me, laughing, snotting over me back and me arse bleeding so the blood's running down the inside o' me legs. Them leavin', footsteps crackling through the fern and myrtle bush, laughing, whooping, doin' up their buckles and buttoning their britches. You fuck little boys too, don'tcha, Mr Sparrow?"

' "Tommo, Tommo! I'm like you," Mr Sparrow wails. "They done the same t'me! The very same! Ask Ikey! He took me from Hannah Solomon's brothel where I were a catamite! He said I were too smart to be raped for sixpence by a turd burglar!"

' "Ikey's long dead," I snap. I don't need Sparrow's begging. I don't want him to be like me, even in this.

'He begins to sob again. "It's true, I swear it's true!" For a moment there I'm almost sorry for him, then I remember Maggie and other things I've 'eard about what F. Artie Sparrow's done if a whore angers him, Maggie ain't the first he's done in.

' "So?" I says, "You knew about the mongrels and you grew up and became one o' them, a mongrel yerself and worse than most. Does that make it right, then?"

'He sniffs and gulps back a sob. "I survived, Tommo. I stayed alive."

' "Me too, only just, but I didn't join the bloody mongrels."

'He is silent for a while, sobbing and wiping his snotty nose, pinching at it with his thumb and forefinger. I don't say nothing, letting him think to himself awhile. Then he slowly raises his head and looks at me. "What you gunna do to me?" he asks, his voice real small.

'I don't even really hear meself saying it, it just come out natural, like I've been wanting to say it since I were seven years old and in the Wilderness alone. "I'm gunna kill you, Mr Sparrow, it's what's long overdue for your kind."

'He begins to sob even harder than before, not looking at me, gulping and choking and taking to the hiccups and all the while begging for his life between his blubbing. I've had enough, so I taps him hard on the head with the blunt o' the axe and he slumps out of the chair to the floor. I stretches him out on his back and goes to work.

'Me head's hurting like hell and I know I ain't got much time, the craving for the poppy is buildin' up and

I'm beginning to shake for the need o' the blessed pipe. I take the Tiki from my neck and lifts his head and puts it round his neck, then my purse with four pounds and several o' me calling cards in it. I put it in his jacket pocket, then me hunter with the ace of spades on the outside lid and the gold sovereign 'anging on its chain which I fits to his weskit pocket and secures the fob.

'I stands back and looks down at him. Matter 'o fact he don't look that unlike me and with a bit o' splashing around in the sea water and after the fishies 'ave a go at him nobody will be able to tell the difference. Not that I expect he'll be washed ashore before a shark gets to him, though you never know with the ship still hugging the coastline.

'Like I said, in me anger to get to him, to get aboard and kill him, I've not thought too much about escaping after. Now me plan's changed. So I put me axe in the holster to my back and lifts him again and carries him up the hatchway, it's harder even than before. He seems heavier somehow and I'm exhausted as I get up the last o' the steps and dump him on the deck. I'm puffing like a bull mastiff after a pit fight and I'm forced to sit and rest. It's still dark, the moon not broken through yet and I've only a few feet to go to the starboard rail.

'I get up and half drags him and then slumps him over the ship's railing and I'm about to lift him over when I remember something Hammerhead Jack once told me on the *Nankin Maiden*. How it comes to me at that moment I can't rightly say, it were not thought out, just comes into me 'ead like before.'

Tommo looks up at Hawk. 'Hammerhead Jack once told me if the Maori want to get rid o' someone with no trace they takes him out to sea and chops off his head, so nobody can identify the phiz and the *moko* markings upon it. "The body float but head it sinks like a stone,

Tommo, eh. No head, no know him!" He gimme this grin so I don't know if he be serious or what. "No meat on head, on body plenty to eat?"

'I'm only glad Sparrow is out to it. It is sufficient he knew before I tapped him that he was gunna die. He'd shit himself at that, I could smell it as I carried him up the hatchway. Even after what he did to Maggie I can't bring meself to wait 'til he come round to tell him the Hammerhead Jack manner o' his death. So I lops him there and then. Three sharp blows at the back of the neck and the head drops into the waves below like a stone and the blood pours out his neck like a pipe's burst, four feet into the air and arches into the foamy brine below, enough to attract a hundred sharks. I wipes the blade on the back o' his jacket then grabs him by the ankles and tips the rest o' him over the ship's rail. Over he goes, a complete somersault and hits the waves spread-eagled. Good riddance to bad rubbish. With the wash against the bow it don't hardly makes a noise. Then I throw up over the rail.'

Tommo pauses at last and Hawk can see that he's been pretending to be calm, but is terribly upset at the telling, never having brought what happened to the surface before. He puts his arm around Tommo's shoulders and holds him against his chest, his brother is shivering and then begins to sob. 'I got them, I got the mongrels, didn't I, Hawk? Maggie would 'ave been happy knowing what I done for her, hey?'

Hawk is himself crying, holding his brother, sobbing for the agony of Tommo's bitter life. His tiny brother just twenty-one years and some months old, now with his life so nearly over. Hawk can see that Tommo's eyes have lost their focus and his twin is shaking violently. 'Do you need a pipe, Tommo?'

'Aye,' Tommo replies, his voice barely above a whisper.

Hawk has grown accustomed to preparing Tommo's opium pipe. The great ball of opium Tommo carried away from Mr Sparrow is almost used up. It is as though Tommo's life is to be measured by the diminishing size of the sticky black paste.

Hawk finds the oil lamp, its glass like an upside-down bell the shape of a lily and lights it; the flame in the centre of the glass looks like a golden stamen looking down into a lily. Then he takes a small clay bowl and fills it with the black paste which he heats slightly until it reaches the consistency of treacle and with a long steel needle he dips into the bowl and winds a small amount of paste onto its end. This he warms over the flame until the small pearl of opium begins to bubble. He places the smouldering opium into the bowl of Tommo's pipe and watches as his twin pulls the opium smoke into his lungs, his very life seeming to depend on it. Each pearl allows only three or four puffs and Hawk repeats the process until the bowl is empty which takes almost an hour. Afterwards Tommo drifts into a deep contented sleep.

Hawk has long since given up trying to stop Tommo from using the poppy. He knows it is the only way to kill the pain that is slowly bringing his twin's life to an end. Carefully he cleans the pipe and the bowl and blows out the lamp and stores it with the little opium that remains. He has no way of obtaining more unless he should visit Auckland and hope to find it on the waterfront. It is a task he is willing to do if his twin survives beyond the last of Mr Sparrow's supply. Though the idea of leaving Tommo for the three, perhaps four, days it will take to make the journey and return fills him with the utmost concern that Tommo may die while he is away.

Now, as his twin sleeps on his reed bed, Hawk covers him with a blanket. 'I loves you, Tommo,' he says softly, 'sleep now awhile.'

The remainder of Tommo's story comes out over the next week or so. Tommo had the presence of mind to retrieve Mr Sparrow's hat, then wearing the scarf about his face as Mr Sparrow had done, he simply assumed his identity. It seems nobody on board had seen the little villain without his hat pulled down low over his eyes and his scarf wrapped about his face. Mr Sparrow did not even want the captain to know his true appearance when he was smuggled aboard.

Tommo left the ship at Levuka and a few days later caught a ketch going to Auckland and found his way back to Chief Tamihana's village and his baby daughter, Hinetitama.

Over the next three weeks Tommo's lucid periods become less and less frequent, and at night Hawk sleeps on a rush mat on the earthen floor beside Tommo's bed. In the morning he carries him outside to do his business and then prepares his pipe. One morning just after sunrise and three months after Hawk's arrival, Tommo reaches down to touch the slumbering Hawk who thinks he wishes to go outside. Hawk rises and goes to lift him, but his brother shakes his head and now Hawk sees that his eyes, his sad blue eyes, are clear and his mind is lucid.

'What is it, Tommo? Water?' Tommo has neither eaten nor taken anything to drink for two days and Hawk reaches down for a small earthenware dish filled with water and holds it to his twin's lips. Tommo's lips are cracked and they tremble with the effort of swallowing so that most of it runs over his chin and down his neck, brightening the emerald-green surface of the Tiki about his neck.

Hawk places the gourd on the floor beside the bed and takes Tommo's tiny hands in his own. 'Do you want a pipe, mate?' His twin's hands are cold to his touch and Hawk starts to gently massage them, hoping to transfer some of his own warmth into his brother's trembling fingers.

Hawk thinks about the hands he holds, so deceptive, clumsy to look at, ugly even. The palms are criss-crossed with white axe scars, several fingers bent and knobbed from being broken and not set back straight from his twin's time as a captive child in the Southwest Wilderness. Yet Tommo's hands are proved so elegant and mercurial when they hold a pack of cards and so certain and deadly when clasped about the handle of a fighting axe. His brother's hands, always his chief mischief-makers, now look innocent and helpless clasped in his own great paws.

'No pipe, not yet,' Tommo whispers. 'There are two more things I must speak of, Hawk.'

'What is it?'

Tommo tries to rise, his hand trembles as he points to the corner of the hut. 'It's buried in the corner, the satchel, Mr Sparrow's. I don't know how much, but it's a lot.'

'Shall I fetch it?' Hawk says.

Tommo shakes his head, 'Nah, just to know it's there. Jewels, everything, a king's ransom.'

'What is it you want me to do with it?'

'Buy land. For the Maori. Buy it back for them from the pakeha, much as you can.'

'You mean in perpetuity?'

Tommo doesn't know the word and he rests for a moment, panting. 'There is a Maori saying, "Until the sun is dowsed in the sea", buy it for them so it can never be took back, much as you can, spend it all.'

'It won't be easy, I'll have to get a land agent and tell him it's for a big pakeha interest.'

'Aye, you do that. Then give it to the Ngati Haua people forever, tell Tamihana it's Hinetitama's, my daughter's gift to her people.'

'And what of her? Will you not want some of it to go to her, some small portion?'

Tommo's shake of the head is barely perceived. 'Nah,

it's tainted.' He brings his hand slowly to his neck and touches the Tiki, 'Give her this, the God Tiki has seen all my wickedness and will protect her from the same.'

'What of your axe, will she have that too?'

'Nah, you keep it, if she should have a son, give it to him.'

Hawk can see that Tommo's strength is fading fast. 'Will you take a pipe now?' he asks. Hawk does not know how to tell Tommo that there remains barely enough of the Angel's Kiss for one more pipe.

To his surprise Tommo shakes his head, refusing the pipe. 'Hawk, I loves you,' his voice has an increasingly hoarse quality and Hawk must strain to hear him. His twin pauses, licking his dry lips, breathing heavily, trying to catch his breath again, 'Hinetitama. Don't let the mongrels get her.'

Hawk, overwhelmed with sadness, places Tommo's hands gently back into his lap, then gathers up his twin in his great arms and begins to rock him. 'Oh, Tommo, oh, sweet Tommo,' he moans. 'Oh, my sweet, sweet brother, I shall guard your little daughter with my very life.' Hawk starts to weep as he feels his twin beginning to slip away from him. 'No, no, stay, Tommo, stay a while,' he chokes. 'Please don't leave me!'

Tommo sighs softly and, safe at last from the mongrels, dies in his brother's strong, loving arms.

Within minutes the first of the death-wailing begins, a great and sudden overflowing of grief, as if by some osmosis the tribe knows Tommo is dead. Those who possess firearms commence to shoot them to announce his passing and show their respect. Chief Tamihana arrives at Tommo's hut minutes later and squats before the grieving Hawk and their noses touch. They hold this nose-rubbing position for nearly ten minutes so that the old chief might show his respect to Hawk and Tommo and their ancestors.

Then he announces the *hui* for the *tangihanga*, the wailing for the dead.

Hawk dresses Tommo carefully and his body is carried to the *marae*, the meeting hut, where it will lie in state, for Tamihana has declared that Tommo must have the honours of an important *rangatira* bestowed upon his death rituals.

Tommo is dressed in Mr Sparrow's clothes and boots since they are of a high quality and have scarcely been worn as Tommo reverted to the Maori fashion of dressing. In his long black Ikey Solomon coat and his fine hat he looks more substantial in death than in life.

In less than half an hour the women emerge from the dark line of the forest, carrying armloads of *kawakawa*, the creeper that symbolises death. This they festoon about the meeting house and wave about themselves in the ritual *powhiri* dance.

The old women appear at the *marae* dressed in black and begin the *tangi*, a dance performed together with a high, uncanny wail and much breast beating to express their grief for the recently deceased as well as to summon all the dead to attend the *hui* in the *marae*.

They surround Tommo, moving in a halting fashion about him, wailing, waving the *kawakawa* creeper and singing '*Haere atu, ka tu ka tangi; haere atu, ka tu ka tangi*' ('Move, stand and weep; move, stand and weep').

Soon men and women from the surrounding tribes arrive at the outskirts of the village and halt, waiting to be welcomed with true warmth as they have come to pay their respects to the little warrior Tommo Te Mokiri, the leader of the now legendary fifty-five fighting axes, heroes of the Maori wars. Chief Wiremu Kingi of the Ati Awa tribe sends a large delegation of mourners but lies sick abed and cannot come himself, though he sends his chief orator to take part in the *whaikorero,* the oration.

Their women wail, showing their sorrow is of a great and appropriate kind and when it reaches a crescendo, the tribal women dancing the *tangi* return this wailing in a most melodious way, '*Neke neke mui, neke neke mui*' ('Draw nearer, draw nearer'). They have been welcomed with the Maori heart.

The women wail while the men weep silently and bow their heads; all about there is the deep hum-wail of grief as the tribe's tears flow for the dead. Soon the old women, those whose beauty has passed and wisdom has become fixed to their faces, lacerate themselves, cutting the skin of their faces and breasts, arms and legs with a sliver of obsidian until they bleed on all the exposed surfaces of their bodies.

The wailing and weeping for Tommo continues for three days to show the extremity of their grief. Their respect for him is witnessed by the copious amount of tears and nose mucus which is left to drip unchecked so that the song '*Na te hupe me nga roimata, ka ea te mate*' ('By tears and nose mucus, death is avenged') may be seen to be true.

There is much oratory performed in this period known as the *mihi*, where etiquette demands that orators are carefully chosen with the appropriate praises and lamentations given according to their rank. Chief Tamihana has briefed a famous orator, a master of genealogy, ancient chants and local history, who has at his command all the appropriate proverbs.

The orator, who Hawk sees is a consummate actor, creates a great spoken drama on the life of Tommo Te Mokiri. He tells of an ancient time when a great and wise king whose name was Solomon married a black Queen of Sheba, a woman of exquisite beauty, and how forever thereafter each generation produced two sons, one black and the other white, a giant and a small man, so people might know that small men and big, black and white, have an equal part in life. At this remark the mourners look to Hawk who stands at seven feet tall, the magnificent General Hawk, their beloved Black Maori, and then at the diminutive body of Tommo, whereupon a fresh wailing commences which causes the orator to stop until he may be heard again. He describes Tommo's exploits in the great battle of Puke Te Kauere where Tommo got the wound that has brought about his death. He even makes the mourners laugh a moment when he tells of how Tommo was saved in the swamp water by having his head against the great arse of a dead British soldier. He goes on to explain that Tommo's ancestor, Icky Slomon, sits on the Council of the Dead as a Maori ancestor and that his advice is no doubt much respected by the ancestors.

Hawk thinks of poor old Ikey sitting among the Maori chiefs of the past where the luxury of roast pork is the daily fare, 'my dear-ing' them with every sentence and trying to teach them the intricacies of cribbage and the Jewish perspective of seeing every point of view in an argument and so defeating it with commonsense.

There is much wailing and nose mucus as the mourners show their appreciation for the dead Tommo Te Mokiri who has left them his seed in the form of the Princess Hinetitama, an infant to be brought up in the Maori tradition in the household of Chief Tamihana.

While Chief Tamihana and his *tohunga*, the priests, do not allow the supreme honour of a chief, that Tommo's heart be cut out and buried separately in a sacred place, forever *tapu*, so that any person who approaches the place of its burial will meet with certain death, they agree that his body may be placed high up in one of the tallest trees in the forest where it will remain until all the flesh has fallen from him. After the women have cleaned his bones and skull, they will be placed in a cave looking to the east where he can forever greet the morning sun.

Hawk remains a further fortnight during which time he takes a Maori ketch to Auckland and interviews several land agents until he finds an American with the improbable name of Geronimo Septimus Thompson, who he believes he might trust. Using the five pound notes in Mr Sparrow's stash he opens a letter of credit with the Bank of New South Wales in Auckland and, visiting the Government Surveyor's office, he studies the land titles abutting the Ngati Haua tribal lands. He instructs Geronimo Thompson to buy out the small farms surrounding it.

'You will offer two times what the property is worth,' Hawk tells him, 'and allow six months or the next crop to come to the landowner before he must vacate. The name of the buyer must never be known, Mr Thompson, do you understand me?'

'But how much shall I buy?' asks the bemused Thompson. 'Is there a limit? Five thousand acres? More? Farmland only?'

'You must buy everything, valleys, fields, forests, hills, mountains, rivers and streams. If you can find a way to deal with the Almighty I wish you to buy the sky as well,' Hawk instructs him, but then cautions Thompson, 'The parcel must be clean, there can be no farms left unvacated in any part of the land you buy except at its perimeters. I shall return in a year and instruct you further.'

'But, but . . .' Thompson splutters, 'such an undertaking will attract attention, if I have no name for the purchaser, how shall I answer?'

'You will buy the land in the name of the Bank of New South Wales and they will hold the titles.' By doing this Hawk has prevented any possibility of Thompson cheating him.

Hawk returns to the tribe and informs Chief Tamihana that he must return at once to Australia. The old chief commands that a great farewell feast be held on the *marae* in his honour.

During the festivities and much to Hawk's embarrassment, Chief Tamihana invites Hawk's old friend, the one-armed, one-eyed Hammerhead Jack to tell the *rangatira*, the elders of the tribe, and the *tohunga*, and all those gathered at the *hui* about the time Hawk saved his life when the great sperm whale had overturned their whaleboat and his arm had been severed by the harpoon line.

'I am not much Maori, with only one arm and one eye, but my *mana* is in my left eye and it would be my privilege to die for my brother, Ork,' Hammerhead Jack concludes at the end of his talk.

The *rangatira* clap and shout their approval of Hammerhead Jack's sentiments. Chief Tamihana has earlier reminded them of the contribution of General Black Hawk, who with his new guerilla tactics, which the Maori call 'the running away war', made the forces of Wiremu Kingi and General Hapurona achieve victories against the British. They have more to add to the collective memory of the giant black man they think of as one of their own.

It is an altogether grand farewell though Hawk is somewhat bemused at how his reputation as a fighting man and as a general has grown in his absence.

'Chief Tamihana, I am honoured to be counted among you, to be accepted as *rangatira*, but surely you speak of a stranger. I have neither the wisdom nor the bravery you bestow upon me. Of the running away war, it was something I learned in books and I cannot take credit for it.' Hawk walks over and stands beside Hammerhead Jack who is seated among the highest of the *rangatira*. 'We have been brothers in war and I could ask for no braver man at my side. At the battle of Puke Te Kauere it was *this* man who was the true general when we fought outside the *pa*.

Without him we could not have succeeded and without him Tommo would have drowned in the swamp. How can I merit praise when it is due so much more to others, to this man, my Maori brother?'

The *rangatira* clap, enjoying Hawk's modesty and his copious praise for one of their own warriors. Hawk promises he will return each year to attend to the needs of Tommo's daughter Hinetitama and to sit with his brothers in the *marae*. He tells them that he knows himself to be a Maori in his heart and is of the Ngati Haua tribe and he wears their *moko* on his face with great pride.

He thanks the *rangatira* and is careful to do the same to the *tohunga*. Priests, Hawk has observed, have long memories for small slights, and finally he thanks Chief Tamihana for the honour they have bestowed on Tommo by giving him the burial rights of a great warrior and for elevating him to the ranks of the *rangatira*.

Hawk will sail in the morning and it is late, with a full moon high in the night sky. Chief Tamihana sees him to the hut they have provided for him in the chief's compound. 'I shall leave you now my friend and we will sail you to Auckland in the morning, I have but one more gift for you which I hope you will enjoy.'

'Gift? I have been honoured beyond any possible merit, Tamihana, I have been given the gift of brotherhood and of your friendship. With Tommo dead there is none I value more than yours and that of Hammerhead Jack.'

Tamihana chuckles softly. 'Ah, Hawk, this is but the gift of one night, an old memory revisited.' With this remark he bids Hawk goodnight and takes his leave.

Hawk is too tired to think what the old chief might mean and gratefully enters his hut. The night carries a cool breeze from the mountains and Hawk wraps a blanket about himself and is preparing to sleep when he becomes conscious of a shadow darkening the door of his hut, blocking out the moonlight.

'Who is it?' he says wearily. He has talked and listened too much for one night and wishes only to be left alone.

'It is me, General Black Hawk, Hinetitama, whose name you have taken for the daughter of Tommo. Do you remember me?'

It is as if time has stood in the same place, for in the moonlight he watches as the woman loosens the neck cord and allows her feather cloak, the sign of a highborn Maori, to fall at her feet.

In the silvered air Hawk can see that she is still as beautiful as when she first came to him. He can remember almost every word Hinetitama said to him that first night so long ago. 'Oh, Black Maori, I have wanted you so very long. I have eaten you with my eyes and I have tasted you in my heart a thousand times. I have moaned for you alone in my blanket and my mouth has cried out to hold your manhood. My breasts have grown hard from longing for you and I have brought pleasure to myself in your name.'

Hawk's throat aches suddenly, for he can think only of Maggie Pye, her sweetness and her brash and unashamed love for him. Maggie so different to this beautiful shadow in the night.

Now the moonlight throws a silver sheen across her skin and he can see the curve of her breasts and stomach. It is as if he is within a dream repeated, each detail the same as before even though so much has changed in him.

Hinetitama crosses the small hut and she lifts his blanket and lies beside him. 'I have never forgotten you, Black Maori,' she whispers into Hawk's ear. She begins to kiss him, as she did before, across his chest and belly, moving lower and lower. Hawk feels himself grow hard. 'Oh, Maggie, forgive me,' he moans silently, for Hinetitama's mouth has reached his trembling hardness and now it engulfs him. Hawk thinks that he will die with the pleasure of her lips and, just when he feels he can bear it no longer, she withdraws and her hand guides him into her so that she now sits astride him. Hawk begins to moan softly.

'Black Hawk, have you learned nothing from your pakeha women?' she laughs. 'You must wait for me, there is a twice greater pleasure when the moment is shared.'

'Aye,' Hawk gasps, and then adds in the Maori tongue, 'But I am only a mortal man.' He can see the flash of her white teeth as she laughs and the fine curve of her neck and the sheen of moonlight as it catches the rounded slant of her shoulder.

'Ah, but did you say this to your Maggie Pye?' She laughs again.

Hawk's eyes open in sudden surprise. 'Maggie! You know of Maggie?' he exclaims.

'See how I have caused you to wait.' Hinetitama laughs again. 'It is not so hard to contain your pleasure when your mind is distracted.'

'Yes, but how? How do you know of Maggie?' Hawk repeats urgently.

'The Maori are everywhere, Black Hawk. Our men are sailors on the whaling ships and those that bring timber to Sydney. Many of our women are widows who have lost their husbands in the wars against the pakeha and so remain barren and unloved for lack of men, some have been taken by the pakeha sailing captains to Sydney.' She laughs. 'As a lover I can't say you have improved, but you have become a great fighter since you left us, a great man who is known by all the Maori in Sydney. You also honoured my tribe when you took Johnny Heki to train you, he is a Maori with my *moko*. Ah, Black Hawk, there is much we know of you, for you are one of us and they are our Gods who protect you now and forever.'

Hawk, taken by surprise at the mention of Maggie's name, has lost much of his tumescence. Hinetitama's voice takes on a mocking quality. 'First you cannot wait for me, now you wait too long,' she teases softly. 'Black Hawk, if you do not make love to me better than this, I shall think your Maggie Pye has taught you nothing.'

With her words and her laughter and her permission to love her free of the constraints of Maggie's memory, she withdraws and lies beside him and Hawk enters her again and now he releases his sadness and his grief for his sweet Maggie and for Tommo's death in Hinetitama's wild and generous loving.

'Ah, Black Hawk, I was wrong,' Hinetitama sighs at last. 'The pakeha woman with the bird in her hair, this Maggie, has taught you well how to please a wahine.' Her lips brush his face lightly and then she rises and picks up her feathered cloak from beside his rush bed and he watches as she moves silently out into the moonlit compound.

'Thank you,' Hawk calls softly after her. 'Thank you, Hinetitama.'

Chapter Two

HINETITAMA

1881–1885

At twenty-one Tommo's half-caste daughter is a great beauty with skin the colour of wild honey and hair dark as a raven's wing. She is small, no more than five feet and one inch, but despite her diminutive frame she has a contralto voice of great power and of a most serene beauty. But from all these gifts from a generous God must be subtracted a spirit headstrong and wilful and a nature as wild as her father Tommo's once was.

Hawk has kept his promise to Tommo that his daughter will be raised to maturity within the household of Chief Tamihana but when she is six years old Hawk's dear friend and Hinetitama's Maori guardian dies and Tommo's daughter is cared for by Chief Mahuta Tawhiao, with the old chief's daughter given responsibility for the young child's daily care.

When Tamihana knew he was coming to the end of his life he wrote to Hawk. The letter is unusual because the old chief, in a missive so serious, appended a note mentioning women's matters, in particular those of a child.

Though Chief Tamihana could well have instructed the letter be sent to Hawk in Tasmania, he wanted his old friend to read it on Maori land while he and his ancestors

45

could look over his shoulder. Hawk was to receive it on
his next annual trip to New Zealand to see Hinetitama
and to supervise the purchase of more land. The letter,
intended for posterity, had been carefully scripted while
the note was in the old chief's mission-taught
handwriting.

April 1866

My friend Black Hawk,

*We shall no longer sit together by the evening fire or eat again
from the same pot. I have now seen sixty summers and it is time for me
to join my ancestors.*

*I am writing this letter to you, Black Maori, so that you will
hold my life on the page and be its custodian and then, perhaps some
day, history will judge me for what I tried to do and failed.*

*I have had a long life for a Maori man, who does not often
see his hair turn white, and who is usually dead while his seed is still
strong in his loins. In my time too many of our brave young men have
died for some foolish tribal war fought out of false pride or from
seeking retribution for some imagined insult.*

*When I was a boy my father sent me to the missionaries to
learn the white man's language and his ways. 'You must see if they have
lessons for us,' he instructed.*

I studied hard and learned to read and write and spent much time with the pakeha's Bible. I learned that it was a good book from a merciful God and I found it so myself. But I was soon to discover that it was the white man's Sunday book only and all the remaining days of the week the pakeha felt free to disobey the commandments of his own God.

It was then that I first realised that the pakeha's word could not be trusted, not even on Sunday, for it was not founded in his mana. That his God was good only for births and burials and his word was as worthless as a broken pot.

I knew then that the Treaty of Waitangi was like the white man's word, and that the Maori would never have justice under the pakeha Queen Victoria or the laws she makes.

When I came to my manhood the Maori people had killed more of their own kind than the pakeha. They had taken the white man's gun and turned it on their own. We have killed more than twenty thousand of our people while the pakeha stood by and watched the Maori die, thinking that soon there would be no Maori to come up against them and they could take all our land for their spotted cows.

And so I grew to be a man and I became the peacemaker among the tribes and then the kingmaker, joining all the Maori under King Potatau te Wherowhero so that we could speak with one voice.

Alas, the pakeha did not want us to stop killing our own and they forced us to go to war with them. It was here that you, Black Hawk, became a Maori warrior and gained great distinction, so that you became a rangatira to be forever honoured in the Ngati Haua tribe and among all the Maori people.

Though we fought with honour the pakeha had too many guns and too many soldiers and we forsook the clever ways of our previous guerilla war, the runaway fighting you taught us and we went back to defending the pa and so were beaten, but remained proud in defeat, a worthy opponent.

Now, as I lie dying, I know that the pakeha, in defeating us, has taken everything from us but one last thing. Our warriors still fight in the hills where no pakeha dare go. They have created a redoubt that holds within it the Maori pride. While we have our pride they cannot destroy our race. I pray that it is always there. Ake ake ake. You must speak for us, you must be my elbow and my backbone, General Black Hawk.

I shall die with a curse on my lips for the white man, for what they have done to my people. But there is one exception, Tommo Te Mokiri, who bought back for us, through your hands, the rivers and the streams, the mountains and the hills, the forests and the glades and the good tilling soil all of which once belonged to our people and which the pakeha conspired to take from us. It is for this that I now decree, having talked through the tohunga to the ancestors, that Tommo Te Mokiri's daughter shall be made a true princess of the Maori people.

I go to my ancestors knowing that the Maori mana is the spirit of Aotearoa and that it will prevail. Ake ake ake. In our hearts we cannot be defeated until the earth sinks into the sea.

I go to my ancestors now, where I shall watch over you like a father watches over his beloved son.

Wiremu Tamihana,
Chief of the Ngati Haua Maori.

To this formal letter Tamihana penned his own note.

My friend Black Hawk,

I have kept my promise and now I deliver the Princess Hinetitama to the care of Mahuta Tawhiao, who will care for her as I have done and see that she is instructed in the Maori traditions befitting her high rank.

She is a Maori wahine in all things save one. She is yet a piglet barely weaned from the teats but already she is as stubborn as an old sow. On more than one occasion I have instructed that she be beaten by the old women in my household for disobedience, but she will not bend to their will, no matter how severe her punishment. I think she

has this from her father, Tommo Te Mokiri.

When the time comes you must find her a strong warrior who

will teach her to be a quiet flowing stream as a woman must be to a man

if there is to be peace in his household.

Her singing has brought me great delight and her laughter is

always among us. I thank you for the pleasure she has brought me in

my old age, she will be a worthy princess of our people.

Your friend,

Wiremu Tamihana.

Hawk has kept his pledge to Tommo and visited Hinetitama every year of her life. Now that she has grown to womanhood he wants her to come home to Hobart, to be with Mary, who wishes above all things to have the company of her granddaughter at her side.

However, to his mortification, Hinetitama will hear of no such thing and asserts her independence, telling him she wishes to go to Auckland to become a nurse.

'But you may do the same training in Hobart, we will find you an excellent opportunity and we will all be together?' Hawk insists.

Hinetitama is silent, her eyes downcast, then she looks up. 'I must stay here, Uncle. I want to go to Auckland to be among the poor.'

'The poor are everywhere, my dear. You will find as many in Hobart as you wish to care for.'

'Maori poor?'

'The poor have no nation, or colour or creed, they are

luxuries they cannot afford. Poverty is the one universal brotherhood, my dear.'

'But I am a Maori. I must be with my own people.'

'Only half, the other is pakeha. Grandmother Mary prays that she might have the pleasure of knowing you, of setting eyes upon your sweet face, before she dies.'

Hinetitama gives a soft deprecating laugh. 'I cannot bring pleasure to one rich old woman when so many poor suffer for lack of attention.'

Hawk is shocked at the bluntness of her remark. 'I would not have looked upon it quite like that. Your grandmother has known the worst of poverty and degradation, she will not condemn you for your desire to work among the poor. You must not judge her so harshly, she wishes only to know you as her only grandchild.'

'Uncle, I mean no impertinence, you have always said I must obey my conscience.'

Hawk sighs. 'Hinetitama, it is your duty to also obey me,' he says sternly. 'I wish you to come to Hobart. Your grandmother wishes it, that is all.'

Hawk sees the stubborn set of her jaw as Hinetitama answers. 'Uncle Hawk, when we were young and you would come to New Zealand every year and we would take long walks, you told me about my father, how he wished me to remain among the Maori, among my mother's people, and then when I came of age to make up my own mind.' She looks defiantly at Hawk. 'I have decided to work among my own people. My grandmother does not need me, they do.'

'Your grandmother has promised me she will do as Tommo wished and that you be included in her will. If you obey and honour her wishes you will become a very wealthy lady. You will be able to help a great many more of your people. Be a little patient, my dear,' Hawk pleads. 'A few years to be kind to an old woman and then you may do as you wish, I will not stop you.'

'Ha! You would bribe me, Uncle,' Hinetitama says scornfully. 'I must sit at the feet of an old woman, I must lick her boots so that I may feed the poor. Is that what you are saying?'

'It is not a sin to be rich and then to spend what you have on those less fortunate than you.'

'And it is not a sin to be poor with strong hands and a good heart. The Maori do not need the pakeha money, their handouts, what we need is to regain our pride. I will do more for them working among them in torn clothes than strutting around in new boots and with an open purse.'

Hawk sees in Hinetitama the same idealism he himself felt at her age and he secretly admires her for her determination. God knows the poor and the destitute among the Maori in the city have need enough for someone of their own kind to care about them. Since the Maori wars things have gone from bad to worse for the indigenous people of New Zealand and poverty, sickness, malnutrition and drunkenness promise to do as much to eliminate them.

But Hawk also has Mary with whom to contend. Mary has never accepted that her only grandchild should be raised among the savages and has railed against it for years. Now he must tell her that Hinetitama will not be coming into civilisation. Hawk well knows Mary's hidden agenda, she wants great-grandchildren, heirs to carry on with the business empire she has so brilliantly begun and Hinetitama is her last chance. And so Hawk, putting aside his conscience, tries for several more days to persuade Hinetitama to travel to Tasmania. But Tommo's daughter is resolute in her decision.

Hawk finds himself between the devil and the deep blue sea. In all conscience he can find no reasonable argument with Hinetitama's ambition. After all, she has

HINETITAMA

no aspirations to be a white person, a tribe she is deeply suspicious of. Raised under the influence of Chief Tamihana she is steeped in Maori tradition and in the knowledge that the Maori have been cheated and swindled by the pakeha. She simply cannot see any virtue in learning to be a proper lady or adopting European values and ways.

As the days go by, Hawk finds it increasingly hard to counter her defiance. Several times his anger at her unreasonableness has reduced her to tears, but she weeps from frustration that he cannot see her viewpoint. Hawk notes that after each such occasion she seems strengthened in her resolve.

Finally, having exhausted every argument and plea, he agrees that she can stay. He has been warned of her stubbornness by Chief Tamihana, but he always felt that because of his love for Tommo's daughter over the years and as her guardian, she would obey him without question. It is not the custom for a subservient female member of a family to disobey the wishes of the predominant male in either white or Maori society.

Hinetitama is trained in the Anglican Mission Hospital as a nurse and shortly after she completes her two-year training she leaves the hospital to work among the Auckland poor. She is unusual in this for she is a Maori princess and her bandages and treatments do not come wrapped in a sermon or a plea to repent. Hinetitama brings only her hands and her heart to the slums, together with the songs of her nation, to remind those who have lost their pride, their *mana*, that they belong to a unique people.

Hawk has now taken to visiting her every two years, for despite his letters pleading with her to visit Tasmania, if only for a period brief enough to satisfy her grandmother, she stubbornly refuses, insisting that her work must come first. Mary, for her part, has grown too old to travel to New Zealand.

Hawk grows increasingly frustrated, but realising the futility of punishing Tommo's daughter by withdrawing her small allowance, he deposits a monthly stipend in the bank to see that she has income sufficient to maintain a small clinic. It is obvious to him that she spends little on herself and that she is much loved and respected by the Maori slum dwellers, though whether she is able to do any good among the poor is problematic. It is, he concludes, probably sufficient that she is there among them, a princess of their own, and that the bandages and the salves do less for her patients than her cheerful and compassionate nature and the fact that they see her as one of their own.

Alas, unbeknownst to Hawk and no doubt because of fatigue and the ongoing frustration of dealing with the poor who never seem to improve in their circumstances, Hinetitama has begun to drink herself. At first she is a tippler, an ale or two taken after a long day and for the opportunity to have a bit of a laugh among those for whom she cares, but as time goes on she discovers the false seduction of cheap gin and becomes more and more dependent on grog until she is unable to do without it in her life. She has inherited her father's weakness and his craving.

While Hinetitama continues to work among the disadvantaged, over a period of two years the drink takes possession of her. With her twenty-fifth year approaching, Hawk arrives in New Zealand for his second visit since she came of age only to discover that the clinic has been closed and that Hinetitama has disappeared.

Hawk seeks out the Maori people in her neighbourhood and asks them if they have any news of her. He is a *rangatira* and his *moko* shows him to be of very high rank, so that they must by tradition tell him what they know. But apart from confirming that she is now always drunk and that the clinic has been shut for several months they do not know her whereabouts.

After several days and nights of walking the streets and enquiring in all the harbour-front taverns, he is accosted by a Maori prostitute.

'You want to know about Hinetitama?' she asks him in the Maori language.

'Yes.' Hawk goes to his purse, knowing that information from her kind is seldom given freely.

'No, I don't want your money, Black Hawk.'

'You know me?' Hawk asks in surprise.

'We are from the same tribe,' she answers simply.

'Ah, you know Hinetitama?'

The prostitute nods.

'Do you know her whereabouts?' Hawk now asks.

'She's taken up with the Dutchman, a gamblin' man, them two's gone to Wellington, last thing I heard say,' she replies.

Hawk continues to question her closely but she cannot help him further though she has the name of Hinetitama's paramour. 'It is Slabbert Teekleman.' She giggles and says in English, 'He is known as Slap 'n Tickle, but he ain't like that, you know, nice? He a bad bugger that one.'

Hawk thanks her and tries to press a half-sovereign into her hand for her trouble. 'I have given you sad news, Black Maori, it would be *tapu*. Hinetitama Te Solomon is a princess of the Ngati Haua.' She points to Hawk's face, to his *moko*. 'I cannot take your money. You are *rangatira*.'

Hawk comes away gratified, thinking that Chief Tamihana may have been right after all, and that the Maori, despite their dispossession, have not entirely lost their pride and dignity.

He hasn't lost his touch and he knows that a gambler can always be found if you know where to look. In

Wellington he visits the waterside pubs and eventually discovers the Dutchman's whereabouts.

Hawk takes a horse cab into the slums of Thorndon and is finally let down in front of a miserable hovel, made of planking, the single window so crusted with dirt that he is unable to see through it into the interior. He knocks on the door, at first politely and then more loudly until, in the end, he is battering at it with his fist. He is about to smash it in with his shoulder when a bleary-eyed man, with dirty yellow hair and bloodshot eyes of a quite startling blue, opens it, though no more than about twelve inches. Hawk sees that he is clean-shaven and still handsome, though he carries several days of growth upon his chin.

'What you want?' the man asks.

'You Teekleman?' Hawk enquires. It is not the sort of neighbourhood where a man qualifies for any status beyond his surname.

'Ja, maybe?'

'Slabbert Teekleman?'

The man ignores Hawk's question, 'What you want, hey?' It is clear he is losing patience and the door begins to close.

Hawk kicks his foot forward, jamming the door open and starts to push it inwards. 'Hey, nigger, what you doing?' the man shouts in alarm. But Hawk has taken him by surprise and pushes the door, his huge shape filling the doorway. Hawk's free hand shoots out and he slaps the surprised man across the face, sending him reeling backwards so that he loses his balance and falls to the floor.

'Get up, you bastard!' Hawk snarls, moving into the hovel so that daylight now pours inwards through the doorway.

The Dutchman gets to his knees and wipes the blood

and mucus from his nose with the back of his hand. 'Please, you don't hit me, please, sir!'

'Where's Hinetitama?' Hawk growls.

'Who?' the man says, though he hesitates a fraction before he speaks and Hawk knows immediately he's covering up.

'Get up, so I can beat the living shit out of you!' Hawk growls again and takes a step towards the Dutchman.

The drunk at his feet pulls back whimpering, scrambling away like a monkey on all fours until he is backed up against the far wall of the tiny room. From the corner of his eye Hawk can see a doorway leading to another room on his left. 'Where's Hinetitama?' he demands again.

The man nods his head to the right and Hawk turns slightly to look at the doorway leading to the next room. 'She dronk.' He gives Hawk a conspiratorial grin. 'Too much the brandy, she Maori, heh?' He shakes his head deprecatingly. 'No goet for grog.'

The doorway has no door and Hawk takes the two or three steps necessary to get to it. Hinetitama is passed out, sprawled naked on a mattress. She is dirty and unkempt with a mass of black hair spread across the top of the filthy mattress. He is too preoccupied to see that her sweet face is unlined and her small, neat body is still firm and beautiful.

Hawk turns back to the man and takes out his purse and throws two sovereigns to the ground. The Dutchman, still on all fours, scrambles after them grabbing one up, testing it with his teeth and then he finds the second coin and does the same again. It is a gesture Hawk will later recall. Then Teekleman grins. 'I go. I don't make no trouble. You see I go now.' He nods his head in the direction of the bedroom door where Hinetitama lies unconscious. 'She go fock herself.'

Hawk for the first time realises that Teekleman is a big man, six foot at the least and perhaps fifteen years younger than him, a strapping fellow who, if he had the heart, the moxie, might be a bit of a handful in a fight. He takes another step forward so that the Dutchman cowers against the wall. He feigns a punch, pulling back his fist, and Teekleman gasps and brings his hands up to protect his face. Hawk sees the terror of a true coward showing in his eyes.

'G'arn, get yer things and scarper, piss off!'

Hinetitama comes screaming through the door to Hawk's left and jumps onto his back from behind and with her arms clasped about his neck she fastens her teeth into his left ear. Hawk has no trouble breaking her grip and she falls naked to the ground. He brings his hand up to where she has bitten him and it comes away bloodied. Then he sees that his shoulder is already covered with blood which seems to be pouring from his ear. Hinetitama has now got him about the leg and fastened her teeth into his calf, snarling like a wild beast. He leans down and pulls her arms away and jerks her up to her feet, then with the other hand holds her about the neck at arm's length so that she is powerless, though she still tries to kick him, lashing at him, but her legs are not long enough to reach him. She is snuffling like a wild animal, too furious to scream. His powerful hand about her throat could easily close down her windpipe and render her unconscious, but she doesn't seem to care, his niece is a hellcat who knows no fear.

'You bastard! You fucking bastard! Leave him alone!' she screams.

In the meantime the Dutchman has taken up his shirt, boots, his violin case and his jacket and hat and is going out the door, fleeing as fast as he can. 'Piss off, you scum!' Hawk shouts after him. 'If you come back I'll break your fucking neck!'

'I go, I go!' the Dutchman cries fearfully.

Hawk has one hand to his ear and with the other holds Hinetitama at bay about the throat. The ear is bleeding so copiously that the blood runs down the back of his hand and down his wrist and is soaking his shirt cuff and saturating the sleeve of his jacket.

Hawk is suddenly conscious that his niece has gone quiet and sees that her eyes are popping out of her head as she tries to breathe. With the concern for the blood pouring from his ear he has inadvertently tightened his grip about her throat and Hinetitama is choking under his grasp. He lets go of her and she falls at his feet, clutching at her neck and coughing, desperately attempting to regain her breath.

Hawk quickly takes off his jacket, bundles it up and holds it to his ear then drops to his knees beside Hinetitama and touches her on the shoulder with the unbloodied hand. 'Are you all right, my dear?' he asks anxiously. 'I'm truly sorry if I've hurt you.'

Hinetitama lies with her knees up against her breast, still gripping her throat with both hands. She has regained her breath and is panting heavily. Her golden body is wondrously beautiful, caught in the light from the door as she turns her head slightly to look up at him. 'Uncle Hawk,' she croaks in a small, plaintive voice and passes out.

Hawk is suddenly conscious that the light has changed and he turns to see two urchins silhouetted in the doorway. The two boys turn to run but Hawk calls, 'Hey, stop! I need your help!' The urchins turn to face him, legs triggered to the ground, ready to flee like scared rabbits at the slightest suggestion of danger. 'Is there a doctor lives nearby?' Hawk asks. Although his own body shields Hinetitama's nakedness, the two boys can plainly see that there is someone lying on the floor.

'Is she dead, mister?' one of the lads asks.

'No, she's fine.' Hawk removes his bundled coat from his left ear so that they see the blood covering his neck and soaked into his white shirt. 'My ear, it's torn, it needs to be stitched up. Is there a doctor hereabouts?'

'There's Mrs Pike,' the other urchin replies.

'Is she a doctor?'

'Nah, I think she's a sort o' nurse,' the boy says, 'fer 'avin' babies.'

'There's a sixpence in it for both of you, go fetch her, tell her to bring her stitching stuff.'

The boys do not move. 'G'arn, be off with you and hurry.'

'Where's our money, mister?'

Hawk sighs and pulls out his purse, allowing the blood to run from his ear, and takes a sixpence from it. 'One now, one when you return.' He holds the little silver coin up to the urchins.

'Throw it here,' one of them says. Hawk throws the sixpence in his direction and both boys drop to the ground in a scramble, pushing and shoving each other out of the way to reach the small fortune at their feet.

'Damn you, get moving!' Hawk barks. 'And close the door!'

One of the lads has secured the coin and they both run off, to return half an hour later with a stout, big-breasted woman who huffs and puffs as she makes her way through the crowd beginning to gather outside the hovel. She carries a leather doctor's bag and shouts, 'Out of the way! Out of the way!' pushing the crowd aside by banging the bag against them until she reaches the door. The two lads are still with her. 'G'arn, be off with you!' she says, shooing them away.

'It's our sixpence, we's got a sixpence comin' from the nigger man!' one of them protests.

'Honest, missus!' his companion confirms.

Not bothering to knock, Mrs Pike pushes open the door. 'Sixpence! You promise them sixpence?' she shouts into the darkened interior. She turns to the two boys. 'Wait here,' she commands imperiously as she steps into the hovel.

Hawk finds the second sixpence and hands it to the nurse who drops it into the pocket of her nurse's pinny and turns to the two urchins. 'You two stand here at the door, I'll need it open to let in the light, don't let nobody come in, you hear? You'll get yer sixpence later when I'm good an' ready.'

She looks over the heads of the two urchins at the crowd. 'G'arn, piss off the lot'a ya! This ain't none of your business.'

In the time it has taken the two boys to fetch the nurse Hawk has found a threadbare blanket and torn a strip off it and bound his head several times around to contain the bleeding from his ear in order to free both his hands. He finds a bucket half filled with water and a tin mug and splashes as much blood from his hands as is possible. Then he returns with a mug of water to find Hinetitama sitting up with her face in her hands.

'Better get dressed, my dear,' Hawk says to her, handing her the mug.

Hinetitama takes it in both hands and drinks thirstily, downing the entire mug without taking a breath. Then she gets slowly to her feet and, bringing her hands down to cover her pubic region, she goes back into the little bed chamber and begins to get into her filthy gown. She has no hosiery or underwear and finally she pushes her dirty feet into a pair of badly scuffed and worn boots and dumps herself in the middle of the mattress with her legs tucked under her and waits. She has not said a word to Hawk since her recovery.

Mrs Pike, it turns out, is the local midwife, which is a stroke of luck, as she well understands how to insert stitches. She does a neat enough job of Hawk's ear, stemming the bleeding and inserting the stitches which run halfway down the ear by using horsehair and what has the appearance of a small darning needle. It is a rough enough job but soon the bleeding stops. 'It ain't pretty but the parts I 'as to stitch in me midwife's work don't need no fancy darning,' she says gruffly, then adds, 'Better than bleedin' ter death.'

Mrs Pike has become aware of Hinetitama sulking on the mattress within the tiny bed chamber. She nods her head towards the door, 'Bite you, did she?' Hawk doesn't reply and Mrs Pike continues. 'Mouth bite ain't a nice thing, could turn very nasty.'

Hawk rewards her over-generously for her work, handing her a sovereign. 'Ta-muchly, that's very good of you, I must say. Don't see too many o' these around here.' She plunges her hand into the bodice of her dress and moments later withdraws it minus the gold coin.

'You won't forget to give the lads their sixpence?' Hawk says.

'It's too much for the likes of them,' she says sternly, 'I'll give threepence each to their mothers.'

'No! I promised it to them. I'd be obliged, Mrs Pike.' Hawk watches as the midwife reluctantly finds the sixpence and hands it to one of the urchins.

'Thanks, mister!' the boy says with alacrity. Plainly he was expecting a less happy outcome at the hands of the bossy midwife.

'Is there some place near we may stay tonight?' Hawk now asks her.

'There's a wee tavern up the road a bit, the Thornton Arms, you can stay there, they've got a bathhouse out the back.' Then the midwife adds gratuitously, 'They'll take

62

niggers, but I don't know about the likes o' her, she's Maori ain't she? 'Alf-caste I'd say lookin' at her.' She sniffs. 'Brings out the worst of both sides if you want my opinion.'

'I haven't asked you for it, missus,' Hawk says softly. 'We are both Maori, and proud to be so.' He smiles, for he is grateful to the midwife, 'I daresay a coin or two placed in the right pakeha's hands will take care of his sensibilities, Mrs Pike.'

'Oh dear, we are the proper gentleman then, aren't we! No need to be uppity,' the midwife reproves him. Then adds cheerfully, 'Well, must be on me way then, plenty to do, folk breeding like mice, makes a nice change to stitch up a gentleman's ear 'stead of a torn pussy.'

The following morning, leaving Hinetitama locked in her room in the tavern, Hawk bathes and, wearing clean linen, visits a Dr Spencer in a more respectable part of town who examines his ear and pronounces Mrs Pike's work rough but adequate. He is a Scotsman in his fifties with a large belly and a talkative manner to go with it.

He chats as he examines Hawk's ear and then treats his wound with a solution of carbolic acid to stave off infection. 'Stitches, sutures we calls them in the profession, fascinating study, what. Been done since time out o' mind, Ancient Sumerians, Egyptians, Greeks, Romans all did much the same as your Mrs Pike, horsehair! Nothing wrong with that, first-class material.' He pauses as he attempts to wipe away a crusting of dried blood. 'Now if you'd have come to me, m'boy, I'd have used catgut, recommended by the great Doctor Lister himself. Easy to work and doesn't break. If this had been a scalp wound I might have tried something else completely, plaiting.' He looks up at Hawk expectantly, waiting for his reaction.

Hawk, who is only half listening to the good doctor's

prattle, feels compelled to say something. 'Plaiting? Like a girl's hair?'

'You heard me right, m'boy. Plaiting. Worked in America once, New York, in the slums of the Bronx where getting your head split open was more frequent than getting a hot breakfast. College chappy, doctor in the Civil War, McGraw, Irishman, nice fellow, apt to drink a bit, hands unsteady, not much chop for stitching, never did it, got his young assistant to plait the hair on either side of the wound together, worked like a charm, union by plaiting, no shaving, stitching, plastering and an excellent result if you ask me, learned it in the American Army, thinks it was probably borrowed from the Red Indians.'

All this is said without a pause and Hawk, feeling he must respond to such verbosity, laughs, puts his hand to his head, fingering his short, negroid, unplaitable hair. 'Not much good if you're a nigger,' he says.

'By George! I never thought of that!' the doctor replies. 'An excellent observation if I may say so, sir.'

Hawk grins, grateful that he has been elevated to 'sir', says quietly, 'From what I've read of the American Civil War it is unlikely they'd have stopped to suture a nigger, Dr Spencer.'

'Quite right, quite right, poor old negro was what the fight was all about though God knows, the niggers don't seem to have gained much benefit from the victory.'

'Doctor, of a more immediate concern, how do I rid a head of hair of lice and nits without shaving it off?'

'Good Lord, m'boy, there's no nits in your hair, I'd have spotted them a mile off if they were there.'

'Not for me,' Hawk replies, growing impatient with the loquacious medical man.

'Oh, in that case you would purchase from any chemist shop a solution of half five per cent oleate of mercury and

64

half ether.' The doctor then proceeds to show Hawk how the delousing might be done.

Leaving the doctor, who has given him a bottle of permanganate of potash to prevent infection to his ear, Hawk takes a pony trap into the centre of town and, with some embarrassment to himself and the young shop assistants concerned, purchases a suitable gown, bonnet, boots, hosiery and underwear for Tommo's daughter at Kirkaldie and Stains emporium. He includes with his purchases a cake of perfumed soap and a towel. As a small apology for his clumsy treatment the previous day, he also buys a bottle of toilet water and a scarf to cover the noticeable bruise on Hinetitama's neck. After these awkward purchases Hawk visits a nearby chemist shop and purchases the delousing solution.

The tavern where they have spent the night has no washing facilities for women so Hawk takes Hinetitama, together with all her packages, to the public bathhouse. He waits outside while she gives herself a good scrubbing down and carefully explains to the female bathhouse attendant how he wishes to delouse her hair.

'Gotta shave it, mister. Ain't no other way. Shave it right orf then wash the 'ead in pariffin,' the woman says.

Hawk produces a florin. 'Do as I say and there's another of these for you, missus.'

The woman sighs, 'It's your money, sir.'

'Oh, and burn her old clothes,' Hawk adds.

'Burn 'em? Seem orright t'me.'

'Just do as I say, please.'

The woman clucks her tongue but protests no further. 'Cost yer sixpence.'

Delousing Hinetitama's hair is a most laborious process involving a towel, the chemist's solution, and a fine-tooth comb, which the woman calls a nit-comb. Tommo's daughter's hair is washed several times but when the process is complete her hair shines long and beautiful.

They sail out of Wellington Harbour on the evening tide, Hawk having purchased the last two available cabins from the Union Steamship Co. The *Wakatipu*, a screw steamer of 1158 tons, will take just five days to reach Sydney.

Hinetitama sulks in her cabin for the first two days. On the third she emerges, having cut and stitched and hemmed the overlarge gown Hawk has purchased for her with needle and thread borrowed from one of the ladies in the next-door cabin through the intermediary services of a young cabin steward smitten by her beauty. It now fits her slender young body and tiny waist almost to perfection. Though by no means mollified, she behaves politely enough towards her uncle while offering no conversation whatsoever to any of the other passengers.

Hawk, for his part, does not expect her to apologise to him or even necessarily forgive him for rescuing her. She has not been asked if she will accompany him to Tasmania and he has, he supposes, effectively kidnapped her.

But as Hinetitama's strong young body recovers, seemingly without any harmful effects from the abuse it has received from bad grog and poor living, her naturally friendly disposition returns and she is soon her cheerful self again, talking to all and sundry and looking a picture.

Hinetitama actually seems hopeful and excited and sings all day, to the enchantment of the Maori crew who soon grow to love her for her informality and friendliness and treat her like the princess they observe she is.

Hawk though finds himself increasingly despondent. First Tommo, a drunkard at fourteen, and now his daughter is well and truly headed up the same path.

Finally, after four days at sea and a day's voyage out of Sydney, Hinetitama unexpectedly comes to his cabin and swears she will take the pledge when they arrive in Hobart.

Hawk affects a great delight at this and embraces her warmly, though not without a sense of pessimism. He is experienced enough not to hope for too much and has come to realise that there is a great deal of Tommo in his daughter.

Upon arrival in Sydney Hawk learns that Mary's own trading vessel, the *Waterloo*, a three-masted trading schooner of one hundred feet, is in port and due to return to Hobart in two days. He informs the captain they will take passage on her back to Hobart.

Hawk has some business with Tucker & Co. and also visits his old friend Caleb Soul who has a thriving business as a chemist and manufacturing pharmacist with several of his own successful potions and prescriptions on the market. The elderly Caleb welcomes him warmly and Hawk learns that he has also opened a large retail chemist outlet with the help of his son, Washington Handley, after whom he has named the business. 'Caleb Soul sounds like the combination of a turtle and a fish, not a good name for a business dealing in potions and cures, Washington H. Soul be much the sturdier proposition,' he explains to Hawk.

Hawk also visits Ah Wong, the Chinaman, and his family whom he rescued at Lambing Flat during the riots. Now a prosperous businessman, Ah Wong imports rice and silk from China. He creates a banquet for Hawk and Hinetitama to which he invites Caleb Soul and his son. After the truly splendid repast he brings in his three sons to be introduced to Hawk. He points to his eldest son, 'He born Lambing Flat you lescue him, his name Hawk,' Ah Wong says proudly. Then he points to his second son,

'Number two son yes please, this Tommo.' Hawk laughs, pleased at the compliment to himself and Tommo. 'Number three son,' Ah Wong continues, 'he name Solomon.'

Hawk grins while Caleb and his son Washington clap enthusiastically, 'Three fine sons, eh, Ah Wong, no daughters then?' Hawk says.

Ah Wong claps his hands and says something to a servant who leaves the room and presently returns accompanied by a young girl of about twelve. 'This me daughter, her name, Maggie Pi Wong.'

Hawk is hard put to prevent himself from weeping and as they take their departure from the little Chinaman Hawk embraces his old friend. 'You're a good bloke, Ah Wong, I wish you well.'

Ah Wong looks up at Hawk. 'You want from me, you get anytime for sure, certainly, by Jove!'

The remainder of their time is spent shopping and going to the theatre, both new experiences for Tommo's daughter and each is an occasion in which she plainly takes great delight. In the David Jones Emporium she chooses her shoes and two new gowns with such enormous enthusiasm that the salesgirls, who crowd about her, are as delighted as she is when she discovers something, no matter how small, to her liking. Her taste is plainly for the exotic and she chooses her gowns for their brightness and eschews the dull browns and blacks and deep blues which are the current fashion. The bonnet she buys is simply a riot of artificial blossoms and gaily coloured ribbons and bows.

Hawk cannot help being constantly reminded of Maggie Pye whom he still misses every day of his life and he takes great pleasure in having his beautiful niece on his arm, who, like Maggie herself, barely reaches his waist. Hinetitama's love for Hawk is too old for her to sustain her resentment at her kidnapping and they seem once again the greatest of friends.

The *Waterloo* possesses no spare cabins and the captain is forced to forsake his own for Hinetitama. He and Hawk join the crew in their quarters. The *Waterloo* trades hardwood and hops with the colony of New South Wales and returns with Scotch whisky and good quality brandy as well as an imported English gin. All is purchased from Tucker & Co. in Sydney to be sold in the fifty tied public houses that The Potato Factory Brewery now owns in Hobart, Launceston, Burnie and throughout rural Tasmania.

The mercantile empire built by Mary Abacus and with Hawk's own considerable business acumen embraces timber concessions, a glass bottle factory, several hop and barley farms, fifty taverns and public houses, fifteen business properties in Hobart and Launceston, the majority shareholding in a tin mine at Mount Bischoff and, as the jewel in the crown, The Potato Factory Brewery, the third largest of its kind after the Cascade Brewery in Hobart and Mr James Boag's Launceston brewery.

Mary, once a convict, is now the richest woman in Tasmania and by virtue of her wealth has made it to the top of the business classes, though she is not yet accepted by the true merinos, a rejection which causes her not the slightest anxiety.

As the sole owner of one of its largest private fortunes and one not to be sneezed at on the mainland Mary reckons she has sufficient status and respect for one lifetime. She is a canny and prudent business woman and everything she touches seems to turn to gold.

Mary Abacus has long since discovered that, in this new land, power and influence are not attached to social status but to money. She lacks only one thing to make her life's work complete, she desperately requires grandchildren to continue after Hawk is gone. Hawk, in turn, has steadfastly put off being married and now it is unlikely that he will father children. Hinetitama is her last hope.

'How shall I match the little savage with a good family even if her dowry should be most attractive?' she constantly laments. 'We must have her here to teach her manners and the customs of civilised people.'

Hawk recalls one momentous occasion when Mary's frustration brought matters to a head.

'Tommo were no judge of what was good for his child,' she announced. They were seated on the porch of Mary's mansion set in the foothills of Mount Wellington. Below them all of Hobart stretched out along the shores of the great Derwent River, which in the late afternoon sunshine lay burnished, the colour of sheet metal. 'How can you let her grow up among them savages when she could be brought up proper with no expense spared and married with a dowry to attract the very best of mannered blood? Why may I not have my own lineage?' Mary Abacus asks petulantly and makes a sweeping gesture with a tiny clawlike hand to include all of Hobart below. 'So they may inherit all this and I may pass away knowing I have worked to some avail!'

'Mama, all this as you put it, is precisely why Tommo wished his daughter to be reared by her own Maori tribe. He would see no virtue in his daughter's marriage to a true merino. Tommo saw only mongrels around him, he found greed and avarice everywhere. Then he looked into his own character and pronounced it weak. "Hawk, there is bad blood in my veins, you must protect Hinetitama from it," he said to me. "We must not allow it to come through. She must stay with her tribe until she is of age, you must promise me this."' Hawk shrugs his shoulders. 'Mama, I promised him as he lay dying. I shall keep that promise until his daughter is twenty-one and I am no longer her guardian.' He sighs and spreads his hands wide. 'Then she will make up her own mind.'

'No, she bleedin' won't! She'll come here to become a lady and settle down and have a family.'

'Mama, that's precisely what Tommo feared most.'

'Feared? Why? This talk of mongrels, bad blood? Is that supposed to be me? Is that what I am, greedy, avaricious? Is that what you think of me?' Mary screams. 'Lemme tell you something f'nothing, my boy, everything you see here, everything we've got, come from hard work, from the sweat of me brow. What we have, I've worked for, day and bleedin' night, nobody's done me no favours! And now you're saying I'm a mongrel! You and Tommo, what I brought up from a pair o' brats in a basket over here t'boot, is accusing me o' being greedy and avaricious! Ha! That's a bleedin' laugh, that is!'

Hawk is long accustomed to Mary's temper tantrums. She runs an empire and has become used to being obeyed without question, to being indulged and fawned on by sycophants. Mary has grown to accept as her right the dominion she has over most other people and has become corrupted, if not in deed, for she is a hard but fair trader, but in thought, corrupted by the power she commands and the unequivocal respect she demands for her every decision. Only Hawk may disagree with her and hope to get away with it.

'No, Mama, you know I think no such thing. What you have achieved in your life is remarkable, but it has not all come about from the sweat of your brow. Tommo is right, there is a part in all of us that may become greedy and avaricious, in each of us there is a mongrel waiting to emerge if the right circumstances prevail.'

'What do you mean? How dare you say that!' Mary cries. 'I have paid me debts to society, I am an emancipist, an honest woman by the letter o' the law!'

Hawk is hard put to continue and tries to make peace with Mary. 'Mama, please don't take it personally. Tommo only wanted that his daughter should be brought up innocent of the white man's ways. He could not forget what was done to him when he was kidnapped and taken to the Wilderness.'

'Yeah, well, that were different, that was Hannah and David, them two evil bastards, they done that to the two of you.'

'Oh?' Hawk replies, one eyebrow slightly arched. 'There's no proof they kidnapped us, but *if* they did, why do you think they did so?'

'Hatred!' Mary spits. 'Them two hated me and Ikey.'

Hawk sighs. 'Mama, it were hatred, yes. But it came about because of greed and avarice, because of what was in the Whitechapel safe. Not just their greed and avarice, yours too. We stole that money, you and me, we stole it.'

'Half of it were Ikey's,' Mary protests. 'Hannah tried to get it all! Pinch the bleedin' lot!'

'But she didn't, *we* did. It was never *our* money in the first place, not even Ikey's half, he didn't leave it to us in his will, we stole it before he died, remember?'

'He died unexpected like. Before you come back from England. But he gave us his part of the combination, that shows he intended we should have the money. I know that's true!' Mary insists.

'Mama, you know that's *not* true! I worked out Ikey's combination from his riddle and you got Hannah's from the orphan school, from Hannah's daughter, little Ann, who inadvertently spilled the beans. The safe was empty when David arrived, the contents taken by me. We stole it all, but for one ruby ring and Ikey's note which I planted in the safe for David to read.'

'Ikey would have given it to us, shared it if he'd lived,' Mary says petulantly.

'Ikey never shared anything in his life, Mama. Ikey accumulated, he added and subtracted, but he never divided.'

Mary, despite herself, smiles at Hawk's concise summary of Ikey's character.

'Anyhow,' Hawk continues, 'even if he had intended to share with us, only half of it was his to share, the other half belonged to his wife, to Hannah.' He pauses for emphasis, 'And we stole the lot!'

'Yes, well,' Mary now says, patently growing tired of Hawk's persistence. 'Hannah and David kidnapped you and Tommo, they sodding well deserved what they got in return. After what they done to us, to me two precious ones, they ain't entitled to a brass razoo!'

'Mama, we can't prove they did it! That it was them that took Tommo and me from the mountain.'

'And they can't prove we took the money from the safe, can they now?' Mary says triumphantly. She clears her throat. 'Let me tell you something f'nothing, Hawk Solomon, I know in me heart and soul that they did it, took the two of you, my precious mites, my two beautiful boys, and ruined Tommo's life.' She stabs a crooked finger at Hawk's neck, pointing to the band of silvered scar tissue formed from the wild man's rope burns about it. 'And near bleedin' killed you!' Then Mary leans into her chair, arching her back and looking at Hawk with ill-disguised scorn. 'Nothing will convince me otherwise, you hear? Them two bastards are guilty as sin! They done it, I'd stake me life on it!'

'Ah, but Hannah and David also know in *their* hearts and souls that we took their money and nothing will convince them otherwise. I daresay they'd stake their lives on it as well,' Hawk says, then adds, 'And they'd be damned right to.'

Mary says nothing, looking down over Hobart to the

Derwent River, the last moments of the sunset now
turning it to gold. There is a lovely calm about the little
city at this hour when the lights begin to shine from the
windows of houses and cottages on the hill behind the
waterfront and from the single row of street lamps that
trace the line of the harbour. 'That money were wrongly
come by in the first place,' she says finally. 'It weren't
gained on the straight, them two never did deserve it, it
were stolen goods, fenced off the poor for a pittance, or
gained elseways in an evil manner in Hannah's vile
brothel.'

Hawk remembers how his heart began to beat faster
and he suddenly found it necessary to take a deep breath
before speaking. He has waited years for this moment and
now when it has arrived the roof of his mouth is suddenly
dry. 'Mama, we must give it back,' he says at last.

Mary can scarcely believe her ears. 'Give it back? Are
you stark, starin' mad, Hawk Solomon? Give it back!
Give what back? Ikey's money? Do me a favour! Over me
dead body!'

'Mama, you have used it to make a fortune ten, fifty
times as big as the one we stole. Think now, if you don't
give it back, then Tommo is right, we must be counted
among the mongrels, among the greedy and the
avaricious. Mama, don't you see? If we do not make
amends we ourselves are sufficient reason why his
daughter Hinetitama must stay with her mother's people.'

Mary leans forward and glares shrewdly at Hawk.
'And if I give it back, only Hannah's half, mind, will you
bring Tommo's daughter to me now?'

'No, Mama, that I cannot do. I have promised my twin
and I must honour my word.'

She pulls back and gives him a short, disparaging
laugh. 'Thought so! Yes, well then them two can go to
buggery, they're getting sod-all from me!' she shouts,

banging her mittened fist against the arm of her chair. 'They get bugger all, you hear me?'

Despite Hawk bringing up the subject of restitution to Hannah and David several times over the years, Mary won't budge an inch and the enmity and the hate between the two families continues to grow.

But now, at last, Hawk is bringing Hinetitama to Hobart to meet the formidable seventy-eight-year-old Mary Abacus, who still runs her brewing and business empire with a grip of steel so that those who work for her dub her Iron Mary.

Mary has had the extreme satisfaction of seeing Hannah Solomon pass away the previous year. She was pleased as punch when David, respecting his mother's dying wishes, buried her in the Hobart cemetery next to Ikey.

Hannah's son, having inherited his business interests from his mother's de facto husband George Madden, has expanded them hugely. David now lives in Melbourne and is a man of considerable wealth. Mary sends an extravagant wreath to the funeral of her mortal enemy with the message attached:

Say hello to Ikey from me
when you arrive in hell!
Mary Abacus.

The day after the funeral Mary purchases the grave lot beside Hannah's. 'So I can keep an eye on the bitch when I'm dead,' she tells Hawk with satisfaction. 'Mark my words, you can't trust them lot, dead or alive!'

Mary, Hawk knows, will be delighted with Hinetitama's unexpected arrival. She will want Hinetitama married as soon as possible and he expects the clash of temperament between the two women in this regard alone to be considerable.

But, in the meantime, he can almost hear Mary saying upon his arrival in Hobart, 'Oh, my precious Hawk, I shall go to my grave a happy woman, I shall have my great-grandchildren to carry on!'

He doesn't quite know how he will tell Mary about her granddaughter's drinking problem. He is doubtful that Hinetitama's taking the pledge will work, she is too high-spirited, too wild to be constrained, and the dullness and pretension of the better folk in Hobart and her stubborn nature do not bode well for the future. Hinetitama, he thinks, will be more than a match for Iron Mary and Hawk does not expect a calm relationship to develop between them.

But he is wrong. From the outset Tommo's daughter and Mary hit it off splendidly. Hinetitama is a Maori in her manners and upbringing where respect for one's elders is a primary consideration. Mary, on her best behaviour for once, seems to like her granddaughter's feisty demeanour. Hinetitama, though always polite, will not be bullied or told what to do and Mary is forced to seek her co-operation in the plans she has for her.

There is, of course, no initial talk of marriage, Mary being much too cunning to shy the filly before the stallion arrives. She merely asks her granddaughter to embrace the conventions of Hobart society. This includes learning how to dress and behave in polite company, the latest dance steps and, of course, the intricacies and mysteries of acceptable table manners. Her rough manner of speaking is put into the hands of Miss Brodie, a teacher of elocution and correct pronunciation favoured by the true merinos. Her pupil's pronunciation is subject to the closest scrutiny, with her vowel sounds given the most attention. Hinetitama takes all this instruction in good humour, she has a marvellous ear and can mimic Miss Brodie perfectly and, if she wishes, she can pronounce her vowel sounds to perfection.

Mary laughs as Hinetitama afterwards takes her through every lesson. Mary has selected one teacher for dress, another for deportment, a third for manners and conversation. These are invariably women with big bosoms and hair drawn back into rigid grey buns, who wear brown or black bombazine gowns and stern bonnets and almost always turn out to be middle-aged spinsters of impeccable character, genteel poverty and in precious possession of an over-pronounced and meticulous English vocabulary.

Hinetitama not only repeats a particular lesson in a voice redolent of her teachers' but she proves to be a clever actress, who takes on their mannerisms as well, often stuffing her own bosom with a small cushion and drawing back her beautiful dark hair into a bun. She will sometimes affect Mary's reading glasses to perfect a likeness.

Her master of dancing is the ancient Monsieur Gilbert, pronounced 'Gill-bear' who dubs himself Professor de Dance and has become a living institution in Hobart. To be tutored by this ageing and doubtfully French dancing master is a prime requisite among the crinolined society and Mary knows she cannot complete her granddaughter's admittedly crammed social education without a knowledge of all the steps in the latest dances practised in the salons of London and Paris.

Although Hinetitama is forbidden to sway her hips in the seductive style of the Maori, she sometimes includes a bit of a swish, a sway and a naughty thrust of the hips into the rigid and pompous dance steps taught to her, rendering them into an altogether different permutation. 'Oh, Grandmother, must I learn this funny pakeha dance,' she laughs. 'It has no joy in it, how can it catch a man or ready him for the joy of a woman?'

Mary delights in these impersonations which usually

take place on the balcony of the big house where Mary always waits at sunset to see the parakeets, her talismanic rosellas, fly over on their way to roost in the trees higher up the mountain. Hawk, in all the time he has known her, has never heard her laugh as much. He can see she is greatly enamoured of her beautiful granddaughter and is even beginning to dote on her. Hinetitama, for her part, tries to co-operate with Mary's wish for her education, but she has won the battle of the dress. While she will accept the dictates of fashion, she simply refuses the dark shades and plain bonnets insisted upon by its arbiters in Hobart. She elects to have her gowns and bonnets made in the brightest of silks and satins and even the cotton dresses she wears during the day are of the strongest colours.

This is all observed with a tight-lipped disapproval from her social *milieu*, who regard her as cheap, and her manner of dressing vulgar and ostentatious, although Hinetitama does not seem to notice, or otherwise care for what the young matrons of Hobart may think of her. As for her various tutors, they gossip endlessly among the older society women. While they may privately accuse Hinetitama of constantly drawing attention to herself with her garish finery and her over-bright smile and lack of dignity in front of her tutors, no one is prepared to point this out to Mary for fear of losing their sinecure. They know that the redoubtable Mary Abacus will accept no criticism of her granddaughter beyond the various problems she has given them to correct.

Mary tactfully dismisses Miss Mawson, the spinster in charge of Hinetitama's wardrobe, paying her over-generously and, without mentioning the matter of fabrics and colour, she compliments the cut and style of the garments the old lady has chosen for her granddaughter. She is secretly pleased that Hinetitama refuses to accept the dull colours of the prevailing fashion. Though Hinetitama is now twenty-five years old she is still a rose in young bud and with her light step, skin colour and raven-dark hair the bright colours suit her very well indeed and Mary thinks will greatly attract the male of the species.

She has also fallen in love with her granddaughter's voice. When her little Maori princess sings to her of a night she often enough causes the tears to run down her grandmother's cheeks for the sheer joy of her song.

Mary gradually begins to introduce males into Hinetitama's life. These are, for the most part, men in their early forties, widowers and bachelors with some breeding or social standing in Tasmanian society. However, Mary has not precluded male members from the more prosperous but coarser business community, who are also invited for sherry and a light supper. With very few exceptions, the men are prematurely bald with stomachs which spill precipitously over their waistlines maintained thus on a bachelor's diet of ale and stodgy food.

Hobart is not a large place and most of the suitors involved share the same clubs or meet at the Wednesday and Saturday races so that the 'Wild Wahine', as one of these hopeful suitors has dubbed Hinetitama, is freely discussed between them. All see her as a filly to be happily mounted and the source of a large and continuing accreditation to their bank accounts. Her dark good looks testify to her tempestuous nature and they roll their eyes in supposed anticipation while speculating on the stamina required to keep up with her primitive savage desires.

But secretly they conclude they are engaged in a simple transaction, no different to a stud bull. In return for their seed well planted, they will have no further obligations and be free to enjoy the fruits of their labour, the abundant dowry that comes with a successful coupling. Hinetitama's half-breed status, they tell themselves, precludes any future considerations or obligations they might be expected to show her as a husband.

Nor is Mary under any illusions. She observes their greedy eyes and reads their sycophantic gestures towards her and the sloppy compliments directed at her granddaughter for what they are and she knows that the only reason the men have accepted her invitation is because of her money.

Despite Mary's extreme wealth her granddaughter is still a half-caste and as Ikey might say, 'Not quite kosher, my dear.' While she hopes for a marriage based on mutual respect she knows this to be highly unlikely. Mary, though anxious that her granddaughter not marry beneath her status, is not looking for perfection. She admits to herself that the potency of the pistol the successful suitor carries between his legs is more important than his looks or even his brains, given her observation that most men seem to be more or less of equal stupidity. She has been told that the Maori blood breeds out and so, if anything, she shows a distinct preference for men of a fair complexion.

But she has not reckoned on Hinetitama's stubbornness. Her granddaughter, while co-operating in most things, refuses to accept any of the suitors Mary introduces. No amount of cajoling or persuasion will convince her and she seems quite impervious to Mary's temper.

'They are all fuddy-duddies and complete ninnies and speak only of commerce, farming, hunting, horses, racing and football. Of commerce I know nothing and of the others I've heard enough after two minutes. They cannot sing or dance and they have no laughter in their bellies like a Maori man. I'd be ashamed to carry their baby in my stomach!'

Mary admits to herself privately that she agrees with

her granddaughter, they are a poor lot, men mostly left over in the first place because of their lack of prospects or character. She thinks of taking her granddaughter to the mainland, to Sydney or Melbourne, where the pickings can be expected to be rather better, especially among the burgeoning middle classes. But first Hinetitama must have a veneer of culture applied sufficiently thickly not to arouse the suspicions of a would-be mother-in-law, that is, until it is too late and the nuptials are concluded. Whereupon the family can happily console themselves with the dowry her granddaughter brings to the marriage.

As the battle of wills rages between the two women Hawk's respect grows for his niece, but he knows the fight is one-sided and Mary will not give up under any circumstances. Even though she is plainly enchanted with Hinetitama she will attempt to achieve her ambition for great-grandchildren at any cost.

Hawk realises that Mary is at deadly serious play with Tommo's daughter. She watches her every lesson and makes her practise what she has learned. Although Mary is conscious of her own lack of grammar and syntax, she has always been a great reader and she is quick to correct a grammatical slip or a mispronunciation if Hinetitama should revert for a moment to her accustomed pattern of speech.

'If you know what's correct grammar, Grandmother, then why do you talk differently?' Hinetitama asks her one evening after Mary has corrected her half a dozen times. It is at the time an innocent enough question but is to begin a conversation which will affect Hinetitama's entire life.

'Too old, my dear, can't teach an old dog new tricks. Never had no time for all that malarky, talkin' posh when you ain't. Folks can take me for who I am, common as dirt, or not at all.'

'Why then must I learn all this stuff?' Hinetitama protests, 'I'm common as dirt.'

'Well my dear, no point in beating about the bush. When you're beautiful *and* rich, rising out of a cloud of dust up into the clean air on nob hill ain't too difficult. All it takes is a few manners and customs learned and a voice that don't sound like a cockatoo. But I must be frank my dear, at twenty-five you're well past the marrying age even though you're a beautiful and desirable woman.'

'But a half-caste, eh?' Hinetitama interjects.

'Yes, no point in denying that. So, if we're going to find you an 'usband of the right breedin' stock, with the right pedigree, it's going to take a fair bit of money and manners. I've got the money but you have to learn the manners. Though, Gawd knows, I've searched the length and breadth of this accursed island and what's available and respectable we've already had to tea and you've rejected the bleedin' lot. The whole bunch o' would-bes if they could-bes! Whatever am I to do with you? Maybe the mainland, what say you?'

'But, Grandmother, if you should find me one, what if I don't love him?'

'Love? Tush! T'ain't necessary. Love's for shopgirls,' Mary says dismissively. Then she becomes aware of the distress in Hinetitama's eyes. 'What do you know about love, eh? You ain't gunna miss what you ain't never had, my dear.'

'But I *have*! I have loved,' Hinetitama protests.

Mary sniffs dismissively. 'That's news to me. Hawk didn't say nothin' about you being in love.'

Hinetitama looks defiantly at Mary. 'Hawk don't know *every* thing about me!'

'*Doesn't* know,' Mary corrects. 'Who've you loved then?'

'Never mind, it doesn't matter!' Hinetitama sulks.

'Yes, it bleedin' does! Tell me, my girl.'

'Why? You wouldn't like him?'

'Like him? What's my liking got to do with it?' Mary sighs. 'I'm an old woman wot's filthy rich, Hawk won't marry and you're twenty-five years old and ain't got a man yet, let alone children!'

Hinetitama looks confused and hurt. 'I don't understand?'

Mary shows her impatience and decides in her frustration to come clean. 'Who's it all gunna go to, eh? Who is gunna carry on with it, with everything I've worked for, built? I daresay Hawk can go on another few years, but what then, leave it to the bleedin' Salvation Army? You, my dear, have no idea of business and don't show the *slightest* interest in bookkeeping.' She looks beseechingly at Hinetitama. 'I simply must have great-grandchildren prepared and ready to take over when Hawk dies.'

'But that will be another twenty, maybe thirty years! You'll be long dead, Grandmother?'

'Not too long, I hope,' Mary sniffs, then she lifts her hands towards her granddaughter showing her crooked fingers. 'But what I did with these, with me own hands, won't be dead! The Potato Factory, me beloved brewery, *must* carry on. I don't care much about the other things, they's nice, but the brewery, that's different, that *must* continue!' She takes a deep breath and gives a resigned smile. 'Now tell me, my precious, who is this man you say you love?'

Hinetitama looks shyly up at Mary and says softly, 'He's a Dutchman, from Holland.'

'A Dutchman, eh? Me old man was a Dutchman,' Mary exclaims. 'A tally clerk down at the East India docks.' She thinks of her poor drunken father and how she loved him despite his constant betrayal and state of inebriation.

'He isn't what *you'd* call a true merino, he isn't the right breeding stock and he hasn't got no . . .' Hinetitama corrects herself, '. . . any pedigree. He ain't . . . isn't what you're looking for, Grandmother.'

Mary ignores her protest. 'Tush, go back a generation or two and we're all scum on this island, even the free settlers come from a pretty dodgy lot, scratch one o' them and you'd be surprised what you find underneath. How old is this Dutchman of yours?'

'Thirty.'

'How tall?'

Hinetitama thinks a moment. 'Six feet and a little bit, I think.'

'Healthy? No coughs in his chest?'

'Yes, he's healthy, no coughs.'

'You sure?'

'I'm a nurse, I ought to know.'

'Got all his teeth?'

Hinetitama laughs despite herself. 'Last time I saw him, yes.'

'When was that?'

'When Uncle Hawk found us.'

'He didn't tell me about no Dutchman?'

'That's 'cause he kicked his arse and sent him packin',' Hinetitama says, her grammar reverting to type.

Mary can be seen to think for a moment, then she draws a breath and says, 'Well, never mind, Hawk never were a good judge o' character.' She pauses. 'Do you still love him?'

'Who? Uncle Hawk? Of course!'

'No, not *him*, the Dutchman.'

Hinetitama nods her head and Mary sees a sudden tear run down her cheek.

'Does he love you?'

'I dunno, he never said.'

'Men never do,' Mary sniffs. She looks wan and lowers her eyes as she thinks of Mr Emmett, the man she loved since the first day she set eyes on him when she'd been in the Female Factory. How, after all the years of knowing him, she had been too shy even to attend his funeral. 'You spend your whole life loving them and never know what they thinks of you,' Mary says at last.

Hinetitama looks up surprised. 'You were in love, Grandmother?' She breaks into a smile. 'You *were*! I *knew* it!' she cries, clapping her hands. 'You were, weren't you, c'mon own up, tell the truth?'

Mary pulls her lips into a small grimace as she tries to conceal her smile. 'Never mind that, my girl, what you don't know can't hurt you. Tell me, do you want to have this man's children?'

Hinetitama is momentarily taken aback by the question and she thinks for a moment, then nods her head. 'I suppose? I never thought about it before.'

Mary's manner is suddenly all business. 'Where is he to be found?'

Hinetitama shrugs. 'Wellington, I suppose. Somewhere in New Zealand, who knows. Wellington's where we left hum. What are you going to do, Grandmother?'

'Why find him, of course.'

'Find hum? Go to Wellington?' Hinetitama says incredulously. 'What for?'

'Him, not hum,' Mary now corrects. 'To bring *hum* over. Why else would I bother to find *hum*, my dear?' she teases smilingly.

'Here? To Hobart?' Hinetitama says excitedly and then, as suddenly, looks forlorn, her eyes cast downwards. 'What if he won't come?'

'He'll come,' Mary snorts. 'Don't fret your little heart about that. In my experience there is seldom a man money can't buy, and he don't sound the sort to be too hesitant.'

'But it's been over a year? What if he's forgot me or took up with someone else, he's very handsome?'

'Forgotten me, and taken up,' Mary corrects without thinking. She gives a cynical little snort. 'My dear girl, he'll be suitably reminded then, won't he? In my experience, wallets, in particular, are a splendid way to jog the memory, provided they are allowed to grow a little in size. If he has married someone else then it may be difficult, but if he merely enjoys different company, then a considerable thickening of his wallet will soon cause him a remarkable loss of enthusiasm for the pleasure his new partner brings him.'

'You mean you're going to bribe him, buy him for me? I don't think I'd like that, Grandmother. That's what you've been doing with all the others.'

'Ah, yes, but you didn't love the others, my precious.'

'But what if he truly *doesn't* love me!'

'Don't you bother your little mind about that right now. We'll bring him over and you can decide for yourself. If he doesn't love you there isn't much I can do about it, is there? Besides you're not the sort to be easily forgot, my precious little lark.'

Hinetitama looks doubtfully at her grandmother, she knows enough to suspect Mary's devious mind is at work. 'You promise me you won't bribe him to say he loves me?'

'No, no, of course I promise,' Mary protests, thinking, if she knows anything about men, how unnecessary it is to make such a promise.

Hinetitama remembers the circumstances in which Hawk found the two of them. It is now obvious to her that he hasn't told Mary about their drunken behaviour or the nature of her lover's profession or their predilection for the grog bottle. She is grateful to Hawk for this, but also finds herself deeply concerned. She has managed to stay clean for more than a year and knows that if Slabbert

Teekleman returns she will be lost. Hinetitama senses that Mary's efforts to bring her lover back to her are likely to end in disaster for them both.

Hinetitama tells herself she has tried to get over her Dutchman, to forget him, but he has been constantly on her mind. Not a day passes when she doesn't ache to be with him. Just as she knows that even though she hasn't touched a drop of alcohol since she fought Hawk in Wellington, she still craves the gin bottle every day of her life. There is something, some evil devil, deep down in her belly, that needs it. She knows she loves her Dutchman with the same senseless and destructive passion. She admits to herself that he is, by every definition, a scoundrel, a profligate, a drunk and a gambler, but it makes no difference. She loves him, loves the excitement of being with him, and she cannot cast him from her mind. Hinetitama, her heart pounding, gives herself one last chance at her own salvation.

'Uncle Hawk doesn't like hum?' she says to Mary. 'He won't permit it.'

'Didn't expect he would,' Mary barks. 'You leave Hawk to me, an' all.'

But Hawk won't hear of a plan to find the Dutchman and return him to Hinetitama. While he doesn't know the intimate details of their love affair, he has witnessed its consequence.

'Mama, he is a drunk and a gambler just like Tommo, only I daresay not as skilled. I found them in a hovel drunk, with her naked and filthy and him a coward who ran away and left with a curse for her on his lips. I bought him off with two sovereigns. Can't you see what will happen if she returns to this evil man?'

Mary is obdurate. 'Well! If that's all you can say. Why, if she's what you say she is, a drunk like her father, has she not touched a drop of liquor since she arrived? She's a good girl, stubborn as a mule, that I'll admit, but I don't believe she'd do anything silly.'

'Mama, there is a weakness in her. He is a drunk and will take her down with him.'

'Nonsense! Besides, men don't always drink from addiction, often it's from despair at their prospects in life. As Hinetitama's husband he shall enjoy the most excellent prospects. He seems from her description to be a strong enough fellow with good teeth and lungs, tall and fair of complexion. He is a musician also, so he may be a sensitive fellow underneath.'

Hawk cannot believe his ears. Mary, the ever wary, who doesn't suffer fools gladly and can pick a charlatan soon as look at him, is now carrying on with such inane drivel. 'About as sensitive as my black arse,' Hawk says, suddenly angry. 'He is a gambler as well as a drunk, even if he could be made to reform from the grog he will remain the other. She, Hinetitama, has a fixation, that is all.'

'She's in love with him, Hawk, same as you were with Maggie Pye.'

For the first time in his life Hawk turns on Mary. 'How dare you, Mama! This Dutchman isn't worth a pinch of dog shit! He's a useless bastard, and up to no good in every possible way.'

Mary looks at Hawk and says unflinchingly, 'You could have said the same thing about our Tommo, now couldn't you? What about Maggie Pye? She was a whore. I was a whore, reduced to the vilest circumstances. Does that make us bad people? Your Maggie was a fine woman, one of the best I've known, but she was still a whore. We can all reform, Hawk. If we are fortunate enough to get a second chance. Hinetitama loves this Dutchman, why can't we give *him* a second chance, eh?'

Hawk, still angry and unaccustomed to defying Mary

or even using coarse language in front of her, wheels around again. 'Mama, I beseech you, listen to me! You don't know what you're talking about. The man's bad, weak, hopeless. He has the look of a gaolbird about him. I simply won't do this to Tommo's memory. Christ Jesus, Tommo asked me to take care of his daughter not to destroy her! I brought her away from New Zealand so she wouldn't ever again have to mix with scum, with rubbish like Teekleman.'

Mary is silent for a moment and then Hawk sees the anger rise up in her. 'Now you listen to me, Hawk Solomon. Tommo's dead, the girl is alive! I can't go thinking about the sensibilities of the dead where the living are concerned. She refuses to marry any of the local prospects and, I must say, I don't blame her, they're a pretty gormless lot. But she *will* marry her Dutchman and time is runnin' out, she's twenty-five years old, not much time left for childbearing and as far as I can see Teekleman has no disadvantages in that particular area.'

Hawk loves Mary with all of his heart but he now believes her power, wealth and arrogance, taken together with her need to create an on-going, living memorial to her life, has totally corrupted her. 'Mama, you mustn't do this, I beg of you. You will destroy your granddaughter, destroy her as surely as you claim Hannah and David destroyed Tommo.' Hawk pauses and takes a deep breath. 'If you persist in this, then I will tell David Solomon that we stole Hannah and Ikey's share of the Whitechapel safe. He will go to the law and I shall testify, admit our guilt and you will be ruined.'

'And you?' Mary sneers. 'It were you who did the stealing, who opened the safe and took what was inside. What will become of you then?'

Hawk shrugs. 'It don't matter. If you let that Dutchman have Hinetitama you will have destroyed me and you have dishonoured my twin!' Hawk sighs. 'What happens next doesn't matter.'

Mary is silent, her hands in her lap, her head bowed. Hawk appeals once more to her. 'Mama, can't you see, what you've done is wonderful, they can't take that away from you, but what happens after you've gone is of no consequence, you can't take it with you, it's all over. Let someone else have the bloody brewery!'

Hawk hears the sharp intake of Mary's breath as she looks up at him. 'Have it? Someone else? A stranger? A man!' she cries. 'Now, you lissen t'me, boy! I built it with me own hands, these stupid, ugly, broken claws!' She throws her hands up in front of her face. 'I've told you how they come to be like this! Men done it, men who wouldn't let a woman have a job as clerk, they done it! Held me down and broke me fingers with their boots, then raped me!' Mary is shaking with anger and tears roll down her cheeks and her nose begins to run. 'The brewery, the Potato Factory, that's me answer to them bastards who done me in at the East India docks! That's me answer to the beak that sent me down. To the vile Potbottom who flogged me on the convict ship and the tyranny of the sanctimonious bible-bashing surgeon Joshua Smiles! Not to mention the utter bastardry o' the male warders at the Female Factory and their soldier friends who lay us on our backs at night and took from us what they wanted! The banks, the fat, pompous bastards in their grey worsted weskits and gold fob chains, in cahoots with the other brewers. "Sorry, Mary, we don't give credit to women," they sneered, then not even bothering to get up and show me to the flamin' door!' Mary takes a breath, sniffs and then continues, 'I'm the first woman in the known world to build me own brewery! To make and name me own beer! You hear that? The first! That's supposed to be men's work ain't it? The male perog-a-tive! Men own breweries, doesn't they? Men with big bellies and bushy curled moustaches!' She sniffs and knuckles the tears from her eyes. 'Well, a woman built this one! Long as it stands with its two chimneys, two fingers o' brick stuck up into the sky for all to see, it says, "Fuck you!" on behalf of every woman what was ever raped and abused and humiliated by a man!'

Mary now points an accusing finger at Hawk, her voice rasps from the anger and disappointment she feels. 'And now *you* want to do the same. The same as them bastards on the London docks. You wish to destroy me.' Her head jerks backwards. 'Why?' she cries, 'Fergawd's sake tell me why? What have I done to you? You who I brought up, loved with every breath in me body. I even *killed* for you.' She suddenly grows very quiet and speaks almost in a whisper, 'My beloved Hawk, I never thought I'd live to see this day!' Mary stops and bows her head and begins to weep softly, 'I am so ashamed.'

'Oh, Mama! Mama!' Hawk cries out in anguish.

Mary looks slowly up at him, her eyes brimming but her voice defiant. 'Well you won't and you can't!' she chokes. 'I'm gunna find that Dutchman and he'll take Hinetitama to his bed and as soon as he's given her a couple of brats it will be your job to see him off this island. What did you say it cost last time? Two sovs, weren't it? Well, I daresay it will take a lot more next time, but I don't care.' She pauses and shouts, 'I WANT MY HEIRS!' Then she brings her hand up and clasps the small gold medal resting, as ever, upon her breast, Ikey's Waterloo medal, 'You know what it says on the back, on this, don'tcha? *I shall never never surrender!* I ain't never and I never shall!' She releases the medal and brings both her hands up to cover her face and weeps and weeps.

Chapter Three

NEW LIFE AND THE
DEATH OF MARY ABACUS

1886–1892

Slabbert Teekleman simply turns up in Hobart one bright late spring morning in November 1886.

Martha Billings, the kitchen maid in Mary's home, hears the bell on the back door and goes to answer it, thinking it must be the butcher boy. She discovers a small man, who looks to be in his forties and is somewhat red-visaged and battered-looking, as if he's taken a bad licking or two in his time. The hair below his dirty cap sticks out at every angle and is in need of a good wash. At the maid's appearance he removes his cap and clutches it to the region of his crotch. Martha now sees that he has a bald pate smooth as an egg.

'Whatcha want?' Martha asks, summing him up immediately as a nobody.

'I've a note, fer Miss Solomon, miss,' the man replies.

'Give it then,' Martha demands, extending her hand.

The man shakes his head. 'Nah, 'fraid I can't, miss. I got instructions see. I got to hand it to her personal.' He now realises he is talking to his own social level and his confidence is restored. He returns his cap to his head. 'Miss Solomon personal.'

'And what if I said that were me an' all?' Martha says

tartly, feet apart, her hands clamped to her waist.

The man smiles. 'Whole town knows who Miss Solomon is, brought back by Mr Hawk over a year now on the *Waterloo*.'

Annoyed, Martha turns and asks the cook what she must do, explaining the man's purpose. 'Well, what are you waiting for, girl? Go and fetch Miss Heenie,' Mrs Briggs instructs, then she pops her head around the door and takes a quick look at the man. 'He don't look like he bites.'

Martha sniffs. 'Wait here,' she orders the messenger.

The man grins slyly, pleased to see the uppity servant girl put in her place by the cook. 'Thankee, missus,' he says, grinning at Mrs Briggs.

'I dunno, young folk don't seem to know their manners no more,' the cook remarks, 'Too much lip that one.' She turns back to the messenger. 'I don't suppose you'd mind a nice mug o' tea and a slice of bread and jam?'

The man smiles, showing several teeth missing with the remainder blackened. 'Thankee, much obliged, missus.'

When Hinetitama arrives he is sitting on the back step with a tin mug of hot sweet tea and a hunk of bread and jam. He jumps up, slopping tea over his hand in his haste.

'Oh dear, you've burned your hand?' Hinetitama cries, concerned.

'Some, not much,' the man replies, plainly embarrassed for creating a fuss.

'Here, let me see your hand?'

'Me 'and's fine, miss. No 'arm done.'

'Cook'll give you another mug of tea.'

'No, miss, it ain't all spilled.' He looks down into the mug. 'Plenty left, thankee.' Then he stoops to rest the mug on the step beside the hunk of bread, wipes his tea-splashed hand on the side of his greasy corduroy trousers, removes his cap and takes a piece of folded paper from its interior. 'Here, miss, I were told to give it to you personal.'

'Thank you, Mr . . . ?'

'Isaac Blundstone, miss, bootmaker by trade.'

Hinetitama smiles. 'Thank you, Mr Blundstone, I'm obliged to you.' She turns to the cook. 'Do we need a bootmaker, Mrs Briggs?'

'Oh, I don't know about that, Miss Heenie. I could ask Mistress Mary, it ain't for me to decide. Food, yes, but not boots, don't know nothing about boots.'

Hinetitama turns back to Isaac Blundstone and looks down at his boots, which are scuffed and in poor repair. 'Bring some of your work, let me see it.'

'Yes, thankee, miss, I do good work.'

Hinetitama smiles knowingly. 'What, down the pub?'

'The pub, miss?' The man looks puzzled.

Hinetitama points to his hands. 'You've got the brandy shakes. You've had a few already, haven't you?'

The man grins slyly, looking down at his scuffed boots and shuffling his feet. 'Hair o' the dog, couple o' heart starters, that's all, miss.'

'Who gave you this?' Hinetitama waves the note. She is excited, for somehow she senses it's from Teekleman, but restrains herself from finding out, fearful of the contents of the note, wanting to know, but not right off, instinctively needing more to add to what might be contained in the note.

'He didn't say, miss. He didn't give no name,' Blundstone lies.

It's been more than a year since Hinetitama's conversation with Mary. While neither she nor Hawk has said a word to her, the servants, the big ears in every establishment, have inevitably gossiped and Hinetitama, who they call Miss Heenie and is a great favourite with them all, has come to know about the terrible row over Teekleman.

'He didn't say, but he shouted you a drink?' She can smell the cheap brandy on his breath. 'What? A nobbler o' brandy, two maybe, where was that?'

'Aye,' Blundstone says, surprised. 'The Hobart Whale Fishery, miss.'

'Card game, was it? You met playing cards?'

Blundstone is clearly impressed with Hinetitama's sleuthing. 'He were, miss. Me? I ain't got that sorta money.'

'Bar fly, eh? Topping up to cadge?' Hinetitama has seen him for what he is, a regular drunk who'll take on the self-appointed task of keeping the drinks coming at a card game and earning his reward in grog both from the publican and an occasionally generous player. It is unlikely, but not inconceivable, that he might not know Teekleman's name.

'He said just to give you the letter, not to say nothing more.'

'Tall, fair hair, blue eyes?'

'Aye, that's him.'

'Foreigner, when he speaks like?' Hinetitama adds, seeking further confirmation.

The man nods again and Hinetitama, satisfied, gives him a shilling. 'There you go then, that'll buy you the whole dog.' She laughs. 'Or you could use it to sole your boots, Mr Isaac Blundstone, the bootmaker!'

Blundstone grins. 'It's me brother what's the bootmaker, I'm what yiz'd call the prod'gil son.'

The note when Hinetitama finally opens it is written in a competent hand which suggests a fair education.

Dear Hinetitama,

Ja, I have come here to Hobart and also I will much like to see you. It goes well with me. I am staying at the Whale Fishery. You will come I hope so.

Slabbert Teekleman.

Hinetitama goes into a real tizz and spends the remainder of the day alone in her bed chamber arguing with herself, alternately tearful and smiling. When she thinks of going back to Teekleman her heart commences to beat rapidly, though she, on some occasions, thinks this must be a certain sign that she is doing the wrong thing and on others that she loves him. By evening, when a maid is sent up to call her down to dinner, she is emotionally wrung out and exhausted. Claiming she doesn't feel well she tells the maid to ask her grandmother to excuse her.

Mary, upon receiving Hinetitama's message, comes hurrying to her bed chamber, 'What's the matter, precious?'

Hinetitama feigns distress. 'I must have eaten something, I feel unwell, Grandmother.'

'Unwell? Your tummy? I'll call Dr Moses.' She seats herself on the side of the bed and takes her grand-daughter's hand.

'No, it's just a small upset,' Hinetitama smiles wanly. 'Best if I don't eat, that's all.'

'You sure then?' Mary asks, looking concerned.

'Grandmother, it's nothing, I'll just rest,' Hinetitama insists.

'You call me if it gets any worse, you promise now?'

'Grandmother, you work so hard, you look tired, it's me should be caring for you!'

'Day weren't no different to any other,' Mary sniffs. 'Can't turn back the clock, I'm gettin' old, that's all, old and cranky,' she adds gratuitously. She bends and kisses Hinetitama on the forehead then rises slowly, though she stands straight as a pencil and, for a woman her age, still has amazing stamina. 'You call me if you feel any worse during the night.'

By morning, with less than a good night's sleep,

Hinetitama knows that she must go to Slabbert Teekleman, that she cannot resist the temptation. 'Oh Gawd, help us,' she says to herself as she brushes her hair prior to going down to breakfast with Mary. 'Please let it be all right this time.'

At breakfast, which is served early, just after six o'clock so that Mary and Hawk can be at the Potato Factory by seven when the brewery workers start, she again has no appetite. Fortuitously Hawk is away on a trip to Burnie so that she and Mary are sitting alone at the dining-room table. Hinetitama goes through the motions of dipping her spoon into her porridge bowl, but eats very little.

'Still no good, eh?' Mary enquires, observing her lack of appetite.

'No, Grandmother, it's not that,' Hinetitama says.

'The note?' Mary says suddenly, her own spoon halfway to her mouth. 'Is it something I should know, girl?'

'Mrs Briggs told you?'

'Not much to tell, was there? She said you got a note. Man come to the back door.'

Hinetitama, unable to contain herself any longer, announces, 'Grandmother, it was from the Dutchman!'

Mary remains silent for a while. Finally she returns the spoon, its contents uneaten, to her plate. 'The Dutchman? Slabbert Teekleman?'

Hinetitama nods, amazed that her grandmother has remembered both his names.

'Well?' Mary demands. 'What will you do?'

'Grandmother, I don't know, I'm that scared.'

'Frightened? Lovesick, more like!' Then, realising Hinetitama is asking for her support, her voice takes on a more sympathetic tone. 'Of course you're scared, my precious. After all, it's been almost two years.'

97

'I'm different now. He may not like me.'

Mary is hard put to conceal her relief, her grand-daughter is not rejecting the Dutchman as she's come to think of Teekleman in her mind. 'Course he will, child, don't you worry your little head about that.'

'Whatever shall I do, Grandmother?'

'Do? Why invite him to supper tonight, of course. What does he like to eat? Mrs Briggs will make it for him special.'

'Like? I don't rightly remember. Meat 'n' potatoes, I suppose,' Hinetitama says absently.

Mary laughs. 'Like all men, eh? We'll get cook to do us a nice roast, roast beef and taties.' Mary is suddenly all business. 'We'll send the carriage to fetch him. Where's he staying?'

'The Hobart Whale Fishery.'

'The Whale Fishery? That's a Cascade pub, one of Delgrave's, Ikey used to go there a lot. Do you think he'll agree to move to one of ours?' Mary doesn't wait for an answer. 'Course he will, won't cost him a bean. I'll send him a note, make all the arrangements. Half-six, most men like to eat early, I don't suppose he's any different, eh?'

Hinetitama agrees, thinking that Teekleman is unlikely to be drunk so early in the evening. She has never seen Mary all of a twitter like this before. Her grandmother is seldom her best in the morning and is usually silent, almost morose, her abacus at her side. Every once in a while she grunts and sends the beads rattling along their wires, then writes a number down on a notebook beside her. But this morning she's plainly in excellent humour.

'But what if *he's* changed also?'

'Well, we'll just have to find out, won't we, my girl?'

'What will Uncle Hawk think?'

Mary shrugs, not denying the probability of Hawk's opposition. 'He ain't here, is he now?'

For a moment Hinetitama wonders whether Hawk's absence hasn't been planned by Mary all along, but she is not accustomed to deceit and silently castigates herself for this uncharitable thought.

'Oh, Grandmother, I'm so excited. Whatever shall I wear?'

'It don't really matter, men don't notice anyway.' Mary grins. 'Unless o' course you wear your birthday suit?'

'Grandmother!' Hinetitama has never heard Mary talk like this before. Then she laughs, she's never felt closer to her grandmother and her anxiety is greatly ameliorated by Mary's cheerful assurance. 'Please, God,' she says to herself, 'don't let him be drunk when he comes.' Then she adds another plea to the Almighty, 'And don't let all this be of Grandmother's doing.'

Teekleman arrives promptly in Mary's carriage at half-past six and is greeted at the door by Hinetitama and her grandmother, who has finally persuaded her grand-daughter to wear a gown of a modest mousy-brown colour, one of the earlier rejects from old Mrs Mawson's attempts to bring her into line with current Hobart fashion.

'Don't want him to think you're too good for him now, do we? He'll be jittery as a race'orse, no point in shying him right off with silks 'n' satins in the brightest colours now, is there? Modesty, my girl, you need never feel it in front of a man for most have less intelligence than you, but you must appear always to show it,' she declares, then explains further, 'Men believe what they see, women what they hear.' Though she herself has chosen to wear one of her best gowns. When Hinetitama remarks on this the old woman grins. 'Modesty and beauty from you, age and riches from me, mark my words, the combination is irresistible to any man who comes a'courting with a death and an inheritance in mind.'

Slabbert Teekleman is well scrubbed and wears clean though not expensive linen. He is dressed in the manner one might expect from a small businessman of the respectable middle classes and wears a plain woollen weskit without a fob and chain strung across his belly. His boots are freshly dubbined, his hair neatly parted and his beard trimmed. He is a big man, only slightly given to noticeable paunch and is still most handsome in his overall appearance.

Hinetitama watches, smiling, as Mary greets him. 'You are most welcome in our home, Mr Teekleman,' she says, offering him her gloved hand. 'Of course, you already know my granddaughter.'

Teekleman, for his part, seems surprisingly at ease, and Hinetitama observes that he appears to be completely sober. 'Thank you, Madam,' he says formally to Mary. Smiling, he bows and only lightly takes her hand. In doing this he is displaying a social awareness Hinetitama is unaware he possessed. Furthermore, his returning smile reveals he has not lost any of his teeth. Turning to her he offers his hand. 'I am so glad we meet vunce more, Hinetitama, that you and your granmutza invite me here to your nice house.'

Hinetitama smiles broadly, her heart pounding furiously, but she is determined not to show her nervousness and to put the Dutchman at ease. 'I've been that worried all day that you'd change your mind and not come,' she laughs, her words immediately relieving the tension.

'Shall we go in?' Mary invites and turns to lead the way into the mansion. 'Cook has a baron of beef fresh from the roasting oven, I feel sure a big man like you has a healthy appetite.'

A week after the Dutchman's arrival Hawk arrives home shortly after sunset and, stopping only to tell Mrs Briggs he will take a light supper in his study, goes straight to the wing of the house he occupies. He is weary and has a light cold and thinks to take a bath and then read awhile before going to bed. But Mary sends a maid to ask him if he'll have dinner with her, the servant girl adding that Hinetitama is out for the evening.

Hawk thinks the invitation curious. It is the custom for both Mary and himself to dine alone after a journey. Mary is well aware of the rigours of a long coach ride and the accumulated weariness of constant travel over a period of several days. Hawk knows himself to be irritable and not inclined to favour company of any sort. He will catch up with Mary in the morning when she will drill him solidly for an hour, wanting to learn every detail of his business trip.

Hawk finds himself especially tired on this occasion. Normally he would have rested somewhat on the ferry from New Norfolk, but upon his arrival at the little river port he discovered the ferry had struck a docking pylon the previous night and sunk in six feet of river water. The captain, being reputed to have been in an advanced state of inebriation, was blamed for the accident.

Now his back ached from the Cobb and Co. coach ride, where, despite paying for two seats as was his usual custom, he'd been jammed in with too many other passengers, among them two stout ladies who seemed to spend the entire trip complaining about the mishap to the ferry and the added inconvenience of the coach, and on several occasions making pointed remarks that 'someone' among them was taking twice the seating space he was entitled to.

'Tell Miss Mary I am wearied from my journey and wish to bathe and be early to bed and will take supper alone in my study. You will give her my apologies and say that I will see her in the morning,' he tells the maid. Then adds, 'Can you remember all of that?'

The servant girl nods and does a poor imitation of a curtsy before taking her leave. Mary's servants are not expected to be overformal in their behaviour, required only to show respect to their employers. 'Had quite enough o' all that bowing and scraping when I were a maid meself,' Mary would say when she suspected a visitor expected a curtsy or a servant to stand to attention as they passed.

Hawk has removed his boots, socks and cravat and released his starched collar from its gold stud. His braces hang from his waist and his shirt cuffs are unlinked, when there is a sharp knock on the door followed immediately by Mary's voice. 'Hawk, I must talk to you! Will you not take tea with me tonight?'

'Mama, I am greatly wearied from the journey, I beg to be excused.'

'Are you decent?' Mary's voice now asks from behind the door.

Hawk sighs. 'Mama, I have removed my boots and I daresay my feet stink to high heaven,' he says, hoicking up his braces as he speaks.

Without further ado the door to his bed chamber is thrown open. 'Hawk, I simply must talk to you!' Mary repeats.

Hawk groans. 'Mama, can't it wait? I am dog-tired. Can we not talk at breakfast, after I am rested?'

'No, it can't!' Mary snaps. 'I would be most obliged if you'd take tea with me. Mrs Briggs will make you something light to eat, a little cold lamb and mustard pickles perhaps?'

Hawk realises that Mary will not be put off, that if he continues they will inevitably quarrel, an experience for which he has an even greater disinclination than his appearance at supper. 'Mama, allow me to take a bath first,' Hawk sighs wearily.

At the dinner table a thoroughly grumpy Hawk hears of the Dutchman's arrival. Mary tells him that, together with his manservant, Isaac Blundstone, Teekleman has been given quarters at The Ship Inn.

Hawk shows his astonishment. 'You welcomed him and gave him a place to stay?'

'Well, yes, it seemed a proper thing to do, given the circumstances,' Mary says, her lips pursed.

'Proper thing? Proper thing to do! Whatever can you mean?' Hawk cries.

'Well, he's Hinetitama's friend, ain't he?'

Hawk shakes his head, not believing what he's heard. 'Mama, what have you done!'

'It were none of my doing, I swear it! He just come 'ere out of the blue.'

Hawk looks at his mother, holding her eyes. 'Don't you look at me like that, Hawk Solomon,' she shouts. 'It don't have nothing to do with me, ask her, she'll tell yer what happened!'

Mary lowers her eyes, averting his gaze. She is not accustomed to explaining herself or of justifying her actions and he senses she feels vulnerable. 'Mama, are you sure? Are you sure you didn't have a hand in this?'

'Course I am,' Mary snorts indignantly. 'Would I lie to you, me own flesh and blood?'

'Good then, you won't mind if I send him packing? I daresay a little more than two sovs will be needed this time, but I shall regard it as money well spent.'

Mary doesn't react as Hawk expects she will, defending the Dutchman's right to stay as long as her granddaughter wants him to remain, claiming that her love for Teekleman must be allowed to prevail. Instead she shrugs, her expression now completely noncommittal. 'You must do what you think best, my dear, I have only waited until you returned.' Then she adds quietly, 'But if you *must* send him off, then don't tell her, let her think he's left of his own accord. Either way it will break her poor heart, but if she knows it's you done it to her again, this time she will not forgive you.'

Hawk is immediately suspicious. It is an altogether too well-rehearsed reply. He senses Mary is at her most devious. She has the same 'butter won't melt in her mouth' appearance as when she confronted the hapless Senior Detective O'Reilly in the mortuary and claimed Mr Sparrow's headless body to be Tommo's. It is at this precise moment that Hawk knows that Teekleman has been bribed in some manner he cannot hope to match. That money won't buy him off. That, whatever the machinations involved in having the Dutchman return to her granddaughter, Mary has rendered Hawk powerless to prevent Teekleman from staying in Hobart.

She has not forbidden him to send the Dutchman packing, so he cannot chastise or even threaten to undermine her by admitting to David Solomon that they stole Ikey and Hannah's Whitechapel fortune. Unless he should kill him, Teekleman will stay and marry Hinetitama. Mary will have her stallion and Hinetitama will be sacrificed as Mary's willing mare.

Hawk is suddenly very angry. 'Mother, you have done a terrible thing, you will destroy her life. She has Tommo's cravings for the bottle, the Dutchman will bring Hinetitama down to his level.'

Mary has regained her calm and reaching for the tea pot she pours herself a second cup of tea. 'I can't imagine what yer talkin' about. She ain't touched a drop in almost two years and he came to dinner sober as a judge, his linen clean, dressed like Jones the grocer, neat as a new pin, and well spoken and polite throughout.' She places the pot down and adds milk and sugar to her cup and commences to stir it, the teaspoon tinkling softly against the edge of the cup. 'I admit he ain't got the social standing I would have liked for the girl, but who are we to talk? We can't help who we are then, can we? Him a foreigner, her a half-caste, you born black, me a cockney born poor as dirt and not much better than same.'

'Mama, Teekleman is a gambler and a drunk, fer Godsakes!'

'Well, we know all about that then, don't we? Had one of those in the family before, haven't we? Didn't stop us loving him though, did it?'

'Mama, that were Tommo, our own flesh and blood, it's not the same.'

'Oh? Why not? She's in love with him, Hawk. You should see them two together. I've never seen her happier, singing the livelong day, carefree as a lark. She loves him all right, as much as we loved our Tommo.'

Hawk now sees that Mary will not be baited, that she is determined to keep her equilibrium, to stay calm. He tries one more time. 'Mama, I told you how I found them in Wellington, he'll ruin her.'

'People change. He's been here a week and he hasn't touched a drop as far as I know, she's been with him most of the time and except for t'night he's had tea with us every day.' Mary smiles. 'Funny to hear his voice, takes me back, just like me old dad's, all them words pronounced wrong and "ja" this and "ja" that, like turning back the clock, Gawd forbid. I were suddenly a little girl again, tricking pennies from young men stepping out with their sweethearts in the Vauxhall Gardens.'

'Christ Jesus!' Hawk suddenly expostulates, then throwing down his napkin he kicks back his chair and leaves the table.

'Ain't you gunna say goodnight then?' Mary calls after him. Hawk knows that he is finally defeated, that Iron Mary has won the day without shedding a single drop of family blood. He goes to bed furious and humiliated, but nevertheless determined to see Teekleman the next day.

The Dutchman proves to be quite a different proposition to the coward he paid off with two sovs and sent packing in Wellington. He is well dressed, just as Mary has described him, and has a definite air of confidence about him. He is shown into Teekleman's rooms, the two best available at The Ship Inn, by a manservant who, despite a suit of new clothes and boots, has the appearance of a drunkard about him, perhaps an ex-fighter gone to early seed. His rubicund nose looks as though it has been rearranged several times in the past and his ears are tight little knots of flesh. The man is plainly not over-acquainted with the duties of a manservant and fails to take Hawk's hat and coat.

Hawk stoops noticeably to enter the room and Teekleman rises from the table he is seated at and where he has been playing a game of solitaire, the cards arranged in sequence on the table in front of him. Hawk's memory goes back to Tommo, to his abiding obsession, how he couldn't for a moment be parted from a deck of DeLarue and at every opportunity would finger them, handle them, splay and spread them as though they were an extension of his own body, which he supposes they eventually became.

'Once a gambler always a gambler, eh, Teekleman?' Hawk says, this opening remark intended to put the Dutchman on the defensive.

But Teekleman is not so easily disconcerted. He smiles and extends his hand. 'Ja, it is goet we meet, Mr Solomon.' He chuckles. 'Last time was maybe not so goet I think.'

Hawk is forced to take his hand and is surprised at the firmness of Teekleman's grip. 'Now look here, Teekleman,

I do not intend to beat about the bush. You are not welcome here,' Hawk announces and then feels slightly embarrassed at how the words have come out. They sound overpompous, like a retired colonel from the Indian Army. 'So why don't you piss off!' he adds, attempting to leaven his statement with an addition of the vernacular.

Teekleman does not reply, but appears to look past Hawk, who now turns and sees that Blundstone is still standing at the door. 'Ja sank you, Blundstone, you go now,' the Dutchman says, waving the man out with a flick of his hand. He watches as Blundstone leaves, closing the door behind him. Hawk is fairly certain that one of the little pug's cauliflower ears is well glued to the surface of the door.

'If it's a matter of compensation?' Hawk now says to Teekleman.

'Mr Solomon, I am here because I come myself.' He points to the cards on the table. 'It is just a game, I do not gamble no more, with the flats I am finish. I have goet job and I have now Hinetitama.' He pauses and grins. 'Is goet, ja?'

Hawk wants to smash his fist into the Dutchman's face, he knows the bastard is lying. 'Five hundred pounds and your passage out of here to anywhere you wish to go. Holland, America, you name it. All I require is that you never set foot in Tasmania again.' He knows he is offering Teekleman a fortune, but he is disinclined to bargain and has made him an offer a man in Teekleman's position would find almost impossible to refuse. The overlarge offer is also intended to assess whether, as he suspects, there may be another agenda and Mary has rendered the Dutchman bulletproof.

Teekleman whistles softly and appears to be thinking. 'That is a lot of money, Mr Solomon.' He looks slowly up at Hawk and shakes his head. 'No,' he says smiling, 'I stay. I do not go.'

As with Hinetitama, Hawk's fears seem to have been unfounded. Teekleman has been given a job as a tally clerk in the brewery and, soon thereafter, is promoted by Mary to foreman in charge of transportation, delivering to the pubs Tommo & Hawk ale, the beer most in demand from the Potato Factory. Mary has been careful to put him to work in an area isolated from Hawk's day-to-day influence and it has to be said the Dutchman acquits himself well enough. Furthermore, he drinks only beer, which seems not to affect his sobriety in the least, only manifesting itself by the increasing size of his girth. Hinetitama, for her part, though besotted by the Dutchman, maintains her pledge.

The Hobart society is soon atwitter with the news of the romance, though the gossips are all in agreement that Mary has been forced to compromise and has come down in her expectations for her 'dark little granddaughter', the euphemism they have privately adopted for Hinetitama. They have neatly reversed the fact that Hinetitama has summarily rejected every island suitor, and now gleefully whisper that the island's more mature bachelors and widowers have spurned Mary's fortune and collectively rejected her granddaughter out of hand. This wildly improbable proposition is, of course, happily accepted and confirmed by the motley collection of males who have been sent packing.

Nevertheless, everybody who is anybody in the local society is waiting anxiously to be invited to the wedding. Mary has promised a desperate and frustrated Hawk that she will wait six months before the couple are joined in matrimony, his hope being that Teekleman will inevitably reveal his true colours. When time expires and the Dutchman proves his worth an impatient Mary announces the couple's betrothal. Hawk now begs that the wedding be a modest affair and even suggests that it take place as a civil wedding.

Mary is appalled at this suggestion. 'How can you deny me this?' she castigates him. 'Me, an old woman, what hasn't much longer for this mortal coil! Who never had the pleasure of seeing Tommo joined and denied the same pleasure by yourself! I want this whole bleedin' island to know me granddaughter is gettin' married! I want guests t'come from the mainland and every publican and his wife on the island what sells our beer, all the workers, down to the most 'umble, with their families and the nobs and the snobs and the true merinos, I want the lot, even the flamin' governor!'

'Mama, the workers and the publicans yes, maybe a grand picnic for them. As for the rest they despise us, they'll come to laugh, you'll be giving them more bitch-faced pleasure than they've enjoyed in years. I doubt also that the governor will accept.'

'Yes he will, he knows what side his bread is buttered,' though Mary secretly doubts that Governor Hamilton will accept her invitation. He's a nice enough cove, but his wife, Lady Teresa, is a frightful snob with her nose held high enough to look down upon Mount Wellington, never mind the hoi polloi. Mary takes a final shot at Hawk's objection. 'You've made me wait all this time, she could be nigh six months pregnant by now! I may not live long enough to see me own great-grandchild!'

Hawk gives a bitter little laugh. 'Mama, if you have to cut the umbilical cord with your own teeth, you'll be at the birth!'

'Yes, well, you're not denying me a proper wedding. Next you'll be telling me you'll not give the bride away.'

Hawk feels he cannot protest any longer. 'May as well be hung for a sheep as a goat,' he grins.

'Good, then that's settled,' Mary says, trying hard to conceal the triumph in her voice.

The wedding is truly a grand affair with the governor in attendance at St David's Church, though not at the reception afterwards, which is held at the racecourse, there being no other venue sufficiently large to contain the crowd. Three dozen oxen and at least four times as many lambs are roasted and it seems all of Tasmania is in attendance. Mary has reluctantly made a concession to the local society members by creating a grand banquet for them in the Members' enclosure.

She explains this separation of the classes to Hawk. 'I don't want the nobs and the true merinos walking about among the mob with the ordinary folks chewing a bit of a chop and having a good time feeling obliged to bow and scrape and thinking they's not just as entitled to be there as the nobs.'

In fact, she only visits the Members' enclosure once, to present and to drink a toast to the bride and groom, whereupon the three of them promptly leave the nobs to themselves, joining the picnic on the course. Hawk, meanwhile, remains with the common crowd.

In the months that follow the wedding not much is worthy of mention. Teekleman, having secured the prize, does not go astray and within a few weeks, almost on cue, Hinetitama announces that she is experiencing nausea. 'Morning sickness,' Mary announces gleefully to the cook, 'a little strained broth if you will, Mrs Briggs.'

On time and with surprisingly little fuss, given Hinetitama's size, Ben Solomon-Teekleman is delivered by a midwife, with Dr Moses standing by, enjoying an excellent Portuguese sherry or two in Hawk's study.

The lack of complication in Ben's delivery will characterise him all his life. He is a happy and uncomplaining baby who seldom cries, a child who is good at sports, gathers friends around him easily, is in the middle ranking at school and is seldom less than cheerful. Later, he predictably becomes a young man who takes life in his stride. Neither boastful nor arrogant and oblivious to the wealth at his command, he is much loved by a wide range of mates and accepted as their natural leader. At five feet and ten inches in his stockinged feet he is neither short nor tall but powerfully built, dark-haired and brown of eye with a hint of Maori about his broad brow and strong jawline. A handsome young man by all appearances, he is also an excellent shot and a natural horseman.

His sibling, Victoria, born fifteen months later, has a difficult birth and Dr Moses announces that Hinetitama will endanger herself if she attempts to have more children. She is as fair as her brother is dark, a blonde with almost violet eyes and with a slightly olive skin. While Mary dotes on both children it is to Victoria that she is most naturally attracted. The little girl, much to Hawk's consternation and her great-grandmother's delight, is stubborn as a mule, and, in Mary's last year of life, at three years old already shows an exceptional intelligence. She sits beside the old woman, doing basic sums on the abacus, the bright beads never ceasing to delight her.

'She's the one!' Mary cackles. 'She's the one!' Mary at the age of eighty-five still has all her faculties intact, though she is becoming increasingly hard of hearing. 'Damned good thing too,' she often says. 'I'm tired of hearing all the nonsense people go on about.' She was never one to suffer fools gladly but now she has become a thoroughly cantankerous old woman, the only exceptions being her great-grandchildren, though even they are sent packing when they become too boisterous for her. She no longer goes to the Potato Factory every day but still insists that Hawk talk the day's business over with her as she takes a glass of sherry and watches the sun setting over the Derwent.

At half-past five in the afternoon and half an hour sooner in the winter she is to be found in her accustomed chair on the porch overlooking her magnificent garden. Further off still the city snatches the last of the late afternoon sunlight and finally she looks out upon the river beyond it, that brightest ribbon of water that first brought her as a young convict woman over sixty years ago to the shores of Van Diemen's Land.

Though Mary enjoys the magnificent sunset and the closing down of the day, that is, on those good days when the ever changing Tasmanian weather allows it to occur, this is not the reason she is at her station at precisely the same time every evening. She waits for the green parrots.

'My luck, here comes my great good fortune!' she shouts as the flock approaches, wheeling towards her, seeming to be skidding on the glass-bright air. Her poor broken hand is clasped around the little gold Waterloo medal that hangs from her neck. Then as the birds pass over she releases the medal and clasps her hands to her bosom, cheering them on as their raucous screeching fills the space above her, drowning out her own calls of delight.

It is a ritual which never varies and which is of the utmost importance to her wellbeing. The very site for her magnificent home was selected over several months of observation and only after carefully determining the exact morning and evening flight path of the rosellas.

Apart from Ikey's Waterloo medal, sent to her in Newgate Prison in a moment of aberrant generosity Ikey himself could never satisfactorily explain, the parrots have always signified her new beginning, her second chance and her subsequent great good fortune.

She now recalls how she first witnessed a flock of parrots in flight as the *Destiny II* was leaving the Port of Rio de Janeiro, the convict transport having called in to take on supplies of food and fresh water before proceeding to Van Diemen's Land.

Mary was hidden behind two barrels at the stern of the vessel, having escaped from the ship's hospital where earlier she had lain in wait for the vile Potbottom, to recover her Waterloo medal which he had stolen from her. The departing ship had reached a point between Fort San Juan and Fort Santa Cruz when she witnessed a flock of macaw parrots flying across the headland, their brilliant plumage flashing in the early morning sun.

As the birds rose Mary could see the Sugar Loaf, the majestic peak that towers above the grand sweep of the bay and dominates this most beautiful of all the world's harbours.

With the flock of macaws captured against an impossibly high blue sky Mary felt a surge of exhilaration. It was the first time during the long and dreadful voyage from England that she held the slightest hope that what remained of her life would not continue in abject misery and end in her premature death.

Her kind were usually dead at the age of thirty-four and some a great deal earlier. With seven years of incarceration on the Fatal Shore ahead of her, she had little reason to expect a life free of misery or, for that matter, of her death not arriving at the normally predicted time.

Then, at sunrise many weeks later, as the *Destiny II* lay at anchor in the D'Entrecasteaux Channel prior to catching the early morning tide to take them up river to Hobart Town, a flock of bright green parrots had flown overhead calling a raucous welcome down to her. From that moment, when Mary had seen the parrots enter her life for a second time, she accepted the emerald green rosella as her good luck, her great good fortune. Never a day in her subsequent life passes without her going out to greet them at sunrise and, as she is doing now, to send them on their way at sunset.

The following morning, for the first time in her new life, Mary fails to rise. She is always up before the servants and when she doesn't appear on the balcony, Martha Billings, who usually stands in the garden where she can observe the birds and Mary at her customary place, goes hurrying to the back of the house and into the kitchen to tell Mrs Briggs.

Mrs Briggs, all bustle and fuss, hurries up the stairs and arrives panting at Mary's bed-chamber door. She knocks tentatively. 'You all right, dear?' she calls softly and then, when no sound comes from the room beyond, she knocks more loudly. She hears a faint call to enter and shyly enters Mary's bed chamber.

Nobody within living memory has ever seen Iron Mary in bed and Mrs Briggs is surprised at how small and frail she looks with the blanket drawn up against her chin. 'You must call Hawk,' Mary whispers.

'Oh my Gawd!' Mrs Briggs gasps, immediately bursting into tears.

'Call Hawk, you silly woman,' Mary rasps.

With her hands covering her face Mrs Briggs runs from the bedroom.

Hawk arrives a few minutes later wearing a dressing gown over his nightshirt. He has already shaved but not yet had the time to dress.

'Mama!' he exclaims as he enters. 'You are not well?'

The sight of the frail little woman almost lost in the large brass and enamel bed leaves him with a deep sense of shock. While Mary is an old woman, such is her character that only strangers note her advanced age.

Those who have been around her for most, if not all of their lives, see only Mary, or if they are among the unfortunate, Iron Mary, but nevertheless both her friends and her enemies regard her as an indestructible force.

'I shall call Dr Moses,' Hawk says. 'How do you feel, Mama?'

Mary lifts her hand. Even though she is in bed, she still wears mittens to hide the deformity of her hands, they are as indispensable to her as her lace sleeping bonnet. 'No, I don't want him fussing about. Will you call Hinetitama and the children to my bedside but first . . .'

Hawk interjects. 'Mama, you are never taken sick, please let me call Dr Moses.'

Mary doesn't bother to answer. 'Hawk, listen to me,' she says, her voice barely above a whisper. She pats the eiderdown beside her, signalling that he should sit beside her on the bed. As Hawk sits, the weight of his huge body sinks the bedsprings, so that Mary is almost in a seated position. 'Now listen to me carefully,' she repeats. 'In the safe in my office is a brown manilla envelope, it's got a black seal, not red like the usual. Open it, read it carefully.' She pauses to take a breath.

'Then in the drawer of the desk you will find a stick of the same black wax. I want you to reseal it, so it's returned just the way it was.' The effort at talking is taking its toll and Mary rests for a moment, her chest heaving with the effort. 'If the Dutchman behaves well, you will give it to him before you die, or leave it to him in your will.' Mary rests again before continuing. 'If he plays up after I've gorn, tell him *you* now possess the document and send him away. Tell him if he returns you will take the appropriate action.'

'Mama, hush, hush, you're not going to die,' Hawk says, alarmed, putting his huge black hand to her brow. It is cold and clammy and his heart skips a beat.

There is a trace of a smile on Mary's lips. 'Yes I am. If *I* says so, that's it then, ain't it? Do you understand what I'm saying about the Dutchman?'

Hawk nods. 'Yes, Mama.'

'Now call Hinetitama and the children in.'

'Mama, I feel I should call Dr Moses.'

Mary sighs and then remains silent for a few moments as though she is trying to decide. 'No,' she says finally, 'I've had enough, I heard the birds pass over this mornin' but I weren't there to see them.' It is said as though it is her final word, no different to her dismissal of some proposition put to her in business. 'Go now.'

Hawk taps softly on the door of Hinetitama's bed chamber then opens the door a crack to look in. She is awake but still in bed beside her husband, who is snoring, his fat belly rising and falling well above the level of his head and the bolster it rests against.

In the years they have been together Teekleman has almost doubled in size, his girth well beyond the possibility of joining his fingers about it. Hawk opens the door a little wider so that his niece might see his face. 'You decent?' he whispers.

'What is it?' she asks, climbing out of bed. She is wearing a cotton nightgown to her ankles and her dark hair falls naturally to her shoulders, seeming not disturbed by her sleeping. Hawk thinks how pretty she looks, though a woman now of thirty-two she still appears to be ten years younger. He wonders, as he has so often done, what she sees in the fat Dutchman, for she seems as besotted by him as ever.

Hawk points to Teekleman and brings his finger to his lips. 'Come to Mary's room,' he says softly and then goes to fetch Ben and Victoria from the nursery.

With Teekleman excluded and the remainder of her little family gathered around her, Mary first kisses Ben

116

and sends him off to his breakfast. She holds Victoria a moment longer. 'You shall have my abacus, my precious,' she whispers before releasing her.

'Are you ill, Great-grandmamma?' Victoria asks in the clear tones of a child. 'Are you going to die?'

'Run along now, darlin',' Mary says softly.

'No! I won't and you can't make me,' the child replies, looking defiantly at Mary.

'Go!' Hinetitama admonishes her. 'Do as Great-grandmamma says.'

'No!' Victoria replies, folding her little arms and walking backwards until her bottom brushes against a small chaise longue and she jumps up and wriggles, with her arms still folded, until she is seated defiantly upon it. She hasn't, for one moment, taken her eyes off Mary.

'Stubborn,' Mary whispers, though it seems more a compliment than an admonishment. Then with a slight gesture of her hand she draws Hinetitama closer so that she is where Hawk previously sat. 'I have made provision in my will for you and the children, my dear. You are to have your own house with servants provided and the income from a trust fund I have set up for the children until Victoria reaches the age of thirty and Ben thirty-two.'

Hinetitama does not appear to grasp what the old woman is saying. 'Grandmother, please don't die,' she cries and bursts into sobs.

Victoria watches Hinetitama crying. 'She can die if she wants to,' she says suddenly to her mother. Then she turns to Mary and announces, 'Great-grandmamma, we don't want you to die, but if you must, then you simply must.'

Mary, increasingly short of breath, still manages a wan smile. She looks up at Hawk. 'She's the one,' she whispers. She lies still for a while then turns to the weeping Hinetitama, 'Now, now, girlie, enough o' that nonsense. Listen to me, I shan't say it again. You shall have the income from the trust fund I have set up for Ben and Victoria, it will take at least until they are thirty years old to learn enough to take over from Hawk. Then they shall each inherit fifty per cent of the trust and you will receive a separate pension.' Mary rests a while, her chest rising and falling in short sharp bursts. 'The principal is *not* your money. *Only* the interest may be used by you and your husband, that is, until they reach the age to inherit,' she repeats. 'Does yer understand?'

Hinetitama, who has her chin on her breast, nods. 'Yes, Grandmother,' she sniffs, though it is unclear whether she does.

'Now I want you to do something for me,' Mary says, reaching for her granddaughter's hand.

'Anything, Grandmother,' Hinetitama sniffs.

'Will you sing me that song?'

'What song?' Hinetitama sobs.

'The Maori one, child, about goin' away.'

Mary nods and Hinetitama suddenly breaks into uncontrollable sobbing. 'Come, come,' Mary whispers. 'None o' that, girl.'

Hinetitama struggles to regain her composure then begins to sing, her voice soft and reedy at first but her lovely contralto gains the ascendancy and a beautiful, haunting melody rises deep and strong.

Hinetitama comes to the end and Mary lifts her arms and hugs her granddaughter perhaps for the second or third time in her life. 'I am most proud of you, Hinetitama, most proud, thank you for my heirs, for Ben and Victoria.' She pauses, then says gently, 'Now you must go, I wish to be alone with Hawk.' Mary turns slowly to Victoria. 'Run along, my precious.'

Victoria jumps from the couch, her small feet landing together with a soft thump on the Persian carpet. She walks the few steps over to Mary's bed and, standing on tiptoe, she kisses her on the forehead, then takes her weeping mother by the hand. 'Come along, Mother,' she commands, leading the sobbing Hinetitama from the room.

Hawk waits until they've left before he resumes his place beside Mary. 'You will keep all the servants,' she instructs, 'they's all of them strays and ain't got no family and nowhere to go, they must have pensions when they are too old to work.' Then she places her hand in Hawk's huge paw. 'I loves you Hawk, I always loved you the most.' Hawk remains quiet, though great tears run down his black cheeks and splash between the cleavage of his dressing gown and onto his dark chest.

After a while Mary asks him to help her up to a sitting position. Hawk does so, plumping and propping the cushions behind her. She leans slightly forward. 'Take it off,' she says slowly. Hawk sees that her Waterloo medal hangs from her neck on its gold chain. 'Keep it for Victoria, give it to her when she comes of age. Tell her how it come about, that it's luck beyond good luck, much, much more, it's her great good fortune.'

Hawk wipes his tears on the sleeve of his dressing gown and reaches over and slips the chain over Mary's head. 'Mama, I will tell her what it meant to you.'

'Tell her about the birds, the rosellas,' Mary says, now almost breathless.

She is silent for almost half an hour and Hawk regains his composure. Every once in a while he can feel pressure from the hand he holds, as though she is about to speak, as though she is gathering her final strength. Then with what must have taken an enormous effort of will, she suddenly sits bolt upright. 'Don't trust the bastard,' she shouts. 'Don't never trust him, yer hear!' Mary, exhausted, collapses back into her pillow.

'Who, Teekleman?' Hawk says scornfully. 'I never did, Mama.'

Mary's eyes open in alarm. 'No! Not him, David, David Solomon!' With this last great effort she closes her eyes and appears to fall asleep.

Around the middle of the afternoon she wakes, though she seems weaker still, barely able to talk. Hawk has sent for Ann Solomon, Ikey's youngest daughter, who at sixteen had left Hannah to be with her father and who has since been cared for by Mary, lacking for nothing and now on a generous pension for the remainder of her life. Ann says her tearful farewells to Mary, of whom she has always been most fond. After her departure Mary calls for Hawk and soon afterwards, with her hand clasped in his, she loses consciousness. Just on sunset, she sighs softly and passes away. Mary has achieved in death what she'd always done in life, gone about things without too much fuss and carry-on.

Hinetitama and the servants will ever afterwards tell how upon the very moment of Mary's death the garden is filled with flocks of emerald rosellas, their terrible screeching rending the air, so that the children and the servants run about with their hands to their ears. The small green parrots land in their many hundreds, some will later say in their tens of thousands, a huge spreading mass of bright emerald and yellow covering the entire surface of the roof and shrouding the surrounding trees and bushes in a whirring of bright feathers. They remain for a full hour, then as suddenly as they've arrived, they depart, leaving the air behind them so still that no one dares be the first to break the silence.

Martha Billings, the kitchen maid, swears on her life that the following morning when she went out into the garden at sunrise, not a single rosella passed overhead. She declares ever after that the little emerald green parakeets changed their path of flight and were never again seen during her time in the big house.

Mary's good luck, her great good fortune, has followed her to the grave, where Hawk later speculates she will lie forever beside Hannah Solomon, quarrelling ceaselessly and giving each other what-for. Though the both of them, he knows, will take time off to lay down the law to a hapless and fervently protesting Ikey. 'Oi vey, I must have a little peace, my dears, a portion of quietitude from your combined vexations, conniptions, quarrelsomeness and cantankery. God forbid I should live through all of eternity in the company of two such raucous and spleenful harridans!'

Chapter Four

HAWK, TEEKLEMAN AND HINETITAMA

Hobart 1892–1893

Mary has left everything to Hawk, that is all but the ten per cent of her fortune bequeathed to Ben and Victoria, the income from it going to Hinetitama until Victoria reaches the age of thirty and Ben thirty-two. Mary failed to explain this disparity between the two ages and no mention is made of it in the document drawing up the trust deed.

Hawk can only assume that Mary believed Victoria was to be favoured. She'd often enough in his presence declared that Victoria was, as she put it, 'the one'.

Iron Mary did not believe in the God-given right of the male gender to take control, leaving the female to fetch, carry, nurture and nourish. She constantly championed a woman's right to look to her own affairs and never relinquished any of her personal power to the opposite gender. She understood the principles of construction as well as any foreman builder and woe betide any carpenter, cooper, brickie, plumber or engineer who tried to pull the wool over her eyes. In matters of accountancy her abacus threatened any tendency to be careless and she knew her beer and its chemistry as well as any brewmaster in the land. While she left the supervision of the company's hops and barley farms to Hawk she nevertheless could gauge the quality and price of the crops as an expert. Iron Mary's querulous eye was everywhere to be found.

It was this fierce sense of independence that led to her constant disparagement and often even to outright hatred. The malevolence felt towards her came not only from the business community in the colony, but also from the chattering females in its society, who saw her as having betrayed her gender. The exceptions were those who worked for Mary, who knew they were better treated and their families more secure than in any other form of employment available on the island. Iron Mary was hard, but she was also fair, there was never any ambivalence about her, you always knew where you stood.

She had even carried the notion of female financial responsibility through to Hinetitama, though she believed her granddaughter practically incapable of counting the change in her purse. Mary made her the trustee for the children's legacy, knowing it was a fairly harmless gesture. Hinetitama could never get her hands on the principal sum while receiving a considerable independent income from it. In her will she had written: *Though you know nothing of bookkeeping, it will be good for you to be charged with this small duty in return for the income it brings you.*

Mary's funeral proved to be one of the biggest yet to be held on the island, though it turned out to be a quite different affair to the one originally intended by Hawk. He decided to give the brewery workers a half-day holiday, informing them they were not duty bound to come to the funeral but that a picnic would be held for their families. However, the workers formed a delegation to ask if they might attend the funeral instead. It was an indication of how they felt about Mary and so Hawk turned what was to be a picnic into a wake. The servants in the big house were invited as well as those publicans and their wives who wished to be present. This was simply a gesture of goodwill, publicans and their wives are seldom included in events of most kinds.

Hawk knew those businesses that depended on the Potato Factory for part of their livelihood would show up at the funeral in their Sunday best. Altogether, he hoped attendance would be kept to a minimum, but now with the workers asking to be at her graveside, it would give things the common touch she would have liked. Mary would have approved of her own people seeing her off without too much of a fuss.

However, Hawk had underestimated the effect her life had had on the people of Hobart and the small towns beyond it. On the day of the funeral the early morning ferries and boats from the outlying districts up and down river were packed and the country roads unusually busy. By noon the common folk had gathered along the route from St David's to the cemetery, removing their caps and bowing their heads as the funeral cortege passed them by. Many wore black armbands or bonnets and it became obvious they had come to say goodbye to Mary Abacus, who, despite her enormous wealth, had retained her common touch and, unlike most of the so-called nobs on the island, never concealed her convict origins. She had given them cottage hospitals, schools and soup kitchens, made work available to the poor and created a widows' pension fund. Wherever a tied pub existed there would be an annual Christmas party for the children of the town or suburb, where no child went without a feed and a gift at Yuletide and, as well, took home a quart bottle of Tommo & Hawk Ale to their parents. She endowed the orphanage and educated and apprenticed its children, finally allowing them jobs in her various enterprises. Half the brewery workers thought of her as the nearest thing they would ever know as a guardian and now they lined the streets. Scarcely a person in the crowd hadn't in some way or another been touched by the little cockney lass who had been transported to the Fatal Shore sixty years before.

The plain folk knew they'd lost someone who could never be replaced in their affections. The *Hobart Mercury* reported:

Hats and caps were removed from the heads of the men and there were copious tears to be witnessed under the bonnets of the women lining the streets to the grave yard. Not an inch of standing space appeared to be available for a hundred yards all about the site of the grave. A great many of the common folk brought informal floral tributes of their own, small bunches and single blooms from their gardens, even wildflowers picked along the lanes. Many brought a single potato as an acknowledgment to her humble beginnings. With due solemnity, they later placed these tributes upon the grave to form a mound of blossom well beyond six feet in height. Mary Abacus never slept under a softer, more perfumed quilt.

There was even talk of the governor coming to the funeral service, but this proved to be a false rumour. Chasms in Tasmanian society were too wide even for Mary to leap, or as Lady Teresa was heard to say at a tea party she attended on the day of the funeral, 'One does not lift one's skirt to step *into* the gutter.'

Hawk, long accustomed to working together with Mary, has none of the usual male reservations about training Victoria to the task of taking over with her brother.

Although she is still a small child, Victoria has shown an intelligence above that of Ben, who seems normal enough in all respects, his natural gifts no more than might be expected from a small boy of seven who rides his first pony.

However, Hawk does not see himself as a mere caretaker, preserving Mary's life's work intact for her great-grandchildren to inherit. He has different plans for the Potato Factory which he modestly and correctly believes he has helped to build.

For some time he has realised there is little chance of expanding their interests much further in Tasmania. Scarcely any sizable enterprises are left in which the Potato Factory does not have a finger in the pie. Mary had often talked of opening a brewery in Melbourne, though she knew that Hawk would need to be there to supervise it and she was reluctant to have him away from her. Now he thinks this may well be the way to go in the future.

Hawk, fulfilling Mary's wishes, allows Hinetitama to purchase a home of her own in Sandy Bay and she and Teekleman and the two children move out of the big house, taking four of the female servants and a gardener and stable hand with them.

Thinking he will be moving to Melbourne for several months at a time, Hawk does not wish to buy or build a new home for himself and the big house is much too large for his needs. Retaining Mrs Briggs the cook and Martha Billings as housemaid, he joins Ann Solomon, at her insistence, in Ikey's old home in the centre of town where she has continued to live after her father's death. It is simply a convenience, two people who have always known and enjoyed each other's company in the most platonic way for the best part of their lives, but, of course, it sets the tattletales a-chattering.

Ann's house in Elizabeth Street, though designated a

cottage, is large enough for them both, with Hawk taking the upstairs rooms where the ceilings are sufficiently high to prevent him from having to stoop and Ann the ground level where there are rooms as well for Mrs Briggs and Martha. Mary's house is converted into a maternity hospital where company workers' families receive free treatment.

The transfer of power and authority to Hawk is surprisingly smooth. Even the acceptance of him as their new adversary by the other brewers and the business community sees not the slightest reduction in their malevolence. A nigger in charge of the Potato Factory is only fractionally an improvement over an independently minded woman.

Mary, who kept most things close to her chest, has always made Hawk the exception and he knows and runs the business well, seeking among his employees and elsewhere for men, and even women, who can be trained to higher positions. Hawk is an altogether more trustful and benign authority at the helm of the Potato Factory.

However, things do not transpire as well on the family front. Four months after Mary's death Mrs Briggs returns late one afternoon from Sandy Bay where she has spent her Thursday afternoon off visiting her friend, Mabel Hawkins, Ben and Victoria's nanny.

Ann Solomon will be out in the evening to a whist drive, a card game with old friends whom she never fails to join on the same evening every week. Thus, it is agreed that Mrs Briggs is not required to prepare a hot dinner for Hawk and may add a quiet evening to her afternoon off. Hawk is happy to be served a cold collation on a tray in his study upstairs. On this particular Thursday, when Martha is sent upstairs with the tray, she is instructed by Mrs Briggs to ask Hawk if he will see her after he has taken his meal.

'Now this is how you says it,' she carefully instructs Martha. 'Sir, Mrs Briggs has a matter o' concern to your good self, which she 'opes to see you about at your convenience, but hopefully after you've taken your dinner tonight.' The cook looks at Martha doubtfully. 'Shall I say it again, or does you understand it? G'arn, say it just like I said.'

Martha repeats the message without missing a word and Mrs Briggs nods her approval. 'Remember, *a matter o' concern to your good self*, that bit be most important, I don't want Mr Hawk thinking I'm bringing him me own troubles.'

'What's the matter o' concern?' Martha asks fearfully. 'Is it something I've done?'

'I'll thank you to mind your own business, my girl. No it ain't, the world don't revolve around you, you know. Though if you're going to be a stickybeak, we might soon enough find something to your disadvantage, 'aven't I seen you ogling Young Benson?'

'Benson!' Martha exclaims. 'Do us a favour! I'll not have nothing to do with him, he's an orphan an' all.'

'So were you!' Mrs Briggs exclaims, surprised.

'Takes one ter know one, don't it?' Martha sniffs, then lifting the tray she leaves the kitchen with her head held high.

Hawk agrees to see Mrs Briggs immediately after he has eaten and when Martha returns to take his tray he asks her to tell the cook to bring a fresh pot of tea and two cups.

He makes Mrs Briggs sit down and pours the tea himself. Then with milk and sugar offered and accepted, he does the same for himself and leans back in his chair, lifting up the cup and saucer. He brings the cup to his lips and takes a sip. 'Now then, about this matter of concern to myself, Mrs Briggs?' Hawk says, smiling.

'Mr Hawk, I hope I ain't interfering in what's thought to be family and none o' my business, but I've been with you and Mistress Mary nigh thirty years . . .'

'Of course not, Mrs Briggs,' Hawk interrupts, 'you *are* family. What is it you wish to say?'

'Well, sir, it's about Miss Heenie, she's been beaten most severe.'

'Beaten?' Hawk asks, shocked. He leans forward and puts his cup and saucer down on the table beside his chair. 'By whom?'

'Mr Teekleman, sir.'

'The Dutchman? Has Dr Moses been called?'

'No, sir, Miss Heenie will not allow it.'

'Who told you this?'

'Mrs Hawkins.'

'The children's nanny?'

'Aye, she's the only one allowed in Miss Heenie's bed chamber.'

'Does she think the doctor is needed?'

'No, sir, Mrs Hawkins knows something of nursing and says it is a matter o' bruises, nothing broken. Miss Heenie is mending well enough, but waits until the marks are gone.'

Hawk leans back somewhat relieved. 'Now tell me, what precisely happened?'

'Miss Heenie's 'usband come home last Monday dead drunk and she and him had a devil of a row.'

'What time was that?'

'Near on midnight. Mrs Hawkins says they was all asleep like and were wakened because o' the shouting and blasphemy.'

'Did anyone get up and go to her?'

'Aye, Mrs Hawkins, she's ever the brave one. But when she got to her bed-chamber door and asks polite if everything be all right, Miss Heenie, who she can hear

129

crying and sobbing, stops and shouts out she's to go back to bed at once. Mrs Hawkins says there were an empty brandy bottle left outside the bed-chamber door.'

'Thank you, Mrs Briggs. I am most grateful to you. I'd be obliged if you'll not speak of it to anyone.'

'No, no, o' course not, sir. And Miss Heenie's servants, they's all been in the family awhile and knows the same, to keep stum.'

Hawk expects the cook to take her leave, but Mrs Briggs makes no attempt to do so.

'Sir?'

'Yes? Is there more I should know, Mrs Briggs?'

'I can vouch for Mrs Hawkins, I've known her all me life, a sainted woman if ever I saw one, but Young Benson he says Mr Teekleman . . . he's been seen in Wapping.'

'In a public house? But that is his job?' However, Hawk knows it is a foolish thing to do. Wapping is no place to be at night and Teekleman would not be expected to visit a pub in its precinct after sunset. In fact, he is forbidden to do so by the company, one of his predecessors having been robbed and stabbed to death in its dark felonious streets some years back and another, not that long ago, robbed and badly beaten. The public houses in this notorious slum district are territorial, places for gangs and villains to congregate, and are not for outsiders after dark.

'No, sir, it weren't in a public 'ouse,' the cook's eyes grow suddenly large and her voice comes down to almost a whisper. 'It were a *gaming den*!'

'What, playing at cards?'

'I dunno, Mr Hawk, a gaming den, that's all what the lad said.' Hawk can see from Mrs Briggs' wide-eyed explanation that the two words 'gaming den' conjure a depravity in her mind almost beyond anything she can comprehend. A place of dark corners, scurrying rats, toothless old drunkards, filthy, scabrous harlots with their bodices ripped down and murderous villains and cutthroats, the detestable dregs of the seven seas.

James Benson, Mrs Briggs' informer, is one of Mary's numerous rescues from the orphanage. A young bloke, street-wise like all of his kind, he is responsible for stabling and grooming Hawk's thoroughbred and taking care of his sulky, bringing it around to the house each morning. During the day he acts as personal messenger at the brewery and, when he's not busy with Hawk's needs, he is expected to do odd jobs around the house. He has only recently replaced Old McDougall, a long term family retainer who passed away a fortnight before Mary. Benson is considered by Mrs Briggs to be a bit too cheeky and forward for his own good and has not yet earned her trust, which Hawk knows is likely to take him several more years, if ever. It is because of this that she offers Benson's information to Hawk somewhat tentatively.

'Wapping?' Hawk repeats.

'Aye, that's where 'e said it were, sir.'

If Young Benson's information is true then Slabbert Teekleman has reverted to being his old self. Hawk hopes that it is only an aberration, done on the spur of the moment or as a gesture of bravado when he is drunk and no longer possessed of a natural sense of caution.

While Hawk hasn't yet thought out the consequences of the Dutchman's actions, a husband's right to beat his wife, or even to get totally drunk occasionally, is not a heinous crime in Hobart society. Or in any prevailing society for that matter, provided always such an incident may be brushed under the carpet and doesn't get out into the public domain except as an occasional whisper at a ladies' tea party. The shame of having beaten your wife does not lie in the beating itself, but in the fact that it is something the common people do and is therefore altogether too plebeian. Or as the French might say, it is simply *de trop*, a black mark against one's good standing in the social register.

Hawk well knows that Hinetitama is quite capable of having instigated the fight when her husband proved to be drunk beyond his normal fairly benign state of inebriation and, provided she is not badly hurt, which doesn't seem to be the case, it may be difficult for him to interfere.

The gambling in Wapping concerns him the most. Hawk has a morbid fear of gambling and its consequences. With the sad life of Tommo always in his mind, he knows that gambling and ardent spirits do not sit well together and the results of combining brandy and cards are almost always disastrous. He can only hope, when he speaks to Teekleman, that it has occurred on this single occasion, the result of a flight of fancy by the Dutchman, and not a deliberate intention, arrived at in a state of sobriety.

Despite Mary's instructions, the ever fair-minded Hawk has not opened the envelope with the black seal left in her office safe. Teekleman has behaved commendably in the past five years and Hinetitama seems happy to remain with him, her wild nature somewhat becalmed by the advent of the children and her temperate surroundings. She has latterly been given the responsibility of overseeing the running of the new maternity hospital, a task Hawk feels sure will utilise her talents as a nurse while keeping her happily occupied.

The Dutchman, for his part, has sired two healthy children and kept his side of whatever bargain he and Mary made. As a result he has sent her contented to her grave, the future of the Potato Factory assured. Whatever it is that Mary held against the Dutchman has either proved to be highly successful in containing his baser instincts, or Teekleman has decided to reform of his own accord. Hawk sees no point in meddling with the past while the present seems nicely intact. Perhaps the only alarming thing about the Dutchman is his stomach, which continues to enlarge to the point where he looks like a perambulating fermentation cask.

Teekleman's rapidly expanding girth seems of no concern to Tommo's daughter. It is, after all, a traditional sign of prosperity among the Maori and an indication that a man is being well cared for by his wife. Hawk tells himself what he doesn't know about the man cannot influence his future judgment, which, as for every other brewery worker, ought to be made on Teekleman's performance and not on his past misdemeanours.

Slabbert Teekleman has risen to be a distribution manager of the brewery. The common name for such a job is a 'cheersman'. A curious job, it entitles him to start at the brewery in the late afternoon where, upon his arrival, he will examine the weekly beer orders made by the various public houses owned by the Potato Factory around Hobart in preparation for his nightly peregrinations.

Over the years, Iron Mary was forced by the rival brewers to build or buy her own public houses as they wouldn't sell her beer in their pubs and successfully bribed or intimidated most of the independents. There was a limit to the number of public houses she could build and, if the company was to prosper, she had to ensure that each of her outlets sold near to its total capacity.

A cheersman therefore has a twofold task, he must be both a bully and a *bon vivant*. It is a task for which the Dutchman is ideally suited, for this ambivalence exists within him. He can be bellicose in the extreme or, if he chooses, he can soon win the approbation of the crowd with the magic of his fiddle playing. As Teekleman increases in size both these negative and positive attributes appear to be enhanced. He is, at once, a bully to be greatly feared and in another guise he seemingly becomes the merriest of company. It is a sweet and sour, hot and cold, merry and monstrous dichotomy seldom found living so conspicuously in one person.

Part of Mary's genius was that she understood this duality in him and cast him in the role of a cheersman. If one of her pubs was not selling the amount of beer expected of it then Teekleman would drop in for a visit. Those publicans unfortunate enough to witness this side of the Dutchman did not easily forget the experience. On the other hand, if a pub succeeded to her expectations, then the publican greatly treasured his visit.

It should be pointed out, in fairness to Iron Mary, that every publican was allowed fifteen per cent of his profits as a means of eventually purchasing forty-nine per cent of his business, a task which should take him about ten years to achieve. Thus it was to his ultimate benefit to increase his sales in what Mary saw as a partnership of mutual profit.

This having been said, she would not tolerate a publican partner who did not give her his very best efforts and a visit by Teekleman in his guise as standover man was the first sign of her displeasure and a warning to the publican to pull up his socks. Eight weeks of poor trading would see him paid out and on the street. The Potato Factory was alone among the breweries in this arrangement, the other brewers using it as yet another example of Iron Mary's stupidity and inability to understand the correct principles of profitable commerce.

Despite the fact that the Wesleyan Women's Temperance League constantly rails against the company for selling more liquor per Potato Factory outlet than any of the other public houses, Hawk continues the arrangement after her death on the basis that the good it does for a publican and his family far outweighs the bad.

Slabbert Teekleman plays a very fine tune on the fiddle and wherever he goes in his second capacity, a good deal of merriment is sure to follow. He seems to know every jig, shanty and folk song to be sung by the light of the silvery moon and if a new one is presented to him, a few bars sung, even if it should be off-key, he will pick up the tune and present it to the crowd as though it was learned on his grandmother's knee. His fiddle seems to have a magical quality of discovery, constantly surprising with its invention and its ability to make his audience happy. It is as though the bellicose bully is himself, while his fiddle is a happiness of its own, a person quite different in nature to the morose bully who clasps it to the curve of his shoulder.

The Dutchman's entertaining presence in a pub of an evening will guarantee to increase the takings fivefold, while his magic fiddle seems to have the capacity to cause sworn enemies to promise everlasting friendship and send the inebriated patrons home bellowing songs to the moon.

Teekleman the cheersman is always accompanied by Isaac Blundstone, who remains within the crowd buying customers an occasional drink on the house so that a sense of good cheer prevails. He is an expert at picking those among the crowd who might not have the means to hang about, but are potentially among the most roisterous. A drink placed gratuitously in such a person's hands will, he knows, be rewarded by the increased approbation of the crowd and in the greatly improved ambience of the pub.

By closing time, the ex-pug is all sails to the wind and must generally be supported to the coach that comes to pick up Teekleman. It is the last laugh of the night as the Dutchman carries his mate under his arm like a sack of potatoes and unceremoniously dumps him into the coach.

While Blundstone is not in the employ of the Potato Factory, the company willingly accepts the cost of his largesse chalked on the publican's blackboard. The Dutchman himself consumes large volumes of beer as a source of encouragement to others to do the same and, as a further part of the entertainment, he will challenge any man to a chug-a-lug, where, it is claimed, he has never been beaten. The presence of both men can substantially increase the takings for the night and is as happy an arrangement as the two of them can imagine while, at the same time, maintaining goodwill and *bonhomie* with the delighted publican.

Perhaps, after all, Mary was right, some people need only to be offered a second chance to grab the nettle and make good. Hawk hears her voice plainly in his mind, 'We can all reform if we are fortunate enough to get a second chance.' He wishes only that her faith in the capacity of humans to turn over a new leaf might have proved as true for his precious twin, Tommo.

'Have Mrs Hawkins or the other servants noticed any change in Mr Teekleman's habits?' Hawk now asks Mrs Briggs.

'Abits, sir?'

'You know, his routine, his comings and goings from the house?'

'I don't think so, sir. He comes 'ome, takes his dinner with Miss Heenie and then goes out, returning very late, it's what he's always done.'

Hawk, of course, knows this to be true. It is said by some that the Dutchman's work brings him a great deal of pleasure in both its aspects, as enforcer and clown, but with the former giving him the greater satisfaction. Though nobody can deny his almost inhuman capacity for ale, and while he may get merry enough when he has imbibed a skinful sufficient to sink six men in a jabbering heap to their knees, he is never said to be out of control or dispossessed of his wits.

'So what was the difference in his disposition on his return home late on Monday night? I mean, apart from the beating?' Hawk asks the cook.

'Don't know nothing about his dispo...dispo... whatever, sir. Mrs Hawkins says they was all asleep like and were woke up because o' the shouting and blasphemy and then the screams and sobbing from Miss Heenie.'

'And that was the same night Benson saw him in Wapping?'

'I can't rightly say, sir, he didn't mention what night it were.'

'Thank you, Mrs Briggs, I am truly grateful to you for coming to see me.'

Mrs Briggs rises from the leather armchair. 'Thank you, sir, shall I leave the pot? I'll bring you a fresh cup.'

'No, no, take it,' Hawk says absently, then sees that he has allowed the cup resting on the small table beside his chair to grow cold. The cook is on her way back downstairs when Hawk calls out to her. He hears her ponderous tread as she turns and climbs the three or four steps she has already descended, then her head pops around the door.

'Yes, sir?'

'Tomorrow morning when Young Benson arrives with the sulky, be so kind as to ask him to come up and see me.'

Hawk sits for some time after the cook has left. His first instinct is to take a cab to Sandy Bay and call on Hinetitama. But it is already well after eight o'clock and his commonsense tells him there is little he can do until the morning. He knows sufficient of Tommo's daughter to decide that discretion is the better part of valour, to go around and make a fuss will most probably create an even

137

bigger one. Hawk thinks she is more likely to take her husband's side than his. Despite Tommo's daughter having mellowed somewhat, scratch her skin and underneath is the tiger she ever was. He'll have to approach things somewhat delicately or she'll be likely to send him away with a flea in his ear.

The following morning when Young Benson comes up to his study Hawk questions him closely. 'On how many occasions have you er . . . seen Mr Teekleman in Wapping at night, Benson?'

Benson, cap in one hand, scratches his scalp, thinking a moment. 'Can't rightly say, Mr Hawk, sir.'

'Once . . . twice maybe?'

'Oh no, it be more than that, they's regulars.'

'They? You mean Isaac Blundstone?'

'Aye. But it's late, see, and Blundstone slumps in the corner too pissed to even fart. It's the Dutchman what plays alone.'

'Plays what, Benson?'

'Poker, sir, and euchre.'

'A game between friends maybe, nothing serious, eh?'

Benson grins. 'Not on your bleedin' nelly, sir! It's Benny the Mill what runs it. I wouldn't say it were what you'd call a friendly game.'

'Benny the Mill?'

'Ben Mildrake, sir, a proper villain.'

'Mildrake? But he's in prison, isn't he?'

'Aye, don't make much difference, school's his, he's still the boss cocky on his patch, the dockside half o' Wapping, Andy Handshake runs the top half.'

'Andy Handshake?'

'Another proper villain, sir, Andrew Hindsheek, but they calls him Andy Handshake.'

'Benson, as a matter of interest, how do you come to know all this?' Hawk now asks.

'Cockatoo, sir. Gets me out o' mischief, keeps me out the pub.'

'What, watching out for the law?'

'Nah, law don't come into Wapping at night, sir. Big game, lots of gelt about, there's villains what wouldn't hesitate to 'elp 'emselves given 'arf a chance.'

'Villains watching out for villains, eh?'

Benson shrugs, and then by way of further explanation adds, 'Wapping, sir. It ain't the nicest place.'

'Benson, I want you to stay stum, say nothing, not even to Cook or Martha, but keep your eyes skinned, let me know when Teekleman comes and goes and whether he wins or loses.'

'The first, that's easy, he ain't of a size to be easy missed, but I dunno about the take home. I'm outside on the corner, a cockatoo, I ain't in the room where they plays, nor wants to be. I keeps me nose clean, less you know the better with them lot, know what I mean, sir?'

'Very wise. Well, do your best, there'll be a sov in it for you.'

'Yes, thank you, sir, Mr Hawk, I'll be waiting with the sulky. Will we be going to the brewery, sir?'

Hawk nods and the young man takes his leave. 'He's sharp enough,' Hawk thinks to himself, 'might warrant watching.' He thinks to find out how well the young fellow reads and writes and whether he has some arithmetic.

Hawk calls for Teekleman to be sent to him when he arrives at the brewery in the late afternoon. A few minutes past the four o'clock smoko whistle there is a tap on the open office door and Hawk looks up to see the huge form of Teekleman almost filling the entire door frame. For all his own great size, the Dutchman must outweigh Hawk by a hundred pounds, which would give him a weight of around four hundred pounds in his stockinged feet.

'Come in, Mr Teekleman,' Hawk calls out. Despite the Dutchman being Hinetitama's husband, Hawk has always kept his distance and addressed the cheersman in a formal manner.

'Mr Solomon, you vant to see me, ja?' Teekleman asks.

'Yes, yes, please, come in,' Hawk points to the ottoman, the only seat sufficiently large to accommodate the Dutchman's corpulence. 'Please be seated.'

Slabbert Teekleman first examines the couch suspiciously, trying to decide whether it will bear his weight. Then he gingerly lowers himself into it, first each cheek in a rocking motion, the leather ottoman sighing beneath the weight of his arse. His thighs follow, either hock clasped and lifted into position with both hands to rest in the correct forward direction, though his knees do not touch, his protruding stomach denying them access to each other. His feet are planted like stout stumps, rooted into the Persian carpet, as if they are his anchor points to keep him seated in an upright position. Finally, in what seems his only spontaneous gesture, he slaps a massive paw down onto each knee. It is a process which has taken a conscious effort and some little time to achieve. 'Ja, that is goet,' he says at last and Hawk senses that a part of the elaborate performance is an attempt to conceal the Dutchman's nervousness.

He rises from his desk and comes to join Teekleman, seating himself in a club chair opposite him. The two big men are strangely contrasted. Hawk, though his waistline has thickened somewhat in middle age, does not carry any excess weight and at seven feet remains an awesome sight. His face, now well lined, wears the fearsome *moko* of his Maori initiation and his hair is beginning to turn grey at his temples. It is an altogether imposing look made all the more incongruous beside the fat Dutchman with his straw-coloured hair, blue eyes and florid complexion.

While Hawk could well pass for the devil himself in any children's pantomime, Slabbert Teekleman might appear as a grotesque perspiring cherub bursting out of his grey worsted suit. The one man exudes sheer power while the other is a testimony to the extremes of self-indulgence.

'Mr Teekleman, while you and I have kept our distance from each other, you should know that I admire the way you have conducted yourself since you arrived in Hobart.'

Teekleman looks surprised. 'I try alvays my best, Mr Hawk.'

'You have been a good husband to Hinetitama and father to her children and I am grateful to you for this.' While this last is not entirely true, Teekleman sleeps for most of the day and sees little of his children and when he does shows no interest in them beyond a pat on the head, it serves Hawk's purpose to commend him. Hawk is thought by both Victoria and Ben to be the dominant male figure in their lives and he is secretly grateful for Teekleman's neglect as it allows him easy access to Ben and Victoria. For their part, the children seem to like Hawk immensely.

'Ja, Hinetitama, she is goet vummen,' Teekleman mumbles. He senses that Hawk hasn't simply called him to compliment him on his success as a husband and father. 'She look after me well.'

'Wapping, what do you know of it?' Hawk now asks.

'Vapping?' Teekleman repeats. 'We have two pub there.' He squints curiously at Hawk, 'You know already this?'

Hawk nods. 'Do you visit them often?'

'Ja, sometimes, like all za others,' he lies, then shrugs, appearing to be bemused. 'This is my job, I think so, no?'

Hawk nods again. 'And lately, have you visited them at night?'

'Alvays I visit za pub at night.'

'Yes, yes, but the two in Wapping?' Hawk persists. 'Have you visited them recently?'

The Dutchman is suddenly silent, he averts his eyes and fixes them down onto his massive stomach so that his numerous chins concertina inwards. He doesn't know how much Hawk already knows or to what he should admit. Teekleman finally glances up at Hawk. Chancing his arm he says, 'Ja, sometimes I go zere.'

Hawk has earlier in the day sent Young Benson to the two company-owned public houses in Wapping, the Lark & Sparrow and the Emerald Parakeet, Mary having named both public houses, the one after English birds and the other after her new land, for her great good-fortune birds, her beloved rosellas. Benson enquires whether Teekleman has visited either at night in recent weeks. The Dutchman is not stupid and if he has taken the trouble to do so he will have a sufficient alibi to argue his case for being in Wapping. But Teekleman has been too arrogant, or perhaps grown overconfident about his nocturnal perambulations, and hasn't thought to cover his tracks sufficiently well. Young Benson reports that neither publican can recall a visit from him after sunset and that both seem surprised at the question, Wapping is one of the few exceptions where a cheersman never visits at night.

'Mr Teekleman, we value your services very highly. Wapping is a dangerous place after dark and I must from now on expressly forbid you entering it after sunset on behalf of the brewery. I believe there is an existing order to this effect. I know that a man of your standing in the community would not normally enter a place like that at night of his own accord and I thank you most sincerely for doing so in the line of duty.' Hawk pauses and then adds, 'I want you to know it is not required.'

Teekleman is forced throughout to hold Hawk's gaze and now he averts his eyes and appears to be closely examining the fingernails on both his hands which are spread out on the surface of his enormous stomach. 'You do understand my concern, don't you, Mr Teekleman? I feel quite sure Mistress Mary, had she been here now, would feel exactly the same. You are, after all, a part of our family and we would not knowingly place your safety in jeopardy.'

The Dutchman looks at Hawk, his eyes drawn to narrow slits. 'Thank you, Mr Hawk, I am not afraid this Vapping. It is not so bad.' He tries to hide his anger at being told what to do by the nigger and attempts a smile. 'Ja, I have been places much verse den dis.'

Hawk returns his smile. 'Ah, haven't we all, Mr Teekleman, but we are neither of us as young and I trust not as foolish as we were then.'

'I go now, ja?' Slabbert Teekleman suddenly asks, anxious to avoid making a direct promise to Hawk. He is perspiring profusely even though the temperature in Hawk's office is by no means inclement. He begins to move on the couch, his hands firmly gripping the edge of the seat while his huge arse starts to wriggle as if to gain sufficient momentum of its own to attempt the enormous effort required to rise. With a great heave he pulls himself slowly to an erect position, his legs wobble dangerously and for a moment seem unable to carry the burden thrust upon them, then he locks his knees and they steady as the distribution of his weight is adjusted and, panting from the effort, he finally stands upright, his hands clamped to the small of his back.

Hawk rises from his chair and, making a deliberate effort to keep his voice calm, says, 'I hear your wife has had a small domestic accident but is recovering well?'

He waits for Teekleman's response. The Dutchman seems to be thinking then says, 'It is not so bad, a few bruise, I think she vill be soon better.'

143

'I am most pleased to hear that, Mr Teekleman. Her welfare is of the utmost concern to me. You will be sure to take good care of her, we would not like her to have another such accident.'

Teekleman, who has been feeling increasingly angry, now seems close to apoplexy at Hawk's implied threat. He has the greatest difficulty concealing his fury and his several chins visibly quake and his face turns the colour of new-baked brick as he struggles to restrain his temper. Hawk has no right to threaten him. He has always hated the schwartzer, who humiliated him in Wellington by buying him off and forcing him to run away with his tail between his legs. Now, like the old hag before him, Hawk threatens to possess his whole life, to rekindle the fear he has lived with for five years.

Teekleman believes that while he had an agreement with Mary, it should not carry over to Hawk. The contract with the black seal has become a life sentence he can no longer endure. He has wealth and protection and even a certain standing in society but remains as much a prisoner as if he was incarcerated in a dank prison cell. It is all too much to bear.

Slabbert Teekleman halts at the doorway and turns to face Hawk, who has returned to his desk and is attending to some paperwork. The Dutchman cannot contain himself any longer.

'Mr Hawk, why you do this, eh? What you want?'

Hawk looks up querulously. 'Do what, Mr Teekleman?'

'Threaten me.'

'Threaten you? How have I done that? I am merely concerned for your safety in Wapping.'

'I think this is *not* true!' Teekleman shouts. 'You know something, eh? Mistress Mary, she speaks to you about za contract?' The moment the word escapes his mouth he knows he has made a terrible mistake, that his temper has allowed him to play into Hawk's hands.

'Contract? What contract is this?'

'A paper,' Teekleman replies. 'Your muthza and me.' His voice is somewhat mollified as he tries to play down the importance of the word he has used.

'I have not seen such a contract,' Hawk says truthfully. 'What does it concern?'

The Dutchman cannot explain any further without exposing himself completely. 'It is nothing.' He gives Hawk a feeble grin, then shrugs his shoulders and spreads his hands wide as if to apologise for his outburst. 'Maybe she loses this paper, eh?' he says. 'I go now, please?'

'No, just a moment, Mr Teekleman!' Hawk says, stepping out from behind his desk and coming towards the Dutchman. 'If you wish I shall look through Mistress Mary's papers?' He halts in front of the perspiring Dutchman, a look of concern on his face. 'An agreement you say? We do not break agreements here, nor do we expect them to be broken. Is there something I should know?'

Teekleman is beaten neck and crop and he raises his hand in a feeble protest. 'No, it is nothing,' he repeats, turning back to the door, though Hawk can sense his enormous frustration, his huge body trembling as he waddles through the doorway.

To a man like Slabbert Teekleman Hawk's subtle approach is a form of persecution he is unable to endure. He would rather feel the sharp lash of Hawk's tongue and have him waving the black-sealed agreement under his nose than to suffer the uncertainty of not knowing how much the nigger knows about his past.

He always thought that Mary Abacus would return the document to him when she came to the end of her life, or that she would destroy it, releasing him from its conditions. When nothing was said for several months after her death, and with no evidence to the contrary, he convinced himself that this was what happened. He was free at last to lead his life without constraint. With Mary's death, Teekleman decided that Hawk was not going to take her place and run his life for him. Now he feels deeply betrayed. After all, he has kept his part of the bargain and sired two great-grandchildren for the old bitch. He has served his sentence and it is time for him to be released.

While he would have been afraid to gamble in Wapping while Mary was still alive, his agreement is not with Hawk. He insists to himself, perhaps not unreasonably, that if he can get drunk on behalf of the brewery he has every right to get drunk on his own account. He will gamble wherever and whenever he chooses and, in the process, choose his own companions. Drunk or sober, he will beat his wife if he desires to do so. It is every husband's duty to keep his wife subservient to him and it is common knowledge that a beating will stop a woman from having ideas beyond her station. It is, he tells himself, a matter of respect for his role as head of the household and he cannot be restrained from exercising it. Hinetitama may be a Solomon, but she is still a half-caste, a reformed drunk and finally only a woman. He, Slabbert Teekleman, is a white man and a Hollander, so he does not have to prove his superiority. In future, nobody, least of all a nigger and a half-caste, will decide how he will lead his life. He has decided that from here on they can both get fucked.

But now Hawk has pulled him up, reminding him that the old shackles persist. It is simply too much to bear and, as he walks away from Hawk's office, he swears he will have his revenge. Halfway down the long corridor, as he passes the stairs leading to the fermenting tower, he suddenly realises how he can destroy the giant black man without placing himself in danger.

It is quite simply done. He knows that Hawk is due to visit Melbourne where he will explore the business opportunities available and is to be gone for four months. Teekleman will wait until Hawk has departed so that he cannot be present to influence Hinetitama, then he'll chuck in his job with the Potato Factory and announce to his wife that henceforth he will make his living as a fiddler working the various taverns at night. With the income from Hinetitama's ten per cent share of the Potato Factory they are wealthy and there is no need for Teekleman to work. He already has a reputation as an entertainer and those taverns and pubs tied to the Cascade and the Jolly Hatter breweries should welcome him with open arms.

'My dear, you are not singing vunce since you granmutza dies, you come with me, we make together beautiful combination, ja.'

With Mary gone Hinctitama has been lonely. Furthermore, her work at the maternity hospital, where she had hoped to practise as a nurse and midwife, has not turned out as she had expected. While the nurses are prepared to have her in the role of owner or even administrator, they will not accept her as an equal who is prepared to work with a birth or a miscarriage in the same capacity as they do. Though they cannot openly object to her presence, they find a thousand small ways to disconcert her and make things difficult.

This proves also to be true with the female patients. Whether or not they have been put up to it by the hospital staff, the workers' wives profess to feel equally uncomfortable knowing that they are being subjected to the ministrations of a member of the late Iron Mary's family.

Despite Hinetitama's lack of affectation, they regard her presence almost as though the formidable old lady is herself delivering their children. As one pregnant wife was heard to say, 'Don't want no rich nob poking around in me pussy.' Her words are repeated with hilarity among the staff and finally reach the brewery itself, where the *double entendre* is a cause for much merriment among the men. When Teekleman hears it told he makes a great pretence of laughing and being seen to be a good fellow who can take a joke, but later relays the remark to Hinetitama who finds herself completely mortified and humiliated.

As Hinetitama has no experience in administration and no pretensions or desire or even the ability to be the hospital manager, she has, with Hawk's help, appointed a matron and a manager, and increasingly has withdrawn her presence, remaining only, at his insistence, on the hospital board.

When Teekleman approaches his wife about joining him as an entertainer she is, as the expression goes, 'ripe for the plucking'. Hinetitama is bored and disappointed and while she loves Ben and Victoria dearly, Nanny Hawkins sees to most of their other needs. Hinetitama still sings to them or tells them bedtime stories of the Maori, but otherwise she is given little cause to share in their lives.

She is a woman of thirty-two with her looks, spirit and libido still retained, but the last two have been much dampened by the routine nature of her daily life. Although she has not lost her affection for her husband, Teekleman's increasing size has rendered him impotent and his nightly absences increase her sense of loneliness and isolation. His recent beating has caused her to believe she has lost his love and, as so often happens, she thinks she must be the cause of his anger and somehow given him reason to beat her.

Hinetitama still works among the poor in the slums of Wapping where, during daylight hours, she is a familiar sight. But whereas her work in Auckland involved rolling up her sleeves and nursing the sick and the frail, the poor of Wapping and some of the poorer part of New Town see her in quite a different light. Before, when she worked among her own people, her work involved bandaging the broken heads of women and children invariably caused by the drunken fists of their frustrated, unemployed and usually de facto husbands and temporary fathers. Acting as a midwife to deliver their babies or trying to keep their half-starved children alive through the vicissitudes of measles and mumps, diphtheria, whooping cough and pneumonia, to name but a few of the childhood diseases rampaging through the slums, she felt then that she was one of their own, who offered them from her heart all she had and they responded by loving her and understood when the grog got the better of her as it had to so many of them.

But here in Hobart, the poor want none of her tender ministrations, she is expected merely to give them a handout. As with the hospital, she is regarded as a member of the Solomon family, rich beyond avarice. Her bandaging, nursing and dispensing of cough syrup and ointment, pills, potions and mustard poultices is scorned as mere pretension, a rich woman playing at being Florence Nightingale. They hold out their hands and ask for money, all the while promising to send for the doctor, but, as often as not, a child remains ill or dies and the money gets spent in the Emerald Parakeet or the Lark & Sparrow. The irony of this does not escape Hinetitama, increasing her frustration.

While she has no illusions about the desperate poor, Hinetitama finds herself increasingly disenchanted with this rich woman's life. It is not one she has chosen for herself and her stubbornness precludes her from accepting it as a compromise role. She has begun to despise money and the life it forces her to lead. She is in this frame of mind when, to her surprise, Teekleman comes down to breakfast. She is accustomed to taking breakfast alone while he usually sleeps to well past noon.

'My God, what is this?' she exclaims as he enters the dining room.

'Morning, wife,' Teekleman says, not explaining and walking over to his chair which has been reinforced to take his enormous weight.

Hinetitama rings the bell to bring the maidservant. 'Do you want something to eat?' she asks her husband.

'Coffee only,' then he points a stubby finger to the loaf of bread on the table, 'and brood.'

Hinetitama cuts two thick slices from the loaf of fresh-baked bread and when the maid arrives orders coffee. 'So what wakes you at this hour?' she asks.

'We must talk, ja?'

'Talk? Haven't done much of that for a while.'

Slabbert Teekleman looks up, his belly is so large that he appears to be seated two feet from the edge of the table but for his stomach, which touches the edge. 'No job no more,' he announces.

'Whatever can you mean?' Hinetitama asks, confused, reverting to the safety of her elocution lessons and the protection of good grammar.

'I give it away, I tell them to stick it up their bums,' Teekleman says, attempting to sound nonchalant.

'What? What did you give away?'

'Me job?'

'What?' Hinetitama shouts, forsaking all pretence at calm.

'Ja, it is so,' Teekleman says more calmly than he feels. He breaks off a small piece of bread and pops it into his mouth.

'At the Potato Factory? You've given in your notice?'

'No notice, I finish, no more work,' her husband announces, chewing on the bread rather more conscientiously than it merits.

'You saw Uncle Hawk before he left for Melbourne?'

'Him? No.'

'Slabbert, what can you be saying?' Hinetitama exclaims, frustrated. It has never occurred to her that her husband isn't well satisfied with his position as a cheersman. After all, it allows him to drink as much as he wishes, and unlike her, he seems able to hold his grog well enough. With Mary's trust fund they are rich and if he spends all his salary on drinks to show what a great bloke he is, what does it matter? She's long since given up thinking of him as her companion and the father of Ben and Victoria. They haven't made love since Victoria was born. 'You didn't tell me you weren't happy. I could always have talked to Uncle Hawk, he'd give you another job if I'd asked him?'

'He found out I were gambling. He don't like that, ja.'

'Gamblin'? That's the one thing!' Hinetitama exclaims.

'Ja, with Miss Mary. It is true. We agree, no gambling. But not Boss Hawk.'

'What does yer mean? 'Course it's the same.'

'Miss Mary sign the agreement, not him. It be her and me, dat agreement. Ja, I have no agreement mit Boss Hawk.'

'What agreement? You had an agreement with Mary?'

Slabbert Teekleman sighs. 'I come here because she bring me, if I don't she tell the police. I go back to Holland, maybe I am hanged.' He shrugs. 'What can I do?'

'What are you talkin' about, Slabbert?' Hinetitama has reverted to her natural vernacular which she finds puts her husband more at ease.

'I kill a man. In Holland. Long time ago. She, Miss Mary, she find out this.' Slabbert Teekleman shrugs. 'We have contract, agreement, black seal on the paper. I give you baby, I don't gambling, Miss Mary, she stay stom. She don't say nothing the police.' Hinetitama can see he is plainly distraught.

'Why didn't you tell me?' Hinetitama cries.

'Ja, Miss Mary say I don't tell you.' Slabbert Teekleman shrugs and grins. 'She give me goet job, plenty beer, plenty money.' He pauses and looks at his wife. 'When Miss Mary is alive it's goet, ja?'

'You mean you didn't come to Hobart because you loved me? I mean, on your own like? Because you wanted to see me?'

Teekleman looks surprised that she would have such a stupid notion. 'Me, I am Hollander, a white man, I do not marry willing a Maori.'

Hinetitama, who has lost all affection for Teekleman, is less upset by this pronouncement than she is about Mary's duplicity. She shakes her head in denial. 'She bought you as a bloody stud! Jesus!'

Teekleman chuckles. 'I do goet job, ja? Ben, Victoria, my cock it is goet, ja, of course, I am Dutchman!'

Hinetitama conceals her contempt for him. 'So, Hawk found yer gamblin'? What, you and the creature Isaac Blundstone? What did Hawk say?'

'He say, night-time I don't go Vapping, it is *verboten*.'

'And so you chucked it in? Gave up your job for that?'

Teekleman is suddenly annoyed. 'Ja, Miss Mary can say this, not Boss Hawk! When she die I am free man, I go where I like.'

'Did she say you were free when she died?'

'No. But I think so. I always think this, ja.'

'And Uncle Hawk threatened you with the contract?'

Teekleman doesn't answer, instead he counters with,

'Why he tell me I cannot to go to Wapping, huh? Wapping, dat is where I can play cards, poker, euchre. It is not fair, he go to buggery, ja.'

Hinetitama sighs. 'Slabbert, don't be a fool. I'll talk to Uncle Hawk about the contract, I'm sure he'll tear it up.' She smiles. 'You've done your part, you give us Ben and Victoria, he'll understand. He won't tell anyone about,' she pauses, 'you know, what happened in Holland.'

Hinetitama is too accustomed to the Maori way to be concerned about the supposed murder. A fight between two men of neighbouring tribes will often enough result in the death of one of them without recriminations, the fact that Teekleman may have committed a murder when he was young, sometime in the dim past on the other side of the world, means little to her.

'No! It is finished! No more I kiss his black bums!' Slabbert slaps his hand down hard onto the surface of the table. 'Potato Factory, no more!'

The maidservant enters with a pot of coffee and Hinetitama waits until she has left again. She pours coffee for her husband, handing him the cup. 'So what now?'

Slabbert Teekleman smiles. 'We stay here. But like before, in New Zealand, I play fiddle in the pub, you sing, we are happy, ja?'

'You mean you gamble and I get drunk?'

Teekleman doesn't deny this. 'Maybe, a little euchre, sometimes poker, for fun, ja. Drunk? No, no, you sing only, no grog. I tell the publican.'

Hinetitama laughs, shaking her head. 'Slabbert, it's been eight years since I sung in a pub!' But Teekleman can see that as she recovers from her surprise she is beginning to like the idea.

'No matter, your voice it is so beautiful.' He smiles. 'We can practise, soon it will be goet again, first class, okey-dokey ja, you will see,' he jokes.

153

Hinetitama thinks of the years ahead of her. The children have tutors, already she sees little enough of them, what between Mrs Hawkins and their lessons at sums and reading. She has given up any prospect of being accepted on equal terms at the hospital and the poor of Wapping don't need her love or compassion. She has come to understand that there is a class system no less deeply felt and practised by the poor. What they will accept with open hearts from their own kind, knowing the struggle it takes to give compassion, they will not take from a rich woman with a hot breakfast under her bustle playing at Christian charity for the sake of her soul.

Hawk comes around whenever he can, but he is very busy and when he does he likes to spend time with the children, who quite plainly adore him to the exclusion of their mother.

Though she belongs to one of the richest families in Tasmania, it isn't exactly a family. Teekleman the Dutchman has no status within it whatsoever, Hawk a nigger, respected to his face with much bowing and scraping, is sniggered at and disparaged behind his back, she is a half-breed, a savage with a doubtful past. What passes for the local society, the nice folk, have snubbed her since her arrival and she has returned the sentiment by ignoring them.

It has been a long, long time since she's had any fun. Whatever she has come to think of her husband, which isn't much, though in the Maori tradition she is bound to him, he still plays a wonderful fiddle and she can still sing in tune.

Hawk will be away for three months or more. If she doesn't like working as a singer in a common public house she can creep back into her safe, cosy, boring nest before he returns and resume her role as the good little mother again.

After all, she tells herself, they don't need the money, they will be doing it for the fun, which is different.

'Do you think we can do it, Slabbert?'

'Ja, of course, my dear.'

'We'll have to practise, very hard. I shouldn't like to make a fool of myself.'

The Dutchman brings the coffee cup to his lips and takes a long sip. His revenge has begun, Hinetitama is back in his grasp. 'Ja, that is goet, Hinetitama,' he says quietly. 'Now you are my wife again.'

The first night they perform together is in the Hobart Whale Fishery and Teekleman's fiddle and Hinetitama's beautiful contralto voice, now mature and rich, complement each other perfectly and fill the public house to the rafters.

It is more a concert than simple tavern entertainment, though the voices of the patrons raise the roof when a shanty they know is performed. Late in the evening when mellowness has not yet turned to drunkenness someone shouts, 'Sing the whalemen's song, "John Rackham"!'

It is said to be the song composed for whalemen by Sperm Whale Sally, a dockside whore of the most sweet temperament and voracious appetite for both food and whalemen. As legend has it, an entire whaling ship's crew could be accommodated by this huge and sweet-singing whore, who could consume a leg of mutton, two plump chickens or a goose and a dozen skinned and lard-roasted potatoes while at the same time drink any man who cared to sit beside her under the table.

It is also said that the gargantuan whore, a great friend of Ikey Solomon, was the true mother of Hawk and Tommo Solomon and died giving birth to them. 'John Rackham' is the song which Sperm Whale Sally composed and first sang in the Hobart Whale Fishery, which has ever since flown the Blue Sally flag in her honour.

The Blue Sally is a flag with a blue sperm whale emblazoned against a white background and was presented to any whaling ship in which a member of the crew had successfully eaten more and consumed more grog in the process than the giant whore and then afterwards still possessed sufficient stamina to receive her favours free of charge.

This little piece of blue and white bunting was considered the greatest of talismans for a successful whale hunt a ship could fly from its foremast and it was carried throughout the Pacific islands, Antarctic waters, South America, the Caribbean, West Indian islands, along the coast of Africa and around the Indian Ocean. The song is therefore of great sentiment to the regulars who frequent the Whale Fishery.

Though the sea shanty has been sung on the seven seas for sixty years it is claimed that it has never been matched in the original voice. Now, with the Dutchman's magic fiddle and the Maori Queen of Song, as Hinetitama has been billed, there is an anticipation that Hinetitama might attempt to equal the original, though of course there are few, if any, still alive who heard it performed by Sperm Whale Sally. If there were, they would be too enfeebled to remember, leastways to make a comparison. Nevertheless, the imagination of the patrons at the Whale Fishery is heightened by the prospect and their pulses are quickened with the thought that tonight they may hear more than they have ever bargained for.

The tavern is brought to silence as the giant Teekleman puts up his hand in acknowledgment of the request. In truth, it has been done at the instigation of Isaac Blundstone, who has prompted a patron to call out. Hinetitama has spent two weeks perfecting the song and so is well prepared to render it.

'Ja, this is a goet, I ask her.' He turns to Hinetitama.

'Perhaps, maybe also, you can sing this song, you think you can remember the words?'

'Yes she can! Yes she can!' the mob chorus back. 'Sing us the Sperm Whale Sally song! Sing "John Rackham"!'

Slabbert Teekleman raises his hand for silence. Then when the pub grows quiet again, though this is not achieved without some effort from the more sober among the crowd shushing those who are not far off drunkenness, Teekleman announces, 'Ladies and gentlemen, I give for you, Princess Hinetitama, the Maori Queen of Song!'

There is much applause, whistling and encouragement, for Hinetitama is, in herself, a curiosity, a Solomon by birth and a member of the richest family in Tasmania who is to sing for them in a common public-house entertainment. Many of the patrons have brought their wives and some of their children who crowd against the wall at the back near the doorway.

Hinetitama acknowledges the crowd. 'Thank you, thank you,' she says, 'I shall try to sing this lovely shanty, I don't know that I can do it sufficiently well and I beg you all to help me please.' Hinetitama has become so accustomed to speaking correctly and she knows she must sound quite the toff to the crowd, but she does not revert to her original accent, knowing it will be seen as an affectation.

She is wearing her brightest gown, an off-the-shoulder velvet in cerise, a bright clear red which shows off the light brown skin of her shoulders and arms to perfection. The hairstyle, worn in the modern idiom, is a swept-up look, gathered like a wide garland about the circumference of the head, with the hair smooth and tight pulled from the centre of the scalp, and turned back and tucked under at the peripherals. But she has ignored this flight of fashion and wears her hair in the traditional Maori style, combed smooth, straight and shining to the waist, a raven-dark cascade which shows not the slightest trace of grey. She wears a double tiara of gardenia flowers, and her lips, left in their natural state, are almost the exact match of her gown. She is still an attractive woman and there are many in the crowd, not all of them men, who speculate how ever Fat Slab, the Dutchman, can have captured such a fragile beauty. There are some among them, with several drinks too many below their belts, who crudely speculate that he must surely crush her, if ever he can get it up sufficient to mount her for a smooey. Another remarks that, with his great gut interfering, his plunger could never hope to reach her pouch.

'You must sing the chorus with me,' Hinetitama appeals to the crowd. 'I shall sing it now, so that you may recall it.' She glances at Teekleman, who takes up his fiddle, and to the first strains of the chorus she begins to sing in a fine, clear voice.

> So take up your doxy and drink down your ale
> And dance a fine jig to a fine fishy tale
> We'll fly the Blue Sally wherever we sail
> And drink to the health o' the great sperm whale!

Hinetitama repeats the chorus twice so those who do not know it, though there are not too many from the sound of the response, may learn the words. Then to the opening accompaniment of Teekleman's fiddle, which appears to be in most glorious form, she begins to sing 'John Rackham'.

> Come gather around me, you jack tars and doxies
> I'll sing you the glorious whaleman's tale
> Let me tell you the story, of death and the glory
> of Rackham . . . who rode on the tail of a Whale

It started at dawn on a bright Sabbath morning
When Lord Nelson's body came 'ome pickled in rum
Every jack tar mourned the great British sailor
And drank to their hero as church bells were rung

I be born to the sound o' the bells of St Paul's
Where they buried the sealord all solemn and proper
That very same day harpooner John Rackham
Rode the tail of a whale around Davey Jones' locker

The watch up the mainmast gave out a great shout,
'A six pod to starboard all swimming in strong!'
So they lowered a whale boat, harpoon gun and line
Three cheers for the crew then the whale hunt was on

John Rackham, he stood to his harpoon and line
'Row the boat close, lads, 'til we see its great chest
Steady she goes now, keep the bow straight
Or this great fearless fish will bring all to their rest!'

The boat's bow, on a crest, held still for a moment
Sufficient for Rackham to make good his aim
Then the harpoon flew screaming to carry the line
And buried its head in a great crimson stain

'Steady now, lads, let the fish make his dive
Then he'll turn for the top and the fight'll begin
Ship your oars, boys, take the ride as he runs
For the Sperm has a courage that comes from within'

Ten fathoms down the fish turned from its dive
As the harpoon worked in, on the way to his heart
Then he spied the boat's belly directly above him
And he knew they'd pay for this terrible dart!

Fifty tons rose as the fish drove like thunder
Like a cork in a whirlpool the boat spun around
The jaws of the whale smashed through its planking
And the sharks made a meal o' the pieces they found!

John Rackham was saved as the fish drove him upwards
He found himself up on the nose of the whale
With a snort he was tossed sky high and then backwards
And landed most neatly on the great creature's tail

'Let me live! Master Whale, I've a child to be born!
Spare my life and I promise to name it for you!'
'That's a fanciful tale,' cried the furious whale
'But how can I know what you say will be true?'

John Rackham he pondered then started to smile
'Not only its name, but its soul to you too!
And we'll make a white flag with your picture upon it
A great sperm whale emblazoned in blue!'

The great fish turned and swam straight to the ship
With a flick of his tail threw him safe in a sail
Then the deadly dart finally pierced his great heart
Now we fly the Blue Sally to honour the whale.

'Everybody now, one last time!' Teekleman shouts. The crowd, flushed by the joy of their own singing, respond even more fulsomely to the final chorus.

So take up your doxy and drink down your ale
And dance a fine jig to a fine fishy tale
We'll fly the Blue Sally wherever we sail
And drink to the health o' the great sperm whale!

There is thunderous applause and much stomping as the final chorus is completed, it has been most beautifully sung and those present cannot imagine how it could be better rendered. Hinetitama is flushed with the excitement and the success of the performance and she is happy beyond words for she has been rescued from a life of tedium and frustration.

Folk crowd around her to offer their congratulations and it is then that Isaac Blundstone, at Teekleman's instigation, places a double of gin in her hands. It is the first drink Hinetitama has had in eight years and as the perfumed liquor slips down her throat her entire body seems to come alive.

Chapter Five

HAWK, DAVID AND ABRAHAM SOLOMON

Melbourne 1893

Hawk arrives in Melbourne on 1 May 1893, the very day of the collapse of several major banks. The banks have long been carrying the euphoric symptoms of gold fever and have finally been struck down by the disease. They have extended credit to too many unlikely projects and explorations devised by dreamers, schemers, believers, confidence men, chancers and those too ignorant to understand what they were doing. The day of reckoning has finally arrived and some of the major banking institutions in the land find themselves victims of their own greed and naiveté. Having over-extended themselves with their incautious lending they are now faced with too many outstanding loans defaulting to have any hope of balancing the books or of continuing to trade. They close their doors to lick their wounds and fail to open them again. Tens of thousands of small depositors lose their shirts and in the process learn that banks are run by men who have no special talent and are as easily infected by opportunity and greed as everyone else. It is a very sobering day for every Australian colony.

Hawk cannot quite believe his luck when he reads in the *Age* that an almost completed brewery project in

Ballarat has come to a halt for lack of funds and that it is the collapsed Bank of Victoria which has financed the project. He thinks perhaps that he may be able to bridge the gap and finance the completion and in return be rewarded with a major shareholding in the new brewery.

To his enormous surprise, the company register reveals that the shareholders in the brewery are David and Abraham Solomon. Hawk appoints a firm of accountants to look into the affairs of Solomon & Co. and discovers the Bank of Victoria holds the combined assets of the company against the loan it has given David Solomon to build the brewery. The irony is that among the many harebrained and unlikely schemes the bank has extended credit to, this one has all the hallmarks of a sound investment. It becomes a case of the good collapsing with the bad.

With its line of credit destroyed Solomon & Co. is effectively insolvent and will be forced to declare itself bankrupt as the collapsed bank cannot finance them to completion. They, in turn, now lack sufficient collateral to secure a loan to complete the brewery project from one of the few banks which haven't gone to the wall. David and Abraham Solomon have the makings of a first-rate asset on their hands but for a simple bridging loan and, in the prevailing climate, they have no chance of obtaining one.

The liquidator for the Bank of Victoria will be most anxious to sell the collateral it holds and Hawk finds himself in a position to make them an offer for the Ballarat brewery and also for the entire assets of Solomon & Co. at a fraction of its true value. This will allow the bank with the sale of all the additional collateral it owns from its other loans to eventually pay its own shareholders five shillings in the pound, one of the more creditable performances within the discredited banking community.

Over the years David Solomon has built the grain and timber business Hannah inherited from George Madden into a fair-sized conglomerate that includes wool, coal, timber, mining stock, cattle, barley, wheat and a quite decent portfolio of Tasmanian real estate.

It is an intelligent diversification not entirely dissimilar to the one Hawk and Mary devised over the years. But whereas the Potato Factory has always bought with cash and never taken a loan, David's shrewd business brain has built Solomon & Co. using very little of his own capital. He has financed each new enterprise by borrowing from the banks and using his existing assets as collateral and security against defaulting. In the past he has always retained sufficient assets to recover if a particular project should fail; in effect, never putting all his eggs in one basket.

Though there have been some close calls, the market has always held up sufficiently long enough for him to redeem himself. David seemed fireproof and the bank had come to trust his business judgment and progressively extended his line of credit.

However, this time David has gambled everything to build the most splendid brewery in the colony of Victoria and has been caught well and truly with his trousers down. Hawk, in looking at the prospects for a new brewery in Ballarat, agrees that if it were to be allowed to come on-line, it would have taken Solomon & Co. from a modestly sized conglomerate into the big league. Instead, Solomon & Co. is effectively finished, dead in the water.

Hawk is forced to speculate as to why, as an enormously wealthy and successful man in his seventies, David Solomon would risk everything he has acquired, simply to own a brewery. For a man who has shown such good business judgment it is a surprisingly naive mistake to make.

Then it begins to dawn on him. It is not done out of simple greed as he'd first supposed. The brewery represents something in David's mind of enormous emotional importance. The Ballarat project has the potential to have almost double the bottling capacity of the Potato Factory. The old man simply wished to show Mary Abacus, before she died, that he was superior. That anything the person he hated the most in the world could do, he could do better.

For a businessman as astute as David, this was a childish thing to have attempted. But in some things perhaps we never mature beyond our ability to hate. Hate fostered in the young often brings with it an enormous sense of inferiority, the need to prove oneself in order to overcome the humiliation one has been made to feel as a child. The brewery was not only to be David's ultimate triumph over the adversity of his childhood, but also to serve as a symbol of the fulfilment of his promise to his mother Hannah that he wouldn't rest until he had wreaked her vengeance on Ikey's whore, until he had beaten Mary at her own game.

The day David heard of her passing he flew into a terrible temper, breaking furniture and raging for two days, at one stage invading the kitchen and throwing the pots and pans about, pouring hot soup over the cat and breaking almost all the crockery and glassware while causing the servants to run for their lives. Iron Mary had once again robbed him, cheating him out of his moment of triumph.

With the imminent collapse of Solomon & Co. Hawk instructs his accountants to act as broker and make an offer for all of their assets. While the liquidator may have made more money had he sold each of these ad hoc, the prospect of taking a large debt off his books in one fell swoop is too attractive for him to ignore and he accepts an offer which gives Hawk control of Solomon & Co. at a bargain-basement price. Within three months of arriving in Victoria Hawk has achieved what he'd anticipated might take him three or four years to build or acquire.

On paper it seems to be a brilliant investment. David's assets are soundly based and simply need an injection of working capital to continue to succeed. The ever cautious Mary had accumulated a large number of investments which could quickly be converted into liquid assets. Although Hawk is forced to use a good deal of these to make the acquisitions, he does not stretch his resources beyond anything he cannot cover if things were to suddenly go wrong.

The speculative profit and loss statement shows the new brewery should be in a net profit situation in three years and, had the bank not collapsed when it did, the brilliant David Solomon would almost certainly have pulled off his gamble and paid back his enormous borrowing over a comparatively short period. Ballarat's beer-drinking population is underserviced and, providing the new brewery produces a beer at the right price and suited to the local palate, it is difficult to see how it will not succeed.

In one major move Hawk has established himself as a brewer of some significance in Victoria. The Potato Factory now owns Solomon & Co. lock, stock and barrel and Hawk is in a position to destroy the elderly David Solomon and his son Abraham. For the second time in his life he has David Solomon completely at his mercy.

His intention is to do no such thing. At last Hawk is able to achieve what he urged Mary to do for so long, to make restitution for the money they stole from the Whitechapel safe, with interest added. In fact, the value of the Solomon & Co. assets, if the new Ballarat brewery is included and paid for, is nearly eight times the face value of the original fortune stolen. Hawk calculates that it is at the very least the equivalent of Hannah's fifty per cent entitlement with a decent interest earned on the money over the thirty-eight years since the theft took place. By returning David Solomon's business to him he will have fully satisfied his conscience.

However, the gesture is, to Hawk's mind, too pretentious. There is yet another way which, if taken, will still save the fortunes of David Solomon and his family and serve Hawk's original intention to expand the Potato Factory onto the mainland.

Hawk decides to create a new holding company to be called Solomon & Teekleman under which he will place the Potato Factory and Solomon & Co. as separate identities. The idea is to keep Abraham Solomon as managing director of Solomon & Co. and David as its chairman, while Hawk remains in the same positions with the Potato Factory. At the same time he would hold the chairmanship of Solomon & Teekleman. David and Abraham, Hinetitama and he will own all the shares in Solomon & Teekleman with the combined profits of both companies reporting to it to be divided among the joint shareholders according to their shareholding.

Even in this division of shares, Hawk is scrupulously fair. The Potato Factory is the larger of the two companies though, with the new brewery coming on-line, he estimates by not much more than eight per cent. He calculates the shareholding accordingly. He gives David and Abraham each twenty-three per cent of the shares of the holding company and then converts the ten per cent of the Potato Factory shares owned by Ben and Victoria under the trusteeship of their mother, Hinetitama, into ten per cent of Solomon & Teekleman and the remaining forty-four per cent goes to him.

What this means in effect is that he is the single largest shareholder and his shares combined with those held in trust for the children will always allow his side to control what has now become a giant corporate entity. As the biggest shareholder Hawk appoints himself the chairman of the holding company.

Hawk, going through David's business affairs, sees that father and son are a good combination, with David the developer and Abraham a clear thinker with a cautious mind, his steady right arm.

As David Solomon is already an old man, Abraham, upon his father's death or retirement, will remain as a steady and wise influence in the company, acquiring and building its affairs so the next generation will inherit a conglomerate on a very sound financial footing. Hawk is aware of Joshua, Abraham's six-year-old son, and thinks how well the next generation would be equipped to take over with Ben, Victoria and Joshua sharing the management tasks.

It is all, to Hawk's trusting mind, a nice combination, with David and Abraham running things in Melbourne and himself in Hobart and all of it under his own reasonably benign chairmanship. Ever the peacemaker, he has entirely forgotten the words spoken to him by Mary on her deathbed. 'Never trust that bastard, David Solomon!'

When David learns who owns his company he makes his previous tantrum seem like child's play. 'That nigger bastard! I'll kill him! How dare he! The ignorant black syphilitic bastard! Mary, yes! Mary were a worthy opponent, I hated the bitch, but she was clever! This is the second time that schwartzer has humiliated me! That stupid, dumb whore's son's got the better o' David Solomon!'

Abraham clumsily tries to calm his father. 'But, Father, he's rescued us? Saved us from disaster?'

'Saved us? What you mean saved us?'

'The company, saved from bankruptcy.'

'By a nigger bastard what's going to make us eat shit! You call that saved? You wouldn't know saved if it were jammed up your fat arse!'

Abraham sighs, ignoring his father's insult. 'No, Father, I don't think you're right, he's a good businessman, he sees that it's better to save us than to let us sink. It's commonsense.'

'What do you know, eh? That one's as cunning as the devil, he's stole from us before, now he's done it again, the bastard has humiliated me *again*!' David drops to his knees and starts to sob then as suddenly he stops and throws his head back. 'FUCK HIM! FUCK HIM!!' he screams. 'I SWEAR ON ME GRANDSON'S LIFE I'LL GET HIM! GET EVEN!' Rising, he rushes into the kitchen then outside to the woodpile where he takes up the axe and comes storming back with the heavy axe over his shoulder. 'Out of my way, out my fucking way!' he snarls at Abraham and enters his study, locking the door from the inside.

He remains in his study for three days and with the axe he progressively wrecks every stick of furniture in it. He accepts only water pushed through a small window and refuses anything to eat. Despite Abraham's constant pleas to come out, it is only after six-year-old Joshua, the apple of David's eye, has cried for several hours outside his study door that David finally emerges.

He is weak from lack of nourishment and the doctor is called and he is given chicken soup and crustless bread and put straight to bed. The doctor recommends that David stay in bed for a week until he regains his strength. But the following morning at half-past six he is up and seated at his usual place at the breakfast table beside his grandson. Since the day he has been able to sit up in a high chair Joshua has taken his breakfast alone with his grandfather.

'Grandpa, are you better now? Why did you break everything? the child asks ingenuously.

'Joshua, my boy, we have lost everything, the schwartzer has taken everything, your grandfather has let you down,' David tells his grandson.

'No, we haven't, Grandpa, I've still got the little wisdoms.' Joshua grins and shrugs. 'So when I grow up I'll be rich, like you said!' The small boy laughs. 'I'll give it all back to you, Grandpa.'

'Rich again? Wisdoms? So much for wisdoms! I am too old and you are too young. That's the only wisdoms we've got!' David brings his hands up to hold his cheeks. 'Oh my God, what shall I do?'

Joshua, seeing his grandfather starting to get upset again, starts to talk. 'Never borrow more than the value of your least important assets,' he declares.

David can't believe his ears. 'And I told you this? I should be ashamed, I don't listen to myself!' he sobs.

Joshua is too young to be aware of the irony of the words he's just recited and begins again. 'When you hire a manager ask him how much he wants, it will always be less than you expect to pay. Then pay him more than he expects in return for owning him body and soul.' Joshua continues, 'Never hire a Jew in case he turns out to be smarter than you or you've married into his family. Roman Catholics have too many children which drives the breadwinner to drink and a drunk can never be trusted to give you a full day's work. Never do business with a handshake, a good contract doesn't have a faulty memory. The eyes in the back of your head must be constantly on the lookout for the knife aimed between your shoulder blades. Hearsay and memory are bad witnesses in a court of law, always write everything down and, if possible, have it signed by the person with whom you are doing business or otherwise a reliable witness.' The small boy stops. 'Shall I go on, Grandpa?'

'Impossible! Impossible! You've learned it all!' David cries, clapping his hands together, real tears now rolling down his cheeks, though he himself doesn't know whether they are from joy at the boy's cupidity or despair at his own impoverished situation.

However, Joshua is enjoying the game and resumes talking. 'If an employee is guilty of doing something wrong in the past, never allow him to forget it in the future. An eye for an eye is what it says in the Bible, but consider a moment, two eyes for an eye, when your enemy is in the dark, he can't hurt you. A bribe only becomes poor business judgment when it doesn't work. On the other hand, a bribe is only a bribe when it's done by somebody else, when you employ it, it is a gratuity in return for something you want. In business a man is always guilty before being proved innocent. Remember, greed is the most important motivation in the human race, forget this and you are out of business quick smart. Revenge is a dish best eaten cold. Never trust anyone except only maybe your mother and even her, think twice and only act the third time, if she is Jewish, the fourth!' David realises that years of breakfast maxims have paid off, the child has learned them as if by rote.

'Enough, enough already,' David cries. 'You are breaking my heart, Joshua!'

Almost from the moment Joshua was born these maxims, and a thousand like them, have filled the intellectual space in the child's mind. David's idea has always been that when his grandson is an adult and forced to make business decisions on his own he will have equipped him with an aphorism for every conceivable situation he might have to face.

Whenever David taught his grandson a new one, he would always end by saying, 'Joshua, my boy, trust nobody except your dog, Spot.' And now, barely stifling his sobs, he repeats the homily and waits for Joshua to complete it.

The child, ever eager to please his grandfather, laughs and claps his hands. 'But always leave a flea under his collar so Spot knows who's the boss!'

It is at this point that Abraham enters the dining room. 'Excuse me, Father, but it is of the utmost importance that I see you immediately.'

David thinks for a moment to send him away, Joshua giving him the first moments of enjoyment since the bank collapsed. Besides it is accepted that his time with his grandchild at breakfast may not be interrupted. But things have changed lately and Abraham's look of concern makes him hold his temper.

'What is it?' David asks, irritated.

'We have a visitor.'

'A visitor? But it is not yet seven o'clock in the morning, tell him to bugger off, come back in two hours.'

'I think you should come, Father, he waits in my study.'

'He, who, why, never mind!' David shouts, slamming his hand down hard onto the surface of the table, but then he rises from his seat and turns to Joshua. 'You're a good boy, Joshua, you've made me proud.

'Who is it?' he now asks Abraham.

Abraham is reluctant to tell his father, afraid that David will not accompany him to his study. 'Father, it is best you see for yourself.'

They reach his study door and David, entering first, very nearly faints at the sight of Hawk seated on the ottoman couch. 'Jesus!' he cries, physically jumping backwards at the sight of the giant black man. 'What the devil!'

Hawk rises, towering over the diminutive David

Solomon. 'I hoped we might have a few words, David,' he says, extending his hand, though not expecting it will be taken.

He is not disappointed and his hand is ignored. 'A few words!' David shouts. 'I'll give you two. Fuck off!'

Hawk chuckles. 'No less than I expected, I see you've inherited your mother's charm.'

David ignores Hawk and turns to Abraham. 'What does the nigger want? My blood? Come to gloat, 'as he? Well, you tell the bloody cannibal we'll have no further truck with his sort, we may be poor but we don't 'ave to join him in the gutter!'

'Father, Mr Solomon has a business proposition, one I think may be to our advantage.'

'I'd like to see that when it's got its jodhpurs on!' David sneers. 'What's he want to do, buy the bleedin' 'ouse? He's got everything else!'

'I already own your house,' Hawk says quietly.

'Please sit, Father.' Abraham leads David to a chair and then gently pushes down on his shoulders to force him into the leather club chair.

David is fully dressed except that he still wears his bedroom slippers with no hose. He slumps in the deep chair with his chin tucked into his chest, looking directly into his own lap. 'Well, go on, get on with it, nigger!'

'I must remind you, David, that my mother, like yours, was a Jew, that makes me a Jew as well, perhaps a nigger Jew, but still a Jew.'

'And she was also a whore!' David snarls.

'But not a whore mistress, like yours was,' Hawk replies, then smiles. 'I don't expect you to be happy at the thought of meeting me, but I had hoped that, after all these many years, our next meeting might be cordial, albeit not one filled with mutual admiration.' Hawk turns to look at Abraham. 'I'm pleased to say your son is not similarly discourteous. Also, I apologise that I have called on you at such an early hour and without prior notice, but I have business of some urgency to discuss which I believe will turn out to be altogether to your advantage. Perhaps a better outcome than the last time we met.'

David is suddenly transported in his mind to the dark, musty pantry in London where together he and the fifteen-year-old Hawk had opened the safe only to find it was empty but for an envelope addressed to himself. Inside was a gold ring set with a handsome ruby and a note in Ikey's handwriting. *Remember, always leave a little salt on the bread.* The remainder of the fortune had disappeared and, while it has never been traced, David knows with the utmost certainty that somehow Mary Abacus and her nigger boy had contrived to open the safe and steal what he correctly believes belonged to his family.

Now the nigger has beaten him again, humiliated him a second time beyond any possible endurance. Hawk destroyed his prospects as a young man and now he has done so again at the end of his life. He has effectively rendered his entire existence worthless.

'Father, Mr Solomon has a proposition to put to us,' Abraham repeats, 'I think we should hear him out.'

'*See* him out, more like,' David snarls. 'G'arn, fuck off, Hawk Solomon!'

Hawk sighs and removes his half-hunter from his weskit pocket, unclips it from its fob chain and clicks it open. 'You have five minutes to save your company and your arse, David Solomon,' he says quietly. 'If after that you are not willing to hear me out I shall leave you. I had no hand in bringing your destruction about and take no pleasure in it, but I will not again lift a finger to help you.' He removes the watch from its chain and places it on the small table beside the couch. 'Five minutes, gentlemen, and then I'm off to mind my own business.'

174

A silence follows that must have continued for a good three and a half minutes. Abraham keeps glancing at the fob watch, believing he can hear it ticking away the seconds, though he is too far from it for this to be possible. Another half a minute goes by and unable to contain himself any further he calls, 'Father!'

With less than thirty seconds to go David, restraining his anger, says, 'G'arn then, get on with it, I 'aven't got all bloody day!'

Hawk returns the watch to its chain and restores it into his fob pocket then proceeds to outline the plan he has for the two companies. After he has completed his explanation, he emphasises that David and Abraham would be left to run their own company, provided always it meets with its expected profits and losses and that all major acquisitions are subject to verification from the chairman of the board of the holding company, Solomon & Teekleman.

'That's you! You the board?' David rasps.

'Ah, yes, a board? Yes, well, I daresay we shall have a board, the two of you, my niece Mrs Teekleman and myself, but I shall make the decisions on the simple basis that I control the most shares.' Hawk smiles. 'We shall, of course, discuss whatever is in contention and I shall greatly value your opinions, but the decisions will always be made on the basis of share majorities, whoever might in the future control the majority of the shares will be chairman of the company.' Hawk is thinking that he must keep young Joshua from ever taking over the new holding company.

'Ha, you will be the boss!' David exclaims. 'Just as I thought.'

'Does that surprise you?' Hawk asks him, but David merely grunts, 'And a woman, another damned woman in the picture!'

'You will find this one less trouble than the last,' Hawk says.

'Why, Mr Solomon? Why have you done this absurd and unnecessary act of generosity?' Abraham now asks.

'Ah, it is a long story, Abraham, and I think no longer worth the telling. Let it suffice to say that I do not believe it either absurd or unnecessary. I am most impressed with the manner you and your father have built Solomon & Co. and honestly believe, while you extended your credit with the bank to breaking point, you did not deserve to lose all you have worked so hard to achieve. Quite simply the Potato Factory hopes to expand its interest into the colony of Victoria and eventually throughout Australia, but frankly we lack the top management to do so. I admit I cannot do it by myself. It would seem stupid in the extreme to lose two excellent businessmen who understand the corporation they run simply because of some old enmity between our families. If we cannot be friends then let us be the best of business partners. I assure you, as your chairman, I shall always try to be fair in my decisions and hear you out. But, if you attempt to cheat me, you will find the outcome an unhappy one for yourselves.'

David suddenly looks up and glares at Hawk. 'It's because of the safe, ain't it? The money you and Mary Abacus stole from our family?'

Hawk sighs and for a moment wears an expression of acute exasperation. He knows himself to be as good an actor as David Solomon and so he points to the ruby and gold ring on David's middle finger. 'The only thing I know to come for certain from that safe you are wearing on your finger.' He turns to David's son who has remained standing throughout. 'Well, what say you, Abraham?'

There is a moment's silence when Abraham looks at his father who has always dominated him. He brings his fist up to his mouth and clears his throat. With his heart racing he looks directly at Hawk, 'I accept, sir, your terms are most generous, most equitable indeed.'

'Accept? What? Without me?' David can't believe his ears.

'Yes, Father.'

'Jesus! Me own flesh and blood!'

'Well, that's it then,' Hawk says, nodding towards the seated David. 'I daresay we'll manage quite well without you, David.'

Abraham looks quickly at Hawk. 'No, no, wait a moment, please!' He addresses David, 'Father, be sensible, for God's sake!'

David does not reply, his eyes directed to his kneecaps. Abraham can see that he is near weeping from frustration and anger. While his commonsense has forced him to make a final appeal to his father to accept Hawk's offer, it also gives him a curious satisfaction to see his father with his back so completely against the wall.

David Solomon has always run roughshod over any opposition including Abraham's own cautionary advice, his sheer aggression, bluff and stubbornness often winning the day, when caution would have served him better in the long run. Now this giant black man has him all tied up in knots. For once the bully has met his match and Abraham knows it to be sinful to feel elated at his father's downfall, but he knows that he will always cherish this moment while never again being able to admit it, even to himself.

Abraham Solomon has, of course, heard of the existence of Hawk Solomon, but always as some dark demon, an evil force castigated with the very breath that carries his name. He had no idea that Hawk was Jewish, for David had always portrayed him as the most primitive of savages. Now this huge black man is not only extending an olive branch to his family but also allowing them to recover from disaster, even to prosper again and, what's more, allowing him to personally regain his pride. For the second time in Abraham's life, he has opposed his father.

On the first occasion it concerned Elizabeth, Abraham's sad, disappointed and mostly inebriated wife. When Abraham decided to bring Elizabeth home to meet his sickly mother, half expecting her disapproval, but hoping that by convincing her of his happiness she would understand his desire to marry a gentile, he went to see his father.

Elizabeth came with impeccable credentials except for the most important one of all, she was not Jewish. She was the daughter of the third daughter of an impoverished English lord who had married a wealthy and well-connected Melbourne financier, who boasted of being a 'Fitz', the illegitimate offspring of royalty at some time in aeons past. Her father had subsequently lost all his money speculating in gold shares on the stock market, but because of his wife's lineage and his own pretensions, the family had maintained its social status among Melbourne's better bred while, at the same time, living in relative poverty.

Simply stating that she was a gentile and then presenting Elizabeth's credentials to his father he waited, expecting the worst, but for once in his life he was prepared to stand up to him. To his astonishment, David Solomon had approved of the match after asking a single question, 'Is she a Roman Catholic?'

When told she wasn't, but Church of England he'd seemed unusually enthusiastic. 'Splendid, m'boy, a bit of goy blood can do us no harm whatsoever.' In what was a rare show of affection he'd clapped his son on the back and asked, 'Has she got big tits?'

Not answering, but nevertheless encouraged by his

father's approval, the following day Abraham brought his intended home. Leaving Elizabeth to wait in the conservatory he'd entered his mother's bed chamber.

To Abraham's surprise David was seated beside his wife's bed when he entered. This came as somewhat of a shock to him as David's habit was to spend no more than a few moments at her bedside after he'd taken breakfast and when he returned at the end of the day from his office in Bourke Street. Rebecca referred to these visits as 'Papa's passion! A peck in the air, a burp, a fart and always the same greeting, "Ow yer going? Orright? Good! Eat something. Too-ra-loo!" ' He would have entered the bed chamber, reached her bed, pecked the air above her head, turned around, spoken, farted, burped and been back out the door before she'd managed a single word in reply.

It was unusual therefore to see David at his wife's bedside in the middle of the afternoon. Abraham had expected to speak to his mother alone and, with the presence of his father, who he assumed must have unexpectedly and untypically come to lend his support, his feelings were mixed. The previous day in David's office he had not talked of loving Elizabeth, nor even of feeling an affection for her, but merely that he had met a girl he liked, a Christian who came from a decent family and he hoped to gain David's blessing to marry her. 'Love' was not a word he knew to use in front of his father, but it was his only hope of success when talking with his mother. Abraham had carefully practised the words he would say to her, but now with his father present, he was afraid they might sound mawkish and pathetic whereupon David wouldn't hesitate to mock him and to make a fool of him in front of his mother. Nevertheless, not one for extemporaneous invention, Abraham decided to plunge ahead with his original plea for her blessing.

'Mama, I have brought someone home to meet you,'

he announced shyly, then clearing his throat added, 'Someone I love with all my heart and who it is my dearest wish to marry. Will you give me your blessing, for I cannot do without it, or her in my life?'

Rebecca clapped her hands, delighted at her son's news. 'Oh, Abie, what wonderful news!' She turned to David. 'To think, all the nice girls I've found for him, the boychick finds one for himself! Her name, if you please?'

'Elizabeth, Mama.'

'Elizabeth?' Rebecca frowned, thinking a moment. 'I don't know an Elizabeth? Not from the reform synagogue, I hope?' She looked immediately suspicious. 'Her surname, if you please?'

Abraham brought his fist to his lips and coughed, 'Fitzsimmons. Mama, she's ah . . . not Jewish.'

Rebecca promptly refused to meet the plain-looking Elizabeth, declaring later that she would rather die than see her only son marry a gentile. She turned and cried loudly to David, 'My son, he wants me to die! I have no time left, but he wants I should die tonight!'

'No, Mama, that is not so,' Abraham cried. 'Give me a chance to introduce her to you, I know you'll change your mind!'

'Not enough boobs to feed a hungry mouse!' Rebecca declared out of the blue, again directing this remark to David. It was true enough, Elizabeth possessed a very small bust, but as his mother was bedridden and had never laid eyes on her, nor David for that matter, Abraham could not imagine how she could have known this.

His mother was a determined woman but she usually submitted to his father's will. He now turned to David for his help. 'Father, I thought . . . ?'

'Stop!' David shouted. 'Not another word! Get rid of the shiksa, you hear! We work with gentiles, we do business with gentiles but we don't marry them! Get rid of the goy!' He looked sternly at his son. 'You hear me, Abraham?' David pointed to the door. 'Out she goes!' Then he added, 'Wait for me in my study after you've sent her home.' Abraham, deeply distressed, hesitated. 'G'arn . . . be off! Oh, and give her a ten pound note for her father, tell him to buy a revolver and use it on himself, he ain't worth a pinch of shit, the stuck up bastard!'

'Thank you, David,' Rebecca cried, taking her husband's hands in both her own and clutching them fondly to her breast. 'I am not long for this world, you must find a nice Jewish girl for Abie before I die, the boy knows from women nothing!'

Abraham, distressed by his mother's stubborn refusal, became even more confused when, upon his return from seeing the tearful Elizabeth to her home, having attempted to comfort her and to assure her that he intended to fight for her, he marched into David's study to have it out with his father once and for all. 'Father, I cannot accept your rejection of Elizabeth,' he cried immediately upon entering.

But before he could continue David held up his hand. 'Sssh! Not so fast, my boy. Not so fast. Close the door. Rejection? What rejection? You have my blessing to marry the girl one hundred per cent.'

Abraham wasn't sure he'd heard his father correctly. 'What? But in Mama's bedroom you . . . ?'

David nodded. 'She's dying, have you no compassion for a dying woman?'

'But why, Father?'

'Your sons will be gentile,' David replied simply. 'It is time we stopped being Jews.'

'Stopped?' Abraham was deeply shocked. 'But we *are* Jews!'

'You are, I am, your mother is, but your children won't be.'

'But Elizabeth could turn, she's agreed to convert. We have already discussed it.'

David looked unblinkingly at Abraham until his son could no longer meet his father's eye. 'She could, but she won't.'

'But Mama? You said yourself, it will break her heart?'

'That's why I wanted to see you, your mother will be dead soon enough.' David shrugged. 'So what's so hard? You'll stay stum until after the funeral.' He gave a philosophical shrug. 'It's not such a long time, just don't shtoop her, you hear? I want your children to be born within wedlock, everything kosher.'

Rebecca died three months later of consumption, much as the family physician had predicted she would. Abraham married Elizabeth and, for the first time in his life, he was truly happy.

When after a year there was no sign of offspring, David started to put on the pressure, demanding that the couple get on with it. When after four years there was still no offspring, David had had enough and he decided Elizabeth was to blame, his son had married a barren woman.

'She must go! Make a settlement, not too much, she has eaten our bread too long for too little!'

But, for the first time in his life, Abraham dug his heels in and stood up to his father and refused. 'Father, Elizabeth is my wife and I love her. If we are not to have children then that's God's will.'

'God's will! God's will! Can't you see the shiksa is too bloody in-bred, she's all dried up inside, look at her tits fer Chrissake!' David, accustomed to having his own way, continued to rant and rave, threatening to throw his son out of the business without a penny if he didn't divorce Elizabeth.

Abraham stayed calm throughout the tirade. 'Father,

it's no use, you may do as you wish to me. Elizabeth is my wife and I love her.'

In the end David had no further recourse. There were no substitute heirs in the immediate Solomon family. Ann, his sister, was a spinster and gone over to the other side, Sarah had married and had two children, girls and both quite dotty, not suitable as heirs and unlikely to find husbands, Mark had gone bush on the mainland and was said to have taken an Aboriginal wife.

Abraham remained David's only hope for a grandchild with the unbanished Elizabeth the obstacle.

David, who himself had married late in life, refused to believe that it might be his own son firing blanks. He knew that eventually he would find a way to get rid of Elizabeth. Equally, he was aware that he was already in his sixties and running out of time. His lack of an heir other than Abraham began to preoccupy him to the extent where he grew morbid and introspective.

As often enough happens with men who suddenly become conscious of the fact that their allotted time in this mortal coil is coming to an end, David began to dwell on things spiritual.

In a man as iconoclastic and venal as David Solomon this was a curious notion in itself, but his spirituality took an even more bizarre twist. His son's declaring that their lack of offspring was God's will began to obsess him. Soon he started to believe that maybe it *was* God's will, that he was being punished by a Jewish God for allowing Abraham to marry a gentile.

Though he was wise in the ways of the business world, he was essentially an uneducated and, at heart, superstitious and ignorant man. Reluctantly admitting to himself that his miserable son and his gentile wife had, for the time being, beaten him, David visited Rabbi Dr Abrahams, the rabbi of the Melbourne synagogue.

Since the death of his wife, Rebecca, and the marriage of Abraham to Elizabeth Fitzsimmons, the Melbourne Jewish community had seen very little of the Solomon family, a problem of some significance as it represented a regular source of funds which had now dried up.

And although Abraham's marriage to Elizabeth Fitzsimmons had created a great deal of delicious gossip amongst the synagogue congregation and was seen as a betrayal of the faith, Rabbi Abrahams, essentially a pragmatic man, was sufficiently worldly to know that religion of any kind cannot exist solely on the piety and pennies of the poor and so he welcomed David warmly.

'A great pleasure to see you again, Mr Solomon. Since your beloved wife's tragic demise we have not enjoyed your attendance at synagogue.'

'Too busy,' David replied brusquely, and then lost no time in getting to the purpose of his visit. 'Rabbi, my son Abraham has been married four years and . . .' He paused and shrugged his shoulders, 'Nothing.'

'Nothing? No children, eh?' The rabbi stroked his beard. 'A shame, it is written, every Jew is entitled to a son.'

David nodded. 'Yeah, well we ain't got one!' he'd snapped, then came straight out with it, 'What would it take for my daughter-in-law to become pregnant?'

Rabbi Abrahams looked surprised. Witchcraft and superstition usually belonged to the poorer end of his congregation. He pursed his lips and spread his hands wide. 'As far as I know, the same as always, a boy and a girl and a feather bed, the rest is God's will.'

David was not in a mood to share the rabbi's homely wit. 'Yes, yes,' he said impatiently, 'that's what I mean, God's will. Can you get God to change His mind? Can you pray for a grandson? A pregnancy *and* a grandson?'

The rabbi shrugged. 'The one is impossible without the

other.' He thought for a moment. 'You want me to pray? To ask God your daughter-in-law should be pregnant?' He stroked his beard. 'Hmm . . . certainly, it's possible to *ask* Him.' The rabbi could not quite bring himself to believe a man as rich and cynical as David Solomon was so naive in spiritual matters as to expect him to be able to bring his personal influence to bear on the Almighty.

On the other hand, Rabbi Abrahams knew an opportunity when he saw one, though he was not quite sure how far he could go with David Solomon. Certainly the rich old man was a gift from a merciful God, that much he knew for sure. And, furthermore, one which didn't come along every day. And so he decided to hedge a little.

'Mind you in this matter, when the girl party is a gentile, there could be er . . . complications.'

David Solomon was delighted. Complications he knew about, whenever money was about to be discussed the word 'complications' occurred frequently.

'Complications, what complications?'

'You see, it is a matter of ears,' Rabbi Abrahams said, thinking on his feet.

'Ears?'

'Will God listen with His Jewish ear or His gentile ear, that is the question?'

'Both!' David exclaimed. 'How much?'

'Both?' The rabbi looked doubtful. 'I must remind you I am a rabbi, Mr Solomon, a Jew. While I have the utmost respect for the gentile ear of God, I am only familiar with the Jewish.' He shrugged. 'Alas, I am permitted to pray only to one ear.'

'One ear?' David thought for a moment. 'How much for one ear?'

Rabbi Abrahams smiled and spread his hands wide. 'We pray always that God will provide a little Jewish school we hope to attach to the synagogue. A little place of scholarship for our children. Maybe even your grandson?' he suggested slyly.

'Send me the plans, get me a quote.' David jabbed his forefinger at the rabbi. 'Though I warn you, I will obtain another myself, we don't want another incident like your predecessor, that villain,' David paused, 'whatsaname?'

'Rabbi Dattner Jacobson,' Dr Abrahams sighed, referring to the rabbi before him who had been publicly accused of lining his own pockets.

'Yes, that crook, we'll have none of that, there'll be receipts needed and shown, down to the last copper nail.'

The rabbi bowed his head slightly. 'But of course, everything must be kosher.'

'So? What about the other ear?' David now demanded.

'The other ear?'

'Yes, the gentile ear? I *must* have both ears!' David announced. 'I can't take no chances.'

The rabbi rubbed his bearded chin once more. 'For a small commission, say ten per cent, for books you understand, in the school, I could talk to the bishop. We could maybe make a little arrangement?'

Arrangements, like complications, were the things David knew most about. 'The bishop?' David shook his head. 'I'll not do business with the Papists, with them damned Catholics,' David said emphatically.

'Not so fast, not so fast, my friend,' Rabbi Abrahams said soothingly. 'My friend the Anglican Bishop of Melbourne, James Moorhouse, I could have maybe a little talk to him?'

'And he's got the *best* gentile ear? Better than, you know, that other lot?' David asked suspiciously.

The rabbi clasped his hands together and brought them to his chest. 'After the Jews, the best,' Abrahams assured him. 'He is a good God-fearing man who, it so happens, needs a new roof on the baptistery of St Mark's. On the other hand, the Catholics have a brand-new cathedral and God would maybe not be so willing to listen to their needs at the present moment.'

'Fifty per cent now, fifty per cent when the child is born, no commission on the goy roof, but a thousand pounds bonus to you if it is a boy,' David said, extending his hand to the rabbi.

'We will pray for the boy through both ears,' the Chief Rabbi promised, accepting David's outstretched hand. It had been a rewarding day. At the very worst half the cost of the new infant school was paid. Furthermore, with half the price of his new baptistery roof on St Mark's guaranteed and, in the process, a firm relationship established with the powerful bishop, it could do the increasingly prosperous Jewish community in the city no harm. Even if the collective prayers were to fall on deaf ears, the ledger for God's work in the city was suddenly in excellent shape.

Precisely eleven months after David's visit to the rabbi Joshua was born. Rabbi Abrahams, clearly not a man to lose an opportunity to capitalise on this wonderful act of nature, accepted David's cheques together with his bonus.

Carefully folding the two bank drafts into his purse, he addressed his source of pennies from heaven. 'Mr Solomon, God has provided you with a fine, healthy boy, but there has been no bris, he has not been circumcised.' He sighed. 'There is even some talk about, a rumour no doubt, that he is to be raised as a gentile?'

David shrugged. 'It's your law,' he replied with a dismissive shrug. 'His mother Elizabeth is a gentile, my grandson is born a goy.'

Rabbi Abrahams had flinched at the vulgar expression. 'Our law, certainly, Mr Solomon. It is true, your grandson is technically a gentile.' He paused. 'On the other hand, if your son's wife, Elizabeth, is willing to turn, to convert to Judaism,' the Chief Rabbi spread his hands and smiled, 'then it would give me great pleasure to personally instruct her in the Jewish faith. Believe me, it would be a happy occasion for the Jews of Melbourne if I could tell the members of the synagogue that the Lord God has provided Abraham Solomon with a fine *Jewish* son and a grandson to the illustrious Mr David Solomon.'

David was unimpressed with the praise and he thought for a moment then announced, 'No, Rabbi, we will leave things as they are, that is the best thing to do.'

The rabbi was somewhat taken aback, in fact, barely able to conceal his dismay, for he had fully expected David to comply with his request. 'But why, Mr Solomon? Your father Ikey Solomon was a Jew, a member of the first synagogue in Hobart, your mother Hannah was a Jew, also your dear departed wife? You are a Jew, your son Abraham is a Jew? God has answered our prayers, you have a grandson. Why?'

David looked sternly at the rabbi. 'Rabbi Abrahams, I am a plain-speaking man and you have cost me a great deal of money. Not only have the Jews of Melbourne benefited, but I have also allowed you to kiss the arse of a bishop of the Church of England. Mind you, I am not complaining, we made a deal, as you say, I have a grandson and you now have your school and the goy bishop has a new roof over the heads of his Sunday Christians.' He paused for a moment and then said, 'Now, answer me this, please, Mister Rabbi of Melbourne. How do I know it wasn't the gentile ear of God that answered my prayers for a grandson?'

That, with his son, Joshua, the outcome, was the very first time Abraham had gone against his father's wishes. Now, with Hawk waiting for David's answer to his business proposition he has once again defied him. Abraham reasons that if his father, coming to the end of his life, isn't able to accept Hawk's generous rescue plan for Solomon & Co. he, with the remainder of his life ahead of him, has no reason to reject it. On the contrary, he knows himself quite capable of running Solomon & Co. on his own and, without the constant harassment and interference of the old man, he relishes the opportunity.

Abraham can feel his ambivalence growing, but nevertheless feels duty bound to ask once more for his father's co-operation. 'Father, I have accepted Mr Solomon's offer, I shall not relent. Will you not do the same?' It is the last time he will ask and, for the remainder of his life, he will bitterly resent having done so.

Ignoring Hawk's presence David looks up at his son and bellows, 'Yes! Damn you! Count me in!' The task his mind has set him at this moment is to leap from his chair, cross the room and leave it, slamming the door behind him. But he is an old man and rising from the deep leather chair is an onerous business, though he does so with as much vigour as he can muster and crosses the room to the door, forcing his old legs to hurry. He turns at the door, 'S'truth! A nigger chairman!' then exercising his bad temper he exits, slamming the door behind him as hard as he may.

'I apologise, for my father,' a red-faced Abraham says. 'It has all come as a great shock to him.'

Hawk looks up at David's son. 'I sense you would have preferred him to stay out eh? Well, never mind, it's settled then.' Abraham will later recall how Hawk had clasped his fingers together and brought his chin to rest upon his hands. Then looking down into his lap he had given a deep sigh. 'Thank God, after thirty-eight years,' he'd heard Hawk whisper.

Hawk loses no time drawing up the documents and in a month they are signed by David and Abraham and notarised. He plans to stay another month so that he might learn all he can about the new brewery, though he has learned that Abraham is more than competent to see to its completion and seems anxious to be allowed to do so. Hawk feels they will get on well enough and intends to be home soon with Hinetitama, Ben and Victoria. He does not think of Teekleman as family, but simply as an obese presence to be tolerated. He has since learned that the Dutchman has left his employ, but thinks little of it. Hinetitama is well provided for and her husband does not need to work to keep his household going. Hawk will sort out any other details upon his return.

However, two days after the completion of the contracts Hawk receives a telegram from Hobart.

TEEKLEMAN DEAD HINETITAMA IN TROUBLE ANN

Chapter Six

THE RETURN OF HINETITAMA

Melbourne 1914

September 25th 1914, the day of the big military march past, is typical of that time of the year in Victoria. It commences with a thin pre-dawn drizzle, clears up a little just as the paperboys hurry in the six o'clock dark to their allotted street corners then persists foul all morning, with flurries of rain and sudden gusts of bone-chilling wind that invert umbrellas and send hats skidding along the mirror-wet pavements.

It is miserable weather even for ducks, and the folk making their way from Flinders Street Station to Parliament House lower their heads into the wind and the rain, with one hand placed upon their sodden hats, the other clasping raised coat lapels tightly about their chests, their children, all except the infants, fending for themselves.

If spring is just around the corner as all the newspapers proclaim, then, on a day such as this, it seems in no great hurry to arrive. However, an ever hopeful nature has already set the sap to rising in the plane trees on Bourke Street and, while they still stand naked like up-ended witches' brooms, a more careful examination will show that the ends of the most slender branches are tipped with tender green shoots.

Where other cities might bemoan a rotten rainy day, Melbourne folk take a perverse pride in its weather, fondly imagining they share a climate with England, a place which, in the current nomenclature, they refer to as 'home'.

It is as if in their minds Australia is considered their temporal abode while England remains the destination of the heart and the true home of the spirit.

Because it is claimed Melbourne has four more days of rain a year than does London, its citizens think of themselves as somehow more English than the other cities with Adelaide, home of the free settlers, perhaps the single exception. So ingrained is this premise, that on a February day when the temperature is as likely to soar to over one hundred degrees Fahrenheit, the better folk of Melbourne feign surprise. It is as though they feel it unfair that the weather should turn on them so.

In the middle of a heatwave a stout Melbourne grande dame, taking afternoon tea in the new Myers shop in Bourke Street and dressed up to the nines in a gown she has sent to Paris to obtain and wearing a fur appropriate to a London winter, may bat the air with a cheap Chinese paper fan and exclaim in a superior tone, 'Whatever has become of the weather, it was never this hot when I was a gal?'

But even the rising temperature is accommodated to the myth of an antipodean England. The top people in Melbourne compare the sweltering heat with their notion of an endless English summer, where larks fly in a high blue sky and brass bands play in rotundas on Sunday afternoon in a park redolent with crocuses, bluebells, lilacs and daffodils, an England of quiet country pubs, cricket matches on the village green and small boys fishing for sticklebacks in the local pond.

This sense of Englishness has been carried even further,

for unlike the impetuous higgledy-piggledy, stumble and tumble of Sydney, nothing has been left to chance. It is a city meticulously laid out in neat squares, the streets and avenues straight and wide with earnest, clanking trams rattling self-importantly down the centre and generously wide pavements which boast of the city's prosperity and sophisticated demeanour. This is a change brought about by the new wealth from Ballarat and Bendigo gold, which has turned the city John Batman founded into the financial capital of Australia.

However, Melbourne in the old century was not a city to make its better-class citizens proud of their rapidly expanding metropolis, the stench of urine from the back lanes being one of the more ubiquitous characteristics of street life. The Bourke Street East theatre district was used every night by hundreds of theatre-goers and citizens of the night as a common urinal. After sunset the stench and extent of the urine running into it and overflowing its gutters made the footpath almost impassable. The smell of horse dung in every street worthy of a name was omnipresent while the generous dumpings of large herds of cattle and sheep regularly driven through the city added to the ordure.

All said and done, it was a dirty but interesting place, with a street population of German brass bands, Italian organ grinders, French hurdy-gurdy performers and Hungarian musicians, hitching posts and horse troughs and hundreds of street stalls selling every manner of wares. As the sun set there was a migration of coffee stalls into the centre of the city, their owners trundling the strange square boxes with funnels sticking out of the roofs and pitching them in a favourite spot where, with charcoal fires blazing, they appeared transformed into a welcoming and well-lit coffee stall. Hawkers were everywhere, loud and declamatory, selling the latest ballads printed on long narrow pieces of paper clipped to a stick they held above their heads. There were cockatoo hawkers selling caged birds, hawkers selling boiled sheep's trotters, small children selling flowers late into the night and fruit and veggie men and women. Barrowloads of crayfish were sold at sixpence a pound raw weight or for threepence more they came ready to eat.

From December to March, the fish season and the hottest time of the year, when the dusty streets were filled with peel and debris, human urine and horse and cattle shit, the city stench reached a malodorous crescendo with the invasion by fish hawkers. These merchants of the sea used the horse troughs to clean their fish, dumping the fish guts into the gutter and after the plugs were removed from their barrows, oyster shells, fish scales, fish heads and slimy water flowed over footpaths and clogged city gutters in a slushy, effluvium tide that damn near brought its citizens to their knees.

But the Melbourne of 1914 has sobered up and dressed its city fathers in dark broadcloth, top hat and spats and the women from the better classes now dress in unseasonable furs and ill-chosen Parisian finery and, with pinkies pointed outwards, hold bone-china cups of tea and mouth the vowels of England.

Neat cast-iron urinals, exact copies of their Paris counterparts, dot the clean pavements and the city council has erected five underground conveniences with closet accommodation at one penny a time should the requirement be to sit down and an extra penny for a wash and brush. Males in a standing position facing the porcelain are not required to pay.

Perhaps the best example of the now repentant Melbourne is its botanical gardens, designed to be precise and orderly by the German botanist, Baron von Mueller. It adorns the south side of the river and is pruned, mowed and dressed in oak and elm and festooned with the shrubs and blossoms to be found in England and Europe with a token display of the parochial flora.

Only the lazy, mustard-coloured Yarra sidling unpretentiously by is Australian, a laconic country cousin of a river come to visit a rich, patronising and wealthy urban relative.

Despite the cold and the wet, the crowd attending the military parade and now standing three deep in Spring Street remain cheerful. Waving little Union Jacks fixed to lolly sticks, their hearts beat collectively for England and the Empire. Someone with a half-respectable baritone voice and accompanied by a lone mouth organ starts to sing the words to the popular refrain, 'Sons of Australia', and when it comes to the chorus the crowd immediately in the vicinity of Parliament House join in.

> *For Britain! Good old Britain!*
> *Where our fathers first drew breath,*
> *We'll fight like true Australians,*
> *Facing danger, wounds or death.*
> *With Britain's other gallant sons*
> *We're going hand in hand;*
> *Our War-cry 'Good old Britain' boys,*
> *Our own dear motherland.*

They have come to cheer on their troops who are marching off to war to fight in a quarrel Mother England helped to start, but one which their colonial sons neither bother to understand nor stop to think about. 'England calls and we answer' are the proud words on most lips. Young lads, barely out of knee britches, fake their age and grow unconvincing post-pubescent moustaches, hoping to disguise their callow youth and pink unshaven cheeks in their eagerness to join the fray. They carry a collective

SOLOMON'S SONG

sense of anxiety that they may miss the so-called 'Grand Picnic in Europe'. The *Age*, the *Truth* and the *Argus* all agree it will be over by Christmas with the German troublemakers taught a damned good lesson by the British Empire.

Not only do the youth answer to the bugle call of the Motherland. Boer War veterans, who should know better, blacken the greying roots of their hair with a diluted solution of boot black. A wag in the letters column of the *Age* notes that never has 'Bluey' been so numerous on Melbourne's streets and in the queues outside the recruitment depots as older men rinse their hair with henna. They all want to join in the mad scramble to fight for a cause more stupid, pointless, morally reprehensible than any in the long quarrelsome history of mankind.

This is a war instigated by pompous German generals with waxed and curled mustachios and their British and French counterparts, who, but for the colour and insignia on their uniforms, can barely be told apart.

Self-important old men, accredited diplomats and posturing politicians, talk of peace and reconciliation while secretly itching to get on with it. In the weeks leading to the assassination in Sarajevo of Franz Ferdinand, the Archduke of Austria, they make and break alliances almost as regularly as the sounds of popping champagne corks are heard in their embassies whenever they celebrate meaningless diplomatic and political initiatives. Some of these barely last longer than the fizz in the champagne they drink in their toasts to peace.

Eventually, with the arcane dialogue exhausted, the pointless assassination of the Archduke gives them all an excuse to declare war. Citing insults more imagined than real as the reasons for taking up arms against each other, these pompous and vainglorious old men have their tailors fit military tunics to accommodate their paunches.

196

If asked, their collective wives, bringing a little commonsense to bear, could have resolved the shambles in a peaceful afternoon around the kitchen table.

The finest, the very best we have to give of our young blood, our tall, strong, colonial sons, will fight for an England they, nor their parents or their grandparents, have ever visited. For some, the last of their forebears to see England had left its shores on a stinking, rat-infested convict ship to arrive in Australia, cowed and beaten.

Now, on this cold and windy September day, to a rousing march played by the bands of the 1st Australian Division together with the 3rd Light Horse Regiment, their fourth-generation descendants wave to their precious sons and brothers who in this passing-out parade each receive the imprimatur of trained fighting man.

David Solomon and his son Sir Abraham sit among the dignitaries on the apron directly above the first set of steps of Parliament House some eight feet above the crowd. David, ninety-four years old, is almost blind and somewhat deaf, a frail old man who must be transported in a wheelchair. Nevertheless, he enjoys the full use of his mental faculties which are mostly employed in voluble cussing and being curmudgeonly. It has been a decade or more since he was last heard to say a good word for anyone with the exception of his grandson Joshua. He turns stiff-necked to his son and declares, 'Is that the band I hear?'

'Yes, Father, won't be long now,' Sir Abraham answers, sensing his growing impatience.

'What's the time?'

Abraham withdraws his half-hunter from his weskit pocket and reads the time out loud. 'Twenty minutes past eleven, give or take thirty seconds of the clock, Father.'

'They're late! Should've passed by at eleven, it's too damned cold to be sitting around.' The old man turns to

SOLOMON'S SONG

face in the direction of the Governor-General standing on the pavement below the steps with Major General Bridges and members of the general staff. They wait to take the general salute. 'Sloppy work! By golly, we won't win the war this way!' he shouts down at their backs.

The Governor-General turns towards David. 'Not you, sir! That fat army chappie in the uniform next to you!' He points an accusing finger at Major General Bridges, a man with a high colour and a distinctly bellicose look about him. 'Your troops, aren't they? Should be on time! Not good enough by half.'

The general is clearly taken aback and turns and points at David Solomon. 'Who is this man?' he shouts up at the Governor-General who is also in the front row of the seated dignitaries. Then without waiting for an answer he turns back to David. 'Sir, you insult me!'

Despite the noise from the street below and the rapidly approaching band, the silence on the podium is palpable. Most of those present know David Solomon is notorious for his plain speaking, an old man who doesn't give a fig for the good opinions of others and, with the increasing loss of his sight, most are aware of his irascibility.

'I demand an apology,' Major General Bridges barks, for the band is now less than fifty yards away and the cheering of the crowd has greatly increased.

David, feigning a deafness of convenience, turns to his son and shouts, 'Eh? What he say?'

Abraham leans close to the old man's ear. 'He wants you to apologise, Father. We must!' He is visibly embarrassed and now takes it upon himself to rise and face the officer. Attempting an awkward little bow, he shouts, 'Sir, we apologise most profusely! No insult intended, none at all, I'm sure.' He smiles weakly. 'The cold, General, my father is a very old man and is rheumatic.'

198

Major General Bridges, only slightly mollified, turns away. The band is almost upon them and he must take the salute with the Governor-General, who has already risen and taken his place on the steps. 'Father, you go too far,' Abraham remonstrates, 'you will need to apologise officially.'

David casts an angry look at his son. 'Apologise? Whaffor?'

Abraham sighs. 'Just don't say anything more, please, Father!'

'It's too bloody cold, I'm freezin' me knackers off, how much longer must we all sit here because of his damned incompetence?' David now says, but the band is upon them and only Abraham hears him. He knows David will continue the altercation with the general just as soon as he can make himself heard again.

'Father, you will do Joshua a disservice,' Abraham shouts into David Solomon's ear. His only hope is to scare the old man into silence with the notion that his precious grandson's carefully planned career in the army might be affected by his rudeness to the general. He knows David will do almost anything to protect Joshua from coming to any harm in the war.

David sniffs and jerks his head backwards as though to refute this notion, but Abraham knows he has won and lets out a sigh of relief. He will send the military man an abject note of apology accompanied by a box of Cuban cigars and once again plead the weather, his father's extreme age and his non-existent rheumatic condition and decrepitude.

Sir Abraham Solomon is a deeply conservative man, deficient in imagination, but meticulous in business procedure and placid enough to have always taken his directions from his mercurial father. Confrontation is not a large part of his character and Abraham, unlike his own son Joshua, both fears and dislikes his father. Often brought to the verge of despair by the old man's unreasonableness, he secretly wishes the miserable old bastard would die, thinking him at least twenty years overdue for the plain pine coffin.

Both he and Joshua have spent their lives attempting to please the old man, but with quite different results. David dotes on his grandson Joshua who can do no wrong in his eyes, while he thinks Abraham, at very best, is an unimaginative plodder with an honest bookkeeper's mind, not at all the sort to advance the Solomon fortunes.

Abraham has spent his life trying to make David proud of him. A naturally shy and retiring man with a passion for racing pigeons, he has, at David's instigation, been Lord Mayor, received a knighthood in 1910, and is now the Grand Master of Melbourne's secret order of Free and Accepted Masons.

These are all positions which David has himself secretly coveted but has made no attempt to achieve. Despite his enormous wealth, David Solomon is aware of his lack of education and the social graces required for public office. His bravado and brusque manner in public are an attempt to conceal a deep-seated insecurity and sense of inferiority he has felt since his early childhood. He is secretive by nature and not at all gregarious, mostly for fear that, despite his wealth, he might be exposed and humiliated as so often happened to him in his childhood.

So Abraham, who has been properly educated in the manners of society, has been forced by the old man to play what is essentially a surrogate role, with his ambitious father calling the shots behind the scenes and taking advantage of the opportunities his son's public persona and position affords Solomon & Teekleman.

As a consequence Abraham has very little sense of his own worth. All his achievements have been reluctant, undertaken only to please the cantankerous old man seated beside him. He is aware that money, placed in the right places and in the right hands, has been the primary reason for his progress in civic affairs. As his father so often says, 'Money will buy you everything, son, except love. The currency of love is soon spent but the money it will cost you never ends.' It is one of David's more benign sayings.

As the mayor of Melbourne, Sir Abraham had the personal satisfaction of having the Solomon family endow the city with a plot of land in St Kilda Road for civic purposes and to finance a new wing for the public library. This sort of largesse could never have emanated from David himself, but Abraham was able to convince his father that the goodwill of Solomon & Teekleman Holdings was at stake. Finally, when it was proposed that the new library wing be named the David Solomon Wing, he agreed even though he had always thought it a crime to educate the masses.

The endowment to the library, in particular, was a quiet source of amusement to Abraham and perhaps the closest he would ever come to avenging himself for the hundreds of humiliations he had suffered at the old man's hands. David Solomon had never read a book in his life, constantly chastising Abraham as a child for doing so. If it had not been for the protection of his mother, Rebecca, his father would have denied him the pleasure of books, believing they softened the mind.

To David, education meant sending his son to the *right* school where he would meet the *right* people and learn the *right* manners so as to be accepted within Melbourne's polite society. It never occurred to him to equate Abraham's education with intellectual progress. Business was all that interested David and he accepted the responsibility of teaching Abraham this himself. In fact, he would later blame his son's conservative business habits and lack of a killer instinct on too much education. 'Too many bloody books when you were a child, that's the problem with you, m'boy!'

Abraham's career as a Freemason was much more to David's taste. While he himself did not join, he liked the idea of a secret society of men who 'scratched each other's backs' and who covertly agreed not to witness against each other in a court of law. He quickly realised how this might be to his advantage, happily accepting that the price of Abraham's elevation was the unspoken promise to employ only Freemasons within the family's vast enterprises. This meant well over two thousand jobs went to the secret brotherhood, which excluded Catholics from its membership. This suited David, too, for he loathed the Irish papists with a fierce and abiding hate. His mother's de facto husband, George Madden, was an Irish Catholic who had treated David and his three siblings, Ann, Sarah and Mark, with a singular disdain and often enough had beaten them or, as a punishment for some imagined misdemeanour, made them go without food for three days. 'You English made the Irish starve, boy, now you can do the same,' he'd say. David had never forgiven the man, blaming his race and religion for their childhood suffering.

Abraham is aware that his father sees him as a far from adequate replacement at the helm of the giant brewing, timber, pastoral and business empire. He knows that he is, at best, the temporary standard-bearer while Joshua is being groomed for the job of ultimately running Solomon & Teekleman Holdings.

Far from resenting his caretaker role, he looks forward to the time when he can hand over to his son and he can get on with his life free from the restraints of business. The only office he cherishes is that of President of the

Pigeon Racing Association of Victoria. Furthermore, he blames his wife Elizabeth's drinking on himself and anticipates a time when he will be able to give her sufficient attention.

With his heart still pounding from witnessing the contretemps between David and the Major General, Abraham folds his arms tightly across his chest in an attempt to crush the anxiety he feels in his gut.

The band is almost upon them with the brass and drums crashing about his ears. Abraham prepares to alert his father that the 4th Australian Light Horse follows. The clopping of 546 horses on the macadam surface of the street and the jangle of their brasses as the mounted troopers move up to take the salute now almost completely drowns out the departing band. Joshua will be the officer riding ahead of the third squadron.

'Is he here yet?' the near blind David cries, grabbing his son's arm. In the din and the cheering of the excited crowd it is impossible to hear him and, besides, Abraham has previously agreed he will tap his father on the shoulder when Joshua's troop appears. David's bony fingers are surprisingly strong as they dig deep into the flesh of his son's upper arm. Abraham sees that the old man's mouth is spit-flecked with anxiety at the thought of not being ready when his grandson passes by.

Joshua's troop rides into sight and Abraham taps David on the shoulder, whereupon the old man brings his hand up to his forehead in a salute intended to be rigid, though his hand trembles so that the tips of his fingers set his ear to vibrating. Abraham sees that the old man is crying and he reaches into his pocket for his handkerchief to hand to him when Joshua's squadron has passed by.

Directly across the street from where the general is taking the salute, black as the devil himself and towering head and shoulders above the crowd, is the magnificent

Hawk. He is unseen by David Solomon, but his presence with Victoria is quietly noted by Abraham. During a lifetime of malice and greed, most of it in the name of sound business practice, David has acquired a legion of enemies who would happily slit his throat if they thought they could get away with it. These men, with perhaps one or two exceptions, do not cause David to lose a moment's sleep. On the other hand, David's personal hatred for the giant black man is beyond the sum of all of the others. Abraham decides his father has caused sufficient trouble for one day.

Somewhat stooped, at seventy-three Hawk still stands near seven feet tall with a snow-white crop of woolly hair and the Maori *moko* markings on his proud and handsome face. He provides a natural curiosity for the crowd who try not to stare too blatantly, but occasionally steal furtive glances in his direction. The smaller children have no such reservations and they gawk unashamedly, clutching the hems of their mothers' dresses until they are pulled away and turned about-face to witness the on-going parade.

Standing beside Hawk, her small white hand in his great black fist, is Victoria, Tommo's granddaughter who now lives with him in Melbourne. He brought her over from New Norfolk at the age of eighteen to further her education. She is a handsome young woman of twenty-five who has served her articles and passed the solicitor's examination, but who does not possess, or even wish to embrace, the restrained manners expected of a girl of her social class and wealth. Victoria jumps up and down in excitement, showing her slim ankles and, every once in a while, a daring glimpse of calf as the mounted troopers finally pass and the companies of foot soldiers hove into view, their band playing the popular 'Skipper' Francis anthem, 'Australia Will Be There'. Among them, in the third platoon from the front, is her brother Ben whom she adores with all the considerable love she can pack into a naturally generous heart.

She has observed Joshua riding by, sitting tall in the saddle and ramrod straight and as dashing as can be, with blue eyes and blond hair, the latter inherited from his mother, Elizabeth. Victoria thinks of him as a cousin, though, of course, he is not a relation, and her heart skips a beat at how very handsome he is in his jodhpurs and trim tunic with the polished leather of his Sam Browne belt. She is aware of the enmity between the two Solomon clans, but as Hawk has never dwelt on it, nor fully explained its reasons, it has not assumed any importance in her mind and she feels free to admire the young officer on the big chestnut stallion.

For an instant Victoria regrets that Ben, a magnificent horseman, hasn't joined the Australian Light Horse but has chosen instead to become a foot soldier so that he can be with all his mates. She can see Ben in Joshua's place, every bit as handsome, though darker where his Maori blood comes through, a little shorter and bigger around the shoulders and altogether stronger looking. Whereas Joshua looks like an illustration of a British officer in *Boys' Own Annual*, Ben has a physical hardness about him that comes from working with his hands on the land where he has spent the last eight years of his life, latterly in charge of the company's hop and barley farms and pastoral properties.

Although a uniform sits well enough on his strong frame, it somehow looks temporary. Ben is his own man and no institution is likely to transform him into anonymous cannon fodder. While Joshua will gain his authority from his status as an officer, the twenty-six-year-old Ben needs no rank to make men defer to him. He has been appointed a sergeant not because he marches any better or shoots straighter, or has, for that matter, any more experience at the business of waging war. Ben is their sergeant because they want to go to war with him at their side. Though he has enlisted in Tasmania and will rejoin his regiment before it leaves Australian shores, he has come to Broadmeadows, the Victorian military camp, to attend a special weapons training course and so is today acting as the sergeant of a Victorian infantry platoon. It is a most fortuitous situation as Hawk and Victoria would otherwise have been forced to take the overnight boat to Hobart to farewell him.

The clatter of horses' hooves begins to fade as the Australian Light Horse passes and the infantry brigade are now upon them, the men marching proudly, their chins slightly raised, boots striking the surface of the road setting up a sharp rhythmic cadence, the bayonets fixed to their rifles gleaming against a leaden sky and their heads turned to the eyes-right position to salute the Governor-General.

Hawk is consumed by pride as Ben's platoon approaches them, though, at the same time, silent tears run down his great cheeks. He has no romantic illusions about the war Tommo's grandson is marching off to fight. He has seen men kill men before in the Maori wars and has learned that there is no glory to be found in the slaughter of humans. His heart is filled with trepidation for the lad he thinks of as his own grandson and loves with all his heart.

Victoria also weeps, but rather more from excitement, for she has no sense of Ben's being in danger. Her brother has held her hand since she was a baby and no matter what childish disaster they faced, she always knew he would bring them through it with a self-deprecating grin and a pat on the head. Now, after showing the Germans who is the boss, he'll return to her unscathed and with

206

that same crooked big smile on his silly gob. They'll all be together again, Grandpa Hawk, Ben and herself, all that is left of the disparate little family Mary Abacus gathered around her during her long life.

Hawk hasn't told Victoria that earlier this very morning he has come away from the Sisters of Charity Hospice for Women in St Kilda where for several weeks he has been watching over a dying Hinetitama.

In the inside pocket of his white linen jacket he holds her will, in which she, of sound mind, and in front of a justice of the peace, the Mother Superior, Sister Angelene, and the parish priest, Father Anthony Crosby, has given her proxy to Hawk, making him the trustee for the ten per cent share Ben and Victoria will now own in the giant Solomon & Teekleman Company.

The voting rights on this ten per cent, which have been unavailable to Hawk for the twenty-one years Hinetitama has been away, are the difference between his side controlling a majority shareholding in Solomon & Teekleman or David and his son doing so.

Hawk promised Tommo on his deathbed that he would always care for his daughter but when he took the boat back to Hobart in response to Ann's telegram he arrived to find that Hinetitama had absconded.

In a state of shock he listened while Ann told him the story of how Hinetitama had taken up singing with Teekleman and was nightly to be seen drunk in one or another of the pubs around the waterfront until she was the laughing stock of the town. She told how Teekleman, in the middle of one of his famous 'skols', that is the drinking down of a pint of ale in a bout with another drinker, a competition in which he had never been beaten, suddenly dropped the tankard of ale and clasped his hands to his chest, collapsing to his knees. He was dead from a sudden and massive heart attack before his forehead struck the wooden floor. Without the giant Dutchman to take her home when she looked like making a fool of herself and despite Ann's efforts to dissuade her, Hinetitama had been on a continual binge almost from the moment Teekleman had died. Like all alcoholics, the single glass of gin placed in her hands by the nefarious Isaac Blundstone had been the beginning of her undoing.

Told in a moment of sobriety by Ann that Hawk was returning to Hobart, she'd that very night packed a few things into a canvas bag and disappeared. Hawk arrived in Hobart on the overnight steamer to discover that she was last seen in the drunken company of Captain Ben 'Blackbird' Smithers of the windjammer *The Fair Wind*, one of the sailing ships still plying between the island and the mainland.

Smithers, a former captain of a whaling ship, was notorious as a blackbirder, plundering the islands in the seventies and early eighties, kidnapping Kanakas and bringing them to Queensland to work in the cane fields. He was never apprehended and, like Teekleman, is a drunk and a thorough scoundrel.

From that moment, Hawk searched Australia and New Zealand, even sending detectives to Canada, the new Dominion of South Africa and the United States of America but to no avail. Somehow Hinetitama managed to evade him.

Just before her disappearance Hawk had concluded the deal with David and Abraham Solomon which relied on her shares and proxy in the new conglomerate for him to be chairman. Unable to utilise her ten per cent shareholding he lost his voting majority in Solomon & Teekleman, giving David and Abraham control of the giant enterprise. When David became chairman he immediately removed Hawk from the Potato Factory and Hawk was reduced to being no more than a large shareholder.

Despite his untimely demise, Hawk never sought to find Hinetitama simply to regain her proxy, but because he was guilt-stricken, forced by her absence to break what he considered his sacred word to his twin Tommo. That is, until he received a note from the Mother Superior of the Sisters of Charity Hospice in St Kilda.

The Sisters of Charity Hospice for Women, St Kilda

14th August 1914

Dear Mr Solomon,

Sir, it is with some hesitation that I write to you.

However, after prayer, I am convinced that I have no choice in the matter and so I crave your indulgence.

In recent weeks there has come into our hospice a half-caste woman suffering from delirium tremens, malnutrition and cirrhosis of the liver, in all, an advanced state of alcoholism from which the doctor does not believe she will recover.

She answers to the name of Mary Gibbons, but says that her true identity is Hinetitama Solomon.

I hasten to add that information obtained from alcoholics is usually not to be relied upon. Except, in the case of Mary Gibbons, at such times when her mind is clear, she persists in asking that we contact you as a matter of urgency. It is not usual for someone in her condition to retain such a persistent and consistent obsession and so I am forced to conclude that it may have some validity.

Sir, we do not believe that God will grant Mary much longer on this earth. If this poor demented soul has had any connection with you in the past, then I can only hope and pray that you will see it in your heart to grant her final wish some priority.

I remain yours, in the name of Our Lord Jesus Christ,

Angelene Denmeade,

Mother Superior – Sisters of Charity.

Upon receiving the letter Hawk makes the messenger boy wait and immediately pens a letter to the Mother Superior thanking her for the information and urging her to give her patient all the medical attention she needs without regard to the costs involved. He adds that she is to be given a private room if such exists and asks Sister Angelene to assure Mary Gibbons that he will visit the hospice that very afternoon. With a penny in his pocket for his trouble and the letter placed under his greasy cap for safekeeping, the lad runs off.

Hawk arrives to discover that Mary Gibbons is once again in a state of delirium. He is to wait almost two days before she recovers sufficiently to see him. He takes lodgings at a bug-ridden boarding house across the road, leaving instructions with the sisters at the hospice that he is to be called at any time during the day or night when she comes out of her delirium.

Close to midnight two days later, Hawk is finally summoned to the bedside of Mary Gibbons. A nun carrying a hurricane lantern leads him through the darkened ward to her bedside. She hangs the lamp on a hook suspended from the ceiling and, without a further word, leaves him alone with Tommo's daughter.

The lantern throws a circle of yellow light over the bed and Hawk sees immediately that the emaciated old hag lying in the bed bears no resemblance whatsoever to the beautiful woman who forsook her two children all those years ago.

But he knows almost at once that it is Hinetitama in the bed. On her face she carries the distinctive *moko* markings of her Ngati Haua tribe and attached to a cheap metal chain about her scrawny neck and resting on the coarse material of her cotton nightgown is Tommo's greenstone Tiki.

Hinetitama is by now fifty-four, though she appears to be at least twenty years older. She has always been small, taking her size from Tommo rather than her Maori ancestors. But now she seems diminutive, a tiny wreck of a woman, her unkempt hair white and her face deeply wrinkled. Her dark eyes are sunk into her skull, though Hawk sees at once that they are clear and follow him closely as he bends over to look into her face. She is toothless and repeatedly smacks her gums together, her once elegant Maori nose and the point of her chin almost touching to give her the appearance of an old crone.

Hinetitama lifts her right hand slightly to acknowledge his approach but it trembles beyond her control and falls back to her side. 'Hello, Uncle Hawk,' she cackles.

'Oh, my dear, what has become of you?' Hawk cries, at once overcome. Tears appear instantly and he reaches for his handkerchief to brush them away. 'Hinetitama, what have I *done* to you!' he cries again in anguish.

'Nuthin', Uncle. I done it all meself. I could never learn t'behave meself. I were always a bad 'un.'

Hawk takes her tiny claw in his hand. Her nails are chipped and broken and while the nuns have scrubbed them clean the brown tobacco stains remain on the first and middle finger of her right hand. 'I searched so hard to find you, how ever did you escape me?'

'Yeah, I know'd that well enough. Always some bugger sniffin' about, askin' questions. Promising rewards.' Her eyes light up and she raises her head from her pillow. Hawk sees there is still a spark of defiance in them. 'But youse didn't get me, did yiz?' She falls back exhausted. 'Nah, it wouldn't'a worked out. It were best I left the young 'uns to you, Uncle. I was never gunna be a good mother t'thum.'

'But, my dear girl, you left everything behind, the most fortunate life. You had so much to live for. Mary's shares made you a wealthy woman. Why did you not come back to claim them?'

Hinetitama sighs. 'Them shares? They's for the brats, had'ta be somethin' good comin' t'them two little 'uns.' She closes her eyes, too exhausted to continue, then in a voice not much above a whisper asks, 'Ow'd they turn out them two?'

Hawk tells her about Ben and Victoria though there is no sign that she is listening or even still conscious. Finally, at the insistence of the nun on night duty, he leaves in the early hours of the morning, with instructions that he is to be called the moment Hinetitama is again lucid.

Over the next week he returns home to dinner each night and leaves soon after, giving Victoria the excuse that he has business which must be conducted at night and continues until too late to return home, which in a sense is the truth. Apart from the occasions when they are allowed to visit Ben, he remains at the boarding house and whenever his niece has an hour or so of clarity he visits her.

Hawk slowly begins to piece together her life, though Hinetitama's mind is too far gone for him to get anything but a sense of her misery and the terribly hard life of a woman who lives rough and cannot get through a day without a black bottle cradled in her arms. To an alcoholic one day is much the same as another, one place as good as another, and the abuse of every kind a poor, drunken woman suffers at the hands of men doesn't alter. She had been abandoned in Cape Town by the nefarious Blackbird Smithers and drifted into a life as a sometime chanteuse, though her drinking made her unreliable as a singer and this soon became a euphemism for practising the oldest profession in the world.

She'd lived in District Six, once the Malay slave quarter, now inhabited by their descendants who had become a mixture of the many races of Africa and were known as Cape Coloureds, a people thought to be neither black nor white and so alienated from either extreme.

District Six is its own private world, in some parts it is still a respectable Muslim community but in others it has become a notorious slum where violence is commonplace and Cape brandy the standard fare for its people. Tucked into a fold on the slopes of Table Mountain, the folk who lived there trusted no authority, kept their own counsel and solved their own problems.

Hinetitama, in the guise of Mary Gibbons, was as safe from discovery and the prying enquiries of any detective under Hawk's instructions as it might be possible had she disappeared into the depths of China. Starting to cough blood and thinking she was dying, she had somehow managed to persuade the captain of a Russian whaling ship bound for Melbourne and thereafter to hunting the whale in the Pacific to give her passage back to Australia.

Gradually Hawk begins to talk to her about her will and makes her see what she must do to ensure her shares in Solomon & Teekleman go to her children. 'It's the one decent thing I done thum,' she says, over and over, 'the one decent thing.'

Hawk tries to persuade her to see Ben and Victoria and tells her that Ben is going off to the war in Europe. But

Hinetitama won't be persuaded. 'Nah, they don't want to see me, an old woman what's a derro. I'd be ashamed meself, them two seein' me like this.' Despite Hawk's pleas she is unmoved, the old stubbornness inherited from Tommo still there.

He'd seen the same wilfulness emerge in the next generation, when Victoria, as a child, would stamp her tiny foot and yell at her nanny, 'I won't and you can't make me!' after which no amount of admonishment or punishment would prevail against her. Now as a young woman Tommo's granddaughter is equally certain of what she believes and, while of an altogether sweet nature, she is not easily dissuaded once she determines upon a course of action.

Ben, thankfully, is too easygoing to get into a bind about almost anything. But with Hinetitama's shares and her proxy safely in his pocket, Hawk knows that the cheerful Ben will not lead the family in the next generation, that he has neither the desire nor the kind of intellect to do so. Victoria, as Mary had claimed from the outset, has the brilliance and the willpower and, yes, the sheer stubbornness required to eventually run Solomon & Teekleman.

Hawk reassures himself that Victoria, with her good looks and the wealth she will bring as her dowry, will find herself a good accommodating husband and that this may somewhat soften her nature. Perhaps she will even marry someone capable of sharing in the running of the giant enterprise Solomon & Teekleman. In the meantime he must keep Abraham as chairman, for he has served the company well and Hawk bears him no animosity, knowing that his demise is entirely the work of David. Even though his father has been retired since the advent of Federation, Abraham is still unable to go against the old man's will.

'What you tell them kids about me?' Hinetitama on one occasion asks him.

Hawk smiles. 'I told them how beautiful you were, a Maori princess, with a voice that could charm the birds out of the sky.'

Hinetitama smiles. 'I could sing good, that's the one thing I had goin' for me.' Then she sighs, 'But the grog and tabacca took it away like everything else.'

Hawk continues, recalling the lovely young girl he once knew. 'I told them how, when I visited you each year in New Zealand, we would go for long walks in the forests and, like your mother, you could imitate the birdsong of every species and that you knew all the names of the trees and the plants of the forest and the flowers in the meadows and along the river banks. How, even at the age of ten, you could set an eel trap or weave a flax mat or a fruit basket and cook me a nice fish dinner.' Hawk sighs. 'You were an enchanted child, Hinetitama, always singing and laughing and up to some sort of mischief.'

'What you tell them, the brats, why I left them, hey?' Hinetitama asks suddenly.

'I said that you were a songbird and couldn't stay in one place for long, that you wanted to sing to all the world and that, with some people, it is wrong to try to clip their wings and keep them in a cage.'

Hinetitama squints up at him. 'And they bought that shit!'

Hawk laughs. 'At first, when they were kids. Later they just accepted you were gone from their lives.'

Hawk did not tell her that when Ben and Victoria grew older and asked him about their mother he had been forced to tell them the truth, that she was wild and wilful and drinking heavily and simply couldn't abide the constraints placed upon her in the narrow Hobart society. That Victoria, in particular, is not the sort who can be fobbed off with a fairytale forever. He thinks how sometimes, much to his embarrassment, she says to him, 'Now I want the truth, Grandpa Hawk. Don't tell me any cock-and-bull story!'

Hinetitama smiles wistfully as Hawk talks, then she sighs and says, 'Let it be, Uncle. Let them think of me like what you said. I could sing too,' she repeats. 'It was the one thing I done good.'

She attempts to sit up, struggling to get her head off the pillow, but she lacks the strength and Hawk calls to a nun for help. The nun brings Hinetitama to a seated position in the bed and continues to prop her upright as there are no pillows with which to do so.

'What is it, dearie?' the nun asks.

Hinetitama doesn't reply and Hawk watches as she slowly brings her hand up to her neck, her trembling fingers plucking at the skin, searching for the chain which hangs about it. Finally she locates it and pulls at it to reveal Tommo's little green Tiki from under her nightdress.

'Take it, give it to the boy. Gawd knows it's done me no good, but it's kept me alive, I suppose that's something, eh? Maybe it'll do the same for him. I wore it 'cause me daddy left it to me, but a Tiki is not a thing for a woman to wear.' She touches the little green idol. 'Take it off, Sister,' then looking up at Hawk she repeats, 'Give it to the boy. Tell him it were his grandfather's and now it's his own good luck.'

Now, standing in Spring Street amongst the cheering crowd waiting for Ben's platoon to march past, Hawk decides not to tell Victoria about finding her mother. The gift of the Tiki amulet has taken place two days before the parade by special permission of Ben's company commander Major Sayers. Ben is expecting to return to Tasmania to rejoin his regiment as soon as possible after the passing-out parade and they may not otherwise have been given the opportunity to say their goodbyes to him.

Ben has completed his special weapons training course which involves in the main the Vickers machine gun, but he has, as well, been trained in the machine guns of the Allies, those of the Japanese, the Belgian Browning and the French Hotchkiss. He has acquitted himself well and has also during his time taken control of training a platoon at Broadmeadows and Major Sayers has made it known that he is most reluctant to lose him.

'It was your grandfather's, Ben,' Hawk says hesitantly, not knowing how Ben will take the gift of the Tiki, perhaps thinking it is a piece of jewellery a milksop might wear. 'I want you to wear it and never take it off.' He doesn't explain any further and Ben, somewhat bemused, puts the Tiki about his neck.

'Dunno if they'll allow me to wear it, Grandpa,' he says a little sheepishly.

Victoria laughs at her brother's apparent chagrin. 'Oh, but it's so handsome!' She steps closer to her brother and takes the Tiki in her hand. 'It's a fat little man, such a pretty green colour too.'

'It's the Maori God, Tiki, the creator of life and, as he is said to have created all life, he is opposed to killing. It was given to Tommo by the *tohunga*, the Maori priests, who first asked the permission of the ancestors, it will protect you,' Hawk says.

'I should so like one just like it,' she exclaims. 'If it belonged to our grandfather it's bound to be good luck, you must wear it always, Ben!'

Hawk laughs. 'It is not an amulet to be worn by a woman, Victoria. Tiki is sometimes thought to be the creation of Tane, a female God, who some say was the real creator of life and that Tiki is the male,' he clears his throat, 'er . . . penis.'

217

Victoria blushes, but then quickly recovers. 'So that's where all the trouble started, is it?'

Now holding Victoria's hand in the crowd, Hawk thinks back on Victoria's innocent remark that the Tiki was bound to bring good luck. Good luck was never a commodity in abundance in Tommo's life, nor in his own, for that matter. With the melancholy he feels at Ben's leaving he begins to reflect on how almost everything he seems to have attempted has, in some way or another, failed or, at the very least, been a source of bitter disappointment to him. He has tried to be a good and honest man, yet those he loved the most he seems to have let down.

He thinks about his beloved twin, Tommo, and of his failure to rescue him when he returned from the Wilderness, tormented, mistrustful and broken in spirit. A fourteen-year-old drunk, mortally afraid of the mongrels, the spectre of whom continued to haunt him all his life, until finally he chopped off their collective heads in one horrific incident when he avenged the death of Maggie Pye.

With Hinetitama's proxy votes now in his possession, this one thing at least Hawk thinks he may be able to rectify. That is, if he should live sufficiently long to train Victoria to take control of Solomon & Teekleman, with Ben there to support her against Joshua, who has always believed that he will inherit the vast conglomerate.

A sense of overwhelming panic suddenly grips him. If Ben does not return what will happen to his beloved granddaughter, Victoria? She has none of the cunning or the guile or even the knowledge to survive against Hannah Solomon's rapacious descendants.

Hawk knows with a deep certainty that David's side, even with the evil old man gone, will somehow contrive to crush Victoria, to steal what Mary Abacus and he have left her. Hawk can barely embrace the thought of this final failure. He suddenly feels older, much older, than the seventy-three years he has lived. His free hand moves to the inside pocket of his linen jacket and his fingers touch Hinetitama's last will and testament. 'Oh God, please let me be doing the right thing this time,' he groans to himself.

Ben's platoon is suddenly upon them and Victoria squeals with delight when Ben, instead of his head and eyes directed to the right in a salute to the general, has turned them towards Victoria and Hawk. And, while his hand has been brought up to slap his rifle stock in the traditional salute, his thumb wiggles in a gesture of recognition and there is a great grin on his gob.

A month after the parade they will go down to Port Melbourne to see him sailing off to King George Sound at Albany, Western Australia, prior to departing overseas in a convoy, but Victoria will ever remember this moment with the band playing 'Sons of Australia' and her brother's thumb saluting them.

Victoria delights in the sight of her brother, the ever cheerful, ever optimistic Ben, marching off to war to put the Germans in their place. She is suddenly aware of being lifted, as Hawk, ignoring propriety, grips her under the arms and raises her high above the crowd so that she might be clearly seen by her darling brother.

After the passing-out parade they are unable to find a hansom cab or, an even rarer commodity, a motor-driven taxi cab, and so return home in the tram where they are packed like sardines in a can with weary folk, their damp clothes steaming in the hot tramcar, carrying sleeping children, returning from the parade. Hawk must bend his head awkwardly to avoid bumping it against the roof and he is grateful when at last they arrive at their stop and are able to walk the short distance to their home.

Victoria, who has hardly spoken a word on the short walk home from the tram stop, pleads a headache from the passing-out parade and goes directly to her room. After the excitement of the parade she is suddenly deeply depressed at the prospect of losing her brother without knowing when or whether she will ever see him again.

A short while later, Hawk, thinking to ask her if she'd care for a cup of tea, pauses at her bedroom door and then turns back at the sound of the broken-hearted sobbing coming from within. Somewhat heavy-hearted himself he retires to his study where shortly afterwards Martha Billings, his housekeeper, comes to inform him that a lad has arrived from the hospice and presents him with the letter the boy has delivered.

'Will there be a reply? Shall I keep the boy waitin', sir?' she asks.

Hawk nods, tearing open the envelope absently. 'Make him a sandwich, Mrs Billings, and give him a cuppa tea. If he's the same lad as before he'll take some filling, he's a lanky lad but thin as a rake.'

'They all looks the same ter me, dirty, smelly and cheeky and always bleedin' 'ungry!' Mrs Billings says. Then ignoring the fact that Hawk is now reading the letter she continues, 'Will you and Miss Victoria be in to tea?' Again she doesn't wait for a reply. 'There's only cold cuts, mind. What with all them going off in the parade, Mr McCarthy's son, Johnny, like our Ben, is also off to fight the Germans. So, without so much as by your leave, he closes the butcher shop and trots off in his Sunday best to see him march in front o' the bloomin' Governor hisself.'

'That's all right, Mrs Billings, cold cuts with a bit of mustard pickle will be just fine.'

'It's not my fault you ain't got a nice roast tonight. Wait 'til I see 'im, I'll give him a piece o' me mind!'

Hawk completes reading the letter and looks up at the old family retainer he inherited from Mary and then from Ann Solomon. Martha Billings is one of the many children Mary rescued from the orphan school and employed. Although young Billings was no different to most of them, hungry with a cough and perpetually running nose, Mary started her in the home and not the brewery. She commenced her employment as a scullery maid and finally, when Mrs Briggs passed on, took over as Hawk's cook. A year later Ann died and Hawk, who could not bear to remain in Hobart with the Potato Factory no longer under his control, brought the plump and perpetually prattling, always complaining Mrs Billings as cook and housekeeper to Melbourne.

As far as Hawk knew Martha Billings had always been a spinster, but Mary, who refused to have a butler, insisted that a cook needed authority over the other servants, and so ought to be a Mrs. She simply expunged Mrs Briggs' spinsterhood. Hawk assumed that Martha Billings had continued this tradition and he never questioned her about her marital status.

Over time Mrs Billings has become so accustomed to this gratuitous addition that whenever she feels sorry for herself, which is frequently, she thinks of herself as a poor widow.

At such times, the man in her imagination is Mortimer, a partner of fanciful character who combines humour, manliness, morals, conscience and kindness with generosity, intelligence and a religious conviction. All of these attributes are of such a high standard that they are well beyond the aspirations of any male who ever lived.

This proves to be a good thing, for Mrs Billings has very little admiration for the living members of the opposite sex who, as far as she is concerned, spill food on the damask table linen and walk into her parlour with mud on their boots. Both crimes are in her mind worthy of the severest whipping if not a lot worse.

Careful not to be seen as potty by her peer group she only talks about her phantasmagorical husband to Sardine, a tabby of no particular breeding, who sleeps eighteen hours a day and will only eat minced lamb and gravy or a nice bit of raw snapper. That is, if she can wheedle a fresh one out of Cox the fishmonger whom she trusts about as far as she can throw one of the sharks, the flesh of which she suspects he substitutes for blue cod.

She has lately taken up seeing a part-time clairvoyant, an Irish woman who calls herself Princess Salome, her alter ego when she's practising her gift of 'the sight', but in the daily domestic answers to the name of Mrs Brigitte Maloney and works as a filleter at the fish markets.

Brigitte Maloney, alias Princess Salome, told Mrs Billings about Cox's shark substitution and so won her trust forever. That, and the fact that Princess Salome demanded the head of John the Baptist on a platter and so obviously shared her deep distrust of men. She could quite clearly imagine John the Baptist coming in from the desert, filthy dirty, his great clodhoppers traipsing dirt around the palace and spilling his food all over King Herod's clean tablecloth. A beheading was a small price to pay in Mrs Billings' estimation.

Mrs Billings is invited by Brigitte Maloney to a free trial seance and when asked about her marital status finds herself forced to admit to being a widow, the alternative untruth being that her husband has abandoned her, an idea which her pride will simply not permit. In no time at all she is in touch with the saintlike Mortimer.

While Mrs Billings greatly enjoys these visitations from the other world her conscience eventually demands that she confess his non-existence to Brigitte Maloney, whereupon the Princess Salome becomes quite angry with

222

her. 'Mrs Billings, can you not see that you were married in another life?' Brigitte Maloney does not wait for an answer from the bemused Mrs Billings. 'So great was your love that no other man, no matter how many lives you may live, can take your dearest Mortimer's place. Perfect love, my dear, is what every woman desires.' She pauses, breathing heavily. 'And perfect love is what you've had!' Now she slaps her hands hard against her cheeks, 'You have had the love of a man who has not been tarnished by life in this mortal world!' The thought is all at once too much for her and she abandons the voice of Princess Salome and begins to talk in her normal voice, 'Oh me Gawd! No comin' 'ome pissed as a newt, no Saterdee night leg over, no chunder on the parlour carpet, no gettin' a backhand when you done nothin' to deserve it, no farting in bed, no gamblin' his wages on John Wren's pony track at Richmond, no bleedin' fist fights!' Then, suddenly remembering her other persona, Princess Salome turns to Mrs Billings. 'You have had a marriage made by God in heaven itself, my dear.'

Hawk has long since ceased to listen to Mrs Billings' prattle. His housekeeper is simply a part of the background noise. Only Victoria can tell her to hush, for it is a toss-up between Sardine the cat and the young mistress as to whom Martha Billings loves the most among the living creatures of this earth.

'It's not that I didn't try, Friday is always a roast,' Mrs Billings persists. 'The tram, by the time it come to our stop, was that full with folks going to the parade it just sailed right past, never mind a poor soul waiting in the cold. I thinks to meself, I might go into town, try that new butcher in Lygon Street, the I-talian. Fat chance! After four trams pass me by without so much as 'ow's yer father, I come 'ome bothered and all f'nothing, me basket empty as a curate's purse. There's no tellin' what's gunna happen next. Mrs Maloney from the fish markets says there's already talk of rationing and doing without!'

Hawk, oblivious to Mrs Billings' prattling, now says, 'Miss Victoria is not to be disturbed. If she's hungry she'll get something for herself later.' He instructs without looking up.

'I'll leave her a nice plate, poor little mite's 'ad a long day of it, all that marching and drums, them horses clopping, boats sailing off.'

The letter Hawk holds is from Sister Angelene to say that Hinetitama is dying and that they don't expect she'll last through the night. It asks if she is a Catholic and whether they should have Father Crosby come around especially to hear her confession.

Hawk, who is dog-tired from the long day, is somewhat confused by this and wonders why Hinetitama, in her lucid moments, hasn't told them herself. He'd left her religious instruction to Chief Wiremu Tamihana, who was educated by the missionaries though never himself became a Christian. Not too impressed with the pakeha God, his old friend probably brought Tommo's daughter up in the Maori way with their pantheon of Gods.

The note concludes by asking him if he wishes to be at Hinetitama's bedside as a comfort to her in her final hours.

Mrs Billings has turned at last and is on her way back to the kitchen when Hawk looks up. 'On second thoughts I won't stop for tea. Will you make me a couple of the same sandwiches you made for the lad?'

Mrs Billings stops and turns, one eyebrow raised in indignant surprise. 'Oh you wouldn't eat what I gives 'im, sir! That's scrag ends o' mutton and yesterday's bread. I'll not be wasting good meat and pickles on the likes o' a poor brat like that!'

'The same for me, if you please, Mrs Billings,' Hawk

224

quietly scolds her, 'I'm sure he's as fond of cold roast beef and mustard pickle as I am.'

'Doubt he's ever 'ad it,' his housekeeper sniffs.

Hawk fans himself absently with the letter he is holding. 'Oh, and tell the lad to wait, he can come with me to St Kilda. There's no need for Brock to bring the motor, we'll take a taxi. Will you please telephone the taxi depot for one and have him waiting.'

Mrs Billings, not at all happy to have been reprimanded, sniffs again. 'Blimey, you'd think it was the boy what's had a bad day.'

In the taxi cab on the way to the hospice Hawk unwraps the sandwiches Mrs Billings has made for him and starts to eat one, expecting the boy to do the same. But the lad continues to hug the parcel of bread and meat he carries to his chest.

'Not hungry then?' Hawk asks.

The lad shakes his head. 'No, mister.'

Hawk smiles. 'You haven't given me your name.' He extends his hand. 'I'm Hawk Solomon.'

'I know,' the urchin says. 'You the biggest nigger in the world!'

Hawk laughs. 'Maybe. In my experience there's always someone who's bigger, smarter, faster, more cunning or more skilled, son.' He takes a second bite from his sandwich and chews it awhile, thinking as he does so that Mrs Billings makes a nice mustard pickle. 'Well, what's the big secret?' he finally asks. 'You know my name, you keeping yours to yourself then, lad?'

'Billyboysmith, mister.'

'Not mister! We've already been introduced, it's Mr Solomon if you please, Mr Smith,' Hawk laughs.

'Billyboysmith,' the urchin says quickly.

'Yes, that's what you said, Billyboy.'

'No I ain't, I said Billyboysmith, it's all together like.'

'Billyboysmith, all one word? Not two, like Billyboy,' Hawk pauses and then says, 'and Smith?'

'Nuh, me mum says it's Billyboysmith because she says that's the bloke she thinks she 'ad me with if she remembers correk.'

'Well, well, now, I don't suppose I'll forget that in a hurry, Mr Billyboysmith,' Hawk says, amused.

'Yessir,' Billyboysmith says, then quickly adds, 'Mr Solomon.'

Hawk finds himself liking the urchin who has tucked himself into the corner of the taxi cab. He is tall himself, a bag of rag and bones, lanky and awkward, and he knows he doesn't belong and is trying to give the giant Hawk as much space as he can so as not to be a nuisance. Hawk realises that there is nothing about the exchange they've just been through which suggests the boy is a smart alec. He likes the way Billyboysmith has stood up for his correct name.

'Got any brothers and sisters?' Hawk asks between another mouthful.

The boy places his sandwiches on his lap and thinks for a moment, then slowly begins counting on his fingers, his lips moving. Finally he nods, satisfied, and holds up both hands with only the thumb of his left hand concealed.

'Nine! Six girls and three boys.'

'Nine?' Hawk says in surprise.

The boy nods again and grins. 'We got one in the oven, there's gunna be ten of us soon.'

'All hungry I expect. Your father working?'

The boy shakes his head. 'He done a runner. They don't stay long them uncles. They gets me mum with a bun then they piss orf. Me mum does washin' fer the nuns, at the 'ospice.'

'It's not much to keep body and soul together, nine mouths to feed and one on the way.'

'We all does our bit,' Billyboysmith says proudly, then adds gratuitously, 'Every time we gets another one me mum says, "Bugger me dead, where'd that one come from?" and then we all got to remember what "uncle" it were so we can put his name onto the baby's name.'

Hawk throws back his head and laughs. 'You mean all nine have a different father, a different surname?'

Billyboysmith grins. 'One o' me sisters is called Gertiebell, that works good, but another one,' he brings a grubby hand up to his mouth trying to conceal his mirth, 'she's called Nellypoop.' He giggles, 'We calls her Smellypoop!'

'Billyboysmith and Gertiebell and Smelly . . .' Hawk laughs again and waves his hand in a gesture of dismissal. 'Billyboysmith, not *Bully*boysmith I hope?'

'No, sir, Mr Solomon, I ain't no bully.' He pauses. 'But I don't take no shit neither, I can fight if I 'as to.'

'And what is it you want to do when you're older?' Hawk asks.

'Same as everyone, fight the Germans.'

'How old are you, Billyboysmith?'

'Fourteen, sir, Mr Solomon.'

'I daresay it will be all over by the time you're old enough to volunteer, lad.'

'It ain't fair, I'd be good at killing Germans an' all, I ain't frightened of no one.'

'Count yourself fortunate, lad, killing isn't a pleasant business.'

Billyboysmith looks confused. 'I'd be doing it for our King and for England, that's good, ain't it?'

Hawk smiles, not wanting to give Billyboysmith a lecture on the morality of man's propensity to kill one another.

'Some say I look eighteen and could join up. You get five bob a day, they says.'

227

'Take my advice Billyboysmith and sit this one out,' Hawk says quietly. He still has two of Mrs Billings' sandwiches and almost half of a third. He lifts the open parcel from his lap and offers it to the urchin. 'Here, Billyboysmith, I'm not a bit hungry, tuck in, mate.'

Billyboysmith's eyes grow large and he puts his own packet of sandwiches on his lap and snatches the parcel from Hawk's hands and places it on his lap beside his own. He takes the half-eaten sandwich in both hands and, bringing it up, tears voraciously at it with his teeth. It is as if he hasn't eaten for a couple of days and, in his haste to get the bread and meat down, he barely chews before swallowing. The half-sandwich gone he looks longingly at the two remaining, then sighs and rewraps them carefully and places the parcel on his lap beside the other. Billyboysmith pushes his thin body back into the corner of the cab and, taking up both parcels of meat and bread, he clutches them tightly to his scrawny little chest.

Upon his arrival at the hospice Hawk hands Billyboysmith a sixpence. Billy has to put the two packages down to accept. 'Gee thanks, mister!' he exclaims in wide-eyed surprise, looking at the small silver coin in his hand as though not quite believing his luck.

Hawk sighs in an exaggerated manner. '*Mr Solomon*, if you please, *Mister* Billyboysmith.'

'Ain't I supposed to be "master"? Master Billyboysmith. I ain't grow'd up yet, though I could be eighteen if I wanted.' Billyboysmith pockets the coin and snatching up the two parcels jumps from the cab. 'Cheer'o, sir . . . er, Mr, uh . . . Solomon,' he teases cheekily.

Hawk calls after him. 'What's your mother's name, son?'

Billyboysmith stops and turns to face Hawk, who is having trouble squeezing his huge frame through the door of the cab. 'It's Miss O'Shea.'

'Miss?' Hawk says surprised, then repeats, 'Miss O'Shea, so what's your surname then?'

Billyboysmith nods. 'I'm Billyboysmith O'Shea. She ain't never been married, so she's just Miss Therese O'Shea, sir, Mr Solomon.' He grins. 'It don't make Father Crosby too happy neither. But me mum says she's buggered if she's gunna have a bunch o' bastard kids from only one bastard so's they grows up to be identical drunks the each as stupid as the other, thank you very much, but no thanks!'

'Billyboysmith, you'd better come and see me next week, see if we can find you a job,' Hawk says.

'Yessir! Thank you, sir . . . er, Mr Solomon, sir,' Billyboysmith stammers, this time overcome, and runs off. 'Goodbye, sir,' he shouts from the darkness beyond the street lamp.

Hawk thinks how he has deliberately preoccupied himself with Billyboysmith so that he will not sink into a slough of despondency. But now he prepares himself for the vigil ahead in the little hospice where Tommo's daughter lies dying.

A week earlier he had ordered a lead-lined coffin of a most impressive nature from John Allison, the city's prestigious funeral parlour, and had instructed that it must be properly sealed for travel and its solid silver handles and other 'furnishings' remain intact and were not to be removed. On the lid he had requested a polished silver plaque to be inscribed:

PRINCESS HINETITAMA,
A DAUGHTER OF THE MAORI PEOPLE

He rings the night bell and then enters the vestibule of the hospice, which, much to his surprise, is lit by a lantern hanging from the ceiling. He sees that Hinetitama's coffin stands ready within it, supported by a carpenter's horse at either end. In the dozens of times he has visited the hospice at night he has never seen a light or a coffin in this entrance, yet death, he knows, is a daily occurrence. The Sisters of Charity are simply too poor to afford to maintain a lantern which has no practical use.

Then it suddenly strikes Hawk that the nuns have put the coffin on display to show off its grandness, to give an air of dignity to their hospice. Death is such a poverty-stricken business here that Hinetitama's coffin lends them all prestige, and even, by their terms, grandeur, an object to brighten their selfless lives. A nun arrives carrying a candle and Hawk is ushered into the hospice ward.

The ward is in almost total darkness but for the candle she carries and a hurricane lamp suspended from the ceiling hook above where he knows Hinetitama's bed to be located. The lamp throws a pale yellow circle of light which extends to include a chair the nuns have placed beside the bed for Hawk's vigil. The night sister bids him a whispered goodnight and retires to return to her cubicle, leaving the remainder of the ward in stygian darkness.

It is a darkness filled with the sounds of the dying. Every once in a while there is a scream or howl from some unfortunate caught in the hallucinatory grip of the DT's. The air around the bed smells of Jeye's Fluid, a common disinfectant, though it is mixed with the smoky oleaginous smell of the kerosene lamp. Permeating everything is the insidious, sweet, slightly putrid smell of death.

There are fifteen beds in the ward, some of which Father Crosby has visited before nightfall. These are the Catholics, selected by the nuns earlier in the day for absolution, the dying who are not expected to last through the night.

If these poor souls believe that, with their sins

confessed and absolution granted, a merciful God will yet save them from the fires of hell, then the others among the dying must feel that Hawk's huge black presence caught, as it is, in the circle of light, can only be a visitation from the devil himself.

The sense of panic and the sounds of fear palpably increase in the darkness around Hawk as they catch a glimpse of the King of Hades, whose white hair and great dark satanic head almost brush the ceiling as he enters and upon whose terrible face, lit by the light of the nun's candle, can plainly be seen the scratch marks of God's wrath. The Devil has come to take one of their kind, but they know that they too will soon enough follow, to be drawn down to where they will be embraced in a halo of light caused by the eternally roaring flames of hell.

Hawk seats himself in the chair beside the bed and takes Hinetitama's tiny clawlike hand in his own. 'How you going, girlie?' he asks softly.

Hinetitama is too weak to reply but Hawk can feel the slightest pressure of her fingers as she acknowledges him. He knows suddenly that she has waited for him to come, fought to keep death at bay until he arrived. He leans forward and says into her ear, 'I told them you were Maori, girlie. Not Catholic or Protestant, Maori, from a tribe that's proud to claim you as their daughter and a princess in your own right with Gods of your own.'

Hawk pauses, trying to fight back his tears and to keep his voice even. 'Because, you see, girlie, we're taking you back to where you belong. Back to Aotearoa, among the giant kauri trees that sweep the skies and brush the howling wind to a whisper in the forest canopy. Back where your spirit will walk through the flowering meadows and listen to the running of clean water over pebbles kissed smooth by a million years of passing by.

'My sweet Hinetitama, I'm taking you back to bury

you with your own people, near where little Tommo sits sleeping in a cave which faces the sunrise.' Hawk gulps back his tears, his voice choked as he continues, 'You'll sing to him all the songs that only a Maori princess may sing. Your voice will be in the sigh of the wind, contained in the mountain echoes, it will become the soft murmur of the runnels made from the melting snow and be heard in the sudden rushing sound of a late afternoon breeze bending the flax grass. We're taking you back, back to your beloved people, where you belong, my little Maori maiden, my beautiful princess.'

Hawk feels Hinetitama's grip loosen and she gives a soft sigh and the tremors in her hands stop forever. The nightmare is over, Hinetitama has gone to join Tommo in The Land of the Long White Cloud.

Chapter Seven

HAWK AND DAVID –
A FIGHT TO THE DEATH

Melbourne 1914

Hawk leaves the hospice in the early hours of the morning of Hinetitama's death. He has had some weeks to reconcile himself to its inevitability and his tears are now turned inward. Even as a poor wretch, ravaged by years of abuse, Hinetitama remained an innocent, with a heart that never seemed to have hardened to a world of grog and the life of a derro. Hawk tries to console himself with the knowledge that she died aware there was someone who loved and cared about her. After placing his large hand on her brow, Hawk rises wearily from her bedside, his heart heavy, his bones aching. 'Tommo, I let you down, I'm sorry, I'm truly sorry, mate,' he whispers. For the first time in his life he feels old. 'Why,' he thinks to himself, 'must I live to see everyone I love die before me?'

He startles the night sister almost out of her wits by handing her a cheque with the words, 'There is more than sufficient in this to install an electric light system, Sister Brigid.' The Irish nun glances down at the piece of paper in her hands, it is for a larger sum than she's ever seen, larger even than the amounts whispered in the most ardent prayers Mother Superior has urged them to address to the Lord to supply their needs.

'Oh my goodness!' she gasps, holding the cheque to her rapidly palpitating heart. 'Mercy be, to be sure, I shall faint.'

Hawk reaches into his purse and takes out a five pound note. 'I would be most obliged if you would see that my niece is dressed in a new cotton nightgown.' He pauses, then adds a little sheepishly, 'Her hair is still beautiful, will you see that it is washed and brushed? I should like it to hang over her shoulders, over the front, like?'

The nun nods her head, still holding the cheque clasped to her bosom. 'I'm . . . I'm sure that will be a pleasure, s-sir,' she stammers. 'To be sure, I shall see to it meself.'

Hawk places the money on the desk beside the nun. 'Thank you, Sister, I shall make arrangements for the casket.'

Sister Brigid, now somewhat recovered, says, 'You'll be wanting to see Mother Superior before you're to be going now. I shall call her if you'll wait a moment?'

'No, no, Sister, it is just past dawn, you're not to wake her.'

The Irish nun looks surprised. 'Wake her? She'll be up having said her rosary and scrubbed her cell. She'll not be lying abed, you can be sure of that now.'

'No, really, Sister. I crave your indulgence. It's been a long night. I shall visit at another time to pay my respects to Sister Angelene and to Father Crosby. In the meantime would you thank her for the loving care you have shown.' Hawk bows his head slightly. 'I am most grateful to you all.'

The nun, still clutching Hawk's cheque, afraid to place it down, smiles and stoops to look through the slot in her cubicle, which looks into the ward just beginning to be tinged with the light of a new day. 'Electric lights? What a grand thing that will be.'

Hawk decides to walk home to Caulfield, a journey on foot of nearly an hour. He has a great deal to think about and sets off at a brisk pace. The sun rises soon after his departure and he removes his jacket, but it is not long before the sweat runs down his neck and he can feel his starched collar grow damp. It is a small enough risk that anyone who may know him will see him, or even be up and about at such an early hour and so he removes his weskit as well and loosens his tie. Comfortable in his linen shirt and braces, he strides onwards.

In the weeks preceding Hinetitama's death, Hawk has done a great deal of thinking about what he should do about Solomon & Teekleman now that he once again controls a majority of its shares. He has kept the knowledge of Hinetitama's reappearance from both Ben and Victoria at Hinetitama's request, but Victoria will want to know how he managed to regain control of the shares. He decides he must tell her and risk her anger at not being allowed to see Hinetitama before she died. More importantly, he is not sure how he will explain the situation in which they now find themselves.

Victoria has never been told of his aspirations for her to succeed him and, increasingly, she is being drawn to the Labor Party and sees her ultimate career in the law as a means to help the poor and the working classes. Hawk is not convinced that she will happily take to the proposition of one day running a huge organisation dedicated to making money for the already vastly wealthy.

She has, of course, some years previously asked him why her surname is included in the company name. He replied that he thought Solomon & Teekleman was a name which constantly reminded everyone of the enmity between the two families, that one day she and Ben would own a large shareholding in the company and it seemed appropriate that their surname be included in it. Victoria had accepted this explanation at the time but she has on more than one occasion suggested that Hawk, at the annual meeting of shareholders, propose that the name be dropped and they sell their shares to Abraham and Joshua.

'Grandpa, I am ashamed of it! People look at me when I'm introduced and say "*The* Teekleman?", some because they are impressed and others because they despise what the name stands for. Either way I am ashamed to be associated with it, to be a shareholder!'

Hawk has always resisted both requests, putting it down to youthful idealism that will modify as Victoria grows older and becomes involved with the company. But he also knows how stubborn she can be. Now that he is potentially back in control of Solomon & Teekleman he may not be able to effectively manage it. He realises that his eventual ambitions for Victoria may be impossible to accomplish and that he, or rather circumstances, have conspired to leave his run too late.

Sir Abraham Solomon and his stewardship, though not spectacular, have been steady and he has done nothing to harm the profitability of the two giant companies under the Solomon & Teekleman banner. The times have been prosperous and both have simply continued to grow, finding opportunities to expand without having to seek them out and at very little financial or decision-taking risk.

Hawk is well versed in the affairs of Solomon & Teekleman, but only as a shareholder. He has been absent from the helm for more than two decades and is sufficiently astute to realise that he knows little of the internal workings of the two companies and may no longer be the right man for chairman. Or even if he is, Abraham Solomon would almost certainly retire if he attempted to take over, leaving him alone to organise the affairs of the conglomerate.

Tom Pickles, who is the managing director of the Potato Factory, has requested early retirement. Pickles, a veteran of the Boer War, was wounded at Spion Kop and now has only one lung working effectively, a condition which is exacerbated by the inclement and unpredictable Hobart weather and a childhood spent in an orphanage where, like most of the children, he showed a propensity for bronchial ailments.

Pickles started his working life as one of Mary's orphans and soon proved to be a cut above the usual lad or lass brought into an apprenticeship at the brewery so that Mary picked him early for better things and trained him to accountancy. He had risen to assistant manager of the accounts department when he enlisted for the Boer War, where he was mentioned in dispatches. He returned to the Potato Factory a war hero and resumed his previous job. With Mary dead and Hawk replaced by Abraham, he soon again showed his original promise and was appointed as the manager of the accounts department. When David retired, Abraham elevated Pickles to the position of managing director so that he himself could assume the title of chairman of Solomon & Teekleman.

Pickles has served the company well but, increasingly, is plagued by chronic bronchitis. The doctor has advised him to move to a more equable climate and has suggested Queensland. It is proposed that Wilfred Harrington, the managing director of Solomon & Co., take his place in Hobart and that Joshua, having completed a year of learning the ropes, be given the same position at Solomon & Co. A neat enough arrangement had it not been for the outbreak of war.

Hawk now thinks that it may be possible to broker a

compromise. He will agree to leave Abraham as chairman and, upon his return from the war, allow Joshua to take up his position as M.D. of Solomon & Co., in return for the vacant position of managing director of the Potato Factory and a position for Victoria as a trainee under Hawk's direction.

This is not altogether wishful thinking. Hawk has some reason to believe it might be acceptable. Abraham doesn't share David's pathological hate for Hawk, and has hinted that he would be willing for him to return as the managing director of the Potato Factory under his chairmanship, but only after David has passed on. Hawk has never pursued this idea, thinking it prudent to wait until David is dead.

However, they badly underestimated David's tenacity and physical toughness. He did not retire for lack of strength or the will to continue, but for the singular purpose of training the fifteen-year-old Joshua to take control of Solomon & Teekleman. Obsessed with this mission he has managed to live through his grandson's puberty and into his adulthood. David at ninety-four is still a force to be reckoned with, though recently he has spoken of seeing Joshua take up his rightful role in the company and, then, in his own words, 'Carking it, being rid of you miserable bloody lot once and for all!'

But just when all seemed in place, with Joshua back from Oxford and having almost completed his mandatory year learning the practical aspects of running Solomon & Co., war is declared in Europe.

David is mortified, instantly flying into one of his infamous tantrums. Lacking the strength to break things with an axe, he demands to be wheeled into the kitchen and has the kitchen maid bring him every plate, cup and saucer in the house and stack them beside his wheelchair. Then, hammer in hand, he has Adams, the butler, read the underside of each plate or piece of crockery to determine its origin. Those pieces made in England, France or Germany he smashes. In the first hour after he has been told of the declaration of war David renders a small fortune in Royal Doulton, Wedgwood, Limoges and Rosenthal as well as a dozen manufacturers of lesser fame into a colourful sea of broken crockery that covers the entire surface of the kitchen floor. Exhausted, he is put to bed mumbling obscenities and the doctor is called. The doctor warns him that another such conniption could bring on a heart attack, to which David shouts, 'Piss off, what would you know, you stupid old fart!'

David takes the declaration of war personally. He sees it as a part of the long-standing persecution he has received at the hands of Mother England. Just another part of the personal vendetta she has waged against him all his life. He tells himself that because of his advanced age she is taking this final opportunity to put the boot in. The first time she got her claws into him was when she'd transported his mother and their little family to the utmost ends of the earth. Now she would see him dead and buried before Joshua assumes his rightful inheritance, she would rob him of this one great ambition and see him die without achieving it. David knows from the moment war is declared that not even he will be able to dissuade Joshua from volunteering to fight for the old whore.

While at Oxford Joshua has trained in the OTC, the Oxford University Officer Training Corps, under the direction of the Royal Oxfordshire Regiment. Now he is raring to return to the grand sport offered by a proper war. He has often enough hinted to his grandfather that had he not been trained to commerce he would have liked the life of a professional soldier. It is a prospect totally abhorrent to his grandfather and one of the very few things that has come between the two of them. David's intention in sending Joshua to Oxford was simply so that he might gain all the social contacts and background he would need as the head of an industrial empire. David knew that Joshua was unlikely to do anything of academic note and thought to sneak his grandson in and out of Oxford without Mother England realising he was there, a colonial son making so little impression that the old bitch hardly noticed his presence. But she'd known all along of his whereabouts and promptly set about corrupting his mind with military gung-ho and carry-on.

David has over the years made generous donations to causes serving the interests of both the conservative and the radical sides of local politics and, by sheer attrition and the ultimate size of the accumulated donations, gained a knighthood for Abraham. Like everything else about his son, in his father's mind Abraham's title is intended to bolster Joshua's credentials, the gentile son of a Jew is a difficult concept to grasp but, in David's mind, the son of a knight of the realm, who coincidently happens to be of the Jewish faith, is quite a different perception and will help to bolster his grandson's credentials as a bona fide gentile.

Joshua, ever dutiful, has enhanced this claim to respectability whilst at Oxford by becoming a surrogate Englishman, a complete Anglophile, adopting the mannerisms and attitudes of the English upper class. While at university he has managed to perfect a set of rounded vowels to match his new-found affectations. The ultimate irony is that David's grandson now considers it his patriotic duty to fight for the country for which his grandfather retains only the bitterest memories and feels the greatest antipathy.

Hawk thinks the miserable old bastard will somehow contrive to keep himself alive until Joshua returns from the war and is seen to fulfil his grandfather's ambition.

He knows also that Abraham is unlikely to agree to his conditions while David is alive and that it is the ninety-four-year-old whom he must convince, a task which he knows will be formidable.

The certain ascendancy of Joshua to chairman has also been a problem preoccupying Hawk for some years. He has never given up the idea of Victoria usurping him for the same position. Even before Hinetitama reappeared, under the terms of Mary's will Ben and Victoria resume control of their ten per cent of the company shares when Victoria becomes thirty, by which time, unbeknownst to David and Abraham, Hawk's side will again own the majority of shares.

Hawk knows that, with his increasing age, Victoria is his only real hope of getting Solomon & Teekleman back under the control of his side of the family. Ben is essentially an outdoors man and his bum sits more comfortably in the saddle than on an office chair. Although he seems to attract the co-operation of those around him, his is a leadership by example and not out of a sense of being superior.

This lack of ambition in Ben has also been apparent to David and Abraham, both of whom have secretly kept a watchful eye on the young man as he was growing up. They are now certain that Ben will never prove a danger to Joshua and have forgotten about him.

But Victoria is an altogether different proposition. When David first discovered that Hawk's granddaughter, then only fourteen years old, used the abacus with consummate skill, he had her progress monitored and forbade his son to admit her at any stage into any aspect of the company. 'She's another one!' he'd raged. 'Another Mary bloody Abacus! She's not to be employed, not until hell freezes over, you hear me, Abraham?'

'But why, Father, she will one day be a major

shareholder, it is as well not to make an enemy of her now. She is still a child but will eventually be a woman, and will marry and have children and assume a woman's place in the home. Surely we have nothing to fear if, when she is eighteen, we bring her into the company where we will be able to keep an eye on her?'

'The abacus!' David shouts. 'Can't you see, it's the bloody abacus!' It is almost as though, in his eyes, the abacus itself is an instrument potent enough to destroy them all. It becomes apparent to Abraham that to the superstitious and ignorant old man, the abacus is a dangerous, almost mystical weapon placed in the hands of a young sorceress who, through some sort of witchcraft engendered by the Chinese counting beads, will triumph over them.

Ignoring the fact that there has only ever been one woman and one abacus, he makes it sound as though there have been a succession of Marys since time out of mind. 'You'll see!' he screams. 'Soon her fingers will grow crooked and her talons grow sharp as a ferret's teeth!'

And so Hawk, unable to place Victoria within the Potato Factory, has her trained in every aspect of bookkeeping and accountancy. After which, she sits for her university entrance examination and wins one of the very rare places for a female student in the law faculty of the University of Melbourne. Hawk, afraid that as the only woman in the faculty she will suffer at the hands of the male students, persuades her instead to gain her articles. By pulling strings, he finds her a position as articled clerk in the office of the prominent city law firm Slade, Slade & Hetherington, in Collins Street.

There are very few women solicitors in Victoria, but Hawk thinks it would be good training for her agile and questioning mind. This proves to be a not altogether ideal arrangement. A female articled clerk is far from welcome in a profession and a clerks' chamber dominated by males. This is even further exacerbated when the other articled clerks in Slade, Slade & Hetherington are confronted by a young woman who is not afraid to express an opinion, doesn't know her rightful place as a female and is a junior. They also discover that she can be inordinately stubborn when she thinks she is right and has the audacity to possess more than a modicum of grey matter and a logical mind to boot. The only other female in the company is the tea lady, Mrs Wilkinson, a timid creature in her late forties in a mob-cap, who addresses the most junior clerk as sir.

Because of all of these things, but mostly because she is female, Tommo's granddaughter is given the work nobody else wants to do. These are inevitably tasks well below her intellectual capacity which she performs generally with her bottom lip tucked under her top teeth, but essentially without complaint.

Her working life filled with tedium, Victoria is hungry for some intellectual stimulus and is astonished when one day Mrs Wilkinson approaches her while she is alone in the firm's library looking up torts for a senior partner and asks her if she would like to attend a meeting of the St Kilda branch of the Labor Party. To her amazement, after a whispered conversation, she discovers the tea lady to be far from the tepid creature she appears to be.

In fact, Mrs Wilkinson proves to be a veritable firebrand who introduces Victoria to the politics of poverty, the rights denied to the underprivileged and the conditions of the working classes. Victoria needs little encouragement to take sides, she has already gained a dim view of lawyers in particular and the business world in general, what Mrs Wilkinson calls 'the lining of fat around the hungry belly of society', meaning by this the world dominated by middle-class males who think themselves superior by dint of money, a privileged upbringing and a stint at Melbourne Grammar.

For the first time in her life, Victoria hears the viewpoint of the other side from men who wear cloth caps and women who cover their heads with cheap scarves and wear knitted jerseys with holes in them, but who nevertheless have fine minds, have read widely and have a mission to fight for the rights of the working classes.

The fact that she is amongst the most privileged of them all in terms of wealth never occurs to Victoria. Hawk has not let her grow up in a wealthy environment nor molly-coddled her in childhood nor ever allowed her to develop a sense of privilege. Brought up on one of Hawk's hop farms near New Norfolk she and Ben have had a natural and easy upbringing, attending the local primary school.

When Ben reached the age of twelve and the limits of the education locally available, Hawk brought in as his tutors Mr and Mrs Wickworth-Spode, recent immigrants to Tasmania. Mr Wickworth-Spode, a graduate from Cambridge, was the retired headmaster of a boys' school in England and a mathematics and history teacher, while Mrs Wickworth-Spode had been a teacher of English and Latin at Roedean, a famous English public school for girls. Both were fanatical gardeners and with a cottage of their own, all the gardening space they could contend with and a generous salary as well, Hawk was able to attract them to the New Norfolk farm.

It soon became apparent that Ben was an indifferent scholar with his eyes constantly turned to the schoolroom window and the promised freedom of what lay beyond. But the ten-year-old Victoria, who would rush from primary school to sit in on the last hour of Ben's lessons, proved to be a naturally gifted learner, in particular with numbers. She would often confound Mr Wickworth-

Spode as her little fingers blurred across the abacus to return an answer to a sum in the time it took a bemused Ben to chew a couple of times at the end of his yellow pencil.

When it was Victoria's turn to come under the total influence of the redoubtable husband-and-wife team, they doted on her and gave their every attention to her education. It was a happy childhood with the rigours of a sound education admirably mixed with the easygoing business of life in the country, and Hawk keeping a sharp eye on their progress when he visited them once a fortnight from Melbourne. Hawk brought Victoria at eighteen to live with him in Melbourne while Ben remained, by choice, in Tasmania learning hop farming, taking over the management and the general supervision of the hop farms when he turned twenty-one. Mr and Mrs Wickworth-Spode retired to the cottage with Mr Wickworth-Spode doing the books for the four estates and Mrs Wickworth-Spode keeping the kitchen supplied with vegetables.

Despite her private tutors and an education which proves to be well in advance of the people she meets of her own age, Victoria doesn't see herself as above her contemporaries. They know her as a young woman with a confident and outgoing personality and friendly disposition.

By contrast, she constantly earns the disapproval of the senior law clerk and even sometimes makes her opinions known in the august presence of one or another of the male partners when she believes an injustice has been perpetrated. She is also prepared to accept their rebukes if she is proved to be wrong, though she seldom lets her emotions override her logic and so she is more often right than wrong, which doesn't endear her to any of the men. If it were not for the importance of Hawk's personal financial dealings with the firm and the fact that her marks in the periodic law examinations are the highest in the State of Victoria, it is doubtful that Slade, Slade & Hetherington would continue to employ her.

Hawk can see that she is unhappy and attempts to mollify her. 'My dear, it is never wise to bite the hand that feeds you, they will not change their ways because you have proved them to be fools. Stay the course, bite your tongue, be patient, your time will come.'

'But, Grandpa, it is not my intention to seem difficult, I wish only that they will be just and fair.'

Hawk laughs. 'Justice requires integrity and there is little enough of that among lawyers. They would sooner get rid of you than have to deal with their own consciences.'

'But it's not fair!' Victoria protests. 'The poor are evicted from their homes so that our clients can build factories on the site rather than find locations where electricity, gas, drainage and roads must first be built. Then they erect sweatshops in which women work for starvation wages!' Victoria has already picked up the vernacular of the Labor Party. 'That is just *one* case I am working on,' she continues. 'What's more they will win. They'll win because there is no one able to oppose them!'

Hawk looks at Victoria shrewdly. 'Have you thought to find out who owned the homes from which the poor were evicted?'

'Of course,' Victoria snorts. 'The rich slum landlords who sell them to the developers at a huge profit but which is still less than what it would cost to develop virgin land with all the utilities to be resourced.'

'Ah, there you have it, the very principle upon which English law is based, the right of property over the rights of the common man. Throughout the history of English law the penalties for damaging property have always been

246

greater than those for harming people. The law has always protected the "haves" and punished those who have nothing. It is very simple, my dear, it is the "haves" who have always made the laws.'

'But, Grandpa, they are hypocrites and the mayor announces to the world at large that they are clearing the crime-infested slums for the benefit of the city when their true motive is to build factories convenient to the city, the railways and the port! The mayor is one of the shareholders in their development syndicate!'

'And what would you have them do? Build homes for the poor with hundred-year mortgages and no interest payments?' Hawk chuckles. 'Ours is a profit-based society with the upper class owning the capital, the middle class utilising it and the working class enduring the consequences. The poor will always be among us and while there is very little profit to a lawyer in defending a poor man's plea for justice, there is a great deal of money to be made out of helping a rich man to exploit him. That, my dear Victoria, is what you are up against and, quite frankly, I don't like your chances.'

'But we are supposed to be an egalitarian society where Jack is as good as his master.'

'In my experience wherever there is a master and a Jack travelling along the same road, it is Jack who carries the master's portmanteau but the master who gets paid for the wares within it. Money, not class, is the equaliser in this country, Victoria, which is perhaps better than class controlling it. No profession understands this better than those who practise at the law.'

Victoria looks up, appealing to Hawk. 'Grandpa Hawk, they are not even clever men, they think to please their clients with sycophantic advice, invitations to the races at Flemington and the cricket at the MCG and suppers of roast beef and claret at the Melbourne Club.

247

They are rapacious, selfish and vainglorious and would step over a beggar rather than throw him a coin. They don't even get their Latin right!' Victoria says in a final expression of her frustration.

'Spoken with all the insight of the very young,' Hawk laughs. 'If brains and Latin were the sole criteria for success in business there'd be a poor living in store for most of us.' Nevertheless, he is delighted with Victoria's strong sense of justice but realises that, while he shares it, his attempts to be just and honest have brought nothing but misery and failure into his own life.

Victoria will often outline a case to him in which she has acted as articled clerk and Hawk learns that she has a capacity to see both sides of a question and draw a quick and accurate conclusion. If ever she should qualify and find herself in charge of handling a case in front of a magistrate, he knows she has a tongue that can cut like a whip and an ability to quickly spot a fool, whether barrister, solicitor, witness, defendant, policeman or magistrate. Victoria may not be a blood relation of Mary Abacus, but she has the same uncanny ability to know what is wheat and what is chaff, what is useful and what is pure hyperbole. Perhaps it is the same instinct Tommo had as a gambler, to know what was real and what was bluff.

At the age of twenty-two Victoria sits for her final law examinations and passes with flying colours. During the course of a celebratory dinner, Hawk, admittedly somewhat reluctantly, points out to her that there may be some future advantage in being counted among the members of Melbourne's society. He adds that while he believes himself not suitable as a black man to make her introductions he can quite easily find the right chaperone to do so.

Victoria is mortified by this suggestion. 'Grandfather,

how could you think such a thing? You of all people!' she cries. 'It is everything I am against! They are the people who exploit the workers, who cheat and lie and rob the poor and you want me to join them?' She is barely able to conceal her anger at Hawk's suggestion.

'Not all of them. Not all rich people exploit the poor,' the ever reasonable Hawk protests.

'I can't think of any who don't!' Victoria snaps, letting her indignation override her logic.

Hawk laughs. 'Well, I can.'

'Who? They're all the same. I see them every day.'

'Well, *you*, my dear, soon you'll be richer than most of them. You don't exploit the poor.'

Victoria is scornful in her reply. 'Tush, the money Ben and I get when we're thirty from Great-grandmother's will won't make us rich?'

'Rich enough, but the money you will inherit from me, I daresay, will make you the richest woman in the nation.'

'But that's obscene!' Victoria cries, then quickly adds, 'I shall give it all away!'

Hawk laughs again. 'It won't make a lot of difference if you do. You and Ben will inherit a majority share in Solomon & Teekleman. As fast as you give it away your wealth will be renewed.'

'But, Grandfather Hawk, they are among the worst of the slum landlords and the developers! Did you know that they employ only Freemasons?'

Hawk nods. 'One of David's little innovations.'

'It's not little. Freemasonry, as you no doubt know, requires some expense which, generally speaking, is beyond a poor man's resources. So David made it a condition that anyone who works for the company must be a Freemason and then the company pays for the regalia and, furthermore, as an incentive to join, the company pays their sick and old-age benefits as well.'

249

'Yes, well, I've always thought it one of the few acts of real generosity emanating from David Solomon.'

'Generosity my foot! You know what that means, don't you? The benefit funds are administered by the Independent Order of Oddfellows, who have strong links with Freemasonry. Grandfather, they are in each other's pockets up to their armpits.'

'I would think that perfectly legitimate. If you're going to pay for the workers' benefits you have every right to choose the friendly society you are going to involve.'

'You still don't get the point!' Victoria exclaims. 'Lots of the company's workers are poor but they are Protestants and now Freemasons. Lots of Catholics are poor but they are forbidden by the Church to be Freemasons. So Solomon & Teekleman deliberately pick their so-called slum areas to buy and then to clear for the building of factories, offices and middle-class homes where the workers' cottages are predominantly Catholic, knowing that their own workers are unlikely to be sympathetic to their plight.'

'My dear, the Freemasons are not villains, in fact integrity, honesty, moral and social virtue are the cornerstones of their beliefs. I feel sure, if they thought Abraham, as Grand Master of the Melbourne Lodge, was forcing his workers to join the brotherhood, they would soon enough do something about it. It is, I believe, one of the strongest tenets of the movement to render practical aid to the less fortunate members of the community. By helping the poorer of his own workers to embrace the brotherhood and by ensuring some sort of sinecure for them in sickness and old age, isn't Abraham doing just that?'

'Yes, but only for his own workers! The unions are powerless to prevent them from going ahead with a particular development by utilising the only weapon they have, to bring the company workers out on strike. As Freemasons, the company employees have elected not to join the various unions. Did you know the company does not employ a single member of a union! Nor can the unions bring the workers from the outside contractors and suppliers out on strike against them, because Solomon & Teekleman are virtually self-sufficient, they largely own all their own equipment and the resources to complete a "slum clearance" as they are so fond of calling it.'

'Just for a moment, let's take the company's point of view. What have they done wrong? You call it exploiting the poor, they call it much-needed slum clearance. They are *not* the government, they are *not* required to make decisions as to what benefits the poor and what doesn't, they are not a social welfare organisation, they are an organisation working within the law to make a profit. Moreover, they can be said to have looked after the welfare of their own employees very well indeed and, furthermore, it is the collective decision of those employees *not* to join a union. I can see that there may be a moral issue here for you and, of course, also for the unions involved, but in the purely practical sense Solomon & Teekleman have done nothing wrong. They are in a commercial sense completely blameless.'

Victoria suddenly stops and brings her fingers to her lips. 'My God, I never thought of it!' She points to Hawk. 'You're one of them, a Freemason, aren't you?' She doesn't wait for Hawk's reply. 'That's why you're defending Solomon & Teekleman, isn't it?'

Hawk laughs. 'Freemasonry is a secret society in that it doesn't disclose its members, but you are quite wrong, Victoria, I am not a Freemason, nor am I defending the company in which both your name and mine appears, but I do try to be a fair-minded and logical human being.'

'But, Grandfather, what I say is true! They have completely manipulated the situation in their favour. John Curtin, the head of the Brunswick branch of the Labor Party to which I belong, says they're virtually bulletproof. Frank Anstey the federal MP says the same. John Curtin says they've got a battery of lawyers ready to defend Sir Abraham's actions every time he passes wind! It's simply iniquitous and this is a company which, in part anyway, you and I own! My name, for God's sake, is Teekleman! How can I hold my head up? How can I live with that?' Victoria cries despairingly.

'Come now, my dear,' Hawk comforts her, handing her his handkerchief, for she has begun to cry. 'It's not as bad as all that, there's still the Potato Factory under Tom Pickles, as decent a man as they come.'

'Tom Pickles! Don't give me Tom Pickles as your example. He is Master of the Grand Lodge of Tasmania!'

'How do you know all this, Victoria?' Hawk asks sternly.

'I heard it at the Labor Party conference last April. From the Tasmanian delegates.'

'Victoria, the Potato Factory has always been a strictly ethical company in its outside dealings, and the workers were always happy. It was your great-grandmother's pride and joy that she neither cheated nor lied in her dealings with others. She would say, "I've done enough o' that in me life and 'ad the same done to me often enough. From now it's all on the square, do unto others what you'd want for yerself."'

Victoria nods. 'According to the Hobart delegate, it's the same there as here, no problems within, with the Freemasonry and health benefits and pension fund thing working, but the company's outside dealings have been described as industrial rape and pillage. All kept very quiet, mind, money and Freemasonry are a powerful combination in Collins Street, but it seems this is equally true of Elizabeth Street, Hobart.'

'Why didn't you tell me how you felt before now?'

Victoria bows her head and is silent awhile, then says softly, 'There was nothing you could do about it.' She looks up at Hawk, her eyes sad. 'I didn't want you to be hurt, Grandfather. You and Mary Abacus built the Potato Factory to be a fair place, a great and good company, you worked so hard to make it the best, now it isn't any more.'

Hawk remembers how, when Victoria was first articled as a law clerk and started to see the lack of corporate morality and greed from the inside and realised she was inadvertently a part of it, he wanted to tell her then that in a few years she and her brother would be the major shareholders again in Solomon & Teekleman, that she would have the power to change things if she eventually became chairman.

But he held his tongue at the time, knowing that it would be eight years before she came of age to exercise her proxy, by which time, with no experience in the company, she would have little chance of competing with Joshua Solomon. He also had to consider that he might well be dead or enfeebled and no matter how brilliant his grand-daughter proved to be, she would have little hope of fighting Abraham and Joshua on her own for control.

Now, with Hinetitama's death and his ability to assume control again and with the declaration of war, everything has changed and the odds have evened up for Victoria. Everything but one thing, Hawk's rapidly advancing age. He is already a septuagenarian and knows he is running out of time. He must move quickly if he is to get Victoria up and running as future competition to Joshua. There is only one way he can do this. He must once again confront David Solomon.

Hawk has no doubt that Victoria will be a match for Joshua Solomon if they compete on equal terms. As two people they are very different. Victoria is brilliant, confident, stubborn with a sharp tongue, perhaps a bit of a bossy boots, but without pretension, loyal and honest and much loved by her friends.

Joshua, on the other hand, seems of an altogether different disposition. On a superficial level he appears somewhat foppish and it would be easy to take him too lightly. But Hawk does not intend to make this mistake, Joshua is David-trained and Solomon-bred and while, on the surface, he may seem the antithesis of his uncouth and irascible grandfather, the old man appears pleased with the job he has done on his grandson and that is warning sufficient for Hawk.

In the year Joshua Solomon has been back from Oxford it is already established among the mothers in Melbourne's social circles that he is the big catch of the season. It seems he has no disadvantages beyond his odious grandfather who, fortuitously, must leave this mortal coil at any time. They titter among themselves and count Joshua's many blessings. He will be rich beyond avarice, is blue-eyed, fair-haired and handsome as can be, he is well mannered and utterly charming, with the affectations and speech of a young English gentleman. To the society matrons with unattached and eligible daughters, Joshua Solomon seems almost too good to be true. To their daughters he is truly to be swooned over. To the patriarchs of Melbourne's business community he represents the new age, the end of the gold-rush mentality with its rough and ready business ways. Joshua is one of the scions who will define business in the new century, just the sort of young business leader to represent the new Melbourne. An Oxford blue in both cricket and rugger where he played in the 1911 Australian rugby tour of

254

England and Wales, starring on the wing in the test against Wales, he now plays cricket for Victoria. He is urbane, bright, educated and informed. While his Jewish father is sufficient reason for him to be blackballed by the Melbourne Club, he has been accepted with alacrity as a member of the Australia Club. Old codgers in the club, witnessing the young man playing at billiards, turn to each other and remark, 'Splendid young chappie. Wish we had ten more young members made of the same solid metal, eh?'

As Hawk approaches his Caulfield home on the morning of Hinetitama's death he knows that he must somehow force David once again into a corner so that he will be made to capitulate. Hawk knows that Joshua is the key. He must pluck David's teeth first, whereupon he will see Abraham about remaining as chairman. But first he must talk to Victoria and then get some sleep.

In the late afternoon of the day of Hinetitama's death the butler, known simply as Adams, enters the sunlit conservatory of Abraham's Toorak home where David Solomon, wrapped in a light blanket, is dozing in a bathchair. The butler stands beside the old man and announces, 'Mr Hawk Solomon has called and offered his card, he requests that he might be allowed to see you, Mr David.'

'Eh? What did you say? Speak up, man!' David shouts, annoyed at being disturbed.

'Mr Hawk Solomon to see you, sir.' The butler raises one eyebrow slightly, not that David can see this clear sign of his disdain. 'A black man, sir.'

'Hawk Solomon to see me? Tell him to go ter buggery!'

'Sir, he apologises for the lack of an appointment but says it is a matter of some urgency.'

'What, *his* urgency or mine? The only matter of

urgency I have is to take a piss. Here, get the bloody chamber-pot.' The old man brings his legs over the edge of the bathchair with some difficulty and places them on the floor. With hands trembling he begins to fumble with his pyjama pants. He can barely see the chamber-pot which Adams now holds at the correct level. 'Tell me when it's pointed in the right direction,' he instructs Adams, 'then close yer eyes!'

'It's about right to proceed now, sir,' the butler says solemnly. He is a big man with a pronounced belly and appears awkward as he bends to hold the chamber-pot at the right height and angle.

After what seems like ages, Adams hears the thin trickle of urine splashing into the porcelain pot. He keeps his eyes shut until the sound finally ceases and then allows sufficient time for David's trembling fingers to return the fly of his pyjamas to a more decorous arrangement. Placing the chamber-pot down, he lifts David's trembling legs back into the bathchair and tucks the blanket around him. 'Bastard ain't worth the piss in that pot!' David snaps. 'Is that all he said, a matter of urgency? A matter of urgency about what, man!'

'Just a matter of urgency, Mr David.'

'Yes, yes, you said that before!' David says impatiently. David thinks for a moment and then decides that he will take this final opportunity to spit in the face of his last great enemy. 'Tell him he's got ten minutes and damned lucky to get it.'

'Yes, Mr David.' Adams bends slowly and picks up the chamber-pot. 'Ten minutes, it is?'

David appears to be looking about the conservatory until his failing eyesight spies a large wicker chair. 'Take that out, make the nigger boy stand.'

Adams, still holding the chamber-pot, takes the chair from the back and drags it behind him as he leaves the conservatory. 'He's not to be offered any refreshment, yer hear,' David shouts at the departing butler.

Clasping his rheumatic hands so as to appear completely calm and in control, he waits for Hawk to be ushered into his presence.

Hawk's shadowy figure stoops to allow him to enter the doorway into the conservatory. 'Ah, Hawk Solomon, you have dared to call at my house when you know you are not welcome.'

Hawk smiles. 'Would you have met me elsewhere, David?'

'Certainly not.'

'Well then, how else would I be able to say what I have come to say?'

'There is nothing you can say that would interest me, so be out with it and then be gone, I am too old to waste what time I have left in the company of a nigger.'

'Ah, my tidings, whether from a nigger or a white man, will cause you no less consternation, David Solomon,' Hawk replies evenly, not in the least upset by the outburst from the old man. He stands relaxed in front of the bathchair, towering above the supine David, who can see him as a soft image, almost a dark shadow, as if he is looking into a badly smudged mirror.

'There is naught you can do to consternate me now, you have been beaten neck and crop these last twenty years. Yer old and yer useless and yer ready to die!'

Hawk's voice is suddenly sharp. 'I have not come to banter, David Solomon, it is you, Sir Abraham and your grandson who have lost, *we* have regained the voting rights to Tommo's daughter's shares, *we* are again in the majority.'

'We? Who the hell is *we*?' David screams. 'Bah! The boy is not worth a pinch of shit, a bloody hops farmer! And the girlie, the little witch, she is like her mother, nothing but trouble. She and her abacus, opening her big gob and wailing about the conditions of the poor. What does she know about being poor, eh? Tell her to come and see me. I'll tell her about poor! Jesus!' He brings his fist up and wipes his mouth with the back of his hand as though to be rid of a bad taste. 'Now the boy's gone to war, you think she'll take over, do ya? What to do, eh? Count the daily takings with her beads?' He stabs a bony finger in Hawk's direction. 'Now you lissen t' me, yer black bastard, no old nigger and a girlie from the farm who plays with beads is gunna take over Solomon & Teekleman. You've got the proxies, has ya? From that half-caste drunken whore who went walkabout and never come back? You've got her will, has ya? And her proxy? Well, well, ain't that grand.' He pauses again to take breath and spit a gob of phlegm into a spittoon placed beside his chair, then he continues, 'So tell me? How you going to do it? How you going to take over Solomon & Teekleman? You are alone and have no one who knows of the workings of the company! Fer Christsake, you've been out of it twenty years! You'll soon be dead yerself and good riddance to bad rubbish! You think that little snot-nose solicitor girl is going to do it on her abacus . . . alone? Ha! Lemme tell you something for nothing, yer full o' bullshit, Hawk Solomon, and I'll see you in hell first!'

'Ah, but before I do, I shall take over as chairman. It will be tenure long enough to destroy your grandson.' Hawk is surprised how well informed David Solomon is about Victoria. It is, he thinks, a great compliment that they should have watched her so closely. He wonders briefly which of the senior partners at Slade, Slade & Hetherington is in David's pocket.

Nevertheless the old man has instantly put his finger on the problem and, if anything, has managed to gain the initiative. Hawk is forced to admire him. At ninety-four his mind is still sharp as a tack. The length and content of his tirade alone would have exhausted a man thirty years his junior.

But David has only paused to draw breath. 'You think the government will stand by and let the third-biggest company in Australia with a dozen major war contracts be managed by an old fool? Allow you to put the troops in jeopardy because you want to punish a young man, an officer of the King, who has volunteered to fight for his country? You think they'll stand by and watch my son Abraham be replaced by an old blackfella who 'asn't done a day's work in twenty years? Do me a favour, will ya? Go away! You're fucked, Hawk Solomon!'

Hawk chuckles, hiding his true feelings. It is pointless, he decides, trying to put his original proposal to the old bastard. David Solomon will not compromise, will never capitulate. To get himself and Victoria back into Solomon & Teekleman will be an enormous fight. They could be saddled with years of litigation and interference from a government bureaucracy protecting its military contracts before they eventually win. And, always, there is the sense of time running out for him. Hawk decides that there is little more he can do but try to bluff his way through.

'All that work for nothing, eh, David? All those years teaching your grandson what you know and Joshua will never again have anything to do with Solomon & Teekleman. Such a pity, such a nice lad they tell me.' Hawk pauses. 'Still, you've got plenty of money, I'm sure you can buy the boy a soft job with a large income in a nice gentile firm, a sinecure so that he might remain the darling of the social set.'

But David is not a bit fazed by Hawk's taunting. He presses the electric buzzer at his arm to summon the butler. 'Bah! My lawyers will have your guts for garters! Now you lissen ter me, we'll still be here, still running things, when Joshua returns to take his rightful place. No country-bumpkin, half-arsed female solicitor who uses an abacus to count and calls herself a bloody socialist is going to take his place.' He cackles suddenly, genuinely amused at the thought. 'The nigger and the farm girl are going to run the biggest private company in Australia!' The smile disappears from his face and he sniffs derisively and, with a dismissive flick of his hand towards Hawk, says, 'Be gone with you, you cheeky black bastard!'

Hawk, remaining calm, ignores David's outburst and speaks slowly, his voice raised so that the old man is certain to hear him. 'I have called an extraordinary general meeting of the directors for tomorrow at 10 a.m. sharp when your son will be asked to relinquish his position as chairman and, of course, I shall see that your grandson, upon his return from the war, finds no position in either company available to him.' Hawk pauses a moment, before adding, 'Victoria Teekleman will replace him and I daresay will eventually become chairman.'

Hawk allows all this to register with the old man and concludes, 'It's our turn now, David, your side is finished. As a director I hope you will be present with your son to witness Victoria Teekleman's acceptance into the company, its latest recruit, the new Mary Abacus. But I don't give a shit whether you attend or not. Tomorrow at ten o'clock sharp I shall accept your son's resignation as chairman.'

The butler comes into the conservatory. 'You wanted something, Mr David?'

'Yes, you will show this impertinent fellow to the door at once, Adams.' David turns to Hawk. 'Be gone with you, Hawk Solomon, I do not wish ever to see you again.'

'Ah, but you will I hope, David. Tomorrow.'

'Be gone! Damn your hide, nigger!' the old man shouts, shaking his fist in Hawk's direction.

Adams steps up to Hawk. 'I'm afraid you must go, my good man. Come along now, we don't want any fuss, do we?' The unfortunate Adams makes the mistake of reaching up to take Hawk's elbow and Hawk, not changing his expression, takes Adams' hand in his own and begins to squeeze so that the butler sinks to his knees, his face turning scarlet and his jowls shaking like a jelly freshly removed from its mould. His expression is a mixture of surprise and agony as his mouth pops open and closed like a goldfish in a bowl as he gasps silently to be released.

'What are you doing!' David demands, not able to clearly see what's going on.

'He's h-hurting me, sir,' Adams says at last.

'Just a bit of good man-ing,' Hawk says softly, and looks down at Adams. 'Come along now, there's a good man, we don't want any fuss, do we?' Still gripping the unfortunate butler's hand in his giant fist, Hawk says to David, 'Tomorrow then. Be good enough to be on time. I shall notify Sir Abraham as well.'

Hawk releases his grip on the poor man gasping at his knees and, bending slightly, takes him by the elbow and helps him to his feet. 'Thank you for seeing me in, Mr Adams. I shall see myself out.'

'We will have the law onto you for this,' David shouts, finally realising what has happened to his butler.

'Oh yes, the law,' Hawk says absently. 'The guts-for-garters men. If you think they will help you, bring all the lawyers in Christendom to the meeting tomorrow. I, for my part, shall bring only one. She should be sufficient to effectively deal with them all, that is, after first adding up their collective fees on her abacus.'

With these final words Hawk turns to depart, leaving the hapless butler to nurse the fingers of his damaged hand by means of squeezing them under his armpit.

'Go to hell, you nigger bastard!' David screams, shaking his fist at the dark shadow he sees as the departing Hawk.

Hawk pauses at the door and turns back to look at the old man and sees that he is weeping, though whether they be tears of temper, frustration or anxiety he can't tell. But with a certainty born out of a lifetime of knowing David Solomon, he knows they are not the tears that flow from remorse. 'Will the wicked old man never die?' he thinks, as he closes the door behind him.

David, in fact, weeps for himself, despite his bravado. He is aware that Hawk is a patient but determined foe and that ultimately his enemy will gain control of Solomon & Teekleman once more. He considers briefly having Hawk murdered, but he is too old and feeble to make the arrangements and Abraham would not countenance any such action. Everything is suddenly falling to bits, first Joshua going off to war and now this.

He has tried so hard to make his grandson everything he himself isn't. Joshua is his alter ego and he is going to die knowing the boy with whom he has worked so diligently and upon whom he has lavished so much affection will come to nothing. David thinks back to the day of Joshua's birth which, in his mind's eye, he sees as clearly as if it were yesterday.

He is standing impatiently outside Elizabeth's bed chamber and when he hears the first mewling cries of the infant he turns the knob on the bedroom door, determined to barge in, but it has been locked from the inside.

'Open this bloody door!' he shouts.

'Sir, I must cut and tie the cord and wash the baby,' the midwife shouts back.

'Bugger that, lemme in!' David throws his shoulder against the door. 'Lemme in, will ya!' he demands again.

But the midwife won't be intimidated. 'You'll stay there until we're ready, sir,' she shouts back.

It is a good fifteen minutes before David hears the click of the key and, without waiting for the door to open fully, he barges into the bedroom, brushing the midwife aside. He doesn't even demand to know the newborn's gender, convinced that whichever one of the ears of God has heard his request, it has also plainly understood that a male child was a mandatory part of it.

David simply walks into the darkened room and makes for the velvet drapes which keep the bed chamber in a semi-darkened state. He rips them open to expose the late morning sunlight.

Elizabeth lies with her infant swaddled and held tightly to her breasts. 'Righto, girlie, let's see him. Hold him up, will ya. Take that bloody blanket off. I want to see the lot of him, all of the little bugger, see he's got everything that should be there and nothing that shouldn't!'

The midwife tries to interfere. 'Sir, she's wearied, the baby is only just born, the mother is weak from the birth.'

'She's always been weak and bloody wearied. Look at her, no bloody tits. How's the boy gunna suckle, eh? Come along, girl, hold him up, let me see the little blighter.'

Elizabeth begins to cry, clutching her infant even more tightly to her chest. 'Father, please go,' she whispers through her tears. 'It's my baby.'

David is genuinely shocked at this idea. 'Your baby? Oh no, you don't! You'll not pull that one on me, girlie.' He points to the swaddled infant. 'That's *my* child. I got him from God and a pretty penny he cost too!' He turns to the midwife. 'You! I'm not finished with you! Hold my boy up, let me see him,' he demands. The midwife, afraid to confront the monstrous man standing in front of her a second time, takes the infant from the weeping Elizabeth and, removing the blanket that covers him, she lies him down on the counterpane, which is folded neatly at the end of the bed. The tiny infant stretches, then balls his fists, screwing up his eyes against the glare which now bathes him in the light, showing the rubbery reddish-brown colour of the healthy newborn.

'See, making fists,' David says gleefully. 'A born fighter already.' He inspects Joshua minutely from head to toe, then, pronouncing himself satisfied with the front, turns to the midwife. 'Turn him over, woman, let's see his tukis.' Finally, having checked Joshua for birthmarks or any other defect, he looks up pleased. 'Good,' he grunts. 'Wrap him up, missus.' Turning to Elizabeth he points to her bosom, 'You'll not feed him with those, girlie. We'll get a wet nurse with big tits. I'll not have him starvin' to death sucking on a couple of bleedin' mosquito bites!'

David leaves just as Abraham arrives, having been summoned from work. Father and son meet at the bed-chamber door. 'It's a boy and he's mine,' David says to his son. Abraham, anxious to be at Elizabeth's side, only hears the words 'It's a boy' as he hastens to be with his distraught wife. This will prove to be one of the few times when the two parents will be alone with their child. David is convinced that the child is his, prayed and paid for, and that Elizabeth is simply the delivery container who, while she is useful, is Joshua's surrogate mother.

At first, Elizabeth objects to David's complete possession of her child but to little avail. David demands that the wet nurse feeds him in his presence so that he is assured the baby receives sufficient milk. He stands beside the nursemaid they have employed to care for the baby while she weighs him every two days, jotting down baby Joshua's weight in a small notebook. As Joshua grows older, David so totally monopolises the child that Joshua's own father seldom gets to play with him. David sees his grandchild as an extension of himself and, from the very first day, he discusses affairs of business with Joshua.

'It's the sounds, see, the sounds of the words. Course he don't understand them, but if they're the sounds he hears about him, he'll get to know them unconscious like, sounds of words like profit, loss, debit, credit, insurance, compound interest, percentage, negotiation, contract. Them's all sounds and words he must later think was born into his head. It don't matter that he don't comprehend yet, it's the sounds, see, like litigation, a lovely sound that, lit-ti-gation.'

'Leave the child alone, Father,' Elizabeth would cry, exasperated at David's almost maniacal preoccupation with her child. 'He's only a baby.'

'Alone? Leave him alone?' David shows his astonishment. 'What do you mean alone!' he yells at her. 'I can't take no chances. It's not my fault there's only *one* of him around.' This last is always said accusingly, guilt is David's speciality and he never hesitates to use it on his daughter-in-law.

Shortly after Joshua's birth, Abraham contracts the mumps which results in him becoming sterile. Despite this explanation for the couple's infertility, David continues to blame Elizabeth at every opportunity for only producing a single male heir.

'You was married four years!' he shouts, holding up four bony fingers in front of Elizabeth's face. 'Four bloody years before Joshua come along, before *I* got him born! Then, only then, Abe got the mumps what made his pistol fire blanks. You and that book-reading bastard who calls himself my son could have made me two more grandsons at least! Instead, you was gallivanting around in the cot using them fancy rubbers!'

'What about you?' Elizabeth objects. 'You had Abraham. That's only *one* child!'

265

'Rebecca was sick. Sick doesn't count!' David yells back at her. 'Four years you waited. You and him having a good time in the cot, eating me out of house and home, never a sick day between you, and at the expense o' *my* bloody grandchildren!'

On one such occasion, when David's tormenting has driven Elizabeth to distraction, she bends down, thumping her knees with her fists and screams at the old man. 'For God's sake, Father, leave us alone. Don't you realise, your son can't even get it up! He never bloody could hardly!'

'What's that?' David cries. Then, realising what his daughter-in-law has just said, adds, 'That's your bloody fault, girlie! Let me tell you something for nothing. There's bugger-all wrong with my boy a good Jewish girl couldn't fix!'

'Well, then find him one!' Elizabeth howls. 'He's no use to me!'

David stops, not believing his ears. 'You'll not divorce him,' he shouts. 'There'll be no divorce in this house, you hear?' He points an accusing finger at her. 'You leave and I'll cut you off without a penny,' he stammers, barely able to contain his anger. 'You won't even find work in a brothel, girlie! I'll see you in the gutter with the dog shit!' Shaking with rage he grabs her by the arm and pushes her so that she stumbles and falls to the carpet. Standing over her, both his fists clenched, his arms rigid at his side, he screams, 'Joshua has got to have a mother, even if it's only to wipe his arse!' Leaving her on the floor, he walks from the room shaking his head. 'Jesus Christ, I should never have let my son marry out!'

And so, in the age-old manner of men holding women captive, Elizabeth, for lack of independent means, is rendered helpless. Nor can she hope to appeal to her husband to stand up to his father. Furthermore, by keeping Abraham busy and, in Joshua's early years, frequently away on business, David prevents his son from attempting to win the child's affection.

David simply wants Joshua for himself and shortly after Joshua is weaned, his cradle is moved into David's bed chamber with the nurse in an adjoining room and a door between the rooms. The cradle is later followed by a cot and then a cast-iron bed. Most of Joshua's waking childhood is spent within bawling distance of his grandfather and when he reaches puberty and, as David tells himself, needs to pull his pud in private, he moves Joshua into the nanny's old room, so that he still has direct access to his grandson at any time of the day or night.

His tutors, the first employed when Joshua turned seven, are Englishmen, gentlemen fallen on hard times. All are paid well above what their vocations might normally command, as David is aware that they will not long put up with his interference, bullying and bad temper unless the reward for their services is sufficiently high to quell their inevitable disenchantment. Even so, Joshua will have four tutors in all before he is finally trundled off to Oxford.

Joshua's first tutor undergoes a routine which will be common to those who follow him. David interviews him in his opulent office, resplendent in the latest Edwardian style, making him stand like a naughty schoolboy in front of his mahogany desk even though the room is amply supplied with an ottoman couch and four comfortable leather armchairs of similar configuration.

'I am not an easy man to please, Mr Smyth, and in the matter of my grandson you will find me even more particular. Whereas you are a gentleman, you should know right off, I am not. I am a rich Jew and I wish my grandson to be tutored as though he were a gentleman and a gentile, a rich goy. Do you understand me?'

Smyth, who has only recently had his impecunious financial position alleviated by David and all his gambling debts paid, is happy to agree to just about any terms the old man wants to impose. He has been promised superior lodgings and a stipend far beyond the abilities of a second-class degree at Oxford, and he can't quite believe his good fortune.

'I shall do my best, sir,' he assures David.

'No, Mr Smyth, you will do *my* best, which I think you will find a bloody sight better than your best. We will begin with elocution. I desire my grandson to speak like a gentleman.' David deliberately adopts a harsher version of his own accent and lack of grammar. 'If he don't talk proper and drops his h's or his g's like his grandfather, you're in for the 'igh jump.'

'I shall take particular care of his speech,' Smyth promises.

'Yeah, whatever, you look after his speech. I want him posh, not dead common like me.' David looks steadily at Smyth until the other man is forced to drop his gaze. 'What you study at Oxford University then?'

'History, sir.'

'History? What history?'

'British. The history of the British Isles.'

'You mean English?'

'No, sir. That, of course, but Irish and Scottish. The Welsh, as well.'

'Well, you'll teach the boy English history, but no Irish. You understand, no Irish!'

Smyth starts to protest. 'Without a grasp of Irish history it is difficult to get a true perspective on England's –'

'You heard me, Mr Smyth. No bloody Micks! No Irish!'

Smyth looks down at his toes, feeling like the schoolboy David has intended he should. 'Yes, sir.'

'And we'll have arithmetic, addition and subtraction, multiplication and division. Reading and writing, o' course, and Latin.'

Smyth looks up. 'I'm afraid I'm a poor Latin scholar, Mr Solomon, never got much beyond schoolboy Latin. I had just sufficient to scrape into Oxford,' he says, with disarming modesty entirely lost on David.

'Well, my grandson will be a schoolboy one day. That's enough Latin for him. All he needs to know is what it says on coats of arms and the like.'

'In which case I feel sure we will manage splendidly,' the tutor replies.

'Mr Smyth, do you 'ave a coat of arms?' Smyth opens his mouth to speak and David puts up his hand, 'No, don't answer that, I know you 'ave, that's why you got the job in the first place.' David pushes himself away from the desk. 'That will be all. You may go.'

'Thank you, sir.'

Smyth turns and walks from the study, conscious of David's rudeness, but telling himself he has no choice but to countenance it. David calls after him, 'Oi, boy, you wouldn't know how to use an abacus, would you? A Chinee abacus, yer know, for counting and doing sums?'

Smyth turns to face him. 'No, I'm afraid not, sir.'

'Hmm, be most useful for the boy to learn.' David smiles for the first time. 'Perhaps we can find a Chinaman to teach him, eh? Knew a whore woman once who used the abacus, fast as bleedin' lightnin' she was. Had these broken 'ands, see, all deformed like, but you couldn't hardly see them when she worked them little black and red beads, beat anyone hollow who was usin' a pen and paper to do their sums.'

'Remarkable, sir,' Smyth replies, unable to think what else to say, though he does wonder briefly what a whore would be doing with an abacus.

'Mr Smyth, one more thing.'

'Yessir?'

'You will be polite to the boy's mother, Mrs Solomon, but no more. You'll not speak to her about his progress or, as a matter o' fact, anything else. If I catch you doing so, you will be dismissed immediately. Do you understand me?'

'Perfectly, sir.'

David has so effectively sidelined Elizabeth that she eventually loses heart and spends most of her day in her bed chamber quietly nursing a gin bottle. He puts this down to the inherent weakness in the gentile strain and is grateful that she no longer makes a fuss. He knows that his own mother, Hannah, and even the sickly Rebecca would have fought him to a standstill and most probably would have won. A Jewish mother has resources of resistance and sheer cantankery to a depth impossible to plumb.

Not that Hannah Solomon much cared about how David turned out, other than to instil in him the same hate she had for his father Ikey and his so-called mistress Mary Abacus. Hannah believed that survival in a world where a Jew was considered even lower than the bog-Irish, depended on money and a heart filled with malice. 'Vengeance is a dish best tasted cold,' she'd say to him. 'They's all bastards, David, all greedy. Only thing you gotta learn is how to be a bigger bastard and more greedy. Know what I mean, son?'

David has few illusions about the sort of man he is. Given his parents, he believes he is the logical outcome of Ikey and Hannah Solomon, two of the more rapacious creatures to step ashore from a convict ship. They were formidable in their capacity to create mischief or to make a shilling out of someone else's misery.

Hannah had been the owner of a dockside brothel, the

most vile in London. She kept small boys and turned them into catamites. Little girls, orphans from the streets of London, were trained by her for the delectation of paedophiles and the most evil of the great city's perverts and sexual predators. She would, for the right price, obtain dwarfs, nigger women, the deformed and even slobbering idiots from the madhouse, whatever the vile preference or sexual proclivities demanded. That was Hannah Solomon, a business woman who didn't stop to weigh the consequences of any perversion beyond the price it might fetch in the market of the depraved. She believed that if there was a need and if she didn't exploit it, someone else would. And in this regard she was probably right. London, at the time, was the greatest cesspool in the known world, and the exploitation of ragged children abandoned by their mothers to live under the bridges and in the underground sewage system was so common as to be ignored by the law.

However, her four children were well cared for and were too young to be aware of their mother's pernicious occupation. They lived in a pleasant, even by comparison to the houses around it, salubrious, Whitechapel house and were minded by a nursemaid, usually a malnourished Irish biddy, grateful for free board and lodging and a few pennies to spend on gin on Saturdays, the Jewish Sabbath, when Hannah remained at home with her children and the maid was given the day off to get drunk.

This cloistered, albeit lonely life as a child came to an abrupt end when David was eight and Hannah was convicted of the theft of a batch of gentlemen's fob watches and sentenced to be transported with her children to Van Diemen's Land. Though the theft of the watches was no less an act of her own rapacity, Hannah believed her arrest and subsequent transportation were the result of a clever plan hatched by Ikey so that he and his whore mistress, Mary Abacus, could steal the contents of a large combination safe hidden under the floor of the pantry in the Whitechapel home.

People who hold themselves to be victims seldom bother to examine the evidence leading to the circumstances in which they find themselves and Hannah was no different.

How Ikey might be somehow able to force open the safe from as far away as America, where he'd absconded, Hannah never bothered to explain. Even after Ikey was recaptured and was himself transported to Port Arthur, so that the safe remained unopened in their boarded-up Whitechapel home, she continued to blame them.

Hannah's transportation and the wealth denied her became the basis for her hatred and bitterness and, as both emotions needed to have subjects for vilification, Ikey and Mary Abacus remained the principals accused of her demise.

It was a bitterness and hatred for his father which she nourished in her oldest son during her years as a convict and, later, when, as an emancipist, she took up with George Madden, a successful grain merchant in New Norfolk.

'You must promise me, David,' his mother would say, 'if I should die before that miserable bastard, Ikey Solomon, your father, Gawd 'elp us, or his whore, you will avenge our little family. What we have become is because of them two and they must pay for what they done to us. Listen to Mama, my precious. Every humiliation, every insult, every misery that has befallen you, every moment you've suffered is to be blamed on those two vile creatures who put us here in this Gawd-forsaken place and stole our money. Rich? We was, filthy bleedin' rich, we could've been nabobs, kings and queens. It's them two robbed us, took everything what was rightly ours!'

She would repeat this sentiment every day of the miserable life David endured. Hannah was nothing if not persistent and persuasive and soon David's young mind had become totally corrupted with a hatred for his father and a loathing for Mary Abacus. They were to blame for all his unhappiness, for the beatings he received at the hands of Madden, for every insult and humiliation he suffered working for him.

'Mama, I swear on your grave, they shall pay,' he would tell his mother earnestly.

'Listen to me, David, my boy. You must learn to be a businessman like George, only better. He ain't too well and I don't suppose he'll last much longer.' She smiled and gave him a sly look. 'He coughs somethin' awful at night and sometimes there's blood comes up. I'm happy to say he won't take physic or see the doctor neither. I know he beats you somethin' awful, but we'll get it all when he passes on. Listen to me, poor folk can't take revenge, only rich. That miserable whore Mary Abacus is getting rich with her brewery and what she stole from us, and she'll be respectable soon enough and she'll come after you, you mark me words. What she done to me she'll do again to you and the others.' Tears of mortification would run down Hannah's face. 'We'll be rubbish and she'll be respectable,' she'd wail. 'It's money what earns respect, we must get what's rightly ours and see her in the gutter again!' Hannah would wipe away her tears and beckon to him, 'Come 'ere then, give us a kiss. You're a clever boy, David. I know you won't let your old mama down. Remember, folk don't ask how you got your gelt, long as you've got it. Money ain't got no conscience, nor should you have.'

Soon David equated the only love and affection he ever received with his ability to hate and as he grew to manhood he saw his business success and the subsequent wealth as the means to enable him to become a bully and to use his power to gain revenge for true and imagined hurts and insults. Throughout his long life, Mary Abacus remained the primary protagonist he must defeat. It was a promise to Hannah he was to keep better than she could ever have imagined.

At the age of twenty-eight he'd conspired with Hannah to kidnap Mary's adopted twins, Tommo and Hawk, in an attempt to blackmail Ikey into giving her his numbers to the safe in Whitechapel. The kidnap plan went disastrously wrong but Hannah comforted herself with the knowledge that she'd blighted the lives of both children forever and had somewhat evened her score with Mary Abacus, who loved the boys more than her life. 'It's no more than she deserves,' she'd sneer. 'Them two brats were bastards born of a fat whore, it's all the bitch could love, a whore's sons.' Then she turned to him. 'It's not enough, David. We cannot rest until we have taken everything from them, you hear. *Everything*, we must have it all!'

When Ikey died, leaving his half of the combination to Mary, Hannah, borrowing the passage money from Madden, sent David to England where the fifteen-year-old Hawk was learning how to grow hops in Kent.

It was agreed that the two families would share the safe's contents, dividing it equally, though David and Hannah had already planned for Hawk to be followed and robbed of his share soon after he emerged from the Whitechapel house.

As David lies weeping in the bathchair, he thinks how terribly he was cheated by Hawk when the safe was opened and shown to be empty. How, over the past twenty-one years, in the twilight of his life, he has clawed back his family fortunes and consigned Hawk and his so-called grandchildren, the last vestiges of Mary Abacus, to emotional oblivion by controlling everything the great whore built with her misbegotten gains. Now, he sobs, the nigger is back again, the perfidious bastard has come back to threaten him and his grandson, to destroy his life's work.

David feels a terrible anger rising up in him. It grows more and more intense and he knows he must release it, break something. He finds the spittoon and hurls it to the ground, though it is made of brass and simply clangs and bounces before coming to a halt. He is too weak to get out of the bathchair and the anger grows and envelops him until his entire body shakes uncontrollably and he cannot find the electric buzzer to summon help. His arms, flapping about like a rag doll, are beyond his control. He attempts to shout but his throat is filled with an anger and a panic that leaves him incapable of more than a gurgling sound. His legs are jumping wildly and still the anger grows until it is now beyond containing so that his last conscious thought is that he is about to suffer a heart seizure and suddenly there is only blackness.

Almost an hour later David is discovered lying on the floor of the conservatory by Adams. He appears to have been thrown from the bathchair. His nose has bled profusely from the impact of landing on the tiled floor. The bleeding has now stopped but the front of his pyjama jacket is soaked in blood. His face is fixed in a state of rictus, a grimace not unlike one of his more unusually cantankerous expressions, though it appears to be permanently in place. When the doctor is called to examine the still alive but completely comatose old man, it is discovered that David Solomon has suffered a massive cerebral stroke.

Hawk is not to know the news about David until a telephone call from Abraham the following morning asking to postpone the boardroom meeting. Abraham, ever polite, simply explains that the old man has had a stroke and that it would be most convenient if Hawk would be so good as to postpone their meeting for two days.

Hawk offers his sympathy to Abraham, knowing that David's son would be aware that he had visited the old man and that the confrontation may well have been the reason for David's stroke. It is typical of Abraham that he should avoid conjecture and say nothing. 'I may be implicated, Abraham. I went to see your father yesterday morning, it wasn't an altogether harmonious occasion,' Hawk tells him.

There is a moment of silence at the other end of the phone before Abraham replies. 'He was very old. Something like this is to be expected. The doctor says he has no pain.'

'How long will he last?' Hawk asks.

'According to the physician, a week, maybe a little more, who knows?'

'Then we shall postpone the meeting until after the shiva,' Hawk says.

'Thank you, I am most grateful,' Abraham says quietly, placing down the phone.

To everyone's surprise the old man regains consciousness and can even sip a little broth or take a cup of tea, though he is unable to talk and the left side of his body is paralysed. The last known words to cross his lips are a curse for his mortal enemy, the adopted son of Mary Abacus.

David Solomon dies quietly in his sleep three days after Hawk's visit and not even the maid, who habitually brings a cup of tea to his bedroom of a morning, has a tear to shed for the old man.

'Missus, he's dead,' is all she says to Mrs Tompkins, the housekeeper, as she returns the tea to the kitchen.

'Who's dead, girl?' the housekeeper asks.

'Old Mr David.'

'Oh,' says the housekeeper. 'I'd better wake Sir Abraham then.' She points to the discarded cup of tea. 'Is that still hot enough to take in with me?'

'Suppose so,' the maid says, 'but Sir Abraham don't take no sugar.'

Chapter Eight

THE SONS AND DAUGHTERS –
VICTORIA AND JOSHUA

1914

Hawk knows little of women's fashions, but senses that the drama of the occasion may be heightened when they meet Abraham if Victoria appears to be the social equal of the sophisticated, popular and good-looking Joshua Solomon. Therefore he tries to persuade her to dress in the style that might be expected of a young Melbourne socialite whose hair is worn in what is known as the short bob, with curls brushed forward over the forehead. A gown typical of the fashion for the very rich is one such as worn by the pretty Miss Vanda Clarke at an afternoon reception at the Clarke home, Winmarleigh, for the dancer Ivy Schilling, 'the terpsichorean with the most beautiful legs in the world'. Miss Clarke wore a peacock chiffon taffeta gown, with draped bodice and tunic of soft lace and ninon, the bodice finished with a deeper tone of blue.

Hawk, reading the *Age*, has somehow stumbled across the photograph of Miss Clarke and a description of her gown and points it out to Victoria at breakfast. 'Perhaps you could wear something like this?' he says casually. 'You know, done up to the nines.' He chuckles. 'It'll fair sock Abraham and his cohorts in the eye, eh?' He stabs a finger at the paper. 'Miss Clarke seems to be the very height of fashion and you, my dear, are much, much prettier than she is.'

Victoria, who is seldom rude, though often forthright, sends him away with a flea in his ear. In fact, she seems to have tried even harder to appear as plain Jane as possible. Tommo's granddaughter has taken to dressing in a manner you might expect to find on any neatly dressed shopgirl in Myers, wearing a plain black dress, a modest hat and a cheap pair of gloves, except that her face is scrubbed clean, with not the slightest trace of powder, rouge or lip colour.

Despite these extreme efforts to appear to be plain, Victoria has inherited the bone structure of her island ancestors and while she is unlikely to be considered pretty by the fashions of the day she is a handsome young woman with her eyes being quite unusual. They are large and almost violet in colour and have a direct gaze. It is as if they contain an innate intelligence of their own even before she has opened her mouth to speak. They are a weapon of which she is not yet aware. As she grows older and assumes more authority, her eyes will often make people confess the truth before she has demanded or even expected it. Victoria's remarkable eyes will serve her well throughout her life.

Her skin, inherited from her mother, is the lightest olive and flawless, though it is clearly not of the much-admired peaches-and-cream perfection usually accorded the English and to be greatly cherished if it is possessed by a colonial femme. To the astute observer, and there are many such among Melbourne's social elite, Victoria's wheaten hair and violet eyes do not deceive them. Her naturally tanned skin shows that she is a half-breed or, among those prepared to be more charitable, at the very least of Mediterranean extract, a lineage barely considered an improvement on the part-Maori she unashamedly claims to be.

Victoria holds herself erect, even perhaps a little stiff-backed, with her chin at right angles to her neck and even though she is only slightly more than average height, five feet and five inches, she appears to be much taller. While she aspires to the uniform appearance of those women increasingly to be found in the ranks of the Labor Party, her deportment, together with her slightly clipped and correct grammar and rounded vowels, both courtesy of Mr and Mrs Wickworth-Spode, will forever stamp her as being different. In England she would be called a 'bluestocking', here she is simply a misfit, neither Friday fish nor Sunday fowl, a socialist by conviction and an aristocrat by demeanour. To the Labor organisers of the day, in particular those men running the trade unions, she is much too frank, clever and over-qualified to be allowed to play a role beyond that of a general factotum or amanuensis. These two positions are regularly reserved for a female fellow traveller in the so-called egalitarian Australian Labor Party and its corresponding union movement. Only the notorious Muriel Heagney has managed to climb further up the ranks of the unions and it is claimed that the price she has paid to achieve this status is sufficient warning to any other female who feels she might like to attempt to follow in her footsteps.

Victoria Teekleman is cursed with a quality men have never admired in a woman and, like her brother Ben, she is a natural leader. James Scullin, the Labor Prime Minister in the first two years of the Great Depression, was once heard to say of her, 'If Victoria Teekleman had been born a man I have not the slightest doubt that she would one day be running this country. Thank God she is a member of the opposite sex and not a Member of the House.'

Hawk smiles to himself when Victoria emerges from her bedroom, ready to depart with him to the city. He decides that he was quite wrong to try to persuade her to pretension. She is attired in a white cotton blouse with a wide lapel, a knitted cardigan, a sensible grey worsted skirt that shows a defiant glimpse of her ankles, woollen stockings and inexpensive black boots. Her only affectation is a cheap black Chinese silk scarf knotted in the manner of a gentleman's tie but worn loosely with the knot well down below the neckline so that the curve of her neck is clearly visible. Her hair is drawn back severely to a bun at the back of her head. Though neatly arranged, it is not much different to a style any washerwoman might affect and upon her head she wears a broad-brimmed Panama hat with only a simple black band.

However, Victoria still manages to look very attractive. She stands perfectly straight, her chin raised to appear just a fraction defiant. Although in her mid-twenties, she still looks too young to be taken seriously. Hawk suspects men will forever underestimate her, as he himself has in how she should appear at the board meeting. He wonders whether she will ever find a man strong enough to contain her, or will it be Mary Abacus all over again?

In Victoria's own mind, her plain dressing and general demeanour is not an affectation. In the time she has been in Melbourne she has come to despise the debutantes and, later, the prattling, empty-headed, husband-hunting young women who make up the unmarried social scene. She consciously does not wish to be included among them, even though her name and the wealth that comes with it condemns her to sit at the very top of the social ladder.

It has always astonished her that the middle-class girls with whom she studied accountancy, typing and shorthand look up to these young socialites as if they were on the silver screen and are perpetually gathering scraps of gossip about them as eagerly as a magpie furnishes its nest with brightly coloured bits. It is a curious fact of life that money bestows on a woman an enhanced perception of glamour, whereas a man is accorded the bonus of a superior mind. People mistakenly think that the very rich are somehow more glamorous or intelligent than themselves.

Victoria is conscious of this cultural sycophancy and her manner of dressing is also an effort to be accepted at face value by those who see themselves as having a lower status than herself. She is similarly troubled that women from the so-called middle and lower classes are terribly self-deprecating and believe that they must be less intelligent than men, so that they dare not assume the same responsibilities or expect equal remuneration for their work.

It concerns her deeply that even when women are doing essentially the same work as men, the female equivalent of the job is somehow thought to be second-rate. In the classes she attended in accountancy where the students were a mix of males and females, the women, knowing her name to be Teekleman, seemed disappointed that she didn't live up to their exalted expectations of glamour. They seemed collectively embarrassed that she topped the classes in every subject, almost as though, by beating the males, she was letting down their gender. It was a paradox she would live with all her life as she urged women to slough their sense of inferiority and take the men on at their own game, and to see the male conspiracy for what it was, merely bluff and balderdash.

She would argue with her female classmates, often exampling Addie Keating, the only woman department head at Myers, who ran the toy department, the smallest and most unprofitable area of the store. Miss Keating built it into one of the most profitable within the giant emporium. She was the first woman to travel alone overseas as a buyer, visiting Japan on several occasions and later Europe, where Sidney Myer allowed her an unlimited bank draft to purchase not only children's toys but also any other merchandise. Victoria would point out that Miss Keating came from an Irish family in Bendigo who were down on their luck, and that she'd started as the humblest fourth assistant shopgirl with no influence but a burning desire to succeed. She took on and beat the men at their own game and earned the respect of the great Sidney Myer, who once told his male department heads that Miss Keating was worth two of any of them.

Victoria would become frustrated talking to her female classmates, who pathetically stared back at her blank-eyed. On one occasion, one of them gathered up the courage to say, 'It's all right for you, you're filthy rich! You don't have to work. It doesn't matter if you lose your job!' which brought acquiescent nods from them all.

Hawk also sees why Victoria has dressed in such a severe way for the meeting with Sir Abraham and his legal and accountancy cohorts. She intends to show them that she is of equal intellectual standing and not a dizzy young thing to be treated in the patronising and jocular manner they are accustomed to adopting with the vacuous friends of their own muddle-headed daughters.

Hawk ineluctably concludes that Victoria, despite her efforts, has probably failed in both these attempts as her youth, handsome looks and natural ebullience completely override any conscious effort of plain-mannerliness. She simply isn't common or plain and no uniform she chooses to adopt will make her appear to be so. Nevertheless, in a business world where young women are expected to be seen and not heard and are usually accompanied by a pad and pencil and a competence in Sir Isaac Pitman's shorthand, Hawk silently applauds her determination not to be categorised or taken for granted.

Bringing Victoria to the boardroom of Solomon & Teekleman has not been easy. In fact, the three days it took for David to die and the additional seven for the shiva, the period of mourning whereby the family of the deceased is required to do no work and to remain quietly at home, have been very welcome. Hawk has needed every one of these days to bring Victoria around to his way of thinking.

Abraham has insisted on the strictest orthodox funeral rites for David Solomon. There is no shortage of visitors to his home while the family sit shiva. Even though David Solomon had few friends, probably not even enough for a minyan, the ten males required to say the Kaddish, the traditional prayers for the dead, Melbourne's Jews have all come to witness for themselves that the old bastard is finally dead and buried in his plain pine box.

Hawk himself attends the funeral and stands in line to offer his condolences to Abraham and Elizabeth. Abraham is aware of his presence long before they shake hands and so has time to compose himself.

'I wish you both long life,' Hawk says, offering a frail-looking Elizabeth and then Abraham his hand. He can see that Elizabeth is flushed and, as he draws closer, smells her distinctly peppermint breath. Hawk hopes only that today's bottle of gin is one of celebration rather than of despair.

Abraham, shaking his hand, says, 'I am surprised you came, Hawk Solomon, though pleasantly or otherwise I cannot yet say.'

Hawk looks at him and replies, 'Abraham, the orthodox burial is also a surprise to me, but your father was too big a factor in my life to be ignored in death. To do so would be to convey the impression that our quarrel continues.'

'Oh?' Abraham's head jerks backwards in surprise.

He looks thoroughly bemused, not sure quite what Hawk means by this final remark, but certain that his mention of the orthodox ceremony means he understands that the prolonged mourning period gives him valuable time at Hawk's expense.

This is, of course, its principal purpose, though there is another which Abraham will scarcely admit to himself. He knows that David would have resisted with every breath in his body the idea of an orthodox funeral.

'Rubbish! It's all superstitious rubbish!' he'd said often enough in life. 'Waste of time! Put me in a plain box and leave me to the worms! No rabbi, yer hear, and *don't* send a donation! That shlemiel Rabbi Abrahams has already cost me an arm and a leg *and* two ears, he's not going to cash in on my corpse as well!'

Now, by going against his wishes, Abraham is consciously asserting himself, getting rid of the last vestiges of his father's influence. That he needs the time to put his legal representatives and accountants to work to see how they might prevent Hawk from taking over at Solomon & Teekleman allows him to deny this second motive to himself.

When the housekeeper woke him with his usual cup of tea and quietly informed him of the old man's death, Abraham had already decided to give his father an orthodox funeral for these reasons.

Putting on his dressing gown and slippers and without waking Elizabeth, who was sleeping in an adjoining room, he took up his mother's prayer book and put it under his arm. Carrying the cup of tea, he went quietly into David's bed chamber.

After David first had his stroke Abraham had taken the precaution of finding his mother's prayer book. Rebecca, when it came her turn to die, had insisted on an orthodox funeral and, finding herself unable to trust her husband in the matters of her death, had schooled Abraham in the rituals to be observed. Abraham now recalls the long vigil at her bedside where he and Elizabeth had taken turns to sit for three days and nights. How, as dawn approached on the fourth day, he'd read aloud the prayer he'd been required to learn by rote. Even now he can hear his mother whispering the words, repeating them back to him as she lay dying. He also remembers how David, in his red silk dressing gown, sat with his arms crossed, looking up at the ceiling with an expression of resigned exasperation. He had refused to sit with his wife except for the briefest periods and had to be wakened when the time came for Rebecca to say her last farewells. Although it was a long time ago, Abraham now tries to recall the ancient rituals involved in Rebecca's death. He knows he has neglected to perform the first three, the candles, the vigil at David's bedside and the final prayer of confession.

However, he is not unduly concerned, thinking that he can make good with the candles and, when the rabbi arrives, it will be easy enough to be seated beside his father's bed, appearing to have been present throughout the night's vigil. With the prayer book at his side, or perhaps on his lap, the rabbi will assume that Abraham, even though David can't speak, has read the prayer of confession to his father.

Abraham knows how important this last act of contrition is among orthodox Jews, but privately thinks how inappropriate it would have been for David Solomon to show the slightest sign of remorse, even in death. For his father to enjoy the radiance of the Divine Presence after death, as is promised to orthodox Jews, seems somehow to Abraham to be a miscarriage of God's justice. Even though, where a distinct lack of saintliness in life existed, provision has been made for the departed soul to undergo a year of chastisement before entering the

Divine Presence, this too seems totally inadequate in David's case. There is a third category, where, according to tradition, only the grotesquely evil qualify for and are subject to eternal damnation. However, Abraham is too honest to place his father in this truly heavyweight division on the scales of wickedness.

Abraham tells himself that his conscience is clear on both counts, the vigil at his father's bedside and the final prayer of contrition. David's stroke has prevented any possibility of a confession and, as for the vigil at his bedside, David was so habitually drugged with an opiate syrup prescribed by the family doctor that he was forced to sleep soundly until well into the morning and it is unlikely that anyone seated at his bedside would even have noticed the moment of his death.

It had been different for his mother. She'd made him rehearse the prayer of confession several times during the week she correctly forecast she would die. 'It is a great mitzvah to be present at the departure of a soul,' Rebecca had told him. 'It will be your duty to request me to confess my sins and I hope to do so with pride.'

She had grown so accustomed to talking about her impending death that the whole family had long since given up protesting. Rebecca tended to get her own way in most things, and it did not surprise them that she would choose the timing of her own death.

'But, Mother, isn't pride a sin?' Abraham remembers teasing her.

'Believe me, in death a little pride does no harm,' she'd said with great authority. 'It's the English Jews got it, not those immigrants from Poland and Russia who do all that lamentation, weeping and gnashing of teeth. That lot, they got no pride!'

'Anyway, what sins could you possibly have to confess?' Abraham recalls humouring her further.

'Sins? Never you mind, my boy! Believe me, I got plenty! You want I should miss you saying the words so I can say them back, my very last words to my only beloved son?' she'd said accusingly.

'Aren't you supposed to say them to God, Mother?'

'Him also,' Rebecca had snapped. Then, finding the confession in her prayer book, she'd marked it with a hairpin. Abraham now sees that the hairpin is still in place after all these years and, not quite knowing why, he opens the book and begins to read aloud the long since forgotten words of the *yezi'at neshamah* in the presence of his dead father. If Rabbi Abrahams asks whether he has performed this particular mitzvah, he won't mention the disparity in time between the death and the reading, explaining only that his father had suffered a stroke and therefore was unable to respond to the words in the ancient ritual of confession.

I acknowledge unto Thee, Oh Lord my God, and the God of my fathers, that both my cure and my death are in Thy hands. May it be Thy will to send me a perfect healing. Yet if my death be fully determined by Thee, I will in love accept it at Thy hand. O may my death be an atonement for all my sins, iniquities and transgressions of which I have been guilty against Thee . . . Hear O Israel: the Lord is our God, the Lord is One.

He completes the prayer and places the prayer book where it can be clearly seen on the bedside table, then he presses the electric buzzer three times to summon the housekeeper.

When Mrs Tompkins arrives, she carries another cup

of tea. 'Nice fresh cuppa tea,' she says, putting it down beside Abraham and taking up the old one.

'Thank you, Mrs Tompkins,' Abraham says. 'Now there are several things I want you to do immediately. I want nine candles, well-used ones if you please.'

'Candles, well used? Oh dear?' The housekeeper appears to be thinking. 'I dunno, sir,' she says, 'I shall have to try and scrounge them from the servants' quarters.' She suddenly brightens. 'Plenty o' new ones in the kitchen, mind, kept in case the electric lights should fail.'

'Yes, yes, thank you, I shall require *only* used ones, the more used the better, and don't remove the wax that's melted down the sides. Do please hurry, Mrs Tompkins,' Abraham urges. 'Oh, and while you're at it, see if you can find me a chicken feather, a small one will do.'

'A chicken feather? Don't have chicken on a Thursdee.'

'From a pillow perhaps?'

'That's goose,' Mrs Tompkins says.

'Yes, well, a feather. Find one, please! Oh, and another thing, tell the maid who irons my shirt every morning to make a tear, a big tear where my heart would be, then to bring it to my bed chamber.'

'Tear your shirt?'

'Yes, yes, tear it.'

'You ain't got no old shirts, Sir Abraham.'

Abraham sighs. 'A good one, Mrs Tompkins, a *very* good one!' he says, showing some signs of exasperation.

'Hmmph!' Mrs Tompkins expostulates, clearly showing her disapproval, then she turns towards the door.

'And tell Adams to take the motor car to fetch Rabbi Abrahams, he knows where he lives.'

'Worn-down candles, chicken feathers, torn shirts and Mr Adams to fetch the rabbi, right then,' Mrs Tompkins mutters unhappily as she leaves the room.

With Mrs Tompkins dismissed Abraham walks into the

reception room where his mother always kept a silver menorah, the traditional Jewish candelabrum consisting of eight branches. He finds it tucked away in a cupboard and takes it to his father's bed chamber, where he places it on a chest of drawers to the left of the bed.

Then he moves a chair beside the bed and leaves for his own bedroom where, fortunately, the maid has not yet removed yesterday's suit for pressing. Drinking the cup of tea, Abraham waits until the laundry maid brings in the freshly ironed shirt and when she goes to pick up his suit trousers from the carpet where he's thrown them the previous night, he instructs her to leave them. Abraham examines the shirt and discovers that the maid, though it was probably Mrs Tompkins, has made a small, almost tentative cut around the area of the heart with a pair of scissors. Abraham gets into his vest and long johns and, pulling on the shirt, examines the tear in the mirror. Deciding that it does not appear sufficiently contrite, he rips it further to expose a goodly area of his undervest. Abraham is a modern Jew and doesn't habitually wear the tallit, the tassled prayer shawl traditionally worn under the shirt. His mother never threw anything out and he wonders if a little rummaging might produce the one he wore at his bar mitzvah but then decides that Rabbi Abrahams is astute enough to know that, in his case, it would be an affectation or perhaps even be seen as a hypocrisy.

He retrieves his trousers from the bedroom carpet and is pleased to see that they give every appearance of having been much rumpled. Abraham pulls them on and hooks the still attached braces over his shoulders. Leaving the starched collar off the shirt, he cunningly inserts a gold collar stud into its topmost buttonhole to give the appearance of a soiled collar removed. Finally adding his weskit, socks and boots he presents himself once again in front of the mirror. The total effect, taken together with the dark stain of his overnight growth, gives every impression of dishevelment; of clothes and man having endured a long night at the bedside of the dying.

By the time the rabbi arrives the candles of varying sizes that Mrs Tompkins has scavenged from the servants' quarters are well alight and look as if they have worn their way downwards throughout the long night's vigil. Adams steps aside at the door to let Rabbi Abrahams into David's bed chamber. The rabbi observes Sir Abraham sitting slumped in a chair at the bedside with his chin resting on his chest, giving an altogether convincing imitation of someone who hasn't slept a wink all night. Abraham, who is not by nature duplicitous, is relieved when the rabbi nods his approval.

'The vigil of a faithful son, I commend you and I wish you long life, Sir Abraham,' Rabbi Abrahams says as he crosses to where Abraham sits. Abraham rises wearily and they shake hands. 'Ah, he has not been touched,' the rabbi exclaims, seeing David's staring eyes and open jaw.

Abraham points to a saucer on the bedside table on which resides a rather small chicken feather. 'Am I not required to wait for you to say the *Baruch Dayan ha-Emet*?' Abraham asks, hoping he has correctly pronounced the Hebrew words taken from his mother's prayer book.

'Oh, you should have done that yourself, then placed the feather to the lips of the deceased to ensure there is no breath coming afterwards, leaving the body untouched for eight minutes only.'

Rabbi Abrahams points accusingly to where David lies with his toothless mouth gaping, his head sunk deeply into the goose-down pillow. 'It is the task of the eldest son to close the eyes and the mouth,' he says, reproving Abraham. 'Rigor mortis has already set in, now it will not be easy.'

'I'm sorry, Rabbi, as I said, I was under the impression he was not to be touched.'

Rabbi Abrahams shrugs and sighs and points to the candelabrum with the stubs of nine candles still burning. 'And the menorah you don't need. Only one candle to be lit beside the dying, nine is an extravagance, one candle is all that is required to symbolise the flickering of the soul. A Jew's death is a simple affair, a rich man and a poor man are equal in death, so in God's law we keep things simple, affordable, a single candle, a pine coffin, death is no time to show off.'

'I'm sorry, Rabbi, it has been too long since my mother passed away to remember all the details.'

'That is two times you are sorry already. It is unseemly to allow such a distinguished man as your father,' he points to the gaping jaw once again, 'to be like this.'

Abraham looks alarmed. 'What shall I do, Rabbi?'

Rabbi Abrahams shrugs his shoulders. 'It is not for me to say, he will not be seen, it is only a private matter, of respect between you and your father.'

'I thought it important not to touch him. I did not think of rigor mortis.'

'So now he has a big mouth to catch flies?'

'I'm sorry, Rabbi Abrahams.'

'Three times now you are sorry. Perhaps next time the telephone, eh? When you know death knocks at the door you take the telephone and call me and I will tell you what to do?'

Abraham knows Rabbi Abrahams has not been fooled by his bumbling attempt to cover up. The good reb has a reputation for both wisdom and shrewdness and in the work of the Lord is not afraid to use an acerbic tongue when he is confronted by a sacrilegious Jew. Even David had, on more than one occasion, ruefully admitted that Rabbi Abrahams got the better of him, that the rabbi had managed to effortlessly loosen his tightly drawn purse strings when no other man on God's earth could have done so.

Abraham, of course, knows the story of the two ears of God and the resultant birth of Joshua. How the rabbi took a natural and perfectly fair advantage of David's obsessive desire for a grandson. After all, it was one of the few occasions anyone can remember when David Solomon got his comeuppance and Melbourne's Jewish community are very fond of relating the story. Abraham himself derived a fair amount of comfort from the tale, for it proved that his father was vulnerable and it pleased him to think that David was made to look foolish for once in his life. But now he has no desire to undergo the same treatment at the hands of the famous rabbi.

'What shall I do?' he asks the rabbi again, knowing that if Rabbi Abrahams decides to advise him, he will by this act alone have attracted a more than generous donation to the synagogue.

'I can show you, but I cannot help. You understand?'

'Yes, thank you, Rabbi,' Abraham says, greatly relieved.

'You will need a linen table napkin and a woman's stocking and also somebody else must be here. Mr Adams perhaps? It is not necessary that this somebody is a Jew.'

'A table napkin and a woman's stocking?'

'For the jaw,' the rabbi explains, 'we must close it, force it into a closed position, then tie it for a few hours so it won't snap open again. The napkin is for the eyes,' he adds gratuitously.

Abraham nods. 'Right.' Then he calls Adams, knowing that the butler will be standing outside the bed-chamber door. The jowly visage of Adams appears around the lintel, 'You called, sir?'

'Get a stocking from one of the maids and bring a linen towel,' Abraham instructs the butler.

'A stocking, sir?'

'Yes, yes, man, do hurry, rigor mortis has set in.'

'Hurry, smurry, it won't make no difference, now is already too late to hurry,' the rabbi looks meaningfully at the hapless Abraham, 'but not too late for due care.'

Adams returns after a few minutes with both items, and no doubt there is much speculation and giggling taking place in the kitchen.

'You must stay to help, Adams,' Abraham commands, glad to be in a position to assert a little authority of his own. 'And see that whoever is given the money for a new pair of hose.'

'Certainly, Sir Abraham. May I offer my condolences to yourself and Lady Elizabeth.'

'Yes, yes, thank you, Adams. Rabbi Abrahams will instruct us now in what to do.'

'If you please, Sir Abraham, you must place both your hands on the top of Mr David's head.' The rabbi turns to Adams. 'And you, Mr Adams, will push from the base of the jaw to close it. Then Sir Abraham will tie the stocking about the jaw and pull it tight to the crown of the head where he will tie it like a bandage for a sore tooth. Do you understand?'

'Certainly, sir, I was a stretcher-bearer in the Boer War,' Adams says a trifle smugly.

Abraham is mortified at the prospect of touching the cold, staring, gap-mouthed face of his father who in death wears an expression not unlike the one he customarily assumed when his temper was out of control and he was looking around for something expensive to break. 'Er, I say, can we not have Adams do it with someone else?' Abraham now asks.

Rabbi Abrahams shakes his head and looks scornfully at him. 'It is a task for a loving son, a great privilege and an honour.'

'But you said it was not a religious act?'

'Not religious no, but loving, yes.'

Abraham sighs and closing his eyes places both hands down on the cold skull of his dead father.

'Push now!' the rabbi instructs. 'Push down!' With his eyes still tightly shut Abraham pushes down and he can hear Adams grunting as he forces the jaw to a closed position. 'Now bring the stocking,' Rabbi Abrahams says, 'cup it under the chin and draw it up over both ears and pull tight, then make a knot.'

Abraham opens his eyes and takes up the black woollen stocking in both hands and as Adams removes his hands from David's jaw he quickly loops it under his dead father's chin and draws it upwards, covering his ears.

'Tight! Pull it tight,' the rabbi explains. Abraham pulls hard on both ends of the stocking and finds his hands are now a good eighteen inches above his dead father's head. 'Keep the strain and make a knot. Mr Adams, bring back your hand on the jaw!' Abraham makes a knot and pulls it tight then makes another so that an almost perfect topknot appears at the apex of David's almost bald skull. Abraham notices for the first time that the surface of his father's skull is blotched with large dark age freckles and is, in appearance, not dissimilar to the skin of an overripe banana. He has a sense of having lost his dignity and feels slightly soiled by the waxy, cold feel of the skin. The too close proximity to death is not at all to his liking.

'Now the eyes,' the rabbi says, he looks suspiciously at Abraham. 'You will do the eyes, it is the duty of the eldest son.'

'No, please, no! I do not feel well.'

The rabbi looks at Abraham in surprise and points to the corpse. 'Not so sick as him! Tradition, tradition, it is a great honour, for three thousand years the Jews . . .'

'No! Please?' Abraham interrupts him.

'Tut, tut, it is not difficult, it is very symbolic, you are closing the curtains of life.' The look of scorn appears again as Rabbi Abrahams looks at Abraham. 'It is a great privilege to make this gesture, to bring peace, rest and tranquility to the dead.'

'No, I simply cannot do it! I can't touch him again, not his eyes.' Abraham visibly shudders.

'I shall do it, sir,' Adams says, addressing himself to the rabbi, 'though I must remind you I am not a semite,' he glances quickly at Abraham, 'but Mr David always treated me as his son.'

'Yes, thank you, Adams, I am most grateful,' Abraham says, ignoring the butler's remark. Like himself, Adams took almost nothing but abuse from his father.

Rabbi Abrahams sighs and then shrugs, it is a gesture which makes Abraham immediately decide to double the already generous donation he intends to give in memory of his father. 'As you wish then, Sir Abraham, it is not a religious task.'

Adams stoops over the bestocking'd head of David Solomon and with a minimum of fuss gouges his thumbs deeply into the cold eye sockets and expertly pulls the lids down over the dead man's eyes. Then taking up the table napkin he twirls it into a narrow strip which he uses to bandage the closed eyelids.

Abraham looks down at the now heavily bandaged head of the dead David Solomon. The tightly drawn stocking has pulled his father's jaw so far upwards that his mouth serves as a hinge and the point of the jaw now touches the tip of his nose.

Rabbi Abrahams rises. 'You will, of course, cover all the mirrors in the house.' He looks about him and spies a mug beside the bed. 'And pour the water from all containers near the dead.'

He leans over to pick up the mug. Suddenly his eyes grow wide, 'Oh my goodness!' he exclaims. 'The teeth! We have locked your father's jaw without putting back his teeth!'

Abraham draws back in horror. 'Oh no, you don't! No way! That's it. I've had quite enough!'

'But, Sir Abraham, the jaw will collapse,' the rabbi points to the dead man's face. 'See already it's not so good, it will be most unseemly, Mr David *must* have his teeth, it is a matter of respect for the dead.'

'So, let it collapse, no one will see him!' Abraham shouts in panic, his voice climbing two octaves. 'He's dead, my father's dead, he's not on exhibition! I'm not going through that again!'

The rabbi shrugs. 'That is true but you are the only son, a great privilege!' the rabbi protests.

'No, Rabbi! You've heard me. I'm absolutely not going to do it!'

'It is not such a nice thing you are doing, Abraham Solomon.' The rabbi smiles, 'But on the other hand, I understand.'

'Thank you, Rabbi,' Abraham sighs, greatly relieved. 'I am not sure I feel well, I wonder if I may be excused?'

'Certainly, Sir Abraham, but first I must say the prayers for the dead, it is important that you be present for these.' The rabbi turns to the butler. 'Mr Adams may now leave.'

With the ancient prayer rituals completed, the rabbi quietly instructs Abraham in his further duties. 'You will wrap your beloved father with a sheet and place him on the floor with his feet pointed towards the door and then you will place a single candle at his head. Before Mr Moshe Sapperstein of the Chevra Kadisha arrives my advice to you is to remove the bandages from his head and eyes so your father will look the way a father should when a loving and dutiful son has properly attended to his death.'

'Yes, thank you, Rabbi Abrahams, I am most grateful.

I shall make a donation in memory of my father if you will let me know how this might best be done. Some useful project perhaps?'

Rabbi Abrahams bows slightly. 'Now is not the time to talk of such matters, but I am most grateful, Sir Abraham, the Lord's work is never completed. We have a great need to build a new synagogue, thank the Lord our congregation grows. Perhaps I may visit you at some time more convenient to discuss this with you?'

'Certainly, Rabbi. I will look forward to your call. We shall telephone for a taxi to take you home, there is a depot not far away, it will not take long.'

'Thank you, Sir Abraham, I must remind you that the body of your father must not be left alone. You or your wife must not leave him until the Chevra Kadisha comes to fetch him.' Rabbi Abrahams looks around the room and points to the menorah. 'I think maybe a small miracle, that is the first time I have seen candles that do not all burn down at the same rate.' Then bowing his head slightly before leaving the room, the rabbi says the traditional blessing, 'May the Lord comfort you with all the mourners of Zion and Jerusalem.'

With the rabbi's departure and Elizabeth seated facing the far wall, her back turned on the shrouded body of David on the floor with his feet pointed towards the door and with one of Mrs Tompkins' brand new candles at his head, Abraham is feeling decidedly better. Tradition, tradition, how useful it can be. Expensive, but useful. Abraham decides he will call Hawk immediately and ask for a postponement to prepare for him and his clever little granddaughter. As he commences to wind the handle on the telephone he thinks that David's timely death is the only true example of consideration his father has ever shown him.

Hawk, putting down the telephone from Abraham Solomon, is almost as grateful as Abraham for the extra time David's death allows him. Victoria is proving extremely difficult to convince that she should work with him at the Potato Factory.

'But, Grandfather, you have been retired these twenty-one years, why would you wish to go back?' is the first question she asks after he has approached her with the proposition he has in mind.

'Not retired, my dear, removed, sacked from the chairmanship of Solomon & Teekleman, you well know the circumstances.'

'Well, yes, but does it really matter?' Victoria says, appealing to him. 'We are well rid of the vile company, they exploit the poor at every opportunity.' She shudders suddenly. 'You know how very much I wish my name wasn't a part of it!'

'But you *are* a part of it, Victoria, and will, someday, with Ben, be its biggest shareholder. The three of us already are.'

'It makes me feel dirty, Grandfather. They are singular proof that we must have stronger unions and a government that is prepared to take away much of the power of the large corporations.'

Hawk sighs. 'The working class will certainly benefit by a stronger union movement and you already have a Labor government, but as long as industry can be relied on to pay taxes, even a Labor prime minister will be reluctant to interfere. While I am all for curbing excesses, wherever they may be, it seems to me that the best way to change an organisation is from within.'

'I should much rather work *within* a trade union to make the changes.'

Hawk laughs, applauding Victoria's quick mind. Nonetheless he continues. 'Think of a corporation or

299

company as a human with many of the same characteristics. For instance, Solomon & Teekleman is formed out of two companies, Solomon & Co. founded by David Solomon, and the Potato Factory founded, as you know, by Mary Abacus. The two, when they came together under the same parent company, were diametrically opposed in their philosophies, in other words they had quite different personalities. Like a husband and wife with different cultural backgrounds who are unable to agree on almost anything. Take David Solomon's company, selfish, greedy, unsympathetic, cunning, vengeful and deeply suspicious of those who work for it, these are the characteristics of Solomon & Co. and are a mirror image of the man who founded it.

'On the other hand, Mary's company, in the light of the times, was straight-dealing, open, hard-headed but responsible for the welfare of those who worked for it. Your great-grandmother never forgot her humble beginnings or what it meant to be poor and so she understood the needs of her people.' Hawk pauses and looks at Victoria, 'Do you follow the analogy so far?'

Victoria nods her head, 'Yes but . . .' She knows better than to interrupt, but simply cannot contain herself.

'Yes but what, my dear?' Hawk asks, a trifle irritated at being interrupted when, to his mind, his explanation is progressing along so nicely.

'The bad swallowed the good! Evil triumphed, as it always seems to do in big business! David Solomon won, didn't he!'

Hawk shakes his head. 'I know it looks that way. But David's control came about by a series of unfortunate circumstances which allowed him to take control, rather than what was originally intended, that someone who believed in the Mary Abacus approach should be at the helm.'

'You mean, of course, yourself?'

'Aye. I failed to ensure my control of Solomon & Teekleman.'

'Because our mother left without giving you her proxy? Is that why?'

Hawk nods again. 'It wasn't evil triumphing over good, it was my own stupidity. I should have been more sensitive to the emotional needs of your mother. I'm afraid I'm a clumsy, insensitive fool when it comes to that sort of thing. Her restlessness was there for me to see if I'd been looking. David Solomon obtained control by default or, if you like, because of my own lack of foresight, and so he proceeded to create both companies in his own image.'

'Grandfather Hawk!' Victoria protests. 'You are not clumsy and you are the least fool of any man I've ever known, you are the most fair-minded, honest and sensitive person I know!' Victoria pauses then lowers her voice, 'But after all that's said and done, that's my *very* point!'

'What is?' Hawk asks. To his surprise he finds himself slightly on the defensive. 'That you think me weak and David strong?'

Victoria sighs. 'No, "fair-minded, honest and sensitive" doesn't mean weak. But you would be the first to admit that they are characteristics largely missing in big business and deeply scorned by the capitalists. You must see the enemy for what they are! They are not going to change willingly but must be dragged kicking and screaming to the negotiating table.' Victoria takes a breath, 'And if they won't come, they must be punished!'

'Spoken like a true disciple of Labor!' Hawk teases. 'The dialectics are fair enough, though the wording a little too revolutionary for my taste. Capitalism as a system has many advantages but it is essentially based on the very human need that most of us have to want more. Greed being perhaps the most primitive of our many human urges, the capitalist system works very well for those who have the money to exploit it.'

'But greed has no right to exist in a modern society, we are no longer primitive, there is enough for us all, we must learn to share our wealth.'

'Unfortunately, right at this moment the capital on which the system is based is in the hands of those new Australian money aristocrats, the Clarkes, the Armytage family, the Fairbairns, Hentys, Mackinnons, Manifolds and Sargoods to name but a few and, indeed, David Solomon and yourself, my dear. With the exception perhaps of the Clarkes and ourselves, who have been generous in their public donations, they all have every intention of having as much as they can get and sharing as little as they can get away with.'

'But they *must* be made to share!'

'Well, perhaps, but remember they were prepared to take the original risks to acquire it. Taking risks should not go unrewarded or no one would take them. Sidney Myer Baevski was once a hawker, a poor Russian Jew who spoke no English when he arrived, working the small country towns for his living. He endured daily ridicule, young boys would throw rocks at him and shout, "Jewboy, Jewboy, take a piece of pork and put it on your fork!" Three months ago, as all of Melbourne witnessed, he opened his new emporium in Bourke Street, the greatest and grandest shop in Australia and few better in the world. All this in twenty years and achieved by taking countless risks. You could say that he deserves the reward of the risk-taker. Must he also be punished?'

Hawk does not wait for Victoria to reply. 'David Solomon was yet another who started out with virtually nothing. Men such as these, poor boys, Irish, Jews,

Protestants, all took risks and some were successful while others failed. It only becomes a problem when the risk-takers are so successful that they control most of the capital, which means they are the only ones who can reasonably capitalise on the essentially risk-free and truly big opportunities that occur in a growing economy such as our new Federation. As capital expands it gains more and more power. Money and power is a heady mixture which very easily leads to corruption.'

'So you agree with me, we need a strong counter-system to control these rich families and consortiums, these money aristocrats?'

'Well, yes and no. Alas, it is my observation that counter-systems, as you call them, tend to acquire the same characteristics and many of the bad habits of the systems they oppose and are therefore often counterproductive. What's more, they are essentially more difficult to remove than big business, because they do not have to survive in a risk-taking world or answer to shareholders.'

'Ha, that may be reasonable speculation, Grandfather. But the unions do have the government of the day to restrain them.'

'Perhaps not as far as you think, let me give you an example, and one I personally experienced. Though I confess it was a little too early for the union movement, it was the start of worker dissent in factories. A Workers' Deputation, as they called themselves at the time, claiming membership of several factories and workshops in the Hobart area, visited Mary Abacus under the leadership of a Scotsman named Hugh Kirk. Kirk was a small-time firebrand and his movement one of many which preceded unionism as we know it today. He had visited Melbourne where he became acquainted with a newly formed group who named themselves the Brewers'

Employes' Eight Hours Association and returned home to aim his sights at the Cascade Brewery and ourselves, urging the workers to unite against the bosses and join "the Association". He was a popular speaker among the working classes and had gained some real success in recruiting members as I remember, by calling one- or two-day strikes and frightening some of the smaller workshop owners. But not, it was claimed, without a fair bit of heavy-handed coercion involving several broken heads among those workers reluctant to join. The Potato Factory was his first incursion into the big league and with his new Melbourne association, Kirk demanded that Mary allow his movement to operate within the brewery.

'"Righto," says Mary, "if that's what my people want then they can 'ave it with me blessing."' Victoria laughs despite herself for Hawk brings her great-grandmother alive for her. He continues, 'Mary points her crooked finger at Hugh Kirk, "But first, let's ask 'em straight. You talk to them, tell 'em whatever it is you wish to say, you know, exploitation o' the working classes, snot-nosed kids begging for pennies on street corners, wife dying in childbirth, father of consumption, leaving ten starvin' kids behind, all the stuff what's been goin' on for 'undreds of years and all now blamed on big business. I promise I won't say nothin'. I'll keep me gob shut tight as a possum's bum. Then we'll 'ave the vote, let 'em decide for themselves. Fair enough, Mr Kirk?"

'"Fair enough, missus," Kirk says reluctantly. Well, Mary calls for the works foreman, Ernie Connaghan. "Mr Connaghan," she says, "stop the brewery, close it down the 'ole box and dice, we're 'aving a meeting o' the workers this afternoon."

'Ernie Connaghan looks like he can't believe what Mary's just said, "Can't do that, Miss Mary, we'd 'ave to steam-clean all the pipes, get the yeast vats started from scratch, build up the fermentation vats, take us all night to get under way again, cost a fortune in lost production, what's more, you know it's impossible to close the malt house, barley's piling up as it is with no place to store it."

'"That all right, missus, maltsters don't belong in the Association," says Kirk.

'"You hear that? Cost a fortune, Mr Kirk. My money, not the workers'." She turns to Ernie Connaghan, "No matter, do as I say, Ernie, er Mr Connaghan, Mr Kirk here is from the . . . what did you say you were?"

'"Brewers' Employes' Eight Hours Association," Kirk replies.

'"Yes, well them. He wants to spruik to all the workers, 'cept the maltsters and the clerks in the front office, whom he don't consider the first brewers and the second to be workers, them wearing stiff collars and all." Mary now turns to Kirk, "So what's wrong with the clerks? You got something against clerks, Mr Kirk? I was a clerk once, still am as a matter o' fact, only a bit better paid than most."

'"Clerks can become bosses, missus. Can't trust a clerk."'

Hawk grins at the memory. 'So we close the brewery down except for the malt house and the front office and all the workers assemble in the dray yard to hear Mr Hugh Kirk. And I have to say he does a damn fine job telling the workers how they are exploited by the owners, blah, blah, blah. He's of a fiery Scots temperament and he works up quite a sweat socking it to the bosses, who in this case is Mary and myself, both of us sitting on a dray cart with our arms crossed listening. Then he says, "Righto, we'll take a vote, like the boss said, all who wants to stop the exploitation by the bosses by joining the Association and getting an eight-hour working day raise yer hands."

'"Oi! Just a bleedin' moment!" Mary shouts. "We'll 'ave none of that, Mr Kirk. A vote you shall have, fair and square, but it will be by *secret* ballot, our people will vote with their consciences not with their bleedin' 'ands. Only them and Gawd is gunna know who they are and 'ow they've voted."

'"That's not how it's done, missus," Kirk objects. "We like things to be kept in the open like, democratic, know what I mean?"

'"Democratic me arse!" Mary says. "Sure you want it open so you'll know the names of those who are *for* you and them's what's *against*. All for the future records, eh? Very 'andy, if I may say so meself, being a clerk an' all. Well, I tell you what I'll do, I'll exercise me own perog-a-tive as a boss and put democracy to work. I'll allow a secret ballot to determine whether the people at the Potato Factory want an open vote, a show of 'ands, or want a conscience vote. Now what say you to that, Mr Kirk? Ain't nothing says that's against the rules, is there?"'

Hawk spreads his hands. 'Well, the Potato Factory workers voted in Mary's ballot that they wanted a secret ballot to decide whether to join Kirk's association or remain as they were. Then they used the secret ballot to say they wished to remain as they were.'

'You mean your workers didn't vote for an eight-hour day?' Victoria asks, incredulous.

'Indeed, they did not, but they got it anyway two months later.'

'Well, Mr Kirk's visit did some good then. But, Grandfather, the Potato Factory was an exception, other companies did, and *still* exploit their workers,' Victoria challenges. 'The intimidation from the bosses experienced by the workers during the Shearers' and the Maritime strikes proved once and for all that the capitalists could not be trusted, that a strong labour movement had to be in parliament, that unionism was essential if the workers were ever to be free of what virtually amounted to a system of bondage!'

'Perhaps, but let me make my point. Perhaps as a consequence of this single incident with Mary, for Hugh Kirk was later to become a very big figure in the Tasmanian and Australian union movement, the unions never allowed secret ballots. Today, coercion and standover tactics are more than common in our trade unions. So you see, my dear, power and corruption are not such a long way away in any organisation. We all want control, the bosses have it by owning the means of earning wages and the unions have it by owning the workers. Mark my words, secret ballots are outlawed by the union movement and the next thing they will do is to make joining a union compulsory. In other words, a worker will not be able to find employment without a union card and, as a registered member, they will not be allowed to vote according to conscience for fear of repercussions, not from their industrial bosses, but from their own union bosses. Furthermore, industry will not be allowed to employ non-union labour.'

'But the union officials will be serving in the interest of the workers, gaining advantages and better conditions for them, why would they vote against such laudatory pursuits? Besides, Mr Curtin says it is a matter of brotherly trust, that a worker must show where he stands at a union meeting, that secret ballots are sneaky and unmanly!'

'Ah, well said, Mr Curtin, how very convenient to the cause.' Hawk gives Victoria a rueful smile. 'But in the end, my dear, it is a matter of freedom of choice. But it is interesting, is it not, that those who have been elected to the House of Representatives achieved this by secret ballot? The so-called common worker must enjoy the right to choose without fear or favour.'

'Oh, I see, the age-old system of divide and conquer. Turn the unions against themselves. Is this then to be the new management weapon?' Victoria snorts.

Hawk looks amused, enjoying both Victoria's lively mind and her strongly held convictions. 'You have the makings of an excellent union leader, my dear.'

Victoria appeals to Hawk. 'But I *am* a member of the Labor Party and I do truly believe they are the solution to the terrible exploitation of the working classes in our country.' Her eyes are sad, as though disappointed that he might not feel the same way. 'Surely you also believe this?'

Hawk smiles. 'Of course. Capital and labour must both be seen to co-exist, to be a viable part of our economy. Both must benefit if we are to prosper as a nation, but there is an ingredient which is essential if each side is to have its rightful share of the good life.'

'And what is that?' Victoria asks.

'Goodwill,' Hawk replies.

Victoria looks genuinely shocked. 'You're not serious? Goodwill? You said yourself, people are greedy and can't be trusted?'

'Well, take Sidney Myer again. He has established a pension fund for his workers, he is a Jew but allows the staff to hold Christian services in the shop at lunch time. He has a choir, a Friday night get-together for his staff, annual picnics and now he has introduced what is called "a spiff", that is, his sales people are paid a penny in the pound commission as an incentive. Is this not the beginnings at least of a caring company?'

Victoria looks appealingly at Hawk. 'You're going to say, when a generous person controls a company and is in a position to make the right decisions, management and trade unions don't necessarily have to be at each other's throats. Is that it, Grandfather?'

'Very good, my dear. If you were to join Solomon &

Teekleman and rise to the top it would be a great opportunity to show your character, to show how things might be different.'

'Well, what about Joshua? He has been groomed to run Solomon & Teekleman virtually since birth?'

'We have the majority now, Victoria. We have the say.'

Victoria shakes her head. 'How could you say that! How is that fair? If he were better than me I wouldn't want to be chairman. I would hate that.'

'Better? How can he be? He is the product of his grandfather, he will run the company much as his grandfather did. There is very little of Abraham and a whole lot of David Solomon in that young man, he would be the devil you know and want to be rid of, Victoria.'

'But I would always have to fight him, he'd never give in.'

'Aye, that's true. If you were a union official you'd always have to fight him and he'd never give in. The proposition I hope, with your permission, to put to Abraham is that he remains overall chairman, that I become the chairman and managing director of the Potato Factory and take you with me to train you to eventually run it. Then, upon Joshua's return from the war, he will take over Solomon & Co., whereupon I retire and you replace me as managing director of the Potato Factory.' Hawk shrugs. 'After that it's your personal donnybrook with Joshua.'

'I see, him with one company, me with the other. So that I can learn to practise what I preach, our ideal of a fair-minded company, and Joshua does it his way. The performances of the two companies may then be compared. What if his is better, and greed and bullying proves to be better than sharing the wealth?'

'Well, that's for you to find out, I didn't say it would be easy. If it's a disaster you could always resign and join the trade union movement,' he teases Victoria. 'A little wiser in the ways of the world by then, I daresay.'

'But, Grandfather, you do believe that fairness and honesty will win the day, don't you?'

'I have always tried to be honest and fair in my dealings in life and to be perfectly frank with you my life has been a failure. But that doesn't mean you will fail. The very predicament we find ourselves in at present, with David having snatched control of Solomon & Teekleman, was because I wanted to be fair-minded.'

'You mean you don't think I can do it?' Victoria challenges.

'No, I didn't say that. I said that I had not been successful. But Mary Abacus was, so why not you?' Hawk replies.

'I have never understood why you wanted to join with David and Abraham in the first place, if as you say their way of doing things was so very different to yours? You didn't need to do it, you were already a huge success and, as I understand it, they were in financial trouble. It's never made any sense to me?'

Hawk sighs. 'Because out of something rotten came something good and then out of that something good has come something rotten again and I am stupid enough to believe it might yet come to something good.'

'Whatever can you mean?' Victoria says, puzzled.

'Ah! It's a long story and one I would only wish you to hear if you decide to come into the company so that I might train you. If you don't I will not burden you with it, it is too long and painful and not worth the telling unless it ultimately helps your determination to succeed where I have failed.'

'Grandfather, that is so very unfair!' Victoria protests. 'You want me to make a decision without knowing its entire purpose?'

'Nevertheless, I want you to decide using your own free will. Whatever you decide to do, I shall accept your decision. If I were to tell you my reasons for wanting you to take your rightful place in the company you own, you may well be persuaded by your emotions and not by your own reasoning. I should not want that to happen.'

Victoria spends the next two days alone, taking her meals separately then announces that she wants to talk to Ben who hasn't, as expected, returned to Tasmania. Four days after the passing-out parade he was told to report to Major Sayers, his Victorian company commander.

The major, a scouse, comes straight to the point. 'Look, Sergeant Teekleman, we need you here. I've spoken to your C.O. in Hobart and he's agreed you can stay with us, though in fairness I 'ave to say he put up a fair bit of fuss, no, more than that, he was bloody angry.'

'But why, sir? It was clearly understood that I'd be allowed to return to my own regiment, to my mates?'

The major shrugged, 'Ard luck, lad, we need another instructor on machine guns. Sergeant Freys, the chief instructor, has been diagnosed with cancer, he won't be going overseas with us.'

'But, sir, there are ten other sergeants all of whom did the course with me, all of them Victorians.'

'It's damned 'ard luck. I know. But there are other considerations I am not at liberty to divulge like.' He points to the ceiling. 'Made higher oop.'

Shortly after Ben's instructions that he is to stay with the Victorian regiment it is announced that the troopships which are to take the Victorians and Tasmanians to King George Sound in Albany will be delayed three weeks. There are no official explanations for this, but a major story in the *Age* speculates, as it turns out correctly, that it is because the prime minister and the war cabinet do not want to send the convoy ships to Western Australia without the protection of the battleships HMAS *Sydney* and HMAS *Melbourne* in case the German navy decides to hunt in Australian waters.

Victoria contacts Ben at Broadmeadows and he requests and is granted forty-eight hours' leave. She books two rooms overnight at a small hotel in the Dandenongs so that she might talk undisturbed with him about Hawk's proposition.

Victoria arrives home at ten o'clock in the evening of the second day and goes immediately to Hawk's study to tell him that she accepts the challenge he has given her.

'I am delighted, my dear,' Hawk says, rising and embracing her. 'But now you must tell me why? I cannot believe that my arguments alone have persuaded you.'

'Well no, not entirely, it was Ben.'

'Ben?' Hawk says surprised. 'I didn't think Ben took much interest in business matters?'

'No, he doesn't, but he's got an awful lot of commonsense.' Victoria smiles. '"Sissie," he said after I'd told him how I felt and what you'd said, "the bloody unions are never going to let you rise high enough in their ranks to really change things. Grandfather Hawk is probably right, there are just as many crooks, greedy and corrupt blokes protecting their arses in the unions as there are in big business. The army's the same, full of bullshit artists that don't know their arse from their elbow. What's more, how far do you think you're gunna get as a woman in the Labor Party, eh? You ain't gunna get into parliament, will ya? A woman in parliament, heaven bloody forbid, she might take her knitting into debate! Do a pair of baby booties when the house is in session!"' Victoria is a fair mimic in her own right and she has Ben's soft drawl down pat. '"But, look at it this way, sis, if you join Solomon & Teekleman and you go against Joshua and you beat him, you can do things your way and make a bloody big difference, possibly change the way business is done in Australia. Grandfather Hawk is right about money and power. Mind you, round this bloody place there's no bloody money, it's just power! But it doesn't always have to make you corrupt, does it?"' Victoria concludes. 'Well, that's what he said anyway.'

'He said that?' Hawk exclaims, impressed. 'And that's what made you decide?'

Victoria nods. 'Now, will you tell me all I must know about the past?'

'First you must eat something. Mrs Billings has left a plate in the oven for fear you'd return and starve to death on boarding-house food. Hawk imitates the housekeeper, '"She'd be a shadow, that one, left to her own! Can't even boil an egg, too busy doin' sums on them bloomin' beads! Young girls these days got nothing in their 'eads what's useful. I don't know what the world's coming to, her goin' off and staying in a boardin' 'ouse!"' Hawk then adds in his own voice, 'Better eat something, though, or we'll never hear the end of it.'

'It was a perfectly lovely little hotel and we had a scrumptious lunch before we left, but a little supper would be nice. Will you sit with me, Grandfather? Have a cup of tea?' Victoria smiles. 'I can make a cup of tea.'

It is nearly two before they finally rise from the table and Hawk has told Victoria the whole story of the two families and the bitter conflict which has always existed between them and the reasons for it. He leaves nothing out. Finally he tells her of Teekleman's death and Hinetitama's demise until she returned to die in the St Kilda hospice and that, with her proxy, they once again control Solomon & Teekleman.

When Hawk has completed the story they both remain silent for some time, Victoria weeping softly. 'It is not too late to decide against joining Solomon & Teekleman. I would completely understand if you are reluctant to carry the burden of such a past. Though Abraham Solomon is a reasonable man, Joshua has been bred to commerce by his grandfather and he may prove equally recalcitrant and unforgiving.'

Victoria looks tearfully up at Hawk and sniffs, 'No, I've made up my mind, I want to be with you.'

'Well then, there is one last task, though more a pleasure than a task.' He rises and goes to his desk and taking a small key from his pocket he opens a drawer and takes out Mary's Waterloo medal attached to a thin gold chain. 'Your great-grandmother asked me on her deathbed to give this to you. It was her talisman, her great good luck. It was only removed from her neck on two occasions, when it was stolen on board the convict ship she came out on by the assistant to the ship's surgeon and when she died. Will you wear it? On the back it says "I shall never surrender", four words which made everything possible for Mary. Will you take it for yourself, the medal and the words?'

Victoria gasps as she is handed the medallion. 'Oh, I know it was wrong, but I was so envious of Ben when he received our grandfather's Tiki. I would so much have liked it for myself.' Victoria, already emotionally exhausted, bursts into tears as Hawk takes the medallion back again and places it about her neck. 'I shall treasure it all the days of my life, Grandfather Hawk. Thank you, thank you,' she says, barely above a whisper. 'I shall wear it with the same pride as did Mary Abacus.'

She goes to bed in the small hours of the morning exhausted but unable to sleep, her pillow wet with tears for the sad past of her family. She sees the dawn light growing through her window and hears the call of the currawongs, always the first of the birds to greet the new day, and then the next thing she knows, Mrs Billings is shaking her. 'It's four o'clock in the afternoon, lovey. Mr Hawk says to bring you a nice cuppa. I've got a nice bit o' fish for your tea and some new taties and them baby beans you likes. I dunno what his nibs thought he was doin' keeping you up so late, you comin' 'ome after a long journey like that. That's men for you, don't think do they, does what they wants, never mind the feelings and welfare o' others, especially us womenfolk!'

Victoria smiles, sipping the tea, her whole life seems to have changed in the last few days but the whingeing rock of Billings can be relied upon to remain ever the same. 'It was my fault, Mrs Billings, he was telling me the story of our family.'

'Hmmph! I could tell you a thing or two meself, but I won't, it's not for me to say, being in service and all.' She points to the Waterloo medal about Victoria's neck. 'Give you that, did he? That were her most precious possession. Never mind the money, it were that she treasured above rubies. Always knew when things were not going good, she'd sit on the porch in her rocking chair 'olding the medal in her broken fist waitin' for them birds.'

'Yes, Grandfather Hawk told me, it was her talisman and her great good luck.'

'Yes, that and them bloomin' parrots. Did he tell you about them green parrots, that were also her great good luck she'd say?'

Victoria shakes her head, trying to recall if Hawk said anything about green parrots. 'No, I don't think so?'

'Well, you saw them yerself, you was three years old.'

'I don't remember. What about the green parrots?'

'Miss Mary, she'd sit on the porch o' the big house in Hobart to watch the parrots come past. They'd fly over the roof going to their roost higher up the mountain. "Here they come, my great good luck," she'd shout for one and all to hear as they passed over.' Mrs Billings warms to the story, happy to be a part of a family legend. 'Your great-grannie, she loved them birds. Well, the day she died, the very minute she went to her peace, the parrots started to come, but they didn't fly over like always, they settled in the garden, on the roof, in the trees, there was more green parrots than there was leaves on the gum trees. Hundreds o' thousands o' them. They made so much racket you couldn't hear nothing, everything was vibrating green. They stayed an hour then they took off, all o' them together. It were like the roaring of the wind, just their wings and the screeching fair blow'd the ears off yer 'ead.

'Well, next mornin' at sunrise I'm in the kitchen garden 'anging out the tea cloths like I always does first thing. I looks up to the porch expecting to see Miss Mary, her in her favourite chair, waiting for the parrots to pass over. But o' course she ain't there this partickler mornin', she's dead, ain't she? But it's time for the parrots to fly over so I waits, remembering the strange thing what 'appened the night before. I waits and waits. You could time them birds on a clock, you could, always ten minutes after sunrise, but they didn't come, didn't fly over. Not that morning, not ever again. The parrots never come back again and if you think I'm lyin' I'll swear it on a stack o' Bibles,' Mrs Billings says. She looks at Victoria darkly. 'The luck's run out, see. That's what happened to Mr Hawk. There's no more luck, it's all been spent by Miss Mary, used up.'

'Oh, I don't believe you, Mrs Billings, that's just superstitious nonsense,' Victoria cries.

'You mark me words, young lady, the luck's run out with the green parrots.'

Hawk and Victoria arrive at the head office of Solomon & Teekleman on the dot of ten o'clock, having waited in the motor car around the corner for five minutes so that they wouldn't appear over-anxious by arriving early.

They are met at the door by Abraham's secretary, a tall, dour man of whom it is claimed that he has never been seen to smile. There is a greyness as well as a mustiness about him as though he has been locked in a cupboard for several years never seeing the sunlight. 'Sir Abraham is expecting you, sir,' he says to Hawk, while managing to completely ignore the presence of Victoria.

'Good morning, Mr Phillips,' Victoria chirps brightly, but receives no response.

Hawk is impressed, she has done her homework and knows the name of Abraham's private secretary, whom he is certain she cannot have previously met. 'I don't believe you've met my granddaughter, Phillips?' Hawk now says. 'Victoria, this is Mr Phillips, Mr Phillips, this is Victoria,' he says smiling. He can sense that Victoria is more amused than upset by Phillips' original rebuff.

'How do you do?' Victoria smiles, extending her hand.

'How do?' Phillips mutters, averting his eyes and pushing forward a limp hand which scarcely touches the tips of Victoria's gloved fingers before being withdrawn. 'Follow me please, sir.'

Sir Abraham Solomon is seated at the head of the table as Hawk and Victoria enter the boardroom. There are three men around the long mahogany table and another is seated away from the table, in the corner furthermost from the door. They all rise. Abraham in his fifties is a balding, corpulent, clean-shaven man dressed in a well-cut, three-piece, dark-navy woollen suit. He wears a black tie and gold tie-clip, and his starched collar seems to cut somewhat into his jowls. Everything about him, right down to his highly polished black boots, starched shirt cuffs and gold cufflinks, bears the hallmark of those who do business in the big end of town. 'Good morning,

317

Hawk, good morning, Miss Teekleman, may I introduce you to my colleagues?'

Abraham turns towards the three men standing. 'Hawk Solomon you already know, this is his grand-daughter Miss Victoria Teekleman.'

'Miss Teekleman, at the far end is Sir Samuel Sopworth, then Mr Bramwell Cumming two chairs up on the right and, next to him, Mr John Miles. Not joining us at the table is Mr Parkin, who will be taking notes as an observer.'

Victoria has heard of two of the men, Samuel Sopworth, who is a famous accountant, and Bramwell Cumming, a notorious barrister known in Labor ranks as the scourge of the union movement. John Miles, whom she hasn't heard of before, has the pinched and fussy look of a successful lawyer, a type with whom she is all too familiar. Parkin is an unprepossessing-looking man in a suit one might expect a clerk to wear, a misfit, and doesn't appear to belong to the same world as the four other men. Though somewhat older, he has a quite startling resemblance to one of the members of her Labor Party chapter, who is a clerk in the railways office in Flinders Street. Then she suddenly remembers that he is also named Parkin, George Parkin, and has on several occasions boasted of his older brother, who he claimed worked in Trade and Customs, and with the previous month's election of the Andrew Fisher Labor government has been made head of department under the Hon. F. G. Tudor, Minister for Trade and Customs.

Hawk has moved to shake each man by the hand, leaning across the table to do so, and when he has completed greeting each of the men around the table, he walks over to Parkin and shakes his hand before returning to Victoria. The men remain standing and Victoria looks at each of them in turn and, smiling, says, 'How do you do, gentlemen, please call me Victoria. It will be easier on us all. Perhaps we can all be seated now, Sir Abraham?'

'Yes, yes, please,' Abraham says anxiously, indicating the two vacant chairs on the side nearest the door. He is a little taken aback by Victoria's unexpected poise. Abraham thinks what an attractive girl she is despite the plainness of her attire and her well-scrubbed complexion. He has grown accustomed to the flighty and fashionable young women Joshua brings home from time to time and thinks to himself that Victoria Teekleman is far more the type of young lady he would prefer to see on his son's arm, unlikely as that is.

The four men resume their seats and Hawk and Victoria take up theirs. On her small notepad she writes *Mr Parkin – Government!* and puts the pad and pencil down in front of Hawk as though she is handing him his notepad. She sees him casually glance down at it.

There is a sudden silence around the table and then Sir Abraham Solomon clears his throat and seems a trifle nervous, glancing first at the two lawyers and then at Sir Samuel, before returning his gaze to Hawk. 'Well, Hawk Solomon, what have you to say for yourself?' Clearly it is an opening line he has practised carefully, though his voice lacks the casual arrogance needed for such a statement. Hawk thinks how much better David Solomon would have used such an opening remark, bringing to it sufficient vitriol to make it hiss like spittle on a hot stove.

Hawk smiles. 'Well, firstly, Sir Abraham, I wish to offer Victoria's and my own condolences on the passing of your father. Although we didn't get on, he was in many ways a remarkable man, we wish you and your family a long life.'

'Thank you, he had a good innings,' Abraham replies and turns and speaks directly to Victoria. 'Thank you, Victoria, I shall pass your kind remarks on to my family.'

Victoria looks directly into his eyes and Abraham cannot help but feel that there is something quite different about Hawk's granddaughter, though he is about to find out just how different.

Abraham, of course, has a clear idea of why Hawk has called the meeting. When Hawk called on him to make the original appointment he'd been out of his office and so Hawk had simply conveyed, through the dour Mr Phillips, a request for a board meeting the following morning, preferably at ten, simply stating that it was on a matter of critical importance to the future of the company.

Abraham, on returning to his office, knew at once that something was afoot and made an educated guess as to what it might be. Shortly afterwards he received the urgent call to return home as David had been found unconscious on the conservatory floor. Later he'd questioned Adams at some length about Hawk's meeting with the old man. Adams, sporting a severely swollen hand, proved to have an excellent, if biased, recall of what had transpired, painting Hawk very much as the villain in the proceedings.

David's funeral and the shiva that followed it has given Abraham time to brief John Miles and Bramwell Cumming and to arrange for Sir Samuel Sopworth to be at the board meeting. Not only is Sir Samuel's firm the accountants for Solomon & Teekleman but he, as does Abraham, sits on several government committees and is, in addition, a member of the wartime Board of Industry. Sir Samuel has also arranged for a high government official to sit in on the meeting as an observer, hence the anonymous presence of Parkin from the Ministry of Trade and Customs.

Hawk says, 'I feel sure you will know why we are here, Sir Abraham. As of this moment Victoria Teekleman, her brother Ben and I hold a majority shareholding in our jointly owned company.'

'Ah, so you would like to resume as chairman, is that it?' Abraham interrupts. But before Hawk can reply he continues, 'Well, it may not be quite as easy as you think.' He nods at Bramwell Cumming, the barrister.

'Ah, yes, by no means an open-and-shut matter. In fact, rather more shut than open I'd say!' Cumming glances at John Miles.

'We are at war, the rules change, Mr Solomon, pertinences more powerful than ourselves are brought into play.' He looks to the end of the table at Sir Samuel.

It is apparent to Victoria and to Hawk that the scenario taking place in front of their eyes is well rehearsed, an act, each player knowing precisely his role. She is witnessing the rich and famous scratching each other's backs. Victoria glances at Hawk and she can see his amusement. 'With the greatest respect, Sir Abraham,' she says quickly, 'my grandfather has not completed what he intended to say.'

Sir Samuel Sopworth ignores her interjection, determined to deliver his lines. 'There is a great deal of government money tied up with this company, Mr Solomon. Contracts that are vital to the war effort and which cannot be placed in jeopardy by any sort of interruption, by a . . . er, palace revolution. The Prime Minister, Mr Fisher, and the Minister of Defence, Senator Pearce, have the greatest confidence in Sir Abraham, they have this very week declared Solomon & Teekleman a vital war industry and, I can assure you, they will not take kindly to any changes in management at the very top.'

'They will simply not allow it!' Bramwell Cumming affirms.

'Quite, quite!' John Miles adds. 'Not to be tolerated. War industry. Too important.'

Victoria thinks how Hawk was right about the pragmatism of politics. Andrew Fisher, the recently elected Labor Prime Minister, is already in bed with the capitalists.

Hawk puts up both hands. 'Gentlemen, gentlemen, a moment please, you have not heard us out. In the words of Mark Antony, "I come to bury Caesar, not to praise him." Except in my case there is no duplicity involved, no dastardly plot, no assassination.'

'What do you mean?' Abraham asks surprised. 'It's been all too clear what you intend to do. Good God, man, do you take me for a complete fool? But you won't get away with it, Hawk Solomon, you'll not be chairman just yet,' he repeats.

'Sir Abraham, I don't think any of you are listening to what my grandfather is saying. Perhaps you may allow him to explain our position fully before you all go off half-cocked once again,' Victoria says in a peremptory voice.

There is a stunned silence, the three men on the opposite side of the table as well as Sir Abraham cannot believe what they've just heard from the young woman seated next to the giant black man.

'Half-cocked! Did you say half-cocked?' Bramwell Cumming expostulates. He leans forward and glares at Victoria, intending to intimidate her. He is a large, heavily jowled, bulldoggish sort of a man with a florid whisky complexion, the school bully grown older but not any wiser for the years he's put behind him. 'Damned cheek, who do you think you are, young woman?'

Victoria meets his threatening stare with a calm, clear-eyed gaze. 'Yes, and now you're doing it again, Mr Cumming. It would be so very accommodating if you simply remained quiet for a few minutes while my grandfather completed explaining our position, as the chairman so kindly requested him to do quite some time ago,' she says in Mrs Wickworth-Spode English, whereupon she gives the fiercely glowering barrister a brilliant and disarming smile.

Hawk is filled with admiration for his granddaughter, for it is immediately clear that the opposition's attempts at intimidation have failed and, furthermore, there seems no rebuttal to Victoria's plea to hear him out. To ignore the request and to talk over it for a third time would not only make them look foolish but show the meeting to have been an utter contrivance.

'Would you mind, gentlemen? It won't take long?' Hawk says in a tone of mock humility, then looks at each man around the table as if seeking his permission to continue.

'What is it you have to say then, Hawk?' Abraham finally asks. The tactic they had agreed upon all along was to get Hawk and his granddaughter riled so that they could at once prove his incompetence as a chairman to Parkin. Abraham has forgotten Hawk's ability to stay calm even in David's unsettling presence and so he is reluctantly forced to admit that, as a tactic, it has failed them miserably. In fact, the man from the government observes that Hawk and Victoria remain the most calm of them all.

Hawk scratches the point of his chin and smiles. 'Well, our proposal as the major shareholders is that you remain as chairman, Sir Abraham.'

There is complete silence around the table and all eyes are on Abraham.

'I see, under what condition?' Abraham says at last.

'Well, none really. None anyway which I feel you will object to.'

'That remains to be seen,' Abraham says, clearly trying to recover his composure.

'Well, with your son Joshua away serving his country and Tom Pickles' desire to retire from the Potato Factory, we propose that I take over the Potato Factory. I will take Victoria with me as a trainee and Wilfred Harrington, I suggest, remains here in Melbourne at Solomon & Co. He is also due to retire in three years so that Joshua will return to take his position as was always intended.'

'And your granddaughter? What happens to her?'

'Ah, she takes over from me at the Potato Factory at the same time as Joshua and in the same capacity, as its managing director. The two of them to be the next generation in charge, with you the father figure, guiding them through the narrows, so to speak.'

Abraham immediately sees the sense in the proposal but also the catch. 'Then, when I retire, you, or your grandson and granddaughter, exercise your majority shares and Victoria here becomes chairman, is that it?' Abraham doesn't wait for Hawk to answer him, 'Well, I'm not at all sure that I am willing to agree to such a proposition.'

'Nor should you,' Hawk grins and turns to look at Victoria. 'My granddaughter here informs me she won't agree to it either.' Hawk takes a breath and continues, 'Abraham, my quarrel has never been with you. I have always known you to be a reasonable man and no fool and furthermore, your father has trained Joshua to run Solomon & Teekleman and, I feel sure, trained him well. You will have high expectations of the lad and he must be given every chance to fulfil them. But not without some stiff competition to brace his resolve. Prizes easily won are as easily lost, and I shall probably be dead when all this comes about anyway. We are asking *you* to make the decision when the time comes. You will appoint the new chairman, and you alone will decide between Victoria and Joshua, awarding the prize to the one who has most clearly demonstrated, in your opinion, the ability to lead the company into the future.'

Abraham looks at Hawk aghast. 'You would have me choose between my own son and your granddaughter? After all that has happened between our two families? After all we've done to you, Hawk Solomon?' He looks up to meet Hawk's eye. 'You would trust me to do that?'

'Aye, I must. If I don't, I cannot go to my grave knowing that I didn't do all I could to right the wrongs of the past.' Hawk sighs. 'I have no choice, I *must* trust you, there is no other way to make peace between us. No other way to finally put the past to rest. The rivalry between our two families has gone on for two generations – must we take it into a third?'

'Bravo!' Parkin calls quietly from the corner where he has been sitting.

Abraham leans forward with his elbow resting on the boardroom table and his hand clasped to his brow. 'My God,' he says absently, almost as if he is speaking to himself, 'this places an altogether different complexion on things.'

'No, not different, finally the right complexion,' Hawk whispers.

But Abraham knows that Joshua is not truly his son, emotionally he is David's boy and David Solomon did not bring up his grandson to accept a fair and even contest. He brought him up to be chairman and Abraham knows his son will accept nothing less. He looks up at Hawk and Victoria, 'I will do my best to make the right decision when the time comes.' Then, turning to face the men around the table and nodding to Parkin, he says, 'Thank you, gentlemen, the meeting is adjourned.'

BOOK TWO

Chapter Nine

BEN TEEKLEMAN

'The Click', Broadmeadows 1914

Ben's battalion has three more weeks at the Broadmeadows military camp before departing by ship for Albany, the small whaling town in Western Australia. This is where the convoy of ships destined to take the Australian and New Zealand forces to Egypt will congregate in King George Sound, a narrow isolated passage of water between the mainland and a ridge of island hills that forms a natural barrier of protection for the tranquil stretch of deep water from the rest of the Indian Ocean.

The last two weeks of Ben's stay in the Broadmeadows camp are comparatively easygoing, although the bugle still gets them up at dawn, followed by morning kit and tent inspection, physical jerks, squad and rifle drill, bayonet practice and, if a route march is not scheduled for the day, an afternoon lecture for sergeants on basic hygiene for the troops. In addition, once a week there is musketry practice on the rifle range, an exercise intended to get the platoon accustomed to the Short Magazine Lee-Enfield, known in the military vernacular as the S.M.L.E.

It is a simple daily routine, designed to be busy enough to keep an infantryman's mind on the job and only made difficult by the constant mud. It has been raining for most of September and the men complain that the mud at Broadmeadows makes everything they do seem twice as hard to accomplish, while kit and uniforms are impossible to keep clean. They are not to know that the mud of Ypres, Pozières, the Somme and a dozen other battlefields will one day make Broadmeadows seem like paradise on earth.

Ben has been seconded to the 5th Battalion, 2nd Australian Infantry Brigade and has been given a temporary platoon consisting mostly of city types recruited in Melbourne. Though initially bitterly disappointed that he couldn't return to Tasmania, Ben makes the best of the situation, the consolation being that he will see a little more of Hawk and Victoria before departing overseas. He has a platoon of young blokes who are keen as mustard, but have limited knowledge and, for the most part, no previous experience with a rifle. He has come to realise that all the other standard military procedures can be taught on a parade ground, but learning how to use a rifle is not something a lad from the city can pick up after firing a few rounds at a stationary target on the rifle range.

Ben has never regarded himself as a typical soldier and while he accepts the need for discipline involved in the mindless pursuit of parade-ground drill and obedience without question, he doesn't necessarily believe that it is the best way to stay alive. Taking the initiative and the ability to improvise have always been a part of his character. He also knows he isn't going to change the army mindset and so he concentrates on teaching his platoon useful skills, most of which revolve around three aspects of life in a trench, food, personal hygiene and knowing how to kill, preferably at a reasonably long range with a rifle.

There is nothing much Ben can do about army rations, though he does take several days' worth of standard rations home to Mrs Billings and asks her to experiment with them to see if she can improve the taste.

Martha is, of course, totally scornful of the ingredients she has to work with. She examines the tin of bullybeef, turning it around in her hands. 'Fray Bentos,' she says reading the label, 'sounds foreign to me, foreign muck is it?' Ben shows her how to turn the key to open the can. 'Never seen such an assortment of rubbish in one tin,' she sniffs. 'Wouldn't give it to me cat.' As Sardine, her cat, eats a lot better than any trooper, Ben thinks this is not too much of an indictment. 'Fat and gristle and not much else, if you ask me! Can't do nothing with this,' Martha whinges.

However, she works hard at making culinary improvements and the results are not too bad, but unfortunately involve several ingredients such as onions, Worcester sauce, tomatoes and a number of other tasty additions that are unlikely to crop up in a front-line trench. But she does create what she refers to as a hurry-curry, which seems halfway practical, as a tin of curry powder is small and long-lasting if used judiciously and not entirely a burden when carried in the infantryman's ninety-pound kit. Furthermore, if a handful of raisins are added to the pot, they plump up a treat and the dish is even further enhanced. Ben purchases two small tins of curry powder for each of the thirty-five men in his platoon. There is a great deal of gratuitous comment about these new field rations and very little of it is complimentary. Curry is a new experience for the city lads and few, if any, of them can cook anything more than the ubiquitous soldier's stew – a rind of bacon boiled in a billy of water. But in the months ahead they will become miserly with the dispersal of their precious tins of curry powder.

However, with the army biscuit and the standard ration of tinned jam Martha Billings creates what will become a culinary triumph in the trenches. To grind down an army biscuit is in itself a major task, because they are so hard. There is a popular myth that, carried in the pocket over the heart, the army biscuit is certain protection against the German Mauser as it is guaranteed to be bulletproof. Most soldiers believe that at the outbreak of war Arnott's, the great Australian biscuit-maker, released a huge warehouse of army biscuits that they'd stored since the end of the Boer War. But the biscuits had grown so hard that they'd defeated even the weevil and couldn't be smashed with the butt end of a Lee-Enfield and so were patently beyond the capacity of the human tooth.

Martha grates the biscuit first then mixes the crumbs with a pinch of salt, a little sugar, baking powder and water until it can be moulded into six small tart-shaped cups. She fills three of these with apricot jam and covers them with the unfilled cups, pressing down gently so that the end result is a flattened disc about an inch high. These are then placed in a billycan with a couple of tablespoons of water in the bottom and the lid pushed firmly in place before being set on the embers of an open fire and baked for twenty minutes.

Victoria pronounces the result inedible but Martha's 'billyjam tarts' eventually become a great favourite in the trenches of Gallipoli and France. They are a major source of comfort to many a young soldier who, standing knee-deep in mud and surrounded by death, with artillery fire whistling overhead, closes his eyes, munches slowly into the hot jam tart, and with a little imagination is transported back to family excursions to the beach and his mum's Sunday baking.

But it is on the rifle, the Short Magazine Lee-Enfield,

that Ben now concentrates. By military standards Ben Teekleman is a misfit when it comes to the popular concept of a platoon sergeant. He is relaxed and reassuring, without the need for hyperbole or the traditional overused vernacular of the soldier with three dog's legs on his shirt sleeve. His easy manner makes his men keen to improve under his direction.

At the rifle range while the other sergeants are yelling, threatening, insulting and cussing the greenhorns in their platoons, Ben spends time with each of his men explaining the basics. He watches them carefully as they fire off a round, correcting their action, 'Give the trigger a gentle squeeze, lad, like squeezing a tit, no, no, don't shut your eyes when you fire!' He shows them how to adjust their sights, how to correct an error or bias in the rifle itself, demonstrating the right way to position themselves to maintain firing for long periods without becoming cramped or shooting erratically. Ben strives to give them confidence in themselves, accepting the mistakes they make as beginners and never humiliating them in front of their comrades in arms.

After the second musketry session Ben makes his platoon sit down in a quiet spot under the shade of a large angophora near the firing range and talks with them. 'Nobody gets to be a good shot in a hurry, lads, I ain't yet come across a bloke who was a natural. To use a rifle properly takes patience and some learning,' he grins, 'even a little love and imagination.' He picks up a rifle belonging to one of the infantrymen and almost immediately the Lee-Enfield takes on a different look in his confident hands, it is as if the rifle and the man have a natural affinity with each other.

'Now this thing is a pretty clumsy weapon,' Ben begins, 'it's a rod of steel and a chunk of wood and it ain't friendly neither, it kicks you if you don't hold it tight enough and jams up on you if you don't oil and care for it properly, just like a flamin' sheila.' The platoon laughs and Ben waits until he has its attention again. 'It's heavy and it's a pain in the arse to carry around. Add a bayonet to it and it becomes a top-heavy spear that can't be thrown and isn't that easy to stick into someone's gut.' He brings the rifle to a horizontal position at about waist height, cupping it halfway along the stock with his left hand and working the bolt action smoothly with his right. Although he is left-handed, he works the action with consummate ease. 'But despite all these obvious character deficiencies, you've got to make this clumsy fellow your best friend.' He pauses, then adds, 'And because your rifle is such a cranky sonofabitch, making friends isn't gunna happen overnight. But like all true friendships, with a little practice and a bit of respect, you'll soon enough be the best of mates.' He looks around at the platoon. 'Any questions?'

'Yes, Sergeant!' An infantryman named Cooligan stands up. He is the smallest man in the platoon and at five feet and six inches only just tall enough to make the first intake. He wears a brush of snowy hair above a cheeky face sprinkled with a million freckles and is already known in the platoon as Numbers Cooligan or, simply, Numbers.

'What is it, Private Cooligan?'

'Sergeant, we are to do range practice once a week while we're here, that's six weeks where we fire off two magazines if we're bloody lucky, that's a hundred and twenty rounds.' He clears his throat and looks about him. 'And the best I've done so far is an outer and I think that must have been by mistake, I must a jerked or somethin'. You see, I've never had a rifle in me 'ands before this. 'Cept for Crow and Hornbill, we're all city blokes, so I'll vouch it's the same with most of us.' He turns to the remainder of the platoon. 'What do you reckon, lads?' There is a murmur of acquiescence and several nods of the head from the other young infantrymen.

'Yeah, well it ain't that difficult to tell,' Ben says smiling. 'Can't expect to hit the bullseye right off. One on the outer rim after your second practice on the range, that's not too bad, Private Cooligan. So what's your question?'

'Well, are a hundred and twenty rounds enough practice to kill a German at three 'undred yards?'

'Well, in terms of not firing a shot in anger, that's about all the firing practice you're gunna get. All I can say is I hope it's enough when the Hun aims *his* Mauser at you.'

'Yes, Sergeant, but what if I miss him?'

'Then you better pray he's had no more practice than you, Cooligan.' Ben pauses, thinking. 'While I admit there's nothing quite like using live ammo, firing a rifle isn't the only way to get to know your weapon.' He looks at the faces around him. 'Remember, it's not the bullet that does the killing, it's you. It's you or the Hun and the difference between the two of you is simply practice with a rifle or a bayonet. Practise holding your rifle, practise carrying it, practise firing it with an empty magazine in all sorts of positions, practise squeezing the trigger ten thousand times until you can do it in your sleep. Practise ejecting a spent cartridge, reloading and firing until you can do it in three or four seconds without taking your eye off the enemy position. Practise hitting the enemy in your imagination.' Ben sees the grins on their faces at the idea of this. 'No, really, I mean it, see the Hun in your mind's eye, see the bastard cop your bullet, see him jerk back suddenly, see him clutching at his gut, see him topple, hear him scream out his mama's name as he sinks to his knees and coughs blood. Do it all in your imagination a thousand times. Get so that's what you see without thinking when you fire a shot in anger. Half the skill of firing a rifle effectively is about total confidence in yourself and your rifle. It's about not having to think about what you're doing.' Ben lifts the rifle he's holding up to his chest. 'You can look at this weapon in two ways, as an extension of yourself, a very dangerous twenty-nine inches or so added to the ends of your arms, or you can regard it as something the army gives you to make your life difficult. You can do what you are required to do at rifle drill and no more, or you can work with it after hours, every spare moment you've got.'

'But, Sergeant, I reckon a man would look a proper galah falling about with an empty rifle, going click, click, click, "bang you're dead", when he wasn't doing rifle drill on parade, like when it's not official, know what I mean?' one of the infantrymen volunteers.

'Unloaded rifle, Private Hamill, a jam tin is empty or full, a rifle is loaded or not loaded, or, if you wish, safe,' Ben chides him without raising his voice. 'Sure, it takes a bit of character to play around with an unloaded rifle. I would have thought that keeping yourself alive would be a top priority and that's what this is all about.' He grins. Ben has the kind of easy smile that gives men confidence. At twenty-six he is only about four years older than most of them but they accept his authority as one might an older and more experienced brother. 'There are only two things that can keep you alive in a battle, luck and good practice. I hope you all have a lot of the former, but before I leave you, I'm gunna make damned sure you've had plenty of the second. Then if you haven't the guts to make a bloody fool of yourself in front of your mates, well, I guess I'll be there to bury you as well.'

There is laughter in the platoon and a sense of increasing confidence. Ben hasn't threatened his men with mindless practice and punishment for errors, so that they get to hate their Lee-Enfields, instead he has made them see how necessary the S.M.L.E. is to their survival.

Ben now points to a lanky private who seems to have more bony angles to his body than ought to belong on a normal human being. 'Right, now we all know Private Rigby here is a damned good shot, better than any of you blokes, certainly better than I am.'

The platoon turns to look at Crow Rigby, a country boy from Gippsland who carries the all too familiar badge of recognition of a volunteer from the bush, a permanent squint from staring into the sun. The young private, not yet twenty, blushes furiously and the fresh crop of acne covering his neck and jawline brightens visibly, his elbows rest on his bony knees and he looks down between his legs. It is obvious that he is not accustomed to praise or even to being noticed in a crowd.

'Good on ya, Crow,' someone says.

Crow Rigby has earned his nickname because of an incident on the very first occasion the platoon is taken onto the firing range. All of them are sprawled on their bellies in the standard firing position, legs apart, feeling awkward and anxious, the butt of their Lee-Enfields unfamiliar, tightly tucked into their shoulders to prevent the legendary kick few of them have yet experienced. Each man has his own target which is about to come up in the target butts three hundred yards away. Their instruction is to fire at a rate of fifteen rounds a minute. There is a great deal of nervous anticipation, every man hoping to give a good account of himself while not quite knowing what to expect. Each has his finger lightly on the trigger waiting for the musketry sergeant to give the command to fire. Moments before it comes, a crow cawing and flapping its wings suddenly alights on the top of a flagpole a good twenty yards beyond the end of the firing range. The bird is still wobbling slightly on its new-found perch when a lone rifle shot rings out and the crow explodes in a cloud of black feathers. At three hundred and twenty yards it is a truly exceptional shot.

Placed on a disciplinary charge and marched in front of his company commander, Rigby is asked if he has anything to say in his own defence. 'Er yes, sir, it come on me like automatic, it's the lambing season back 'ome, crows'll peck the eyes out a newborn lamb, can't 'ave one o' them buggers hangin' 'round the paddock, can you, sir?'

Rigby was given only six days' picket duty and then selected to do a special training course as a company sniper. This is his first day back with his platoon.

'Private Rigby, how many times do you think you've fired a rifle, not a S.M.L.E., a rifle of any sort?' Ben asks him.

Rigby is too shy to look up and keeps his eyes on his boots as he thinks, then answers carefully. 'Crikey, Sergeant, I dunno, I been doin' it since I were knee 'igh to a grasshopper.' He squints up at Ben briefly, 'Thousands and thousands o' times, I s'pose, I reckon 'bout six shots a day, though maybe that includes a shotgun, I been doin' it since I were five year old. Awful lot a crows, snakes, and rabbits 'anging about on the selection, Sergeant.'

At the mention of crows the platoon breaks up.

'Thirty-two thousand, eight hundred and fifty times he's fired a rifle against our possible hundred and twenty,' Cooligan shouts out, sending the platoon into fresh gales of laughter.

'Thank you, Private Cooligan, that's very encouraging. Right, now let's be serious for a moment.' Ben, crooking his forefinger, beckons to Cooligan. 'Come here, lad.' The young private gets to his feet from the back and steps between several of the men, zig-zagging his way forward, placing his hand on their shoulders to get to Ben. 'Righto, take your cap off, Private Cooligan.' Numbers Cooligan removes his cap, placing it on the ground. Ben takes a clean handkerchief from his pocket, twirls it into a strip about two inches wide and blindfolds the infantryman.

'Oi, what's 'appening?' Cooligan cries.

'Right, Private Rigby, c'mere!' Ben says not answering.

Crow Rigby unfolds his legs and, rising, walks over to Ben. 'Take Private Cooligan over to the tree, stand his back and head against the trunk.'

'Righto, Sergeant, will I tie his hands?'

There is laughter. 'No, he's going to need them to cover his goolies,' Ben says calmly. 'Now, Cooligan, don't move a muscle, that's an order, ya hear?'

'What you gunna do, Sergeant, shoot me?' Cooligan asks tentatively.

'No, lad, you'll be as safe as if you were in your mother's arms.'

'Do I have to, Sergeant?' the young infantryman pleads, instinctively knowing that somehow his courage is to be tested. 'I promise I'll shut me trap next time!'

The platoon all laughs uproariously. 'Yes, I'm afraid you must, Private Cooligan, it's an order.'

Crow Rigby takes him by the hand and leads him the twenty or so feet to the trunk of the large old gum tree and positions him as Ben has directed.

'Now hold your hands over your privates, lad. Don't want you catching cold, do we?' Ben's voice is perfectly calm. 'Don't move until I tell you. You understand, don't even twitch yer nose?'

'Yes, Sergeant, but I ain't happy, Sergeant.'

'Not supposed to be, you're in the army now.'

Ben stoops over his kitbag as he speaks and from it he removes Tommo's fighting axe. Before anyone can quite realise what's happening, he has straightened up and the axe has left his hand in a whirring blur. It lands with a soft thud, its blade buried in the trunk of the tree no more than half an inch to the side of Cooligan's head and directly above his left ear.

'Shit, what was that!' Cooligan howls as the remainder of the platoon gasps in collective astonishment. To his credit he has not moved.

'Right, Rigby, remove his blindfold,' Ben instructs.

The lanky country lad plucks at the blindfold, his country calm gone, his hands trembling from the shock of what he's just witnessed. Cooligan opens his eyes. The axe handle is sticking out beyond the left side of his nose, but he cannot see the axe clearly as it is so deeply embedded that only the head and a small section of the blade are exposed.

'Jesus!' Cooligan yells. His knees give way under him and he collapses to the ground.

There is complete silence from the rest of the young infantrymen, then someone says softly, 'Jesus and Mary!'

'Right, Cooligan, well done, lad, stand up,' Ben commands.

'Can't, Sergeant,' Cooligan whimpers, the after-shock of the experience bringing him close to tears.

'Come, come, it wasn't that bad, what you can't see can't hurt you, stand up, lad,' Ben says soothingly.

'Sorry, Sergeant, I mayn't, I've pissed me trousers,' Cooligan says in a distressed voice.

Cooligan's confession that he's wet his pants breaks the tension and the platoon roars with laughter, though as much from relief as mirth.

'Shut up! That's enough!' Ben barks suddenly, bringing the platoon to instant silence. Then turning to Cooligan he says, 'Don't blame you, lad, a lot of blokes would have shit themselves.' He rummages around in his kitbag and pulls out a spare pair of khaki trousers. 'Here, take these, lad, get to the latrines, clean up, then back here on the double.' Ben's sharp, emphatic orders help to jerk Cooligan back into action. 'Eyes left, all of you!' He hands Cooligan the spare trousers. 'Up you get, nobody's looking.' Ben turns back to the platoon. 'So what do we do about that, gentlemen? We give our comrade in arms three cheers for being a bloody good sport, eh?'

To the cheers of the platoon the miserable Cooligan, covering the wet patch to his front with the help of Ben's spare trousers, legs it for the latrine block.

'Private Rigby, fetch the axe,' Ben now commands. The country lad retrieves the axe, though not without some difficulty. Ben goes to stand where previously Numbers Cooligan stood blindfolded. 'Righto, Rigby, you've got a good eye, now do the same to me,' Ben says evenly.

Private Rigby hops from one leg to the other, his head buried into his right shoulder and appearing to be all bones and acute angles. 'I can't, Sergeant,' he says at last.

'Why not, lad?'

'I might miss, Sergeant,' he says, grinning.

The platoon, a moment before brought to a nervous silence, now cracks up again.

Ben steps from the tree and, going over to his kit, he removes a small cork dartboard of the type a child might get as an inexpensive extra in a Christmas stocking. It is about half as big again as a human head. He walks back to the tree and fixes the board to the trunk at roughly the same position occupied by Cooligan's head.

'You first, Rigby, and then the rest of you. Take the axe and throw it at the target, see how you go, eh? Ben has now reached the position where he previously stood to throw. 'Imagine it's your only weapon and that there dartboard is an enemy head. Fritz is coming at you in a bayonet charge and he is no more than a few feet away, ten, fifteen feet, you've got maybe two or three seconds. Righto, Rigby, go for your life.'

The young blokes are clearly taken with the game and, with some jostling to get to the front of the queue, quickly form a line behind Crow Rigby, who now takes careful aim, not bothering about the imaginary bayonet-wielding German advancing. Taking a great deal more time than the three-second maximum, he sends the axe flying and they watch it tumble head over handle through the air. To his credit the blade actually fixes into the tree trunk, though almost three feet above the dartboard and somewhat to the side.

'Better hope he was a very fat German sitting on a horse, Private Rigby,' Ben says.

'German general, Sarge, big 'orse, seventeen hands,' Crow Rigby says.

'Well done, anyway. Who's next?'

Rigby and one other young infantryman are the only ones who manage to get the blade of the axe into the tree, while the others either miss the trunk or the head of the axe bounces off the trunk and falls to the ground. They have almost completed the exercise when Cooligan arrives back wearing Ben's trousers. He has rinsed his own under a faucet and now carries them bunched up in his right hand. He sees instantly what's afoot and can't wait for his turn to come. With the rest of the platoon watching, he weights the axe in both hands, then gripping it firmly he takes careful aim, pulls it well back beyond his right shoulder and lets it go with a furious swinging action. Tommo's fighting axe twirls several times in the air and comes to land about twelve feet up at the conjunction of the trunk and the first of its branches, but at least it bites in, the blade sinking solidly into the rough bark. The platoon claps and whistles.

'Real big German on a ladder bird-nestin', Sarge!' Crow Rigby drawls slowly.

Ben thinks what a great temperament young Rigby has

for a sniper. 'Righto, gather around, gentlemen,' he now says and waits until the platoon is once again seated on the grass in front of him. 'Thank you, Mr Cooligan, you're excused tent inspection in the morning and may kip in an extra half hour.'

'Lucky bugger!' several of them shout.

'Thank you, Sergeant, that's thirty minutes, precise, I take it?'

'Aye, thirty-one and you're on a charge. Now, what have we learned from that little exercise?' Ben asks.

'That it's easy to get yerself kill'd with an axe, Sergeant?' calls a private by the name of William Horne, the second of the country lads in the platoon, who is predictably enough known as Hornbill. He is a big, strong lad, six foot two inches with a pair of shoulders that would make him a good ruckman. He is also a reasonable shot, though not anywhere near the class of Crow Rigby. His chief distinction is that, using a pair of pliers and a length of baling wire or a hammer and nails, he is able to fix just about anything that gets broken in a mechanical or carpentry sense.

A small sample of Hornbill's ingenuity occurred when Ben introduced Martha's culinary ideas to his platoon while they were away on a four-day route march. The bullybeef hurry-curry was initially only a limited success as they had not yet been deprived for long enough of the memory of half-decent food to fully appreciate it. But the exception proved to be the billyjam tarts, although they almost came to a premature halt when someone pointed out that they had no way of rendering army biscuits to fine enough crumbs for the required doughlike mixture. That is, until Hornbill was consulted.

'No rucking problem,' he declares and promptly produces a six-inch nail from his kit. 'Always carry one o' these, best bloody tool there is after the one nature give you.' Then, using the steel end of the haft on his bayonet, he hammers an empty jam tin flat. With the six-inch nail he soon pierces the flattened tin with dozens of holes, hammering the nail point through the tin plate and forcing a perfectly burred hole on the opposite side surface which proves to be no different in function to a normal household grater. Hornbill then takes out his wire-cutter which is standard issue and snips a small length of fencing wire from some farmer's paddock and cunningly fashions it into a handle for the grater. 'There you go, good as gold,' he pronounces to one and all.

Private Horne's Gallipoli grater will eventually become a stock item in every trench along the Gallipoli Front, although the Turks, finding them abandoned in deserted trenches, can never quite work out what the hell it is the Diggers needed to grate. They conclude that they can't be bug rakes as the handles are not sufficiently long for them to be back scratchers for the lice they generously share with the enemy.

In civilian life Hornbill is a timber cutter and hails from Coffs Harbour up in northern New South Wales. It seems he was on a visit to Melbourne to help out his uncle when war broke out. His uncle owns a pie cart which he positions nightly outside Flinders Street Station. Or, put into Horne's own slow drawl, 'The old bloke's rheumatiz was worryin' him a treat and me Aunty Mavis took crook so she couldn't push the pie cart from their 'ome in Fitzroy of a night. So I come down to the big smoke ter give 'em a hand 'til she got better again, then the ruckin' war come and I joined up with you miserable lot.'

'Yes, Private Horne, the fighting axe can be a lethal weapon in the right hands,' Ben smiles, 'but I don't suppose there'll be too many of them on either side in this war.'

'Reckon I'd 'ave one o' them 'stead of a bayonet any

time,' Horne drawls. 'Not much you can do with a bayonet, it don't even chop timber good.'

Ben ignores this last remark as it will necessitate a lecture on the uses and abuses of the infantry bayonet. He runs his eyes across the sitting infantrymen. 'Anything else we may have learned?'

'Practice, Sergeant? Everything takes practice.' The answer comes from a serious-looking lad named Spencer, with the stocky build, dark hair and obsidian eyes of his Welsh ancestors. He has a naturally scholarly look about him, enhanced by the fact that he is constantly found wearing a pair of reading spectacles and with his nose in a book. He passed the required army eyesight test simply by memorising the complete eye chart and is known in the platoon as 'Library', as he always seems to know the answer to every question they are collectively asked.

'Right, Private Spencer.' Ben would have preferred someone else to have come back with the answer. He is concerned that rather than think for themselves, too many have come to rely on young Spencer to answer for them. He picks up the axe and absently strokes the slightly curved blade with the ball of his thumb. It is severely blunted from its recent mishandling by the platoon and he thinks how it will take him most of the evening to hone it back to its former razor-sharp cutting edge. 'This is a fighting axe,' Ben pronounces, holding it above his head. 'It was used in the Maori wars around 1860 against the British by my grandfather's platoon, the Tommo Te Mokiri.'

'Your grandfather was a Maori, Sergeant?' Numbers Cooligan exclaims in a surprised voice.

'No, my grandmother was. My grandfather was a first-generation Tasmanian, a timbergetter like Private Horne here, but from the Southwest Wilderness. He perfected the use of the fighting axe for the Maori and made it a very effective weapon.'

'He fought against the British, Sergeant?' Spencer asks quietly.

'Yes, Spencer, the British aren't *always* on the side of God. But that's enough o' that,' Ben says, impatient to continue. 'The point I'm trying to make is that Private Rigby here is a great shot because he's practised most of his life. I guess I can do what I did to Private Cooligan for the same reason. I too have practised throwing a fighting axe for most of my life. Throwing it sixty, perhaps more, times a day since I was seven years old.'

'How old are you, Sergeant?' Cooligan now asks.

'Twenty-six, Cooligan, and prematurely aged by having you in my platoon asking unnecessary questions.'

Cooligan hardly hesitates. 'Sixty times a day, shit that's four hundred and sixteen thousand and one hundred times you've thrown that axe, Sergeant.'

'Thank you, Cooligan, I thought by now you would have learned not to be a smart arse!' Ben pauses and looks about him. 'So that's my point.' He indicates the gum tree with a jerk of his head, 'I apologise for showing off back there, but it's my job to try to keep you alive against the odds. If you can use a rifle better than the enemy it may just one day save your life.' Ben pauses again and spreads his hands. 'So don't despair, you ain't gunna be a marksman right off. Private Rigby here is just as much an amateur with the fighting axe as you are with the Lee-Enfield.' Ben shrugs. 'So there you go, practise, practise, practise. There's few that's born to do anything instinctively except to suck on our mamas' tits.'

This brings a few titters from the seated platoon, but Ben isn't through talking yet. 'Remember, you don't have to be able to hit the badge on a German soldier's cap at a hundred yards to kill him. A metal jacket will make a fair bit of mess wherever you hit him. Remember, you've got a target as big as yourself and the enemy has the same, so always conceal as much of your body as possible. If you've practised holding a rifle, firing it, spending time with your S.M.L.E., then, when you're firing at the enemy, the accuracy will come to you soon enough. Statistics gathered in the Crimean War and again in the Boer War show that only one in one hundred rounds fired will cause any sort of damage, that is, find its mark. You can improve on that statistic. The platoon that uses its concerted and practised firepower effectively and aims accurately is the one most likely to stay alive. The enemy is least likely to directly attack a section of the trenches where the firepower is accurate and sustained. Now, do you understand me, you blokes? Get to know your rifle and you may just come out of this war alive.'

Over the subsequent weeks Ben's platoon is constantly jeered at, the other platoons in the battalion and the company chiacking them mercilessly. They become known as 'Trigger Clickers' because of the manner in which they constantly practise with an unloaded rifle. There is even a chant some wag has dreamed up.

Tiddly-winks young man

Get a woman if you can

If you can't get a woman

Get a Trigger Clickin' man!

However, on the final occasion Ben's platoon appears on the firing range, they achieve the highest aggregate ever scored at Broadmeadows. Moreover, Numbers Cooligan has taken the opportunity to run a book at the camp, betting that the Trigger Clickers, now abbreviated among themselves to 'The Click', who have come to take pride in their nickname, will beat any other platoon in the camp at final range practice. He offers the attractive odds of three to one and he isn't short of punters willing to have a bet as some platoons consist of mainly country lads who know their way around a rifle. After the big win he shares his takings with the others, making every man in the platoon two pounds richer, eight days' pay after deductions.

'So what if you'd lost, Private Cooligan?' Ben enquires while graciously accepting the two pounds Cooligan proffers after the shoot-out.

'No way, Sergeant, I give the scorer at the shooting range two quid to gimme the total score of every platoon in the battalion for all six times we've been to the range. By the time we got to the last practice we was an average of thirty points ahead o' the second best, that's a fair margin to play with.' He pauses and taps one forefinger against the other, explaining, 'Now, with Crow Rigby shooting a possible one hundred or near as dammit every time we go out,' he taps his forefinger a second time, 'and taking into consideration that one or two of us is gunna go off the boil, so deduct say, twenty points, we'd still 'ave won hands down. It's averages, Sergeant, numbers don't lie.' He pauses. 'A champion 'orse don't win every race he runs, but if you know the form of all the 'orses in the race and put him in accordingly, lemme tell ya, he ain't gunna get beat too bloody often.'

'What did you do in civilian life, Cooligan? I seem to recall you were a strapper, that right?'

'Nah, I only said that because I 'oped to get into the Light Horse, Sarge, fancied them emu feathers in me hat.' He continues, 'But they found out soon enough I couldn't ride, never been on an 'orse in me life. Bookmaker's clerk, Sergeant, me uncle's an on-course bookmaker at Flemmo. I pencil for him. Cooligan's the name, numbers is the game!'

Ben waves the two pound notes Numbers Cooligan has

given him. 'Well, thanks for including me in, Private Cooligan.'

Cooligan's hair, like all the others', has been cut short back 'n sides but he's managed to persuade the camp barber to keep the front a bit longer so that it looks like he is wearing the hairy part of a snow-white shaving brush above his brow. He constantly smooths it with his palm as he talks, 'Well, matter a fact, Sergeant, The Click was, well we was 'oping, you know, that you could sort a spend it with us? Two quid each in our pocket will go a long way to drown a man's sorrows durin' a night on the town before we embark on the slippery dip. Lads reckon that'd be real good, you know, a final beer or twenty before we all leave 'ome?'

'You're on. Name the time and the place, I'll be there.'

'Hornbill, er . . . Private Horne, says his uncle will lay on the pies at cost price and throw in the sauce bottle, so we thought we'd meet at Young & Jackson's, the pub with the bollocky sheila painting above the bar. Know it, Sergeant?'

'She's called Chloe, yeah, I know it, what time?'

'Tuesday, seven o'clock, er . . . nineteen 'undred hours, Sergeant,' Numbers Cooligan says, clearly chuffed that Ben has accepted their invitation.

It is October 16th, just five days before the battalion will depart on the *Orvieto*, part of the fleet assembled to transport the troops across the Great Australian Bight to Albany and then eventually across the Indian Ocean via the Suez Canal to Britain.

Ben spends as much time as he can with Victoria and Hawk, both of whom are becoming increasingly aware that the war in Europe is not going to be over by Christmas, as all the newspapers confidently predicted when war was declared.

The war of movement had started with the retreat from Mons, where in the first weeks the German successes caused consternation throughout Britain and the Empire. The Germans swept everything before them to come within fifty miles of Paris before they were finally halted by the French and British Expeditionary Forces at the battle of the Marne. But it was achieved at a terrible cost to the Allies, two hundred thousand killed, wounded or missing in September alone, eight thousand dead at the battle of Le Cateau, by no means the biggest battle fought, yet more had died here than Wellington had lost at Waterloo. The battle of Ypres, still going on, promises ten times as many. Slowly it is beginning to sink into the consciousness of thinking Australians that this is no grand excursion in Europe to which the flower of our young blood is being invited but a bloody slaughter such as the world has never witnessed before. They wonder how Britain has managed to involve herself in such an ungodly mess.

With the Turks closing the Dardanelles and thus denying Russia access to the Mediterranean via the Black Sea, it now looks increasingly likely that they will declare themselves on the German side. Most Australians give little thought to what might be. The glory of a young nation proving itself in battle is still the ideal most hold dear to their hearts. As far as the hoi polloi are concerned, all the Allied casualties prove is that we'd better get the 1st Division over there in a hurry so that our lads can have a go and show the Germans what good colonial stock can do in this made-to-order stoush.

The morning of October 21st brings a cloudless dawn which will later be followed by bright sunshine. Victoria rises early and, putting on her dressing gown and slippers, pads through the silent house towards the kitchen to make herself a pot of tea. Passing Hawk's study on the way, she sees his light is still on. She taps on the door which is slightly ajar and pushing it open a little further sees Hawk at his desk writing.

'Grandfather, you're up early?'

'Hmmph, what is the time, my dear?' Hawk asks absently, not looking up or pausing from his writing.

'It is just after five, not yet completely light.' Victoria then realises that the curtains are drawn and Hawk is still dressed as he was the previous evening. She knows her grandfather to be a meticulous man who bathes and changes into a fresh suit and linen every morning. He'd once explained to her that most folk think of black people as being naturally dirty, 'It comes with the chocolate colour, my dear.' From some deep sense of inferiority which he has long since overcome in other things, he has accustomed himself to change his suit and linen every day and, sometimes, if the day has been hot, twice a day. 'You haven't been to bed, have you, Grandfather?' she chides.

'Couldn't sleep,' Hawk says brusquely, putting his pen away and turning stiffly to smile at her, rubbing the back of his neck with a huge hand. She sees his weary face and realises that he is now an old man, it is only his enormous size that still gives him the impression of strength. She has also noticed that the joints of his fingers have become swollen and nobbled with arthritis and that he has taken to holding his pen awkwardly, though, typically, he has not said anything about the pain he must be experiencing.

'Oh, what's going to happen? Will Ben be all right?' she asks in a tremulous voice.

'I hope so, my dear, though it's looking less and less like the grand picnic in Europe the recruitment posters so ardently promised our lads, the great adventure.'

'Grandfather, can't we do what Abraham's done for Joshua Solomon and find a nice safe position for Ben so he doesn't have to fight? Surely you have the influence, if Sir Abraham can, then you can too!' Victoria cries in sudden despair.

Hawk raises his eyebrows in surprise. 'My dear, we don't know for sure that's the case with Joshua, all we know is that he's one of the few selected to go to England for further training, a singular honour I believe.'

'Yes, to be on the staff of one of the fat old generals! What is it? Liaison officer? It's not fair. Why should he get away with it?'

'Well, someone has to do it. Joshua has been to Oxford, he knows the English and their ways extremely well. Why, he's almost become one of them and he's a clever young man to boot. I'd say he was an admirable choice as a liaison officer, wouldn't you?'

'Grandfather, you know what I mean, it was fixed!' Victoria reproaches him. 'It's not like that at all!'

'Well, we can't prove that and nor should we try to. As for Ben, how do you think your brother would feel if we even attempted to remove him from the coming fray?'

Victoria sniffs defensively. 'He needn't know,' she shrugs, tearfully.

'Don't be foolish, Ben would most certainly know. He's not a lad to be easily fooled. Besides, you of all people with your egalitarian Labor views, how could you suggest such a thing? Even if we could, it would be grossly unfair to use our influence in such a manipulative manner.'

Victoria begins to sob. 'I'm sorry! I'm *so* sorry, but I *can't* help it, I don't want Ben to die!' she howls, and rushes towards the seated Hawk, curling up on her grandfather's lap and, like the little girl he used to comfort when she was upset, she weeps against his chest.

'There, there, my dear, we simply have to hope for the best. Ben's a sensible lad and knows how to keep his nose clean. He won't go looking for trouble.'

'Oh, Grandfather Hawk, I have such a terrible feeling,'

Victoria sobs. 'Ben never lets anyone do what he can do himself! He'll want to fight the Germans all on his own,' she whimpers.

Letting her weep for a while, Hawk finally reaches into his pocket and hands her his handkerchief. Victoria dries her eyes and then blows her nose. Rising from his lap she stands before him, her eyes red-rimmed and now level with his own. Hawk, with a sense of shock, sees the same sudden blazing defiance in them he has only before seen in Mary Abacus. It is a defiance that brooks no possible compromise.

'Grandfather, so help me God, if Ben dies and Joshua comes home unscathed from some cushy job behind the lines,' Victoria pauses, and in a voice and accent that is more evocative of Mary than her own, declares, 'may Gawd 'elp him!'

Chapter Ten

THE DEPARTURE

Albany, Western Australia 1914

Never before have the Melbourne docks seen a day like October 21st 1914. For the past three days eleven troopships carrying nearly eight thousand men and three thousand horses have departed for Albany, with the Orient liner *Orvieto*, the fastest and the largest ship, departing last. Dock workers are bleary-eyed, having worked double shifts during the several embarkations. Exhausted tugboat captains are hoarse from trying over four days to make some sense of a convoy of ships where each vessel is preoccupied with a hundred tasks at once and seems to have neither the time nor the nous to complete any one of them correctly. It is madness and mayhem and anyone who pretends to know what they are doing is indulging a fevered imagination.

Yet somehow the troops say their last farewells to weeping mothers, sisters and tearful girlfriends. Sons, brothers and sweethearts are embraced one last time and urged to look upon the evening star with the knowledge that their loved one will be on the front porch every night they remain apart, gazing at the same heaven's light and praying for their safe return. Gravel-voiced fathers suck in their stomachs and comport themselves in what they imagine is a military posture, gravely shaking the hands of their sons, exhorting them not to let the family name down. 'Go to it, son, show the Hun what we Aussies are all about, there's a good lad, your mother and me are real proud of you.'

'We've drawn the short straw, lads,' Ben tells his platoon after returning from the sergeants' briefing on the departure. 'We're on the *Orvieto* and so is the top brass, General Bridges and the entire collection of red tabs.' He continues, 'If we should go to the bottom, Australia's part in this war is over. You'll have to watch your dress, mind. It'll be spit and polish all the way and your saluting arm won't get a lot of rest neither.'

'She's an Orient-line ship, Sergeant, there'll be cabins and all, even a ship's library,' Library Spencer pipes up.

'Sure, Private Spencer, though I can't see you loungin'' about in a club chair doing a lot of reading, it's steerage for such as you lot, real cosy accommodation. There's two extra bunks built into each cabin and when you're lying down, there won't be enough room between you and the bottom of the next bunk for a highly polished cockroach to squeeze through. One good thing, though, the chow's likely to be a bit better, the high-ups tend to like their tucker, but I daresay the standard will drop a little towards the bottom of the stew pot. I hope you've all brought your curry powder?'

Hawk and Victoria are up early to see Ben off, though they are aware that he will not be permitted to break ranks to meet them. Victoria has obtained a pre-war photograph of the *Orvieto* from somewhere and has marked the exact spot where Ben must stand, roughly midships with the second funnel directly behind him. He is to wave a red silk scarf she has given him, while Hawk, with his head and shoulders well clear of the crowd, will do the same. Hawk and Victoria both count themselves fortunate that the departure has been delayed and over the past three weeks have taken great delight in enjoying more of Ben's company.

Victoria, teasing Hawk, puts the delay down to the generosity of the new Labor Prime Minister, Andrew Fisher. As it will later show she is not that far off the mark. The two German battleships the *Gneisenau* and the *Scharnhorst* visit the capital of Samoa which is only 1,580 miles from Auckland and 2,570 miles from Sydney, and the German light cruiser *Emden*, of the same squadron, is known to be in the Bay of Bengal. Fisher thinks they are much too close to send an unescorted convoy around the coast of Australia. The government of New Zealand shares his opinion and it is decided to send the *Minotaur* and the Japanese light cruiser *Ibuki* to escort the New Zealand troops to Albany. This strategic decision, as well as organising escorts for the Australian contingent from Queensland, New South Wales and Victoria and yet another from Hobart, is the cause of the delay.

Of course, no official explanations for the hold-up are given, as newspapers are forbidden to comment and, as is ever the case in wartime, the wildest rumours spread like a bushfire.

The postponement proved to be a trying time for the men of the A.I.F. They had already said their goodbyes to loved ones and friends and their anticipation was at fever pitch. These were young men trained and ready to go to war, anxious not to miss out on the fray. Now they were thrown back into basic training and the inevitable boredom of repeating the drills and exercises they had long since completed.

In the course of the three-week delay there had been two or three false alarms and any amount of speculation until the troops began to doubt if they would ever get away. A new word for these endless rumours was coined among the Victorian contingent which would go into the Australian language. In the Broadmeadows camp the rear of the sanitary carts that pumped out the latrines carried the name of the manufacturer, Furphy. The rumours became known as 'furphies', in other words a whole load of shit.

The delay also put a heavy strain on discipline. Broadmeadows camp was some ten miles from Melbourne. To an infantryman accustomed to route-marching this distance two or three times a week, carrying a rifle and full kit weighing some ninety pounds, wearing only his uniform and a little change jingling in his pocket, the city was considered a mere stroll down the lane. Army rules required every soldier to be in his blankets by half-past nine but men and officers in their hundreds thronged the streets and eateries of Melbourne until the early hours of the morning during the weeks prior to departure.

Ben, taking the opportunity to visit Hawk and Victoria, was often driven back to Broadmeadows and deposited half a mile or so from the camp at around two. On these occasions Victoria would give her brother a last hug, just in case something happened, or the latest rumour proved to be true and they weren't able to see each other again.

On the morning of Ben's departure, she has accumulated three weeks of tearful farewells and is, herself, somewhat exhausted by the process.

The *Orvieto* is docked at the Port Melbourne Pier, which is just off the main road that fringes the bay, and Hawk and Victoria arrive to find a large crowd already gathered on the road. It is a great disappointment to the crowd that the dockside itself has been placed off limits to civilians. The general grumble is that, in the sea of khaki lining the decks, sons and lovers are too far away to be clearly identified. Nevertheless, there is a great deal of shouting and banter going on, people fashion megaphones from folded newspaper and call out names in the direction of the liner at the top of their voices. 'Good on ya, Billy Thomas!' 'Lucky bugger, Kevin O'Shea!' 'Give me compliments to the King, Danny!' 'Give the Kaiser a kick in the arse from me, lads!' 'Up the mighty Crows!' 'Paris oo la la!' What with the noise of the troops embarking together with the rattle, clank and whine of chains, winches, crane engines and the general mayhem of getting under way, it is unlikely these messages can be heard on board, but they greatly amuse the crowd and do much to quell its disappointment at not getting closer to the liner.

Towards noon the ship's horn gives a baleful blast to warn the dock workers and maritime officials on board to go ashore. Perhaps it is the mournful sound of the ship's horn or the sense of imminent departure, but there is a sudden collective murmur from the crowd which quickly turns to a roar, like a dry river bed suddenly brought into flood. Almost as one the crowd surges forward, the guards stationed on the perimeters of the wharf are brushed aside and helpless to prevent the general stampede onto the wharf.

Hawk and Victoria are carried along with the crowd. To resist would be downright dangerous. So, when the time comes for the tugs to finally pull the giant liner away from its berth, they have a clear view of Ben waving his red scarf more or less from the prearranged position. Hawk waves back with his scarf and it is evident that Ben has seen them, though the noise from the crowd makes it impossible to communicate with him. The liner is pulled away from the dock while a lone tug holds her stern steady and in a surprisingly short time the giant ship is moving to the combined cheering of the huge crowd and the soldiers on board.

Ben is at too great a distance to see that his sister, though waving both arms frantically, is howling her heart out. His last view is of Hawk's snowy hair and the dark dot that represents his face. Hawk is standing head and shoulders above the crowd, still waving the red bandanna. He tries to make out Victoria's white straw hat but she is lost in the sea of bobbing heads and waving hands. Ben, who does not think of himself as either religious or sentimental, whispers quietly to himself, 'I love you both, God bless and keep you safe until I return.'

Ben's prediction is right, his platoon is bunked down in the deepest recesses of steerage with five men in a cabin that would have seemed cramped to three fare-paying passengers. Their kit takes up most of the room and only two of them can occupy the cabin at one time. When it comes to going to bed, three must wait outside in the corridor while two undress and slip into their bunks to allow the next two to do the same. There is no porthole and the ship's laundry is located twenty feet further down from their nearest cabin. They are informed that it will be at work twenty-four hours a day, sending a blast of steamy heat down the corridors every few minutes, so that the sides of the tiny cabins are always damp from the humidity.

Ben quickly realises that the stifling conditions will make rest impossible and loses no time locating a place on deck where his platoon can sleep. He finds an area aft between several large wooden packing cases that is ideal for the purpose as it catches the breeze and will comfortably take twenty-four members of his platoon. Six men will need to remain, one to each cabin to protect their kit, which means every member of the platoon will do cabin duty once every five nights. He sketches out the area and writes down the precise location and pins it on the board in the sergeants' mess, claiming the area at night for No. 2 Platoon, B Company.

Later that afternoon a sergeant named Black Jack Treloar from D Company in the 5th Battalion who is in charge of a platoon of sappers approaches Ben as he is walking down the corridors on D deck. Treloar is a big raw-boned man who affects a dark stubble even when closely shaved. He is known as a bully and has earned his three stripes in the permanent forces where it is said he was once the cruiserweight boxing champion of the Australian army. Drawing up to Ben, he blocks the narrow corridor by leaning against one side and stretching his arm out to bring the flat of his palm against the other. A large semicircle of sweat can be seen under his outstretched arm.

'G'day, Black Jack,' Ben says cordially, 'I hope your blokes scored better cabins than mine, we're in a real shit-hole, hot as blazes, can you believe it, twenty feet from the bloody laundry.'

'Nah, same,' Treloar says, not moving his arm. 'Matter of fact, that's what I want to see you about, Sergeant.'

'What, a sergeants' deputation? Can't see them making any changes, we're foot soldiers, mate, this is the army, besides I'm told the ship's chocka.'

'Yeah, but I hear you've found a nice little space on the deck for your lads to kip down?'

'Yeah, that's right,' Ben jerks his head, indicating the corridor and the cabins behind him. 'Them cabins are not fit for man or beast, put five blokes in 'em and they're jammed closer together than a tin o' sardines.'

'Yeah, right,' Treloar says dismissively. 'Well, I reckon you should share that space on deck, let my platoon in.'

'Love to, Jack, but I can't even fit all my own lads in, six o' them will have to kip down in the cabins, take turns like.'

Black Jack scratches his nose. 'That right, eh?' He looks at Ben. 'That's not good, mate.'

'I daresay there are other places on board, shouldn't be too hard to find a spot.'

'Nah, all took. But I saw your place first, just didn't bother ter make a fancy pitcher and stick it up in the mess, reserve it like?'

'Well, that's tough, Black Jack, but you know the rules, mate. If you got there before me, you should have told us, or posted a confirmation on the sergeants' noticeboard, like I did.'

'You teachin' me to suck eggs or something, Teekleman?' Treloar growls. 'Watch yerself, son, I'm permanent army, not like you lot of toy sergeants from the militia.'

'Sergeant Teekleman or Ben, take your pick, Sergeant Treloar, but not "son" or "Teekleman".'

Treloar chooses to ignore Ben's rebuke. 'You a Tasmanian, ain't yer? Touch o' the tar too, I hear. That's two counts against you in my book, son.'

'I told you, don't call me "son", Black Jack.'

Treloar places his head on the biceps of his outstretched arm and grins dangerously. 'That so? You're asking for it, ain'tcha?'

'Asking for what?'

'A hiding.'

'What? From you!'

'Yeah, none other?'

'What for, Black Jack? The space on deck?'

Black Jack taps Ben's chest with a forefinger then returns his hand to the wall. 'I've 'eard about you bastards. What's it they calls yah? Yeah, that's right, Tiddly-winks young man!' The big sergeant laughs. 'How many pretend Huns have your mob wiped out, or is it killed with an axe? I hear you're pretty 'andy with an axe. You a woodchopper then? Plenty o' them in Tasmania, mostly idjits I hear, droolers.' He smiles unpleasantly. 'If you want my personal opinion your platoon are a bunch o' fuckin' boy scouts.'

'When I want your opinion, Sergeant, I'll pull the chain. Now I'd like to pass if you please?' Several infantrymen have come up the corridor intending to pass and are held up by Black Jack and Ben blocking the way. They hold back, waiting. 'There's men want to pass, Sergeant, we can continue this later in the mess, if you want?'

Black Jack looks up at the half dozen men, but his arm remains firmly jammed across the narrow corridor. 'G'arn, piss off you lot or you're on a charge. G'arn, scarper!'

'Take the port-side stairs, lads,' Ben calls after the retreating soldiers.

'Tell you what, Sergeant Teekleman, I hear there's to be boxing on the foredeck, entertainment for the men. What say I fight you for that deck space, three rounds, winner takes the space. Can't be fairer than that now, can I?'

Ben listens with his eyes fixed on his boots and then looks up slowly, meeting the other sergeant's eyes. Treloar stands about six feet two inches with Ben around five ten but just as broad about the shoulders as the sapper. Treloar has a pronounced beer gut, which gives the impression of his being a lot bigger than Ben. 'Well, I reckon there's nothing to be gained by fighting, Sergeant Treloar, that deck space belongs to my platoon and a stoush isn't going to change that.'

'G'arn, it'd be first fight o' the voyage. A good example set for the men, couple of N.C.O.s having a friendly stoush, boxing gloves an' all, nobody gets too badly hurt, encourage them to do the same, 'stead of pullin' their puds in their bunks at night.' Treloar waits, bringing his head back from resting on his arm. 'Yeah, I thought so, you're a bloody coward, ain't ya?'

'You heard me the first time, Treloar, it's no deal, you're not getting our deck space and two sergeants having a blue is bloody stupid.' Ben's eyes suddenly narrow. 'Now, me being a Tasmanian with a touch of the tar brush, just what did you mean by that?'

Treloar shrugs. 'Ain't too hard to work that out, now is it? Reckon you blokes from the Apple Isle are all cousin fuckers, snot-nosed droolers.' He pauses and nods his head, 'And you, mate, they tell me there's a touch of the Zulu in ya. That right, is it?'

'Zulu?'

'Yeah, nigger, African Abo!'

Somewhat to Treloar's surprise Ben grins and slowly shakes his head. 'You've got a real nasty mouth, Treloar, but you may have half a point there. You see, we Tasmanians go to a fair bit of trouble not to mix our blood with shit from the mainland. As for the other? I'm half-Maori and bloody proud of it, just like I am of being a Tasmanian.'

'I've been to yer little island, son, it's the arsehole o' the known world.'

'Oh yeah? Just passing through, were you?'

There is a sudden burst of laughter from behind Treloar's back. He is unaware that several infantrymen have come up again and are standing behind him waiting to pass. It is obvious most have heard a fair bit of what's been going on. At Ben's put-down of the bully sergeant they prove unable to contain their mirth.

Treloar spins around, furious. 'G'arn, fuck off!' he shouts at the men, but in doing so he is forced to drop his arm so there is space for Ben to pass him.

Ben smiles at Treloar. 'I've got to be off, Sergeant, urgent rifle-clicking practice with my platoon.' Ben stands aside to let the six waiting infantrymen through first. He can feel his shoulder pushing against Treloar's chest and moves backward a little harder than necessary. 'C'mon lads, through you go.' Then he turns around to face the big man once again, 'Been real nice talkin' to you, Sergeant.'

'Yeah, yeah, you'll keep, Teekleman,' Black Jack Treloar growls. 'I'll be lookin' for you, mate.'

Ben has taken three or four steps down the corridor but now stops. 'I'm not hard to find, Sergeant, try leaving a note on the noticeboard in the sergeants' mess.'

The first two days on board are spent settling in, cleaning the Broadmeadows mud from their uniforms and polishing their brass while at the same time, in the ship's parlance, 'getting their sea legs', which proves to be a good thing, for even in the relatively calm seas Numbers Cooligan is sick as a dog while, surprisingly, the remainder of the platoon seems unaffected.

Cabin inspection is followed by physical jerks on the main deck and then breakfast. After which there is rifle drill and musketry practice, though no actual firing takes place. The day then takes on a familiar routine which will continue in much the same way when the convoy sets off overseas. With route marches and many of the other tedious and time-consuming tasks eliminated for want of space the time is taken up with specialist training. Men are selected for all the arcane occupations demanded by a killing machine and are turned into signallers, sappers, machine-gun operators, snipers, clerks, stretcher-bearers and just plain soldiers with a little bit of everything thrown in, though the fundamentals of army discipline are maintained throughout the five-day voyage.

However, talk of the corridor confrontation between Sergeants Ben Teekleman and Black Jack Treloar has spread through the ship. There is a great deal of speculation as to who would get the better of whom in a fight. The fights are on every night in a ring set up on the foredeck and named by the troops 'The Stoush Palace'. It proves to be the most popular entertainment on board and Black Jack Treloar is always there, sometimes acting as a referee and on three occasions even entering the ring himself.

On the first occasion he knocks out his opponent in the opening round and on the next occasion the referee ends the fight in the first minute of the second round, awarding it to Treloar on a t.k.o., the third is another knockout towards the end of the second round. Treloar is a fighter who likes to work the ropes, pushing his opponent into a corner and letting him have it with a barrage from both fists, relying on his strength and aggression to batter through his opponent's defence and put him on the canvas. All three bouts end with a spectacular uppercut and Numbers Cooligan, pronouncing himself an expert, calls Treloar 'a one-punch Johnny'. Treloar's flailing fists invariably force his opponent to his knees while he hangs onto the ropes, whereupon the sapper sergeant takes great delight in delivering the coup de grâce to his undefended chin.

There is something about the way Black Jack fights that makes the audience yearn for an opponent who will take him on. All of the men who climb into the ring with him are game enough but have little previous experience of the sport. They are big blokes, but generally clumsy with their fists and don't know their way around the square canvas. Some may know how to mix it well enough in a pub brawl but getting the hang of the Marquis of Queensberry's rules and a pair of ten-ounce boxing gloves proves quite another matter. It is obvious that Treloar has the advantage of previous experience in the ring as well as being enormously strong in short bursts. He is the undisputed heavyweight champion of the *Orvieto*, though the audience is reluctant to talk him up.

After the confrontation in the corridor, Ben's name is most often cited as the opponent they would like to see, though it is not known whether Ben is a boxer and even if he was he would be a light–heavy, giving Treloar at least a twenty-pound advantage in the ring.

After the way Treloar has disposed of his opponents there are no more contenders for the heavyweight division but there are few outside his own platoon who believe he has earned the title fair dinkum and it is plain he is neither respected nor admired. There is something of the braggart about him, he is rough trade and his platoon of sappers, who are going to war with picks and shovels, is made up of men who have been labourers all their lives and fit much the same description. By way of contrast they take great pride in their fighting sergeant and they begin to taunt Ben's platoon, giving it the sobriquet 'Sergeant Chopper and the Bang Bangs'. Passing a member of Ben's platoon they'll aim an imaginary rifle and say, 'Bang bang you're dead!'

It is childish stuff but nevertheless humiliating and, while none of Ben's platoon will say so, they all secretly wish Ben was as effective with his fists as he is with an axe and that he'd climb into the ring and give Treloar the licking he deserves. They do not have any doubts about their sergeant's courage but would like him to be the instrument of Treloar's demise, bringing the incident in the corridor to its rightful conclusion with the good bloke triumphing over the bully.

Though Ben has won the war of words, the men hunger to see the living shit beaten out of Black Jack Treloar so that there will be no more conjecture. With young warriors the word has never been mightier than the sword. It is not only the incident in the corridor that gives the speculation impetus but also the fact that Ben Teekleman has on a second occasion single-handedly put

Treloar's platoon in its place, though unfortunately it does not directly involve Black Jack Treloar.

On the third night out at sea when Ben's platoon is bedded down on deck, six members of Treloar's platoon, no doubt with his tacit approval, decide to teach Ben's platoon a lesson. The story has become somewhat embellished in the retelling, receiving a good start towards mythical status at the hands of Numbers Cooligan, whose accurate accounting is strictly reserved for arithmetical calculations.

However, Library Spencer has written the incident down in the illicit diary the army has forbidden soldiers to keep. His version is without the Cooligan flair but has the virtue of being scrupulously accurate.

They are crossing the Great Australian Bight with the sea uncharacteristically calm and with a full moon in a cloudless sky making the deck seem almost in daylight. Around one in the morning Crow Rigby, who has been placed on guard duty by Ben, sees six men approaching, carrying what can be clearly seen as pick handles. He shakes Ben awake. 'Reckon we've got visitors, Sergeant,' he says quietly.

Ben rises quickly. 'How many?'

'Six, they've got pick handles.'

Ben takes Crow Rigby by the elbow and guides him behind a large packing case lashed to the deck so that they can't be seen by the advancing men. The six would-be attackers move forward in a half-crouch, with one of them four feet or so ahead. He holds his hand up as an indication to advance slowly and quietly. When he is close enough to the first of the sleeping men, Ben leaps from behind the packing cases with an ear-piercing cry and Crow Rigby sees for the first time that he carries his fighting axe. Before the forward man has time to lift his pick handle Ben has jabbed the blunt end of the axe handle hard into the attacker's mouth, taking out several

367

of his front teeth in the process. The soldier gives a startled howl and before he has time to sink to his knees Ben has reached the next man, slapping him on the side of the jaw with the axe head and sending him sprawling to the deck, the pick handle flying from his hands. The third attacker has managed to get the pick handle above his head and as he brings it down Ben parries the blow by holding the fighting axe at each end, then in a lightning-fast gesture he scrapes the axe handle along the pick handle and down onto the hands of the third attacker, breaking his grip and his fingers so that the pick handle clatters to the deck and the man lets out a cry of sudden pain. The axe handle swings up in a curve and smashes into the man's face and there is an audible crack as his nose breaks and he is thrown backwards by the force of the blow to land hard on his arse.

The first two men lie moaning and sobbing sprawled on the deck unable to rise as the third attempts to get to his knees, clutching at his face with one hand while steadying himself with the other. Ben turns to face the next in line but the remaining three attackers turn and flee for their lives.

'Shit!' Crow Rigby says softly, it has all happened in less than fifteen seconds. The rest of the platoon, wakened by Ben's bloodcurdling yell, are barely out of their blankets and on their feet, still somewhat bleary-eyed, when the fight is over. The platoon watches in noisy amazement as the three men on the deck try to get to their feet.

'Quiet, everyone,' Ben commands. 'Help these men to their feet. Private Crow, Private Horne, you too, Private Cooligan.' He is puffing slightly from the sudden rush of adrenaline, but his voice remains calm. The platoon watches in silence as the three privates pull their attackers to their feet and they see for the first time the extent of the damage the axe has done to their collective physiognomies. 'Fuck me dead!' Cooligan says, expressing it adequately for them all.

Ben addresses the three men. 'You all right, lads? Can you walk?' All three nod, the blood from their faces dripping down their chins and onto the deck. 'Righto, no names, no pack drill. Tell the M.O. in the morning that you fell down the stairs or you had a stoush, whatever.' Ben points to the three pick handles lying on the deck. 'Pick those up, lad,' he says to an infantryman named John Parthe who is referred to by the platoon as Muddy. Then turning back to the three wounded sappers he says, 'We'll keep the pick handles, tell your sergeant if he wants to recover them he can post a note on the board in the sergeants' mess. Got that?' The three men nod unhappily, two now have their hands clamped over their mouths, the third over his broken nose. The blood oozing through their fingers can be clearly seen in the moonlight. 'Righto, on your bicycles. As far as No. 2 Platoon, B company, known to one and all as the Clicks, are concerned nothing happened tonight, right? Or would you rather face the C.O. in the morning?'

The three soldiers shake their heads and turn away, stumbling into a half-trot, their hands still clamped to their faces as they make for the hatchway at the far end of the deck. Ben turns to his platoon. 'Let's get some sleep. Well done, Private Rigby, you're off guard duty, get some sleep. Private Spencer, you're on guard.' Ben glances in the direction of the three departing men. 'Stupid bastards didn't even have the sense to wait for a dark night.'

Numbers Cooligan laughs. 'London to a brick them buggers won't be back.' He turns to Ben. 'I has me doubts we can sleep after that, Sergeant.'

'It's an order, Cooligan,' Ben says, stooping to pick up his own blanket.

'Jesus, why don't they issue us with them fightin' axes instead of a stupid bloody bayonet?' Hornbill says ruefully as he wraps his blanket about him. 'Germans would shit 'emselves!'

While Treloar has been strutting his stuff in the boxing ring, he has been careful to avoid Ben. The story of the incident has inevitably reached the other sergeants who approach Ben for confirmation, but all he will say is that there has been a little rough and tumble on deck and that it has been sorted out to everyone's satisfaction.

The three men from Treloar's platoon, reporting to the ship's hospital the following morning, claim to the medical orderly that they had been negotiating the steel steps down a hatchway in the dark when the man at the rear missed his footing and collided with the other two, sending them all crashing below decks. A later inspection would show that two light bulbs were missing over the offending steps, though the ship's doctor, examining them, pronounces himself mystified that no other bruises appear on their bodies. 'You've been fighting, haven't you? What were you using, knuckledusters?' When the men deny this the M.O. shakes his head. 'I'll have to have confirmation from your sergeant, who's your sergeant?'

'Sergeant Treloar, sir,' the sapper with the broken nose and whose name is Brodie replies, being the only one of the three able to speak.

'Treloar, the boxer?'

'Yessir.'

The doctor waves a hand, indicating their faces, 'And you're sure this didn't come about in a fight?'

'No, sir.'

'I'll have to hear that from your sergeant.' The M.O. turns to one of the medics. 'Send a message to Sergeant Treloar to report to me at once.' He looks at Brodie. 'What's your company?'

'D Company, sir, Sappers.' The medic nods and leaves them.

Black Jack Treloar arrives twenty minutes later and confirms that the men are telling the truth and blithely signs the medical report. The M.O. shakes his head, 'I'm not at all sure I shouldn't take this up with your C.O., Sergeant, damned peculiar fall.'

Treloar looks directly at the doctor. 'I agree, sir, and would have thought no different, but it happened on the hatchway stairs aft and I just happened to be close, so I seen it meself. Them bulbs, the lights were missin'.'

'Why weren't the men brought in right away, there's always a doctor on duty?'

Treloar chuckles quietly. 'Well, you know how it is with young lads, sir? They're in the A.I.F. First Division, they didn't wanna be seen as milksops, sir.'

'Sergeant, I've a good mind to put you on report, you have a duty to look after your men, these are not minor injuries!'

'Be obliged if you wouldn't, sir. The lads begged me. They didn't wanna be seen as the laughing stock, there's a lot of pride in the sappers, sir. Fallin' down stairs, it'd be humiliatin', sir.'

'A fair whack of stupidity too, if you ask me!'

'No, sir, with the greatest respect, *pride*, sapper pride, not stupidity, sir.' Treloar would like to put his boot into the M.O.'s groin, silly bastard wouldn't know what side was up. He's only a bloody captain, he thinks, straight off civvy street and now he's playing the fucking warrior doctor.

'Well, I'll overlook it this time, Sergeant Treloar, though it's against my better judgment. Don't let it happen again or I'll see your C.O. is involved.'

Treloar jumps spontaneously to attention and salutes, 'Yessir! Thank you, sir!'

'Dismissed,' the M.O. says in a weary voice.

The three men are placed in the ship's hospital for two days, Brodie to have his nose reset and his hands placed in plaster and the two others, Matthews and Jolly, requiring copious stitches to the lips and mouth and the extraction of several broken teeth, which will be done by the ship's surgeon. There is no dentist on board because in the first A.I.F. intake the standard of recruiting was set so high that a single tooth missing in a recruit's mouth would disqualify him.

Ben, hearing in the sergeants' mess that the three men have been hospitalised, goes to see them late on the afternoon of the day following the incident. On arrival he asks a medic if he can see the three men from D Company.

'You'll have to see Sister Atkins first, Sergeant,' the medic replies.

'How do I do that?'

'Wait here, I'll fetch her.'

Ben is made to wait, standing in the ship's hospital corridor for nearly twenty minutes before he sees Sister Atkins approaching. He has a mind to say something, show her he's a trifle miffed, but a nursing sister, without apparent rank, is given the status of an officer and so he decides to keep his trap shut. Moreover, as she draws closer, she smiles at him and Ben feels his heart skip a beat. A troopship is an unlikely place to fall in love but Ben knows with certainty, even before she has spoken, that he must make every endeavour to develop a closer acquaintance with Sister Atkins. Please, God, don't let her have a sweetheart somewhere, he says to himself, knowing full well that anyone as pretty would not go unattended.

'Yes, Sergeant, I'm told you wish to see the three men who came in this morning?'

'Yes, Sister.'

'Are you their sergeant?' Her voice is light and bright and she smiles again so that the question doesn't appear to be overly officious.

'No, er, they're involved with my platoon, I just want to see if they're all right,' Ben replies a little sheepishly.

'Well, they're not going to die, Sergeant, if that's what

you mean? But they've had a nasty fall.' She puts her head to one side as though she is examining him more closely. 'We don't usually allow visitors.'

'I won't take long, Sister.'

Sister Atkins laughs. 'I'll say you won't, five minutes is all you'll get.'

'Thank you, Sister.' He is suddenly desperate to think of something to say that will impress her but his mind has turned to mashed potatoes.

'Right, follow me, Sergeant er . . . ?'

'Teekleman, Ben Teekleman, Sister.' Then he adds gratuitously, 'From Tasmania.'

'Tasmania? How nice. I have a cousin in Tasmania, though I don't suppose you'd know her, Lucy Atkins?'

Ben is walking beside her and he receives the slightest whiff of lavender water which is enough to send his head spinning. 'Don't suppose I do, but there was a Lucy Atkins in primary school once?'

'Oh, sure, your sister's best friend, was she?'

It is obvious that Sister Atkins has not gone unnoticed on the ship and is up to all the tricks men play with a pretty woman in an attempt to prolong a conversation. 'No really, in New Norfolk, red hair, green eyes, lots of freckles, her mum and dad ran, still do I suppose, the drapery shop.'

Sister Atkins stops, her eyes grown wide. 'My goodness, Sergeant Ben Teekleman, you *do* know my cousin Lucy!'

They have reached the ward door and Sister Atkins enters first and steps ahead, Ben following two or three steps behind her. The ward contains some twenty men. There has been an outbreak of flu on board and there have been several cases of pneumonia as a consequence. Ben silently bemoans the fact that they have effectively come to the end of their conversation.

Sister Atkins stops at the last three beds. 'You've got a

visitor,' she says cheerfully. The three sappers sit up in bed and from their expressions it is fairly apparent to the nursing sister that Ben's arrival doesn't exactly thrill them. 'Hmmph, you don't seem too happy about it?' she says, straightening up Brodie's blanket.

'Thank you, Sister,' Brodie says without enthusiasm. The space between his eyes and mouth is swathed in a large bandage, while the damage to the swollen lips of the other two soldiers is uncovered and the ragged criss-cross of stitches can be readily seen.

Sister Atkins turns to Ben, 'Five minutes. Well, I must be off, there's no rest for the wicked.'

Ben is suddenly desperate and he takes his courage in both hands, 'Can I see you, Sister, meet again, talk about Lucy?'

Sister Atkins' pretty lips form a perfect 'O'. 'No, Sergeant, you cannot, you know the rules,' she replies and, turning on a well-polished heel, she exits the ward watched all the way by Ben.

'Bad luck, Sergeant,' Brodie says, happy that Ben has been put in his place. 'Good sort, though, ain't she?'

Ben turns back to the men, remembering suddenly why he's come, 'Oh, g'day, lads.' He glances at the doorway, 'Yes well . . .'

Brodie nods towards the two beds on his left. 'Them other two can't talk, Sergeant, stitches inside their mouth and tongue.'

Ben clears his throat, 'I don't suppose you've ever heard a sergeant apologise, so I won't. But next time you get an order for a night attack at close quarters, point out to your sergeant that it's a full moon, will ya.'

Brodie drops his eyes. 'We was only havin' us a bit of fun, Sergeant.'

'What? With pick handles?'

'Yeah, but we was only gunna hit to the body like,

through the blankets, nothing too harmful, plenty o' bruises but nothin' broke. Surprise yiz and get out before youse could do anythin'.'

'That what your sergeant told you, was it?' Brodie doesn't reply and Ben continues, 'In my experience, Private . . . by the way, what's your name?'

'Brodie, Sergeant,' he indicates the two beds to his left with a nod, 'Matthews and Jolly.' The two men nod curtly, unable to speak, though their eyes show them to be less than friendly.

'Yes well, as I was saying, the essence of surprise is concealment, the enemy has twenty-twenty vision the same as you, Private Brodie, you could've read a newspaper on deck last night.'

Brodie glances down at his lap. 'Yes, Sergeant,' he says in a small voice. Then to Ben's surprise he looks up, 'It were wrong, what we done. Your mob didn't do nothin' to us and we didn't find that place to kip down before you done, neither.'

Ben smiles. 'Well, one apology deserves another.' He looks at all three men in turn, 'I'm sorry I hurt you, lads, surprise attacks generally cause an overreaction.'

Brodie looks up at him. 'Not to worry, Sergeant, me nose's been broke twice before by me old man and he didn't never say sorry neither.'

'Yeah, well, what say you, lads? Best to keep our mutual aggression for the Hun.'

'Jesus, Sergeant, when I saw that there axe o' yours, I damn near shit me trousers.' He pulls his hands from under the blankets and Ben sees that they are both in plaster. 'Four broken fingers and me nose ain't too bad, I thought me time was up for bloody certain.'

Ben laughs softly then suddenly grows serious. 'We're all in this war together, lads, if I can help you at any time, I hope you'll come to me.' Conscious that he may have

embarrassed Brodie he looks down at the sapper's plaster-
of-Paris mittens. 'Don't suppose you'd care to shake hands
on that, Private Brodie,' he teases. Ben is suddenly aware
of a tug to the back of his tunic and he looks round to see
both Matthews and Jolly have their hands extended. 'No
hard feelings?' he asks. They both shake their heads and,
in turn, clasp his hand in a firm handshake. Then he
shakes Brodie's plaster cast ceremoniously, both of them
laughing. 'Well, I guess my five minutes is up, lads, better
be kicking the dust then, eh? Cheer'o, nice to meet you
again under friendlier circumstances.' Ben walks away
down the centre aisle of the ward.

'Good luck with the sheila, Sergeant,' Brodie calls after
him. 'I reckon you ain't got a snowball's 'ope in hell.'

'You'll keep, Private Brodie,' Ben calls back and there
is general laughter in the ward.

The five-day voyage to Albany is without further
mishap. In the parlance of the sea, it has been plain
sailing. In the way of the army the days become routine,
even somewhat boring, so that by the time the ship
reaches the tiny whaling port the troops feel as though
they've been at sea for several weeks.

What a sight the fleet presents as it lies anchored in the
tranquil waters of King George Sound, set against a
smudge of distant island hills. Twenty-eight ships carrying
twenty thousand young men, Australia's young blood,
hand-picked like some exotic fruit to be as perfect as can
be, the tallest, straightest, strongest we have to give. They
are not to know that they leave as surrogate sons tied to
the apron strings of Mother England, but will return as
Australians, sons of a nation confident and individual,
having completed its final rites of passage.

Chapter Eleven

PEREGRINE
ORMINGTON-SMITH

Leaving Home 1914

If Peregrine Ormington-Smith had enlisted as a raw recruit, he would have been culled from the queue outside the recruitment depot. If by some mischance he'd made it inside, he would have stumbled at the very first hurdle, the all-important eye-test. Ormington-Smith wears spectacles, the lenses of which closely resemble the bottom of a ginger-beer bottle.

In military terms Second Lieutenant Ormington-Smith is a dud, plain and simple. Peter Pan would have been a more effective platoon leader. There is simply nothing about him that inspires confidence. He is so hopeless there is a fair bit of speculation that he is the reason Ben's C.O. contrived to keep Ben in the Victorian outfit.

It is difficult to see how Ormington-Smith could possibly have passed muster when the battalion commander was selecting his junior officers, unless nepotism or some other major influence had been brought to bear. Like most sergeants, Ben has grown accustomed to the often mystifying decisions of senior officers, nevertheless he finds it impossible not to believe that any experienced senior officer even wearing a blindfold would instantly conclude that Peregrine Ormington-Smith has a very precarious hold on the practical skills required to navigate his way through life. The battalion commander, Colonel Wanliss, has obviously passed the buck to his C.O. in C Company, Major Sayers, an Englishman from Liverpool, who, in turn, has duck-shuffled it on to his most competent sergeant. Ben Teekleman is to be Ormington-Smith's surrogate nursemaid.

Sayers has on one occasion come close to admitting as much, hinting it was the fault of his battalion commander. 'It's got naught to do with you, Sergeant Teekleman, it's . . . well, it's just the way things sometimes are in the army.'

'With respect, sir, the excuse that there are too many sergeants in the 12th Battalion is bulldust. We have five more platoon sergeants than we need in this battalion.'

'Oh aye,' his C.O. admitted, 'more a question of personnel, officer personnel.' He looked meaningfully at Ben. 'Influence higher up, if you get my drift.' He left it hanging in the air like that, making Ben cope with the hapless junior officer, knowing that the stumble-bum was the reason why he couldn't join his mates in Tasmania.

One of life's paradoxes is that people who are temperamentally ill-suited to a particular vocation actively seek it out. It is as if they want to prove to themselves that they are not who they seem to be. For instance, an irascible and short-tempered person becomes a shop assistant, a tram conductor, a teacher, a football referee or a museum guide and in the process makes a terrible hash of things. Conversely, a timid or congenitally shy person elects to be a policeman, a clergyman, an auctioneer or a choirmaster, with the same disastrous results. These perverse decisions to practise what one is patently ill-suited to preach seems to have no rational explanation and simply emphasises that our perception of ourselves is seldom, if ever, to be trusted.

In an effort to understand where Peregrine Ormington-Smith was coming from, Ben asked Victoria to dig into the second lieutenant's background. She came back with the information that his father had been a colonel on the headquarters staff of General Roberts in the Boer War and was one of the heroes of Mafeking.

The family settled in Australia in 1901 because Peregrine, an only son, suffered from a bronchial complaint and, on the advice of a Harley Street specialist, they moved to a warmer climate. He was just fourteen when they arrived and, shortly afterwards, the colonel purchased a sheep property near Warrnambool in the Western District of Victoria. In Victoria's words the family is 'quite uppity', with Lucinda Ormington-Smith, 'quite a gel', quickly making her mark on the Melbourne Ladies' Benevolent Society and the Red Cross committee.

Young Peregrine somehow stumbled and mumbled his way through Geelong Grammar, where he was the subject of routine persecution because of his impossible Christian and family names, his toffee-nosed English accent and his inability to master even the fundamentals of cricket or football. His chest cleared up and he matriculated, but without distinction. Soon after, much to his father's dismay, he elected to study art at the National Gallery School. After this, little is known of his whereabouts except that he was thought to have become 'some sort of a bohemian'. Quite simply, Peregrine Ormington-Smith began life as a failure and seems to be continuing on in the same vein.

Ben's very first task was to try to persuade his lieutenant to keep in step, for on occasions Ormington-Smith confuses his left with his right. Even when he does march in time, he seems to develop an awkward sort of wobble, his head jerking forward, followed by his shoulders, then his hips and finally his long Ichabod Crane legs. All in all, his body gives the appearance of being jointed in a manner quite different to that of most homo sapiens.

Ormington-Smith stands a reedy six feet and one inch in his stockinged feet but, unlike the angular Crow Rigby who is all horn and hide, he is built on a skeletal frame so rickety in structure and sparse of muscle and meat that a sou'wester blowing with only the slightest malice would knock him on his arse. At the one extremity he has two left feet, both of them size thirteen, while at the other he is almost completely bald. People seeing him in full uniform shake their heads in disbelief and grow fearful for the defence of the country. It is also apparent that the tailor who fashioned his uniform admitted defeat early on in the cutting and stitching process, for his tunic, despite the efforts of his Sam Browne belt to hold it down, hangs from his body like sacking on a scarecrow and his trousers end two inches above the top of his boots.

But it is the lieutenant's voice that marks him for genuine disaster. As high-pitched as a girl's, words issue from his mouth with machine-gun rapidity, so that they bump into each other, some of them breaking in half and joining together as they collide, with the result that Ormington-Smith seems to speak a language which resembles English in tone but makes almost no sense. No doubt this manner of speech has developed as a consequence of the chiacking he received at boarding school for his plummy British accent.

The platoon is forced to master this new language which Library called 'Truncation'. They have learned to respond to sounds rather than meaning. As an example, the word platoon comes out as 'oon', attention as 'shin', eyes right, for some reason, always comes out as 'shite', forward march as 'farsh', and dismissed as 'mist' to name but a few. Library Spencer seems to be the only one in the platoon to understand him without too much difficulty.

'How come you understand him?' Muddy Parthe once asked him.

Library shrugged. 'I don't know, I just can.'

'It's got to do with him reading all them books,' Numbers Cooligan explained. 'Library's that fast when he's readin' that the words come into his mind all blurred, bumping and squashing together, same as the lieutenant speaks.'

Eventually Library Spencer produces a dictionary of the Truncation language which even Ben is forced to swot up.

However, Second Lieutenant Peregrine Ormington-Smith, christened 'Wordsmith' by Library but soon enough adapted to 'Wordy Smith' by the platoon, does not have a malicious bone in his body. And on those not infrequent occasions when the platoon responds incorrectly to one of Wordy Smith's mysterious commands, he doesn't seem to mind too much. At first their apparent ineptitude brought down the wrath of the company sergeant-major and Ben was obliged to cop a fair bit of aggro until the cause of the confusion was corrected by learning Truncation.

Whenever Ben places a member of the platoon on a charge for some army misdemeanour it becomes fairly pointless parading him in front of Wordy Smith for sentence. The lieutenant simply appears anguished and, often biting his nails, he looks appealingly at Ben, sighs and says 'Kitchooty'. This means the offender is to do a day's kitchen duty peeling potatoes or at the handle end of a broom. Kitchooty eventually comes to mean whatever Ben considers to be an appropriate punishment.

The platoon regards Lieutenant Wordy Smith as a kind of invisible presence who depends entirely on Ben to guide their destiny and get them all, including himself, safely through the war. They don't, as might be expected with soldiers who are not much older than schoolboys, take the piss out of him. They accept that they have a sergeant whom they trust and an officer who, while being totally inadequate, doesn't interfere, which makes for a reasonably uncomplicated army life.

In the sergeants' mess Wordy Smith's disinclination to be involved in the daily affairs of the army is considered an ideal situation and Ben is thought to be a lucky bastard. Since the time of the ancient Romans, sergeants have come to the conclusion that the art of war cannot afford the luxury of an officer class and the A.I.F. is no different, regarding the rank of second lieutenant as the lowest possible form of life.

Lieutenant Wordy Smith's reluctance to issue orders and to restrict himself only to those parade-ground commands which are mandatory for a one-pip lieutenant makes running the platoon comparatively easy for his sergeant. As a consequence, Ben must do most of the administration work normally the duty of his platoon commander. Sheer incompetence, and the fact that it is easier to perform around him than to include him, has given Lieutenant Ormington-Smith a soft ride in the army.

All Wordy Smith ever desires is time to write or paint in watercolours. But even in this he is peculiar and contradictory. Without his spectacularly thick spectacles he is certifiably blind, yet his art concentrates exclusively on wildflowers, but only those too small to be noticed in the normal course of observing nature. Using a sable brush which contains only three or four hairs, he will paint no flower in nature that is larger than a tunic button, specialising in those to be found in decreasing sizes down to exquisitely beautiful specimens no bigger than the circumference of a single, minutely small blossom from the pale blue pin-cushion plant. His paintings of tiny green hood, spider and pink cockatoo orchids found on a route-march location show him not only to be a very fine watercolourist but also a very competent botanist. It is as though Lieutenant Wordy Smith is doing some sort of penance for a previous life, one which requires him to find the most difficult way possible to accomplish everything he attempts.

Together with his paintbox and diary, which doubles as his sketchbook, he carries a very large magnifying glass and a small laboratory microscope, the first to locate and the second to unlock the secret details of a myriad of dwarf flora. Wordy Smith paints, identifies, catalogues and writes about floral specimens which one might spend a lifetime crushing underfoot without ever being aware they existed. His field excursions are spent almost entirely on his knees within a radius of ten feet of a plant, crawling through rock and scrub with his nose and magnifying glass inches from the ground and his scrawny bum sticking up in the air. His trousers, despite any amount of washing, always show brown stains at the knees. In an attempt to get him onto the parade ground looking half decent, Ben asked Martha Billings to make him a set of padded leather kneepads to wear on his rambles. When Ben presented these to him, he blushed to a new hue of scarlet, his mouth working to find the words to say thank you, but only managing an assortment of small explosive sounds involving spittle. Finally he gave up and simply reached out and touched Ben's shoulder. He now carries the kneepads in the side pockets of his military tunic, which makes him look as though he is perpetually poised to take off and fly.

The *Orvieto* slipped into its West Australian anchorage on King George Sound late in the morning of the fifth day out from Port Melbourne. There were now twenty thousand men and seven thousand, eight hundred and thirty-four horses on board thirty-six ships, who consider themselves fully equipped, trained and ready to go into action.

However, yet another delay caused them to remain at anchor. A rebellion by conscripted Boer forces in the Cape Colony had raised the possibility of Australians being used for garrison troops in South Africa. It seemed the Afrikaners among the South African recruits, many of them still harbouring bitter memories of their defeat by the British in the Boer War, saw no reason to fight for Mother England. Germany had been one of the very few friendly nations to the Boer Republic during the bitter conflict, supplying them with arms and much-needed medical aid and, if they were going to fight at all, the rebellious men would have preferred to do so for the enemy side.

General Botha, who had himself fought on the Boer side against Britain but now commanded the South African forces, managed to suppress the uprising. The convoy of Australian and New Zealand troops was free at last to sail, bound for the Western Front to play their part in a war that was going increasingly wrong for Britain and her allies.

The giant convoy leaves on the first of November and this time it is an almost silent departure, with the townsfolk from Albany lined up on a mountain ridge almost too distant to be seen. Once clear of the Sound, the Australian ships travel in three long lines, about a mile apart, with a gap of approximately eight hundred yards between the vessels in each line, while the New Zealand ships follow in a double line observing the same ratios. The convoy is escorted by the three Allied cruisers, HMAS *Melbourne*, HMAS *Sydney*, *Ibuki*, and with a fourth, the HMS *Minotaur*, leading the convoy.

The New Zealand troopships had been painted light

grey with a small number inside a star at the bow and stern, but the Australians had been less conscientious, leaving their vessels in their original colours, potential sitting ducks in daylight, even obliging the enemy with a large square painted on the bow with which to identify each vessel and supply a perfect target at which to aim. They are almost a week out to sea before someone in the fleet realises that the larger passenger liners and, in particular, the *Orvieto* with the general and staff on board, are conveniently lit up like a Christmas tree for any German cruisers hunting at night. From this point on, the strictest blackout conditions are observed. In an example of Navy overkill which goes from the sublime to the ridiculous, the troops are even forbidden to smoke on deck on the premise that a match struck on a dark night can be observed by a strong pair of field glasses at a distance of four miles.

On November 7th the convoy receives the news that the two German battleships the *Scharnhorst* and the *Gneisenau* have met a British squadron off the South American coast close to Coronel and that the British cruisers *Good Hope* and *Monmouth* have been sunk. There is suddenly a sobering sense of vulnerability among the general staff with the realisation that a single German cruiser, were it to get in among them, could wreak havoc with the three parallel lines of Australian and New Zealand ships. If, for instance, the enemy warship managed to sail into any one of the corridors separating the Allied ships, every ship would instantly become a sitting target for the Germans, while the four Allied cruisers would virtually be unable to fire a clean shot at the enemy for fear of hitting one of their own convoy in the crossfire.

On the night of November 7th, the Cocos Islands thirty-six hours of sailing away, all lights are extinguished in a practice drill involving the entire convoy and its four supporting cruisers. Sleeping on deck is forbidden, members of the crew pad about the ships in bare feet and complete radio silence is maintained. The Cocos Islands are considered a danger point, since the German battleship *Emden* was last known to be prowling in the vicinity of the Bay of Bengal and is quite capable of reaching the convoy.

To make matters worse, at dawn the following day the *Minotaur* signals to Major-General Bridges on the *Orvieto* that she has been ordered on other service and disappears in the direction of Mauritius. The presumption is, because of the losses of two British cruisers off Coronel, she will be needed to escort a South African convoy from the Cape. The Australian and New Zealand convoy is left with only three cruisers and the *Melbourne* takes the *Minotaur*'s place at its head. They now have a cruiser ahead and one on either beam but nothing to protect them if the *Emden* creeps up at night from the rear and gets in amongst them.

The sun sets gloriously on a smooth sea bringing with it a calm and warm night. They are due to pass fifty miles east of the Cocos Islands in the early hours of the following morning. Ben is unable to sleep in the hot cabin and goes on deck for a spell of cooler air just as the moon rises at eleven-thirty. The sea is smooth as glass and he can see the dark hulls of the convoy, like a great herd of silent and determined behemoths moving on their way. The *Ibuki*'s huge smoke plume is clearly visible in the moonlight. Ben remains on deck for an hour before being discovered by a ship's officer and ordered below. He lies in his bunk thinking of home, of Hawk and Victoria, Hawk growing visibly older, and it occurs to him with a sudden start that Hawk may not be there when he returns home. Depressed, he conjures up in his mind the soft cool dawn of a Tasmanian summer morning and then thinks of the adventure to come. He wonders whether seeing Britain and Europe will change him, though he can't conceive of ever wanting to leave the Tasmanian wilderness with its fast-flowing creeks and the deep-flowing rivers fronted with blue gum and blackbutt that had stood tall and majestic when Abel Tasman the great Dutch navigator passed the island more than two hundred and fifty years before. The trees now tower for almost three hundred feet, brushing the canopy of low cloud that settles above the forest just before it begins to rain. He can't imagine anything comparing with that, no cathedral in Europe could be a grander sight to his eyes. The lights of Paris or London could never compare to a vermilion bushfire raging through the mountains at night. Eventually he falls asleep listening to the throbbing of the ship's engines and the plash-plash of the waves hitting the side of the ship as the convoy moves undisturbed through the warm tropical night.

Summer dawn in the Indian Ocean is as beautiful a display as nature is capable of putting on, with the pink-streaked dawn as sharp as a maharaja's ruby. As the new day breaks, the siren of the *Orvieto* gives a sustained hoot, the convoy is, at that very moment, swinging round the Cocos Islands and the most critical point of the voyage appears to have passed.

At 6.24, the cooks are breaking eggs and beginning to fry the first rashers for breakfast in the galley when the wireless operators of several of the convoy ships and the three escorts receive a short unexpected message. It comes through very loud and clear as if sent at no distance whatsoever and simply reads 'KATIVBATTAV' which makes no sense. Two minutes later the message is repeated. Then the wireless station on the Cocos Islands is heard calling, 'What is that code? What is that code?' No answer follows, but ninety seconds later the same coded call is made, though only once. The next signal to come through is from the Cocos Islands calling the *Minotaur*, which does not reply as she is well out of radio range on her way to Mauritius. The Cocos wireless station tries again and this time adds, 'Strange warship approaching.' The *Minotaur* is, of course, again unable to answer and shortly after the station sends out a general call, 'S.O.S. Strange warship approaching,' and suddenly falls silent.

HMAS *Sydney* is detached from the convoy to hunt for the enemy, leaving the convoy with only the *Melbourne* and the Japanese light cruiser *Ibuki* to protect the convoy. If *Sydney* doesn't find her quarry and the enemy cruiser sneaks up on the convoy, all hell will break loose. With a German warship in the vicinity, discovering the convoy's whereabouts isn't going to be too difficult. The *Ibuki* burns two hundred tons of coal a day and an ever-present pillar of dense black smoke tumbles high into a cloudless sky and is visible forty miles away. A determined enemy warship with a good set of guns and a well-trained crew, if it can get in amongst them, is capable of sinking at least half of the convoy before it is finally dispatched.

The entire convoy witnesses the *Sydney* leaving them and it doesn't take a lot of imagination from the men to know she has gone to meet the enemy. The day is to be treated like any other on board, with physical jerks, inspections, parades and rifle drills as well as the scheduled lectures, but at every opportunity the men's eyes are turned out to sea.

Just after breakfast a message is sent from the *Sydney* to say that she has sighted the enemy ship which is steaming northward and could conceivably cross the convoy's track. The *Ibuki* immediately requests permission from Captain Silver of the *Melbourne* to join the *Sydney* in the impending battle, but this is refused.

Both warships now move to a point far out on the port beam to be in the best possible position if the enemy ship approaches, the *Melbourne* slightly ahead of the convoy and the Japanese ship at its centre.

At 10.45 a wireless message is received from the *Sydney*: 'Am briskly engaging the enemy.' Most of the men on board are convinced the enemy must be the dreaded *Emden*, the German cruiser most often mentioned in Australian newspapers as taking a terrible toll on British merchant ships in the Indian Ocean. At 11.10 comes a signal: '*Emden* beached and done for.'

The news, despite the effort of General Bridges to keep it subdued until more is known, spreads like a bushfire through the transports, and there is tremendous pride among the men that an Australian warship has tasted first blood and come out the victor. Whatever activity is taking place on board is thrown into chaos and finally an order from General Bridges gives the troops a half-day holiday.

However, the convoy is not out of danger, the *Königsberg*, the *Emden*'s sister ship, is still thought to be hunting in the Indian Ocean, and that night there is another blackout for the ships. The captains of the transport ships hate the blackouts because they make sailing in a convoy dangerous, with the ever-present risk of one ship ramming another. But the following day news arrives that the *Königsberg* has been definitely sighted off the coast of Africa, at much too great a distance to reach them. From that point on it is plain sailing to Colombo, where they meet up with the *Sydney* again. The prisoners taken from the *Emden* are transported to various troopships, the wounded hospitalised, with the captain of the *Emden* coming on board the *Orvieto* together with several of his officers. The troops are not permitted to go ashore at Colombo and, after coaling and taking on fresh water and supplies, the convoy sails for Aden.

Several days out from Colombo, Lieutenant R. G. Casey, one of the officers in charge of the prisoners, asks Captain von Müller, a tall, thin aristocrat, what he would have done if he had sighted the convoy.

Excessively polite, von Müller replies in an English with very little accent. 'If I had got up to you I should have run alongside her,' he points to the *Ibuki*, 'and fired a torpedo. Then in the confusion I would have got in among the transports. I would have sunk half of them, I think, before your escort came up.' He shrugged. 'I would have been sunk in the end, I expect, I always expected that.'

It is generally agreed that his chances of approaching unobserved on such a bright moonlit night would have been a thousand to one. It is also agreed among the Australian officers who get to know him that he is just the sort to attempt it.

At Aden, while most of the ships are anchored in the harbour, the *Orvieto*, with the Australian High Command on board, docks. Aden proves to be a busy port. Troop transports, either making for India with territorial troops or returning from there with British regulars or native troops, seem to be coming in or out all of the time. On the day the *Orvieto* arrives there are fifty-seven vessels in the harbour and the dusty streets of Aden, set against a backdrop of bare red hills, throng with soldiers.

A small contingent of officers from the *Orvieto* is sent ashore to perform various duties, one of which is to see that the mail from the *Orvieto* is delivered to the Aden Club for posting. Sixteen infantrymen are picked to carry the mail bags to the club where they will be placed under lock and key until they can be put on board a ship returning to Australia. Six of the Click platoon, as they are now known, are among the lucky men selected for the mail patrol. Muddy Parthe, Crow Rigby, Woggy Mustafa, Numbers Cooligan, Hornbill and Library Spencer all draw the lucky short straw, with Wordy Smith as one of the two officers in charge of the ship's mail.

None of the lads has been overseas and, except for Woggy Mustafa, whose father hails originally from Lebanon, they have never seen an Arab and know nothing about the exotic world of the Arabian Nights although, at a pinch, they might admit to having heard of the Pyramids.

Library, of course, knows a fair amount about the Arabs and the British presence in Aden, none of which is considered useful and he proves absolutely hopeless when it comes to the important stuff like brothels, booze, belly dancers and what food is safe to eat, whether the beer is cold and if it gives you gyppo guts.

However, Numbers Cooligan reckons that human nature being what it is, every city has a place where you go to get into trouble and they'd find it soon enough. 'All them what wants to get pissed and plugged, bring your frenchies and follow me,' he declares at the bottom of the gangplank. They are to wait on the wharf for the mail bags and for Wordy Smith to arrive. Ben has given Crow Rigby an exact map to the Aden Club in case Wordy gets them lost.

'Who says we're gunna be allowed any free time?' Hornbill asks.

'Officers have been given the whole day ashore, with my powers o' persuasion, Wordy Smith's not gunna make us return to ship before sundown,' Numbers Cooligan answers confidently.

'Reckon we should do, yer know, a bit o' sight-seeing first,' Crow Rigby says. 'Get to know the lay o' the land, like?'

'Whaffor? We seen it comin' into the harbour, it's a

shit-hole.' Cooligan gives a couple of exaggerated sniffs, 'Can't ya smell it?'

'Shit, Cooligan, that comes from that dead dog over there,' Hornbill says, pointing to a dead mongrel lying some fifty feet upwind from them, three crows are already busy pecking at it.

'Fuckin' 'ell, they've even got 'em here!' Crow Rigby exclaims.

'Well, that's yer proof then, ain't it? We 'aven't come fifty feet and we've hit our first dead dog. Plenty more where he come from, mate!' Numbers Cooligan says ominously.

'What do you think, Woggy?' Muddy Parthe asks. 'Yer old man come from 'round these parts, don't he?'

'Lebanon, it ain't like this, we're Christians, mate,' Woggy protests, then adds, 'Me old man says you got to go to the bazaar.'

'Did you hear that, lads? That's a flamin' expert opinion, Woggy's old man says the bazaar. Righto, them what's coming, onward Christian soldiers!'

Lieutenant Ormington-Smith arrives and shortly afterwards the mail bags are lowered by crane. Crow Rigby, on Ben's instructions, takes command and, with each of them carrying a sack of mail, they head for the gate. The provost sergeant at the gate salutes Wordy Smith with the merest touch of his red-banded cap, examines their passes and tells them not to drink the water or any soft drinks and gets the cheerful reply, 'Righto then, Sergeant, if you insist, we'll stick to beer!'

The Arabs waiting hopefully at the gates follow the lads all the way to the Aden Club where Wordy Smith has simply followed Crow Rigby who, in turn, has assiduously consulted Ben's map. Numbers Cooligan, who has been walking alongside Wordy Smith at the rear, gives the thumbs-up sign as they reach the club.

The veranda of the Aden Club, with canvas awning down and electric ceiling fans working overtime though it isn't much past ten o'clock in the morning, is already packed with Australian and British officers off the various ships, the Australians busy getting their laughing gear around a cold and splendidly foaming ale, while the British seem to have a preference for a drink called 'Gin and it'.

The lads from Ben's platoon, trying hard to remember what a truly cold beer tastes like, soon realise they are unlikely to be given the opportunity to find out at the Aden Club, and take the mail bags to the club secretary's office. With Wordy Smith watching, the canvas bags are locked into a back room with no windows which seems to contain several bags of potatoes and onions but little else. The club secretary gives Wordy Smith a receipt, but Crow Rigby politely takes it from him, folds it and places it in the breast pocket of his tunic for safekeeping.

Wordy Smith leaves them at the entrance, having arranged with Crow Rigby to meet them back at the club no later than five o'clock that afternoon.

They all salute him. 'Thank you, sir, have a beer or six for us, won't you, sir,' Numbers Cooligan advises their platoon officer.

Wordy Smith taps the small canvas kitbag he carries, 'No, no, cliffproms splendspes, whato!', which Library translates when they are out of earshot as 'No, no, cliffs promise splendid specimens, what ho!' Library adds, 'He's got all his stuff in his kitbag and he has his kneepads in his tunic. He's taken the day off to paint his flowers.'

'Do you think Ben knows?' Muddy asks.

'Jesus, Muddy!' Numbers protests. 'It don't matter, not for now anyhow! Let's kick the dust, the bazaar awaits such as us with wonders to behold!'

They walk down the quiet, neatly raked, white-gravel

driveway bordered by brilliant red cannas and clipped lawns, shaded by poinciana trees, and out of the gates of the snooty club grounds into the harsh sun and baked earth where Britain's orderly influence ends and Arab chaos begins.

Once through the gates, the lads are immediately engulfed by men in long white robes importuning them, plucking at their tunics and presenting their wares, most of which appear to be of a recreational kind. All of the offers begin with the words 'You want . . .' 'You want jig-jig, soldier?' 'You want my sister? Very clean. You only first time, British guarantee!' 'You want jig-a-jig show, only one dinar, mans and womans, donkey and womans, very nice for you.' 'You want dirty postcard? Only one dinar, six, you pick also.'

'Ere, give us a gander at them postcards,' Hornbill says to an Arab, who has a dozen black and white pornographic postcards which he loops in a two-foot arc from one hand to another. The cards instantly stack into his left hand and he deals the first one to Hornbill as though a croupier in a Biarritz casino.

The card shows a bald bloke with a waxed and curled mustachio, he is barrel-chested with a protruding beer gut and is completely bollocky except for his socks and suspenders. He is chock-a-block up the back of a large female who is on all fours. She is looking directly at the camera, her face devoid of any expression. The centre of her lips is painted into a small bow, which extends above and below the lip line, with the remainder of her mouth visible on either side of the bow. The outlines of her eyes are heavily made up with black kohl and the eyebrows appear to have been shaved or plucked and then painted back in a more intensely arched line with the same substance. Two darkish circles of rouge are apparent on the cheeks of a face powdered a ghostly white. Her hair is swept up in the style of the Victorian era, the whole effect giving her the appearance of a tarted-up possum.

'Shit, it's him again!' Hornbill exclaims as they jostle to have a squiz.

'Him, who?' someone asks.

'Me uncle's got some o' these pitchiz,' Hornbill explains, 'he got 'em from some sailors who were pissed and broke who swapped them for eight pies and a bottle o' sauce.' He stabs a finger at the man in the picture. 'It's the same bloke, me uncle's got twenty o' them postcards, that fat bloke's in all o' them and here he is again!' Hornbill shakes his head. 'No matter what possie he's in, he don't never take off his socks and suspenders.' He turns to the Arab and hands the postcard back. 'Let's see the others, mate? I bet fat Fritz is in 'em all.'

'How do you know he's German?' Numbers Cooligan asks.

'Sailors told me uncle they gets them postcards in Munich, it's the world capital o' dirty pictures and absolute filth.'

'Gee, I'd like to go there,' Cooligan says wistfully.

'Well, you probably can when we've conquered the buggers,' Crow Rigby says.

The Arab hands Hornbill the bunch of postcards and he shuffles through them all, the others jostling and craning their necks to get a clear look. Although the fat female changes from time to time, the bloke with the socks and suspenders is in every one of them. As if to confirm Hornbill's uncle's assertion, one of the poses shows him riding on the back of a buxom Fräulein, who is on all fours. She has whip slashes painted crudely on her enormous bum and he's holding a riding crop aloft and wearing a German officer's spiked helmet and, of course, the ubiquitous socks and suspenders with a set of Spanish spurs fitted to his heels.

'There you go, told ya didn't I, bloody German!' Hornbill says triumphantly.

'Ten dinar,' the Arab says, holding up ten fingers, 'very cheap, special price for you!'

Crow Rigby looks at the Arab and shakes his head sadly. 'Sorry, mate, we'd be happy to buy the lot off yiz if only Fritzy weren't wearing them crook-lookin' socks!'

Hornbill hands the man back his postcards and, laughing, they depart for the bazaar followed by what is obviously, even to the untuned infidel ear, a string of profanities in the Arab lingo.

At the end of a long day of dust and noise, a thousand importunings, strange smells, exotic wares, high-pitched wailing music that seems to drill through the eardrums, too many beers too weak to make them drunk but which sweat back through the pores of their skin within minutes of consumption, it's almost time to get back to the ship.

They've all bought several cheap brass and enamelled trinkets which they fondly think their mums or sisters will find romantic and exotic. They stop for lunch at a cafe in the bazaar and order mutton, potatoes and chickpeas, which Library assures them is ridgy-didge because it all comes out of the same simmering pot and all the germs have been killed. After this Numbers Cooligan tries a small brass cup of Arabic coffee, thick and sweet, which he pronounces to one and all as delicious, but which collides with the warm beer, lamb, potato and chickpeas and persuades the resident contents of his stomach to retrace its steps so that he is violently sick in an alleyway a few minutes later.

They also visit three brothels, the first two have a line of British tommies and Indian troops in turbans a hundred yards long and they decide to try somewhere else. While the queue at the third is shorter, the brothel is in a mean street where they come across another dead dog. Far from the glamorous velvet-draped and silk-cushioned bordello they'd fondly imagined, the brothel turns out to be several small dark rooms, each of which is curtained off into four partitions only just large enough for a man to be placed in a horizontal position on a dirty mattress. Crow Rigby and Hornbill would certainly have had their heels intruding into the next-door partition.

Moreover, the Arab sheilas, except for darker hair and a somewhat duskier skin tone, are dead ringers for the ones on the postcards and even Numbers Cooligan, the only one who hinted of having had previous experience with a woman, decides to give them a big miss. The mandatory lecture Ben has given them about venereal disease suddenly comes into sharp focus. Losing one's virginity is one thing, but being sent back home with a dose of the clap or something even worse is quite another.

Finally, with a little more than an hour to go before they have to retrace their steps to the Aden Club to meet Wordy Smith, they each part with a dinar, a day's pay, to see a live show advertising itself in crude lettering painted onto the surface of a doorway:

Belly dunce Snakes

Plise pulled the bell.

'Whatcha reckon, lads? Must be a classier sort of joint, no wogs trying to get us ter go in,' Cooligan says.

'Most likely the opposite, the rock bottom,' Library Spencer suggests. 'Even the Arabs must have some personal standards.'

'I reckon with them whorehouses we've already hit rock bottom, we've got nothing to lose and if Crow or Hornbill gets bit by the snake it'll only make 'em 'omesick! What say we go in, eh?' Cooligan says, obviously feeling better after he'd emptied himself out in the alley.

'Yeah, shit, why not? I'm game if you are,' Muddy says.

'You ring, Hornbill, you're the biggest,' Woggy suggests.

Hornbill steps up to the door and looks for the bell which is nowhere to be seen. 'There's no bloody bell,' he calls out.

A short piece of dirty rope protrudes from a hole in the door directly under the lettering. 'The rope! Pull it!' Library offers.

Hornbill tugs on the rope and, without any apparent sound, the door is flung open by an old man sporting several days of white stubble on his chin, wearing a battered top hat and greasy tailcoat together with pyjama trousers and a pair of embroidered slippers just like the ones Muddy has bought for his mum in the bazaar.

'Ladies and Gentlemans, belly dunce, welcome!' he says, bowing with a flourish. 'One dinar, plise, welcome, welcome!' There must have been a peephole in the door or something, because the old man couldn't possibly have responded so quickly to Hornbill's ring.

'Is that one dinar for the lot, squire?' Numbers Cooligan asks hopefully.

'No, no, naughty man!' the old man says, chuckling and shaking his finger at Numbers' joke. 'Six dinar, you come all, very wonderful belly dunce.'

'What about the snake?' Crow Rigby asks.

'Very, very wonderful snake also!'

They look at each other for affirmation and then Crow nods, 'Yeah, bugger it, let's go.'

The old man stands, blocking their way. 'You pay me now, gentlemans.'

'We pay five dinars for six, fair enough, Abdul?' Cooligan offers.

The old bloke shakes his head. 'Very wonderful belly-dunce snake, six dinars, five dinars belly dunce not take away clothers.'

That settles it, with the promise of a bollocky belly dancer the old man has instantly cancelled Numbers Cooligan's need for a bargain and each of them hands over a dinar, which the old bloke slips into his pocket.

They are led down a dark passageway with half a dozen soot-eyed children with runny noses staring at them silently from passing doorways. Two of the smallest, both boys, wear no clothes and have protruding little stomachs, their tiny brown spigots pointing to their pathetically thin, dirt-encrusted legs.

'Classy joint orright,' Crow Rigby whispers. 'Smell the cat's piss.'

'No cats here, mate, we had 'em for lunch,' Numbers Cooligan replies.

The end of the passageway leads directly to a door which, in another life, was once painted fire-engine red but its brilliance has long since faded to a mostly purplish-brown, the paint peeling in parts to show a dirty white undercoat. The old bloke removes Muddy's mum's slippers and places them at the door. 'Very, very welcome, gentlemans.' He points to Woggy's boots. 'Please to take off the shoeses.'

They look at each other, uncertain. 'If he scarpers with our boots we'll get our pay docked and a month's kitchooty,' Woggy warns.

'Crikey, we've come this far, we might as well have a Captain Cook!' Hornbill protests. 'Besides, even Library could take the old bloke in a blue.'

'We could keep them on our laps,' Library points out, ignoring Hornbill's remark.

They sit down in the passageway and remove their boots and puttees and the old man opens the door using a key tied to the end of his pyjama cord. 'Please to enter, gentlemans.'

'We're not gentlemen, we're Australians,' Crow Rigby drawls, hugging his boots.

They enter a small room roughly the size of your average suburban bedroom. Two hurricane lamps with red-tinted glass, hanging from the ceiling at the far end of the room, cast a pinkish glow over a platform, which is about four feet square and eighteen inches high, and covered with a fitted carpet of Arabic design. The carpet is worn through to the boards at the centre where the belly dancer has obviously performed a thousand exotic gyrations. The platform and the wall directly behind it are vaguely outlined in pink light while the remainder of the room is in almost total darkness and smells of sweat and stale Turkish tobacco.

'Sit, gentlemans, you like coffee? Arab coffee, very, very wonderful, only two shekels!'

They all laugh. 'No thanks, Abdul, Mr Cooligan here may accept your kind offer, but we'll give the wog brew a miss if yer don't mind.'

Their eyes have grown accustomed to the dark and they can now see that the earthen floor is covered with several small overlapping carpets onto which have been thrown eight or nine leather cushions. They all sit down cross-legged facing the stage, preferring to sit directly on the carpet rather than the greasy cushions, their boots resting on their laps.

'On with the show, Abdul, chop, chop!' Numbers Cooligan calls, trying to sound cheerfully confident, though secretly sharing with the others the thought that they've almost certainly blown a day's pay on what, judging from the surroundings, promises to be a real dud bash.

'I fetch-ed belly dunce,' the old man announces and

disappears through the door, closing it behind him and, by doing so, further adding to the gloomy atmosphere.

'Shit, what now?' Muddy asks.

'Look, there's ashtrays,' Hornbill announces, reaching out and holding up a large brass bowl he's found on the perimeter of the carpet beside him. 'Anyone got a smoke? I'm out, smoko'll help kill the stink in 'ere.'

Woggy Mustafa fumbles in the top pocket of his tunic and produces a new packet of ten Capstan and foolishly hands it to Hornbill, who removes one and passes the pack around. 'Hey, fair go, fellas! That's me last friggin' pack!' Woggy protests. The packet is returned to him five cigarettes short. 'Jesus! Youse bastards all owe me one, ya hear, the next butt bot's mine?'

'I thought you said your mob were Christian? That's blasphemy, mate,' Numbers Cooligan says, happily lighting up. In the flare of the match he discovers that he too possesses one of the large brass ashtrays.

The door opens and the old man enters, staggering under the weight of a large wooden box with a beaten-brass speaker horn extending from it and reaching into the air well above his top hat. He is followed by a woman clutching to her enormous bosom what appears to be a wicker laundry basket.

'That's for the cobra, I seen it in books!' Muddy says excitedly.

'That's only in India, Muddy,' Library corrects him, 'the fakir uses a flute to entice the cobra out of the basket.'

'Well, the old fucker's maybe gunna do the same here,' Muddy persists.

'Fakir, Muddy, an Indian holy man,' Library laughs.

The woman, undoubtedly and disappointingly the belly dancer, is almost as wide as she is high and wears a red velvet cape which reaches down to her ankles. Even in the dimly lit room it looks much the worse for wear, the hem edged with dirty tassels, several of which are missing, like teeth in a broken comb. The velvet material to which it is sewn is worn down in mangy-looking patches and seems to be attached around her neck by a hook and a curtain ring. It gives every appearance of an old embassy or theatre curtain at the fag end of its life, pensioned off to do the best it can. The fat belly dancer also sports a pair of Muddy's mum's slippers with her big toe protruding through the pointy end of the left slipper.

The old man, wobbling violently at the knees, places the gramophone carefully down to the side of the stage and, staggering back a step or two, is caught in a violent paroxysm of coughing, puffing and wheezing so that he is forced to sit almost doubled up on the edge of the little platform. Finally he seems to recover whereupon he clears his throat and hoicks into a brass spittoon on the floor four feet from him.

'How's yer ashtray goin', Hornbill?' Numbers Cooligan calls as he suddenly realises what the brass bowls placed on the mats are intended for. 'Don't stub yer butts in the bottom of 'em, lads, they may not be empty.'

The old bloke has now recovered sufficiently to wind up the gramophone, then lifting off the lid he sets the turntable going and places the needle arm down onto the thick bakelite record. His hands are shaking like a first-night actor and there is the familiar high-pitched scratching sound as the needle misses its intended groove before gaining traction.

A high-pitched wail, redolent of the music they'd been hearing all day in the bazaar, issues forth, though it seems to be coming from a great distance in fits and starts, as if it has been tortured by being pulled out of the guts of the machine and threaded piecemeal through the enormous brass speaker. The wailing is of such an indeterminate sound as to make it impossible to decide the gender of the singer.

The old man climbs onto the stage and stands beside the woman, who, while being no taller than him, is three times as broad and occupies most of the available space. To maintain his balance, he is forced to rest one leg on top of the basket and his hand on the edge of the gramophone.

The belly dancer hasn't moved since her arrival. She stands with hands clasped in front of her, staring resolutely into the dark. If she can see them she gives no indication. Her face from the eyes down is covered with one of those masks they've seen all day on women in the bazaar.

'Jeez, they all look like nuns planning a hold-up,' Crow Rigby exclaimed on first seeing a group of women in the bazaar. The belly dancer's mask isn't black, though, but is made of a shiny pink material which reminds Hornbill of his mum's knickers.

When they asked Woggy at the bazaar what these masks were called he shrugged. 'It's a face apron,' he claimed, which seemed a fair enough description.

Above the belly dancer's shiny pink face apron appear two hard-as-anthracite eyes buried into kohl smudges, which cover her eyelids and extend into the eye sockets and upwards to end a quarter of an inch below her painted-on eyebrows. She too is a dead ringer for Hornbill's uncle's postcards. Only her jet-black hair is different, either naturally so or deliberately teased. It consists of an enormous frizzy mop which flops in an eight-inch halo about her face and reaches down to touch her shoulders.

'Ladies and Gentlemans, Dames en Heeren, Madame, Monsieurs, Boyses and Girlses, I give you very, very wonderful belly dunce!' the old man announces, as though addressing an audience of several hundred, throwing his head backwards and forwards with the effort, an emphatic spray of spittle exploding into the pink light.

On cue the fat lady comes alive and, with a theatrical flick of the wrist, she unhooks the curtain ring securing the cape and flings it aside in the direction of the old bloke who has stepped from the platform just in time to cop the lot. The heavy cloak hits him on the side of the head and knocks him arse over tit.

This brings a big laugh from the audience but is completely ignored by the belly dancer who is now revealed clothed only in two faded gold tassels which hang from nipple cups glued to her enormous breasts and a pair of Ali Baba pantaloons that balloon to her ankles from her waist. The pantaloons are of the same material as the face apron and Hornbill's ma's bloomers and shimmer in the light.

The belly dancer appears to have a three-tyre thickness of blubber over her stomach and now each of these rotates to the music as she begins to grind her enormous hips. Then, with all her wobbles moving more or less in the same direction, she bends forward slightly and, grabbing her left breast firmly in both hands, gives it a violent twist which sets the tassel rotating. Whereupon she repeats the same exercise with the right tit and now she has everything going, tassels whirring, stomach wobbling and hips grinding as the six lads look on in startled amazement.

It is a bizarre enough sight and they almost feel they've had their money's worth in sheer grotesqueness when the old bloke, having untangled himself from the velvet curtain, lifts the basket lid.

'Bring on the snake! Let's see the snake!' Numbers Cooligan calls out.

'Yeah! The snake! The snake!' the others chorus.

But instead of the snake the old bloke pulls out a bottle about eighteen inches high into which is fitted a long cork. He places the bottle on the stage in front of the gyrating, swirling, tassel-rotating, belly-blubbering, hip-swinging dancer, who miraculously, given her weight, stands on one leg and whips off one side of the pink pantaloons and then the other, not missing a beat.

There is a gasp from the darkness, none of them, except perhaps for Numbers Cooligan, has ever seen 'it'. And, in this case, 'it' is almost a match for her hairdo. 'It' is a thigh beard of monstrous proportions and, like some dark, tangled creeper, it straddles the top of her legs as solid as tree trunks.

Tassels still swinging and everything else going as well, she lowers herself down onto the bottle and using 'it' she neatly extracts the cork from the bottle and with a tremendous flick of her hips the cork flies into the air and is neatly caught in the old bloke's top hat. 'Very, very wonderful belly dunce!' he shouts gleefully.

There is cheering and clapping all around at this amazing display of dexterity and Numbers Cooligan for a start is rapidly becoming convinced they're getting their money's worth and then some. But there is more to come.

'Shit!' Crow Rigby suddenly whispers in a voice loud enough for them all to hear. 'There's a bloody snake in the bottle!'

They all crowd forward to see that the bottle indeed contains a snake curled at the bottom which is now beginning to rise. With everything still moving to the wailing cacophony, which seems a little less scratchy towards the centre of the gramophone record, the belly dancer lowers herself onto the bottle neck and neatly grasps it. She lifts the bottle and arches backwards until she is almost parallel to the surface of the stage. To everyone's horror the snake, about eighteen inches long, moves forward out of the neck of the bottle into the external furry darkness.

'Holy Mary mother of Jesus!' Woggy exclaims, while the others are too gob-smacked to say anything. The dancer, still gyrating and wobbling, though the tassels have now come to a stop, lowers the bottle to the carpet and continues to dance, turning and whirling several times until it seems impossible that her sheer weight and momentum will not throw her from the tiny stage. Then she begins to slow down until she faces them again, her hips undulating slowly, stomach barely wobbling to the music, and opening her mouth she slowly pulls the snake out. In a trice it is wriggling in her hands, its head darting forward, its tongue testing the air, as she holds it triumphantly above her head.

In the weeks to come the eighteen-inch snake will take on python-like proportions and the tit tassels will whirr like Crow's old man's windmill in a stiff breeze. The belly dancer's hips will expand to the size of a buckboard on a sulky and her breasts will become bigger than Easter Show watermelons. They have had their money's worth ten times over. Tired but happy they return to the Aden Club to rendezvous with Wordy Smith.

An hour later they are still waiting for the lieutenant to arrive. Numbers Cooligan finally persuades the reluctant white-uniformed guard in a red fez at the gate to allow him to enter the club to see if the lieutenant isn't waiting for them on the veranda. Most of the Australian officers have already departed for the ship, while those preparing to leave pause only long enough for a final soothing ale. They claim not to have seen the platoon commander all day. At half-past six the lads return to the ship and are put on a charge by the provost sergeant at the gate for staying out beyond the limit on their day passes.

Crow Rigby finds Ben and reports the missing Wordy Smith.

'He may have returned on his own,' Ben says, shaking his head. 'Dozy bugger.'

But Wordy isn't in his cabin or the officers' mess and Ben returns to the lads. 'Did he say anything when you left him?' he asks.

'Yeah, Library translated, he said something about "splendid specimens on the cliff",' Numbers Cooligan says.

Library corrects him. 'No, no, cliffproms splendspes, whato! Cliffs promise splendid specimens, what ho! He had his things with him, in his day kitbag.'

'Any of you men have any experience cliff climbing? Or rock climbing?' Ben asks.

'Yeah, Sergeant,' Hornbill volunteers, 'I come from mountain country, I done a fair bit.'

It is almost seven o'clock before Ben gets permission from his C.O. to leave the ship. They've obtained a length of rope from the chief petty officer, two torches and batteries from the quartermaster and a first-aid kit from the ship's hospital. Sister Atkins, obliging with the latter, seems pleased to see Ben again.

There is only one set of cliffs, to the right of the port as you enter the harbour, though hills stretch further back from them. Ben isn't sure whether he hopes Second Lieutenant Peregrine Ormington-Smith has stuck to the cliffs and probably killed himself or gone into the mountains and become lost. The cliffs seem to be the logical place to start the search, are not too extensive and rise above the sea no more than a couple of hundred feet.

By the time they arrive it's almost dark and Ben sends Hornbill to one end of the top of the cliff face while he takes the other, instructing that they'll meet in the middle, all the while looking downwards and shouting out in the hope of making contact with Ormington-Smith.

Almost ten minutes later Ben hears Hornbill screaming, 'Sergeant, over here!'

When he arrives Hornbill is on his stomach, shining his torch directly downwards. From where he is standing Ben can't see anything and so he joins Hornbill and shines his torch to double the beam. About thirty feet down, Wordy Smith is seen sitting on a ledge looking upwards, squinting into the beam of light. One of his boots and socks has been removed to show a large white foot.

'Doangle!' he shouts at them.

'He's done his ankle,' Ben says quietly. 'Shouldn't be too hard to get him up.'

'Let *me* go, Sergeant?' Hornbill offers.

'Nah, I want the bastard to owe me,' Ben says. 'You reckon you can pull him up if I go down and rope him?'

'Sure, Sergeant, if I can't you can tie him and come back up and we'll sort him out together.'

Ben searches for a while until he finds what seems like the best way down to the ledge. He'll need both hands so he can't take the torch and will have to rely on Hornbill lighting the way for him from the top. It takes him no more than five minutes to reach the lieutenant, whereupon Hornbill lowers the rope and Ben, balanced precariously on the narrow ledge, ropes Second Lieutenant Peregrine Ormington-Smith up and ties his kitbag to the rope as well. The lieutenant seems quite overcome and finds it impossible to get any words past his lips. 'Don't talk, just hang on tight while we get you up,' Ben instructs him.

Making sure Ormington-Smith is secure he calls to Hornbill to have a go at pulling him up. But thirty feet is a fair drop and even though Wordy Smith in appearance seems as light as a bag of chook feathers, without a tree or rock to anchor the rope his weight is too much even for a man as strong as Hornbill to pull up alone.

'Wait on, sir,' Ben instructs and makes his way back up the cliff. It is hard going in the dark and he loses his footing and several times a clatter of small rocks crashes down the cliff face into the sea below. Finally, he crawls back over the lip of the cliff and lies for a moment to recover.

Between them they haul their platoon commander back up and after regaining his breath Ben examines the lieutenant's ankle. It is badly swollen but doesn't appear to be broken, though it is doubtful he will be able to walk. 'We'll manage between us, can you hop on one leg, sir?'

Ormington-Smith nods, it is past eight o'clock and dark, the moon not yet up as they move out with Ormington-Smith between them, his arms clasped about their shoulders and utilising his good foot to hop. They have gone no more than a hundred yards when he suddenly stops, resisting their efforts to move forward.

'What is it, Lieutenant, need a rest?' Ben asks.

'Sketbook!' Wordy Smith says.

'Sketbook? Oh, your sketchbook?'

'Leftit.'

'You what?' Ben can't believe his ears. 'You left your sketchbook? Ferchrissakes, where?'

'Clif-ace.'

'The cliff face, on the ledge?'

Ormington-Smith doesn't reply but gives out a desperate cry, like a child suddenly threatened with a backhander from his father. He removes his arms from their shoulders and, turning, hops back towards the cliff face.

'Bloody hell, we'll get it in the morning!' Ben shouts after him, but Ormington-Smith, as though possessed, keeps hopping frantically towards the cliff face in the dark.

'Shit, he'll kill himself,' Hornbill shouts and together

they set off after the lieutenant who has almost disappeared in the dark and is managing a remarkable pace hopping on one leg.

They reach him at last and Ben wrestles him to the ground, but the scrawny subaltern seems possessed and he is hard put to restrain him. Ormington-Smith is whimpering and sniffling like a child as Ben finally subdues him. 'Sketbook!' he howls again.

'Take it easy now, Lieutenant,' Ben says, trying to calm him down, rising and then lifting him to a seated position. He reaches for the first-aid kit slung across his shoulder, takes out a bottle of water and, unscrewing it, hands it to Ormington-Smith. The lieutenant gulps at the bottle greedily, most of its contents spilling down the front of his torn tunic. 'You all right?' Ben now asks as the bottle is handed back to him, he can see that the lieutenant's hand is shaking violently. Ormington-Smith nods and then suddenly begins to weep quietly.

'Oh, shit!' Ben says softly, almost to himself. Then, in a calmer voice, he addresses his platoon commander, 'We're going back, sir, even if I have to carry you over my shoulders. We'll be back for your sketchbook in the morning.' He turns to where he thinks Hornbill is standing. 'Private Horne, help me get the lieutenant to his feet.'

There is no reply.

'Hornbill, you there?' Ben shines the torch and sees that Hornbill isn't where he supposed he was standing. 'Private Horne!' he shouts into the darkness. 'Where the fuck are you!'

'Coming, Sergeant,' Ben hears Hornbill's voice some distance away.

'Get here will'ya, at the double!'

Hornbill comes panting up in the darkness and Ben shines the torch into his face. 'Where've you been?'

Hornbill doesn't reply but hands Wordy Smith's sketchbook to the hapless lieutenant sobbing at Ben's feet. 'There you go, sir, safe and sound, no harm done.'

Ben is almost too angry to speak. 'You could have killed yourself, yer stupid bastard,' he shouts at Hornbill. 'What for? A bloody useless sketchbook, full of pictures of flamin' flowers no one can see!'

'Sorry, Sergeant,' Hornbill says, in a contrite voice, then nodding his head to indicate the lieutenant at Ben's feet, he adds, 'Them flower paintin's, they's everything to him, Sergeant.'

Wordy Smith has managed to get to his feet, hugging the sketchbook and standing on one leg sniffing. Both turn to look at him. 'Thank you, Private Horne, thank you,' he says quietly. 'This sketchbook is more important to me than my life, but not more important to me than *your* life.' It is said in a steady, perfectly modulated voice, not a single word bumping into another or joining together. Peregrine Ormington-Smith will never have a problem with his speech again.

Chapter Twelve

THE CALM BEFORE
THE STORM

Egypt 1914–1915

The new and articulate Wordy Smith, while being on crutches for the next ten days, is a changed man. Though it cannot be claimed he has made the transition from hopeless to competent, he has, at least, decided to make up for his previously arcane speech patterns and almost total lack of communication by telling his platoon everything he hears in the officers' mess. Or so he claims.

Ben, who has cause to visit his cabin from time to time, does not let on to the platoon that Peregrine Ormington-Smith shares a cabin with the military liaison officer to the ship's wireless room. Nonetheless, Second Lieutenant Peregrine Ormington-Smith is simply incapable of being deceptive and with a slip of the tongue on one or two occasions his source of information is discovered by the platoon. The wireless subaltern, it seems, has grown so accustomed to Wordy Smith's inability to articulate that he talks quite freely about the messages coming through, airing his opinions on what goes in and out.

Ben realises that his platoon officer, if discovered, will be placed in an extremely awkward position, not quite a court martial as he can hardly be accused of supplying information to the enemy, but he will still be in considerable trouble. He finds himself in a real quandary, as a sergeant he must co-operate with his officer, while at the same time he is responsible for the immediate welfare of his platoon.

Even though the information from 'Wordy's Wireless', as the platoon has dubbed the lieutenant's cabin mate, cannot, in this instance, be said to be critical to their welfare, there is a very sound principle involved which every sergeant in every war ever fought would understand. It is simply that the more hard information you can get from an officer the more likely you are to prevent him from doing something stupid which may get you all killed. After years of saying as little as possible, Ormington-Smith must be actively encouraged and Ben decides to swear the platoon to secrecy.

'No leaks yer hear? We've got this on our own. If it gets out where the lieutenant is getting his information he's up shit creek without a paddle and so is Wordy's Wireless, the ultimate source of our information. We're sitting pretty, lads, so shut yer gobs. That's an order.' Ben looks searchingly into the eyes of every member of the platoon, extracting a silent promise from each of them. 'Righto, Private Cooligan.'

'Yes, Sergeant?'

'You run the two-up school on E deck and you're a bookmaker for the Tuesday-night fights, ain't ya?'

They all laugh and Cooligan colours. 'Me, Sergeant? Never! The army has cured me o' me wicked ways. All I wants is to fight Herman the German.'

'Right, there will be times when the information we get from Wordy's Wireless has to get out to the rest of the ship so, Private Cooligan, you're our official mouth, our Gob Sergeant.'

'What's that mean, Sergeant?'

'When stuff comes from Wordy's Wireless that needs to

get to the rest of the ship, you're it. But don't make it look that way, you mix what's real with a fair amount of bullshit, just the way you did a moment ago – you know, but you don't know, you heard, but you're not sure where, something somebody said, putting two and two together, could be wrong but . . . It's a question of mixing the right amount of fact with the correct proportion of crap. Can you do that, Private Cooligan?'

'Can a crow fly?' Crow Rigby quips and they all laugh.

'No, no, I'm serious,' Ben says. 'It takes a fair amount of imagination and at least a pint of Irish blood in yer veins to do it right and Cooligan's got both. What do you reckon, Private?'

Cooligan is flattered. 'I think you just done me a spot-on character reference, Sergeant. Gob Sergeant, eh? Is that a promotion, Sergeant?'

Wordy's Wireless proves to be a real bonus for the Click platoon and adds greatly to their reputation, they now become a valued source of information. Numbers Cooligan performs the role of chief rumour monger with a special brilliance, instinctively understanding the age-old Australian adage that bullshit baffles brains. The information tidbits Ben allows for dissemination spread outwards at an alarming speed and, in a matter of an hour or two, the entire ship knows the latest news. Numbers Cooligan is soon much sought out for information by blokes from the other platoons and, in the nature of these things, anything they know is given to him until there isn't a lot happening on the ship that isn't known to Ben.

However, the very first piece of information Second Lieutenant Peregrine Ormington-Smith brings to the platoon is not from Wordy's Wireless but the officers' mess. Upon hearing it, it is the first time the enlisted men have felt anything but excitement at the prospect of getting stuck into the Hun.

The day after they leave Aden for the Suez Canal and thereafter Britain, Wordy Smith tells them the horrific news brought back by the officers who spent the day at the Aden Club while he went specimen hunting on the cliffs. Several months previously two British battalions of regulars stationed in India, each a thousand men strong, passed through the port on their way to the Western Front. Like those from the *Orvieto* it was an occasion which saw some of their officers visit the club. Now members of the club have received letters from two of the officers who survived to say that one of the battalions has been reduced to three hundred men and the second has been almost completely annihilated.

The news comes as a shock to the thirty thousand Australians and New Zealanders who, from the very beginning, have regarded the war in Europe as a grand opportunity to prove their worth as fighting men while, at the same time, seeing Europe and Britain with their mates. They are suddenly sobered by the thought that they too are destined for the same killing grounds that have butchered both regiments. Herman the German is proving to be less of a pushover than they've been led to believe.

If the minimum recruiting age for men had been put at fifty, saving the young men for breeding and for work, the old men on both sides would have soon enough found another way to resolve the conflict. Young men, though, have always possessed a sense of immortality which their elders have exploited since time out of mind. The notion that they are invincible appears to be a part of the young warrior's genetic code. In a peacetime society this is further evidenced by the fact that almost eighty-five per cent of all violent crime is performed by men under the age of twenty-eight. The young male seems to need an outlet for his aggression and, in the process, believes himself to be bulletproof right up to the moment when a high-velocity Mauser bullet churns his innards to mincemeat.

Sobering as the news of the two devastated battalions is, it doesn't seem to greatly affect the desire of the young Australians to fight the Germans but now there is a rumour gaining notoriety on board that the British High Command does not fully trust the Australian irregulars, or believe that men can be trained effectively to fight a war in twelve weeks. This, in their minds, is especially true of the Australians, who, on the last occasion they fought beside British troops, gained a reputation for often ignoring the commands of their senior British officers. In truth, this only occurred in the Boer War on no more than half a dozen occasions when it became apparent to the Australian Mounted Rifles that the British officers, untrained in the guerilla tactics required in South Africa, were attempting to fight a war in the African bush as if they were back in the Crimea.

Britain has always depended on the career soldier who never questions orders. The Australians, faced with similar bush conditions as at home, and living a not dissimilar lifestyle to the Boer enemy, quickly adapted to the hit-and-run commando style of warfare, much of which was conducted in the saddle.

The British regulars took a hiding against the Boer irregulars, whose commandos were made up mostly of simple farmers with virtually no previous military training. But, like many of their Australian counterparts, the Boers rode like the wind and could shoot a man between the eyes at a thousand yards. They could attack a British unit and be twenty miles away before the British had time to pack up and move out in pursuit. In the peculiar African conditions they proved too elusive for the highly trained, rigidly disciplined British regulars, who found it difficult to adapt to this new kind of warfare. Only by sheer force of numbers and the personal understanding and leadership brought to the battlefield by that great general, Lord Roberts, did Britain finally succeed. By the time the war ended in victory for the British forces the Boers had been outnumbered six to one.

The rumour now doing the rounds on board the ships of the convoy is that Britain will use the supposedly under-trained, ill-disciplined and second-rate Australians in India and Egypt as garrison troops. This will relieve the British regulars, at present occupied in this task, to fight in the *real* war on the Western Front. To further substantiate the rumour, news comes through that the Turks have sided with Germany and have declared war on Britain and her allies. The average soldier on board has no trouble making one and one equal two and reaching the conclusion that the Australian troops will be stationed in Egypt.

So when Wordy's Wireless tells them the day after they leave Aden that General Bridges has received instructions by wireless that they are to proceed to Britain, there is a palpable sense of relief. The news spreads as if carried on the stiff nor'easter blowing that morning and by the time the official announcement is made most of the troops on board see it simply as confirmation. Those who first got it from Numbers Cooligan are beginning to show a growing respect for his sources.

However, on a day filled with contradictory news, night brings a further instruction to General Bridges. The *Orvieto* is to sail ahead of the convoy to Port Said. The same message is received by Major-General Sir Alexander Godley, the commander of the New Zealand force headquartered on the *Mauganui*. The two ships are to proceed at their own speed to Egypt.

Wordy's Wireless has suffered a stomach complaint and has been confined to bed for two days when the message comes through so Ben doesn't receive any advance notice from his lieutenant. Therefore it is a tremendous surprise to the troops when the *Orvieto* breaks away from the convoy and sails off on its own. Numbers Cooligan, newly appointed Gob Sergeant, is unable to supply any explanation, which, strangely enough, confirms his status among the troops, as knowing everything seems improbable and is also highly suspicious.

Fortuitously, Wordy's Wireless recovers from his stomach ailment and is back on deck the following evening, safely ensconced in the wireless room when a late telegram arrives for General Bridges from Sir George Reid, the Australian High Commissioner in London. Wordy Smith reads it to the Clicks at the breakfast parade fully two hours before it is officially announced to the troops on board.

GEN. BRIDGES.
HQs FIRST AUSTRALIAN DIVISION – ORVIETO.
MESSAGE FOLLOWS:
UNFORESEEN CIRCUMSTANCES DECIDE THAT
THE FORCE SHALL TRAIN IN EGYPT AND GO TO
THE FRONT FROM THERE. THE AUSTRALIANS
AND NEW ZEALANDERS ARE TO FORM A CORPS
UNDER GENERAL BIRDWOOD. THE LOCALITY
OF THE CAMP IS NEAR CAIRO.
GEORGE REID – AUST. HIGH COMMISSIONER. U.K.

The decision is met with utter consternation. When the change in plans is made known to the troops they boo loudly and stamp their boots on the deck to demonstrate their disapproval. To the average soldier the arithmetic is irrefutable, the declaration of war by Turkey and the order to proceed to Port Said can mean only one thing, they are to be used as garrison troops against the Turks.

Ben and his platoon, like every volunteer in the A.I.F. and together with the New Zealanders, have a burning desire to prove their mettle on the Western Front. Nothing short of this is acceptable to them. The soldiers of both antipodean nations take a quiet pride in the fact that they are the finest specimens their people can supply to the war machine, and unspoken, but in their minds, is the notion that they deserve to go against an enemy worthy of their calibre. For them the Turks are simply a bunch of wogs to be kept in line.

General Bridges is forced to issue the exact contents of the telegram together with a personal explanation. He strongly emphasises the particular section of the telegram which stipulates 'AND GO TO THE FRONT FROM THERE'. This somewhat, but not entirely, mollifies the men. There is already a sense of distrust between the private soldier and the officer class which is part of the Australian personality. The convict against the prison warder, the shearer against the squatter, the trade unionist against the capitalist, the people against the politician and, now, inevitably, the foot soldier against those who are placed over him.

The explanation for the diversion, couched in the usual official military language, is essentially correct, but it does nothing to subdue their misgivings. In the eyes of most of the troops it is a heap of bullshit and they suspect the British High Command is going to leave them stranded in Egypt to face the Turks. They are simply told that, due to the early onset of winter in Britain, the site on Salisbury Plain, which is intended for the encampment and further training of Australian and New Zealand troops, has not been adequately prepared.

Three weeks after they arrive in the camp in Cairo a more satisfactory explanation comes out. Wordy Smith once again has come to the rescue. It seems he has an uncle who is a major on the staff of Lord Kitchener, the Minister of State for War. In a letter to his nephew in Mena, the Australian camp just outside Cairo, he gives a much more colourful account of the reasons.

Wordy Smith, perhaps a little naively, simply reads the letter to his platoon.

6th December 1914

Dear Peregrine,

How very disappointed your Aunt Agatha and I are that we shall not be able to give you a warm welcome on your return to England. We remember you as a fine fourteen-year-old lad. Your father assures us your bad chest has completely cleared up in Australia and we greatly looked forward to meeting the strapping young man you've undoubtedly become.

However, we are fast learning that during a period of war the best-laid plans of mice and men are apt to be frustrated. My job is no more important than any other entrusted to the rank of major in the War Office, but it has the singular advantage of bringing me into frequent contact with Colonel Chauvel, the Australian representative with the W.O.

And what a splendid chap he is, straight as a die and not in the least pretentious. It is said he is a disciplinarian and a stickler for protocol and correct military procedure, though I have not seen this side of him. He seems happy enough to mix with the lower officer ranks here at the W.O. and is often to be seen having a beer at the local, where he is fond of pronouncing the English beer as 'tasting like warm piss'.

It was during just such an occasion that he told me in his own colourful vernacular why the Australian and New Zealand contingent have been diverted for further training to Egypt.

As the official explanation doesn't differ in essence, but rather in detail, I am confident that Col. Chauvel's version doesn't transgress the O.S.A. (Official Secrets Act 1912).

I shall try to put my amateur theatrical experience to work to capture the tone and manner of his dialogue, as I feel sure it will amuse you. I apologise in advance if it doesn't ring quite true to your acquired Australian ear.

The following conversation takes place with yours truly and the colonel after the third pint of 'luke-warm piss' or, if you like, best British bitter:

'Harry, didn't you mention you had a nephew back home who enlisted with the A.I.F.?'

'Yes, sir, my brother William's son, we were greatly looking forward to seeing how the lad has turned out, he had a rather nasty chest problem when he left England.'

'I shouldn't worry about that, lots of sun and good red meat, soon fix his chest, pity you won't see him. [Takes a sip of LWP.] Good thing, though, would've been a complete shambles.'

'Oh?' I say, not understanding how meeting you could possibly lead to a shambles.

'The weather, the camp, bloody impossible,' he exclaims.

'You mean on Salisbury Plain, sir?'

'Well, that's just it, isn't it? Bad enough for your own troops and the Canadians, you're accustomed to the mud and the cold, but our blokes are not used to that sort of thing.'

'You mean it doesn't rain in Australia, sir?'

'Well, it doesn't piss down twenty-four hours a day, day in and day out, until you're up to your bollocks in mud!'

'Well, how will they be at the front?' I ask cheekily, 'That's nothing but mud, sir?'

'Hmmph, I daresay they'll do a damn fine job when the time comes, but that's a purely academic observation, the poor buggers would all have been dead from pneumonia long before they ever got to France! Half the Canadians who are encamped on Salisbury Plain are crook, and the others are rioting in the streets of Salisbury!'

'Crook?'

'Yes, down with flu or pneumonia and the other half are close to rebellion. They were promised huts, heated huts for the winter, and they're still in tents, which at night are cold enough to freeze the balls off a brass monkey. What's more, they have no hope of getting better billets until the spring.'

'I'm sorry to hear that, sir. What a good thing the old man changed his mind and sent your lot to Egypt.'

'Had it changed for him, you mean?'

At this last remark I raise my eyebrow somewhat. Chauvel is superior in rank to me and I don't wish to point out that Lord Kitchener is not inclined to listen to the opinions of or be persuaded by a junior officer. 'Well done,' I say, deciding discretion is the better part . . . etc.

'Good God, man, not me! Georgie Reid!' Chauvel exclaims. 'I reported the conditions on Salisbury Plain to him and he telephoned his nibs on the spot for an appointment.'

In case you are not aware, Peregrine, Sir George Reid is your Australian High Commissioner in London, and is well known for his casual disregard for the niceties of diplomacy.

However, being in the W.O., I know that access to the Field Marshal's room by telephone is impossible to obtain. Not even the Prime Minister would think to call him without prior warning and I daresay that pretty well goes for the King as well.

But I wasn't to know that Kitchener makes an exception with

Sir George. It seems he enjoys the Australian's disregard for protocol, especially his ability to tell a good after-dinner yarn and generally play the buffoon. (Clever man, what?) Col. Chauvel calls it 'being a larrikin' which is, I believe, a uniquely Australian expression meaning a number of things, both good and bad. It would appear that being a larrikin (good) allows Sir George to get to the great man at any time and to freely discuss subjects which few would dare to broach.

Col. Chauvel then went on to say, 'Georgie saw Kitchener the following morning with my report and told him our convoy would be passing Egypt in a few days. That there was no time to lose, the Australian troops must be diverted to Egypt at once, and on no account be allowed to come to England where they would only increase the already unmanageable congestion.'

I must say Sir George Reid must be a remarkably persuasive chap, because Kitchener immediately advised the Australian government and the plan was adopted in a matter of hours.

So there you have it, dear fellow, straight from the horse's mouth.

While your aunt and I will be disappointed not to see you, it's been a beastly winter, freezing winds from the north, with January, and possibly snow, yet to come. I don't imagine, with such short notice, that things are all they should be in your Cairo camp – I'm told there's a great shortage of tents – but the prospect of wintering on Salisbury Plain is not one I would wish even on the Hun. You are far better out of it.

The newspapers here have expressed the view that the Australians and New Zealanders are disappointed with the decision not to bring you to England, being of the opinion that the diversion to Egypt means you will not fight on the Western Front.

I am inclined to think this is not correct, as you are much needed in France, where things are not going as well as they might. All things considered, a bit of the Australian 'larrikin' (good and bad) might be a jolly good thing.

The first time I was stuck in a military office job was during the Boer War when I begged for an active-service posting but was refused. Once an office wallah always one, the War Office is unlikely to give me a company command in this one, so it is going to fall upon your shoulders to follow in your grandfather's (Crimea) and your father's footsteps and to represent the family at the sharp end. I want you to know that your aunt and I are extremely proud of you and we wish you and your platoon the very best of luck.

That's about all I have to say, old chap. Agatha asks me to send you our Christmas greetings and to tell you to make sure you visit the Pyramids. (Isn't your camp close by?) She also says I must take care to inform you that the damage to the face of the Sphinx was *caused when Napoleon's troops used it for cannon practice. She has*

never been fond of the French – 'Too much side and front but essentially

lacking in substance.' She also sends her love and asks you to write a

postcard. Though, I daresay, not one showing the Sphinx.

> *With my very best wishes from your uncle Harry;*
>
> *Harold Ormington-Smith, Major.*

There is some amusement in the platoon at Wordy Smith's Uncle Harry's perception of his nephew, but they feel included and complimented that Wordy would think to read the letter in its entirety to them. Uncle Harry seems like a good sort of bloke despite being an officer and his nephew is so completely inadequate to the task that the Click platoon simply cannot harbour the suspicions they instinctively reserve for the officer class.

None of them can possibly imagine Second Lieutenant Peregrine Ormington-Smith performing as a fighting man, issuing the order to go over the top and, with whistle in his mouth and revolver in hand, leading the charge against the enemy. They look to Ben to lead them with the vague notion that Second Lieutenant Ormington-Smith, with his kneepads firmly secured, his bum in the air and his magnifying glass inches from the ground, will be off somewhere finding his flowers to paint.

'London to a brick, if he's wounded it will be in the arse, a bullet through both cheeks,' Crow Rigby says at tea on the evening they reach the Suez Canal.

'We ought to paint a face on his bum,' Numbers Cooligan ventures. 'For his own protection. Bloody sight better getting a bullet through both them cheeks than the ones higher up.'

They see the Sinai Desert for the first time stretching away to the foot of the Arabian hills, painted pink in the sunset.

'It looks bloody lonely,' Muddy Parthe remarks. 'Yiz wouldn't want to fight in a place like that, would youse?'

The *Orvieto* is put on alert as they approach the ninety-nine-mile canal cut straight as an arrow through the desert and it is thought that they may be fired on by the Bedouins from the east. But instead, in what remains of the daylight, they see the first evidence of the Allies, a tented company who have created a series of small sangars with sandbagged breastworks in a semicircle, the loopholes in the breastwork facing outwards from the canal. Any enemy attempting a surprise attack at night would be met with an outer ring of barbed-wire entanglements. Behind the breastworks, as a fall-back position, are a line of trenches and, behind these, the tents for the men. It is the first sign they've seen of any serious commitment to wage war and there is a great deal of shouting, which brings a number of Indian soldiers out of their tents and up onto the banks of the canal. They are soon followed by two British officers with baggy khaki shorts which fall to well beyond their knees. Shouted greetings are exchanged and they learn from two English officers that they are the Indian Army, the 128th Native Infantry.

'You'll probably join us here soon,' one of the officers shouts.

'Not bloody likely!' a chorus of Australian voices shout back. 'We're off to Britain, mate!'

For the first time the men on board get an actual sense of being involved in something bigger than the A.I.F., a war where others, like themselves, have come from the far ends of the earth to fight with them. It is one thing to be told you are a part of something larger and quite another to experience it.

The *Orvieto*'s original destination of Port Said has now been changed to Alexandria, where they arrive just a few hours ahead of the first ships in the convoy. On the morning of December 3rd, the 3rd and the 5th Battalions entrain from Alexandria for Cairo. They cross the Nile delta with the annual floods rapidly subsiding in the burning sun so that the Nile flats are a brilliant green. People in long white robes are working the fields with wooden ploughs pulled by oxen. A woman walking ahead of a male on a donkey catches their attention.

'Hey, wait a mo! Ain't it supposed to be the other way around?' Crow Rigby says suddenly.

'What yer talking about?' someone asks.

'The bloke on the donkey, ain't the Virgin Mary supposed to be on the donkey?'

'Shit, you're right,' Numbers Cooligan exclaims. 'Look at bloody Joseph, you'd think it was him up the duff, Jesus!'

'It's just like being in Sunday school with all them pictures they show you o' these parts,' Woggy now says.

'You should know,' Cooligan says. 'They're your kin folks, ain't they, Woggy?'

'I told yiz, we're Christians, them lot's Arabs, mate.'

'What say you, Library?' Hornbill asks.

'Well, it's all academic, ain't it? There were no Christians at that time, Woggy's ancestors were either Arab or Jewish.'

'There you go! I told ya, didn't I, Woggy's a bloody Arab, no risk!' Cooligan says triumphantly.

It is nightfall when they finally reach the outskirts of Cairo. Seen from the railway carriages it seems to be a big, untidy-looking city.

Hornbill sticks his nose out of the carriage window and sniffs. 'Smells crook,' he announces. 'Me uncle says every city has a smell, it's mostly from the food.'

'Melbourne don't smell o' meat pies, mate,' Cooligan says.

'Flinders Street Station does, you can smell me uncle's meat pies the moment you get off the train and all the way across Flinders Street.'

'Hornbill's right,' Library says, 'it's the oil they use for cooking mixed with the spices. We smelled it in the bazaar in Aden, though not as bad as this.'

'Wonder if they've got any belly dunces and snakes here,' Crow Rigby says.

The belly dancer and the snake has by this time been told so many times and in increasingly lurid detail that even the six who were present are becoming convinced that the snake was several feet long and the belly dancer's weight around the four hundred pound mark with the three spare tyres around her belly big enough to fit out a Leyland truck.

'There'll be nothing to beat that ever,' Numbers Cooligan says emphatically. 'We'll go to our graves remembering that, lads.'

The train pulls into a railway siding specially built for the Australian troops in the heart of Cairo. The idea is to show the Australian colours by marching both battalions down the broad European streets with the bands playing 'Sons of Australia'.

The buildings on either side of the grand central avenue, some of which must have originally been quite impressive, are now dilapidated, with the stucco damaged, the paint peeling, and the windows dirty. They look as though they've not seen a lick of attention since the day they were built, which is probably true. The whole scene resembles a sort of huge stage set, for the streets have been cleared of traffic and the people, for the most part, have been told to stay indoors. So the hard crunch of boots, the sounds of the bands and the shrill commands against the backdrop of crumbling buildings seem contrived and theatrical.

They pass the Kasr el Nil Barracks where the sound of the bands brings out the Lancashire Territorials of the 42nd Division, who rush across the parade ground to cheer the Australians on.

'Jeez, take a look at 'em, they're all dwarfs,' Hornbill says out of the corner of his mouth. 'I always thought, yer know, the Brits were big blokes.' Indeed the soldiers from the north of England, recruited originally from the coal mines and the cotton mills, are tiny compared to the average Australian and New Zealander, who are astonished to find that they are, for the most part, a head taller than their British counterparts.

'It's meat,' Library Spencer explains. 'Not enough protein in their diet.'

'Meat? Don't they eat meat?' Muddy Parthe asks, astonished.

'Well, not enough, that's why they're so short.'

'Hear that, Numbers, yer mum didn't feed ya enough chops when you were a young 'un. That's why yer such a short arse!' Muddy says gleefully.

Numbers doesn't reply for a moment and then announces, 'Bullshit, I had a chop every mornin' f'breakfast since I was two years old, that's six thousand, five 'undred and seventy chops I've ate, mate!'

'Not enough, mate,' Muddy says, feeling smug.

They pass the barracks and cross several bridges and then march along a long avenue built on a causeway, which starts at Gizeh and runs for five miles all the way to the flooded flats of the Nile. It is almost full moon and towards the end of the avenue when they approach the edge of the desert sand they catch their first sight of the Pyramids etched clear and massive as they rise from the desert. The causeway finally ends and they are marched

430

onto a newly laid road, bathed in the light of a glorious moon, which seems to disappear into the desert.

'Hey, you blokes, lookee there!' Crow suddenly exclaims. 'Flamin' gum trees!'

Indeed they are passing a magnificent group of gum trees standing alone in the desert. A sudden breeze blows up and the sound of the wind high in the trees, like waves crashing on an Australian beach, makes them all suddenly terribly homesick.

'How'd they get here then? Big bastards too, been there a while I can tell ya,' Hornbill, the timber expert, says.

'The eucalypt is the most adaptable tree in the world, it can grow almost anywhere,' Library Spencer calls out. 'They plant it in arid regions to prevent the soil blowing away.'

'Righto, lads, keep the chat down,' Ben calls.

They now see that the avenue of gum trees is planted as a part of the Mena House Hotel, which they soon pass and continue marching onwards until they come to the first valley of the desert and, in doing so, almost bump into the Pyramids standing majestic in the moonlight, taller than any building they've ever seen.

It is here, on a lonely stretch of sand, under a star-sprinkled sky, the great Pyramids casting dark shadows over the pale moonlit desert, that the battalion receives the command to halt.

They are sweating from the exertion of the ten-mile march from the centre of Cairo, so only after a while do they realise the night has grown very cold. They haven't washed or eaten a square meal since they left Alexandria and they're tired and hungry, but mostly tired. Several tins of bullybeef are opened to share around, but most are too exhausted to think of food and roll themselves in their grey army blankets preparing to sleep. Tomorrow they will begin the task of setting up camp in a place where someone has had the good sense to plant Australian gums in the desert.

'Plantin' them gums,' Cooligan says suddenly, 'I reckon it were one o' them prophets they has round 'ere, like in the Bible. He come to them Pyramids to pray like, you know, to one o' them Egyptian Pharaoh Gods and he gets this message back, sorta like a prophecy, the Pharaoh God tells him about us comin' 'ere. So off he goes at the trot and plants them gum trees to mark the occasion.'

'Jesus, Cooligan!' Crow Rigby calls from his blanket.

'Him too! He could've walked right where you're lying, mate, givin' out them loaves and fishes. Bloody old this place, I daresay every bastard in the Bible's been here. Moses . . .'

'So where's this prophet of yours gunna get the gum-tree seeds?' the ever pedantic Library Spencer asks.

'He's a prophet, ain't he? He waves his stick and strikes the ground and says abra-ca-bloody-dabra and, there you go, flamin' gum trees!'

'Ah, shurrup, Numbers! Can't yer see we're all buggered,' Woggy Mustafa calls.

'I thought you said your lot was Christians an' all!' Numbers Cooligan says, wrapping himself in his blanket against the night chill. As always he manages to have the last word.

At the end of twelve days the 1st Australian Division, infantry, artillery, ambulances, transport and the divisional Light Horse occupy the site at Mena which stretches for nearly a mile up the desert valley. The New Zealand infantry brigade and mounted rifles with all their support companies are camped at Zeitoun, on the northern outskirts of Cairo, while Joshua Solomon's regiment forms part of the 1st Light Horse Brigade, together with all its supporting units, at Maadi Camp on the edge of the desert south of Cairo.

At first the Australians discover that only eight and a half thousand tents exist for thirty thousand men. Britain, whose responsibility it is to see that they arrived on time for the A.I.F., has slipped up on the job. In the first few weeks most of the infantrymen are obliged to dig themselves dugouts, which they cover with their waterproof sheets. The officers' messes consist of large, sprawling Arab desert tents contracted from Greek merchants, who seem to be in charge of many of the more prosperous aspects of Business in Cairo.

With the rainy season over, sleeping in the open desert doesn't seem at first to be such a hardship. But there is a downside none of the top brass has foreseen – the desert goes from blazing hot during the day to bitterly cold at night and an unexpectedly high ratio of men are hospitalised with pneumonia until ordnance manages to procure and issue extra blankets to the men.

Over the next few weeks the tents arrive from Britain, pipes are laid to pump water around the camp and the general infrastructure required to create a large working army takes a surprisingly short time to build.

Soon the tents stand in long, straight rows, and to give the men a sense of some permanency in the desert sand and also to prevent it blowing into the tents, the fronts of these are often aproned with whitewashed stones and sown with green oats. 'Desert lawns, mate, so's you won't be 'omesick,' Crow Rigby tells Library Spencer the first time they see one, whereupon they plant their own so that the platoon's tents have a nice neat look.

The roads between the tents are also neatly marked out with whitewashed boulders. Whitewashing stones and roadside boulders becomes the local equivalent of kitchooty. Spacious mess-rooms are erected for the men and the ramshackle grandstand belonging to an abandoned racecourse is turned into the ordnance store.

433

Finally the tramway is extended from the causeway to the edge of the camp.

In no time at all, an Arab shanty town grows up along the perimeters of the valley. And while no houses, brothels or grog shops are allowed, shops of every other description tumble along roads and appear in self-created alleyways. The shops are constructed of bits of tin and box wood, canvas and any material which can be brought to the site and erected in a hurry.

An Arab merchant will arrive in the morning with a donkey cart piled high above his head, and his wife and a helper sitting on the top of the impossibly secured load. By evening, with a bit of hammering, nailing, tying and stretching of canvas and the laying of Turkish carpets, a new shop will appear on the desert sand.

Every imaginable service is suddenly at the disposal of the men, laundering, dyers, tailors who can whip up a brand-new uniform in half a day from army cotton drill mysteriously obtained, news vendors, photographers with painted backdrops of camels set against the Pyramids when the real thing is only a matter of yards away, dubious antique dealers, trinket shops, restaurants with stove pipes jutting out of their canvas and beaten tin roofs with live chickens and ducks out the back, for the slaughter of, bootmakers, carpet sellers, and every few shops there is a tea-room with a crudely painted sign, 'Australians System Afternoon Tea', as opposed, presumably, to 'English System Afternoon Tea'. Miraculously, scones and strawberry jam are available, the former somewhat leaden but the jam surprisingly good, though clotted cream is not on the menu.

Before the winter is over, the little valley that contains the vast tombs of a civilisation more than four thousand years old, and where Numbers Cooligan's biblical prophet first smote the gum trees into existence some fifty or so years ago, has become a dusty, thriving, bustling small city with all the smells and sounds of the Arab bazaar.

Hawkers are everywhere, small boys shouting 'Eggs-a-cook!' 'Oringhes!' 'Boots-i-clean!', selling hard-boiled eggs or oranges and working as boot blacks. Some with dirty postcards call out 'Jig-a-jig-a-look!' The coffee sellers and lime-juice vendors shout their wares and merchants stand outside their shops and beg passers-by not to miss the opportunity of a lifetime and to come inside. On one occasion, when the six 'Aden lads', who are now such firm mates that they seldom go anywhere without each other, are ferreting around the makeshift alleys of the Mena bazaar they are approached by an urchin selling dirty postcards, announcing them as 'Jig-a-jig-a-look!' Hornbill suddenly shouts, 'Betcha a bob Herman the German's in 'em all!'

'You're on,' says Numbers Cooligan as they crowd around the young boy. Sure enough, there he is, the same fat-gutted, curled-moustached kraut, with his balding hair parted down the centre of his skull and brought to two little wings above his eyebrows, bollocky, except for his socks and suspenders and, as usual, chock-a-block up a plump black-eyed woman.

'Told yer, didn't I!' Hornbill says triumphantly, holding his hand out for Cooligan's shilling.

While they are in Egypt, the name Anzac is born out of circumstances less than romantic. General Sir W. R. Birdwood, a British general stationed in India, is appointed by Lord Kitchener to be in overall command of the Australian and New Zealand troops and leaves India immediately to take up his posting. His job is to train the Australians and New Zealanders into a concerted and united fighting division. Before departing he writes to General Bridges and asks him what he proposes they should call the Australian Division when it is united with the New Zealand Brigade under his overall command.

Bridges proposes 'Australasian Army Corps', but the New Zealanders object to this. To them it smacks too much of Australia and not enough of The Land of the Long White Cloud. They finally settle for the rather clumsy mouthful, 'Australian and New Zealand Army Corps'. Soon afterwards, the clerks in ordnance take to identifying goods received by the initials Anzac, which soon enough becomes the accepted acronym. Thus, in a simple and uncomplicated way, a legend is born.

General Birdwood, as it turns out, is an excellent choice as the commander of the two forces, for he lacks much of the fuss and nonsense and the reliance on due ceremony to which most of the ageing British generals are accustomed and which they demand as their God-given right. His easygoing outlook and genuine regard for the troops under his command will make him popular with the Australians and New Zealanders, who resent the rigid authority the British troops accept without questioning. He seldom if ever judges a man by the shine of his boots or deprecates him for the roughness of his voice or whether he salutes or addresses an officer with the right amount of respect, and actively discourages this form of sententious bullying.

He clearly understands that, in the Australian and New Zealander, he is dealing with a different sort of man. The antipodeans possess a genuine abhorrence of taking pains with their appearance beyond what is tidy and functional.

As General Birdwood once remarked to General Bridges, 'They're tall enough and big enough and, I daresay, more than brave enough, to make splendid guardsmen, but they'd never tolerate the spit and polish!'

To the amazement of their British counterparts, the Australians love fresh air and cold water and, together with their refusal to adopt an obsequious attitude to officers of almost any rank, this distinguishes them from a great many of their counterparts in the various armies collected under the Allied banner.

But it isn't all sweetness and light at Mena camp. Never at heart regular soldiers, Australians off duty consider themselves civilians, full of high spirits and looking to amuse themselves by taking every opportunity to make the most of their time away from home. Like Napoleon's troops and those of earlier British regiments stationed in Egypt, the Australians write their names on the Pyramids. They have money in their pockets and, after two months of being cooped up in transports without being allowed ashore at Colombo or Aden, they have adventure in their hearts. This makes for a highly combustible combination as they invade the bright lights of Cairo and Heliopolis, which proves not to be a city designed for the entertainment of young men and is lamentably lacking in respectable diversions such as sport, theatre or outdoor recreation.

Shepheards and the Continental Hotel, the only two sources of any sort of European culture, are, by tradition, reserved for officers, which leaves only the cafes, the bazaar where some are taught to smoke hashish, and the brothels and sex shows for the men. In the cafes the mostly Greek proprietors serve them poisonous arak and gut-wrenching meals and the brothels, with few exceptions, are diseased and dirty. Fired up with arak and a sense of being out on the town, the young men willingly follow touts to 'exhibitions' of the vilest nature.

The Clicks, led by Numbers Cooligan, set off in search of grand adventure. The tram from the camp is so overloaded with laughing and boisterous men that soldiers are piled onto the roof and bunch out from either of the two entrances, clinging to each other for dear life, all the way to the centre of Cairo.

437

'If you think Aden was good wait till we get to Cairo,' Numbers Cooligan promises those in the platoon who hadn't been fortunate enough to be present at the now legendary Belly Dunce and Snake performance in Aden.

'How do you know it will be better? I thought you said Belly Dunce and Snake couldn't be bettered?' Library Spencer reminds him.

'Yeah, the best of its kind. But here they're real serious, mate. It stands to reason, don't it, Aden's a pisspot city compared to Cairo. The bigger the pot the more piss it holds, get my drift, gentlemen!' Which is about as close as Cooligan has ever come to a serious aphorism.

Carrying two months' wages in their pockets they show not a scintilla of resistance when an oleaginous tout, with a pencil moustache and dark rings around his eyes deep as a boxer's bruises, persuades them to see a woman copulating with a donkey. On a second occasion, another local low-life leads them to a large room which is more or less in darkness, with a single spotlight positioned over a small stage, under which and, in the presence of several hundred troops, a woman with pantaloons made of a diaphanous net material with the crutch missing, does the splits, picking up shilling coins which the troops throw onto the stage using only her 'it' muscles.

The one curious aspect of this basically boring performance is that she continues picking up a copious number of coins without apparently ever depositing them anywhere. They leave when, to the general hilarity and agonised cries of the performer, some bastard, using a pair of tweezers and a couple of Swan Vesta matches, heats a coin to an almost red-hot condition and throws it onto the stage.

'Shit!' Hornbill says when they're back in the alley. 'That was a shit thing to do, even if she were no lady!'

Numbers Cooligan appears to be thinking, 'If she's

done the splits two times a minute, that's every thirty seconds, and what they thrown on the platform was a shilling each time, 'cause she didn't pick up nothing less, then she's making two bob a minute!' He looks at them all. 'Shit, that's six pounds an hour! Jesus, and we felt sorry for her an' all!'

'Yeah, but what I want to know is where all them coins went?' Woggy Mustafa says.

'Where do you expect? In her purse o' course,' Crow Rigby replies.

In the cold light of morning, with their heads pounding something terrible from the previous night's poisonous arak and after a good few of them have freed their stomachs of the atrocious Greek cafe meal taken at some time during their carousal, they collectively decide to give the dirty part of Cairo's night life a big miss.

Belly Dunce and Snake, whether personally witnessed, or given the benefit of Numbers Cooligan's phantasmagorical version, has set the standard by which they now judge these things. Cairo, as far as Ben's platoon is concerned, has been permanently eclipsed by the little pisspot bazaar in Aden.

They also stay away from the brothels, apart from visiting one or two to take a quick squiz at the sheilas, who turn out to be dead ringers for the woman portrayed in various compromising positions connected to the ageing male appendage belonging to the socks-and-gartered form of the ubiquitous Herman the German of Hornbill's uncle's dirty postcards fame. Thus both the virginity and, with Cooligan, improbably, the exception, the physical health of the thirty members of Ben's platoon remains intact.

Ben, who has attended a sergeants' course on sexual hygiene, hasn't attempted to frighten them, as have so many of the junior officers or sergeants lecturing their respective platoons on venereal disease. He simply says, 'Get a dose and it's a free ticket home, lads. Then they're gunna write to your mum and tell her why you've been sent back. And you, Private Cooligan, could well be the first to go home.'

'Me, Sergeant? Never. Pure as the driven. Left me darlin' at 'ome!'

'Who's that, the cat?' Crow Rigby asks.

The behaviour of Ben's platoon is no more than high spirits. They're all big lads with too much energy, who wouldn't harm a flea unless they found it on their own person.

However, there is a much more serious aspect of behaviour among the Australian contingent – drunkenness, attacks on the local population, desertion, stealing and the wilful destruction of property. There comes a point when the excuse of high spirits among young men bent on having a good time will no longer wash with the senior military and they call for an account.

The supreme commander of the Allied Forces in Egypt, General Maxwell, draws the attention of General Birdwood to the matter and he, in turn, refers it to General Bridges, who writes to the troops appealing to their finer spirit and their country's good name abroad.

What follows is a pronounced improvement, but by early in January some three hundred men of the 1st Division are absent without leave, roaming about Cairo drunk and disorderly, thieving from the local population and defying the local authorities. In the British army this constitutes desertion and they are liable to be imprisoned or even shot, but under Australian law shooting a soldier isn't allowed, nor, for that matter, is it even contemplated and smacks rather too much of the colonial past.

However, General Bridges institutes an investigation and somewhat to his surprise discovers that the trouble comes, to a very large degree, from the older soldiers, mostly veterans from the Boer War or men who have not been born in Australia, though a young Australian-born criminal element is also present.

Bridges, in a covert message to officers of every rank, asks for their suggestions as to what might be done.

Wordy Smith tells Ben. 'You know what I would do, sir,' Ben says at last.

'What?'

'Well, we know it's not lads such as our own who are the villains.'

'That's right, it seems to be the older men, mostly ex-military and, they say, a young criminal element.'

'Yeah well, they're only a tiny fraction of the A.I.F., a pinch of sand in the desert, why don't we just send them back home?'

'What, cashier them?'

'Isn't that only for officers?' Ben asks.

'No, I don't think so, but what you mean is send them home in disgrace?'

'Well, yeah. Most, if not all, of the young lads are here to fight the Hun, they're volunteers and damn proud of having been chosen for the privilege. Let's send the troublemakers home, discharge them from the army altogether, we don't need 'em, all they're doing is giving the rest of us a bad name.'

Second Lieutenant Peregrine Ormington-Smith claps his hands gleefully. 'I say, that's splendid, Sergeant, it's almost bound to work.' He looks at Ben admiringly. 'You know, you really ought to be an officer, Sergeant Teekleman.'

Ben is genuinely appalled. 'Thank you, sir, with the greatest respect, I would consider it a demotion.'

Wordy Smith persists, 'I know you could do my job a lot better than I can, in fact mostly do. More importantly,

I most certainly could not do yours. So, in a manner of speaking, I suppose it would be a demotion.' He looks at Ben steadily. 'Sergeant, it's a truly grand solution, but I can't submit it in your name to the C.O.' Ben now sees his platoon officer is visibly blushing. 'He'd . . . well, he'll know I've been talking to . . . er, other ranks, that I've abused an officer confidence, so to speak.'

Ben grins. 'Go for your life, sir. They'll probably think you're crackers.'

Wordy Smith grins back. 'Nothing new in that, Sergeant.'

But it doesn't turn out that way. Major Sayers takes the suggestion to his battalion commander Colonel Wanliss, who moves it further up the ladder to his brigade commander Brigadier M'Cay, who finally presents it to General Bridges. The three hundred men are sent back to Australia in disgrace, accompanied by a letter to the Australian press from Bridges explaining the reasons why they are returning. Except for the comparatively minor incidents which occur in every army, this very largely settles the issues of hooliganism, criminal drunkenness and violent and inappropriate behaviour by Australian troops in Egypt.

Working on the premise that a young man who is physically exhausted is less inclined to get up to mischief, General Birdwood sets about turning the Australian Division and the New Zealand Brigade into a concerted fighting force. While he stipulates the training required he leaves it entirely up to General Bridges and his Australian and New Zealand officers to undertake. Bridges works his men intensely hard and the training in the desert often goes for twelve or fifteen hours without respite. They march and fight mock battles and do manoeuvres under the glaring desert sun until the shirts cling to their backs. Often they find themselves caught in a dust storm brought on by the howling winds of the *kamsin*. In the first two weeks the average loss of weight over this period is almost eight pounds a man.

Ben is quick to cotton on to the recurrence of a problem which affected his men in their first three weeks in the desert. His platoon, along with their company, will often stop for a rest at sunset, their flanelette vests so wet they can be wrung out by hand. Then, the moment the sun dips behind the highest dunes, an icy breeze will begin to blow. The youngsters, exhausted from eight or ten hours of manoeuvres, think the breeze a blessed relief as it dries the wet vests clinging to their backs. In a matter of days nearly two hundred troops are down with pneumonia and several die. Ben's platoon is bearing up well but Wordy Smith has developed a bad cold and is having trouble keeping up.

Ben visits his C.O. to see if they can be issued with sweaters. Major Sayers sees the sense in this, but upon enquiry discovers that ordnance has no sweaters. The British army, whose responsibility it is to supply the cold-weather uniforms, has, perhaps understandably, not considered that troops training in desert conditions will require warm clothing. It will take several weeks before they can be ordered and transported from Britain and even longer if they are to come from Australia or New Zealand.

Ben calls Numbers Cooligan and Library Spencer to his tent the following morning. 'Right, you two will go on sick parade tomorrow . . .'

'Whaffor, Sergeant?' Cooligan asks before Ben can complete the sentence.

'Don't jump the gun, Private Cooligan, and I'll explain.'

'Yes, Sergeant, sorry, Sergeant.'

'You'll go on sick parade, I've already spoken to the

sergeant on duty and he'll give you a chit, permission to miss tomorrow's manoeuvres, bronchitis. Then I want you to go into Cairo, maybe you could try the Arabs in Mena first, see if you can buy thirty-two pullovers, all of them large.'

'What, jerseys? What colour, Sergeant?' Library asks.

'Not sure we'll be given the luxury of a choice, the essential thing is that they're warm and that they're large. Be too much to expect to find thirty-two large *khaki* sweaters for the use of. Oh, and try not to pay more than ten bob a piece.'

'Yes, Sergeant . . . er . . . and the money?' Numbers Cooligan asks tentatively. 'That's sixteen quid.'

'Isn't that about as much as you've made on that two-up school you run behind the Y.M.C.A. shack of an evening?' Ben asks.

Numbers Cooligan visibly pales. 'Er . . . ah . . . shit . . . ah, what game is that, Sergeant?' Then quickly recovering, says, 'Matter a fact, I'm dead broke, skint.'

Ben hands Library Spencer four oversized white English five pound notes. 'There's plenty enough there to buy 'em and to cover your expenses, don't come back without the goods, lads, *and* I wouldn't mind some change neither.'

The two lads return to their tents. 'Shit, how'd he get twenty quid out the army?' Cooligan asks.

'He probably didn't,' Library replies.

'Whatcha mean? Ya reckon he's payin'? Out his own pocket? Twenty quid? No flamin' way, mate!'

'His name's Teekleman!'

'So?'

Library Spencer sighs. 'You ever drink Tommo & Hawk beer?'

'Sure, it's a good drop. Ballarat.'

'In Victoria it's made by a company called Solomon &

Teekleman, they own the brewery in Ballarat among another squillion things.'

'That's him?'

Library nods. 'Not him personally, his family.'

'Shit hey!' Cooligan jerks his head backwards, looking at Library quizzically, 'G'arn, yer bullshittin' me? The beer? That's *him*? Jesus H. Christ!'

Numbers Cooligan and Library Spencer arrive back at Mena camp with an Arab boy who looks to be about twelve years old, leading a donkey carrying a large hessian-wrapped bale half the size of a wool bale on its back. They pull up as the sun is setting over the Great Pyramid and just as the Clicks return, exhausted from an eight-mile march into camp after all-day exercises in the desert. The men drop their kit and rifles and flop down on the sand beside the donkey while Cooligan and Library Spencer help the boy unload the bale.

'How'd yer go, lads?' Ben asks.

'Good. Real good, Sergeant.'

'Righto, let's take a look.'

Cooligan cuts the string tying the bale together and it flops open to reveal a large pile of high-quality khaki pullovers. Library and Numbers Cooligan are both wearing Cheshire cat grins.

'Khaki, Sergeant! Hows about that, eh?' Cooligan says, proud as punch.

'Well done, lads!' Ben exclaims. He is clearly impressed.

'Library 'ere done it, Sergeant,' Numbers Cooligan says in a rare moment of modesty.

'We both did,' Library says, unaccustomed to the praise. 'I did a bit o' thinking and Numbers did the bargaining.'

'Egyptian police, Sergeant. Library thought it out and we went to their headquarters in Cairo, cost a bit but we got the donkey and the boy buckshee.'

Ben is busy counting the pullovers and now looks up, 'There's fifty-two here.'

Numbers Cooligan shakes his head. 'Yeah well, I thought I'd make an investment of me own like, Sergeant.'

'How much did you pay for these?'

'Eight bob each, Sergeant. Cooligan did the bargaining,' Library repeats proudly.

'Yeah, but it become a bit complicated see,' Cooligan says hurriedly. 'Eight bob each, plus the two pound we give the police lieutenant and the quid we give the sergeant in their ordnance, then the ten shillings for the cop at the gate who let us 'ave the kid what's just been nicked fer stealing the donkey, and then just when we's loaded up . . .'

'Hold it, Private Cooligan!' Ben commands. 'Why is it that I somehow know it's all gunna come to exactly twenty quid?'

'Just a mo, Sergeant, or I'll forget where I was . . . oh yes, just as we's about to say "Oo-roo, ta-ta", with the donkey loaded an' all, the lieutenant comes out, the same bloke what's already done us for two quid, and says it's three quid for the police captain or the deal is off!' Cooligan looks at Ben. 'I tried to argue that we done a deal, Sergeant, but he don't want to know. Then I says, "Righto, no deal, gi's back the money!" I'm thinkin' like, yer know, ter bluff him. "No no! No money you get back! Three pound. The captain very hungery!" he says, looking real nasty. They's a bunch o' crooks, that lot, Sergeant, villains to the last man.' Cooligan gives a disdainful sniff and continues, 'Then there's four shillin's for a binder, just lamb and rice at a Greek's, two beers, one and six, a shillin' for the hessian and the string, sixpence for a bunch a carrots for the donkey,' Cooligan smiles benignly, 'and a shillin' to the Arab lad who stole

446

it. And, oh yeah, I nearly forgot, two bob fer me and Library's tram fare to town in the first place.' Cooligan finishes, 'There yer go, Sergeant.'

'And that's precisely twenty pounds,' Ben repeats, a touch sardonic.

'Yeah, that's right, Sergeant?' Numbers says quizzically and looks a trifle hurt at Ben's seemingly critical tone of voice. 'We didn't charge nothin' for walking the ten miles back to Mena with the flamin' donkey!'

'Well done, you two,' Ben says and turns to Numbers Cooligan. 'And your investment? I thought you said you were skint?'

'Yeah well, I come good all of a sudden, like overnight.'

'What, the tooth fairy come?' Crow Rigby asks.

Ben laughs with the others.

'It was me own money, Sergeant!' Cooligan protests fiercely. 'Fair dinkum! I'll swear it on a stack o' Bibles!'

'It's true, Sergeant,' Library Spencer says hastily, nodding his head as further confirmation. 'He had to borrow a quid off me.'

'I wouldn't doubt you both for a moment, lads,' Ben says good-humouredly, then points to the twenty pullovers he's set to one side. 'What do you think you'll get for those on the black market, Private Cooligan?'

'You mean here in the camp, Sergeant?'

Ben nods.

Numbers Cooligan, clearly relieved that he's not in trouble, thinks for a moment, his head to one side, hand stroking his chin. 'I reckon fifteen bob a piece, Sergeant, no sweat.'

'Well that's real bad luck, Private, because I'm buying them from you for eight shillings each. We're changing over to the British system of organising a platoon and a company, there's twenty more lads coming in with us. I owe you eight quid for the remaining twenty pullovers, you'll have it in the morning, Private Cooligan.' He faces the seated platoon. 'Righto, grab a pullover each and make sure you have them in your kit tomorrow. Yeah, I know it's extra weight, but if I find any of you lads without 'em, it's two days kitchooty.'

General Birdwood, on instructions from the War Office, changes the old system of company formation used by the Australians to the one adopted after the Boer War by the British. Whereas there were formerly eight platoons to a company, around two hundred and seventy men with supporting staff, they now organise into four platoons and two hundred and twenty-eight men to a company, the bigger platoons still remaining under a single subaltern.

There is a fair amount of consternation at the news of this reorganisation in the Clicks, who have always seen themselves as somewhat special and have become a very close-knit unit. Furthermore, there are now four extra subalterns in the company, second lieutenants over, and the fear is that Wordy Smith, who is plainly the worst of them all, is going to be taken away from them. While the extra men mean more work for him, Ben doesn't want to lose Peregrine Ormington-Smith. It must be one of the few occasions in military history where the men feel charged with the responsibility for maintaining the poor services of their platoon officer.

Crow Rigby voices their fears to Ben when they are out in the desert the following day. Wordy Smith has sloped off to look under a large overhanging rock some hundred yards away, no doubt seeking out some invisible-to-the-naked-eye desert flora, so the infantryman is free to speak. 'Sergeant, with this reorganisation, does that mean we're gunna lose, you know, Wordy . . . er, Lieutenant Ormington-Smith?'

The others wait anxiously for Ben's reply. 'Can't say, Private Rigby, not much we can do about it anyway.'

'Couldn't we like . . . go to the C.O. and ask him, say we'd like to keep him, Sergeant?' Hornbill asks.

Ben clears his throat, and appears a little embarrassed. 'It's . . . well, it's not the sort of thing a sergeant can do, lads.'

Put this way, they all get the message right off, a sergeant can't be seen kissing the arse of an officer, no matter how he feels about him. That means the men can't do so either.

'There's only one thing the army might take into consideration?'

'What's that, Sergeant?' Muddy Parthe asks.

'Well, with this new formation the platoon becomes the real fighting unit in the army. In the field, once the battle is closed and we're in the thick o' it, the platoon has to be an independent unit. So company commanders and the like get to know which platoons work best for what fighting job. For instance, you lads have been trained with a heavy emphasis on the rifle, I'm trained in the machine gun as well, British Maxim and the French Hotchkiss, so they'll see us as a fighting arm. I think we're potentially a good one, we can already bring more firepower to bear on the enemy than most. But we lack sappers. So, if I'm not mistaken, we'll be given a bunch of lads with shovels to round us out.' He pauses and looks about him, then goes on. 'Now if we can show Major Sayers and Colonel Wanliss and Brigadier M'Cay and some o' the brass looking on when we're on manoeuvres that we're a shit-hot unit, the best there is, well they're not going to change the subaltern, are they now, lads?'

'Jesus, Sergeant, sappers joining us? You mean like them bastards what tried to attack us on board ship?' Muddy Parthe asks.

'Well, yes.'

'More than possible,' Library Spencer says, 'Black Jack Treloar's been sent home.'

449

'Nothing trivial I hope?' Crow Rigby quips.

'One o' them three hundred disgraced, them what give us a bad name,' Woggy adds a little self-righteously.

'How come I don't know this?' Cooligan laments. 'I'm the Gob Sergeant, I'm supposed ter know everything!'

'No, mate, Library *knows* everything,' Woggy says.

'That's enough, lads, but yes, Sergeant Treloar's platoon is one of those to be broken up and redistributed. I've asked for at least three of them, Brodie, Matthews and Jolly.'

There is a stunned silence.

'But . . . but they were . . . ?'

Ben cuts Muddy Parthe off before he can go any further, 'Yes, the three who went to hospital, they're joining us with some others and I want you to make them welcome. And, by the way, Private Spencer, it's *Sergeant* Black Jack Treloar to such as you.'

'Jesus, now I've flamin' 'eard everything,' Cooligan gasps.

'That's enough, stow yer mess cans, it's time to move out. Private Mustafa, go fetch the lieutenant, make sure he doesn't leave anything behind.'

In the next few weeks the expanded platoon throws itself into training as if it is real war, though this is not uncommon with the 1st Division, all of whom want to make their mark. The young Australians are positively itching to go to war. The new blokes from Black Jack Treloar's platoon work as hard as the rest of them, even harder on occasions. They're naturally fit, accustomed to pick and shovel work, big, strong lads, perhaps a little basic, but tough as teak wood and scared of nothing. Like a journeyman boxer who always finds himself the sparring partner to the champion, they yearn for a chance to shine on their own.

Slogging it out in the desert is bloody hard work and

the new members of the platoon give no quarter and ask no favours. Ben though is remorseless, and when the new group gets back to camp or bivouac in the desert at night he has them behind a rifle, sharpening their skills, making them catch up with the Lee-Enfield. They don't complain, which is rare for young soldiers, and from their actions it seems as if they are somewhat ashamed of Black Jack Treloar and want to make up for the bad reputation they've earned. The axe incident on the deck of the *Orvieto* has given them tremendous respect for Ben and, now that they find out he's a good bloke as well, they feel privileged to be in with the Clicks.

Brodie is an instant hit with the members of the old platoon and is immediately christened Brokenose, his hooter now considerably flattened on a face that could never be pretty but which is seldom less than cheerful. He and Library Spencer hit it off together a treat and are soon good mates. This first comes about when Brodie wanders aimlessly into the Y.M.C.A., a ramshackle hut in the camp where the men can write letters home, and observes Library seated at a table writing.

'Whatcha doin' then, Library?' Brodie asks.

Library is too polite to point out that it must be perfectly bloody obvious that he's writing a letter. 'Writing home.'

'Shit hey?' Brokenose Brodie seems genuinely impressed. 'Wish I could do that.'

'Well, what's to stop you? Sit down, there's plenty o' paper, pencils, it's a free world, go for yer life.'

'Nah, can't, me old folks don't read.'

'Well, that doesn't matter, mate, somebody can read it to them, a neighbour?'

'Nah, wouldn't work.'

'Why not?'

'They's ashamed like. Too proud.'

Library looks up at the huge form of Brokenose Brodie. 'You can't write, can you, mate?'

'Course I can!' Brokenose says proudly. 'Me name.' Whereupon he takes up a pencil and on a scrap of paper he laboriously writes *KEVIN BRODIE* in the script of a seven-year-old schoolchild. 'There yer go,' he says, smiling, 'me moniker!'

'That all you can write?' Library enquires softly.

'And me army number!'

Both break up at this and somebody at another table calls, 'Shush!'

'Can't read neither, eh?' Library asks in a half-whisper.

Brokenose Brodie shakes his head.

'Wanna learn?'

'Too old, mate, I ain't got no brains, I'm a fuckin' ditch digger, ain't I?'

'Don't matter, I'll teach ya.'

'Yeah? So I can write 'ome?' Brokenose Brodie says, then he seems to have a momentary doubt. 'Me folk still can't read. Fair dinkum yer reckon yer can do it?'

'Not me, you. *You* can do it, Brokenose.' Library extends his hand which is immediately lost in Brokenose Brodie's huge callused paw.

The training the troops receive at the hands of General Bridges, though vigorous, is simply the traditional British army training from an outdated manual. Little or no advice comes to them from the Western Front, where a new kind of war is raging. The Australian and New Zealand officers must rely almost entirely on drills, tactics and manoeuvres written at another time for war in another place and after this use their own initiative.

The men are also showing that they can think on their feet and make decisions at the N.C.O. and even at the basic infantry level. It is somewhat disconcerting that when, in the mock battles they fight, the officer is killed, the platoon carries on as if nothing untoward has happened. They seem to cope with most situations they are thrown into with an almost cavalier carry-on-sergeant approach.

The troops of the 1st Division have toughened, their bodies almost black from exposure to the Egyptian sun. At the end of January a further ten thousand five hundred new Australian troops and two thousand New Zealanders arrive with Colonel John Monash in charge of the 4th Infantry Brigade. They are fine specimens all but they appear soft compared to the desert-hardened Australians and New Zealanders. Nobody in the War Office seems to have asked themselves whether troops trained to fight in the desert in wide-open spaces under a cloudless sky will be able to adapt to the trenches of Flanders and France. Just how these sons of Australia will react in an actual battle is anyone's guess.

In Europe the men are learning to fight in trenches, often up to their knees in mud on battlefields covered in early morning mist or in a perpetual haze of smoke from heavy artillery shells and mortar attacks. Meanwhile, the Australians and New Zealanders have never seen a bomb or been subject to, or even heard, the roar and thunder of a sustained artillery attack, or the whine of a shell passing overhead, nor, in fact, experienced anything beyond the pop-pop of the 18-pounder field gun a four-man crew can drag into position. Most have never even seen a periscope and few of the thirty thousand men have fired a shot in anger except perhaps at a crow or a dingo. About the only thing they can be said to understand with a thoroughness of purpose is barbed wire and how to crawl through it. Furthermore, most of them can use a Lee-Enfield rifle with some skill and the bayonet attached with a singular and determined efficiency, that is, if you consider an unprotesting bag of sand the equivalent of an enemy.

Nevertheless, the intelligence shown by the men as they work their way on their bellies around a knoll or mount a night attack prompts a senior regular-army English officer, newly arrived to take up a position as adviser on Birdwood's staff, to remark, 'A better division than the 1st Australian together with the New Zealand Brigade has never gone to battle.'

When the platoon and company exercises are completed, Ben's platoon is singled out as one of the three best in the 1st Division. Wordy Smith receives congratulations for their conduct in the field and a personal letter of commendation from General Bridges. In part the letter which Wordy Smith reads to the platoon says:

My only regret is that we did not have an enemy and a battle at hand to test your platoon, for I feel certain you and your men would have come through with flying colours.

That evening after tea the 'belly dunce and snake six', plus Brokenose Brodie, who now makes a regular seventh member of their mob, are seated in the soldiers' mess when Crow Rigby suddenly says, 'Hey, wait a mo, what if, after all our 'ard work keepin' him safe from himself, Wordy Smith gets a promotion?'

'Dead right!' Numbers Cooligan exclaims. 'We wouldn't know how to operate without him! He's like being a champion jockey what's always been given an unfair handicap and is gunna show the bastards he can still win the flamin' race!'

'Nah, it couldn't happen,' Library Spencer says. 'Not even the general is *that* stupid.'

There is a momentary silence whilst they all think

about this and then Crow Rigby mutters, 'I dunno, I'm not so sure about that.'

'What?'

'The general.'

Around the middle of March, rumours are coming thick and fast. The British navy, in an effort to aid Russia by creating a supply line through the Bosphorus, fails when her ships are unable to force their way through the straits of the Dardanelles. Like everyone else, Britain has underestimated the Turks and arrogantly assumed the Dardanelles at their narrowest point will be easily breached by her navy and they will sail on to bombard Constantinople and force Turkey out of the war and so, in a military sense, kill two birds with one stone.

The failure of the navy's attempt to force the straits makes a land attack on the peninsula almost inevitable. Though little of this is reported at the troop level, Wordy's Wireless is still working. News is fairly freely discussed in the officers' mess and Wordy Smith briefs Ben daily on what he hears.

The 3rd Brigade has disappeared a month ago and Wordy's Wireless has it that they're in Lemnos practising landing from the sea. Furthermore, Sister Atkins scribbles a note to Ben to inform him that Jolly and Matthews previously from Sergeant Treloar's platoon need to see the army dentist now that their gums have had time to heal properly. In her note she mentions that the nurses have been ordered to get sunhats, which, she says, seems rather curious as they are all working indoors.

Much as Ben tries to see some special message and encouragement in the note which will enable him to make another advance to Sister Atkins, he is forced to concede that hers is simply a duty performed in the interest of the two lads. The sunhat information is couched as though she thinks it is a wonderful example of bumbling army bureaucracy. Ben knows it is strictly forbidden to fraternise with someone of officer rank, but in a moment of lovesickness he seriously contemplates catching pneumonia so that she might be brought to his bedside.

Much of this rumour and speculation about an imminent invasion is given out via Gob Sergeant Cooligan in the hope that it will attract further confirmation from other sources. In the Mena camp Wordy's Wireless has lost none of its potency and has developed into a sort of highly sophisticated rumour cross-reference system. Library Spencer is charged with monitoring what comes back after a soundly based Gob-Sergeant rumour is circulated.

It is surprising how much information can be gathered in tiny scraps from the observations of clerks, the military police, the officers' mess, the soldiers who drive the top brass around, even the barber who cuts the hair of the officers at General Hamilton's headquarters at Shepheards or the corporals and privates who operate the various telephone switchboards. In fact there are a hundred different sources, the note from Sister Atkins being an excellent example of one of them. They learn how, when it is all co-ordinated, it is often possible to get surprisingly close to the truth. The proverbial grapevine has always worked in the army and what Ben is now doing is trying to create a sturdier and stronger vine with further-reaching tentacles.

For want of a better system it works pretty well and they soon develop an instinct for what is true. They firmly believe they're going to fight the Turks somewhere along the coastline of the Dardanelles sometime in early April, though for a while they think the Australians are going to invade Alexandretta and are surprised when this comes to nothing as it qualified on almost all fronts as sound information.

Meanwhile, the Turks have launched a raid on the Suez Canal and although they are repulsed by the British and Indian troops, it becomes apparent from the reports sent in that they are no easy-beats. A new respect is growing for the fighting capacity of the Turkish soldier and they are no longer considered a second-class fighting force unworthy of the Anzacs.

Almost by sheer fluke the training they have undergone in the desert is not entirely redundant, the terrain around the straits is known to be hilly and, though hardly equivalent to the desert, it would appear they will be fighting a war in the open. Besides, they have grown accustomed to climbing steep dunes and rocky ridges and it will be a nice change to have firm ground under their feet as they advance against the enemy. And advance they will. There is not a single man from general to trooper and soldier who doubts for a moment that they will destroy the enemy, even though the Germans are training the Turks.

The first of April is a Thursday, still three days before the leg-weary platoon can expect a day off. Ben comes out of his tent at dawn to another cloudless sky. Though it is still cold, the sun not yet risen, he knows the temperature will climb above a hundred and ten degrees before noon. They are involved in a field day out along the burning dunes which he doesn't much look forward to.

Ben, sick to the back teeth with Egypt, wonders how long it will be before they leave for the Peninsula to fight against the Turks. In the dawn light he takes from the breast pocket of his tunic the letter he has received from Victoria in the previous day's mail. He has already read it half a dozen times but does so again. Rubbing his forefinger and thumb along the edge of the paper he imagines his sister writing it, a cool breeze blowing off the Derwent rustling the curtains as it enters gently through a bright, sunlit window. She will be seated at Mary's old desk, which she tells him Hawk has removed from the Potato Factory and brought to her small study in Ann Solomon's Hobart cottage which she and Hawk now occupy.

Hobart

5th February 1915

My dearest Ben,

You must be thoroughly sick of receiving a letter from me with almost every overseas mail arriving in Egypt, I simply cannot help myself. My mind is so constantly occupied with thoughts of you that my only comfort is to sit down at Mary's old desk and write to you for the sheer relief of getting my thoughts down on paper. I pray each night that you are safe, though God does not seem to be listening, if what's happening at the front is any indication.

Grandfather Hawk says much of what is happening in France is being kept from us. Heaven forbid, what we do hear is horrific enough and, while it may seem unpatriotic, every day you are kept away from the battlefield means another night I can sleep without wondering whether the morning will bring bad news.

I'm sorry to sound so pessimistic and not my usual cheerful self (the newspapers urge us always to sound cheerful when writing to the troops), but Grandfather Hawk brought back the news last night that Joshua, who has already been promoted to captain, has been transferred to be second in command of an ordnance company and is unlikely to see any fighting.

Abraham Solomon, who is visiting us here in Tasmania for a few days, says it is because of his thorough business training, they need men like him because the logistics of war supply require good, sound business principles. In your own words, all I can say is 'Bulldust!' We know perfectly well somebody has pulled strings! And pulled them b . . . . y hard too! It all seems so unfair that he should get a cushy job safe from harm and you will eventually be sent to the front line to fight the Hun.

I can almost see you smiling, I know you wouldn't change places with him for all the tea in China. But please! Please! I beg you to be careful. I simply couldn't bear it if you got wounded, especially knowing you-know-who was safe and sound counting tins of bullybeef.

In a more cheerful vein, I am going up to Launceston next week to see about opening a new warehouse. We are taking a bit of a drubbing from the James Boag Brewery because we sometimes run short of T & H beer in the local market and they, being on the spot, are quick to take advantage. I must say they are keen as mustard and we will have to be on our toes if we are going to keep our share of that market. *Grandfather Hawk also wants me to look at a small factory turning out woollen blankets as he thinks he can get a contract from the government for supplies to the troops training here in Tasmania.*

He seems a different person now that he is back in control again and looks years younger with a definite spring in his step. I simply don't know where he gets his energy! I am learning a great deal from him, though the thought of taking over if he should pass on is frightening, he is so wise and patient and is completely in control and on top of things. For my part I remain confused and I still have no clear idea of all we own, what's more I am led to believe Tasmania is the smaller part of S & T. We went for a spin in the new Wolseley tourer on Sunday and Grandfather Hawk pointed out a dozen buildings and factory works which he said we owned. It's really quite daunting.

I must end now as this has to catch the mail boat to Melbourne to connect with another travelling via Suez. I have become quite the expert at shipping routes since your departure.

Mrs Billings sends her love, she is knitting you a pair of gloves and seems to be taking ages. Sardine the cat has developed a permanent nose drip and she speaks of little else, being quite sure that 'he is not long for this mortal coil'. She is comforted by the thought that her dear moggy will join her sainted husband, the immortal, though never existing in actual human form, Mortimer Billings. She

460

says to tell you that if you should be cooking rice to add prunes to it as they prevent constipation and give the rice a nice savoury flavour! They should be soaked in water overnight and then the rice cooked in the prune juice together with the prunes. She has never quite gotten over, as she sees it, her appointment as Cook to the Australian Forces Abroad and tells everyone she can earbash for long enough about her billyjam tarts!

Grandfather Hawk says he will write to you at length next week, but to tell you the hops crop is looking splendid this year and everyone on the estate asks for news of you. They all send their love and best wishes, he also sends his love.

Will you get the chance to go to Luxor, I believe it is well worth the visit and, looking at the map, is not far from where you are?

Please try and stay away from the fighting as long as you are able and give my regards to your platoon, they seem like such nice lads and I am sure are very fond of you. I cannot imagine you being a strict sergeant who they have cause to fear. Taking twenty more young soldiers under your wing must be an added worry though. Grandfather Hawk says sappers can be a rough lot. I hope this is not true in your case? The desert sounds beastly hot, as usual the weather here in Hobart changes five times each day and I despair of ever wearing the right clothes when I go out to work of a morning.

I miss you terribly!! Write if you can, I constantly long for news of you.

> *Your loving sister,*
>
> *Victoria.*

P.S. Please make sure you always wear your Tiki, I know it's all superstitious nonsense, but our mother said it will keep you safe and she was half-Maori and we are a quarter. I don't know what that's supposed to mean, but just wear it because it's in your blood!

V.

The bugle sounds reveille and Ben goes over to the cook-house to get a mug of hot water in order to shave. Upon his return he sees Brokenose Brodie fully kitted outside his tent, seated on an empty ammunition box with a slate on his lap busy writing. Ben can see by the way he holds himself that the process is one of a most earnest endeavour.

'Mornin', Private Brodie, what are you up to?'

Brokenose looks up. 'Doin' me 'omework, Sergeant. Library's learnin' me to read and write.'

'Good on ya, Private. Soon be writing home to the folks, eh?'

Brokenose Brodie grins but then immediately goes back to work. 'I'm sorry, Sergeant, I can't talk,' he says, his head bowed over his slate. 'I were that tired last night I didn't get me 'omework done and Library's gunna kick me arse from 'ere to Jerusalem!'

The platoon's day is spent out in the desert in a mock battle with the 4th Light Horse Regiment combining with the 1st and 2nd Infantry Brigades to attack one of the high desert ridges. The Light Horse, sent in first to seize the ridge, get there before the enemy, but the 1st Infantry Brigade advancing up the other half of the ridge is held up and the Light Horse are placed in an unsustainable position. If the enemy should reach them before their own infantry they do not have the firepower to hold the position. Ben's battalion with the 2nd Infantry Brigade, who are meant to advance behind the Light Horse, seeing their position is in jeopardy, advances at the double to the top of the ridge faster than seems possible to the two brigadiers, M'Cay and MacLaurin, who are jointly directing the battle. They now see the long line of each company showing dark against the white glare of the sand dunes as they suddenly spring into existence, sweeping, one line after another, across the hillside to take it and bring the fight to an end. A British officer, observing, turns to M'Cay with the comment, 'Could not have been better.' It is apparent to everyone that the Australians are thoroughly trained and ready for the fray.

Late that afternoon when the troops return to camp, instead of being dismissed, they remain on parade and the officers are told that the Australian 1st Division is moving out, and all but the Light Horse and the Mounted Rifles are going to the front. They are to proceed immediately with the evacuation of the Mena camp.

A tremendous cheer goes up as each company is informed. The young infantrymen break rank and are seen clapping each other on the shoulders and backs, sending their slouch hats and caps high into the air. There is no possible way they can be brought to heel. They have waited too long for this moment. This is what they've worked for. At last the time has come for the colonial lads to prove their mettle against a real enemy.

The Anzacs are ready for war.

Chapter Thirteen

THE LANDING

Gallipoli 1915

'Righto, get this into your thick heads,' Ben says. 'We know they'll be waiting for us, it's never easy to invade from the sea, the defender on land always has the advantage and in this case there is every likelihood of high ground involved. That means they'll be looking down on us.'

Ben's platoon is gathered together on a sheltered part of the deck of the *Novian*, one of the transports carrying the Anzacs to Lemnos. They are a day out from Alexandria, hugging the coast of Asia Minor, the weather turning increasingly foul. Ben's platoon is seated under a tarpaulin on the deck where Lieutenant Peregrine Ormington-Smith, together with Ben, is briefing them.

Although they are not supposed to know their destination, there isn't a man in the Australian 1st Division who doesn't have a fair idea of where they're headed after the Greek island of Lemnos. In Library Spencer's words, 'A man would have to be a bit of an idjit not to know that it'll be somewhere along the coastline o' the Dardanelles and that we're gunna get as close to the Narrows as possible.'

'Let me give you an example of what we might expect,'

Ben continues. 'We'll probably wait until the moon goes down.'

'Yeah, we've already seen what 'appens when you attack in bright moonlight,' Numbers Cooligan says, obviously referring to the axe incident on the *Orvieto*. Several of the men look at Brokenose Brodie, Matthews and Jolly.

Brokenose brings his big paw up and rubs his flattened nose. 'Yeah, it ain't the best idea,' he says a little ruefully, 'buggers can see yiz.'

Ben ignores the remark, though it gets a laugh. 'The moon should go down around three o'clock, maybe a bit later. That will give us a little more than an hour of darkness to get the men into the boats and start for the shore. The idea will be to land well before sun-up, but with the dawn light to see by. We'll want to be clear of the water and the beach before sun-up so the enemy fire can't pick us off in broad daylight. Hopefully we'll be up and onto the higher ground and engaging the enemy, which will be made a great deal more difficult because the sun will be at their backs and we'll be looking directly into it.' Ben looks at the men about him. 'That's the first wave going in.' He stops, not knowing quite how to tell them. 'But we're not going to be with them, lads, we're going in on the second wave.'

There is a groan from the platoon and it is obvious they are bitterly disappointed, Hornbill and Crow Rigby and several others bury their faces in their hands.

'Ain't that bloody typical, eh?' Numbers Cooligan howls. 'The best there is they leave for seconds.'

When Lieutenant Ormington-Smith told his sergeant of this decision Ben had been forced to conceal his own disappointment. Had he been allowed to rejoin his Tasmanian battalion he would be in the 3rd Brigade and among the first ashore.

'It stands to reason the 3rd Brigade will be the first to land,' he now says. 'They've been at Lemnos a month practising, we're bloody lucky to be in the second wave. So, don't get your knickers in a knot, Private Cooligan. If things go wrong, as they mostly do in battle, going in on the second wave won't be no Sunday school picnic.'

'But, Sergeant, what if them first lot, the 3rd Brigade, do all the fighting and there's none left for us?' Hornbill says and most of the others shake their heads, the possibility too awful to contemplate.

'That won't happen, lads, Johnny Turk is defending his homeland and we're the invaders. What's more, they've got the high ground looking down, they're sitting pretty.' He continues, 'Now, let's get this straight once and for all, the worst thing we can do is underestimate the Turk. In a moment the lieutenant here will tell you a bit about these blokes and it ain't bullshit neither, but let me first give you an example of the logistics involved, paint you a picture of what could happen.'

Ben turns to Crow Rigby. 'Private Rigby, you're an enemy sniper, you're nicely dug in say four hundred feet above the beach and let's say at a distance of three hundred yards. It's broad daylight, seven o'clock and the sun well up, bit of smoke around from the guns but you can see clearly enough. You're watching as our battalion jumps from the boats and starts to wade up to their waists towards the beach, maybe a hundred yards through the shallows. It's gunna take an hour to get all the men onto the beach and into the scrub. Now here's my question. How many men do you reckon, as a lone enemy sniper with telescopic sights, you can take out in a minute?'

Crow Rigby thinks for a moment then squinting up at Ben asks a question himself. 'I've got an offset mounted MKIII Lee-Enfield, right? With an Aldis No. 3 sight on Holland & Holland mounts?' While he has been trained as a sniper, Crow Rigby has elected to stay in the platoon, but his careful question now reflects his meticulous training.

'Well, technically speaking, no, you're the enemy remember, you'll be using a Mauser which is a better marksman's rifle than the S.M.L.E. and the best of your German optics and mountings are as good as, if not better than, any we've ever made.'

Crow Rigby nods. 'Righto, if I had Woggy here to spot for me, I reckon I could get a real good shot off every ten seconds, Sergeant.' He nods again. 'Yeah, that shouldn't be too hard. In theory anyway, it's a big ask in practice.'

'Strewth! Three hundred and sixty dead or wounded in an hour,' Numbers Cooligan shouts. 'That's our whole flamin' company and half another one!'

There is a stunned silence as the men think about what Crow Rigby has just said.

'And that's just the potential of one sniper,' Ben says at last. 'Gawd knows how many they'll have, and, as well, every other Turk not busy fighting off the 3rd Brigade will be emptying his rifle in the direction of the beach, not to mention their gun batteries and their machine guns.'

'Shit, eh?' Brokenose Brodie says. 'And I thought they was just wogs!'

Ben smiles. 'As Private Rigby says, that's in theory, I don't believe any sniper has ever achieved that many kills in one day.'

'Sergeant, the sun, even if it were up an hour or so, would be shining directly into Crow's eyes,' Library Spencer points out rather pedantically. Ben thinks he would probably make a good officer one day.

'Well said, Private Spencer, so let's hope like hell it ain't a cloudy day like today. But that's not the real point, we'll be sitting ducks blind Freddy couldn't miss. All I want you to get into your noggins is that we're fighting a *real*

467

enemy this time and we'll be at a distinct disadvantage. What's more, if you ever get close enough to use your bayonets, it won't be against an unprotesting sandbag.' He looks about him at the men seated on the deck. 'So when we hit the beach don't stand about chewin' the fat, concealment is everything, once up into higher ground we'll probably be digging like wombats, we'll use whatever cover is available and we're not, I repeat, we're not, any of us, gunna try to be heroes! I don't want any of you lads winning a flamin' medal, because it will probably be given to your mum posthumously.' Ben turns to Wordy Smith. 'The lieutenant is now going to give you a bit of a history lesson, it's just as well to know something about the enemy's past form.'

'Yes er well, thank you Sergeant Teekleman, I er . . . yes, ah . . .' Wordy Smith begins, then clears his throat and looks about nervously. Nobody takes any notice, his apparent nervousness stems from the old Wordy Smith who hasn't entirely conquered the mannerisms that went with his previous persona. Among these is the habit of looking at his boots as he talks.

Lieutenant Peregrine Ormington-Smith begins again. 'Yes well, the Turks, better known in history as the Ottomans, created an empire that lasted just six years short of four hundred years. Until just three years ago they still held Greece, Macedonia and Crete. For the greater part of these four hundred years they controlled all of the Middle East from Iraq to Tripoli, they captured Malta, besieged Vienna and controlled all of the Balkans and south-eastern Europe as far as Budapest.' Wordy Smith reels off these names and places quite oblivious to the fact that the platoon, for the most part, probably hasn't heard of many of them. 'Their navy, well actually the Turkish-Egyptian fleet, under Admiral Ibrahim Pasha, terrorised the Mediterranean until it was finally defeated at Navarino by the French, Russian and English under Vice Admiral Sir Edward Codrington on the twentieth of October 1827. But even after this, none of the great powers were keen to take on such a brave and fanatical enemy on the land.' Wordy Smith clears his throat before continuing. 'For a good deal of this time Russia saw Turkey as her greatest enemy and fought her constantly in an attempt to gain access from the land-locked Black Sea into the Mediterranean. Constantinople guarded the entrance to the Bosphorus and from there into the Sea of Marmara, down the Dardanelles into the Aegean and finally the Mediterranean. Russia never succeeded.'

'Yeah, sir, but all that Otto-Empire, like you says, that was a long time ago, we seen the Muslims in Egypt, they ain't much chop?' Hornbill suggests.

'Wogs in pyjamas,' Numbers Cooligan adds dismissively.

'It's true, the Turks are Muslims, but that's where the comparison ends. They are a fighting nation who goes to battle in the name of Allah. When a Turkish soldier dies in battle he believes he goes directly to Paradise, they are not a people who are afraid to die. Australia has been in existence for one hundred and twenty-seven years, to these people that's the day before yesterday. Believe me, they didn't give up when the Romans invaded, or the Crusaders, the British, the French, the Russians.' Lieutenant Ormington-Smith pauses, perhaps realising that the history lesson is going a bit beyond most of them.

'That right,' Ben interjects, 'so they ain't gunna be shitting their britches now, they'll be thinking we Australians just hatched from the latest batch of eggs in Farmer Brown's chookyard.'

'I should also remind you,' Wordy Smith continues, 'no more than a few weeks ago in an attempt to force their way up the Dardanelles the combined might of the British and French navies pounded the Turkish forts guarding the

Narrows with everything they could throw at them.' Then borrowing his vernacular from Ben the lieutenant concludes, 'And got their arses soundly kicked by the Turks once again.'

There is some laughter at this last remark for it is the first time the platoon has ever heard Wordy Smith express himself in anything but the most correct manner.

'These here Dardanelles where we's goin', Lieutenant,' Muddy Parthe asks, 'is they the same ones Russia tried to get and where the Poms and the Frogs got their arses kicked?'

'Quite right, Private, the Turks have been defending this narrowest part successfully for four hundred years.'

'So that's why we're goin' there, eh? To kick their arses back,' Brokenose Brodie exclaims, pleased with himself for seeing the plot so clearly.

It is probably the first time that the platoon truly knows why they are fighting the Turks and although Sir Ian Hamilton, the supreme commander of the campaign, is better informed than Muddy Parthe, his attitude to the Turkish soldier doesn't appear to be vastly different from that of Hornbill or Numbers Cooligan.

Surgeon-General Birrell has come to him to point out that he hasn't sufficient hospital ships and medical supplies to care for the wounded and has no way to get them off the beaches unless he uses the ships' boats. He is sharply rebuffed by Hamilton who tells him the need to get stores and equipment ashore as quickly as possible takes priority over wounded men.

Hamilton, if he assumes a low casualty rate, has obviously forgotten Europe's long and bloody history against the Turks. As it turns out, very little serious thought seems to have gone into the evacuation of the wounded by the staff officers at his H.Q.

Hamilton's order to the surgeon-general can only be

seen in one of two possible ways, either it is a lack of concern for the welfare of the men fighting under his command or he has a low opinion of the fighting capacity of the Sons of Allah.

If the first supposition is correct he is not the only general in this war to have a laissez-faire attitude to the number of men killed and wounded under his command. If the second, which is unlikely, for it is common knowledge among the officers who openly tell their men that casualties could be as high as thirty per cent, then quite simply Hamilton is guilty of gross incompetence. A good commander, given the time, is charged with planning a correct outcome for these components without having to sacrifice one for the other.

On their arrival on the island of Lemnos, just thirty miles from the Dardanelles, the weather hasn't improved. In fact, it is worse, with a strong wind blowing up a rough sea in the large but essentially shallow harbour at Mudros. This, in effect, means a postponement of the April 21st invasion. In the deeper, more treacherous waters of the Dardanelles, there would be no hope of successfully unloading the boats and getting troops ashore under such difficult conditions.

The wind continues for two more days, only moderating somewhat on the evening of the twenty-third. Meanwhile the men are made to practise getting into the small boats from their transports in the choppy conditions of Mudros Harbour. Even in the comparatively shallow water this proves to be a tricky exercise.

Just after noon on the twenty-fourth, the *Novian*, carrying the 5th Battalion together with the Brigade H.Q. and the Indian Army Mule Artillery, sails from Mudros to the Bay of Purnea on the northeast of the island. Although they sail into a stiff breeze all the way, the weather seems to be clearing and by sunset it has practically died down. Squinting into the setting sun, they see five battleships in line astern, slowly heading for the Dardanelles and a place which will eventually become known simply as Gallipoli. On board are the 3rd Brigade who will make the initial assault before the sun rises over Asia Minor.

After the moon sets, Ben's own transport slips its mooring and under a bright moon, sails the thirty miles to the spot on the map where the Anzac landing will take place. They arrive just as the 3rd Brigade is being lowered into boats, each man carrying ninety pounds of kit and equipment on his back. Many of them must climb down the steep sides of the battleships using rope ladders that are swinging wildly from the weight of the frantically clutching soldiers ahead of them, most of whom are fortified with a liberal supply of rum. Even with the practice they've undergone at Lemnos it proves a difficult and trying procedure, as it takes place in the inky darkness and with the added strain of what lies ahead. Fifteen thousand men are going into battle for the first time, in complete silence, jumping into little boats, which, to their great good fortune, are barely bobbing on a glass-calm sea. These are young men from a nation of beer drinkers, their heads a little fuzzy from the unaccustomed rum, each wondering to himself if he'll be good enough, courageous enough and won't let down his mates.

At 3 a.m. the moon sinks beyond the horizon. The cliffs they could clearly see under the moon now disappear in the pre-dawn darkness. The night is so densely dark that you can almost touch it. Only the soft pulse of the battleship's engines sends a slightly hollow sound against the hull to remind you that you are not alone.

It is a curious thing to be alone. You have become

accustomed to being identified by your group, your brigade, your company, your platoon, but most of all by your mates. Those blokes you have trained with, who crawled sweating beside you in the sand under the blazing desert sun, to whom you clung, bunched together, on the platform of the tram to Cairo, got drunk on arak in the bazaar, laughed and backslapped, chundered in an alley that smelt of piss and shit while your mate steadied you, jeered, chaffed and constantly mocked each other. You no longer belong to your own silence, this is your true identity now.

Each of you sits silent and remote, realising that the problem is the silence itself. That your mates are mostly known to you by the noises they make, the pitch of their voices, the nature of their wisecracks, their stupidity, shrewdness, shyness, boastfulness, bullshitting, modesty and easygoing comradeship, the expressions they use to announce themselves, their weaknesses and their strengths, never allowing you to see their fear, the fear you now feel yourself and think it must be yours alone.

All these things have been constantly with you for the past few months, they have become as familiar to you as rifle drill so that you can't imagine yourself as a separate part of the whole, or them as no longer a part of your life. And now, when you have to face the moment of truth, they are silent, you are silent, all the touchstones are gone. The familiar voices you have come to rely upon are gagged, the whingers and optimists, the cynics and those who believe with something that shines in their eyes, they're all silent in your rum-heated heart. In the pre-dawn chill there is only the creak of the rowlocks and the slap of a wave against the hull of the wooden lifeboat and the soft pulse of the engines within the dark hull looming up beside your fragile wooden boat.

You are aware for the first time since you stood in the

recruitment queue that you are alone, the hard flat wooden seat under your arse turning it numb and the pack on your back the only extension of yourself you are aware of. One towel, one extra vest, socks two pairs, greatcoat, cap, comforter, a change of underclothing (must die with clean underpants, remember throw away the pair you shit yourself in), three empty sandbags rolled up and neatly tied onto your shovel at the back. Three days' rations – two tins of bullybeef, Fray Bentos (doesn't sound Australian), three pounds of hard biscuits (the ones left over at Arnott's from the Boer War). Then the little white bag of iron rations tied around your neck, half an ounce of tea (no fuckin' billy), two ounces of sugar and a jar of extract of beef. Two hundred rounds of ammunition, your rifle and bayonet, the killing load three times as heavy as the food that will hopefully sustain you for the next seventy-two hours, that is if you're not shot right off coming out of the shallows with this heap of shit resting on your shoulders.

In the moonlight you clearly see the cliffs and the land rising steeply from the sea and the fall of land to flatness on the end to the north of a place the Turks called Gaba Tepe on the map, the obvious place to come ashore. But now you only face darkness.

It is a blackness where you know men with cold hands and broken fingernails blow on their clenched fists and wait, their rifles and machine guns oiled, barrels cleaned, spare magazine clips and ammunition belts in reserve, for you to announce your arrival on their land, their beloved country.

They are waiting on the same hills, facing the same coastline where their ancestors fought the Greeks and the Romans, and where they repulsed the Infidel Crusaders carrying their tortured Holy Cross before them into battle, their emaciated bodies and fair peeling skins burnt a crimson colour and their hard, hollow eyes fixed on the cross, prepared to die in the name of the Prophet Christ. Then there were the strutting French and the pompous British, both braided in gold and uniformed in red and blue, both nations vainglorious and arrogant to the point of infinite stupidity. And always, there was the bearded Russian bear trying to shoulder his way through the narrow and jealously guarded sea lanes, never quite learning that he faced a formidable enemy who never failed to singe his fur and send him scurrying back to the safety of the Black Sea.

And now, with spring arrived and the hope of the new wheat already greening the land, the tender shoots broken through the winter-hardened clods and the first of the scarlet poppies in bloom on the thistle and weed-fringed edges of the fields, comes a new tribe of men. Giants with loose shoulders and gangling, easy strides, infidels who have come from somewhere near the bottom of the earth and who are determined to destroy you, murder your innocent children and rape your wives.

And so once again the Turks must defy their entry and, in the name of the Prophet, show them their sharp, snarling teeth and be prepared, as always, to die fearlessly in the name of Allah and so gain a place in Paradise.

The boats are in four long lines, with a little coal-fired pinnace, its stack billowing smoke into the dark night, responsible for towing each line. It is infinitely slow work and, except for the soft throb of the steam engines on the sturdy little boats, one would marvel at the quiet. How can so many young men remain so still when they know that one in three of them may die before the sun sets again?

Suddenly the smokestack of one of the pinnaces sets fire, the leaping flames sending a signal of their arrival for miles, the mirror-calm sea reflecting the orange fire across a wide bay. Shit, if a match struck can be seen at sea for two miles then this inferno must be clearly seen in Constantinople itself. Yet there is no response from the cliffs lining the shore, which, as they draw closer, loom up like dark, unwelcoming shadows. The silence, the fucking silence, remains.

There is a shout, sudden and clear across the water. 'You are going the wrong way, bear over.' But no correction is made and the pinnace ahead maintains the same slow, determined, pulsing course. The voice calls again, 'Bear right, bear to starboard,' but to no avail, there seems to be an inevitability about where you will land, as though the rudder on the pinnace is stuck and it can only move directly ahead. Like all the other men in your boat you wonder what the suddenly shouted instruction must mean. How far are you off course? What will be the consequences? In the dark, how the hell does the voice know, you can't see him, how come he can see you? Why won't the pinnace bear to starboard, to the right, where in the moonlight you supposed the flatter ground to be? Any idjit can steer a flamin' boat in water calm as a mill pond.

And then the pinnace cuts the boats loose and the rowers take over, moving slowly in to the beach, the men behind the oars grunting and sweating in the dawn cold, their oars splashing as the waves created by the prows of the landing boats begin to build up.

The sudden, sharp flash of a searchlight in the distance, then another, both in the direction of Cape Helles, neither reaching you. And at last a half-heard instruction, 'Righto, lads, over the side.' The leap and the obscenely loud splash that follows as you hit the water, the relief as your boots touch the bottom. Tiny waves lap around your waist, your rifle is held above your shoulders as you attempt to wade ashore. Still dark, still safe, though the sky is beginning to lighten, the water cooling, tickling your balls. Then a single shot from the dark cliff ahead, its echo filling the silence so totally that it seems to resonate against the wall of stillness.

And then, in the words of Lance Corporal Mitchell, in the 10th Battalion, 'The key is turned in the lock of the lid of hell.'

Several of the landing boats are scythed by machine-gun fire, killing most of the men on board. Shrapnel pellets rain out of a dark sky, wounding and killing a great many of the men, the young, bright-eyed soldiers of Australia, alive at one moment, preparing to jump, and dead the next. One soldier remains seated as his comrades leap over the side, his sergeant, last but himself to jump, sees what he thinks is panic in his eyes, terror freezing him to the thwart. He reaches out to touch him, their eyes seem to meet for a moment and then the soldier topples forward into the bottom of the boat. He was dead all along, killed without a whimper, the bullet not even disturbing him in his seat. And the bullets and shrapnel pellets fall like summer hail.

The troops thresh through the water, some of them half-panicked but, trying to keep their heads, attempt to fix their bayonets. There isn't any point in firing a shot at the blank, dark wall ahead. Strict orders. 'No rifle fire is to be employed before broad daylight. The bayonet only.' Some stumble against a submerged rock and fall face-first into the surf, the kit on their back slamming them down like a fist to the back of the head, their arms and legs pumping adrenaline to get them up again. Others hit sudden unexpected depths and flailing desperately in the water their packs suck them downwards, mere arms lack the power to pull them back to the surface and they drown wearing full kit in a ring of bubbles. Others drop to their knees in the water with a soft exclamation, a low curse or a surprised bellow as a Mauser bullet smashes into them. They don't see the hole, the size of a baby's tightly clamped fist, or feel the churning together of lung and windpipe and bits of bone as the enemy's bullet enters their chest. The enemy has their range and, even without being able to see clearly, fires into the dark mass of men struggling towards the narrow strip of beach below. Ben is quite wrong, this isn't work for a sniper, this is shooting fish in a barrel. When the dawn finally comes, the surf is seen to wash a frothy deep pink onto the pebbled beach.

The order is for every man to fall in and fix bayonets. It goes further even than this, each man, with his free hand, is to hold onto the sleeve of the man beside him on a beach no more than thirty yards wide. In truth, if anyone had been stupid enough to obey this command it would be the equivalent of being deliberately lined up in front of a firing squad. 'Here you go, Johnny Turk, take your time, aim true, we'll die brave men, steady and stupid to the last.'

Instead, the troops, many of whom toss off their packs as they reach the beach, shouting like demons, rush for the cliffs, men of every company, every battalion hopelessly mixed, sergeants and officers scattered, yelling for their own blokes. Nobody listening. A Turkish battery, concealed in the half-light from the guns of the battleships who commence to pound the cliffs, bursts shrapnel over the landing troops unmercifully. Ears are not tuned to commands, orders have no significance, no meaning, the men no longer know what to do and there is no single command which can possibly make sense. Their briefing has never encompassed or anticipated anything like this. They have landed a mile further north than was intended and, instead of a steady climb, no higher than a good desert dune, they face cliffs and high ground on which no army could or would, in their right mind, contemplate an invasion. In military theory, the Anzacs are defeated before they have fired a single shot in anger.

And so, as the light grows stronger, the Anzacs climb for their lives. The beach behind them is littered with bodies and discarded packs as the men run for cover across the pebbles. Hanging around for orders is certain death, there is no military manual for this, no precedent. And so it becomes a matter of climb or die, clutching onto bush and thorn, root and rock. Boots scuff the hard red soil, sending pebbles and small rocks avalanching onto the beach below. One thought in every soldier's mind is to get off the beach, find cover, move upward, hope you see the bastard before he sees you. Stuff the bayonet, stuff a clip into your rifle. Ram one into the breech and get as far away as possible from a beach which is maybe four hundred yards long but no wider than your mum's backyard and packed with soldiers like newborn chicks in a hatchery.

The immediate slopes ahead of them are very abrupt, rising higher to the north like the walls of some eroding Crusader castle, gaunt canyons are set back slightly further from the beach and appear to be unclimbable. Once up on the slopes it quickly becomes obvious that they are a far more difficult proposition than supposed as they are broken by deep ridges, curving narrow valleys and eroded soil carved into red crumbling gullies twisting in and out of almost inaccessible funnels. Rock outcrops and deep basins, the whole of it, with the exception of the rocky, eroded gullies and cliffs, is covered with dense scrub, much of it vicious thorn. It is a virtual paradise for snipers who, having first had time to study the more likely routes to the top, can position themselves to tremendous advantage. It is not the height of the various ridges that is extraordinary but the steepness and abrupt changes of direction and the general slope which make it almost impossible for advancing infantry and virtually inaccessible for practical or co-ordinated artillery fire.

The entire battle area from extreme north to south is a mile and a half in length and exactly a thousand yards from the beach to the furthest point. In all, it is an area no larger than three-quarters of a square mile. Unbeknownst to many of the urgently climbing troops they often enough rush right past snipers, concealed in the bushes and behind rocks, who take their time to pick their kill.

The sun is well up by seven-thirty when the second wave comes in to run a well-aimed gauntlet of shrapnel, sniper and machine-gun fire. Those on the outer extremity of the beach will lie in the wash and the sun for two days before they are removed. Others, drowned by the weight of their packs, will float to the surface in the next few days. The boats and rafts bringing in supplies will become accustomed to the soft thud of a body as they bump it aside, for if there is no time to attend to the wounded, there is no space left in their minds for the dead.

Ben loses five men from his boat, Matthews and Jolly among them as they sit together one row behind him. Matthews is hit in the throat and, pitching forward, spews blood onto the pack of a soldier named Parker seated on the thwart next to Ben, who grabs him before he pitches against Parker. Warm blood spews over Ben's fist and he sees that the Mauser bullet has torn open Matthews' throat and lodged in his spine. Matthews seems to be looking directly into Ben's face. The soldier's eyes remain bright, alive, for a moment longer, then as suddenly glaze in death. Ben lets him fall forward onto the wooden grating on the bottom of the steel boat, the private's rifle bumping against his arm.

Numbers Cooligan, his eyes wide with terror, grabs Jolly as he's knocked backwards by the force of a machine-gun bullet, another of which catches one of the navy rowers on the port side. The sailor slumps forward, still clutching his oar until the movement of the boat tears it from his lifeless hands. Both men are killed instantly.

'Oh, Jesus,' Cooligan cries, then begins to sob, his hand holding the dead Jolly as though it is permanently clamped to his collar. The young naval midshipman in charge of their boat signals to Ben that it's time to disembark into the shallow water.

'Righto, lads, into the water, keep your eye out for me as we come ashore!' Ben is surprised at how steady his voice sounds, for he can feel his stomach clutching in fear and Matthews' blood sticky between the fingers of his left hand. 'Cooligan, leave him!' Ben shouts. 'He's dead. Get into the water, will yah!'

Ben makes a quick count as the men leap overboard, he is the last to leave and sees that five of his platoon plus the naval rating are slumped or have fallen. All appear to be dead for none of them moves, and the remaining fifteen of the twenty fighting men in the platoon make it into the water. Twenty yards to his left is another boat drifting helplessly, at least half of its complement dead or dying. Several of the oars are missing though two are stuck in the rowlocks, causing the boat to turn in circles. Ben jumps into the water which comes up to his waist. Shrapnel pellets send puffs of water and spray around him everywhere, the whine of bullets stings the air and the entire stretch of water running up to the beach ahead of him is plopping like sudden rain on a pond. He trails his left hand in the water, trying to wash Matthews' blood from his hand, and is barely aware of the thunder of the guns from the battleship sending salvo after salvo into the heights where it believes the Turkish positions to be. The threshing of the water about his pumping legs is by far the greater sound. Bodies are floating everywhere and he bumps against several. Closer to the beach he hits a pebble bottom, the small round pebbles causing his boots to slip and slide, but he manages to maintain his balance as he reaches the wash.

The beach is littered with early morning corpses lying sprawled as though asleep in the hot sun. Others, only just wounded, are crawling up the beach. Directly ahead of him a soldier lies on his stomach in the wash and Ben sees that a large piece of shrapnel, probably a razor-sharp section of a shell casing, has neatly sliced off his pack without having touched the man, its straps still attached to his shoulders. He has either been knocked unconscious or the shock of the impact has made him think he is dead, but left with his face in the wash he is likely to drown. Ben grabs hold of the webbing attached to the man's shoulders and pulls him up to his knees. There is a sudden gasp and gurgle from the man as he opens his eyes. 'Jaysus, I thought I were in heaven an' all!' he says.

'Keep running, Irish, and you'll live to fight another day!' Ben hauls at the webbing again and the man stands up. 'Git the hell out o' here, lad,' Ben shouts, and pushes him forward across the pebbly beach. Ahead he catches sight of the huge lumbering shape of Brokenose Brodie, his rifle held high above his head as if a signal for others in the platoon. Then he sees Cooligan, Spencer, Rigby and Mustafa all running up to the big man. Horne and Parthe, usually found with the others, are missing from the group. He is not aware that he is shouting, 'Number two platoon, come, come!' though it is quite impossible to be heard above the enemy fire.

This time there is a great deal less confusion on the beach. Several officers doing duty as guides stand calmly some thirty feet from the water's edge and with shrapnel bursting in the air over them they read the shoulder patches of the men as they stumble ashore and immediately direct them by way of hand signals in the general direction of their companies. It is apparent at once to Ben that they have landed too far to the right, too close to the Gaba Tepe end of the cove where the Turkish field guns can more easily reach them. Moreover, the part of the slope they have been briefed to attack is some considerable way to the left of where they now are.

He looks for Peregrine Ormington-Smith, who was in the second of the three boats carrying the platoon. All Ben can see are men milling in confusion, but groups like his own are beginning to bunch and he runs towards the five members of his platoon that Brodie has managed to gather together. On the way an officer sees his shoulder patch. '5th Battalion to my right, Sergeant,' he shouts, pointing. Ben reaches the five men gathered at the top of the beach standing in comparative safety under a slight overhang to the cliff face.

'Righto, lads,' he puffs. 'Packs off for the moment, take a break, the company's down this end,' he says, pointing south to a small fold between the ends of two ridges running parallel down to the cove. 'We'll move out as soon as you've all caught your breath, but scatter wide, nobody within four or five feet of the other, no bunching, you hear? Avoid other groups, a sniper will always go for the biggest target in his sights.' They rest up for five minutes, watching the confusion on the perimeter. There are some troops walking, trying to show they're not afraid or perhaps too dazed and confused to know any better, others have unclipped and discarded their packs and are running down the beach for dear life. Ben looks at the five men. 'We're shitting ourselves, that's an order, when you get back onto the main part of the beach, run like scared rabbits! Packs on, let's be off, lads, full pack, everyone, the only thing we leave behind is our flamin' footprints.'

'And a shit-streak or two,' Crow Rigby quips.

The lads arrive to find Lieutenant Peregrine Ormington-Smith with all twenty members of the platoon in his boat present. Remarkably, his landing boat made it onto the beach without a single casualty. They have taken shelter hard against a clay bank within the slight fold made by the two ridges, which now contains a mass of confused men. Officers are checking shoulder patches and trying frantically to sort them into their correct companies.

Wordy Smith tells Ben that they witnessed the third boat carrying the remaining ten members of their platoon take a direct hit by a large shell. The boat simply disappeared in a huge flash. The only evidence of its existence comes with the afternoon tide when several dozen broken and splintered oars with various landing boat numbers marked on them are washed up onto the shore. They are gathered, with other combustibles, by members of the Engineers Unit stationed at Hell Spit and piled up outside the depot to be used as firewood.

Among these are the oars belonging to the landing boats ferrying B Company of the 7th Battalion. Heading in to the beach on the second landing, four of the boats somehow managed to drift or were mistakenly rowed to the outside perimeter of the cove, coming under the direct fire of four machine guns. All the rowers were almost instantly killed and their oars were smashed or lost overboard. The boats then drifted helplessly, making the troops in them an easy target for the machine guns. The few who managed to abandon ship and get to the shore were cut down. Only two men in the four landing boats survived, crossing the pebbled beach and hiding in the scrub, where they were rescued two days later.

'I cannot tell you how immensely pleased I am to see you, Sergeant, a chap has been terribly concerned,' Wordy Smith says, extending his hand. Ben takes it in his own and the lieutenant shakes it over-vigorously. In his excitement he has unconsciously reverted to the syntax and accent of his English public school.

'Who've we got, sir?' Ben asks, still panting heavily from the sprint. He rapidly counts the men. 'Thirty-four, one missing, five dead in my boat and the ten who took a direct hit in the third, we should have thirty-five.'

To everyone's surprise, Wordy Smith starts to call out the names of every member of the platoon. He knows which ten were in the third boat and abstains from naming them and as he calls the name of each of the four dead in Ben's boat, Ben simply says, 'Didn't make it ashore, sir.' When he's called all the names and each man has answered he pauses and says quietly, 'Private Horne is missing, let's hope he eventually finds us.'

Ben now calls out, 'Privates Flynn, Phillips and Spencer, step up!' Library and the two others move to stand in front of Ben. 'Where are your packs, lads?' Ben asks.

Library elects to speak for them. 'Dropped them, Sergeant.'

'Where?'

'On the beach,' Phillips says while Flynn nods.

'In the water, Sergeant, I . . . I panicked,' Library admits miserably, his head bowed.

'Back onto the beach you three, pick up a discarded pack, a full kit, nothing missing, shovel or pick axe as well. Did you drop yer rifles?'

'No, Sergeant!' the three of them chorus.

'Now bugger off, and get back here at the double . . . and keep yer flamin' heads down!'

The three members of the platoon return humping packs, Library Spencer with a shovel and the other two with picks attached. 'You're on a charge, the three of you,' Ben says. 'We'll sort it out later.'

The situation, by the time the 2nd Brigade arrives in the second wave, is perilous. Earlier, the men of the 3rd Brigade who had survived the landing made no attempt to find their companies, but in the total confusion they set out in isolated groups, 'penny packets', to climb after the unseen enemy. As they attempted to scramble up the rocky cliff face and steep ridges beyond, the Turkish snipers picked them off willy-nilly. Soon enough, some of the most intrepid of these unattached groups reached the first ridge, their shapes silhouetted clearly against the skyline. Those coming behind them, thinking at last they were seeing the enemy, fired at them. Suddenly those keenest and in the most advanced positions found themselves sandwiched between the Turkish snipers still higher up on the second ridge and their own rifle fire coming from below. Many of them perished in the hail of misdirected bullets.

However, instead of waiting for their own troops to catch up with them, they are driven on by the fact that, from time to time, they witness the enemy vanishing into the dark tangle of gullies ahead of them, their shooting dying away, and so they think that victory must be close at hand. They thrust further and further inland, isolating themselves completely. They are encouraged in this perception when some of the Turkish soldiers, seeing the Australians catching up, throw down their arms and surrender. But the attacking soldiers, determined not to be slowed down by taking prisoners, simply shoot them and continue on in pursuit.

The advancing troops are unaware that the Turks, not expecting a landing north of the Gaba Tepe headland, only have a single company guarding the slopes. But not far behind Sari Bair, the very topmost ridge and the most important objective for the Australians, there are several companies of Turkish reinforcements who are no more than half an hour's marching distance away.

Just before five o'clock Turkish shrapnel begins to burst among the troops along the ridges and shortly after nine the enemy reinforcements arrive. The Anzacs near the top of the second ridge see them advancing towards them. The Turkish counterattack moves up the valleys, outflanking the Australian outposts on their left, driving the scattered groups backwards and in the process killing a great many men of the 3rd Brigade.

The Anzacs are not to know that the keenest among them would reach no further than their initial attack in the hours immediately after dawn on the first day until after the surrender of Turkey in 1918. Someone had blundered terribly. Strategically the landing at Gallipoli had failed.

Hamilton, the supreme commander, has vastly underestimated the enemy and, to boot, possesses a sense of geography that is to cost his Australian and New Zealand troops dearly, not to mention the English, Indians and French who also die like flies in what, within the context of the total war in Europe, is considered a relatively minor diversion.

In Australian and New Zealand terms it is a terrible sacrifice. As young growing nations, they can ill afford a vital part of their life seed to be sacrificed in places with names such as Baby 700, Lone Pine Hill, Courtney's Post, Quinn's Post, 400 Plateau, The Nek and what will, in time, become known as Anzac Cove.

But now, with the sun not long up, the Turkish troops have been reinforced and are advancing from the heights above the Australians. The first Australian wave is pushed back predominantly on the left flank where they dig in, hoping to hold the line. The Anzac forces in the centre and the right, or southern, flank are increasingly being sucked into the left flank, thinking to reinforce the line where the fighting appears to be the fiercest.

Subsequently, the centre and southern flanks become too thinly manned and are exposed to a Turkish attack, threatening disaster for the whole assault.

It is here, on the southern flank, that the 2nd Brigade coming into the beach in the second wave will be sent. This time, despite the fierce hail of artillery, shrapnel, machine-gun and rifle fire, which is considerably heavier than the reception given the 3rd Brigade in the first wave, the troops are directed to an assembly point, which proves relatively safe from enemy fire.

Here they are organised into their companies or assigned to new platoons if their own has been decimated. The act of reassembling is by no means all calmness and order, instead it is a process of stop–start, with officers screaming commands at confused troops, their own senior officers frequently countermanding their instructions in a similar manner. But somehow the officers and N.C.O.s given the task of organising the troops back into a fighting unit manage to get a sufficiently concerted force together. This allows the brigade commander, Colonel M'Cay, to assemble the means to reinforce the scattered remnants of the 9th Battalion, who are grimly holding their positions on the southern flank against a now increasingly fierce Turkish counterattack.

Shortly after eight o'clock in the morning with the 5th Company in reasonably compact order, Wordy Smith returns from a short briefing. Major Sayers, their company commander, gives the platoon officers their map co-ordinates and tells them they will be advancing up the southern flank known on the military maps as 400 Plateau where they will reinforce the 10th Battalion from the first wave who have been damn near decimated.

'Packs on, bayonets fixed, let's get out of here,' Ben tells his platoon. Whereas the platoon officer would usually give the order to march out, such is the understanding between

Peregrine Ormington-Smith and his sergeant that they simply communicate quietly with each other, with Ben, for the most part, instructing the platoon. Anyone looking on from the outside would assume the incompetence in Wordy Smith still exists. However, since leaving Lemnos the platoon commander has shown that he is not beyond the task of leading his troops. He simply understands he has a first-class sergeant who knows the ropes and who will consult him when needed. Peregrine Ormington-Smith is without the slightest pretension and the relationship between the two men is completely free of rivalry.

Moreover, perhaps because of his countless forays into the wild to find the specimens for his flower paintings, Wordy Smith will show that he has a capacity to read the nature of the terrain and that he can anticipate what is to come in the field with uncanny accuracy.

The platoon now begins to climb the steep and arduous slope. With their packs on their backs it is an enormous struggle up the narrow tracks and they find it difficult to keep up with those platoons that have abandoned their packs on the beach and carry nothing but their iron rations about their necks, their rifles with bayonets fixed, and a little spare ammunition.

'S'not bloody fair,' Numbers Cooligan gasps. 'Look at them other bastards, rifle and just their webbing, ammo pouches, water bottle and iron rations, bugger-all else.'

'Ah, stop whingeing, Numbers, it's your fault anyway,' Crow Rigby calls.

'My fault! Shit, why?'

'With a pack on yer back yer can't run away, Ben knows this and so as not to embarrass yer, we've all got to carry 'em.'

'Ah, you're fulla bullshit, Crow. I'll soon enough be watching your skinny arse fleeing back down towards the beach, no risk, mate.'

'No flamin' way, mate, it's much too dangerous down there.'

And so the usual silly young-bloke banter and jocularity goes on among them, to keep their minds from dwelling on the battle to come. On their way up through Shrapnel Valley they pass several hundred dead men and soon realise the danger they face. The stark reality of warfare is beginning to sink in.

The first of the reinforcements under M'Cay, mostly the men without packs on their backs, arrive at the lip of the plateau. His orders are to advance across it so that they can get in with their bayonets among the Turks on the third ridge. With no telephone wires yet laid the brigade commander is unaware that the rest of the line at the centre and the north is pinned down with no hope of advancing and that for him to cross 400 Plateau and, on his own, attack his objective, the third ridge, is pointless. He can't possibly outflank the Turks who are too well dug in on the high ground above the plateau.

The sensible thing to do is to simply dig in and become the southern part of the front line, to stop just before reaching the lip of the plateau and take cover on the reverse slope. M'Cay sees at once that the plateau is covered with the bodies of the 9th Battalion from the first wave. With all their officers dead, the scattered elements remaining have dug in under the lip and are simply trying to survive the Turkish onslaught from the ridge beyond the plateau.

Deciding he has fresh troops and is part of a front line committed to advance across the full front, Colonel M'Cay believes he has no option but to take his men across 400 Plateau and to dig in on the other side if it should become necessary.

This proves to be a suicidal decision as the Turks on the higher slopes are reinforced, far better organised now, and virtually concealed from the Australian forces. The numbers no longer stacked against them, the Turks can stand and fight. What the Australians thought was cowardice in the Wog army was simply tactical prudence, they are in a position to call all the shots and if M'Cay attempts to cross the plateau his men are, almost certainly, dead meat.

Ben arrives with his platoon soon after the first of the 5th Battalion troops are being fed over the rim and told to cross the plateau. Crawling up to the rim, he can immediately see what is taking place. The men attempting to cross are being cut down in waves. Not only are they subject to a hailstorm of Turkish rifle and machine-gun fire, but heavy artillery from behind the third range is raining down on them, cascading scythes of white-hot shrapnel cutting them to pieces.

'We should dig in here under the lip, sir. Then, if we have to, cross the plateau tonight,' he says to Wordy Smith, who has crept up and now lies beside him.

Peregrine Ormington-Smith nods. 'It's not just crossing, Sergeant, unless I'm very much mistaken this plateau dips down into a gully, a basin at its end.' He points to the plateau running away from them. 'This flat ground is like the handle on a spoon. Not only do the Turks have us at their mercy as we cross down the handle but what's left of us will simply be herded like sheep into the spoon. For them it's like looking down into a street jammed shoulder to shoulder with people, every shot they fire will hit someone.' He looks grimly at Ben. 'If we persist in this, the entire battalion is likely to be wiped out, possibly the brigade. I'll see if I can find the C.O., get further instructions, it's sheer madness to continue like this. In the meantime, carry on, Ben . . . oh, er, Sergeant.'

'That's all right, sir, matter of fact, I've been meaning to talk to you about that. It seems to me that while we're fighting, that is in the course of battle, me referring to a soldier as "Private" followed by his name is too wasteful of time, far better to say his surname or even his Christian name and, well, vice versa, they can call me Ben or Sarge. All of this strictly applying only within the platoon, of course?'

Wordy Smith laughs. 'Peregrine, or for that matter Ormington-Smith, is hardly an abbreviation, Ben.'

'Right. In your case, sir, why don't we simply continue with "sir", it's the quickest of the lot.'

The lieutenant nods, not looking up. Ben can see he's thinking, then he faces him. 'I wouldn't . . . er would you mind? I mean, I'd rather prefer to be called Wordy.'

'Seems like a bloody silly conversation to be having with the shit hitting the fan all around us,' Ben says. He slides down the slope, pushing himself backwards on his belly until he is sufficiently far down to stand erect without exposing his head above the rim. 'From now on it's just names among us, no more sergeant or lieutenant or private, just whatever we're called among ourselves.'

'Righto, Ben,' Numbers Cooligan calls quick as a flash.

'You'll keep, Cooligan,' Ben says as a Turkish shell bursts alarmingly close, sending shrapnel whining over their heads. 'Let's dig in, lads, ain't it grand we brought our picks and shovels.'

'Bastard's right as usual,' Crow Rigby sighs as he unties his shovel from the back of his pack. 'What about them poor bastards who didn't bring nothin', eh Numbers?'

'What gives me the shits is he didn't ask me for *my* permission to call me by me Christian name!' Numbers Cooligan says, conveniently changing the subject.

'Ah, you're fulla shit, Numbers,' Woggy Mustafa says, bringing his pick axe down into the hard earth at his feet.

'Is that a Wog or a Christian opinion coming from you, Mustafa?' Numbers Cooligan asks, picking up his shovel and starting to dig.

'It is a truth that crosses all religious boundaries,' Crow Rigby laughs.

They begin to dig in furiously and, almost as if by telepathy, others on their left and right, those who possess the good fortune to own a pick or shovel, start to do the same.

Brokenose Brodie is wielding his pick with an easy rhythm and Library Spencer beside him is shovelling the clods away as fast as possible as they work in concert, though plainly Library is unable to keep up. He rests for a moment, exhausted, leaning on his shovel. 'I wonder where Hornbill got to?' he says suddenly. The five friends working in the same proximity all stop abruptly, it is as though they have been waiting for someone to bring it up and by voicing their own thoughts Library has somehow admitted the likelihood that their mate is dead, copped one, killed on the beach or in the water.

'Ah, he'll turn up,' Muddy Parthe volunteers at last. 'Look't me, I got lost comin' ashore, separated from youse blokes.'

'Yeah, but in *your* case we was hoping it was permanent, that you'd decided to join another platoon,' Numbers Cooligan remarks.

'Ha bloody ha! If I did, it would be to get away from you, mate.'

Nothing further is said and they return to their digging.

The slaughter taking place on the plateau no more than a few feet above their heads is now apparent to every soldier. The troops are rapidly becoming conscious that going over the lip on 400 Plateau means almost certain death. They all think that if they can wait until nightfall and cross they will be able to get among the Turks with their bayonets.

With their trench no more than eighteen inches dug into the hard red clay, Wordy Smith returns. He is grim-faced as he talks to Ben. 'We're all ordered over the top, Ben. The C.O.'s got his orders. Colonel M'Cay says nobody stays behind and insists on pressing on with the attack, his intention is to take the third ridge before nightfall.' He shrugs. 'It seems we'll be letting down the advance of the centre and the left flanks if we remain here and dig in.'

'The centre and the left flanks are advancing?' Ben asks, sounding doubtful. 'Do we know that for sure? There are no telephone wires up yet, no communication?'

Wordy Smith shrugs helplessly. 'No, it's only assumed.'

'Assumed! Fucking assumed!' Ben cries incredulously. It is the first time anyone has seen him blow his stack and he quickly reins himself in. 'Bloody M'Cay looking for a promotion or something, is he?' he adds bitterly. He turns away from Wordy and looks upwards to the Turkish positions and says quietly to himself, 'As Ikey Solomon would say, "He's fucking meshuggeneh!"'

Platoon officers, brandishing their Webley revolvers above their heads in some macabre form of battlefield tallyho, followed by their men, continue to pour up over the rim, attempting to cross 400 Plateau. By now, less than half an hour after their arrival, the entire area of the plateau is littered with new corpses, a second sacrifice to add to the Turkish killing orgy. Only this time there are vastly more Turks on the slopes above them.

Wounded men, abandoning their rifles, attempt to crawl on their hands and knees back to the safety of their comrades. In the process, they are picked off by the Turkish snipers. Often two or three bullets hit a wounded soldier, his body jerking with each impact, then he lies still, sprawled, spiderlike, with his face against the hard ground, quivering like a rabid dog shot in the street. In a matter of moments his wounds are set upon by a thick swarm of flies. One soldier still crawling back towards the rim has taken a direct hit in the face and the blood pours from his nose, his mouth, even his eyes, though this can scarcely be seen as the flies completely obscure what's left of his features, turning the entire front surface of his smashed and broken head into a blank, black, buzzing horror.

The Indian Mountain guns are firing willy-nilly into the ridge directly above them and are seemingly as effective as a popgun fired at a brick wall, their aim too unco-ordinated to do any real damage to an enemy well dug in and damn near invisible.

It makes absolutely no sense when crossing the plateau to return the rifle fire, it simply delays the run for cover and, besides, there is nothing to aim at. Firing bullets, even machine-gun bullets, into a blank mountainside is a fruitless occupation. The only way they can possibly hope to engage the enemy is by means of a bayonet charge at close quarters. And if Wordy Smith is correct, they won't ever get that far up the slope. In the unlikely event that they make it across the plateau, the handle of the spoon, in any numbers, the spoon is waiting to dish them up piecemeal to the Turks.

'Stow your picks and shovels, get your packs onto your backs, lads,' Ben now orders, then bends down and ties his shovel to the back of his pack and hoists his kit onto his shoulders. Those who watch him are strangely comforted by the sight of the Maori fighting axe in its holster on the side of his pack, a more inappropriate and useless weapon for the circumstances they are about to encounter can scarcely be imagined. But it is their proven talisman and they take heart from it. They also see a red bandanna tied to a buckle on the back of his pack. It is the one given to him by Victoria to wave from the deck of the *Orvieto* when she and Hawk came to farewell him. 'Righto, don't bunch, yer hear?' Ben instructs them. 'Stay well apart, it's no more than a hundred yards across, we can do it in thirty seconds flat, keep low, don't run in a straight line, you all know the drill.'

He turns his back on them and it appears as though he is buckling the chest strap of his pack. None of them see him pull the little green Tiki from beneath his shirt and briefly touch it to his lips. Ben turns and looks at Wordy Smith. The lieutenant nods. Ben turns back to the men. 'Right then, follow me, lads. Keep yer eyes fixed on the red rag at my back, we're going over now, we'll all meet on the other side.'

'Precisely what "other side" is that?' Crow Rigby says softly to himself and watches as Numbers Cooligan makes the sign of the cross.

Chapter Fourteen

BEN AND COMPANY

Shaking Hands with the Shadows

Ben's platoon is positioned on the southern side of 400 Plateau and looking over their shoulder they can see the low black promontory of Gaba Tepe as it intersects the wide arc of Suvla Bay, its Aegean waters sparkling in the bright morning sun. The plateau is covered with low gorse-like scrub, reaching not much above the waist, though it grows in patches with open ground between. It is good cover for a soldier remaining still, but not well suited for forward movement. Directly ahead of him at about four hundred yards is perhaps the narrowest section of the plateau which begins to slope away to an area known as Lonesome Pine, the name of a popular song. This name for the gently sloping hillside came about because among the juniper and scrub stands a single stunted pine tree. Lonesome Pine will soon enough be changed to Lone Pine in the way that Australians have of chopping any extraneous syllable from a word without changing its essential meaning.

Wordy Smith points out to Ben that this southern slope, protected somewhat by the Gaba Tepe headland to the south and positioned at a slightly oblique angle to the sea, doesn't get the full force of the wind. This, in turn,

497

means the juniper and scrub are higher and grow in bigger and denser clumps than on the flatter section of the plateau. He reasons that with the land falling away from the third ridge a man's height is even further reduced, making him a slightly smaller target for the enemy rifle and machine-gun fire. It means they must move in an arc rather than take the shortest route across the plateau.

Ben estimates this will add perhaps another hundred yards to the distance, another four or five minutes of exposure to the hellfire coming from the Turks. But to counterbalance this, Wordy Smith suggests they will avoid falling into the spoon where they can easily be killed, the proposition being that machine-gun and rifle fire is instinctively aimed at the most obvious and nearest target and artillery fire where the greatest force is concentrated.

Ben agrees that the plan is the better of two fairly poor options. He is first over the rim, followed by Wordy Smith and the remainder of the platoon, who are staggered left and right at an interval of approximately four yards between each man. They have practised this drill in the desert where little concealment exists and advancing troops are trained to break into a haphazard formation of single-man targets.

Once on the plateau they can see it is literally covered with the bodies of the dead infantrymen and most of the dead soldiers are already black with flies. Many of them belong to the 3rd Brigade but, after only half an hour of coming over the rim, M'Cay's 2nd Brigade is dying at a much faster rate than during the early morning slaughter. The men trying to cross the plateau form a perfect target for the Turkish artillery, who actually look down at the Australians in a semicircle of heights from Battleship Hill in the north to Gaba Tepe in the south.

If one can imagine an amphitheatre, the plateau becomes its stage and the seats near the top are the enemy artillery positions from which all movement and space on 400 Plateau can be covered. To take the analogy further, the audience in the Greek amphitheatre are the Turks, with rifles and machine guns, and the Australians are the hapless actors.

The Turkish gunfire from the ridge is even more concerted than on the beach. The guns on the plateau have gained a steady rhythm and every thirty seconds a salvo of four shells falls, covering a large part of the plateau as a moving garden spray might water a lawn. Two enemy batteries, one at Chunuk Bair in the north and the other at Scrubby Knoll in the south, are the deadliest. Depending on where the largest concentration of Australians appear on the plateau, these two batteries shorten or lengthen their range like a fire hose playing on flames. The result, no single salvo is missed.

It becomes apparent to M'Cay after the very first troops are sent over the rim that the attempt to get his 2nd Brigade across must fail. A simple estimation of the dead already lying on the plateau after the initial attempt by the 3rd Brigade must tell him that there can be no front line to reinforce. Simple arithmetic indicates there are too many factors against him, the combination of Turkish firepower and the vastly superior and impregnable position they hold on the ridge directly above him means the odds are hopelessly stacked against him. His troops, pouring, as they mostly do, from the handle down into the bowl of the spoon, become, in effect, sitting ducks, unable to do anything more than attempt to conceal themselves from the Turkish guns directly above them. The likelihood of any of them mounting a further attack on the Turkish positions simply does not exist.

Colonel M'Cay is slaughtering his men, thinking only to slavishly obey his misdirected orders without accepting the responsibility to call it off. His men can never reach and effectively reinforce the isolated pockets of the decimated 3rd Brigade who are dug in beyond the plateau and now find themselves pinned down by the Turks. The first rule in the military handbook is that in a rescue operation you do not sacrifice more men than you hope to save.

M'Cay should dig in along a line on the plateau and wait until nightfall for the isolated pockets of the 3rd Brigade to join him in the trenches he has prepared. It is a strategy any junior subaltern could devise and it would save the lives of countless men.

Thus begins a day in which the Turks, far from admiring the courage of the Australians, wonder at the stupidity of the infidels and the commanders directing them. They take great heart from what they witness on 400 Plateau. This is an enemy to be laughed at. Even the humblest Turkish recruit knows that stupidity, even brave stupidity, seldom wins battles.

Stupidity in the time of war is usually put down to a lack of critical information by those responsible for it. It takes a long time for history to point an accusing finger at an errant and inadequate commander, and by then it is usually too late and he is out of the firing line or has been promoted to a higher rank.

Commanders who substitute men for ideas and approach a battle with complete disregard for saving the lives of the troops under their command almost always turn battles into killing fields without being granted victory as the prize.

On the first day on Gallipoli, from the beach landing in the pearl-grey dawn to the splashed and brilliant sunset over Asia Minor, nearly four thousand men are killed, countless others are wounded. The majority of these deaths occur at two places, on the landing beach and later on 400 Plateau.

Once the foolishness of invading Gallipoli had been decided upon, the attrition rate caused by landing from the sea onto a well-defended shore could scarcely be avoided. It is a price an invading army must expect to pay. But the slaughter at 400 Plateau was not necessary.

However, the manner of fighting the Turk on the Gallipoli Peninsula demonstrated on the first day on 400 Plateau by the brigadiers M'Cay and, to a slightly lesser extent, MacLagan sets the pattern for the Australian commanders on several other occasions.

Gallipoli was always intended to be a diversion, a ploy to make the Turks think that the main attack was to come from the high ground to the north so that they would concentrate their strength and effort on the Australians while the British and French invaded the flat ground south of Gaba Tepe.

In the end, seven months later, two hundred and forty thousand men will have been wounded, over forty thousand killed on the Allied side. The Turks never counted their dead, except in counting them fortunate, for they had been grasped to the bosom of Allah as heroes and consigned to Paradise. But it is estimated that they suffered much the same attrition rate as those who dared to invade their ancient land.

And so more than half a million young warriors were wounded or died in a series of battles and endless skirmishes that never reached further inland than a man could walk at a brisk pace in half an hour from the pebbled beach and which, in the overall scheme of things, didn't amount to a fart in a hurricane.

Ben doesn't rush things, making use of whatever cover is available, effectively using the gorse and scrub or a sudden dip or hollow in the terrain and making a dash across the open ground in between, resting up under the cover after every dash. It is careful progress where time is not the principal ingredient and after a while the platoon grows accustomed to the procedure and uses it skilfully.

However, this method of crossing contrasts strongly with the one adopted by a great many of the men who attempted to make a singular dash for it, running in a more or less straight line directly into the path of the remorseless enemy fire.

It may have been that the men were not properly briefed on the distance they needed to cover to get across the plateau or they lost the leadership of their officers who knew at what pace to take them out. Whatever, in the sudden decision to send them over the rim, a great many soldiers did not appear to have thought out how they might sensibly cover the five or, in some cases, six hundred yards across while carrying a rifle and a ninety-pound pack.

Distance in hilly terrain is easily misjudged anyway and the plateau may have seemed much shorter than it proves to be. Men set off, running for their lives, and soon enough they find themselves brought to an untimely halt, not just by the enemy, but by their own physical exhaustion.

Many bend to grab their knees, gasping for breath unable to move forward. Being stationary or slow-moving targets, they hardly merit the attention of the snipers with their Mausers and telescopic sights, who concentrate mainly on killing the officers. Instead, they become easy targets for the more modest shots among the Turkish infantry and are certain kills for the barking enemy machine guns.

The wounded have to fend for themselves. Officers, those few who haven't been killed or wounded, are forced to press on and not endanger the remainder of their platoons by stopping to check on their wounded men. The wounded beg pathetically for help or plead to be taken back to the line. Others simply cry out for their mothers and some lie down and die, shivering in the blazing sun as the cold hands of death embrace them. They are fraternising with death, shaking hands with the shadows as the Anzac saying goes. While some of the men do stop to help a mate in trouble there is little they can do except attempt to take them back behind the lines and, as often as not, they join the dead or lie wounded beside a comrade.

Ben loses two men in his platoon, both from shrapnel pellets, which even concealment in the scrub cannot prevent. Private Woodridge and Lance Corporal Phillips are killed instantly and Ben stops to empty their tunic pockets. He's made each man in his platoon write a final letter home and place it together with any other small personal mementoes, such as family photographs, medallions or keepsakes into the left-hand breast pocket of their tunic. Every member of his platoon has been instructed that should a mate be killed beside him, whenever possible he is to remove the contents of his tunic pocket and carry it with him. Under Library Spencer's tuition even Brokenose Brodie has managed a short letter to his parents. He is inordinately proud of this final missive and often reads it to himself or to anyone else prepared to listen. The joke among the platoon is that the letter will be worn out by the time he dies and one of them will have to look up Brokenose's mum and dad to recite to them what it contained.

Dear Mum and Dad,

I am dead when I write this. Our sargent says I must be.

You musint cry, you hear. I am not wirth the tears.

I don't think I will go to heaven. But who no's. The Turk all go there, its called paradice so maybe God will sent me up there to fite them again and get even for gettin meself killt. Dad you is forgived for

beltin me a lot.

> *Your loving son,*
>
> *Wayne Brokenose Brodie.*

P.S. Brokenose is me name here and I can read real good now.

A little further down the slope as they are crossing open ground Hornbill makes a sudden appearance on their left, his legs and arms pumping as he crosses over to them, yelling the while, though his voice is drowned in a sudden burst of shrapnel. He comes to a halt, panting violently just as they reach the cover of the scrub and Ben sees that he is wearing a bandage wrapped about his forehead. 'G'day, Sergeant, 'ullo, sir,' he pants, looking at Ben and Wordy Smith.

'Get yer flamin' head down, Hornbill, and stay ragged!' Ben shouts.

They proceed another hundred yards or so downhill and reach the stunted pine tree where Ben decides to swing to the left into the slight incline on Lone Pine, which leads to the southwestern extremity of the plateau. The juniper and scrub grow thickly here and reach above their heads so that they can walk upright for a good hundred yards or so, carefully making their way through the bush. Perhaps, because of the extra camouflage provided, the enemy firepower is not coming as thick and fast on this perimeter. Ben realises that they appear to be largely alone, and that few Australians have selected this section, thinking it the furthest away from the objective.

Wordy Smith, who has reached the edge of the tall scrub on Ben's right, suddenly calls out, 'Trenches ahead, Ben!'

They hit the ground and wait, expecting at any moment to see all hell break loose from the direction Wordy Smith has indicated. They can now clearly see the mounds of packed red earth some fifty yards ahead and more or less directly in front and above them. The Turkish trench running a good twenty yards or more has been dug into the brow of the hill to cover a wide arch, the centre of which embraces the whole of Lone Pine where they lie, to the right looking down at Pine Ridge and the left over the bottom section of 400 Plateau. The rear of the trench must also look over what became known as Legge Valley to the north and Anderson Knoll to the south. This trench, Ben reasons, must be the most distant point forward from the heights the enemy dominates. In fact, it is one of the very few positions in the Turkish defence that might be vulnerable if attacked with a sufficient force of determined men who can get close enough to use their bayonets. But now, much more importantly, if they are observed and an enemy machine gun guards the entrance to the trench ahead of them, they stand no chance of surviving. Ben has led his men into a trap from which there appears to be no escape. They cannot retreat back up onto the higher ground of the plateau and if they move further south they must cross open ground where they'll be cut to pieces by the Turkish machine guns. If they use their rifles they have no effective target, bullets don't bend into trenches, so their only hope will be to fix bayonets and charge.

Ben calls to Crow Rigby and Woggy Mustafa to crawl forward. 'Woggy, have a look willya, you've got the best eyes in the battalion, see if you can see any movement, any at all. You, Crow, get your telescopic sights onto those trenches, see if you can see anything as well, if you do, don't fire.' He turns to Muddy Parthe, who is nearest to him. 'Pass on, fix bayonets.'

After a minute or so Crow says, 'Can't see nothin',
Ben.'

'Three Turkish bodies at two o'clock,' Woggy says,
'legs stickin' out the bush.'

'Sure they're Turks?'

'Yeah, their boots, leggin's, they're not us.'

Crow Rigby swings his sniper's sights to where Woggy
has indicated. 'Yeah, he's right, three o' the bastards, flies
buzzin' over them, they's dead orright.'

Ben turns to the lieutenant and to his amazement sees
that he is clawing at a ground shrub with the tiniest bright
pink blossoms. Wordy Smith stuffs the specimen into his
tunic pocket and Ben sees that the pocket is filled with
floral bits and pieces which his platoon commander has
collected on their way across the plateau.

'Wordy, I'm gunna take a squiz, see what's happening.'

'No, Ben.'

Ben looks at Peregrine Ormington-Smith in surprise.
'Uh?'

'I'm going.'

'No, sir, it's best if . . . well, you're the platoon
commander, the lads need you to lead.'

'That's a laugh, Ben,' Wordy Smith says.

'Officer should stay with his men, sir,' Ben says,
reverting to formality.

'It's an order, Sergeant,' Wordy Smith replies sharply,
cutting him short. 'If we get out of this mess it won't be
from my leadership and the men know that.' He rises to
his knees and removes his pack. Ben sees that his tunic
pocket is overflowing with floral specimens and thinks he
must be the only officer in the history of warfare who is
risking his life with a tunic pocket full of wildflowers.
Wordy Smith starts to move forward out of the cover of
the juniper and scrub which on this section of Lone Pine
appear to have been slashed to not much higher than knee

height to increase the line of sight from the trench on the brow of the hill.

Ben grabs Peregrine Ormington-Smith by his Sam Browne belt just as he is about to set off. 'Stay to your left, Wordy, there's more cover, take your time.' He adds, 'We're not going anywhere except straight to hell if that trench is occupied.'

Wordy Smith nods and crawls out of the cover of the tall scrub and juniper into the much lower scrub. His attempt at the leopard crawl on his elbows and knees makes a mockery of the idea that this position presents the most difficult head-on target for an enemy. His long legs push his bum into the air and it now bobs up and down above the juniper and presents a target any sniper could hit without pausing to take aim.

They watch, all eyes glued on Wordy Smith's bobbing bum as he draws closer and closer to the trenches. The scrub has been completely cleared for the final fifty feet up to the trench and the platoon commander must come to a halt before he gets to the edge of the gorse. Hopefully he will be close enough to see if it is occupied, though Ben cannot imagine how, if it is, they haven't spotted Wordy's perambulating movement through the scrub.

'Get ready to charge, lads. Packs off, we'll go to the right, don't bunch, wait for my command.'

They can see that by attacking from the right Ben is trying to maximise every second they have, hoping that by drawing the enemy fire, Wordy Smith will give them time to jump to their feet and get a few yards closer before the Turks in the trench spot them coming. Brokenose Brodie nudges Library Spencer at his side and points silently towards Ben. Library sees that Ben has his Maori fighting axe slung in its holster across his shoulder. 'Them Turks gunna pay dearly,' he whispers.

But Library Spencer knows that Brokenose Brodie's

optimism is ill-founded, the chances of thirty-five men taking the trench by charging front-on over fifty yards is pretty bloody slim. If there is a machine gun facing them, then their chances become zero. He can feel the pressure mounting. If Wordy Smith makes it close enough to the trench to listen for sounds of movement and then makes it back unobserved, which, with the bobbing of his bum above the bushes, is highly unlikely, they may need to wait until nightfall before attempting to move out unobserved.

To everyone's astonishment, Peregrine Ormington-Smith suddenly stands up in the scrub some fifty feet from the trenches and, revolver in hand, his long legs taking surprisingly long strides, he proceeds to run up the final steep slope and onto the embankment to the trench, jumping directly into it.

'Holy Mother o' God!' Numbers Cooligan exclaims, as they all rise at Ben's order to charge.

They are in the open running when the lieutenant's head emerges again and, waving his arms, he indicates for them to come forward. 'Halt, lads!' Ben shouts. 'Get back! Fetch yer packs! You, Brokenose, bring the lieutenant's. On the double, we're still exposed! Packs on and run fer'it!'

Three minutes later they are all safely in the trench, for the first time out of the line of fire. They have crossed 400 Plateau and are now on its lower end at the very topmost point on Lone Pine.

The trench is even longer than it seemed and curves around to the south, following the contours of the ridge, and Ben, barely pausing to catch his breath and remove his pack, nods to Hornbill to follow him. 'Bring your rifle,' he says, though he leaves his own and unslings his fighting axe and removes it from its holster.

With Ben leading they turn the corner into the southern

section of the trench and immediately come across the body of a Turkish soldier, then several more. Most appear to have been bayoneted, some shot, and soon enough they come across a dead New Zealand soldier and then three more and another eight Turks. The trench is a little deeper at this end and leads into a section with a roof constructed of pine logs. Ben looks into the interior and, although at the extremity it is too dark to see, four or five feet in he makes out the shape of a machine gun stripped down. The moveable parts are laid out on a square of canvas and beside it is a dead Turkish sergeant. The attack on the trench by the 3rd Brigade must have caught the Turks by surprise, and unable to use their stripped-down machine gun.

Hornbill, who has climbed onto the firing platform to look over the southern end of the trench, calls suddenly, 'Come, take a look, Sergeant.' Ben withdraws from the covered section and climbs up beside him. What they see is a dozen or so Turkish soldiers lying dead on the slope and among them three more New Zealanders. Then a little further on they see three more sets of legs protruding from the scrub, they are the three dead Turkish soldiers Woggy has seen previously.

Ben returns to the timbered-over section of the trench, which appears to have been used as some sort of storehouse and is perhaps where an officer slept, the rank-and-file Turkish soldier being thought vastly inferior to his officers. As his eyes become accustomed to the darkness, stacked against the wall he sees a dozen boxes of ammunition and a bag of flour and, more importantly, a barrel of water, a neat pile of firewood and beside it what looks like a tin of kerosene. He moves still further inwards where it is virtually too dark to see without a light and is about to lean his axe against his leg while he finds his matches when suddenly a hand grips his ankle.

Ben kicks away violently, jumping back in fright, his heart racing. The back of his head knocks against a hurricane lamp suspended from the ceiling and his arm is instinctively brought up ready to strike downwards with the axe.

'Don't shoot!' a voice cries out of the dark.

'Strewth! You gave me a fright,' Ben calls out. 'Who are you?'

'New Zealand.'

'Shit, you gave me a scare,' Ben says. 'Better come out.'

'Can't, mate,' the voice answers. 'Me leg's broke.'

'Hang on, Kiwi, we'll come and fetch ya, how bad is it?'

'Bullet through me knee.'

'There's a lamp here somewhere, just hit my flamin' head on it, just a sec, I'll light a match.'

Ben strikes a match and locates the hurricane lamp which is still swinging slightly. In the flare he catches sight of the shape of a big bloke seated on the floor, the light from the match briefly shows his blood-soaked trousers and puttees where he's been hit in the area of the left knee.

'Hornbill, get in here,' Ben calls.

'You'll need to find some oil, it went out a while back,' the New Zealander says.

Ben hands the lamp to Hornbill and points in the direction of the small water barrel. 'I think there's a tin of paraffin over there, see if you can get this going.' By now his eyes have adjusted sufficiently to the dark for him to clearly make out the shape of the soldier, though his features are still lost. He moves over and squats on his haunches beside the man, and removing his water bottle he holds it to the soldier's lips. The New Zealander grabs at the bottle and drinks greedily. Ben hopes the water in the barrel he's seen earlier is fresh or he'll be without. He removes the flask from the soldier's lips and takes a small sip before fixing it back to his webbing, though he can feel it is almost empty. 'Owyer goin' then, lad?'

'I could use a smoke, mate.'

Ben calls over to Hornbill, 'You got a tailor-made, Hornbill?'

'Nah, roll me own?'

'Roll one for our Maori friend here, will ya.'

'Hang on, Sergeant, I'll 'ave a light goin' in a sec.'

'How'd you know I's a Maori?' the New Zealander now says.

Ben hears Hornbill strike a match and the room momentarily lights up and he sees a canvas stretcher against the wall. Hornbill trims the wick of the lamp and hangs it back on the wire hook fixed to the log ceiling and the area is filled with a soft light.

'I didn't, mate. I was just bein' a smart arse. Matter o' fact, I'm a quarter Maori myself.'

'Yeah?' the soldier says, then suddenly winces, stifling a groan.

In the lamplight Ben now clearly sees that the wounded soldier sits in the corner, his back against the far wall with both legs straight out. He has torn his trouser leg away to expose the wound and in the blood and gore Ben observes that the kneecap is still intact and that the Maori appears to have been hit below the knee, the bullet smashing through the tibia and the fibula bones. He has done several courses in first aid in the field and thinks the bullet must have missed the posterior tibial artery or the Maori lad would have been long dead from loss of blood.

'It ain't your knee, mate, just below. Lucky that, been the knee, surgeon would've chopped yer leg off.'

'Me granddad didn't have no arm, one eye missing too, maybe it run in the fambly hey,' the big man says, trying to keep calm.

Hornbill bends over both of them tut-tutting about the

Maori's wound while he rolls a hand-made, then licks the edge of the cigarette paper and places it in his mouth and lights it. He takes a quick draw on it himself and passes it to the New Zealander. The light from Hornbill's match, brighter and closer than the soft light from the lamp, reveals a broad, heavily tattooed face and Ben is suddenly and painfully reminded of Hawk and home and his beloved sister, Victoria.

'Thanks,' the Maori says. 'Much obliged hey, man.'

'Bring us the lamp, lad,' Ben instructs Hornbill, 'then go tell the others the trench is clear. Tell Wordy Smith to post a sentry, top, centre and down here both sides and to heave the Turks overboard. Leave the four Kiwis, we'll think what to do about them later.' Hornbill brings the hurricane lamp over and places it beside Ben. 'Oh, and leave your first field dressing with me.'

'Jeez, I'm sorry, Sergeant, I'm wearin' it,' Hornbill says sheepishly.

'Oh, yeah, I forgot. What happened?'

'Shrapnel pellet when we was landing, it ain't much more than a graze, but it fair knocked me out, when I come to I couldn't find yiz so they pushed me into a platoon in A Company. Stretcher-bearer bloke done me 'ead.'

'Nice to have you back, Hornbill.'

'Me too, Sergeant. I can tell ya, I were *that* upset losing yiz.'

'Count yerself lucky, lad. We were all shitting ourselves back there, at least you were out of it for a time,' Ben teases.

Ben turns to the big Maori. 'You blokes issued with a first field dressing?'

'A bandage?'

'Yeah.'

'In me pack.' The Maori tries to reach over for his pack and inadvertently moves his leg. 'Oh fuck!' he yells.

'Steady, lad, sit still, we'll get it.' Ben looks at Hornbill who is about to depart and nods towards the New Zealander's pack.

'Sorry, Sergeant, don't mean t'cry out.'

'Not to worry, lad, be my guest, your leg's bust real bad, but it ain't your knee and that's good.' Ben doesn't tell him that the chances of getting him back to the beach are pretty slim, in fact, for all of them. Hornbill hands Ben the bandage from the soldier's pack. 'I'll need two or three more o' these and a couple of pieces of wood for splints, get the field dressings off the four dead Kiwi blokes, get back here as soon as you can.'

'Sergeant, can we get a brew goin', there's water and firewood back there, against the wall?'

'Yeah, sure.' Ben glances at the Maori. 'Like a cuppa?'

The big man nods and tries to smile through the pain. 'Me mum says nice cuppa tea fix most thin's.'

Ben calls out after Hornbill, 'Tell the lads to break out rations, eat something! Oh, and if the dead Turks have water bottles, take them before you toss 'em over the top.'

He turns back to the Maori. 'I'm gunna do the best I can with this, mate, but it won't be much, clean it a bit, bandage it, fix a splint, that's about it for the time being.'

'Thanks, Sergeant.'

'It's Ben. We don't stand on ceremony here. Ben Teekleman.'

'Jack Tau Paranihi,' the Maori says, extending a hand that's almost twice the size of Ben's.

They shake hands. 'Nice t'meetcha.'

'Same,' Jack Tau Paranihi says.

'They issue you with anything to take, Jack?' Ben asks, tearing open the bandage.

'Take?'

'Pain for the use of?'

'Nah.'

'Same as us, eh, not even a flamin' Aspirin.'

Ben uses the gauze pad that comes with the New Zealand bandage to clean out the wound, which has thankfully long since stopped bleeding. He tries to remove the large bone splinters from the wound, which starts up some superficial bleeding again that he staunches. He knows he must be hurting the big soldier, but apart from one or two winces the New Zealander is stoic throughout. 'I'm goin' ta bandage it pretty tight and it's gunna hurt, so hold on, Jack.'

Ben takes out his own field dressing and places the gauze pad from it on the Maori's wound. The Australian field-issue bandage appears to be of a slightly heavier gauze than the New Zealand one so he uses it instead, winding it tightly just below the knee. With the first wrap around Jack Tau Paranihi gives a loud involuntary cry and then grabs hold of his shirt front and stuffs it into his mouth, biting down hard, his eyes tightly closed as he fights back the pain.

'There you go,' Ben says at last. 'At least the bloody flies can't get in. We'll fix a splint for you soon, lad, get you a brew. Have you eaten?'

'On the shup this mornin'.'

'We'll get you something.'

'There's food in me pack hey,' Jack Tau Paranihi says, 'bullybeef.'

Ben shakes his head. 'Only the flags and the badges change, the bloody tucker in every army is the same shit!'

'Sergeant?'

'It's Ben, mate.'

'Ben, where's you get that there axe hey?' Jack doesn't wait for Ben's reply. 'That axe Maori, man, fightin' axe from me own tribe, it's got the markin's.'

'It was my grandfather's, he fought in the Maori wars in 1860.'

'He took it from a dead Maori warrior?'

'No, no, you don't understand, he fought *for* the Maoris.'

'Shit hey? Your granddad, he was a Maori you're a quarter of?'

'No, he was a pakeha, my grandmother was a Maori, her name was Makareta.'

There is a moment's silence and now Jack Tau Paranihi asks, 'Your granddad, he frum Tasmania?'

'Yes, how'd you know that?' Ben asks, surprised.

'Tommo Te Mokiri?'

'Shit, *yes*!'

'His brother, General Black Hawk, and hum, Tommo Te Mokiri, he taught us to use the fightin' axe, they big warriors in my tribe. Not just mine, all the Maori tribes hey.'

Ben points to the tattooing on Jack Tau Paranihi's face. 'Jesus, I thought I recognised the *moko*, it's the same as Hawk's.' Ben thinks back on the stories Hawk has told him. 'Your grandfather, you said he had an arm and an eye missing, did it happen on a whaling ship?'

'Yeah, Black Hawk rescue hum from a whale.'

'His name, was it Hammerhead Jack?'

'That's hum. He give me his name.'

They both shake their heads and laugh, Jack Tau Paranihi for a moment forgetting his pain. 'Jesus, that's weird, here of all places, eh?'

Hornbill returns shortly afterwards with two flat planks taken from one of the ammunition boxes and three more bandages from the dead New Zealanders. Wordy Smith returns with him and Ben introduces him to Jack. Both men then help Ben with the splints so there is no further time to discuss the amazing coincidence.

Ben, with the help of the two others, begins to set the splints. Jack is stoic throughout, biting on the webbing strap of his ammunition pouches, his brow sweating profusely, eyes dilated from the intense pain. 'Steady, lad, steady now,' Ben says as he tries to push back the shattered fibula bone before applying the splint. Blood runs from the corner of the big Maori's mouth as he breaks a tooth biting down on the webbing. It is finally done. 'There yer go,' Ben says, 'sorry, mate.'

Jack Tau Paranihi spits out the tooth and some blood. 'Can't be helped, mate,' he says as Ben gives him his water bottle again and this time the Maori empties it. 'You a good bloke, man, like the ancestor.' Ben is not aware that, by this remark, he means his grandfather Tommo, who is now a Maori ancestor pretty high up in the rankings.

Wordy Smith produces a brown medicine bottle from the canvas haversack across his shoulder. 'Take a sip, Jack, about a tablespoonful.' He uncorks the bottle and hands it to the Maori who does as he's told and hands it back. 'Should help a bit,' Wordy says, returning the cork to the bottle.

'What is it?' Ben asks, pointing to the bottle.

'Tincture of opium,' Wordy replies. 'It helps to have a little botanical knowledge, used to be known as laudanum.'

'Where the hell did you get it?'

'Cairo. I had it mixed, it's almost straight opium, should keep Jack here quiet for a while.'

Ben looks at Peregrine Ormington-Smith quizzically. 'You don't . . . er, you know, take it yourself, do you? I mean, like for normal?'

'Good God, no!' Wordy Smith exclaims. 'I've seen what it can do, some of the chaps in art school got addicted to it, it's rotten stuff, but great as a pain killer. I'm a natural coward, Ben, if I get hit I want to die peacefully.' Ben realises that Wordy's willingness to share the bottle with a strange soldier belies this remark, that

Wordy has brought the bottle along for the use of the platoon.

'It works good, man,' Jack Tau Paranihi exclaims. 'Thanks a lot, sir.'

'It's Wordy . . . Wordy Smith, Jack.'

'Mate, we're going to move you onto that stretcher, you'll be better off lying down,' Ben says. 'You all right?'

Jack smiles. 'Don't feel a thung.'

'Good, then we'll do it now.' Ben points to Jack's ammunition pouches and webbing. 'We'll take that off, you'll be better without it.' He nods to Hornbill, who helps the Maori remove his webbing and then moves behind him with his shoulders against the back wall, gripping the big man under the armpits. Ben instructs Wordy Smith to hold the legs together at the ankles and he takes hold of Jack by looping his arms under his bum. 'Righto, one, two, three, *lift*!' The huge man must weigh in the vicinity of two hundred and eighty pounds, maybe more, as they move him the few feet over to the camp stretcher.

'Shit, yer ain't small neither,' Hornbill, a big man himself, says, breathing hard from the effort.

'Lock forward,' Jack Tau Paranihi says.

Hornbill nods. 'Rugby,' he says, explaining to Ben and Wordy Smith.

Later Jack explains how they got to the Turkish trench. It seems the New Zealanders had landed on the beach at roughly the same time as the 2nd Brigade and like them had expected to fight to the north on Baby 700. But his landing boat had become unsecured, breaking away from the steam pinnace towing it, the tow rope possibly severed by a piece of shrapnel. They had been forced to row ashore, landing to the right, the Gaba Tepe side. Half of his boat had been hit by shrapnel pellets and machine-gun fire and those not dead or wounded, sixteen of them, had

517

been bunched together with the Australian 6th Battalion in a company under Captain Hooke. 'Like the pirate in that story,' Jack Tau Paranihi said at the time. They'd crossed over a series of spurs leading down from the southern edge of 400 Plateau, five in all, the last, Pine Ridge, being the tallest. Each of the ridges led into deep gullies and the small New Zealand group, sticking together, somehow became detached from the rest of the company after entering a deep gully between what would later be known as Snipers' Ridge and Weir Ridge. Losing contact they pressed on and eventually found their way alone onto Pine Ridge and decided to go up it. It was the steepest of all the climbs, but fortunately one on which the scrub grew mostly higher than a man's head and so they were able to conceal their approach. They'd surprised a group of about ten Turks near the top who were carrying water and supplies and, as Jack put it, 'got in among them'. The Turks made a run for it and they chased them up the final slope. The guns of the British cruiser *Bacchante*, firing on the battery on Gaba Tepe from the bay, were making such a horrendous racket that the Turks in the trench couldn't possibly have heard them approaching. Foolishly thinking themselves safe, they appear to have posted no sentry on the southern side and the New Zealanders had almost reached the trench before the Turks realised what was happening. Nevertheless, they'd managed to kill four of the bayonet-charging Kiwis at close range.

'But then we was among thum with our bayonets,' Jack Tau Paranihi explains. 'Thum Turks didn't have the stomach for that stuff and they're out the top end o' the trench like jack rabbits and gorn f'their lives down the slope out back! I jump into the trench and see the part what's covered, there's a Turk next to a stripped-down machine gun, but he, or somebody, must'a had a rifle, 'cause as I stuck hum there's an explosion and me leg crumples under me and I don't remember nothink more. When I come to, all me mates'a gorn.'

Ben reasons that the remainder of Jack's New Zealanders, unaware of him lying wounded in the dark recess, had moved on in their attempt to find their company or to follow after the escaping Turks.

Ben and Wordy Smith now talk about their position. To press on over the hill into the valley beyond where the 3rd Battalion lies pinned down will bring them back into the Turkish line of fire. Moreover, not long after they've arrived at the trench the Turkish fire over Lone Pine and further south along Pine Ridge has grown much heavier and artillery and machine-gun fire is whistling over their heads. They are not to know that the Turks have spotted the 12th Battalion pushing towards Pine Ridge and a little later the 6th coming over the southern spurs. This means that Lone Pine is not only receiving aim from the Turks on the Third Ridge but also catching the bullets and shrapnel pellets which miss 400 Plateau. Ben and Wordy Smith were lucky they took their platoon across the plateau when they did. Half an hour later, they would have been in the very centre of a maelstrom of bullets and artillery fire. Leaving the trench now means almost certain death.

Ben calls the platoon together. 'We're staying put, lads, moving on is pointless and suicidal. Our objective was to cross the plateau and try to engage the enemy and we've done the first and we'll attempt to do the second from where we are. There's a good position to mount a machine gun on the northern end of the trench and although it's a fairly narrow trajectory across the valley onto the Third Ridge we can hit the enemy from here a bloody sight better than firing at them pinned down from behind a rock.'

'Machine gun? Where we gunna get one o' those?' Numbers Cooligan asks.

'There's one in the shed back there with the wounded Maori, stripped down, it's a French Hotchkiss, the Turks have got quite a lot of French weaponry.

'Yes, but will we know how to use it, Ben?' Library Spencer asks.

'Yeah, I reckon. I covered all the Allied machine guns when I did a special weaponry course at Broadmeadows, the German ones too.' Ben adds, 'I admit, I've never actually stripped one down, matter of fact this one is the first I've seen in the flesh so to speak, but I remember the system.' He hesitates, 'I think . . . hope.'

'She'll be apples,' Hornbill says. 'I reckon if I can get the blighter assembled we'll know how she works orright.'

Towards noon the machine gun is ready but for a part in the firing mechanism. Hornbill calls Ben, 'Lookee at that, willya. Bastard's perfeck, except for the one small part.'

'What are you trying to say?' Ben asks.

'Well, we're fucked, it's a small high-tensile steel spring behind the trigger, without it we can't fire the bastard.'

'Can't you make one, get it out of a rifle, modify it?'

Hornbill points to a Turkish Mauser and one of the New Zealand rifles, which are Lee-Enfields same as the Australians'. 'I've tried that, no good. The Frogs don't do things like other people.'

Wordy Smith comes over. 'What seems to be the trouble, Ben?'

'Spring in the trigger mechanism's missing, without it the bloody thing won't work.'

Wordy doesn't pursue the usual litany of questions – the have yous or did yous – knowing full well both Ben and Hornbill will have covered all this. He thinks for a moment then looks at Hornbill. 'The sergeant!'

'Huh?'

'The Turkish sergeant Jack here took care of, wasn't he working on the gun?'

'Probably, he was right next to it when I done him in,' Jack calls from his cot. He has had another tablespoon of Wordy's medicine and is reasonably comfortable.

Without so much as a by-your-leave, Hornbill is up the ladder and over the top. They both jump onto the firing platform and peek over the edge. Hornbill has found the dead sergeant where they tossed him overboard. He's rolled down from the top of the trench about ten or fifteen feet and now Hornbill rolls him onto his back and is going through his pockets furiously.

'Nothin',' he says at last, looking up at them.

'Get back up,' Ben says, then, 'Wait on, look at his fist, left fist.'

From where they are they can see the dead Turk's left hand is closed.

Hornbill commences to pry it open. 'Gotcha!' he calls suddenly and turning runs up the red-soil embankment and climbs down the ladder back into the trench. 'Bugger me dead, it were in the bastard's hand all the flamin' time! Imagine that, hey!' He has a huge grin all over his gob as he turns and looks directly at Wordy Smith. 'Blood's worth bottlin', Wordy. How'd yer think o' that an' all?'

'Nine times out of ten it would have been a bloody silly suggestion,' he says modestly.

'Fuckin' genius, mate,' Hornbill says, happily squatting beside the machine gun again.

In another ten minutes, with the rest of the platoon, barring the six sentries, crowding around, Hornbill has the machine gun ready. They've discovered more ammunition stored in boxes in other parts of the trench and they have sufficient to keep pumping away all day if they can get it to work.

Ben slips a strip of cartridges in carefully, trying to remember the steps involved in loading it up, then resting it on the parapet he pulls the trigger and nothing happens. Ben curses and examines the machine gun closely. 'Anyone know what "Firm" means?' he says suddenly. 'Firm with two "e"s?'

'*Fermé*, it means "shut" in French,' Wordy Smith says.

'The safety catch!' several of them call simultaneously. Ben pushes a small lever which doesn't look as though it should be pushed or tampered with and then pulls the trigger. A burst of machine-gun fire fills the air to the cheering of the platoon.

They fill a series of sandbags and place them on the northern end of the trench with the Hotchkiss barrel protruding from it with a sufficient arc to cover the section of the Third Ridge known as Scrubby Knoll within their range, and further south to Anderson Knoll. Standing on the firing platform the machine-gunner can see out quite clearly while still being well protected by the sandbags. To the immediate right Ben constructs another sandbag barricade for Crow Rigby and Woggy Mustafa, which duplicates the area covered by the machine gun.

'They're going to cotton on sooner or later where our machine-gun fire is coming from and they'll put a sniper onto us, try to take him out, Crow. How far do you reckon it is across the valley to the ridge?'

Crow Rigby looks through his telescopic sights, and after a few moments says, 'About fourteen hundred yards, Ben.' He turns to Woggy, 'What yer reckon?'

'Twelve hundred and fifty the most,' Woggy says. They have learned in the desert that you can bet Woggy Mustafa against a tape measure. He has a wonderful eye, and when he isn't observing for Crow Rigby he takes a turn with the sniper's rifle. Ben has promised him that if they ever take out a Turkish sniper and can retrieve his

Mauser, and with Hornbill no doubt able to fix the mount to fit the Lee-Enfield, the German telescopic sight will become his.

The men, having eaten and enjoyed a brew, are now much more optimistic and some of them privately wish they could push on, go after the enemy. They've all been scared crossing the plateau, but the adrenaline rush as they fixed bayonets to charge the trench has made them realise that it is the only occasion they've had to assert themselves. Up to this moment, all they've done is stumble through scrub and climb over rocks under a hail of shrapnel and enemy rifle and machine-gun fire but haven't, as yet, fired a single shot in anger. The Clicks are still virgin soldiers even though seventeen of them are dead with only Hornbill having the distinction of being slightly wounded.

After five hours, around two o'clock in the afternoon, M'Cay is at last beginning to realise that he cannot hope to relieve the decimated 3rd Brigade and establish a new front at the base of the Third Ridge. The 400 Plateau lies thickly spread with bodies and he cannot yet claim a single gain or pretend to have inflicted any real damage on the enemy. The closer he gets to the Third Ridge, driving his troops into Wordy's 'spoon', or as it is now referred to by its military name, The Cup, the easier it becomes for the enemy to slaughter them. The Turkish shrapnel and rifle fire have steadily become more intense as each hour progresses and, with it, the danger of crossing the plateau increases.

In M'Cay's defence it must be said that at no time does he have effective artillery to help him. Churchill's assurance that the British battleship guns standing off the beach would pound the enemy positions remorselessly proves entirely wrong. They are less than useless and, if anything, present a danger to the Australian troops without inflicting the slightest damage on the Turks. They are soon abandoned, used only to fire at Gaba Tepe in the forlorn hope that they might destroy a gun battery thought to be positioned there.

The brigadiers, M'Cay and MacLagan to his north, have only rifles and machine guns firing at an enemy, whose whereabouts he can only hazard a guess at. It is popguns against brick walls all over again. For a short period M'Cay has enjoyed the morale-boosting effect of an Indian unit with four small mountain guns positioned two on either side of White's Gully immediately behind 400 Plateau. The battery is commanded by Captain Kirby and at five minutes to noon it opens fire on the Third Ridge.

Although the sound of their own artillery giving the enemy a little of their own back cheers up the Australians, the Turks, clearly able to see Captain Kirby's battery from the heights of Battleship Hill, simply turn their own artillery onto them and by half-past two the Indian battery is put out of the reckoning. Now the Turks increase the pressure on the plateau, The Cup and, further south, in Legge Valley, on Lone Pine and Pine Ridge. The Australian lambs are being systematically led to the slaughter.

Ben's platoon starts firing the machine gun across Legge Valley shortly before noon. By this time the 6th Battalion, to which Jack Tau Paranihi and his New Zealanders were hastily seconded to reinforce the remnants of the 3rd Brigade, are having a torrid time at Pine Ridge and within Legge Valley. As the afternoon wears on they are driven back and in some parts are surrounded by the Turks coming down from the Third Ridge, who can see an opportunity to move around Pine Ridge and up Lone Pine. If they can do this in any numbers they will surround the Australians fighting on the southern section. Moreover, this will mean that the northern section will be caught in a pincer movement with no hope of escaping. For the Australians and New Zealanders the Gallipoli campaign will effectively be over on the first day.

It soon becomes apparent to Ben that firing at the Third Ridge, while attracting return fire from snipers and creating a contest between Crow Rigby and his team-mate Woggy Mustafa and four Turkish snipers on the Third Ridge, isn't making a great deal of impact. Then he sees the Turkish troops coming into Legge Valley to engage the Pine Ridge front. At last he has a target and the platoon concentrates their fire on the Turks moving in numbers through the scrub. The machine gun works all afternoon to devastating effect, manned by Ben and Hornbill and Brokenose Brodie who has been loading ammunition strips. Hornbill eventually falls from the platform out of sheer exhaustion, and tumbles into the trench fast asleep. Ben too has been forced to sleep.

With Ben working the machine gun, Wordy Smith has taken over command of the rifle fire, manning the side of the trench looking down into the valley with fifteen men while the other fifteen sleep. Three of the men on duty cart ammunition, make tea, prepare rations and fill the machine-gun strips. Even Jack Tau Paranihi is put to work filling machine-gun strips. He has received a spoon of Wordy's medicine every four hours which has managed to relieve much of his pain. By mid-afternoon the trench is working as a highly efficient unit and each of the men has killed or wounded to their certain knowledge a handful of Turks. All the Broadmeadows drill, the ceaseless concentration of handling a rifle, has come to fruition. The Clicks, with fifteen rifles firing at a maximum rate well in advance of perhaps any other platoon on Gallipoli, are almost the equivalent of a second machine gun.

On several occasions the Hotchkiss, together with the concerted fire directed at the same target by Wordy's rifles, forces the Turks to scatter and retreat when they are at the point of reaching the Australian line.

Soon a Turkish gun on the Third Ridge tries to get their range and the ridge just below the trench is pounded all afternoon with shells. Clouds of dust often obscure their line of sight. Rifle shots whistle over their heads and sniper fire constantly hits the sandbags, but miraculously never enters the three narrow slots through which the Hotchkiss and Crow Rigby fire and Woggy Mustafa observes. Crow and Woggy have taken to picking out the Turkish officers, doing to the enemy what their snipers have been doing all day to the Australians on 400 Plateau. They've taken out more than thirty, Woggy's incredible eyes calling the shots and Crow Rigby placing them. Used this way, Woggy's eyes are worth several rifles firing at the enemy.

Ben knows that sooner or later they will either take a direct hit or sufficient shrapnel will explode over the trench and wipe them out. At four o'clock in the afternoon this happens at the southern end of the trench and while most of the shrapnel pellets rain down on the covered section, six of the platoon are killed. Ben orders their bodies to be taken into the shed, as the covered section is now known, so that the trench remains uncluttered. 'We'll grieve them later, lads,' he says, knowing that it is only a matter of time before it happens again and they are all killed. Ben is rapidly coming to the conclusion that there is no escape from Gallipoli other than to be killed or wounded. Victory is simply out of the question. He now has only one objective, to inflict as much damage on the enemy as he is able before he dies. Two more of the platoon are wounded, though not too badly, Library Spencer has a chunk taken out of the fleshy part of his arm and a lad from Geelong, a quiet bloke known to all as 'Moggy' Katz, who played for the Geelong reserves, has lost the tip of his little finger. Wordy Smith proves to be a dab hand with a field dressing and both men continue to man a rifle, with a spoonful of Wordy's medicine to comfort them.

Towards dusk Ben observes that the Australians in the valley below are pulling back and that the Turks are coming after them. In the indifferent light it is becoming more and more difficult to use the machine gun effectively and he is convinced that the Turks will attack them after dark. They have done an enormous amount of damage with the Hotchkiss and any Turkish company commander will want to stop them. Ben is about to pack it in when a Turkish sniper hits the barrel and casing of the Hotchkiss, putting it out of action. Hornbill is called to have a look and shakes his head. 'Barrel's bent, ain't no way.' In the dark and without the machine gun Ben realises they are even more vulnerable to attack.

With the light failing fast, they suddenly observe a soldier coming towards them from higher up on the plateau. The man, running down the slope without a pack, is obviously a messenger. He waves his arms, shouting, 'Fall back, fall back!' With nightfall the Turkish rifle fire seems to have temporarily stopped, only the artillery continues to pound the plateau higher up.

Ben turns to Numbers Cooligan. 'Go get that man, bring him in.'

The soldier, a lance corporal named Penman, explains that the Australians are moving back across 400 Plateau to the original crest and that Sayers, Ben's company commander, has pulled back from a position near the Daisy Patch and reorganised what's left of the 5th Battalion and an assortment of others. Commanding the battalion, he is positioned on the rear slope of White's Valley. 'You're not to try to join him, he wants you to pull back down Pine Ridge where the 6th is pulling back and needs help.'

'How did you know we were here?'

Lance Corporal Penman laughs. 'We seen what you blokes been doing all day to the Turks in the valley. Major Sayers says there's only one platoon in the 1st Division can rapid fire at the rate you can and keep it up all day. He just said, "Tell Lieutenant Ormington-Smith and Sergeant Teekleman well done, we'd love them back with us when he's through rescuing the 6th Battalion."'

'He always did have a black sense of humour,' Wordy Smith says.

'Well, machine gun's buggered, I guess we're no better here than on Pine Ridge, maybe we'll get to look a Turk in the eye before the night is out,' Ben says.

'I'll be coming with you,' Lance Corporal Penman says.

'Good, we lost our "one stripe" earlier, that would be useful, one thing though, we don't stand formal here, what's your name, Lance Corporal?' Ben replies.

'Ben,' the corporal says.

They all laugh. 'Sorry, Corporal, but I'm afraid there's only one Ben in this platoon, we'll have to call you something else.'

'Nibs! Nibs Penman!' Cooligan offers, pleased with himself.

'Nibs then?' Ben asks the corporal.

The corporal shrugs. 'Suits me fine, probably won't be around long enough to hear it much anyhow.'

'Subtle or what!' Crow Rigby cries.

'Aw shuddup, Crow!' Cooligan calls. 'Just 'cause you ain't clever like me!'

'Righto, let's pack up,' Ben calls. 'It's dark enough to get going and the moon won't be up for a while. We're taking Jack with us on the stretcher, I want four men on it. Nobby, Brokenose, Macca, Keith, you blokes first, change every ten minutes with someone else. There's still a little water left in the barrel, fill your water bottles, it could be a long night. Everybody have something to eat now, you've got ten minutes before we pull out. Moon will be up soon, we want to get going.'

The platoon moves out down Lone Pine. The artillery fire has ceased over this part of the battlefield and to the south and while it is a welcome relief it is also a sign of danger to come. The Turks are about to mount an attack on the southern spur. Their plan obviously is to move around Pine Ridge, where the remnants of the 9th Battalion of the 3rd Brigade and the 6th Battalion of the 2nd have been fighting all day and are greatly weakened.

Ben and his platoon make their way down the slope and south to Pine Ridge without any fire directed at them. Perhaps the worst aspect of the trip is the scrub they must move through in the dark. On the southern side of Lone Pine and again on Pine Ridge the gorse is heavily mixed with thorn scrub and their uniforms and puttees are torn to pieces. Jack, lying supine on the stretcher, is, seemingly, one long scratch, the thorns having damn near ripped him apart. By the time the moon is up they have made their way down to the extreme northern end of the spur where it connects with Lone Pine and here they come across a captured Turkish gun-pit linked with a series of trenches which are occupied by Captain Daly of the 8th with a handful of men all exhausted from the day's fighting. They welcome Wordy Smith with open arms.

'Frankly, we're about done in,' Daly tells Wordy. 'We've thirty-five men and half of them wounded. With your mob in reasonable shape we may be able to hold the bastards off, though I think you'll need to break your platoon up. There's a handful of men under Corporal Harrison and Lance Corporal Kenyon in a Turkish trench about a hundred yards to the north, I doubt if they can hold on without help. We've heard down the line of what your lads have done today, I guess we were the beneficiaries down in the valley, twelve men with your firepower could make all the difference.'

Ben asks Wordy Smith to recommend that Crow Rigby be promoted to corporal on the spot. He has lost Mooney, his corporal on the third landing craft that morning and Phillips, his lance corporal, on the plateau, but is reluctant to send Nibs Penman since he doesn't even know the names of the men who would be placed under his charge. Daly, when he is told Crow Rigby is a sniper, immediately agrees to the promotion.

Crow asks Ben if he can take Woggy Mustafa and Numbers Cooligan. Ben agrees and picks the other nine, though none of them seem too happy to be broken up as a unit. 'Give 'em hell, lads, this is your chance to look the Turk in the eye,' Ben says and for a fleeting moment wonders how many of them he will meet again.

Ben can see that Daly, who is wounded, and his lieutenant, an officer named Derham who is actually asleep in the trench at his feet, are exhausted and soon after discovers that both have been wounded. He quickly sets about organising the defence of the gun-pit which is situated in a separate trench behind the front one. It is occupied by a rag-tag of mixed platoons from the 9th, 8th and 6th under Lieutenants Levy and Hooper, both of whom are wounded. Ben breaks up his platoon once again, sending ten of the men to the forward trench and keeping eight in the gun-pit.

Wordy Smith reports to Captain Daly and outlines to him what they've done. 'Sir, there's a lot of Turkish ammunition lying about in crates. I'd like to move it under the section of the trench that's covered?'

Daly agrees. 'Go ahead, Lieutenant, 'fraid we're too bushed to attempt it.'

Wordy Smith sets out to put a detail together to move the crates and returns some few minutes later with two men carrying a Turkish machine gun between them. 'Look what I've found,' he says excitedly to Captain Daly.

Daly sighs. 'We know about it, Lieutenant. Nobody knows how to use the bugger, could've been a godsend.'

'It's a Hotchkiss, sir, Sergeant Teekleman and Private Horne have been manning one like this all day.'

Daly looks amazed. 'Something good had to happen in all this, thank God you came.'

A machine-gun post is hastily constructed out of sandbags near the pit furthest to the south, with Hornbill standing behind Ben to feed in the ammunition strips. Almost on cue the scrub and juniper a hundred or so yards below the gun-pits are set on fire, the Turks hoping the fire will reach the gun-pits and explode the ammunition.

But a God who has been anything but kind to the Australians all day changes the direction of the breeze and the blaze turns back on the Turks, forcing them into the more open ground where they can be clearly seen in the moonlight.

The men in the trenches now realise that they are vastly outnumbered by the enemy who have their bayonets fixed and are charging up the slope towards them. It is one of the few occasions all day when the Australians own the high ground. 'Let them come closer,' Ben yells. 'Don't fire!'

One Turk some ten feet in front of the rest is shouting, 'Allah! Allah!' and is caught mid-word on the third 'Allah' by Crow Rigby, who picks him off from the trench fifty yards from Ben and they all see the man's head explode in a black burst. The remainder of the Turks come charging on, the Prophet's name on their lips, shouting, wildly excited, their bayonets gleaming in the moonlight.

'Don't fire, lads,' Ben shouts again. 'Steady! Steady, lads. Wait until you can see the fucker's eyes.'

At a range of about fifty yards Ben gives the order to fire and opens up with the machine gun. The Turks in the front drop like rocks in a quarry blast and the next line follows and then the next. Seemingly in moments bodies are stumbling and tripping over each other and yet they come, there are no cowards among them. The battle lasts no more than ten minutes, the machine gun and the remorseless rifle fire simply cuts the Turks apart. Finally, with some of the Turks having reached almost to the edge of the gun-pits, they fall back. There are more than two hundred of the enemy lying on the black, smouldering apron left by the fire they'd started earlier. Occasionally a small flame from the spent fire momentarily leaps into life and snatches at the rag of a uniform, sending thin ribbons of white smoke spiralling into the moonlit night.

Captain Daly turns to Wordy Smith, his exhausted face barely capable of creasing into a smile. 'I've never seen rapid fire like that before, your lads certainly know how to handle a rifle.' He turns to Ben. 'Well done, Sergeant, I guess the machine gun was the difference, eh? I doubt we could've held them off otherwise.'

Ben, exhausted himself, grins. 'Bloody good thing the Turks have a habit of leaving them lying around, sir.'

A little later the enemy organises a second attack, but it is no more than a show of defiance. Hornbill, now manning the Hotchkiss, gives them heaps and they soon lose the stomach to try again. What is left of the attacking force withdraws back over the valley to the Third Ridge.

At about 11.30 p.m. Daly receives orders to pull back to the original line at the rear of 400 Plateau. Ben's platoon, though nearly as exhausted as the rest of the men, carries no wounded with the exception of course of Jack Tau Paranihi, Library Spencer and Moggy Katz.

They are all badly scratched by thorns and in the days to come almost every soldier who fought across the plateau will suffer from scratches that fester badly. Ben's men are nevertheless in the best shape of any of the men in the gun-pits and so they accept the responsibility for carrying the seriously hurt and wounded men back to the line. Ben, seeing how burdened they are with the wounded, wants to destroy the Turkish machine gun as it will require two men to manhandle it and a third to carry the tripod.

However, Lieutenant Derham and one of his men who is not too seriously hurt elect to take it with them. 'It's saved our lives once and it might do so again, we can manage it, sir,' he says to Captain Daly.

The little party of fighting men under Daly trudge slowly back over Lone Pine. About halfway to the rear they come across a soldier with a broken leg and Derham and his offsider abandon the Hotchkiss, which Hornbill quickly disables, hurling several of its parts into the gorse, and they take the man with them. Light rain begins to fall and the air grows a little cooler. They arrive behind the lines a few minutes before midnight.

So ends the first day of fighting on Gallipoli. They stand exhausted no more than thirty yards from where they'd started digging in behind the rear lip of 400 Plateau shortly before nine that morning. Ben's platoon finds itself with nineteen men dead and three wounded and those still standing barely have the strength to remove their packs. Bruised and cut, their uniforms torn, their faces and arms blackened with cordite and dust, they fall asleep on the damp ground at their feet.

If they can think at all, which is doubtful at this stage, they will be aware that they've killed men they could see, and will never again look at life through the same clear, clean eyes. They have undergone a process of corruption they will be unable to explain and which will cause them to cry out in the small hours of the morning. While some may grow old, where they have been and what they have seen will only ever be acknowledged by a sidelong glance, a knowingness, a look in the eyes of a mate. There are no words for what happens in the organised slaughter of men. It is a thing they've shared, a glory they've felt and a shame they will know all the days of their lives. While they have fought valiantly and with great pride, they have voluntarily lifted the lid to hell and plunged inwards. And, in the process, they have taken a terrible hiding from the proud Turks, whose ancient land they have dared to violate.

GALLIPOLI

Had he never been born he was mine:
Since he was born he never was mine:
Only the dream is our own.

Where the world called him there he went;
When the war called him, there he bent.
Now he is dead.

He was I; bone of my bone,
Flesh of my flesh, in truth;
For his plenty I gave my own,
His drouth was my drouth.

When he laughed I was glad,
In his strength forgot I was weak,
In his joy forgot I was sad
Now there is nothing to ask or to seek;
He is dead.

I am the ball the marksman sent,
Missing the end and falling spent;
I am the arrow, sighted fair
That failed, and finds not anywhere.
He who was I is dead.

– Dame Mary Gilmore

Chapter Fifteen

THE ATTACK ON
LONE PINE

Gallipoli and Alexandria 1915–1916

GALLIPOLI

10th December 1915

My dearest Victoria and my esteemed Grandfather Hawk,

This letter is to be shared between you and is, alas, long overdue. I had hoped to get something to you in time for Christmas but several factors intervened of which I will presently write.

I did manage a scrap of paper to Victoria in mid-November wishing you both season's greetings, I hope you received it as there has been no mail from you these three weeks. Something is going on down at the beach and the mail does not appear to be coming in or is not being distributed. The men are ropeable, letters from home and the regular copy of the Bulletin is what makes life tolerable for us.

Sitting here in a dugout carved out of the cliff face like a gull on its nest and writing by candlelight has no feel of Christmas whatsoever. I met a cove yesterday who has occasion to visit the ships in the bay below and he told me that the thousands of candles from these little shelters where troops bunk down at night give the impression of Christmas lights. I believe it's also been most inappropriately called 'a fairyland of lights'. Although I can vouch there is very little peace and goodwill to all men to be found on the Gallipoli Peninsula at the moment. There may be a few wicked goblins about but there are certainly no fairies.

To further the idea of Christmas coming, we have had the first snowfall of the year. As there has been no issue of blankets, it is bitterly cold. (Did you buy the blanket factory in Launceston?) Coming after the severe summer heat with very little autumn weather to warn us, the snow, the first most of the lads have ever seen, has been disastrous. We are told nearly eleven thousand troops have been treated with frostbite, bronchial conditions and the like. Several hundred men froze to death on the night of the first fall. Even the snow, it seems, has sided with the Turks. I must end this for the time being as we are to go out on patrol at dawn and I must try to get some sleep. I will take up again tomorrow.

PALACE HOSPITAL

1st January 1916

My dearest Hawk and Victoria,

You will see from the above address that my luck has changed, or has it? I lie on a bed in the sunshine, looking over the coming and going of warships and transports in the harbour below, knowing that I am not, for the present, going anywhere.

Your mail sent to Gallipoli has caught up with me at last and I have a pile of eight letters from you, Victoria, and have taken to rationing myself with one each day. Two also from you, Grandfather Hawk, very precious and much cherished. The constant flow of letters from home has kept me sane and I don't quite know how I would have managed without them. My platoon looked forward to them as much as I did. I was in the habit of reading relevant bits to them and, towards the end, I feel sure they regarded your letters as if they had themselves received them. It is now obvious why they were not received on Gallipoli as they would have arrived over the period we were preparing to evacuate, though, of course, I didn't know this at the time I started this letter.

I have taken a bullet to the stomach which occurred on the last day on the peninsula, in fact only six hours before we pulled out. It is not as bad as it might seem, it was not a direct hit, but a ricochet and has lodged sideways near my spine. The doctors have not operated and there is some talk that I may be sent to England where the facilities for removing it are better. Though I have some pain, it is nothing compared to that suffered by most of the men here and I count myself fortunate. They have shaved my head and I am able to wash my body every day, it is quite the most wonderful experience.

You must both forgive me if I return to the subject of my letter to you from Gallipoli, now three weeks ago. I fear it will be a long one as I have much to get off my chest. You would do well to read it in dribs and drabs to avoid tedium. It is now even more important to me that I write it all down. So, with your permission, I shall finish it, though thankfully in the past tense. This morning, for the first time, I have been able to reflect on being alive and am not yet quite sure how I feel, though I think I am grateful and, perhaps, as the saying goes, time will prove to be the great healer it is supposed to be. And now I shall continue.

What a change has come over us since we first sailed from Egypt keen as mustard to get to the Turk and to show him what it meant to come up against Australians. At the time, I am ashamed to say, we had little opinion of the fighting ability of our foe, thinking him just another kind of gyppo with a broad yellow streak running down the centre of his back. We referred to him, as we did the Egyptians, as 'wogs' and often enough as 'dirty wogs' and yearned to be dispatched to France to fight the German soldier whom we regarded as a white man like us and therefore a worthy foe.

It seems quite astonishing to me that this was only seven months ago and in so short a period I could go from such youthful arrogance to the person I have now become. No matter what you are told at home, the Turk has proved to be a brave soldier who is not afraid to die and loves his motherland as we do ours. He has also given us a thorough trouncing and, although I shall always be proud of the way we fought on Gallipoli Peninsula, the Turk has no less reason to feel proud that he defeated us. You must believe me when I say we were not easy to beat and that we never gave up, not even at the very last disillusioned moment.

2nd January

It seems strange lying here in the winter sunshine without the constant crackle of gunfire or artillery shells bursting over my head. The biggest disruption to the peace and quiet is the occasional mournful sound of a ship's horn in the harbour below or the clatter of the tea trolley down the hospital corridor.

Now that it is all over and I lie once again between clean sheets, I want to put down a few bits 'n' pieces. I do so not because they are important, but because there are ghosts in my life which must be laid to rest. So many of my mates are dead and I must speak for them and the battles they fought in. I feel at last able to write about the previous months. I, who always stared out of the window when old Mrs Wickworth-Spode tried to get me to put my thoughts to paper, now wish to set the record straight as far as I was concerned in the Gallipoli campaign.

Some day, they'll write the history of what happened in the Dardanelles but my mates won't be in it. They will not be included in any report, which will tell instead of plans and attacks and the doings of colonels and generals seeking vindication for actions taken that were foolish and unwarranted and which resulted in thousands of good men dying needlessly.

But Gallipoli was never about charts and logistics or the vainglorious careers of our military leaders. It was about young lads doing the best they could, giving the best they had, showing courage and humour and a love for their mates that was always decent and honest and true. Somebody has to tell of them. I will write about my own men, but you could substitute their names for many others, the young blokes who came to Gallipoli who fought and believed until the last. They were the best we had and I doubt we shall ever fully recover from their loss. Wordy Smith once told me that lads like these, strong and brave, most nearly a foot taller than their English equivalents, are the genetic seed from which a people is made. When you see a thousand young lads strewn across a battlefield, their bodies filled with maggots as they rot in the sun, it is difficult not to feel bitterness and despair at the terrible waste. I am not yet thirty years old though I feel twice this age and when I see an eighteen-year-old lad lying dead or calling out for his mother while he holds his intestines in his cupped hands, I cannot think of any cause that can justify such destruction. I'm afraid the old easygoing Ben has been changed, forever, though I doubt for the better.

And so I am writing down what happened to my mates while it is still fresh in my mind. I will write their proper names at the end of this letter and I want you to find their families and read this letter to them so they know what happened to their sons and can be proud that they raised such men.

But, first, now that it is over in this part of the world, though we still fight the Turk in Egypt, I must tell you of our life on Gallipoli. I have written to you of the landing and the first few days and so I intend to take up from there. Oh, by the way, I was mentioned in dispatches over the incident with the Turkish machine gun late on the first day. I have lost touch with Captain Daly who put me up for it, though I hope they have seen fit to give him the Military Cross as he deserved a medal far more than I deserved the 'mention'. I must say I was a bit embarrassed by it all but the platoon took it in the right spirit and said although there is no ribbon for it, if there was they'd each take turns pinning the ribbon above their tunic pocket. Quite right too, if I got a mention all of us should have.

After the first fierce fighting, when we were eventually driven back and we dug in on a front line that never really changed much for the duration of our stay, things sort of settled down a bit. The fighting went on in pockets, sometimes fierce and sometimes simply an attack on a patrol, or we'd come across a dozen or so Turks up to no good and give them hell. The artillery from both sides (though mostly from the Turk who was better equipped than us in this regard) went on for most of the daylight hours and so did the snipers. On one such day Crow Rigby and a Turkish sniper exchanged shots for four hours until our man seemed to have got the last shot in because we heard no more from the beggar higher up on the ridge. Such contests were common enough and we took a win from one of our own snipers to mean we were superior, like a football match where your side wins against a hated team.

Oh, how we despised their snipers who made walking out in the open in daylight always a dangerous occupation and who forced us to do most of our chores at night when we were exhausted. The biggest *danger was going down to the beach to fetch water for the platoon and I lost three men doing this. Ducking or falling to the ground became a habit almost as common as brushing flies from the corners of your eyes. I found myself on one occasion clawing the ground when someone near me snapped a plank of wood free from a bullybeef crate. Without thinking, our ears were tuned unconsciously to the Turkish artillery fire. The snipers' bullets never really stopped and silence was unknown to us, the crackle of rifle fire, the whoosh of a shell passing overhead or the sharp crack, bang and whirr of shrapnel pellets raining down was the only constant.*

3rd January

Yet, after the first month, we became so accustomed to these conditions that the men pronounced themselves bored. The only one of us who seemed remarkably adjusted was Peregrine Ormington-Smith who somehow found flowers still growing on ground that was cratered by artillery shells and churned to dust. He would sit quietly in his dugout with some specimen the size of my little fingernail under his microscope and paint it, making copious notes beside it as though this tiny blossom was of the greatest importance to mankind. The man was quite impossible.

The rest of us soon forgot those first few days after the

landing when we were too stunned to think and wished only to get off the peninsula and never fire another shot in anger again. In the long period of tedium after the first onrush the thing we hated the most was not being able to see the enemy while they, perched higher up, on the ridge and cliff faces, could look directly down on us. We constantly told ourselves that if only we could fix bayonets and have a go then we'd soon enough have the better of them.

I know you must find this difficult to understand, but day-to-day living conditions were so tedious and difficult that the men thought of fighting, even dying, as a kind of relief from the tension. Most had become quite indifferent to losing their lives. Wordy Smith said it was a type of insanity brought about by battle fatigue and the extreme tension of being shot at all the time without being able to effectively shoot back. He may well have been right. We are different now, none of us the same nice lads who left home ten months ago. Death was such a common occurrence that it seemed almost as normal to us as staying alive. We came to see the business of staying alive not as good management but purely a matter of luck.

But always there was a hunger for victory, to do what you could when you could, so that those who followed you had a better chance. Every day wounded men returned to the trenches, not because it was critical that they did so, but because they had begged the hospital or first-aid post to be allowed to fight with their mates. They had quite lost the ability to see themselves as individuals, but only as a part of a unit that was not complete without them nor they without it. This changed after Lone Pine, Quinn's Post and the Daisy Patch, where there was so much slaughter and where we lost so many of our mates that those of us who were still alive felt completely isolated and unable to go back to the slaughter. It was as if a part of us had been removed, disabling us as fighting men. I shall tell you later of these three battles which took place in August.

4th January

Victoria, you must excuse my not pandering to your feminine sensibilities, but I want you and Grandfather Hawk to get a clear picture of how things were here in the summer (June, July, August) and still were right to the end, except that we suffered less from flies and disease in the cooler weather.

I tell you these things not because I want you to take pity on the lads but so that you can understand the life of an ordinary soldier here on Gallipoli. We left Australia not caring what the war was about, it was a chance to fight for King and Country to show what we were made of. Now, with so many dead and so little resolved, I must question why men go to war against each other. If you are to marry and have sons of your own I pray that you will teach them war is a hell to be avoided.

If my life is to be spared there are some things I can never talk about. This is not because I caution myself not to do so, but because men who must kill each other are not given the words for how they feel afterwards.

Not that I regret having come, and if I must die I am prepared to do so, but now I want to know why my country needs to take my life from me, I must know what the higher cause is for which they offer me as the sacrifice. Why all this killing is necessary? On the battlefield, to stay alive was never more than a passing thought, because there was nothing we could do beyond occasional commonsense to increase the probability of survival. We all believe now that it is only a throw of the dice if we come out of this fighting inferno alive or dead. War is a game of chance. A matter of luck.

When a man is shot and killed where you yourself stood moments before, you put it down to luck. God does not get the credit, He loved the man who died as much as you, but it is Lady Luck who is thanked. I confess that each morning as my eyes open to another day it has become my habit to reach for the Tiki about my neck and to hold it to my lips a moment. I do this every bit as earnestly as a Roman Catholic might kiss a crucifix. I do the same before going on patrol or into battle and I do it again last thing at night. Just as our mother said, I have come to believe in it as much as our great-grandmother believed in her Waterloo medal. This little green man that hangs about my neck has become my great good luck and I should be vexed if I lost him.

Let me give you a bizarre example of how our minds were affected in this matter of luck. We all took turns to go down to the bore near the beach for our daily ration of water, that, by the way, was the most precious of substances on the ridge. We were given a third of a gallon each day, which in the heat was only just sufficient to keep us from dehydrating. I tried to save a mugful for my ablutions etc. With this I had to shave, wash and, if I was careful not to make the water soapy, to get a boil up for half a mug of dirty-water tea. Anyway, I digress. As I was saying, the business of going down to fetch water (each man had to carry four gallons up the ridge on his own) was a slow dangerous journey with a number of rest stops where enemy snipers, ever alert, waited to pick us off. Half a hundred troops died this way every week.

On the way down from our position to the bore near the beach, along a steep rocky path lay a dead Turkish soldier whom the maggots had cleaned out, and a bit of a bushfire, started by shrapnel, had smoked the carcass to a black, leathery affair of taut skin stretched over bone. He lay right beside the path on his back with one blackened arm and hand straight up in the air as if he was appealing for mercy.

Well, one evening Numbers Cooligan and Woggy Mustafa were sent down on water detail and, passing the dead Turk, Numbers pointed to the blackened carcass and told Woggy that his Irish grandmother had once said that shaking the hand of a dead man brought incredible good luck and the promise of a long life.

'Yeah?' said Woggy. 'God's truth?'

'Would I tell you a lie?' said Cooligan.

'Course you would,' replied Woggy.

'Well, I ain't,' Cooligan said, 'I swear it on me granma's grave.'

Woggy was taken in by the apparent seriousness of the oath and solemnly shook the dead Turk's hand. Of course, when they got back to the line Numbers couldn't tell us quickly enough about Woggy's nocturnal greeting of the dead Turk. It was a big laugh shared all round and Woggy got a hard time from the rest of the lads except Brokenose Brodie, who asked Cooligan if what his grandmother told him was fair dinkum 'cause he swore it on her grave.

'She ain't dead,' Cooligan said, thinking this hilarious. 'No grave to swear on, mate!'

Well, the next time Woggy was on water detail he went with Andy Anderson, a big lad from St Kilda. Woggy passed the dead Turk and stopped and solemnly shook his hand. On the way back Andy was killed by a sniper. A week later Woggy was on water detail again, this time with Moggy Katz, same thing again, Mustafa shook the dead Turk's hand and a little further down the path Private Katz took a sniper's bullet through the left shoulder. Then another detail on water duty got shot and we had one dead and three wounded in our platoon.

From that time on every member of the platoon going down the path shook the dead Turk's hand. News of the hand soon spread and it wasn't too long before everyone in the company passing by was shaking the hand. Until one day it dropped off, whereupon some wag pushed the hand into the crevice of a rock to the side of the path so that the fingers protruded outwards. To the very day before we fought at Lone Pine in August, every soldier passing by on that particular path touched the blackened fingertips for the luck he thought it would bring him. The black hand, as it became known, assumed a deep significance to those of us on the ridge and I confess to touching it myself.

5th January

Of the many vexations that beset us this past summer the flies were the worst. The greatest relief that came our way was not when the enemy ceased to attack, but when the colder weather killed off the flies.

I first saw the flies on wounded men in April, and thought I had never witnessed such a gross thing, but they were a mere buzzing aggravation compared to what was to come in June, July and into the hot weather of August. We did not always observe the strictest standards of hygiene in the trenches, which fell far short of the standards we were taught before we left. But then it was always supposed there would be water available, whereas we had too little to spare for cleanliness.

The men went for weeks without a wash and the fleas and lice were a constant plague so that every two days we wore our uniforms inside out in the hope that the sun would fry the lice. Every week or so a dozen men from the platoon would go down to the beach where we bathed in the salt water. If you didn't mind a shrapnel pellet plopping beside you every once in a while it was well worth the effort. There were no waves to speak of and it was a bit like bathing in a salty pond, and the cool water of the Aegean after the blazing heat up on the ridges was glorious. We would go in in our uniform and this killed the immediate fleas and the lice, though not the eggs which hatched in the seams and seemed impervious even to being smoked over a fire.

If cleanliness is next to godliness then this was a most unholy place. There was no way we could keep utensils clean other than to lick the surfaces. But always the flies were so thick that to spread a bit of jam on a hard biscuit was to double the weight of the biscuit long before it reached your mouth. You would think there were enough corpses lying around to satisfy them, but still the flies came. We would speak with our hands clamped over our mouths and those who had colds and runny noses soon took the skin from their top lips in the constant attempt to brush away the flies.

I saw one soldier driven to madness in just such a circumstance that he smashed his fist down upon his own nose, breaking it, and the instant flow of blood attracted a swarm of flies so thick that his head could scarcely be seen. I covered him with a bit of a flour bag and he wept uncontrollably for an hour before he could be attended to and we sent him to Lemnos for three days so that he could rest his nerves.

The flies brought sickness which spread throughout the trenches. Our sanitation was not good, as it was never wise to walk to some quiet spot during the day and where there were latrines the queue was an hour long. The men suffered terribly from dysentery and other intestinal ailments and the trenches often went uncleaned with merely a shovelful of soil to cover what a man couldn't help doing when he was down with the squirts.

The rate of sickness, better contained in the cool weather, was far greater than the number of wounded and the men grew weaker each day while the tasks at hand, apart from the fighting, sapped our energy. As well as carrying water up the steep slopes, we made bombs from jam tins, as the bomb factory on the beach could not keep up with the need. We were in constant demand to provide burial parties and no day *passed when we weren't called upon to dig further trenches or to help the saps with the tunnelling towards the Turkish lines. We had no relief, no diversions, no back lines, no rest and we existed almost exclusively on iron rations. This frugal diet, intended as an emergency to take into battle, became our daily fare for all the months we were there, with only an occasional hot meal to break the monotony of hard biscuit, bullybeef, jam and a little tea. Tell Martha the fame of her billyjam tarts has spread far and wide.*

Fleas, lice and flies, dirt and sickness, monotony and always death were our only constants. Death was everywhere. The dead lay under every bush, piled up in rotting heaps, scattered over open ground, and there was a stench beyond any imagining. Turks and Australians rotted equally well under a blazing sun and while the Turks seldom gathered their dead for burial, many of our own could not be reached. They will lie where they have fallen until this terrible time has passed and we can return to bury their bones in quiet graves where the birdsong can be heard once more.

6th January

Yet throughout all this, only a few soldiers surrendered to their afflictions though there were some malingerers and some with self-inflicted wounds, but they were few and far between. Most carried on when they were too weak for any sustained attack. They still thought of victory and wanted to be with their mates. In my platoon not one man dishonoured his nation nor did anything to shame his family name.

I do not say this with false pride, we are well past such shallow and empty sentiment. We were resigned to die and the reason I did not write was simply that I could not imagine what I could say to you. Like all the men who landed here during April I had shaken hands with the shadows and, in my own mind, was already dead. When Moggy Katz was taken off the peninsula with a Mauser bullet through his shoulder he screamed out, not in pain, but in fury that he was leaving and that he had a right to die with his mates. We all knew this feeling.

And now I must tell you of the battles we fought and won and lost and then lost and won and lost again. Late in July we were alerted that we were to make another major assault. Those of us who had been on the peninsula from the beginning accepted the news philosophically. We had long since given up the idea that we could win with one decisive battle. The Turk was too well placed to be dislodged and too numerous to be defeated even if we could kill twice as many as our own dead. Besides, we were ourselves too weakened to sustain an all-out fight to the finish, except to be almost certainly defeated. For us there was only one of two possible endings, we would either be killed or, mercifully, wounded, and our wounds would take us from that dreadful place. Victory was no longer a likelihood in our minds. Yet those who had arrived later looked forward to the coming battle, as we had once done. We had all grown to manhood with tales of glory and honour on the battlefield and this was their turn to prove their courage. They thought us almost certain to win and were most eager for the fray.

We now know that while we thought this a major battle for supremacy of the heights above Anzac Beach, it was only intended as a feint. We were to draw the Turkish reserves from the planned landing at Suvla Bay, the flat ground a mile to the north of our beach, for the twenty-five thousand British New Army troops.

We were to attack the Turks at Lone Pine where they occupied some of the very trenches I had occupied with my platoon on the first day. Now four months later we would try again to take what had been ours within hours of landing. At two-thirty in the afternoon of August 6th we filed into a secret underground trench dug by the sappers for the attack. Three companies, each from a different battalion, formed the front line just sixty yards from the Turkish trenches, though the flat ground between ourselves and the enemy was covered with barbed wire. Another thirty yards in the rear were two companies which would immediately follow us.

Though young men's heads are filled with the derring-do of a bayonet charge, rushing up to an enemy who is dug in and firing from the safety of a parapet at a mass of men who must cover sixty yards *before they can become combative is sheer foolishness. I am convinced that my own platoon alone, facing two hundred men rushing at them from this distance, would have eliminated them by means of rifle fire before they ever reached the point of hand-to-hand combat. Add a single machine gun to such a mix and it is lambs to the slaughter.*

7th January

At about four o'clock our artillery began to pound their trenches and almost immediately the Turks replied with a bombardment of their own. In the artillery department they always had the better of us and soon shells were raining down, their Howitzers causing great craters in and around us, shrapnel pellets thick in the air so that men waiting to attack and those in the supporting trenches were dropping everywhere. There was nothing quite as frustrating when, with bayonet fixed, you were waiting for the whistle to take you over the top and then were taken out of the play before you could get out of your trench.

My platoon was waiting with me, the miracle was that we still had twenty-six of the original complement with us, these old hands mixed with the new chums to keep them steady, though the new recruits seemed to need no encouragement and were calm enough. In the front, the first over with Wordy Smith and myself were Crow Rigby, Numbers Cooligan, Woggy Mustafa, Library Spencer, Muddy Parthe, Hornbill and Brokenose Brodie, who, by the way, could read at quite a pace and was always to be seen with a tattered copy of the Bulletin in his back trouser pocket. He would pat the magazine at every opportunity to confirm his status as a man of letters.

How these stout fellows had managed to come through everything with hardly a scratch was beyond me, they never ceased to chaff each other and were always first into everything going. Though I was proud of my platoon and especially their ability behind a rifle, these seven had become a fine fighting unit with a reputation for the firepower they could put down together with a Lee-Enfield. All the practice at Broadmeadows and on the Orvieto and subsequently here had paid off handsomely. There had even been some suggestion, Captain Daly and Major Sayers I think the instigators, that if we had come out of this the six lads, with Crow Rigby as their corporal, would have been taken back to Egypt to show the new brigades what it meant to use a Lee-Enfield correctly.

It is best, I've found, not to speculate about these things and to take each day as it comes. Though, I confess, if I had been in charge I would have culled men such as these from the bayonet charges where they could be mowed down from the parapets without firing a single shot. They were too valuable behind a rifle. Though, of course, we are all cattle in this abattoir we called Gallipoli.

We were to go over together when the whistle went at five-thirty. Waiting was always the worst time, to be sitting ducks while the shrapnel burst overhead, a veritable cloudburst of deadly pellets, and at any moment you imagined that you would take a direct hit. We had stacked our packs behind the lines so that we could run with all our might, water bottle and ammunition pouches and iron rations all that we carried. We expected to fight well into the night and sewed white calico patches to our sleeves and backs so that we could be seen in the dark by our own men. Of course, this proved just as handy to the Turk who could now distinguish us from his own.

8th January

The whistle went and we were over, it was too late to be afraid now. The new chums were shouting out, 'Here come the Australians!' Some were even singing and all rushed forward as though it was a race at a Sunday school picnic. To use an expression coined here at Gallipoli 'all hell broke loose', it was not yet dark enough to conceal us and a fire started by shrapnel on the Daisy Patch lit us up clearly enough for the waiting Turkish machine guns. Sixty yards at a Sunday school picnic is not much but now it seemed a mile or more. Machine-gun fire, artillery shells, lyddite, hand-thrown bombs and a wall of rifle fire rained down on us. Men fell on either side of us, some sprawled over the barbed wire so that others coming from behind simply used them as mats. I glanced to either side of me and to the back to check my platoon. The ground all the way back from the trenches where we'd started was littered with the bodies of our men, some of whom had taken no more than a single step forward before dying.

We had already decided to go for the trenches we'd occupied as we knew the layout with the covered section at the southern end. We'd make for this part so that we couldn't be fired directly upon and then we'd come down from the roof of what we'd previously called the shed and jump into the trench. We'd rehearsed this carefully and I'd drawn a map of the dugouts, communication trenches and saps with each man allocated a place to enter and fight. Even the new recruits knew the layout of this particular section and where they should go. Wordy Smith with his long legs was the first over and onto the roof, closely followed by Crow Rigby. The roof was almost safe as the Turks were firing forward and would have had to turn halfway around to fire directly at us. In the confusion they seemed not even to see us about to descend from the roof of the trench down into them. It was exactly how Jack Tau Paranihi had described the way the New Zealanders had taken the trench on the early morning of the day of the landing.

I looked back over the ground we'd just covered to see if there were any stragglers from our platoon, a quick look seemed to indicate that we'd lost a few in the charge and I could only hope that they were wounded and not killed. But what I saw about thirty yards from the trench was Woggy Mustafa trying to come forward, his chest a splash of crimson. He would rise to his feet, take a few steps towards us, then fall and rise again.

Suddenly I heard a cry of anguish from Numbers Cooligan, 'Woggy! The bastards! The f . . . ing bastards!' Whereupon he dropped his rifle on the roof of the Turkish trench and ran straight back into the melee, pushing some of our own troops aside as he ran against the tide of oncoming men and flashing bayonets. He reached Woggy who had risen again and now fell into Cooligan's arms. Cooligan was one of the smallest men in our platoon and Mustafa one of the biggest, but the little man hefted him across his shoulder and, turning, ran towards us. He was no more than five yards away from where we stood when a Turkish machine gun turned on him and cut them both to pieces at the foot of the parapet.

I am not sure what happened next. I know we were down into the trench from the roof. I was not conscious of dropping my rifle nor that I had unslung my fighting axe from the holster at my back. All I can remember was seeing the machine-gunner deliberately turn his gun on little Cooligan and the next thing I knew was that eight Turks lay dead between me and the machine-gunner. And then, apparently he saw me and turned the machine gun into the trench but before he had the barrel around in an arc sufficient to aim at us the axe had left my hand and split his head open, cleaving his skull in half from the brow down to his mouth.

Later Wordy Smith told me that I had pushed them all aside as we'd jumped into the trench and my axe had taken the throats of eight terrified Turks standing between me and the Turk who had killed Numbers Cooligan, my eyes never leaving the machine-gunner. The remaining Turks, about twenty in all, seeing me coming at them with the axe, could quite simply have shot me. Instead they turned and fled for their lives. We'd won our section of the trench and the men moved on to clean up the Turks who'd hidden from the artillery bombardment in several small tunnels, communication trenches, the shed and the saps, killing another seventeen of the enemy.

For my part, I can claim no heroics, I was not conscious of what I was doing, my fury overriding any caution or commonsense. In truth, I showed poor leadership. I only tell you this so you will know the power of shock and grief and the disregard one has for one's own life in such circumstances.

Numbers Cooligan showed the real courage. By going out to bring his mate back in he had no earthly chance of surviving. Our little Gob Sergeant had thought only to bring Woggy back in, to allow him to die with his mates. We pulled them both back into the trench and cleaned them up the best we could and put them in the shed so when the sun rose in the morning they would be in the shade and hopefully away from the worst of the flies. I will see that they get proper graves. I emptied their pockets so that I could remove the letter they'd been instructed to write home. Woggy had left his envelope open and attached a scrap of paper to it asking for his crucifix to be taken from his neck and included in his letter addressed to his mother. To my surprise Numbers Cooligan's letter was addressed to me. I opened it to find twenty pounds and the following note:

> Sergeant Ben Teekleman.
> Dear Ben,
>
> I don't have no parents as I was an orphan boy. The bloke at Flemmo racecourse was not my uncle and a real bastard. But I have you and Wordy Smith and seven other brothers now — so will you use this money what's my ill-gotten gains and when it's all over have a beer or ten on me. Tell the lads no bloke ever had a better bunch of brothers and I loves you all. Also, tell Woggy I'm sorry for the hard time I gave him, he is the best Christian I have ever known, bar none, I swear it on my granma's grave (whoever she was!).

It's been a real pleasure, mate.

Wayne Numbers Cooligan
Gob Sergeant, No. 2 Platoon, B Company, 5th Battalion,
1st Division A.I.F. Gallipoli, 1915.

9th January

If we had hoped for a respite after taking the trench we were to be disappointed. We'd clearly driven the enemy from Lone Pine but at a terrible cost, Woggy Mustafa and Numbers Cooligan were but two of thousands who eventually died, a thousand men or more on the first day. The order was to hold on and to expect a counterattack and, indeed, we were not let down in this regard.

They came at us from the start and what followed were three days, wave after wave, of the fiercest possible fighting, a great deal of it at close quarters and with a bayonet, the cruellest of all the weapons and the only one where we touched the man we killed. Often we could feel his hot breath on our faces, and as he died clutching his stomach, the Turkish lad would cry out for his mama, as our own had. I confess with a degree of shame that I found the fighting axe to be a much more efficient weapon than the awkward rifle with its clumsy knife attached to the end of its barrel. Grandfather Tommo's skill with the axe, passed somehow on to me, has, I believe, saved my life on several occasions and, of more importance, has helped to save others. It must have proved a very effective weapon in the Maori wars.

We learned from the enemy the nastiness of hand-thrown bombs. They have a small bomb about the size and shape of a cricket ball which they throw into our trenches. It has a nasty explosion which can kill but will mostly blow off a foot or blind you. At first we found these very awkward to handle and used to drop a sandbag over them to prevent any damage. But then we discovered that the fuses were fairly long and that we could pick them up and throw them back at the enemy. They soon enough cottoned onto this and made the fuses shorter so that we had to either catch them in mid-air or move very fast to throw them back for they would take anything from one to five seconds to explode. The men became quite expert at it but, alas, losing a hand was a common enough occurrence.

We have our own version of this little weapon, empty jam tins packed with explosives and any pieces of metal found lying about. These are manufactured at the bomb factory on the beach or by the men in the dugouts and they are just as effective. The men call these bombs 'the hissing death', for the hiss and splutter of the lighted fuse.

For three days and nights we stood face to face hurling these bombs at each other or charging with fixed bayonets. All the while both sides were sending down a veritable hailstorm of rifle and machine-gun fire. Furthermore, when the enemy were not attacking they bombarded us with a constant barrage of artillery shells. There was not even five seconds of continuous silence in the three days of fighting and we were exhausted to the point of collapse, the men taking turns to sleep although the fighting was raging around them.

Even this had its problems, the dead were everywhere, the Turks' and our own. We had no time to remove them from the trenches and no possibility of burying them, they were piled four or five deep in our own trench and even higher in others. Throwing them over the side meant we were unsighted, unable to look over them from the rifle platforms as they piled up in front of the trenches.

If a man, too exhausted to lift his rifle, needed a spell there was little choice but to sit on a dead man. My men slept with the dead as mattresses.

The stench of bodies rotting in the sun was unbearable. We managed to find six gas protectors to help with the smell, and these were shared, an hour at a time, to bring relief from the terrible smell. By the third day of fighting there were more dead than alive and I had lost thirty men in my platoon and every single one of Numbers Cooligan's 'brothers' had joined him in death. As each died beside me I prayed that I would be next. Now I shall have to drink out Private

Wayne 'Numbers' Cooligan's twenty quid on my own. I hope to stay drunk for a month if it will help just a little to kill the terrible sadness which consumes me.

Wordy Smith is also dead and I am still too numb to mourn him and them beyond crying in my sleep. I shall try, for the sake of their parents, to tell you how each of them lost his life, though I have not the strength to do so today and will try again tomorrow.

10th January

I shall begin today with the statistics of Lone Pine. On the ninth of August the Turks had had enough. Or perhaps they realised that the main threat to them was the British who had landed at Suvla Bay. We did not know this and fought as if the war must end right where we stood, as if it was our own personal responsibility. We had killed six thousand of them in the three days of fighting and we had lost two thousand three hundred dead and wounded. Our own dead lay thickly spread on Lone Pine where, when the burial parties came to fetch them, the maggots dropping from their bodies were gathered in bucketfuls.

Lone Pine was thought to have had the bloodiest hand-to-hand fighting of the war and continued for three days. But on the day following our attack on the Turkish trenches several skirmishes to the north also occurred which, in their own way, were every bit as tragic.

I was not there, of course, still being occupied at Lone Pine, but I have heard about them from some who were, those precious few who lived. I must assure you there is not the slightest exaggeration in any of the details.

The 8th and 10th Light Horse regiments were called upon to take a position known as The Nek, a ridge about fifty yards wide at the Anzac front line and thirty yards or so at the Turkish trenches, so that any bayonet charge from our lines would have the effect of forcing troops into a bottleneck, concentrating their numbers for the Turkish machine guns and rifles. Our trenches and those of the Turks were only twenty yards apart, not much deeper than the average suburban backyard. Five Turkish machine guns covered the ground between them, not to mention the Turks in their own trenches armed with rifles.

The Light Horse were new troops on the peninsula with no old hands among them. This was their first great battle and, like us, they were anxious to make their mark. They told themselves they must prove their mettle and show they could fight as well as their countrymen whom they had watched from the heights to the north as we mounted the attack on Lone Pine the evening before. Bright-eyed and bushy-tailed they stood, four lines of one hundred and fifty men each were to attack at two-minute intervals, their objective the Turkish trenches immediately to their front and the maze of trenches and saps on Baby 700 directly behind the Turkish front line. These trenches to the immediate rear of the Turkish front line were critical to their own attack and were lined with machine guns capable of halting the Australians in their tracks. The idea was for the artillery to pound the Turkish front line and their trenches behind it mercilessly to the very moment of the charge by the Light Horse. In this way the Turks would not be able to get into position before our troops were in among them with their bayonets. Timing was everything, the artillery would halt at four-thirty and at the same moment our men would be over and running.

At 4.23 the artillery stopped, seven minutes short. Three minutes that would cost us countless dead. Seven minutes in which the Turks could get into position, two deep, in their front trenches with their rifles ready, fire a few bursts from their machine guns to clear them and then simply wait for us to come.

Incredibly the Australian officers in command didn't abort the attack. Instead they played by the formula set out and waited the seven minutes. At four-thirty on the dot the whistle went and the 8th Light Horse scrambled from their trenches yelling blue murder. They had barely taken the first step when those soldiers at the front buckled and fell as the machine-gun fire and the Turkish rifles cut them to ribbons. Yet on they went. Twenty yards is not a long way, but they got no further than five yards and not a single man made it to the enemy parapet.

The second line, waiting, saw the fate of their mates but they never flinched and stood the allotted two minutes, many of the dead from the first line lying at their feet where they'd tumbled back into the trench, some clasping at their ankles, begging to be helped. The Turks were jabbering, excited, not quite able to believe the brave stupidity they'd just witnessed. Then the second line went over the top and, like the first, advanced little more than a few paces before they fell in great heaps over the bloodied bodies of their comrades who had died two minutes before them. The wounded tried to move from under the dead bodies, some howling their anguish, others calling for their mothers, but most too stunned to do anything but crawl back. A few made it, most were cut down a second time as they crawled away.

One wonders at such stupidity, but there was so much of it at Gallipoli where men too brave for their own good took orders from officers too stupid to rescind them. Men were fed like fodder into the mouth of hell.

The 10th Light Horse obediently filed into the places of the 8th. By now the men knew they must die, but reckoned still that they must run with all their heart as swiftly as their legs would carry them and so die with honour going forward into the attack. 'I do not want to die running away,' one of the lads was heard to say as he stepped up to wait for the order to go over the top.

'Boys, we have ten minutes to live,' their commanding officer Lieutenant-Colonel Springthorpe told them, 'and I am going to lead you.'

The men shook hands with their mates and when the order came they sprang from the trenches, jumping over dead bodies. Even the Turks could not believe the foolishness as they once again chopped them down to a man. Incredibly, the fourth line followed and they too tumbled into the blood-soaked dust as the attack was finally completed in a terrible defeat. They never stood a chance from the first to the last man dead. Two hundred and forty Light Horsemen lay dead or dying in an area no larger than a tennis court. They lie there still, we left them when we escaped from the peninsula, unable to retrieve them for burial. Of five hundred and fifty men who stood waiting in the trenches for the whistle to blow their lives away, only forty-seven answered to their names at roll call. The battle had lasted less than half an hour.

As the Light Horse lay dying, with the wind howling in the peaks above them, plainly visible from The Nek were the British troops at Suvla Bay making their evening tea. But this is not an indictment of the English who fought valiantly and died in greater numbers even than us, but of their leaders.

When summer comes again the bones of these gallant Light Horsemen will whiten in the sun along with so many others we could not bury with a Christian prayer. No doubt fat officers with bristling moustaches will sip port in clean uniforms at the Shepheards Hotel in Cairo, their chests ablaze with medals and garnished with campaign ribbons while they talk of the glory of this battle, and others like it. These are the names that will tumble carelessly from their lips, Quinn's Post, the Daisy Patch, the New Zealanders at Chunuk Bair. (What splendid fighting men they proved to be.) They will speak with pride that two hundred men attacked the Turks' trenches on Dead Man's Ridge and suffered one hundred and fifty-four casualties, and that fifty-four troopers of the 2nd Light Horse attacked Turkish Quinn's and all but one died. At German Officer's Trench, three hundred of our men went forward with bayonets fixed and one hundred and forty-six lost their lives. These are the only attacks after Lone Pine I heard of at first hand, but dozens of others like them took place and all of them failed. They failed, not because they lacked a full measure of courage, no soldiers ever fought harder or with more determination, but because good fighting men cannot make up for the gross incompetence of those who lead them.

Perhaps I am being unfair for I have become bitter with the months of senseless fighting, but it seems to me that having, in the very first instance, made the wrong decision to attack the Gallipoli Peninsula, those who led us tried to vindicate themselves and enhance their careers by sacrificing the lives of the men under their control. How very much more sensible it would have been if our leaders had let us live to fight a better campaign elsewhere where, in return for courage and determination, there was some small hope of victory.

The Turks, for their part, were simply defending their motherland. How happy they would have been if we'd simply packed up and gone home. When we finally did, they let us go with hardly a shot fired. Make no mistake, we now talk of fooling them, as though our nocturnal escape was somehow a great vanishing trick in a game of blind man's buff. Even some sort of victory. But they knew well enough that we were leaving and were happy to see the last of us. Enough blood had been shed on both sides.

It is claimed their own dead number eighty-nine thousand and ours twenty-nine thousand. One hundred and eighteen thousand men lie dead and no explanation for any of it is sufficiently plausible to convince the mother of a single Australian lad that he died for something of value. We did not die for King and Country or for some great human cause, we died because of the vanity of old men. It should be as plain as the nose on any father's face that his son was murdered. Make no mistake, this was senseless slaughter, men led like cattle to the abattoir, yet we will praise the colonels and the generals and the field marshals and give them more ribbons for their chests.

Speaking of such things, I was visited in hospital yesterday by a major from staff H.Q. who informed me that I am to receive the DCM for the axe incident on Lone Pine. I told him I had no use for it as it cannot bring my mates back to me. He told me not to be so ungrateful and that I was insulting the King.

'Sir, have you led a charge where you lost your entire battalion?' I asked him.

'If I had, Sergeant-Major, I would wear the medal my country gave me with pride.'

'And I, sir, will wear mine with the deepest sorrow.'

'That is enough from you, Sergeant-Major,' he replied. Then, moustache bristling, he turned on his heel and strode from the ward. I have no doubt that the loudest explosion he's heard in this war is the popping of a champagne cork.

I neglected to tell you that I have been promoted to sergeant-major.

11th January

I intended to write about the lads and the way they died, but yesterday, after the major's visit, I had no stomach for such writing. I do not know if I can do so today, we will have to see if I have the hand to write it without the shakes.

WORDY SMITH

I will begin with Wordy Smith, Lieutenant Peregrine Ormington-Smith, the most unlikely soldier on the Gallipoli Peninsula. I have with me his book of flowers and while the last page is soaked in blood the beautiful little blossoms in the spray he was painting have, with one exception, miraculously escaped the bloodstains. They peep around the patches of brown that often smudge the ink where he has written his notes. Every page is filled with his paintings, right up to this last bloodstained page. Above this half-completed watercolour he has written Ulex europaeus. *But it looks to me just like the blossom of the bloody furze bush that has given us such trouble. As you will see, it is plain enough to look at and only Wordy Smith could see virtue enough in it to want to paint it. I am sending his precious book to you, as he told me on two occasions that if he should die I was to have it. It is my most ardent hope that you will find some place of scholarship where it may be placed in perpetuity.*

Wordy Smith died as he would have liked, quietly and without any fuss, though he was a hero. His last moments were spent not with a rifle blazing at the enemy but with a paintbrush in his hand. He had taken a much-needed spell from the fighting and had settled with his microscope and box of paints in one of the communication trenches. Earlier in the day I had watched as he saved enough water from his precious daily ration to half fill a small tobacco tin so that he could use his watercolours. When I emptied his tunic pocket it contained several sprigs and the heads of dead flowers he had somehow gathered, though God knows when he could have done so over the last four days of fighting. He left no letter for me to send on to his parents though. Like Numbers Cooligan, there was a note addressed to me personally.

Gallipoli 1915

Dear Ben,

You are to keep my sketchbook and if my parents should make a fuss please show them this note. They did not care for the notion that I desired to be an artist and, in their possession, it will only remind them of the son who did not turn out well.

For my part, knowing you and the lads has been the very best period of my life. Now that I am dead I am able to say this, whereas alive you may have thought it sentimental and over-effusive.

And now I require a personal favour. I am the beneficiary of a small bequest left to me by my grandmother in England. I wish you to use it to establish a bursary at my old art school. It is to be called The William Horne Art Scholarship.

By going back to retrieve my sketchbook from the cliff face at Aden, Hornbill changed my life. Perhaps some budding artist in the future may study in a little more comfort because of what Hornbill so generously did for me.

Will you thank the lads for putting up with me, they are a grand lot and no officer ever was more privileged than I to have them in his platoon?

As for you, Ben, I do not have the words sufficient or laudatory enough to express my love and admiration.

Yours ever,

Peregrine Ormington-Smith,
Botanical Artist.

CROW RIGBY

Crow Rigby once said to me that when he was a kid he was considered the best shot of the young blokes in the district and won the blue ribbon at the local rifle club three years running and had developed a bit of a swollen head. His father heard him brag of it to someone and that night drew him aside after tea. They sat on the veranda for a while looking out over the dry paddock in front of the house, the old bloke sipping at a glass of milk stout. Finally his father looked up at him and said, 'Son, no matter how good you are at something, remember, there is always someone who is better than you.'

Corporal Crow Rigby died after he had been exchanging shots with a Turkish sniper for an hour and the Turk got one through and put a neat hole into the centre of his forehead. Crow would have admired the shot for it was painless, clean and decisive. He'd met his father's 'someone' who was better than him. Like Cooligan, Crow was terribly upset by the death of Woggy Mustafa whom he saw as his eyes. He came to me afterwards and said, 'Ben, I've got a confession to make.'

'I'm not a flamin' priest, mate,' I remember saying. 'What is it?'

'There was this sniper having a go and I got him in my sights, easy shot and I reckon we could have gotten to him after without too much danger.'

'So?'

'I let him go.'

'Why'd you do that?'

'Woggy. He would have got his Mauser telescopic sights.'

'What are you trying to say, Crow? That you didn't want another sniper competing with you? You wanted to keep him as your eyes? What?'

'Nah, he'd 'ave been the best there is, better than me any day of the week, I wouldn't have minded that.'

'Well, what then?'

'It would have been me made him a sniper and I couldn't bear to know that.'

I don't think I understood fully what he meant at the time. Crow Rigby was as fine a man as nature can make with a mercurial riposte that never went without a laugh. If a man may be judged by the laughter he brings into the world then he and Numbers Cooligan must sit equally on the throne of top-notch blokes.

Crow never shirked his duty either and volunteered on more than one occasion when one or another of the men was down with the squirts to do their water duty, often getting back after midnight from the long climb up from the beach. Once when I could see, like all of us, he was dog-tired, I told him I'd send someone who'd just arrived back from Lemnos after scoring three days' leave for a comparatively minor wound. He'd protested, 'Nah, I need to wash.'

'Why ever,' I'd asked, 'you're no dirtier than any of us?'

'Not my body, Ben, my soul. I must go down to the sea to wash my soul.'

'Your soul?' I remember being a trifle embarrassed, it was unlike Crow to talk in this manner and so I remained silent.

Seeing I didn't understand, he kicked one scuffed boot against the other. 'Ben, as a sniper I've killed at least two men every day *we've been here. It's not like in a battle or an attack when we're all fighting for our lives, it's seeing some bloke, some poor bastard, it doesn't matter that he's a Turk, who's carrying water to his mates or squatting to do his business behind a bush, seeing him in my sights and thinking I must make a clean shot so he dies well. After a while, mate, well it just sinks in what you're doing, you're murdering men, like they was vermin back on the property. You're not killing in the heat of a stoush, but in cold blood.' He shrugged. 'It's inside you become dirty, Ben, your soul. When I go down that path to the beach to collect water then I'm just like one of the blokes I shoot every day, I'm in a sniper's sights and that helps to wash a little of the dirt off my soul.'*

Crow Rigby was a country boy without much education but he was probably the deepest of us all. I shall miss him dearly. I enclose his letter to his parents unopened, though as their sergeant, in the absence of Wordy Smith, I am supposed to read it. There was too much of the private bloke about Crow Rigby to want to know what he said to his parents. Perhaps you, or Grandfather Hawk, will take the motor and deliver it to them and, at the same time, read those parts of this letter you think suitable. Let them know that he was as fine a man as this country has ever produced and that we buried him facing into the sunrise, so that he would see nothing but the light in his eyes.

HORNBILL

Hornbill asked me to read his letter after he'd written it, anxious that it be correct. I recall well how he put it at the time.

'I ain't had much education, Ben, I left school when I were nine and me father went timber fetching and took me along when me mum died of the T.B. Timber and fixin' things is all I know and I've not had much occasion to write to nobody before. Me uncle with the pie cart and me Auntie Mavis with the "artyritus" are the only relatives I got and they don't go in much for letter writing. Still an' all, if it's gunna be me only letter, I mean the first and the last one ever they's gunna get from me, I reckon I ought to get the bugger wrote properly, eh, Sergeant?'

Hornbill died manning the Hotchkiss machine gun during a counterattack by the Turks on the evening of the second day on Lone Pine. The enemy made a concerted effort to put our gun out of action, concentrating all their fire on the machine gun. I guess we must have been doing too good a job with the weapon that had killed Numbers Cooligan and Woggy Mustafa. Hornbill swore he'd take out twenty Turks for each of their lives and I feel sure he succeeded. They threw everything at us, firing and coming in with bayonets. We must have killed thirty men, three getting right up to us, one of them close enough to bayonet Hornbill through the chest before we shot them all. Hornbill, gripping the Turk's bayonet in both hands, ripped it out of his chest with a roar, and at the same time fell over the machine gun, using his body to protect it. He must have taken twenty Turkish bullets to his head and chest, though I feel sure he was already dead when this happened. He saved the machine gun and we continued to use it to the very end of the battle.

Hornbill, 'Mr Fixit', never had a bad bone in his body and he died thinking of his mates. I have put in a report in the hope that he will be decorated posthumously for his bravery, though I can almost hear him saying, 'Me uncle would wear the flamin' thing selling pies and tell everyone he won it for puttin' up with me Auntie Mavis and her "artyritus" all them years.'

Dear Uncle Mick and Auntie Mavis,

I am writing this to say goodbye because I am dead. They would have told you by now but I wanted to tell you myself. It was nice knowing you both and I hope you can sell your pies for many years to come and make a quid. I have made some good mates here, blokes I'm gunna miss a lot. We give the Turk heaps, but he give us some back too. It weren't an easy fight.

Try to remember me sometimes.

Your nephew,
Private William Horne, 1st Div. A.I.F. Gallipoli.

Please explain to Hornbill's auntie and uncle that the letter I took from his tunic was torn to shreds and soaked in blood, that is why I have repeated it here.

MUDDY PARTHE

Every platoon has to have a whinger and Muddy Parthe was ours. He could complain better than anybody else about almost anything. Hornbill, listening one morning to Muddy complaining about the sunrise, shook his head, 'He's got real class, lissen to the bugger, just lissen to what he's doing to the bloody sun comin' up.'

Muddy was squinting into the sun. 'Bloody sun, shines on them first, don't it? Warms their 'ands so the bastards can pull the trigger sooner, shines down into our eyes so we can't see 'em. They can see us though, bloody sun's on their side, I'm tellin ya.'

Bullybeef:

'We got to eat this shit and that's why we've got the squirts, bloody stuff rots our guts, don't it? Lookee here what it's called, Fray Bentos, you think that's the name o' the manufacturer, don't yiz. Well, it ain't, see, it's from Argentine where they speak Spanish, don't they?'

'Jesus, Muddy, what you trying to say?'

'Well you take the word "Fray", it's them trying to speak

English, they don't know the word "chewed" so they say the bloody meat is "frayed".' He took up a lump of bullybeef and pulled it apart with his fingers, the thin red streaks of meat looking exactly as if they'd been chewed before. 'See, what's that look like, it's been chewed before, ain't it?'

'You're beginning to sound like Cooligan, mate,' Woggy Mustafa says.

'So what about "Bentos"?' Library Spencer asks. 'What's that supposed to mean?'

'Simple, mate, it's them Spanish trying ter speak English again – Bentos, "Bent arse", they didn't know how to say "squat" so they say "bent arse", it's their word for squatting down to 'ave a crap. You've got ter bend your arse to have a crap, don't yer? What they're saying is that what we're eating is "frayed bent arse", chewed shit. And don't you think the army don't know it, we been eating shit ever since we got here.'

'For once you may have a point, mate,' Crow Rigby was heard to remark.

Muddy Parthe died throwing one of their bombs back over the parapet. He'd picked up two Turkish bombs and thrown them back and then one came looping through the air and the fuse must have been cut very short, or a Turk had thrown back a bomb that we'd already thrown back, because as Muddy caught it in mid-air, his hands in front of his face, it exploded. It didn't kill him instantly though. He was blinded and his face was smashed terribly. There was nothing we could do. Wordy Smith poured some of his opium medicine down his throat, where his mouth once was, and he died half an hour later. I can only hope without any pain.

Muddy Parthe was a brave man, he knew that sooner or later a Turkish bomb must get him, that his luck would run out. But it was his job to watch for the bombs and return them to the Turks and it was the one thing he never once complained about. I shall miss his colourful whingeing. When we were going through a hard time, to hear him complain often made us feel a whole heap better. No platoon should be without a Muddy Parthe.

I am enclosing Muddy's letter with this one unopened, though London to a brick he's complaining in it about something.

BROKENOSE BRODIE AND LIBRARY SPENCER

I must write about these two men together for they cannot in my mind be separated. Brokenose loved Library Spencer with all his heart and soul. I mean, of course, in a completely manly way. It is hard for a male to talk about loving another but I cannot avoid the word simply because there is no other appropriate word to take its place. Library made Brokenose Brodie realise that he was more than just a ditch digger, that he was someone who could read and write and hold his own in company. Library told him of people and places and things that would leave him gob-smacked with amazement and the wonder of it all. He discovered that he had a prodigious memory and would take it all in. Brokenose was not stupid, only ignorant, and with Library as his mentor he was like a sponge soaking it all in. He wanted to know everything and as Library Spencer knew everything there were never two mates better suited. Library Spencer, the teacher and reader who loved facts and the truth, and Brokenose Brodie, the pupil who could never get enough of either.

In the tedious hours in the trenches we would often become bored and frustrated, but never those two. They spent hours together with Spencer teaching Brokenose to read and write, Library Spencer using his precious copy of Great Expectations as the big man's tutor. Library once told me that Charles Dickens was the greatest writer of them all and, if Library said so, who was I to protest that old Wickworth-Spode thought it was Shakespeare. Anyhow, towards the end Brokenose could read from the great man's book with barely a hesitation.

I suggested on one occasion that he should rewrite his letter home, but he shook his head. 'It was wrote right for them. If I done it better they'd be ashamed they didn't do the right thing by us kids.' Brokenose Brodie, while trying to make up for a life in a dirt-poor family, didn't want to make them feel bad. 'Being poor an' ignorant with too many brats ain't nobody's fault, it just happens to some folks,' he'd once said to me.

Brokenose was the oldest of eight children, who were constantly abused and beaten by a drunken Irish father who worked as a casual labourer at the abattoir. I remember him telling me about his parents. 'Me old man worked maybe three days a week and so we ate mostly quite good, 'cause he'd bring scrag ends and offal 'ome. Saterdee and Sundee, though, we didn't eat nothing we couldn't steal, because me dad and me mum were dead drunk. Me mum couldn't take no more with him and us kids and she'd get stuck in the gin bottle.'

Library was brought up by his mother, a quietly respectable piano teacher who always encouraged him to read and to act like a gentleman. He once told me that he had read every book in the St Kilda library and many of them three or four times over. He never spoke of a father and I can only assume he never had one present in the home. Library was the school swot, the scholarship kid who didn't or couldn't play sport, the brat who knew everything and was bullied because of his brains. Until he joined the army he had never had a friend, had never been admired by someone his own age. He was the loner, the quiet bloke, until Brokenose Brodie, big, clumsy, eager as a puppy and filled with admiration and love for the man who knew everything, came into his life. There was never a couple more oddly paired or one that worked better in friendship.

Library Spencer, like Hornbill, died when three Turks managed to get over the parapet into our trench, one of them stabbing him through his back and heart, the bayonet's point coming out of the front of his chest. Brokenose turned around to see if his mate was all right just as it happened. His roar, or perhaps in the confusion and noise I imagined it, seemed to rise above the rifle and machine-gun fire. He dropped his rifle and lunged at the Turk who had his foot planted in the small of Library's back and was trying to pull his bayonet out. The huge man grabbed the hapless Turk by the throat and lifted him clean off the ground, snapping his neck like a chicken. I saw one of the other Turks coming for him and hurled my fighting axe, the blade cleaving the man's skull. Brokenose bent over the fallen Turk and grabbing my axe by the handle he pulled it out of the dead man's head. Screaming, he jumped onto the firing platform and vaulted over the lip of the trench, charging down the embankment straight into the attacking Turks. He killed six of them before they chopped him to pieces with bullets and bayonets.

I don't think Brokenose would have wanted to live without Library Spencer in his life. Both men died having known that they had a pride and a purpose, the one no longer a loner, the other no longer thinking himself useless. The teacher who knew everything and the pupil who wanted to learn everything there was to know together forever. We buried them next to each other, Mr Dickens' book in Library Spencer's hands and Brokenose hugging his slate and stylus. It was a partnership made in heaven where both men are now looking down at me as I write this.

How very much I shall miss them all.

Your loving grandson and brother,

Ben.

P.S. I have written all the names and addresses on a separate page.

B.

R.I.P.

Second Lieutenant Peregrine Ormington-Smith

General William & Mrs Lucinda Ormington-Smith

Holyoak Farm

Warrnambool, Victoria

Private William Thomas Horne

Mr Mick & Mrs Mavis Horne

14 Lambeth Place

St Kilda, Victoria

Private Wayne Cooligan

(Notify only) The Superintendent

Melbourne Orphan Asylum

Dendy Street

Brighton, Victoria

Private Joseph Mustafa

Mr Joe & Mrs Sarah Mustafa

9A Arthur Street

Coburg, Victoria

Private John Heywood Parthe

Mr John & Mrs Shirley Parthe

15 Vere Street

Collingwood, Victoria

Private Colin John Spencer

Mrs Gladys Spencer

51 Alma Road

St Kilda, Victoria

Private Kevin Sean Brodie

Mr Seamus & Mrs Maude Brodie

14A Wight Street

Kensington, Victoria

Corporal Peter John Rigby

Mr Roger & Mrs Sandra Rigby

'Lyndale'

Roadside delivery

Wooragee, N. E. Victoria

GALLIPOLI

The days will come when men will stand upon the shores,
Of Suvla Bay and Anzac where the fierce sea roars,
Amazed that mortals under such tremendous fire,
Landed at all, and, having landed, could retire.

Men will embark at Anafarta's sandy bay,
Under the peaceful skies of some soft summer day,
And picture to themselves that time, not long ago,
When all the hills were guns, and every rock a foe.

Bits of barbed wire will peep at them from out the grass
And waken up their slumbering memories as they pass,
Old speechless cannon look them in the face,
And ask them are they fit to stand in such a place?

Yes, other men will gaze upon the silent beach,
And thoughts will crowd about the hills too deep for speech;
Sorrow and pride will come and take them by the hand,
To those heroic graves in that forbidding land.

No need for polished marble there, nor sculptor's art,
To tell the world of Australasia's glorious part;
In quiet village church and in cathedral old,
Let the immortal deeds in glass and stone be told.
But at Gallipoli the place will tell the tale,
The yellow sands, the rocks, the beetling cliffs, the gale;
Why carve New Zealand's name on lonely Sari-Bair,
Or tell old frowning Krithia who lie buried there?

Nations may pass away and other nations come,
But time's destructive hand will never mar their tomb;
Those mighty monuments for ever will remain,
The everlasting witness of a deathless fame.

– W. S. Pakenham-Walsh, 1916

Chapter Sixteen

JOSHUA, BEN AND SISTER ATKINS

London and the Western Front 1916–1918

Thus far Major Joshua Solomon has had what every concerned parent would describe as a 'good war' in as much as he has spent it well behind the front line, first in Mena and then in France. Anybody who spends a war ordering boots and bullybeef won't die a violent death, which is a comforting thought to Sir Abraham but one which rankles constantly with his son, the heir to the chairmanship of the giant Solomon & Teekleman conglomerate.

Being the officer commanding an army ordnance company, the chief margarine merchant as the front-line troops call his kind, does not fit in with how Joshua sees himself. From the moment he was plucked unceremoniously out of his Light Horse regiment in Egypt he has done everything he can to be transferred to a fighting battalion.

Joshua is no fool and, while he has been unable to prove that it wasn't sheer bad luck that found him placed in the army ordnance corps, he has a pretty good idea that his grandfather, the deceased David Solomon, may have had something to do with his posting to a safe haven.

His applications to be transferred to a front-line

battalion are sent in monthly and are just as routinely refused. In truth, he is damned good at his job and may be said to have contributed significantly to the efficiency of war supplies reaching the front both at Gallipoli and later in France. So much so that he has been promoted to the rank of major, a rare occurrence in an ordnance outfit where promotion is almost unheard of and where officers tend to die in their beds.

Joshua's life in a British ordnance battalion has become as predictable as if he were working eight to five in the city and catching the five-thirty train to Tunbridge Wells each night.

Having bathed and changed into his mess kit, six-thirty every evening finds Joshua in the officers' mess with a gin and tonic in his hand. The pre-dinner small talk among the battalion officers is occasionally interrupted by the crump-crump of distant artillery and at seven o'clock, feeling slightly tipsy but with the sharp edges of the day somewhat smoothed over, Joshua will gulp down the last of four G & T's before going in to dinner.

Dinner, served by a dour, white-coated corporal, a Welshman whose surname, predictably enough, is Thomas, invariably consists of a pot roast rather too well done for Joshua's liking or an occasional leg of pork bartered or purchased from a local farmer. The inevitable mediocrity of the evening meal is somewhat compensated for by an excellent bottle of French red debited to Joshua's mess account. Finally, dessert and coffee are served while the port is passed around. Though there is a war raging just five miles to the north, with the dead too numerous to count, life in the officers' mess of an ordnance battalion in the rear echelon is very little different from the mess routine of peacetime in the barracks at Aldershot.

Colonel 'Tubs' Henderson, Joshua's battalion

commander, referred to by his officers as 'the old man', is a regular-army officer and veteran of the previous war who enjoys all the characteristics of a Boer War officer, including a sanguine complexion and enlarged proboscis brought about by his fondness for the bottle. However, he never drinks alone and is fond of saying, 'A chap who drinks alone is a pisspot. Bad habit. Bad habit. Solitary, not up to scratch what?'

No matter how ordinary the food, Colonel Henderson has never been known to complain about it. In fact, he completely ignores Corporal Thomas until after he has served coffee and whatever passes for dessert, always something out of a tin from one of the colonies. Thomas' choice of tinned fruit then prompts the same question from the old man every night. 'The fruit, Thomas? Which of our allies do we have to thank for this munificence?'

'The Union of South Africa, sir,' Thomas will reply mournfully. 'Will you take tinned cream with your peaches, sir?'

'Jolly good show, yes, yes, just a drop, ha ha, don't want to drown the African sunshine in the fruit, do we?'

Joshua has come to dread those nights when tinned pears are served. These invariably come from Australia and while the colonel's reply to Thomas always remains the same, with the only change being that Australian sunshine replaces the African, it means that Joshua will almost inevitably be selected to remain behind to share the colonel's after-dinner carafe of port.

Corporal Thomas, also regular army, waits until the port is passed around and the toast to the King is pronounced, then he retrieves the carafe (always from the left) and refills it to the brim.

Together with two fresh glasses and a small silver bell he places the newly filled carafe in front of the old man and then, taking one step back from the table so that he stands behind the colonel's right shoulder, he stamps his right boot to rigid attention. 'If that will be all, sah!' he announces at the top of his voice, bringing his hand up in a smart salute.

'Yes, yes, Thomas, don't fuss,' comes the invariable reply. With Thomas departed, Colonel Henderson looks around the table and fixes a bloodshot eye on one of his company commanders. 'Captain Carruthers, a word in your shell-pink,' he'll say, whereupon the remaining officers, barely able to contain their relief, will hastily scrape their chairs backwards and retire from the table, leaving the old man and the hapless officer of his choice to drink out the brimming carafe.

On a bitterly cold night in mid-January 1916 pears are served for dessert and Joshua finds himself selected for the after-dinner port run. He sighs inwardly. No officer has ever escaped before the carafe was empty. If he's lucky it may take an hour, but if the colonel is in a melancholic mood with the conversation punctuated by long silences it could take as long as two. By the time the last glass is swallowed the old man's conversation will have deteriorated to an almost incomprehensible mumble, always involving the Siege of Mafeking, where it seems Henderson was appointed the senior quartermaster.

However, the mention of Mafeking is always the signal that the evening is coming to an end and the little silver bell may be rung with impunity to summon Gunner Morton, the colonel's batman. Gunner Morton will enter, come to a smart halt, salute and say, 'Permission to transport you to your billet, sah!'

Tubs Henderson, slumped in his chair, will give the soldier a desultory salute and offer the same arm to Gunner Morton to raise him from his chair, whereupon Morton will lead the colonel quietly off to his billet, a cottage on the outskirts of the small French village of

Albert, some two hundred yards from the front gates of the ordnance depot. Many a young officer summoned to the port run of an evening, unable to rise after the colonel has made his departure, has been discovered asleep under the mess table by Corporal Thomas the following morning.

With the weather outside bitter, Joshua had hoped to retire to bed early with a book and a bottle of Scotch. He makes a mental note to renew the pound note he'd slipped Corporal Thomas some weeks earlier, together with the suggestion that he go easy on serving Australian pears for dessert. With a second toast to His Majesty and the royal family and an additional one to the speedy defeat of the Hun, he waits, ruby glass in hand, for the colonel to open the after-dinner conversation.

'I say, young Solomon, you're a damned curious case what?' Henderson begins.

'Case? Curious? How, sir?'

'Well, you're a strapping lad, damned fine specimen, all the right qualifications, Oxford, rugby and cricket blue, not at all the type to be found in an ordnance outfit.'

Joshua, realising that, like himself, the old man is a little worse for wear, replies carefully, 'Are you not happy with my work, sir?'

'Good God, lad, not at all! Quite the opposite. Good heavens! You've done a splendid job. Splendid. Promoted to major, almost unheard of what.'

'What is it then, sir?'

'Young, fit officers like you don't usually end up in an ordnance battalion. We're a bunch of old crocks here, jumped-up senior clerks and depot men in uniform.'

Joshua smiles, unable to disagree with this assessment of the officers in the battalion. 'Well, sir, I really can't say. As you know, I've put in for a transfer to a fighting battalion every month I've been here.'

'Quite right too! You deserve your chance to have a shot at the Hun. At your age I'd feel the same way, old boy.' The colonel takes another sip from his port glass and looks up at Joshua. 'I've put through your request for a transfer every time you've made one and, well, it's tantamount to bumping my head against a brick wall. Damned curious what?' He holds up his port glass and sniffs, then squints over its rim at Joshua. 'Tell me, Major Solomon, are you being saved for something?'

'Saved, sir? Whatever can you mean?'

'Politics? Only son? Heir to the throne? That sort of malarky? Never come across anything like it in my life. Not British, you know. Sort of thing they do to a maharaja's son in the Indian army. Not the done thing here.'

'I can't imagine what you mean, sir?' Joshua says again, knowing himself to be tipsy and so trying to keep the annoyance out of his voice.

'Are you quite sure?'

'Of what?' Joshua asks, now consciously restraining his temper.

'Well, I finally grew curious myself. Not usual to have a request refused when it's signed by the battalion commander. Bit of an insult, actually. Slap in the face. Know a chappie in the War Office. We clerks, you know, stick together. Asked him to dig around. Came back to me all hush-hush. You're not to be moved. Stay where you are for the duration. Nothing *I* can do about it, old chap. Orstralian Government. Official request to the W.O.'

This is all the confirmation Joshua needs to act and he immediately writes off to his father. In his letter he threatens Abraham, telling him that if he doesn't have the order rescinded he'll not return to Australia after the war, stating that he'd be ashamed to do so. He points out that his grandfather has left him sufficient funds to live comfortably in England for the remainder of his life, a prospect that would not make him unhappy. In addition he adds:

Father, please understand, this is no idle threat. While I respect you greatly, I deserve the same chance to serve my country as any private soldier and that means carrying a weapon into battle against the enemy.

If you do not see to it that my grandfather's interference is removed I shall write to the Age, the Sydney Morning Herald and the Bulletin. If you think you can buy their silence then I will write to the Truth, who has long waged war against our family and would relish the opportunity to run a piece as follows.

I shall tell them that while others lay down their lives for their country the rich and privileged such as me issue bootlaces and count cans of bullybeef in perfect safety five miles behind the front line.

I will not hesitate to add that I have weekend leave to Paris and a private automobile to get me there, where I have occasion to enjoy champagne suppers with beautiful young mademoiselles while my countrymen die in the mud and stench of the trenches.

Furthermore, I shall not be above using the anti-Semitic angle to all of this. 'Rich Melbourne Jew's son ... etc.' You know how much the Truth hates Jews and niggers.

Please, Father, take me seriously in this. I have been trained by my grandfather and I will fight you the way he would have done and you may be sure I shall win.

I wish also to be transferred to the 5th Battalion A.I.F. and not the Light Horse as previously. There are sound reasons for this, the 5th contains the public school company which includes many of my friends.

Although, with the rank of major, I am more likely to command another company in the 5th, it will still be within the same battalion. When, after the war, we all return to Melbourne, it will be most useful for business purposes as all the top families are represented.

Please, I beg you, do not let me down in this endeavour, Father.

Yours respectfully,

Joshua.

Though mortified by the general tone of Joshua's letter to him, Abraham Solomon takes his son's threat seriously and realises at the same time that Joshua's ruthless attitude towards him will make him an ideal opponent for Victoria when he returns to civilian life. Moreover, his transfer to the 5th Battalion, if it can be arranged, will not be an altogether bad thing. If he should return as the conquering hero with the rank of major, having faced the Boche in the trenches, it will do him not the slightest harm in the Melbourne business community. The newspapers claim that the worst of the fighting is over in France and that things are relatively quiet on the Western Front. Some sort of medal will sit nicely on his son's chest.

Abraham is beginning to realise that Joshua will not have it all his own way when he returns to Australia. Victoria Teekleman is showing a natural aptitude for business. Increasingly she is being allowed by Hawk to do things her way and the results are impressive. The Potato Factory is growing at better than a ten per cent rate per annum so that the Tasmanian-based company will soon be more profitable than its Victorian counterpart under the Solomon & Teekleman banner.

Hawk's granddaughter is proving to be bold but not foolish in her business ventures and Abraham is forced to admire her intelligence and application. Starting with a small woollen mill in Launceston, which Hawk had given her on her own in the first months she'd been placed under his direction, she has, in just under eighteen months, built it to a size where it is now a major supplier of blankets to the Australian army. In addition she has recently lobbied for and submitted, without any help from Hawk or himself, a government tender for the supply of army greatcoats for the troops fighting in France.

John Parkin, the permanent head of the Department of Trade and Customs, who sat in on the conference when Hawk and Victoria first confronted Abraham with Hinetitama's shares, dropped Abraham a note after the successful contract.

Parliament House

Melbourne

15th January 1916

Dear Sir Abraham,

This morning I was able to write to Miss Teekleman in Hobart to inform her that her tender for the manufacture of greatcoats for our forces abroad has been accepted by my department. While

doing so I was reminded of the meeting in your office.

I must say that I was impressed with the way Miss Teekleman

conducted herself on that occasion and again during our recent

negotiations. She strikes me as an exceptional young woman and well

exemplifies the old adage that we should trust our hopes and not our fears.

I trust you are well,

Yours sincerely,

John Parkin

Department of Trade and Customs.

The factory, which has hitherto employed twenty men and seven women, now has two hundred employees, all but sixteen of them female. Using the excuse that the able-bodied men are increasingly away at the war, Victoria has trained young women in the most previously unimagined capacities. She has them working as successful drivers, mechanics and machine operators, occupations traditionally thought only suitable for men. Furthermore, the clerical staff are also all women, with the exception of the chief accountant, who is an old retainer at the factory. Her appointments include a recently retired hospital matron, fearsome by reputation, named Mildred Manning, who has become her general manager.

When Hawk indicated some doubt about the wisdom of this appointment, Victoria responded sharply, 'Grandfather, if Mildred Manning can run a hospital filled with sick people she can run a blanket factory filled with healthy young ones. She's well accustomed to working with nurses and other female staff as well as handling men, who, if you want my opinion, constantly interfere to very little effect on the boards of hospitals anyway.'

The maternity hospital started in Mary Abacus' home for the wives of the employees of the Potato Factory Brewery has, over the ensuing years, become a general hospital. And while it has been taken over by the state, the brewery has an entitlement to a seat on the hospital board. Hawk has given this position to Victoria and she has made it known to him that the old fogies who sit with her on it, all of them men, do nothing but create obstacles.

When the unions complain about the female bias in the blanket factory, Victoria invites the ten most senior union officials involved in the combined trade unions active in Launceston over for afternoon tea. Needless to say they are all men and the affair, which quite incidentally includes tea and cake, features libations of a somewhat stronger and more spirited kind. In addition, there is a case of beer for each of the men to take home afterwards.

After the officials have had a few tipples Victoria points out that she is acting well within the trade-union charter and that factories employed in essential war industries can recruit from anywhere they wish and are not restricted to union labour. She then informs them that every one of her employees carries a fully paid-up union membership card. After she promises to pay the transport and accommodation for three local union officials as delegates to the Trade Union Congress to be held in Melbourne, they leave, assuring her of the utmost co-operation and giving her three resounding hip hip hoorays.

Victoria has also expanded beer production in the

Tasmanian brewery and Tommo & Hawk beer has made significant inroads into the South Australian market, taking a ten per cent market share from West End, the well-established Adelaide brewery, which has hitherto successfully fought off all outside competition.

Abraham has been forced to conclude that Joshua will need every resource at his command if he is to succeed his father as chairman of Solomon & Teekleman.

Moreover, Abraham privately thinks the deal David made to keep Joshua away from the fighting was quite wrong and that money and title should not be allowed to buy such privileges. Accordingly, he sets about undoing the elaborate network of safeguards that David, even in his apparent dotage, put together, marvelling in the process at the old man's Machiavellian mind.

Joshua finally receives his transfer to the 5th Battalion in March 1916 and is given command of C Company.

On the 25th of January 1916 Ben Teekleman arrives in England on the hospital ship *Gascon* and is transported from the London docks to the 3rd London General Hospital at Wandsworth where a number of Australian military surgeons and nurses are stationed. Nearly ten thousand Australian wounded have been sent to Britain, and this hospital, and the London War Hospital at Woodcote Park near Epsom Downs where Australian medical staff have also been transferred, are working around the clock with the operating theatres running in shifts, twenty-four hours a day.

It is a week before a surgeon is available to see Ben, and then only because his admission sheet shows that he has been mentioned in dispatches twice and is to be awarded the Military Medal. This is not to say that he has gained preference over cases more urgent than his own, but only over those of equal importance where his credentials as a war hero have shuffled him to the top of the pile.

He is interviewed by a weary-looking doctor with a colonel's insignia on his epaulets, who introduces himself quietly as John Mockeridge. He appears to be in his early fifties and, asking Ben to be seated, apologises unnecessarily for not having had time to shave the two-day growth he scratches absently as he talks.

'You've got quite a record, Sergeant . . . oh, I beg your pardon, Sergeant-Major,' the surgeon corrects. 'I'm . . .' he looks up, 'well . . . impressed.'

'Impressed?' Ben says slowly. 'It's only stuff they give you if you've been stupid enough to stay alive.'

'I'm sorry, Sergeant-Major Teekleman, I had no intention of offending you.'

'No offence taken, Doctor. It's just . . .' Ben doesn't finish the sentence and shrugs instead.

'Well then, let's see what's doing, you'll have to forgive me, I've been operating all night and haven't had the time to read my case notes.' Ben sits silently as Mockeridge reads. Finally he looks up. 'It appears from the X-rays that you have a bullet lodged near your spine, could be tricky, would you mind if I examine you? You'll need to take off your uniform, leave your undershorts on.'

Ben finds himself disarmed by the man's pleasant manner, it is not something he has seen in a military doctor before, or any doctor, for that matter, where arrogance and a disregard for a patient's feelings are the usual distinguishing characteristics.

Ben removes his clothes and the doctor points to his examination table. Making Ben lie on his stomach, he prods gently around the jagged purple scar where the bullet has entered. 'Most fortunate, the object appears to have entered sideways with a loss of momentum. A Mauser bullet coming in clean would most likely have severed your spine and entered your stomach. They're a higher-velocity bullet, slightly bigger calibre and do more damage than a Lee-Enfield.'

Ben is impressed. 'Yeah, it was a ricochet, the bullet came off a rock.'

'Well, there you go,' the doctor says, 'a spot of luck, but we're not out of the woods yet, old son.'

'What do you mean, Doctor?'

'Well, it doesn't feel too bad, but it could have damaged the nerve casing around your spine. Fortunately it has not penetrated through the wall of your stomach. Sometimes taking these blighters out causes more damage than leaving them in. Is it very painful?'

'I wouldn't say it's a lot of fun, Doctor, but I'm learning to sleep on my stomach.' He looks directly at the doctor. 'I'd rather you had a go at taking it out.'

'A lot of pain, eh?'

'I've seen blokes in a lot worse.'

'Well, if I leave it in you'll be sent back home?' Mockeridge offers.

'And if the operation doesn't work I'll be sent back home in a box, is that it, Doctor?'

The surgeon shakes his head. 'No, nothing quite that bad, but you could be a paraplegic, you'd be sent home in a wheelchair.'

'Or it could work?'

Mockeridge nods his head. 'Or, as you say, it could work and you'd soon enough be fit as a fiddle, though I don't suppose you'd be too keen to get back into the thick of things?'

'On the contrary, Doctor, I've seen all my friends die while the Turk quite rightly defended his homeland against us. We were the invaders, the enemy who came to take his home away from him. But in France I'll be fighting *against* the invaders, the Germans. I reckon that's different. I must go back and finish the fight or my mates will have died for no good reason.'

'Hmm, I've never heard it put quite that way,' Doctor Mockeridge says. He pauses and scratches the growth on his chin then brings his hands together, his chin resting on the tips of his fingers. 'As I said, Sergeant-Major Teekleman, it can be a tricky operation, there's a thirty to forty per cent chance it won't turn out well.'

'Those are better odds than I've had in a while,' Ben answers, 'but either save me or kill me, I don't fancy spending the rest of my life as a cripple in a wheelchair. I'd be no use to anyone that way.'

The surgeon looks shocked. 'I can't do that, Sergeant-Major, I can only do the best I can to remove the bullet whatever the consequences. Are we agreed I should try?'

'Agreed. Thank you, Doctor,' Ben says softly. 'Will *you* perform the operation?'

'If you can wait another week, Sergeant-Major Teekleman?'

'Sure.'

Mockeridge writes out a prescription. 'Here, take this to the hospital clinic, it will help with the pain.'

Ben is operated on a week later and wakes up after the effects of the chloroform have worn off to look directly into the hazel eyes of Sister Atkins. 'Good afternoon, Sergeant-Major Teekleman,' she says, looking down at him.

Ben blinks. 'I must have died and gone to heaven,' he mumbles, still not quite in control of his own voice.

'Now, now, enough of that,' Sister Atkins chides, though her eyes are smiling.

'Am I a cripple or what?' Ben asks her.

'Cripple? I should think not. You'll be running around like a puppy in a few days.'

Ben smiles. 'This is a surprise. Last time we met was on the *Orvieto*, do you remember?'

'No, of course not!' she teases him. 'There are so many big, clumsy sergeants pestering me.' She gives Ben a mock sigh, 'How could a girl possibly keep up with all their names?'

'Yeah, thought so,' Ben says. 'Talking about names, may I call you Sarah, Sister? I mean not here, not in the hospital . . . er, other places.'

'Other places? How did you know my name, Ben Teekleman?'

'I had my sister contact your cousin Lucy in Tasmania.'

Sarah Atkins looks surprised. 'Just to find out my Christian name?'

'Well, a bit more, really. I hope you don't think me impertinent?'

Sarah Atkins brings her hands to her hips. 'Now what am I supposed to say to that?' She suddenly parodies her own voice: '*No, Sergeant-Major, I don't think you're impertinent, please go ahead, find out all you can about me, it's quite all right.* Umph! You men are all the same, you think you're God's gift!'

'I've upset you, I'm sorry, I apologise, I had no right,' the words tumble from Ben's mouth.

'No right is quite correct, Sergeant-Major!' Sister Atkins says sternly. 'I must remind you once again that I am a captain and you are a warrant officer, the army forbids any fraternising between us. You know the rules as well as I do.' She pauses and then continues, 'Now you've just been through a nasty op and you really must get some rest. You'll be allowed up in two days and then you'll be in a wheelchair for a few weeks before you're allowed to walk. In a month or so, barring complications, you'll be up and about. In six weeks you'll be allowed to leave the hospital grounds for a few hours, you may even be well enough to go into London. In which case you'll need an escort, someone to be with you in case you have a turn, *and*, if you're a very good boy and promise not to pester the ward sister, then Sarah Atkins, the cousin of Lucy Atkins, the well-known Tasmanian blabbermouth, *may* volunteer for the job. Do I make myself perfectly clear, Sergeant-Major?'

'Yessir!' Ben laughs. He can't quite remember when he has been as happy.

'Now try to sleep, Ben Teekleman,' Sarah says, smoothing his blanket and tucking it in at the side. 'I shall call in to see how you are before I go off duty tonight.' She turns and, in the neat crisp way he'd first seen her walking away from Brokenose Brodie's hospital bed on the *Orvieto*, she walks towards the door.

'Sister! Captain Atkins!' Ben calls out.

Sarah Atkins looks back at him. 'What is it, Sergeant-Major?'

'Thank you. Thank you very much.'

'Will you please rest now or I shall be angry,' she calls, though Ben can see the corners of her mouth twitch as she struggles not to laugh.

A week later with Ben now in a wheelchair there is a ceremony at the hospital which Lord Kitchener himself visits to present to twenty of the Australian convalescents ribbons and medals for valour while serving in Gallipoli.

Kitchener reads a prepared speech, fumbling with his glasses and then equally with the words which are high-flown, pompous and patronising.

Sarah Atkins, watching, sees Ben's head sink lower and lower as he slumps in his wheelchair as if to make himself smaller. Anyone looking at him, though thankfully all eyes are on the great field marshal, will clearly see that he is embarrassed and upset and his face is beginning to colour.

She then looks at the other Australian wounded lined up in the front row in various stages of convalescence, two of them have been carted out onto the lawn still in their beds with a saline drip beside them, and their expressions are no different from Ben's.

Sarah becomes conscious that the turgid speech is filled with sentimental rubbish which might work at a convocation of middle-aged English choirmistresses but which is highly patronising and insulting to the Gallipoli wounded forced to listen to it.

She has nursed these Australians before and was on the hospital ship, the *Gascon*, when the wounded started coming in on the first two days after the landing. Barge after barge filled with wounded men arrived at the ship's side and had to be refused since the medical staff of six doctors, seven nursing sisters and thirty-eight medical orderlies were unable to cope with the influx.

Sarah's mind goes back to the time on the *Gascon*. One barge had waited at the ship's side in the rain for five hours, from six until eleven that night, the men in it having lain on the burning beach a further twelve hours or more, their arms and legs smashed, skulls cracked open, features reduced to a pulpy mess so that nose and mouth are simply bloody holes filled with pink froth and bubbles. Some have gone mad in the sun and now cackle and scream, while others beg to be killed or are silent, staring, completely traumatised. Those who die are pushed down onto the duckboards under which the blood leaking from the wounded sloshes and splashes up through the wooden slats. And still the barges arrive.

One young lad comes on board just as Sarah has completed bandaging the head of a soldier. He seems unharmed, though he has his hand cupped over his left eye. Seeing her, he comes over, stumbling against some of the wounded, apologising. 'Sister, it's me eye!' he cries and removes his cupped hand slowly and Sarah sees that he holds his eye in the palm of his hand, though it's still attached to a membrane that stretches some four inches from where it disappears within the bloody socket. 'Can you save me eye?' the young soldier cries again. 'Please, Sister, can you save it, I'm a sniper and they won't want me now!'

A doctor, one of the six on board, passes at that moment. 'Cut it!' he yells. Sarah looks at him, momentarily stunned. 'With your bloody scissors, woman! Cut the membrane, dammit!'

She takes the scissors from her pocket and snips the membrane so that the lad now holds the eye unattached in his palm. Blood from the empty socket starts to run slowly down his dirt-streaked cheek. 'What do I do with it?' he cries in a panic.

'Here, give it to me,' she says, stretching out her hand. Taking the eye from him she can't think where to put it and so she drops it into the pinny pocket of her uniform. 'Have you still got your field-dressing pack?' she asks and when the young soldier nods she instructs him to take it out and use the swab on his eye. Then, in an impatient voice she will forever afterwards regret, she says, 'I haven't the time to do it myself, there are others worse off, I must go, you'll just have to manage somehow.'

The boy looks down at her, the blood from his eye running into his mouth and over his chin. 'Thank you, Sister, I'm sorry to be a nuisance,' he apologises.

Sarah recalls how she worked all night with the surgeons while the remaining doctors tried to cope with the wounded who didn't require immediate surgery and who could be sutured and bandaged and whose shrapnel pieces could be removed from more superficial wounds. However, the doctors found themselves often enough removing fingers and toes, and on one occasion an ear, on the spot while the soldier's mates held the patient down, with part of his tunic stuffed into his mouth so he could bite on it.

By dawn the pile of arms and legs in the operating theatre was stacked to a height of four feet, leaving just enough space for staff to move around the operating tables. The orderlies were unable to keep up with the removal of severed limbs or find a place to store them. Soon it became apparent that what room there was on board was needed for the living, and the ship's small mortuary was packed with the dead. But the severed arms and legs could not be allowed to decay in the heat, so, together with other bits and pieces, they were thrown, unweighted, overboard. For weeks afterwards they washed up on the beach at Lemnos ten miles away and as far as Alexandria, more than a hundred miles from the beachhead at Gallipoli.

By morning the unventilated ship's hold and the decks carried eight hundred casualties with every nook and cranny packed with wounded men, most of them still unattended to. The rest of the medical staff worked to save the lives of the more critically wounded except for a single orderly who handed out water and cigarettes and occasionally lit a fag or held a tepid mug of water to the lips of a soldier too sick or unable to use his hands.

For the most part, the normal nursing duties were left to those soldiers more lightly wounded who procured the few blankets available, less than fifty, changed dressings, made tea and prepared what food there was for their mates, often going short themselves.

These same men, without complaining, performed a further duty they would never have contemplated in civilian life. The ship's toilets were inadequate and soon clogged hopelessly. With no bedpans available, piles of newspapers were handed out so that the men could defecate on a sheet of newsprint, which was then wrapped into a parcel and thrown overboard. As one wag was heard to remark, 'Most of what's in the newspapers is a load of shit anyway.'

Yet, once on board, those in pain were stoic to the extreme, barely wincing when shrapnel was cut out or lesions stitched. Others waited patiently for surgery, often slipping in and out of consciousness. The ship sailed at morning light, its hold crammed with wounded men, not an inch of deck space available to fit another casualty.

Sarah was transferred to the No. 1 Australian Hospital at Heliopolis where she nursed in a constant state of organised chaos and where the relationships between the Australian soldiers and the nurses more resembled the feelings between brothers and sisters than those of medical staff and patients. In the five months she stayed before being sent to Britain, Sarah lost thirty pounds in weight. She had regained half this amount by the time she met Ben again, yet he thought her nothing but skin and bone and talked constantly of fattening her up.

Now, as she stood listening to the platitudinous nonsense from the old, tired warrior whom all England so loved and worshipped and watched Ben's terrible discomfort, tears began to roll down Sarah's cheeks. She knew it was wrong to love Ben, that he would soon be gone, back to the horrors of France where his chances of returning to her were even slimmer than they'd been at Gallipoli. 'Ben Teekleman, I love you,' she whispered through her tears, 'please don't die.'

When it became Ben's turn to receive his medal she watched as Lord Kitchener bent to pin it to his chest. Then she saw the old man suddenly jerk his head back in surprise and drop the medal into Ben's lap and immediately move on to the next man. She saw that Ben was weeping softly.

Later he told her what had happened. Lord Kitchener, noting Ben's two mentions-in-dispatches and the Military Medal he was about to pin to his chest, remarked, 'Well done, you've had a good war, Sergeant-Major.'

To which Ben replied, 'Your Lordship, there is nothing good about this war, except that good men are dying because of the arrogance and stupidity of the old men who lead them.'

It is to Lord Kitchener's credit that nothing was done about Ben's remark. Those hearing about it from Kitchener's aide-de-camp, who held the medal cushion at the time, simply think it typical of the uncouth Australian soldier who refuses to salute his superiors and deserves the contempt with which the English military regard the rancorously undisciplined antipodeans.

Sarah Atkins, though having to maintain her distance while Ben is in the hospital, spends a few minutes with him each day after she has completed her shift. She will pull a screen around his bed and allow him to kiss her, though only briefly. Soon they both long for the time Ben will be well enough to be allowed an eight-hour leave pass from the hospital so that she can accompany him to London where they will be on their own. But his wound proves stubborn and his recovery is painfully slow.

The day of their first freedom, when it finally arrives in early April, though still cold, is filled with spring sunshine. Sparrows chirp cheekily on the pavement outside the hospital where Ben and Sarah wait for their trolley bus and people smile at them as they pass.

Sarah is dressed in civilian clothes just as if she is a soldier's sweetheart, which indeed she is. She's borrowed a pale blue winter coat from one of the English nurses so that she doesn't have to wear her army coat which will give away her officer's rank. Ben can hardly believe how pretty she looks and when she puts her arm in his he can feel his heart thumping madly.

Sarah has packed a picnic lunch and, after getting off at the Embankment, they walk along the Thames, stopping to admire Big Ben and the Houses of Parliament and visit Westminster Abbey, after which they cross Horse Guards Parade and enter St James's Park. The ground is still too cold to sit on, but Ben removes his army greatcoat, spreading it on the grass and Sarah lays out the lunch. 'It's only hospital sandwiches and a raisin bun,' she apologises, 'but I managed to scrounge an orange and I've brought a thermos of tea.'

'As long as there's no tinned meat?'

Sarah laughs. 'Cheese, lettuce and onions or apricot jam, take your pick, either way you're in trouble?'

'Trouble? Why's that?'

'The apricot jam will make you too sticky to kiss and the onion too smelly,' she teases him.

Ben smiles happily. 'No kiss, no afternoon tea.'

'Afternoon tea? There's only three cups in the thermos.'

'At the Ritz, my dear.'

'Whatever can you mean?'

'Victoria, my sister. It's all arranged. We're to have afternoon tea at the Ritz.'

'Your sister is at the Ritz? The Ritz Hotel? Isn't that very posh?'

'No, she's simply arranged it. Sent them a telegram, I suppose. Victoria can arrange anything, anywhere at the drop of a hat, for all I know she probably did it through the High Commissioner's office who would have sent a flunkey round.'

Instead of looking as pleased as he'd expected, Ben now sees that Sarah has an unmistakeable look of panic on her face. 'But, Ben, places like that are only for the nobs, the very rich. How will we know how to behave? What fork or spoon to use?'

'It's only afternoon tea, Sarah. Sandwiches and cakes, a pot of tea and a glass of champagne. We can pretend to be nobs for an afternoon, can't we?'

'You can't pretend to be a nob. You either are or you're not, the very rich are different, you can always tell, they're not like you and me. The people in those posh hotels can see a couple of country bumpkins coming for miles.'

'Is that so?' Ben laughs. 'Do you know something, Captain Sarah Atkins?'

'No? What?'

'You're a horrid little snob.'

'Me? No I'm not! If you'd ever been in a place like that you'd know what I mean.'

'Oh? Have you?'

'No, of course not. But I've seen them at the pictures. There are at least four different glasses on the table and more knives and forks in one place-setting than we've got in the kitchen drawer at home.'

'Not for afternoon tea, surely? A cup and saucer, a tea pot, a plate for the sandwiches or cake and a glass for the champagne, maybe a cake fork, oh . . . and a teaspoon.'

'A cake fork? There you go. Now there's a fork made especially for cake?'

'Yeah, on one side the tines are joined, to create an edge for cutting through the cake, or a tart or flan.'

'How do you know all this, Ben Teekleman?' Sarah asks suspiciously.

'I saw it in the pictures,' Ben fibs.

'It's not funny, Ben. You're not a woman. You don't feel these things. When you grow up having to make your new dress by unpicking someone else's old one, when you see a pretty pair of shoes in a shop window and know you have to buy the plain pair with the sensible heels that will last you all summer because you can only have one pair, when as a young nurse there are holes in your spencer and your stockings have darns on the darns, you soon learn your place in life and it isn't with the nobs.' She pauses and looks at him with her big hazel eyes. '*And it isn't having tea at the Ritz.* I'm not ashamed of being who I am, I don't want to be anyone or anything else, I'm very happy being me. It's only that I'm sensible enough to know I can't have everything or that having everything is even good for me.'

'You could always marry a rich man, you're way, way pretty enough and quite the nicest person I know?'

'I don't want to marry a rich man, I want to marry a man who loves me and me him. I could've if I'd wanted, there's been two or three officers who have proposed to me, from nice families, quite well-to-do, too.'

Ben shakes his head. 'I wouldn't marry an officer if I were you, my dear. Never know where they've been. In my experience they're a very shallow type of person.'

'What do you mean? *I'm* an officer, Ben Teekleman!'

'Well, nobody's perfect,' Ben answers. 'It's afternoon tea at the Ritz for the likes of us, my girl. Fatten you up. Two country bumpkins from New Norfolk and Toowoomba, to hell with the nobs, what do you say, eh?'

'Are you sure, Ben?' Sarah says, still looking doubtful and suddenly feeling dowdy in her borrowed blue coat, sensible brown lace-up shoes and heavy lisle stockings.

'Come here, Sarah Atkins,' Ben commands and takes her in his arms and kisses her, oblivious of who might be looking. 'I've never been surer of anything, I'm only a sergeant-major, but will you marry me?'

'Oh, Ben. I love you so very much.'

'When? Next week?'

Sarah pulls away from him and is silent for a while, staring at her hands which are folded in her lap. Then she looks up. 'No, Ben, after it's all over. After the war. I'll marry you and have your children and love you forever, but no one has the right to marry while this is going on.'

Ben too is silent, then he takes her by the hands and looks into her eyes. 'Sarah Atkins, will you marry me the day after armistice is declared?'

Sarah smiles. 'On the very hour, Ben Teekleman, while they're still ringing the church bells.'

'We need a glass of champagne to celebrate and I know just where to get one.'

'The Ritz? Are you quite sure, darling?'

'Don't you know sergeants-major are never in any doubt about anything, my dearest?'

Chapter Seventeen

BEN AND JOSHUA 1916

'If any question why we died,
Tell them, because our fathers lied.'
– Rudyard Kipling

In May 1916, after spending a month at the Monte Video Convalescent Camp near Weymouth, Ben is sent back up to London to A.I.F. Headquarters where the medical officers at Horseferry Road pronounce him, though not without a fair amount of persuasion, fit for France. ('Sergeant-Major Teekleman, you've done enough, there's plenty to do here in England to see you out.') He is finally issued with his travel documents and a forty-eight-hour leave pass to commence at five that afternoon. It has only just gone noon which means Ben has five hours to kill and the chief medical officer at the depot kindly signs him out, 'Go on, hop it, lad, enjoy yourself,' thus adding the extra time gratuitously to his leave.

Ben calls the hospital at Wandsworth from a telephone box on Horseferry Road and asks to speak to Sister Atkins, hoping Sarah may be able to spend the extra time away with him. He asks to be put through to surgery and when a man's voice answers, presumably a hospital orderly, he asks again for Sister Atkins. 'She's been called into surgery on an emergency,' the voice says.

'Damn!' Ben exclaims.

'You wouldn't be Sergeant-Major Ben Teekleman by any chance, would you?' the voice on the other end enquires.

'The same,' Ben replies.

'Righto then. She's left a message to say if you've been given your medical clearance for France and have a leave pass she'll meet you at the Eros statue in Piccadilly Circus at four o'clock this afternoon. Don't worry, Sergeant-Major, she's a grand lass even if she is an officer, good luck to you. There'll not be a word spoken about this.'

'Good onya, thanks mate, tell her I'll be there with knobs on,' Ben says this cheerfully so that the voice on the other end won't sense his disappointment. It would have been the icing on the cake to have the extra time to spend with Sarah.

He smiles to himself, remembering how he'd practised the way he would ask her about sharing his forty-eight-hour leave with him. He'd worked up and rejected a hundred different approaches in his head, though shortlisting some of them first and expressing them aloud to himself, trying to imagine what her reaction would be. At the same time, he'd invented cover-up sentences if she refused. One of these emerged as a favourite: 'It was in poor taste, my dearest, I am so very sorry, Sarah,' which seemed to Ben to have a touch of dignity and even sophistication to it and was a damn sight better than simply mumbling, 'Sorry, it's just that I was hoping . . .' which was probably what he'd end up saying because he'd be so nervous and shamefaced he'd forget the rehearsed apology.

When the time came Ben approached the subject carefully. 'Sarah, my dearest, when I go to France I'll have forty-eight hours' leave, do you think you could get the time off?' Then before she could reply he chickened out and quickly added, 'The . . . er, I mean, the daylight hours and some of the evening, you could take a taxi back to the nurses' hostel?'

He was afraid to look at her, afraid of the rejection and of the disappointment he'd see in her eyes. Instead, she took him by both hands so that he was forced to look at her. 'Ben, I'm not a virgin, there was someone when I was sixteen, a boy my parents were keen on, whose father had the general store.' She paused, her lovely eyes fixed on his own. 'Are you very angry?'

'Angry?' he replied. 'No, just very relieved. Seeing we're confessing to each other, nor am I a virgin, though it wasn't the storekeeper's daughter, it was the wife of the farmer next door and I was fifteen at the time.'

'Does that mean it's all right for me to stay the night with you?' she asked a little tremulously.

'Only if you insist,' he laughed, then added, 'I'll try to find the name of a nice hotel.'

Whereupon she opened her handbag, took out a small piece of folded paper and handed it to Ben. 'One of the English sisters at the hospital gave it to me. She says it's nice and clean and not expensive, a boarding house in Paddington. She says the lady who runs it understands about soldiers going to the front and calls it "Doing my little bit for the war effort".'

Ben took the note and wrote to the woman, enclosing a pound note which was the tariff for two nights including a breakfast of soft-boiled eggs, toast and marmalade and a cup of tea.

With four hours to spare Ben has a sudden inspiration, or, rather, he received a letter from Victoria the previous day in which she asked him when he intended getting engaged. His letters over the last two and a half months to her have been filled with Sarah of whom Victoria obviously approves as she demanded to have a snapshot.

They'd found a small photographic studio in Penny Lane and he'd sent off a nice photo of them both. In her latest letter she'd written to say how thin he looked and urged him to eat more and then continued: *You both look so happy and your Sarah is quite the prettiest woman, probably much too good for you. My urgent advice is to become betrothed as soon as possible so she can't get away.* Victoria, as usual, had it all planned out.

There's a rather nice shop in Albermarle Street named Garrard's which you may care to visit. They will, I feel sure, have a good assortment of engagement rings. I am enclosing a cheque from Grandfather Hawk on Coutts Bank for one thousand pounds, with it is a letter to the bank authorising you, on proof of your identity, to cash it. You should be able to get a simply splendid diamond ring for about three hundred pounds, three or four carats at the very least, and I urge you to spoil her rotten with the remaining money. Take her shopping to Simpson's or Harrods of Piccadilly in Knightsbridge, a pretty dress, nice shoes, she will choose her own underwear and you won't like the hat she chooses (men never do). Dare I suggest a glamorous nightdress as well? After all, my dearest brother, you are in London and in love and should make the most of it.

Oh dear, I do so worry about you going to France. I know it's not fair to say so, but I cannot help myself, I pray you fail your medical, though just sufficiently to be sent home to fully recover your health or, at the very least, so that you are given a tour of duty away

from the front.

News recently to hand from Sir Abraham is that Joshua has

been transferred to a fighting unit and is no longer in an ordnance

battalion. He didn't say which one, but he seemed pleased. Men are so

stupid. Though, on the other hand, you already know how I felt about him

escaping the fighting, thinking some special arrangement had been made.

I'm glad I was wrong and Joshua goes up considerably in my estimation.

With several hours to spare before he is to meet Sarah, Ben visits Coutts Bank, identifies himself and cashes Hawk's cheque. He immediately opens an account in the name of Sarah Atkins for four hundred pounds and hails a taxi to take him to Albermarle Street where he is deposited at the entrance of Garrard's the jewellers. The top-hatted, brass-buttoned and overcoated doorman looks him over suspiciously as he steps up to the doorway and blocks Ben's path. 'Do you have an appointment, sir?' he asks somewhat imperiously.

'No, do I need one?'

'It is not unusual, sir. Are you quite sure it is Garrard's the jewellers you are looking for?'

'That's two questions in a row and we haven't even been introduced. A bit of a nosy parker, ain't ya?' Ben says, leaning on his Australian drawl. 'What is it? That I'm not an officer?'

'Orstralian are you then, sir?'

'That's right, mate, and bloody proud of it. Are you going to let me in or is this conversation going to go on 'til dinner time?'

'I'm sorry, sir, I only wished to avoid embarrassing you.'

'I'm an Australian, I can't be embarrassed.'

The doorman grins at this and opens the door. 'Beg pardon, sir, I 'ope you find what you're looking for.'

'So do I, mate,' Ben says, entering the shop where he is approached by a stout man who has every appearance of having just stepped out of a very hot bathtub. He is an even-coloured bright pink from his shining pate to his clean-shaven chin and has the palest blue eyes Ben has ever seen. His baldness is fringed on three sides with a neatly clipped curtain of snowy hair. Dressed in striped pants and morning coat, his starched white shirt set off with an electric blue silk cravat, the man appears to be in his mid-fifties or perhaps a little older.

He, too, now approaches Ben with one eyebrow slightly arched and then Ben sees that his eyes go to the colour patch on his shoulder with the bronze 'A' for Anzac and immediately the man's expression changes. 'Good afternoon, sir, may I be of service?' he asks, bringing a pair of folded pink hands up to his chest.

'Thank you, yes, I'd like to see a ring.'

'A ring? And what sort of ring might that be, sir? A signet ring for your good self? A wedding ring, do I hear wedding bells? Or is it, yes, I have an instinct for these things, an engagement ring?'

'Engagement. For my fiancée,' Ben says, then corrects himself, 'to be, that is.'

'Our congratulations, sir. A diamond, is it?'

Ben nods. 'Yes, please, not too big, I don't want to, you know, embarrass her.'

The floor manager, or whoever he is, for he is plainly senior to the other staff who seem to be standing around trying to look busy with only one other person in the shop, smiles despite himself. 'Sir, it is my experience that a young lady is seldom embarrassed by the size of the diamond on her finger.' He seems to hesitate a moment then says in a not unkindly manner, 'I do hope we can accommodate you, sir, but I must tell you that there has been rather a rush on our diamond rings of late and we have no stones left under thirty pounds. Perhaps you could try Hatton Gardens, I am told that there you may obtain what is called a "soldier's stone", a very nice little ring for under five pounds.'

Ben smiles to himself. Unlike the doorman, at least this old bloke is trying to let him down lightly. 'I'd like to see a two or three carat, round brilliant cut, a "D" flawless, forty-six-facet diamond set in twenty-two-carat gold, nothing too fancy, mind. Like I said, I shouldn't want her to think I was trying to show off, but if I cop it in France, my girl will have a bit of a legacy.' All this information comes from Victoria's letter to him and Ben is quietly proud of the authoritative manner in which he delivers her instructions.

The shop assistant, despite an attempt to retain his composure, is obviously taken aback. 'A "D" flawless? Yes, of course. Certainly, sir.' He gives Ben a small bow. 'My name is Johnson, Jack Johnson, I am the manager here at Garrard's.'

'Jack Johnson, same as the heavyweight champ, eh? Nice to meet you, Mr Johnson.' Ben stretches out his hand. 'Ben . . . Ben Teekleman.' Johnson accepts Ben's hand in a surprisingly firm grip.

'Teekleman? Teekleman? Name rings a bell.'

'Oh, yeah,' Ben says doubtfully. 'Not too many of us Teeklemans about.'

'May I suggest a private office, Mr Teekleman? Perhaps a cup of tea, not quite the sherry hour, but perhaps we can send the boy out for a beer?'

'Cuppa tea be nice,' Ben says, suddenly enjoying himself.

He is shown into a small oak-panelled office which is obviously set up for no other purpose than to show important clients the shop's premium merchandise. It has two heavily studded, uncomfortable-looking club chairs upholstered in green Spanish leather with a small display table between them. A second, slightly larger table is placed to the left of his chair and Ben correctly supposes this is for the tea service. There is a picture of the King on the wall as well as the Garrard's *Letters Patent Royal* framed beside it. The carpet is of a slightly lighter shade of green than the chairs.

'Please, do sit down,' Johnson says, indicating one of the leather chairs, then, 'If you'll excuse me just a moment, Mr Teekleman?' Jack Johnson bows slightly again and leaves, to return several minutes later waving a sheet of paper triumphantly. Walking behind him is a pale, sickly-looking, pimply-faced young assistant, also in morning dress, carrying a tray draped in black velvet.

'Ah, here it is, I thought so, I have a letter from Miss Victoria Teekleman of Hobart, Tasmania, received . . . let me see,' Johnson glances down at the letter, 'two weeks ago. In it she suggests we may have the pleasure of a visit from you.' Johnson looks up, plainly pleased with himself. Whatever Victoria has said in the letter has given him all the confirmation he needs to provide Ben with the full Garrard's favoured-client treatment.

The young assistant sets down the tray upon which are placed several tiny envelopes. Jack Johnson, sitting in the remaining chair, opens the tiny flap of one of them and rolls a diamond onto the velvet tray, 'A lovely Kimberley blue–white of two and a half carats, Mr Teekleman.'

'No, no, you misunderstand me, Mr Johnson. I wish to see a ring. You see, I need it this afternoon. I only have forty-eight hours' leave before I go to France.'

'It is most unusual to make up jewellery with a stone of this quality without first ascertaining the customer's exact requirements,' Johnson says a little primly.

'My exact requirements are a ring with a diamond,' Ben points to the beautiful gem sparkling on the velvet cloth, 'bigger than that one and in about an hour.'

Johnson appears to be thinking, then comes to a decision, 'I have an order made up for a client,' he pauses and then, unable to resist the temptation to name-drop, adds, 'well, actually it's the Duchess of . . .' He pauses again. 'Well, never mind, it is not required until late next week when she comes up to stay at Claridges'.' Then he adds gratuitously, 'She has given over her London residence to the military, I believe.' Johnson frowns suddenly. 'Oh dear, a complication occurs to me.' Ben remains silent. 'If I recall correctly, it has two baguette diamonds to the side of the main stone?'

'May I see it, please?' Ben asks.

'Why certainly, sir, though on the hush-hush, we shouldn't like it to get out, I believe it's a surprise for her daughter.'

'Tight as a chook's bum,' Ben says.

'I beg your pardon, what was that, sir?'

'I promise not to mention it to the duchess or her daughter,' Ben grins.

'Well then,' Johnson says, 'if you are prepared to accept this little rearrangement, we can remove the canary diamond at present in it and replace it with the one of your choosing. The transfer will take no more than half an hour, sir.'

'Splendid, Mr Johnson, let me see the ring.'

Johnson presses a small electric bell set into the oak panelling and a few moments later the same pimply-faced lad appears. 'I want you to bring me Number 400 from the safe, and ask Mr James to accompany you.'

The young bloke departs and Ben points to the envelopes on the velvet tray. 'Perhaps you can show me more of these, Mr Johnson.'

Over a cup of tea, which arrives shortly after the

departure of the young shop assistant, Ben selects a beautiful three-carat diamond. The lad returns with a small brown envelope and Johnson spills the duchess's ring onto the velvet surface.

Ben picks it up and examines it in a perfunctory manner, it is immediately apparent that it is a beautiful ring. 'Yeah, this will do nicely,' he says, laying the ring back down on the tray.

He waits for the three-carat diamond he has selected to be set into the duchess's ring, whereupon he pays Johnson two hundred and seventy-five pounds in large, white five pound notes and obtains a certificate of authenticity and a receipt from the now entirely obsequious Mr Johnson.

'If it doesn't fit you may bring it in for an adjustment in the morning, Mr Teekleman,' Johnson assures Ben as he walks him to the door. A few paces short he suddenly halts. 'I couldn't help but notice your Anzac "A", sir. My son, Roger, was a corporal in the Royal Engineers and was killed three days after landing at Suvla Bay.'

'I'm sorry to hear that, Mr Johnson, the British lads fought most gallantly, I'm sure your son died bravely,' Ben says, not able to think of anything more comforting to say to the old man.

'It's been a real pleasure serving you, sir,' Johnson says, 'I'd like to think my son had a sergeant-major such as you to lead him into battle.'

'And you, sir,' Ben says genuinely enough, 'a pleasure also. I don't imagine too many N.C.O.s come into your shop. Your doorman ought to leave the judgment of those who do to you.'

Jack Johnson laughs. 'I very nearly got it wrong myself, Mr Teekleman. We have learned to be cautious about judging the Americans but, I regret, we still have a rather patronising attitude towards the colonials. You have taught me much this afternoon.'

Ben shakes his hand. 'No hard feelings. I've got the duchess's ring for a princess, can't do better than that now, can you?'

This time Ben elicits a smart salute from the doorman.

Ben, with the 'almost' duchess's ring safely in his pocket and with Mr Jack Johnson's mention of Claridges', has a sudden idea and hails a taxi cab. 'Claridges', please,' he instructs the driver.

The desk at Claridges' proves more accommodating than his initial reception at Garrard's, though Ben is also somewhat wiser. 'I'd like to book a suite for two nights and will pay for it in advance,' he says to the desk clerk.

'Certainly, sir,' the man says, 'I shall ring for our manager. What name shall I say?'

'Teekleman, and don't tell me my sister has already written to you?'

'I beg your pardon, sir?'

'No, it doesn't matter.'

'Very well, sir, will you require the newspapers in the morning?'

'Only *The Times*,' Ben says grinning. 'Does it carry the football results?'

'Certainly, sir, though I should include the *Telegraph* in that case, it has much the better coverage. When can we expect your party to arrive, sir?'

'About seven o'clock. Skip *The Times*, I'll take the *Telegraph*.'

'Very well, sir, seven o'clock.'

Ben arrives at Piccadilly Circus with half an hour to spare but enjoys watching the people and the large red buses which seem to pass every half-minute or so. There are several dozen soldiers and sailors and a host of civilians all waiting for someone. Somewhere close by a military band plays, though he cannot see it. It is a perfect spring day in May and Ben plans to walk with Sarah to St

James's Park and find the tree where they had their first picnic. The precious orange had been carefully peeled by Sarah and shared quarter by quarter between them. Tea at the Ritz afterwards had been a painless experience, with the head waiter being especially attentive. After two glasses of champagne, Sarah, who admitted she had never tasted it before, got the giggles and later, on the bus returning to the hospital, she fell asleep against his shoulder. Ben simply couldn't remember when he'd felt as happy.

Although he's been keeping his eye on the arrival of every red bus Sarah comes up behind him, slips her arm in his and says, 'Hello, soldier, don't I know you from somewhere?'

'Ha, you'll need to do better than that, young lady,' Ben says. 'Will you take afternoon tea or shall we walk?' He kisses her lightly on the forehead and takes her small portmanteau. Waiting to cross the road, he sees that Sarah has borrowed the same blue overcoat as before.

'Let's walk, I've been in a stuffy operating theatre all day and when I opened a window on the bus half the people in it suddenly cleared their throats and rattled their newspapers so fiercely that I hurriedly closed it again. The English can be very intimidating.'

'See that shop over there,' Ben says, pointing at Simpson's. 'We're going to buy you a nice new coat and a dress that hasn't been worn by someone else, the prettiest shoes in the shop and a smart new hat.'

'Oh, Ben, I don't still wear hand-me-downs, that was when I was young and living at home. Now I can afford to make my own, you're not to spend your army pay on me. Besides, do you have any idea what a good winter coat costs these days, it's iniquitous!'

'We'll manage somehow,' Ben says. 'Come along, girl, there's not a lot of time and we have to get to St James's

Park as well, the crocuses and daffodils are out and there's a patch of bluebells I want you to see.'

'Oh, I see, been there with someone else, have we?' Sarah teases.

'No, the bobby on the beat while I was waiting for you told me. I asked him the directions to St James's Park and he said, "Ah, the royal park, grand time to go, sir, daffs and crocuses are out and there's bluebells under the elms, with a bit of luck the King's tulips will just be coming out." Ben adds, 'Ah, "the darling buds of May".'

'That's very pretty, Ben,' Sarah exclaims.

'It's Shakespeare, compliments of Mrs Wickworth-Spode, my English teacher. It's about all I remember, that and, "There is a tide in the affairs of men . . . "' Ben doesn't complete the phrase as they've reached the doors of Simpson's.

'Welcome to Simpson's of Piccadilly, madam, sir,' the doorman says, nodding his head and opening one of the several polished brass and glass doors for them to enter.

'All the doormen look like Russian generals,' Sarah says, when they are out of earshot.

'The Brits love a uniform,' Ben says, then takes Sarah by both hands and looks into her eyes. 'Now, there is only one rule you have to promise to observe,' he says sternly.

'What?' Sarah asks, looking suddenly serious.

'You have to pick out exactly what you like without having a sticky at the price tag. And no cheating, you hear?'

'But, darling, what if you're embarrassed?' Sarah looks about. 'It's an awfully posh shop?'

'I've already told one person today that I'm Australian, so I'm incapable of being embarrassed.'

Sarah laughs. 'I'm beginning to think I know very little about you, Ben Teekleman. Perhaps I shall write to my cousin Lucy and ask her to have a bit of a stickybeak. See what she can dig up on the Teeklemans.'

'Well, before she discovers I'm wanted for an armed bank robbery, let's agree to my shopping terms, eh?'

Sarah, somewhat apprehensively, chooses a lovely camel-hair overcoat, the temptation to look at the price tag is almost overwhelming. 'What do you think?' she says, spinning around in it as she pulls the lapels up to her cheeks.

'Terrific,' Ben says, pleased at the happiness on Sarah's face. 'That the one you want?' Sarah smiles and nods and he thinks she looks not a bit like a hardened nursing sister who has seen almost as much death and destruction as he has. 'Righto,' he says to the shop assistant, a pleasant-looking woman in her forties with prematurely grey hair drawn back into a severe bun, 'we'll take the coat.' Ben turns back to Sarah. 'Now choose one for your friend.'

'What, a coat?' Sarah is thunderstruck.

'She's let you use hers every time we've been out,' Ben explains. 'You choose one you think she'll like.'

After purchasing the two coats, two day dresses, a pair of pretty shoes and an evening ensemble with a second pair of grey velvet evening slippers which Sarah describes as 'simply divine', Ben makes her wear the coat out of the shop. As he pays for their purchases he gives the shop assistant his surname and asks her to send all the parcels to Claridges', though he does this while Sarah is busy changing back into her clothes. Then he gives the woman another twenty pounds. 'Ma'am, I wonder if you could, you know, choose a nightdress, silk or something, and some o' that . . . on French . . .'

'Lingerie?' The woman smiles. 'It will be a pleasure, Mr Teekleman. But you've given me too much, fifteen pounds will be ample.'

'You've been very kind and helpful, would you buy yourself something nice?'

'Thank you. It's been a pleasure, I hope the two of you are very happy,' the shop assistant says, smiling.

Sarah emerges from the changing booth wearing her new coat which sweeps down to her ankles in the latest fashion. 'How ever are we going to carry everything?' she says.

'It will all be sent to your hotel, madam,' the shop assistant assures her. 'We'll send your suitcase on with it and the gentleman's kitbag.'

'Hotel? It's a . . .'

'Yes, I have given her our address,' Ben says, cutting Sarah short.

Outside again they walk towards Knightsbridge. 'What say tomorrow we do Hyde Park?' Ben says.

'Oh, Ben, that was so kind, buying a second coat for Linda Newings, she'll be thrilled to bits.' She snuggles into him as they walk, her arm clasped about his own. 'I've never owned anything as nice, I do love you so.'

Most of the warmth has gone from the spring afternoon sunshine by the time they get to St James's Park but the light is still good and they stop to admire the policeman's bluebell patch and wonder at the clumps of daffodils and crocuses that simply grow willy-nilly out of the emerald grass. Ben spreads his army coat on almost the same spot they'd sat before, having to move it a couple of feet to avoid a patch of lilac-coloured crocuses.

They settle down on his coat and Ben takes Sarah in his arms and kisses her. 'Oh, my God, I nearly forgot!' he suddenly exclaims, pulling away from her and, on his knees, begins to frantically pat the surface of the greatcoat in a parody of panic. 'Thank goodness!' he sighs, at last stopping, his hand held over a patch of coat.

'What is it, Ben?' Sarah asks, alarmed.

Ben turns, enjoying his tomfoolery. 'Sarah, while I'm down on my knees, will you marry me?'

'I already said I would, whatever's gotten into you, Ben?'

'So we're engaged, it's official, right?'

Sarah frowns. 'Well, yes, I suppose? It's wartime, Ben, I don't want you to make any promises to me you may regret later.'

'But, nevertheless, you agree to be engaged to me?' Ben persists.

'Of course, silly, why do you think we're spending the night together? I'm not a loose woman, some cheap floozy, you know.'

Ben has found the opening to the pocket of his greatcoat and now produces the little black box. 'Sarah Atkins, will you marry me?' he asks, resting on his knees in front of her. He opens the lid of the little box to reveal the diamond ring.

'Shit!' Sarah exclaims involuntarily, jerking her head backwards in surprise. Wide-eyed, she brings her hands up to her mouth, horrified at what she's just said, 'Oo-ahh!'

Ben throws back his head and laughs. 'Is that all you have to say?' He pushes the little box towards her. 'Go on, it's yours.' Sarah takes it tentatively and Ben sees that her hand is trembling violently. Then she suddenly begins to sob, clutching the box to her lap in both hands. She sniffs and brings her right hand up and knuckles the tears from her eyes, sniffs again and then begins to weep, letting the tears run unabashedly down her cheeks and into her lap.

'I'm so sorry,' she says tearfully at last.

'Here,' Ben says, offering her his handkerchief.

Sarah dabs at her eyes then blows her nose, looks down at the ring and starts to cry again, dabbing at her eyes again. 'Oh, Ben, it's the most beautiful thing I've ever seen,' she chokes.

Ben takes the box from her hand and removes the ring. 'Here, let's have your finger,' he commands.

'Which one?' Sarah, still tearful, cries in a sudden panic. 'What hand, I forget?'

'How should I know, every girl is supposed to know that from infancy!' Ben teases. He points to her left hand, 'The one next to your pinkie. That's where they said it goes in the shop.'

Sarah holds her hand out and Ben slips the ring onto her finger, and it is a perfect fit. 'There you go, you're booked for Armistice Day. You have the hands of a duchess, my love,' he says, savouring the private joke. The light is beginning to fade and it has grown quite chilly. 'We need to celebrate,' he decides. 'A glass of champagne is called for immediately.'

'The Ritz? I'm no longer scared of the cake fork.'

'Nah, let's try Claridges'? Victoria says it's a better pub.'

'Does Victoria know everything?'

'Just about,' Ben says.

'Will she like me?'

'It's compulsory.'

'Last time the champagne made me squiffy, it was lovely.'

'C'mon, we'll take a taxi, it's too cold to walk, besides I don't know how to get there from here.'

At Claridges', in the manner of all good hotels, the desk clerk greets him by name. 'Good evening, Mr Teekleman, good evening, madam, I trust you've both had a pleasant day?'

'Yeah, it was lovely, thanks,' Ben replies and wonders momentarily how the clerk knows his name as it isn't the same man he met earlier.

'Your parcels have arrived, sir, and have been sent up, will you be dining in the hotel this evening, sir?'

Ben turns to Sarah, who has a bemused look on her face. 'What do you reckon, Sarah?'

Sarah is too surprised and confused to say anything.

'Tell you what,' Ben says to the desk clerk, 'we'll have

it in our suite. In the meantime, will you send up a bottle of good French champagne.'

'Certainly, sir, dinner in your suite, I shall send you up the menu. Do you have a preference in champagne?'

'No, what would you choose?'

'I shall consult the cellarmaster, sir. You may depend on him. Shall I show you to your suite?'

'Thank you.'

They follow the clerk and Sarah nudges Ben. 'What's happening, Ben? Tell me!'

Ben allows the clerk to go further ahead. 'Well, you know how you got a bit squiffy on champagne last time at the Ritz, well, I thought we'd just stay on and get even squiffier. They say if you can get a girl squiffy enough . . . ?'

'Ben Teekleman, how dare you!' Sarah giggles.

Sarah is like a little girl at her first birthday party when they get into their suite where all her shopping has been neatly laid out on the huge bed. Soon the bedroom is in chaos as she once again opens all the boxes. The shop assistant has chosen a beautiful dove-grey silk nightdress with a matching peignoir, and, knowing Sarah's shoe size, she has chosen an elegant pair of slippers with a charming little heel. Sarah blushes violently when she opens the ribboned box of lingerie. 'Ben Teekleman, what have you done! Turn around at once.'

Ben turns his back and Sarah takes each neatly folded item out of the box. 'Darling, they're positively wicked, I can't possibly wear these!'

'Oh well, we'll take them back in the morning then, I'm sure the nice lady who looked after you won't mind, we'll swap them for a dozen each of good sensible spencers and bloomers, shall we?'

'Don't you dare! I've never seen anything as beautiful in my life.'

In the middle of unpacking her shopping a waiter

arrives with the champagne in an ice bucket. 'Sir, our cellarmaster, Mr Boddington, hopes that you will accept this with his compliments. It is a 1908 Dom Perignon, a particularly good year and the last bottle he has of that vintage. He lost a son at Gallipoli and this is a small tribute to the Australians.'

'That's very decent of him,' Ben says, slightly taken aback. The English are such a curious mixture of aloofness and warmth, a hot and cold people who constantly surprise.

'May I leave the menu? You may telephone when you are ready for dinner. We ask that you allow half an hour for preparation. Will you choose the wine now so that it may either be chilled or decanted?'

'Would you give Mr Boddington my sincere thanks and please offer him my commiserations, the English lads fought with pride and determination at Gallipoli. I would be happy to have him select a good bottle of red.' He calls to Sarah, 'Red wine all right with you, dear?'

'Lovely!' Sarah calls back, though she cannot remember ever having tasted red wine.

After the waiter departs Ben turns to Sarah. 'That's twice today I've heard of an English lad's death at Gallipoli. We forget that the English lost nearly twice as many men as we did in the Dardanelles campaign.'

Sarah moves over to Ben and puts her hands about his waist, leaning back and looking into his eyes. 'Darling, let's not even think about the war for the next two days. I don't want to go out again, perhaps Hyde Park tomorrow, there are too many people in uniform on the streets, too many reminders of where we've been and where you have to go.' She stands on tiptoe and kisses him lightly on the nose. 'I know this is all make-believe, a fairytale. I can't imagine how you've managed to do it and, what's more, just this once I don't *want* to know.

I just want to be with you for the next forty-eight hours.'
She smiles. 'And then if they throw us in gaol, I won't
mind in the least. I love you, Ben, with all my heart. Right
now, at this very moment, I am happier than I've ever
been and you haven't even made love to me yet.'

Ben takes her in his arms and kisses her deeply and
then draws away, still holding her against him. 'Sarah,
I want you so badly and have done so since the moment I
saw you on the *Orvieto*. I confess, I have made love to
you in my head a hundred times, no, many more times
than that.' Ben can scarcely contain himself, his hardness
pressing against Sarah's slim body. They kiss for a long
moment until Sarah, in turn, gently draws away. Ben can
feel his heart pumping, he is nervous, not quite knowing
what to do next, waiting for Sarah to encourage him.

'Ben, let me have a bath, darling. Change into my
lovely new things. We'll have a glass of champagne when
I come out? But I don't want to get too squiffy, I want to
love you just the way I am now.' Ben watches as she goes
into the bathroom and closes the door behind her.

Suddenly he is depressed. He tells himself he is simply
a bit weary. He's been up since dawn and taken the 6.15
train from Weymouth to London and then the
underground to Horseferry Road. The waiting around,
the anxiety of covering up during his final medical
examination, where he knows in his heart of hearts he
isn't fully recovered from his wound and the subsequent
operation has taken its toll. He tells himself it is mostly
the time he's been off his feet. The strength hasn't
returned, he simply isn't as fit as he ought to be. His
wound still hurts and he wonders if it will always be with
him. Then there's been the excitement of the engagement
ring and the shopping and the strain and emotion of
finding himself alone at last with Sarah. It is as if he has
stretched out his arms to take something more than just

the war and has had them suddenly filled with something too heavy for him to carry.

He aches to make love to Sarah but at the same time he keeps bumping into the images of the lads in his platoon. Crow Rigby squinting down the telescopic sights of his Lee-Enfield, Brokenose Brodie reading Dickens, his lips moving all the while, brow furrowed in concentration, Wordy Smith painting his delicate tiny blossoms with a brush that appears to contain no more than two hairs. Cooligan, Numbers Cooligan, being argumentative, making a bet, taking one. Woggy Mustafa defiantly Christian, Muddy Parthe working up a good complaint, Library Spencer quietly correcting a fact, Hornbill, smiling, fixing something or other, always tinkering. It is as if the love he feels for them in death keeps intruding into his life, even into his love for Sarah, as if they are somehow participants in the present, perhaps competitors, equally admiring of Sarah, sharing her with him. He wonders if he can love and live without them, whether they have become so much a part of his personality that Sarah will be taking them to bed with her, in some weird ritual in his imagination he doesn't fully understand. They will be her lovers forever while he looks on, Sergeant Ben Teekleman, who managed to kill them all and stay alive himself.

Ben pours himself a glass of champagne, watching the bubbles settle in the glass. Outside his window he can hear the starlings settling in for the night. What a racket they make, an urgency to find a place on a branch or twig, a terrible squabbling in the elm trees, life persisting, tiny wings beating the air with a furious energy, a thousand tiny throats demanding their own brief span, resisting death, fighting it for all their worth.

In those moments of silence on Gallipoli, when both sides had had enough, there had been no birdsong, only the occasional mournful caw of a crow feeding on human

carrion. 'Crows. Why is it always the vermin that follow
you?' He can hear Crow Rigby saying it. The urgency of
starlings had gone out of the air at Lone Pine, The Nek,
the Daisy Patch. The charnel fields stank of death, the soil
was soaked in it, drowned in a muddiness of young blood.
There was so much death about, it became more natural
than being alive. Can he now change back again and feel
his need for life returning? Can he wipe death from his
mind, replace it, even for forty-eight hours, with the life
she brings him, the renewal she promises him with her
sweet body? Is this woman, any woman, enough? Ben feels
corrupted, guilty, ashamed even to admit such a thought,
for he knows he loves Sarah more than his own life. Yet
the thoughts of death, of decay, of the past, engulf him.

Ben has his back to the bathroom door, facing the
window when Sarah calls out to him. He rises. She is
dressed in the silk nightdress and peignoir though her feet
remain bare, her toes peeping from under the hem of the
dove-grey silk. She has brushed her hair and tied it back
with a brown ribbon. Her face is scrubbed clean of any
make-up. As Ben draws closer he sees the light scattering
of freckles across the bridge of her nose and the upper
part of her cheeks. Her mouth is slightly open and her
hazel eyes are filled with love for him as her arms reach
out and she starts to unbutton his tunic. 'Come, darling
Ben, come and make love to Sarah.'

Ben entrains at Victoria Station for Dover to catch the
troopship to Boulogne and from there to the 1st Division
base at Étaples, where he is kitted out with a cold-weather
uniform and given, in addition, a tin hat and gasmask. He
is also required to undergo a further ten days of training
which includes the use of the gasmask and a
demonstration and lecture on the effects of phosgene gas.

This is the first of several differences from the

conditions Ben had experienced in Gallipoli. For a start, there had been few gasmasks at Gallipoli, and those that could be found were used for only one purpose, to give the troops some relief from the stench of rotting corpses. Any platoon able to obtain a single gasmask to share among them treasured it. If there was one thing every soldier who returned from Gallipoli would remember until the day he died, it would be the stench of the charnel fields where the dead on both sides lay unburied and forsaken.

Ben's headquarters are near the village of Armentières where he is to report to his battalion commander Lieutenant-Colonel Le Maistre who has replaced Colonel Wanliss, who was wounded at Gallipoli. The battalion commander, much to Ben's extreme embarrassment, welcomes him to his dugout some eight hundred yards behind the lines with, 'Well, well, here cometh the axeman!' Ben thinks for a moment that Le Maistre may be chaffing him, but realises almost immediately that the words are spoken in genuine admiration.

Le Maistre points to an ammunition box. 'Sit, please, Sergeant-Major, I've been through your papers and you're just the sort of chap we need. Though, of course, you'll be short of experience in this sort of trench warfare, but then we all are. Different. Quite different to Gallipoli and you'll find it will take quite some getting used to. Thank God, the weather is being kind at the moment. Except for the deeper bomb craters which never seem to entirely dry up, as you can see it is rather dusty. One big shower, though, and we're all back up to our knees in the infernal mud.' He briefly ruffles the papers on the small table at which he is seated. The table and the hard, straight-backed wooden chair with it, appear to have been appropriated from a farmhouse kitchen. Then Le Maistre looks over at Ben. 'Now, much as we'd like to have you here, brigade headquarters thinks differently, that's the problem coming in with a reputation, you can't slip in quietly, as I'm sure you'd rather do, eh?'

'Sir, I am not an experienced sergeant-major, in fact I'm new to the job, I'll be happy to be the dogsbody around the place, earn my crown.'

'No, no, you'll be given your own company just as soon as you return, you're far too experienced a soldier not to be leading men in combat. It's just that brigade headquarters want you to join a special training group, in the 27th Battalion, being conducted by the 7th Brigade. They're a West Australian outfit, damn fine, too. The Joan of Arc Company.'

'Joan of Arc? That's a new one, sir.'

Le Maistre grins. 'I said that deliberately, Sergeant-Major, hoped you might pick up on it. The battalion has, it seems, a great many members of a West Australian family named Leane. They're all enlisted in the same company, so that the C.O., two of the subalterns, several N.C.O.s and God knows how many enlisted men are all Leanes. In other words, the company is,' he pauses and then continues, 'made of all Leanes, Maid of Orleans, hence the Joan of Arc Company.'

'Very clever, sir. Can you tell me what I am to do in the 7th?'

'Yes, you'll be with selected members of the 27th and 28th Battalions to be trained as scouts and as a raiding party. I'm not quite sure what this entails. It seems you are to be instructed in a raiding technique perfected by the Canadians near Messines, last November. Two officers,' Le Maistre glances at his notes, 'yes, here it is, Lieutenants Conners and Kent of the 1st Canadian Division have been seconded to assist as training instructors.' Ben's commanding officer looks up at him. 'I'm sure it will prove to be very useful stuff when you return to us, Sergeant-Major.'

'When will that be?' Ben now asks.

'Haven't the foggiest, old chap. Rather sooner than later I hope, the 5th are in a big offensive planned for some time in July and I want all the experienced men I can find. I have an inexperienced C.O. in D Company, decent sort of chap but he has spent most of his war in ordnance, we're thinking of putting you in with him.' He brings the papers in front of him together. 'Thank you, that will be all, Sergeant-Major Teekleman, report to the Provost Sergeant, who'll give you your clearance and papers for the 27th Battalion part of the 7th Brigade. You're to report to Captain Foss.'

Ben rises and, coming to attention, salutes. Le Maistre grins suddenly and looks up from the table where he is seated. 'Oh, I almost forgot, you're supposed to have volunteered for this assignment, Sergeant-Major, so take extra good care of yourself. Remember, you belong to the 5th Battalion.'

Ben finds himself in a special unit, which simply becomes known as 'the raiding party' and consists of some sixty men and six officers. It is divided into two sections, one responsible for the left half of the attack, the other for the right. As the unit isn't much bigger than a standard platoon, each half is allocated a sergeant, and though Ben is of a higher rank he is asked if he'll act in the lower capacity for one of the teams.

Captain Foss, a big, ebullient man, nearly six foot four inches in height and a good two hundred and eighty pounds in weight, looks and acts naturally as a leader, or, put into the colloquial language of the men under him, 'he doesn't carry on with any bullshit'. He introduces Ben to the West Australian volunteers.

'Righto, this is Sergeant-Major Ben Teekleman, he's a ring-in, a Victorian from the 5th Battalion, 2nd Brigade, but a very welcome one.'

'Tasmanian, sir,' Ben says promptly and the men laugh.

'Tasmanian, eh?' says Foss. 'Well, in that case, if you have any doubts about him you are advised to look at his ribbons, he has earned his crown the hard way but has volunteered to act as the sergeant for our right section. I guess you'll get to know him soon enough, as for me, I'm bloody glad to have him on board.'

Ben, accustomed to big men and himself about average height for the Victorians, finds that he is much shorter than these West Australians. They are magnificent specimens, few of them are under six feet one inch while most are taller. They're hard and well trained and at first he finds the going tough. After almost three months spent on his back, he has lost much of his fitness and the first few days leave him exhausted, so much so that he wonders if he should tell Foss he's not up to scratch.

The whole of the raiding party is withdrawn to a rear area along the railway line between Armentières and Wavrin where they are trained as if they are a football team preparing for a grand final. Each section is subdivided into right and left trench parties, parapet parties, intelligence, linesmen, messengers, telephonists, scouts, stretcher-bearers and covering parties. The Canadians have worked it all out, learning from bitter experience, and they prove to be excellent instructors.

The men's first task is to dig a replica of the German trenches copied carefully from photographs taken by an aeroplane sent over especially for the task. Each night they practise the raid, learning to co-ordinate the various tasks and sections quickly without talk. The Canadians believe that silence, hitherto never attempted, is a critical aspect for the success of the raid. While the practice works well, the aerial photography isn't detailed enough to tell how effectively the trenches are protected, or what state the barbed wire is in or if there are any other obstacles other than craters.

Two nights before the raid Ben is still not satisfied with his fitness. Though considerably hardened by the rigorous work of the past couple of weeks he goes for a run in his full uniform, carrying a wire-cutter and the weapons he will take with him on the night of the raid. He runs along the railway line, passing five or six hundred yards from the German trenches they are to attack. On a sudden impulse he crosses the railway line into no-man's-land and finds himself moving in a circular direction towards the right-hand side of the enemy lines.

At first it is not a conscious decision, he simply wants to feel the nature of the ground they will pass over on the night of the raid. But soon he is taken by the notion of getting as close as he can to the first line of German trenches. Foss, their commander, had some weeks earlier done the same thing, ending up close enough to see that the trenches on his left (the German right) were protected by barbed wire in poor repair and that they were vulnerable to an attack. It is on this premise that the raiding party is being undertaken.

However, it is not known if the right-hand sector is in the same poor condition and this is the area Ben will be moving into with his men. Progressing from one ditch to another, he slowly makes his way to the German lines, eventually coming to the lip of a bomb crater in which there isn't the usual pool of muddy water. He jumps into the crater, a large one that brings him at its extreme end to a point no more than ten yards from the parapet of the enemy trench. He can actually hear someone shouting out a command and a loud '*Jawohl!*', the reply from whomever the direction is intended for. Someone is playing a mouth organ and in the darkness Ben can see a thin curl of wood smoke coming from the trench.

He crawls out of the crater and examines the wire, which is newly constructed, well tied down with stakes hammered into the ground in an ordered pattern and calculated to make it very difficult to penetrate. But further up to his left the newly laid wire suddenly ends and the old wire is partially pulled up in preparation for the laying of a new pattern. However, there appears to be no sign of work taking place or spare bales of wire lying about. The ten-yard gap where the old wire has been ripped up is quite sufficient to put his section through. It seems the Germans have simply run out of wire and are waiting for more to arrive, their ordnance no more efficient than that of their British counterparts.

Ben makes his way back behind the lines and the following morning reports his findings to Captain Foss.

'You're a bloody idiot, Sergeant-Major Teekleman, but thank you.' He thinks for a moment. 'This means Lieutenant Gill can bring four scouts with him to the left-hand sector to cut the wire and guide us through and we'll send only one along with you to your section. Are you quite sure you can find your way through the gap again?'

'It will be around the same time as last night and, if anything, a little lighter, shouldn't be a problem, sir.'

Ben salutes him and turns to depart when Captain Foss calls out, 'Sergeant-Major?'

'Yes, sir?'

'Bloody beauty, mate.'

During the last week in May and the first few days in June the artillery has bombarded the sector to be entered but not so heavily that the Germans will think it a precursor to an attack on their section. The idea is that they should regard the artillery action as routine, their turn to cop a few medium trench mortars. This may well have been the reason why work was stopped on repairing the barbed wire.

June the fifth is the night set aside for the attack and the raiding party is given a special set of clothing. They are fitted out with English tunics that contain no badges or identification marks, these being thought to be by far the most common on the battlefield and identical for every English unit. If any of them are killed, the enemy will gain no information from looking at their insignia. Their faces are blackened and their bayonets painted, though the scouts, messengers and carriers, as well as the bombers, will carry revolvers instead of rifles.

They are also issued with a device called a 'knobkerrie', which ordnance will later refer to as a 'life preserver'. This short, stout stick with a knob on the end, in this instance a heavy iron bolt, comes out of the previous century and the Zulu Wars in South Africa. The knobkerrie was used in conjunction with an assegai, a short fighting spear, by the Zulu Impi and used well the knobkerrie is a highly effective weapon at close range. A blow directed to the head will quite easily kill a man. Ben declines one of these, explaining that he would prefer to take his Maori fighting axe and Captain Foss quickly agrees. Ben also shows his section how to use the knobkerrie as a fighting stick in the Maori manner, a skill learned from Hawk as a child. Utilised correctly it can ward off a bayonet attack and, at the same time, kill the attacker.

They are all issued with black plimsolls to quieten their footfalls on the hard ground, though later, with even small falls of rain, these will prove impractical in the muddy ditches and craters of no-man's-land. Finally, an idea from Gallipoli suggested by Ben is adopted and they wear white armbands on either sleeve, covered with similar-sized black ones, which are to be ripped off to reveal the white when they begin the attack.

The two Canadian instructors, both of them extremely popular with the Australians, request permission to come on the raiding party but Foss refuses. 'Jesus, imagine if one, or both, of you blokes got killed because of something stupid my boys did. We'd have a diplomatic incident on our hands the like of which would see me demoted to the rank of corporal, if I was bloody lucky.'

The plan is for Ben and another scout, a lad named Wearne from Donnybrook, a small town southeast of Bunbury, both with wire-cutters, to move up to the gap in the wire and, if it is still there, wait for Gill and his scouts to cut through their section of the wire to the left. If the gap has been repaired, Ben, using his electric torch, is to signal for another wire-cutter to join them. On the command of Captain Foss, who is to move up the centre between them, the attacking units of the two sections, situated in a rifle trench some way back in no-man's-land, are to move up into position. Both sections of the raiding party will then mount the attack, entering the German trenches together.

The concept behind the raid is not to capture the German trenches but simply to surprise and harass them, killing as many of the enemy as possible in the time allotted, and then to withdraw, leaving the Germans feeling vulnerable and demoralised. This will give the Australian infantry, who have not yet experienced a full-scale battle in France or are not familiar with this type of trench warfare, the confidence that the Germans can be intimidated and their trenches entered almost at will. After the fierce and bloody resistance of the Turks at Gallipoli when the Anzacs attempted to raid their trenches, Ben wonders privately how successful this tactic will be. When he questions the ever-ebullient Foss, he is told that the fighting is different here and that a raiding party is not a tactic used in France and will come as 'quite a surprise to the Boche'.

Ben and his scout, Wearne, and Lieutenant Gill and his three scouts leave the rifle trenches just after nine-thirty at the first sign of darkness. At this time of the year the night lasts only until 2.15 so they are aware that the whole operation must be concluded in under four hours. All goes well and Ben and Wearne, following the ditches Ben previously used, reach the gap in the wire without any trouble. At the same time they lay a magnetic wire so that their section of the raiding party can find their way safely home.

Things at first go well in Lieutenant Gill's section. They make comparatively short work of cutting through the dilapidated defences. Gill and a scout named Tozer lie on their backs and cut a front path through the wire, while those behind them expand it. So that the clicking of the wire-cutters can't be heard by an alert sentry, they do not entirely cut through each strand, a skill that comes from much practice. Later the wire can easily be snapped by hand. Gill and Tozer have cleared a passage almost through the German wire when they see that it is destined to come out directly under an enemy listening post. In fact, a man in a spiked helmet now peers over it, apparently looking over their bodies directly below him and into the darkness beyond. Both lie frozen, hardly daring to breathe. The sentry must have been made aware of something because moments later two other heads appear and some discussion takes place. Then, as suddenly, the heads of all three disappear beyond the parapet.

Gill and Tozer, hoping that the other two scouts working further back will have seen the Germans, wait another ten minutes before they begin to withdraw, inching backwards, wriggling their way through the wire, joining those parts further back where they have been forced to cut it. By now it is half-past eleven and Lieutenant Gill, using his electric torch at an angle and in such a manner so that its beam cannot be detected by a German sentry, signals Ben to withdraw.

By the time Ben and Wearne arrive back at the assault group and are, shortly afterwards, joined by Gill, Tozer and the other two scouts, it is nearly midnight, too late to attempt and complete the raid.

The excursion isn't entirely wasted. They have learned a fair bit and at the same time on the following night the raid is repeated. This time, at 11.15, the artillery and medium trench mortars open up and appear to be shelling the German positions considerably to the north and south of the one Captain Foss and his raiders will attack. The raiding party moves into position and with the wires already cut the previous night they are, hopefully, in a much better position to attack. During the day medium trench mortars have played on the area where the wire has been cut to discourage the Germans from looking too closely at it or to repair the section on Ben's side. At 11.25 the guns are switched onto the trenches Foss and his men will attack and they are heavily bombarded for ten minutes. The direct fire into the trenches ceases and a box barrage to either side and the rear is formed around the position to be attacked. This is so that no German reinforcements can be brought up from the rear or the side trenches.

It takes only two minutes for the assault party to reach the German trenches and to leap into them with Captain Foss, revolver in one hand, knobkerrie in the other and a whistle in his mouth, leading the attack. The Germans, thoroughly cowed by the bombardment minutes earlier, are found hiding in dugouts and anywhere else they think themselves to be safe.

A large German sergeant comes out of a dugout brandishing a bayonet and goes straight for Foss, who has moved to Ben's end of the trench. Foss doesn't see him at first but turns as the German has his hand raised with the bayonet above his head. The raiding-party leader hasn't even had time to bring his revolver around to fire, when the German simply crumples to his knees, the blade of the Maori fighting axe cleaving the back of his skull. He falls, his head actually bumping against the toe of Foss's plimsoll. Foss looks up to see Ben grinning at him ten feet away.

However, most of the Germans are caught completely unawares. The Australians go to work with their bayonets though none of them finds it necessary to use their 'life preservers', their bolted stick, except for one incident when a prisoner attempts to escape and one of the Anzac raiders, his blood up, chases him and brains him with his knobkerrie.

In just under five minutes six Germans are captured and the remainder killed. The raiding party withdraws without a single Australian being killed or injured, though later two of the scouts are killed when an enemy mortar lands among a group retreating back to their own lines.

The Germans grow much more skilled at resisting the raiding parties in the weeks that follow, but the raids are a source of great pride among the Australian infantry. Although the credit for inventing them must be given to the Canadians, the lads nevertheless see their raiding parties as an original contribution to the war in France.

Ben returns to the 5th Battalion where he becomes the sergeant-major of D Company under the command of Major Joshua Solomon and where he will also train several raiding parties.

Foss, when Ben reports to him on the final day before returning to his battalion, shakes his hand. 'I owe you a big one, Ben,' he says simply. 'Thank Christ for the Maori blood in you.'

On the morning of his arrival Ben reports to Joshua in his dugout. Unlike the British, Australian officers share the trench accommodation with their men and Joshua has a small covered section, though open on both sides, to himself.

'Welcome, Sergeant-Major Teekleman, I am as surprised as you may be at this co-incidence.' Then he adds quickly, 'Though not unpleasantly so.'

'Thank you, sir,' Ben says. 'Co-incidence and war seem often enough to be partners.'

'I feel sure we will work well together, perhaps we can set our past aside, what say you?'

'It never bothered me that much, really, sir, I was mostly out of it. In the army you soon enough learn to accept a bloke for what he is.'

'Splendid, then that's settled. I will expect you to be forthright at all times.'

'Thank you, sir, but, with respect, I don't think you mean that.'

Joshua raises one eyebrow slightly. 'Oh, why is that?'

'Sir, our jobs are different, I'll do everything I can to help within that knowledge.'

'I can't imagine what you mean, Sergeant-Major Teekleman? But let's leave it at that.' Ben can see that Joshua is annoyed with him, but is sufficiently restrained not to take it any further.

Ben knows from experience that as the senior N.C.O. in the company he cannot be in Joshua's pocket nor have his company commander too dependent on him. He has learned from bitter experience that his judgment must be his own. He has an unspoken right to re-interpret orders if they are plainly headed in the wrong direction. A sergeant-major is the intelligent go-between, a conduit with a filter at its end and not simply a messenger between the officer and the men. Joshua's inexperience is already showing.

'I want you to create an effective raiding party in the company which I will expect to lead, it ought to be fun,' Joshua now instructs Ben.

'Yes, sir, I shall draw up the requirements right away, you may find yourself rather busy though, it's a big commitment.'

'About time, I wasn't fortunate enough to be at Gallipoli.'

After Ben has been dismissed he ponders the goings-on in Joshua's head. 'Fun' is a strange word to use about a raiding party, designed to kill the enemy at close quarters, whereas the word 'fortunate' is not an expression anyone having been through Gallipoli is ever likely to use. Then he recalls how they all were at the beginning and realises that Joshua's war hasn't yet begun for him. He is as anxious to be blooded in battle as they themselves were. Joshua is a greenhorn and Ben senses that he will have to watch him very, very carefully or his C.O. will soon be dead.

However, Joshua proves to be a quick learner and keen to take over the leadership of a raiding party, even impatient to have them get under way on a real raid. Ben, though, is more cautious. The Germans are quick learners and they have repaired their wire, laid the odd booby trap and rattles on the wire, mounted extra guards around the clock and, now, as the initial bombardment ends, they rush to stand to order. The chances of catching them off guard are increasingly rare.

Ben suggests to Joshua that he, and not his company commander, should lead the first raid. 'Sir, if you're both an observer and one of the scouts you'll gain a great deal of experience on the job, after which you will be able to take over.'

Ben is aware that he is stepping out of line, but Lieutenant-Colonel Le Maistre has asked him to train a raiding party in each of the companies and he feels responsible. In his mind it is not right to put an officer without combat experience in charge. He has chosen half of his raiding party from men who were at Gallipoli while the other half are new recruits and he feels an obligation to the old-timers and a responsibility for the new. He doesn't want them led by an officer who has never been in a bayonet charge or killed a man in the heat of battle. Joshua can overrule him if he wishes, but Ben hopes he is mature enough not to do so.

Joshua is silent, chewing at the ball of his thumb. Finally he looks up at Ben. 'I know you think I lack the experience to lead men, Sergeant-Major, and you may be right, though how shall I gain it, if not by leading them? I shall lead the raiding party.'

'Very well, sir.'

'Moreover, you will not be on the raid.'

Ben looks at Joshua, astonished. 'I'm not sure I heard you correctly, sir?'

'You will not accompany me on the raid, there is only room for one leader, we have trained two sergeants. That will be all, Sergeant-Major.'

Ben wants to tell him not to be a fool but knows he can't. 'Very well, sir, as you wish.'

'No, Sergeant-Major, there is no equivocation, it is an order.'

The raid takes place two nights later and is a disaster, eleven men are killed and three taken prisoner, with no loss to the Germans, who have seen them coming and led them into a trap. It is Gallipoli all over again. As they rush the parapet the Germans open fire, and if not for a ditch close by, the casualties would have been much worse.

One of the sergeants tells Ben that they were caught in the open under a German parachute flare not fifty yards from the trench they were meant to attack. Instead of falling to the ground or standing quite still, Joshua ordered them forward. 'Blind Freddy would have seen us coming,' the sergeant told Ben.

A second raid is scheduled four nights later but fails to reach its objective, Joshua pulling them out sixty yards from the German trenches when a German machine gun begins to fire somewhere far to their left.

The next two raids he cancels and then allows Ben to take over when a query arrives from Le Maistre asking why his company has not maintained its quota of raids. Ben takes a raiding party over to a different section of the German line. This part of the line dates from 1914 and a number of solid and large German blockhouses were built. He avoids these as virtually impregnable, designed to resist heavy artillery. Some of them are large enough to accommodate a hundred men. The trench he attacks is approached by using a sap, which he manages to enter by cutting the wire and crossing silently over a covered section of the main trench, entering the saps to the rear where two Germans lie asleep. They die silently, Ben using his fighting axe to cut their throats. Neither would have felt a thing. He signals his men to follow and they come into the main trench from the back and take a dozen Germans completely by surprise, killing them all. It is all over in less than five minutes.

Ben is not to know that *der verrückte Australier mit der Axt*, the mad Australian axe man, will in the ensuing weeks become legendary in the German lines where he is greatly feared. Like the stories among the West Australians, Ben's exploits are hugely exaggerated. In his own right he has inadvertently become a major propaganda item for the Allies. The mad axe man does more to undermine the morale of German trenches and strike fear into every soldier's heart than anything a conventional raiding party can hope to do. Imagination is always more powerful than truth.

The success of the raid only emphasises the way the men are beginning to feel about Joshua, though nobody says anything to Ben or even to their own sergeants. In the way a good N.C.O. knows these things, it is becoming apparent to them that their C.O. hasn't got the stomach for the bayonet and it is now common enough when a raiding party is proposed for the men to bet among themselves that Joshua is going to ring it, another way of indicating a man is a coward without having to come right out and say it.

Joshua has also been drinking steadily, bringing a bottle of Scotch into his dugout with him at night and having very little to do with his subalterns, who, like him, are new to the job and in need of guidance. Increasingly he prefers his own company and while he performs his duties reasonably well, he is often thick-tongued and ill-tempered in the morning and apt to bawl his junior officers out in front of the men. His four subalterns learn to avoid confronting him until noon. Ben more or less takes charge of the company, guiding the platoon commanders quietly, never usurping their authority while keeping an eye on the welfare of the men.

The raiding parties are now almost exclusively under his control and, while he takes care to train each of the subalterns to take command, he is never far from them in a raid, ready to suggest the next move if he thinks they are undecided. The company, despite Joshua, soon earns a reputation for mounting effective raiding parties. In this way the morale of its men remains high and Joshua's lack of leadership is of less concern than it might ordinarily have proved to be.

And then, on July 24th, the Allies mount a major attack at the village of Pozières. For the Australians it is their first taste of trench warfare in France, their blooding against the Germans. The raiding and harassing, or as Le Maistre calls it 'the terrier at the ankles', stage is over, they are going to cross a section of the Hindenburg Line.

The Australians are, he assures them, going to do what no Allied army has yet managed to do. To take, cross and hold the German positions on the northern, far side of the village of Pozières and possess their front line.

The Anzacs, having taken the village on July 24th, now extend their attack during the small hours of the morning on the 25th. They do not know that the Germans also have plans to re-take the village fourteen hours after they've lost it. Both sides are planning attacks at the same time.

The Germans have been bombarding the village all day, which is rapidly being reduced to a heap of rubble, but cease at seven on the evening of the 24th.

At eight o'clock the 5th Battalion, led by Lieutenant-Colonel Le Maistre, enters Black Watch Alley, behind the position previously held by that great Scottish Regiment, and prepares to mount the first part of a double attack on the German lines. This is to be a frontal assault to the south of an old Roman road which serves as a reference point for the attack.

Ben and Lieutenant Gray, one of the company platoon commanders who has especially distinguished himself during the raids, creep out after dark carrying tape and pegs and together mark the northern end where the attack is to start. The 7th Battalion, who are to go into the attack with the 5th, are to peg the southern end but, for reasons that never become clear, do not do so and they are consequently not sure where the starting line to commence their attack is intended to be. On the heavily cratered surface of no-man's-land it could be virtually anywhere.

The 5th move out, with Captain Leadbeater in charge of the leading company, and Major Joshua Solomon at the head of D Company beside him. Ben sends the men across the open ground to the starting tape, briefing

Joshua just before he takes his company across. Joshua is plainly drunk and Ben quietly instructs one of the platoon sergeants, a Gallipoli veteran, to stay with him. 'Ben, fer'chrissake, mate, I've got a platoon of greenhorns, they're gunna need me to hold their hands.'

'Timbo, you get the C.O. into position or it's your arse, mate. Put the bastard in front and tell him to run.'

At 1.50 a.m. the two companies from the 5th are in place with the two others lined up in the rear. So far the exercise is copybook. The enemy, if they sense there may be someone there at all, simply cover the area with the usual casual rifle and machine-gun fire.

At 1.58 the 1st Australian Division artillery places a heavy curtain of shrapnel on the front trenches of the German lines and the guns of the 34th Division pound the second line of trenches. After only two minutes, thought to be sufficient to send the Germans in the front trenches scurrying for cover, the shrapnel bombardment stops, though the heavy guns firing on the German rear lines continue for another twenty minutes.

Le Maistre gives the signal for the front two companies of the 5th to advance across a front that is heavily pockmarked by shell craters so that it is damn near impossible to keep to a line. Moreover, the Germans, instead of cowering for cover because of the curtain of shrapnel, are waiting for them and their machine guns start to cut the two advancing companies to pieces.

Then, almost immediately, the enemy artillery comes in. The 5th, advancing parallel to the German front line is thrown into wild confusion, breaking into groups who lose the line of attack, some making for the southwest, others for the northwest.

Ben simply stands in one spot, calling his company in and eventually ending up with the greater part of it, though two officers and at least one platoon have become lost. Joshua is nowhere to be seen. Ben has a fair idea where the German trenches are and joins up with Captain Lillie, known as 'the Pink Kid' as he is close to being an albino, who has distinguished himself at Gallipoli. Lillie takes charge and they rush the German position to find that the garrison have fled, leaving only their dead behind.

The instruction is to hold the front line and not to move on to the second and so Lillie gives the order to consolidate and to start to dig in. Despite the chaos, they've achieved their objective and must now wait for the second attack to advance. At 2.25 the barrage on the German second line of defence is lifted and Leadbeater on the left of Ben's company decides against orders to advance.

'Shit, what's he doing?' Lillie cries. 'We're supposed to consolidate.'

'We don't have a choice now, sir, we have to go with him or the Boche will come around him,' Ben says.

Lillie reluctantly gives the order to advance and the whole force sweeps forward towards the German rear lines. To their surprise there is little resistance and where they believe the lines are they see nothing but churned earth and craters. The Allied bombardment has been so heavy that all traces of the German trenches seem to have been wiped out. Eventually, judging by the number of German dead and the equipment lying about, they realise that they have reached the second line and Lillie, reporting the capture, instructs the troops to dig in. They have achieved more than has been asked of them and have done what Le Maistre has demanded. They have taken a section of the Hindenburg Line which has never before been breached. Moreover they've done it without having to look a single German in the eye.

But their victory is shortlived. The Germans now move

in. The Welsh Borderers, a British regiment responsible for their extreme right, meets heavy machine-gun fire and is forced back, losing nine of their twelve officers and seventy-four of their men. They are intended to be the support for the Australians on the right. On Lillie and Leadbeater's left, the 7th Battalion hasn't arrived and only one platoon has made it to the German second line of defence. They join Lillie and the left flank is completely exposed along with the right. Lillie and Leadbeater, the two officers in command of the 5th, are also exposed on either flank with the attacking Germans about to encircle them, coming around on the left and right to once again occupy their own former front line and trap the 5th Battalion behind the German lines.

Ben points this out to Captain Lillie, who, having come this far, is reluctant to turn back. 'Sir, they'll be up our arses like a rat up a drainpipe before we know where we are.'

Just then a message comes through to say that Leadbeater has been killed and his company is in disarray, all its officers having been killed as well.

'We're falling back,' Lillie decides. 'Ben, get the fuck over there and bring them out, we'll pull back to the first German lines and try to hold them there.'

Ben, sensing the direction the Germans might be taking to recapture their own front line, orders Lieutenant Fitzgerald, another one of his raider officers in charge of the 5th Battalion bombers, to move up onto their flank to guard it as he withdraws Leadbeater's company. Fitzgerald, though an officer, accepts the order and doesn't muck about in moving into position on the left flank to protect Ben's withdrawal.

The Germans, using their own bombers, fight to break through Fitzgerald's defence. The Germans have a lighter bomb which can be thrown a further distance than the one possessed by the Anzacs. To make up for this deficiency Fitzgerald and his bombers dash across the open ground so that they can overcome the disadvantage, thus constantly exposing themselves and at the same time drawing nearer to the German bombers.

In the meantime Ben pulls Leadbeater's company back into the German front-line trenches where he joins up with Lillie. Their flank is still vulnerable to the German attack, which is being halted by Fitzgerald's men, though it is only a matter of time before the enemy break through.

'Sir, they'll be breaking through and coming down their own trenches to get us,' he tells Lillie. 'We can't pull back across no-man's-land, they'll cut us off long before we make it. We'll have to stay here and fight it out. We have maybe half an hour if we're lucky to build a barricade to block their advance down the trench from the railway line. We can fight them from behind the barricade with bombs, it's about our only chance.'

Captain Lillie nods. 'Get the men onto it. By the way, Sergeant-Major, what happened to Major Solomon, he's your C.O.? I could use a little help.'

'I've not seen him, sir, must have been caught up in the confusion when the Boche opened up at the start.'

Ben puts the men to work, building a barricade in the trench, using bits of timber and any German equipment they can find lying around. They work feverishly, knowing it is only a matter of time before Fitzgerald's bombers are overrun.

In fact, Lieutenant Fitzgerald, venturing once too often into the open to hurl a bomb, is killed by a machine gun. Shortly after, Gray, who had earlier laid the starting tape with Ben, is also killed as well as two more of the bombers. The barricade, though, is more or less established.

The fight begins.

At the barricade the surviving bombers and those who can crowd in with them throw until they think their arms must surely fall off. The Germans keep coming, hurling their own bombs. Ben positions six snipers who are given the job of shooting the hands off the Germans as they are about to throw bombs over the barricade. They fight for an hour, the Germans only a matter of feet away on the other side of the barricade. The 9th and the 10th Battalions arrive and at last some of the 7th to reinforce the exhausted and wounded men from the 5th.

They manage to mount a Lewis gun for a while, aiming it directly down the trench at the Germans, mowing them down before it is destroyed by a bomb. One of the officers of the 10th moves with another Lewis gun into a cross trench which effectively prevents the enemy from coming over the top of or around the barricade.

On the Australian side the bombers, by now everyone who still has the strength to throw, are standing on the bodies of their mates to get to the Germans on the other side.

At half-past seven, with the men close to collapse, Captain Oates of the 7th arrives with three platoons from his battalion and drives the Germans back almost to the railway. Then a second barrier is built higher up in the German trenches and a T-sap is cut on either side of it to create a broader front and make bombing and rifle fire easier. After two more attacks the Germans withdraw to beyond the railway and the Australians remain in possession of the German front-line trenches almost to the railway line.

It isn't everything Le Maistre has hoped for, but they've achieved more than any other advance on the Germans since the beginning of the war. They've breached the German Line for the first time and now they are holding it.

They have little time to celebrate. The Germans are not going to let the Australians breach their lines. Realising that all their own troops are out of Pozières and can be cleared from the immediate area, they commence to bombard their former front line, making it impossible for those who hold it to retreat.

What follows proves to be the heaviest and most prolonged bombardment of the war. The length of the line the Anzacs hold is just over four hundred yards and contained in it is the whole of the 1st Division, some eight thousand men who cannot advance or retreat and are trapped under the maelstrom of German artillery.

Those who cannot find cover have little hope of surviving. The Germans, who are using their own survey maps of their former trenches, are laying down such accurate fire that whole sections of a trench are often simply wiped out. Men disappear, with arms and legs and heads torn from their bodies. Hundreds, soon thousands, of torsos and limbs and heads are scattered everywhere.

So accurate and intense is the fire that some officers lead their men out of the trenches, preferring to take their chances in the open. Dust rises in clouds that can be seen for miles and the day is turned into dusk.

Oblivious of the bombing, rats now cover no-man's-land in waves, seeking out the corpses, gorging on the flesh of dead men until they simply drag themselves across the ground or lie panting covered in blood and gore.

Ben's section of the trench is hit, killing twenty men who just disappear, and he finds himself cut off from Lillie with just a handful of men a little further down. Some fifty men are now in his section of the front line. Towards the end of the newly exposed section is a blockhouse, not much bigger than a small outhouse but solidly built, probably a place to store ammunition. Dead men lie at its entrance and one wall has been completely covered in someone's blood and brains. Ben moves down to it and pushes open the door. Inside he finds five men, one of them Joshua Solomon, who cowers in the far corner, his knees hugged to his chest. As the daylight floods in he starts to whimper.

'Sir, you had better come out,' Ben calls to him.

Joshua shields his eyes against the light with one hand. 'No way! No way! I'm not going out there,' he cries. 'I don't want to die. Please, I don't want to die, Ben. Save me. Please save me!' He looks about him wildly. 'Sergeant-Major, I order you to save me!'

'C'mon, out you get,' Ben says to the other men, 'how long have you been in here?'

'I dunno,' the soldier replies. 'Since last night I think.'

'Last night? What time last night?'

'When the Germans started to fire on us?'

'What, you mean just after we started forward?'

'Yes, Sergeant-Major, we lost our direction and then we come across this and crawled in.'

'And him?' Ben points to Joshua.

'He come later, Sergeant, about two hours later, he was pissed.'

'Righto, you bastards have done no fucking work, you're gunna have to dig.' He indicates Joshua. 'Leave him there, come on, move your arses!'

The bombardment continues all day and Ben knows that if the shelling continues they will all die, but he sets his men to digging, thinking it better than keeping them idle. 'If we get a direct hit, we're history,' he tells them honestly. 'If we can dig deep enough we may have a chance, dig for your lives.'

As they dig they find the recent dead, mostly limbs and bits and pieces. They throw them over the side, tossing a dead mate's severed head over the parapet like a melon, their hands often wet with blood and gore. And still they dig, their lives depending on it.

Ben prays that they can last until nightfall when he tells himself he's going to have to get them out. At about six o'clock the dust is so heavy that it is prematurely dark. Ben decides he cannot wait. They have had one or two near misses with the trenches on either side of them taking a direct hit, some of the bodies being blown so high into the air that they sail way over their heads. One of Ben's men is killed when a torso lands on his head, snapping his neck. It is only a matter of time before the German artillery find them.

He calls his men together and points to a blockhouse some sixty yards away. It has been reduced to rubble by the bombardment and seems at first sight to be even more vulnerable than the trench in which they are hiding.

'I've been right up to one of those, most have a section underground, we're going to go for it. If I'm wrong we're dead, if I'm right the section underneath may give us a level of protection. I'm giving you a choice, you can stay dug in here and hope for the best, maybe the bombardment will soon be over. Or you can come with me. We'll be fired on trying to make our objective and I can't promise I'm right.' He looks about him. 'If I'm wrong we won't get back, lads. I want you to understand that, there is no return, we won't be able to get back to this trench and we'll all almost certainly die.'

'What if the bombardment stops? We could be safer here than trying to cross over to that blockhouse?' someone asks.

'Quite right, lad, but if I were the Hun and I had us pinned down like this I don't think I'd stop firing until I had so pulverised the position, no further resistance was possible. That's what I'd do. But I'm not the enemy and, frankly, I don't know. I'll give you five minutes to decide. Those who are coming to the right, get your kit together, those staying to the left, my suggestion is to keep digging.'

Ben leaves them to decide and goes to the little blockhouse where he has left Joshua. 'Come on, we're getting out,' he says.

'No, no, I don't want to,' Joshua cries.

'Right, I'm going to count to ten, if you're not out of here by then I'm going to shoot you,' Ben says and commences to count. At the count of five Joshua has crawled out on his hands and knees. Ben jerks him to his feet, but he immediately collapses the moment he is left on his own. Ben reaches down and grabs him under the arms and pulls him back onto his feet. 'You better learn to stand in the next two minutes, we're moving out.' He props Joshua up against the wall of the trench and leaves him.

Nearly two-thirds of the men are standing to the right with their gear. They're a sorry-looking lot, the fight gone out of most of them. 'Come on, sir, we're going,' he calls to Joshua.

Joshua takes a step away from the wall and collapses. Ben turns to two men, veterans he's known from Gallipoli. 'Partridge, Collins, take the C.O. between you.'

Partridge looks at Ben and spits on the ground. 'Fuck him, Ben.'

Ben grabs him by the front of his shirt. 'That's an order, like it or not, he's our fucking C.O., he's coming.'

'He's not worth it,' Collins says, but they both take Joshua and support him.

'Right, we're out of here, it's yonder blockhouse, every man for himself. Go for it, lads!'

There is a mad scramble out of the trenches and Ben waits for Partridge and Collins to manhandle Joshua out. 'What's fucking wrong with him, eh? Bloody legs look all right to me,' Partridge complains again. Whereupon Joshua, seeing himself exposed, jumps to his feet and runs for the blockhouse. 'I should shoot the bastard!' Partridge says.

'Stop whingeing and get going,' Ben orders and sets out at a trot himself. The dust is now so thick that it is akin to fighting through a dust storm and they reach the blockhouse without being fired on. Visibility cannot be more than twenty feet.

Ben is correct, they find a hole in the ground which leads into an underground section of the blockhouse that is untouched by the bombardment. It is sufficiently large to house them comfortably and the men, exhausted and frightened, collapse.

'Righto, break out your rations, see if there's a stove or a fireplace somewhere so we might get a brew up,' Ben instructs one of the corporals, handing him his electric torch.

The man returns in a few minutes, 'Found the cookhouse, a stove, wood and an urn. No water, though, Sergeant-Major.'

Ben doesn't know where he's heard it, but now he says, 'Look under the floor near the stove. Wait on, I'll come with you.' Sure enough, in the centre of the small room used for cooking is a flagstone set in the floor and upon lifting it they see a steel tank of water and a rope with a bucket attached hangs from it. They find six storm lanterns and the interior of the room where the men are gathered is soon lit, dimly but sufficiently for them to see each other and to prepare their field rations. There is a huge sense of relief among the men. The bombardment outside continues and every time a shell falls close the noise within the blockhouse is so intense it hurts their ears.

During a slight lull between salvos Ben calls them to attention. 'Righto, we're not out of this yet.' He indicates the four men he'd found in the blockhouse earlier. 'You four, you'll stand sentry duty for the next four hours. The rest of you eat and get your heads down, have a kip while you may.'

Ben tries to sleep himself but cannot and he takes out a writing pad and pencil and starts to write to Victoria.

My dearest sister Victoria,

I am writing to you from a German blockhouse we have captured near a village called Pozières. You will no doubt read about it in the weeks to come as it is the first major offensive the 1st Division has undertaken in France. The whys and wherefores are not important. What is, is that I feel sure that I won't be coming home to you. That this is the end. The Germans have us pinned down and there is no getting out.

Curiously, it is also the end of a long story because Joshua Solomon is with me, the two of us in the same battle. But, as I write this, he cowers in a corner whimpering to himself. The poor fool cannot, I believe, help himself. What is happening to us all is well beyond cowardice. You do not call a man a coward for being afraid to go over the top when the whistle blows, be he a company commander or a private. He has seen all his mates killed and then all his new pals killed, and, then, because the idea of friendship becomes impossible, mateship now too awful to contemplate, the replacements are received as blank-eyed strangers, who come at night to huddle beside you in the trenches. These are no longer seen as men, only as numbers in a well-thinned roll call after each skirmish into enemy lines. New recruits are no longer seen as whole, but become assorted parts, eyes, skulls, arms, legs, torsos, scraps of unidentified meat. They simply become flesh new-opened, gaping, bloody stumps where once strong arms held their sweethearts close or firm-muscled legs kicked a football and ran shouting urgent instructions across a flat green paddock under a blue sky.

The men who sit huddled in the dust and carnage beside you in the trench become torsos cut off at the waist, like open-mouthed fairground clowns. Heads lolling with fatigue on your shoulder are in your mind already disembodied, tomorrow's 'dirty melons' you are sent out to gather from the mud after each attack. Only the rats are real, they waddle like fat butchers at a meat market and choose the choicest human parts, the intestines, the haggis of hate.

My dearest sister, I do not expect to return from here. The German artillery has us trapped and it has continued now all day and I daresay will do so all night. It is not too hard to understand why our cousin Joshua cowers in a dark corner sucking at an empty bottle of whisky, which he won't relinquish.

It is to drown the noise, the booming, cutting, whining, whooshing, whistling, exploding, blunt and bloody, neverending noise that goes into the senseless slaughter of good and honest men.

And so the male line of our two families will die, here in a charnel field in France. All the hate, all the fierce endeavour, all the malicious greed, come to an end.

Now I want you to do something for me. Kiss Hawk, tell him I love him, and always have. Of all the men I have met in my short life he has always shown me that to be fair and just and honest is the way of a true man. I often think how men fight to put themselves first but he always put himself in the second place. Great-Grandma Mary once told me as a small child how he loved our grandfather Tommo above all sensibility and would have gladly laid down his life for him.

Alas, he has not got the right complexion to blush as you read this to him, but there is no longer need to hide my feelings. You say in your last letter that he grows frail, his huge shoulders stooped, his hands crooked with arthritis, his eyes, his great dark eyes, grown rheumy, but his mind still clear and clean to the intellect. I shall not see him out, I shall not be there to stand by his grave and weep for him. But you will do it for me. Never was there a man I loved as much. Never was there a man who was better at being a member of the human race. In those moments when I have been overcome with despair, and there have been many such as the one I face at this very moment, I ask myself, 'What would Grandfather Hawk do?' and always it becomes clear, he would do the right thing by his mates, by his fellow human beings. I must do the same. My dear Grandfather, if I should die, as I think I *shall, I can say only this, you have given me the strength to die with dignity. No better man than you ever lived.*

And you, my dearest, I love and cherish you to the last moment of my life. Be brave and good and strong. I thank you and love you with every breath in my body for what you have been to me.

And then there is Sarah, my beloved Sarah. Will you give her half of my inheritance and take care of her when she returns? Treat her as if she was my wife, for I have loved her with my body and my mind is filled with her presence every day. No man could want more than she has given me. Love her, Victoria, as you love me.

And now it is goodbye to the three of you.

I love you all, with all of my heart. Death cannot change that.

Ben.

Ben has barely completed the letter when Partridge comes up to him. 'The C.O.'s gorn walkabout, mate.'

Ben doesn't understand at first. 'What are you talking about?'

'He's ripped off his gear and gorn, tin hat and revolver, screaming like a banshee, told you the bastard wasn't worth bringing.'

'You didn't stop him?' Ben asks.

'Stop him, three of us tried, he's gorn mad, he just knocked us aside, next thing he was out the entrance.'

Folding the letter, Ben finds an envelope and addresses

it. He places the letter in the envelope and seals it. Then he puts it in his kit. 'Partridge, you're a useless bastard, but promise me one thing.' Ben points to his kit. 'Inside are two letters, one is addressed to my sister in Tasmania, the other to my fiancée, if you get out of here you see they get them. Tell my sister I said to give you a hundred quid.' Ben grabs up his pad and writes.

Victoria,

> *Pay this bastard Partridge a hundred pounds when he delivers my letter.*

> *Ben Teekleman.*

'There you go.' He hands the note to Partridge.

'Hey, wait a moment, Sergeant-Major, you're not going after him, he's gorn mad, he's a flamin' looney!'

'It's a long story,' Ben says and, taking up his Maori fighting axe, he starts for the entrance. There is a brief lull in the bombardment and he turns to the men. 'There's just a chance the Germans will stop in the early hours of the morning and we'll try to beat a retreat. If it does, get out of here and make for our lines, it's your only hope, lads, take it, don't stay here.'

Ben walks into the open, it is now around ten o'clock at night with the German bombardment lighting up the battlefield in huge flashes as the heavy shells land, sending up towering pillars of dust that catch the light. It is like a scene from hell and he looks to where his trench was before they made it across to the blockhouse. There is nothing to be seen except craters, the lads who stayed are almost certainly dead.

Ben is not concerned about machine guns, there is too

much dust. He hopes only to find Joshua cowering somewhere. He doesn't know why he's gone after him, something simply tells him he must. That if he doesn't he will be dishonouring himself, Victoria, Hawk. It doesn't make a lot of sense. But by now nothing does any more. Somehow, something is coming to an end, something dark and ugly and too long in his blood.

A shell explodes about fifty yards ahead of him, lighting up the whole area, cutting through the dust, and then he sees Joshua. He is naked, walking towards the village of Pozières. He has crossed a section of trenches where the German front line stood, now pounded into nothing. Where men a few hours before crouched and hoped, there are only craters and death and the rats scurrying everywhere.

Ben starts to run towards Joshua. Stumbling, he falls and feels his face scrape against the dirt, losing his tin hat. He doesn't try to find it but rises and continues running. Joshua has disappeared into the darkness. But another shell lands and lights him up again. His nude body wearing only the tin hat seems enlarged, bigger than the landscape itself. His nudity is somehow visionlike, as though he is an angel who has come among them, or is man, naked, pleading, asking for the carnage to end, for a new beginning, a new start. Adam looking on the battlefield for Eve.

Ben keeps running, his breath beginning to hurt in his chest. He realises that he is very tired but he moves forward. Another shell bursts and he sees Joshua. This time he is standing in a shell crater and is up to his waist in dirty water. At last Ben comes upon him. Joshua has his revolver and he is firing repeatedly at the body of a dead German strung up on a roll of barbed wire. The German is long dead, his body rotting. An arm falls off and rolls down the side of the crater into the water, and still Joshua fires.

Ben runs into the crater and, taking Joshua's hand, he pulls him out of the hole. Joshua screams as though in pain. On the bank Joshua clutches at his ankle, crying like a small child and Ben, using his torch, sees that his ankle is broken. He lifts him across his shoulder, not quite sure where he finds the strength. Then he begins to carry him across no-man's-land.

Ben carries Joshua for fifty yards and then rests and picks him up again and carries him a little further. Twice a machine gun opens up and he can hear the bullets as they strike the ground near him. Still he continues, resting and carrying. It takes him nearly an hour to cover the six hundred yards. A pistol is fired from the direction of the village, from the Allied lines. He can see men starting to run towards him, his own people. The light seems to hang in the sky forever, bright silver light, sharp, clean, and beautiful. He thinks of Sarah, her body touching his, making love, the soft whimpering sounds she makes and then a sudden lull in the bombardment and into it a single cracking sound, like a twig breaking, as the sniper's bullet hits him. Ben feels himself sinking, melting with the weight of Joshua's body. And he hears Sarah sighing, he is caressing her cheek with the back of his fingers and she looks at him and sighs, 'I love you, Ben, more than my life,' then the darkness comes. Joshua Solomon is mad. Ben Teekleman is dead. The story is ended.

Lest We Forget

A Note on Sources

I and my research team have made extensive use of the wonderful resources of the State Libraries of Victoria and New South Wales and also those of the Australian War Memorial. Numerous texts and reference books have been consulted to confirm dates, names, facts and the overall historical accuracy of *Solomon's Song*. My debt to C. E. W. Bean's *Official History of Australia in the War of 1914–1918* (1921–1942) is obvious. Bean not only edited the twelve volumes of this monumental history but wrote the text of six volumes himself and also produced a most readable one-volume abridgment published in 1946 as *Anzac to Amiens* (Australian War Memorial, Canberra).

Other books used include:

Patsy Adam-Smith, *The Anzacs*, Nelson, West Melbourne, 1978.

—— *Prisoners of War: From Gallipoli to Korea*, Ken Fin Books, Collingwood, 1998.

Australian Dictionary of Biography, 1851–1939, Melbourne University Press, Melbourne, 1966.

The Australian Handbook and Directory for 1874.

A.G. Butler (ed.), *The Official History of the Australian Army Medical Services in the War of 1914–1918*, vol. 1, Gallipoli, Palestine and New Guinea, Australian War Memorial, Melbourne, 1930.

Ruth Campbell, *A History of the Melbourne Law School, 1857–1973*, Faculty of Law, University of Melbourne, Parkville, 1973.

Michael Cannon, *Land Boom and Bust*, Heritage Publications, Melbourne, 1972.

—— *The Long Last Summer: Australia's upper class before the Great War*, Nelson, Melbourne, 1985.

Graeme Davison et al., *The Oxford Companion to Australian History*, Oxford University Press, Melbourne, 1998.

Peter Dennis et al., *The Oxford Companion to Australian Military History*, Oxford University Press, Melbourne, 1995.

Bill Gammage, *The Broken Years: Australian soldiers in the Great War*, Australian National University Press, Canberra, 1974.

Gregory Haines, *The Grains and Threepennorths of Pharmacy: Pharmacy in New South Wales, 1788–1976*, Lowden Publishing, Kilmore, 1976.

R. F. Holder, *Bank of New South Wales: A history, 1817–1970*, in two volumes, Angus and Robertson, Sydney, 1970.

H. Aubrey Husband, *The Student's Handbook of Forensic Medicine and Public Health*, 6th ed., E. & S. Livingstone, Edinburgh, 1895.

John Keegan, *The First World War*, Hutchinson, London, 1998.

Henry Kissinger, *Diplomacy*, Simon & Schuster, New York, 1994.

The Longman Handbook of Modern British History, 1714–1950, Longman, London, 1983.

Philip E. Muskett, *The Illustrated Australian Medical Guide*, in two volumes, William Brooks, Sydney, 1903.

L. M. Newton, *The Story of the Twelfth: A record of the 12th Battalion, A.I.F. during the Great War of*

1914–1918, 12th Battalion Association, Hobart, 1925.

Margaret Orbell, *The Illustrated Encyclopedia of Maori Myth and Legend*, Canterbury University Press, Christchurch, 1995.

Stephen Pope and Elizabeth-Anne Wheal, *The Macmillan Dictionary of the First World War*, Macmillan, London, 1995.

Hilary L. Rubinstein, *The Jews in Australia: A thematic history*, William Heinemann, Port Melbourne, 1991.

Anne Salmond, *Between Worlds: Early exchanges between Maori and Europeans, 1773–1815*, Viking, Auckland, 1997.

Sands & McDougall's Directory of Victoria, Sands & McDougall, Melbourne, 1890–1930.

Elizabeth Scandrett, *Breeches & Bustles: An illustrated history of clothes worn in Australia, 1788–1914*, Pioneer Books, Lilydale, 1978.

G. H. Scholefield, *A Dictionary of New Zealand Biography*, vol. 1, 1769–1869, and vol. 2, 1870–1900, Dept. of Internal Affairs, Wellington, 1940.

Michael Symons, *One Continuous Picnic: A history of eating in Australia*, Duck Press, Adelaide, 1982.

Tasmanian Post Office Directory, 1885–1890.

Fred Waite, *The New Zealanders at Gallipoli*, 2nd ed., Whitcombe and Tombs, Auckland, 1921.

Walch's Tasmanian Almanac for 1885, J. Walch & Sons, Hobart, 1885.

THE POTATO FACTORY

Always leave a little salt on the bread . . .

Ikey Solomon's favourite saying is also his way of doing business. And in the business of thieving in thriving nineteenth-century London, he's very successful indeed. Ikey's partner in crime is his mistress, the forthright Mary Abacus, until misfortune befalls them. They are parted and each must make the harsh journey separately to the convict settlement in Van Diemen's Land.

In the backstreets and dives of Hobart Town, Mary learns the art of brewing and builds The Potato Factory, where she plans a new future. But her ambitions are threatened by Ikey's wife, Hannah, her old enemy. The two women raise their separate families, one legitimate and the other bastard. As each woman sets out to destroy the other, the families are brought to the brink of disaster.

A thrilling tale of Australia's beginnings, told by master storyteller Bryce Courtenay

TOMMO & HAWK

Brutally kidnapped and separated in childhood, Tommo
and Hawk are reunited at the age of fifteen in Hobart
Town. Together, they escape their troubled pasts and set
off on a journey into manhood. From whale hunting in
the Pacific to the Maori wars of New Zealand, from the
Rocks in Sydney to the miners' riots at the goldfields,
Tommo and Hawk must learn each other's strengths and
weaknesses in order to survive.

Along the way, Hawk meets the outrageous Maggie
Pye, who brings love and laughter into his life. But the
demons of Tommo's past return to haunt the brothers.
With Tommo at his side, Hawk takes on a fight against all
odds to save what they cherish most. In the final confrontation between good and evil, three magpie feathers
become the symbol of Tommo and Hawk's rites of passage.

**An epic tale of adventure and romance from Australia's
bestselling author, Bryce Courtenay**